CW01011066

1 MONTH OF
FREE
READING

at

www.ForgottenBooks.com

By purchasing this book you are eligible for one month membership to ForgottenBooks.com, giving you unlimited access to our entire collection of over 700,000 titles via our web site and mobile apps.

To claim your free month visit:
www.forgottenbooks.com/free797466

ISBN 978-0-332-94800-3
PIBN 10797466

THE

RAMBLES

AND

SURPRISING ADVENTURES

OF

CAPTAIN BOLIO.

BY DELLA.

EMBELLISHED WITH THIRTY-TWO ENGRAVINGS.

LONDON:

PRINTED FOR THOMAS TEGG, 73, CHEAPSIDE;

TEGG AND CO., DUBLIN; R. GRIFFIN AND CO., GLASGOW;
ALSO, J. AND S. A. TEGG, SYDNEY AND HOBART TOWN.

1839.

Directions to the Binder for placing the Plates.

RAMBLES OF CAPTAIN BOLIO.

CHAPTER I.

"'Aye, Sir, by the rood he was a soldier,
And one more brave did never draw a sword;
And yet, withal, he was a man of whims,
Of fancies singular, and most eccentric,
Whereof his son did plentifully partake.
But hist, hist, you'll hear anon."

CUSTOM is invariably an arbitrary and very frequently an outrageously tyrannical master, to whose imperious mandates we are compelled to do homage, and yield obedience, *nolens volens.*

Bowing to such indisputable and justly revered authority, I shall not, as otherwise perhaps I might have been tempted to do, send forth my hero like an unexpected and unfathered bantling, into the world, but by a hasty sketch of his family, birth, and character, give to him a literary existence, and then proceed to introduce him to all who may feel interested in his history, by recounting some of the observations, scenes, and adventures of his eventful life.

Captain Claudius Bolio—such was the cognomen by which our hero was distinguished from a host of Bolios, all springing as it would appear from one great stock—was the youngest son of a nobleman of ancient and honourable family, but of comparatively limited fortune, that is, when the support of rank and title is taken into the account as an item in current expenses. His sire was Count Dornato Sebastian Bolio; he had rendered himself famous both by intrepidity of con-

B

duct and military skill, during the fearful struggles for liberty which took place at the period that those distinguished individuals, Columbus and Vasco de Gama, led the forces of Spain against his native country. The sanguinary scenes which were witnessed by the republic of Venice, when the tide of wealth, pouring into the exchequer of its adversary from the new-found world, gave to it a power which neither popes, princes, nor sultans had ever possessed, to unsettle and overturn the tranquillity and liberty of that unfortunate people, and the boasted independence of the ruined state, are known, it is presumed, to most of our readers. Then it was that Count Bolio, with the remnant of his fortune, and a small family, fled from the tyranny of the council of ten, and took up his residence in the general rendezvous, or common receptacle of every thing good, bad, and indifferent,—ENG-LAND!

It has been asserted, that in the constitution of a hero the elements of cruelty or of eccentricity are invariably found. How much 'soever such statement may be, in the gross, opposed to plain matter of fact, it is certain that no small quantum of the latter was possessed by Count Bolio, and which became a kind of heir-loom to his son the Captain.

During one of the scenes of conflict in which the Count was engaged, himself and his regiment were subjected to the unpleasant endurance of what in vulgar parlance is called " short commons ;" that is, their rations were light in quantity, and " like angel visits, *few* and *far* between."

Hunger has been known to quicken the genius of *literary* men, and therefore, perhaps for the advantage of the million that are benefitted by their labours, they are generally kept sharp set; and why the same effect may not be produced by the same cause upon *military* men I know not; it is at least possible that in the present case it did so. The Count well knew the superstition which existed among the Spanish troops, and determined to practise upon their credulity for the advantage of himself and those who were enduring with him the twitchings of hunger.

About this perod two men of the Venetian legion had been detected in an attempt to desert to the enemy, and in consequence were advanced to the somewhat unpleasan popularity, which they no doubt would have thought " more honoured in thebreach than in the observance," of being riddled by the balls of some half-score of their comrades

The Count caused it to be extensively circulated, that the apparitions of the two unfortunates were in the habit of making nightly visits to some of those who had formerly been their companions in arms, and displaying various feats of ghostly eccentricity in their presence. The story flew like wild-fire, and, from the piquets of the Venetian, passed to the piquets of the Spanish forces, and operated as he wished and expected. What a troop of his soldiers could not have effected, his tale of phantasmagoria accomplished.

Several head of fine cattle belonging to the enemy grazed most temptingly within sight of the Venetian lines. To obtain at least a few of these was a point of considerable consequence to the Count and his followers, and he determined for once to risk a somewhat daring manœuvre to accomplish his object. In pursuance of this purpose, and as soon as the ghost tale was sufficiently spread, himself and a brother officer arrayed themselves in what appeared spectral habiliments, and, under cover of a clouded moon, stole forth at midnight,—

"The hour so fam'd when spirits love to walk,
And pay earth visits from the world unknown,"

and stalked directly towards the Spanish lines, while a select party stood prepared to receive the booty when obtained, or render such assistance as circumstances might require. With solemn gait they approached the spot where the objects of their ghosly visit grazed, making deep and continued moanings of the most unearthly kind. The Spanish piquets beheld the approaching spirits, and trembled like the conscience-stricken Mede of old; and as they crossed themselves piously, and repeated as devoutly as friars their paternosters and avemarys, the Count and his fellow sprite broke two vessels each, in which they carried an equal number of flambeaux. The sudden glare of the lights, and the furious and grotesque attitudes into which they threw their distorted bodies, increased the terror of the half-dead soldiers, and roused at the same time the grazing cattle, who, tossing their heads wildly, and lashing their sides with their tails, fled in disorder from their fiend-like pursuers, and in a few minutes afterwards they were safely lodged in the custody of the friends of the Count; while the praying Spaniards, discovering the trick which had been played upon them, turned from supplicating the virgin mother to give vent to bitter execrations against the cattle-stealing ghosts.

A variety of similar well-managed feats were performed by the eccentric Count, which, were I to enumerate them, would swell into volumes more in number than those which contain the adventures of the knight of De la Mancha, and of such a character as would put to shame for romantic interest the exploits of that justly renowned champion. As, however, I do not intend to become the biographer of the Count, but of his son, I shall turn from all further reference to them.

It has already been observed, that on the overthrow and degradation of the land of his birth, the Count fled from Venice to England. Here he purchased an estate of some considerable extent, and although he retained the *title* of Count, he assumed the equally respectable and often more useful character and conduct, of an English gentleman. In his experience the words of prophecy were fulfilled, "The sword was turned into a plough-share, and the spear into a pruning-hook." Two of his sons still retained posts in the army of their native country, and continued to do so until after the treaty of Campo Formio, when Venice was ceded to Austria.

In the charming spot, on the borders of the sylvan county of Dorset, where the Count and his lady had taken up their residence, the hero of my tale came into the world; and as he was the last born, so he was, as in all such cases it generally occurs, the pet of his parents. He had scarcely attained the fourth year of his existence when the good old Count his father died, and Claudius became the complete idol, and of course spoiled child, of his only surviving parent. He had not entered his teens when his inherent eccentricity, and his love of adventure over-leaped the bounds of decorum, and displayed themselves in rather glowing colours.

The greatest possible care was taken in the improvement of his mind, and in order that a good and substantial, as well as elegant and classical education should be possessed by him, a gentleman of first-rate talents had been engaged as his private tutor. Unfortunately the temper and staturd of the teacher of the dead languages were held as a deaft letter in the estimation of young Bolio: the former was soi- and gentle as a lady's *should* be, while the latter was as de minutive as a full-grown dwarf's *would* be.

Claudius had not reached his thirteenth year when he could, and in point of stature did, look down upon the man of letters, and in consequence of the wildness of his disposition not unfrequently played him some wild and elfish tricks.

On one occasion they were enjoying themselves on a fine piece of water, which formed a branch of the river Stour, and passed through the grounds attached to the family mansion, when the oft disputed topic of Hannibal's crossing the Alps, as to whether the conqueror of the land of song entered Italy by passing mount St. Bernard, or by the mount Cenis, called into exercise all the fiery temper of the pupil, and for a moment ruffled the placid spirit of the mild tutor himself. Master Claudius, however, cut short the argument by seizing his opponent with a fierce and disrespectful grasp, and plunging with him into the element of the fishes. This would in all probability have been the last, as well as the first *serious* exploit of young Bolio, had it not been for the gardener and his assistant, who, hearing the plunge in the water as well as the shriek which the terrified tutor sent forth, hastened in another boat to the spot, and with the aid of a boat-hook dragged them, like a pair of flat fish, to *terra firma.*

This, it must be allowed, was an auspicious commencement in Claudius' adventures, and for this act of violence and audacious breach of discipline, he was most righteously sentenced to perform a protracted and disgraceful act of penance, rather than attend to which he would almost as soon have been condemned to suffer an *auto de fé.*

The penance referred to consisted of three distinct parts. In the first place it was enacted that he should crave forgiveness of his insulted master, in language and attitude denotive of sorrow. Secondly, he was to live upon the unpalatable fare of bread and water for the space of one whole day and night, or four-and-twenty entire hours; and lastly, to endure the pangs of solitary confinement for the same space of time in a lofty apartment at the back of the house.

Now it should be known that our hero had been wont to revel in those tales of chivalry and romance, of which his father's land is the foundation of so rich a supply, both -

"In simple prose and soul-exciting verse;"

the consequence was, that he glowed with the irrepressible ardour of uninstructed youth to become himself the hero of some wonderful incident. The eccentricity of his father appeared at the instant to live and blaze within him. He had

long panted for an opportunity to display his origin by some
deed of novel nature, and now an occasion fully according
with his wishes was fairly presented. It appeared to him
(albeit he might have been wrong) that he was loudly called
upon, by concurring circumstances, to enact the hero of his
own romantic brain.

How to avoid the first part of his degrading and cruel sentence, as he termed making an apology for the outrage he
had committed, he was puzzled to determine. That he
would *not* make it, however, he was fully determined. At
length the moment arrived when the fiery ordeal was to be
endured. The *little* tutor summonsed him to the hall of
audience, into which, on this special and important occasion,
the drawing-room of the mansion was converted. There
sat the pedagogue in all the plenitude of official dignity, and
there too, on a sofa, reclined Claudius' lady mother, half-
inclined to remit the sentence altogether, and yet, ostensibly,
to see that the first part of her son's punishment was duly
inflicted, nothing being extenuated, nor aught added in
malice.

" My object, Master Claudius," commenced his instructor,
"hem! my object, Sir, in desiring you should endure the
punishment which awaits you, is not dictated by passion or
revenge; hem,—the hope that it may lead you in future to
see the impropriety of yielding to a spirit which, if not at
once checked, cannot fail to be a fruitful source of unhappi-
ness to you through life, alone influences me; hem,—Lady
Bolio, your affectionate mother, acquiesces with me in the
propriety of the sentence passed upon you: hem,—the first
part of which is, that you make an apology befitting the
offence committed. Hem! come, Sir, the apology." Claudius hesitated, the tutor still urged, and gravely raised his
staff of authority. This, in the eyes of Claudius, looked
very like a signal of attack, and feeling as indignant at a
threatened blow as an ancient Roman would at receiving a
lash, he thrust a hand into each of his trousers pockets, and
with the speed of lightning drew forth a rotten egg from
each, which with equal celerity he hurled at the head of his
master, declaring, as he did so, " I will never make an apology to such a *hemming thing*." The first shot took full effect,
striking dominie full on the *os frontis*, while the stinking
contents of the effective missile filled both his eyes, and prevented the infliction of the intended chastisement. Lady

page 15

Bolio, alarmed, rung the bell violently for help, and, with the assistance of two or three servants, the refractory youth was consigned to the place of solitary confinement. The means by which he managed to escape the other parts of his sentence will, with other grave matters, be given in the following chapter.

CHAPTER II.

"His conduct discovered nothing but the violences of youth and obstinacy. He seemed to be equally haughty and indolent. Nobody knew his real character; he did not even know it himself."—*Voltaire's Charles XII.*

OF the power of perseverance to surmount the greatest difficulties, many memorable instances are on record. My reader may have in his recollection the case of De Latude and his companion, D' Alegre, whose wonderful escape from the Bastille in 1756 is so notorious :—if such should be the fact, no surprise will exist in their minds that Master Claudius Bolio, prompted by the same love of liberty, should resolve upon ceasing to be a captive with all possible speed.

No sooner was the door of his prison fastened upon him than the active energies of his mind came into full play to find out some means of escape. The only window in the apartment, which was a large one, was so well secured by iron bars as to forbid all hope of egress in that direction. Every pannel in the heavy wainscoting was carefully examined in the forlorn hope of discovering a secret spring, but in vain The lock of the door was next inspected, but, as it was a mortised one, and he possessing no implements with which to pick it, he was obliged to give up his last faint expectation of leaving his cage that way. One only pathway to freedom remained unexplored, and to that his circumstances, and not his will, directed him; this was none other than the self-same way by which the heroes of the Bastille, referred to above, left their unpleasant residence,—the chimney.

Having determined in his own mind, whatever might be the consequence, or by whatever means effected, to leave the place in which he was now held, he waited with feverish impatience the approach of night, when, under the cover of darkness, he might put his determination into execution without being noticed.

Hour after hour passed with fatiguing monotony, when, as the hall clock struck seven, approaching footsteps announced a visitor. Presently the key turned in the wards of the lock, the hinges creaked ominously, the door opened cautiously, and in popped the head of Mr. Ferule, the tutor, as if to reconnoiter the enemy's camp before he ventured to enter. Like a lion held at bay, Claudius scowled upon the man of letters, while his eye flashed fire, and looked a haughty defiance where he should have expressed sorrow. "I have come, Master Bolio," said Mr. Ferule, as he cautiously entered the room, "at the request of your mother, to know if you yet repent you of your intemperate conduct, and are disposed to make a suitable apology for the same, as well as promise never again to be guilty of such disgraceful outrage."

"You may return, Sir," replied the incorrigible culprit, haughtily, "and assure my mother that I will never disgrace my father's name by making professions which I do not feel."

"Consider, Master Claudius," interrupted the tutor, in a conciliatory tone, "consider well what you are doing."

"I have considered," retorted the youth, with more asperity than prudence, "and warn you, Sir, to consider how you provoke me further, or— "

"Well, well, Master Bolio," echoed Mr. Ferule, drawing one foot backward cautiously, "if you are determined to persevere in your course, the effects must fall upon your own head; you thus spurn the affection of your mother, as well as my disposition to forgive your past conduct, and compel us to execute with more rigour than we intended the punishment awarded you. The servant will presently bring your supply for the night, and then you will be left until the morning, to reflect upon your misdoing." So saying, he stepped towards the door, and was in the act of closing it after him when his rash pupil seized a china jug which was half-full of water, and threw it so furiously at the head of the tutor, that, if it had been as well directed as the egg which he discharged in the morning, it would have sent him to the tomb of the Capulets, or some other place of repose; fortunately, however, he only received the contents of the vessel in the form of a shower-bath; the jug struck against the closing door, and was dashed to pieces, while Mr. Ferule made good his retreat. Once more the door was fastened, and Claudius was again left to his solitary cogitations.

What was the precise nature of the report, made and delivered to Lady Bolio, of this fresh instance of her son's violence,
is not known; all that has transpired is, that in half an hour
after the man of letters had hasted dripping-wet from the place
of conflict, a servant entered the prisoner's room with a fresh
supply of bread and water, and bidding him a "good night,
Sir," left him to make his first essay in chimney-climbing.

As all necessary precaution had been exercised to keep our
hero safely in, so he now resorted to all possible means to
keep all intruders out, in order that he might not be deterred
from making preparations for his escape. Two strong bolts,
one above and the other below, favoured him in this particular; and having drawn them with a noiseless care, he proceeded to his task. He was aware that some help would be
necessary to enable him to descend from the gable-end of the
house to the ground, and he therefore commenced the unmak-
ing of his bed, and then taking the cord with which the sacking was laced, he tied them together, and found he possessed
a sufficient number of yards to lower himself beyond danger.
This done, he replaced the bed and bedding in the best way
he could, and sat down until the hour should arrive for him
to commence the execution of his scheme of folly.

Never were hours considered so long before by Claudius.
Time, to him, appeared almost suspended in its flight. At
length the period at which the family usually retired came,
and he heard, with pleasurable emotions, the doors of the
several chambers close one after another, until all was quiet
as the grave. Having fastened one end of the cord to one of
his legs, that his hands might be left free, he commenced his
sooty expedition. After incredible labour, and almost suffocated by heaps of condensed smoke through which he groped
his way, he felt the sweet refreshing air of heaven play about
his temples. Scarcely breathing for fear of detection, he
stepped upon the roof of the house, and having drawn up his
cord, fastened it carefully round the chimney from which he
had emerged, and commenced sliding down the steep declivity,
rendering the rope through his hands as he gently descended.
Nature seemed to be in conceit with young Bolio's design;
for, as if to aid him in his rambling propensities, the wind
blew with loud and gusty violence, so that any little noise
which his progress over the tiles might have occasioned, was
completely lost amidst the noise of the elements.

All went on well for the first five minutes, when an unex-

pected accident occurred which threatened to prove fatal to
his life as well as to his project.   The knot which he had
made when uniting the two cords gave way, and he flew down
the remaining portion of the inclined plane with a rapidity
such as scarcely any power of steam could have accelerated,
and, like a flying imp of darkness, descended to the ground.
A loud shriek, and a brief·prayer, the latter uttered with evident fervour, roused Claudius from partial stupor ; but, without waiting to learn whence the unexpected sounds proceeded,
he jumped upon his feet, and fled through the grounds to a
neighbouring copse, where, seating himself on the trunk of a
fallen tree to recover his breath, he first began to think seriously what course he should now pursue ; and there, for a
few moments, we must leave him in order to account, satis-
factorily, for the sounds which he heard, when, with more
speed than he intended, he left his place of durance vile.

In the family of Lady Bolio, there resided a young lady of
some personal attractions, who filled the important station of
companion to her ladyship.   She was a very Diana in look
and language, so very discreet and timid, so innocent and
bashful, that a look even of doubtful import from one of the
opposite gender confused her beyond expression, while a gentle word, whispered in her ear by a gay visitor at the hall,
crimsoned her face with blushes, and·almost threw her into
hysterics.

Who does not know the jealousy of little minds ?—Who
has not felt its sting ?—Great ones are not always and entirely free from it ; and where this hydra of passion is indulged, whatever may have given it birth, or on whatever
subject exercised, then—

> " Our innocence is not our shield,
> They take offence who have not been offended ;
> They seek our ruin too, who speak us fair,
> And death is often ambush'd in their smiles."

Miss Pinwell, the lady's assistant, was not the first, nor
will she be the last who have experienced this poetry of truth.
There were certain females in the establishment, who, in the
spleen of their natures, had dared to whisper unkind things
of her ladyship's favourite.   They appeared to have learned
from young Hamlet the more effectual method than by speaking plainly out, to stab and slay ; hence, with a

> " head-shake,
> Or by pronouncing of some dubious phrase,
> As, *well we know*,—or, *we could, and if we would*,

Or, *if we list to speak,*—or, *there be, and if there might,*
Or such ambiguous givings out,"

they intimated that she was not quite as cold as ice, or as pure as snow.

It is indeed a fact that Mr. Ferule, the tutor, had been suspected of having made some impression upon the precise Miss Pinwell; but then, it was only suspicion, none had ever seen a glance of the eye or a wooing smile bestowed by her upon him;

" But with such general warrantry of heaven
As purity itself might give."

Now, it certainly was not the business either of Mr. Ferule, or of Miss Pinwell, to enlighten the minds of the establishment on matters of this nature, or *perhaps* they could have done so. It is *possible* they could have unfolded a tale which would have exceeded even the fertile imaginings of the whisperers around them; but the maiden could keep a secret as well as do other things.

On the night that Master Claudius broke from his incarceration, the kind consenting fair one had yielded to the pressing solicitations of Mr. Ferule to meet him in the garden behind the house when the family had retired. How many times before the same favour had been granted, at the same "witching hour," I feel no obligation to decide; on the night in question they did meet, and,

"Oh night of ecstacy, when shall we meet again ? "

Had just escaped the tutor's lips as he pressed the yielding Miss Pinwell to his heart, when Claudius made his rapid descent from the roof of the house, and fell upon them both. The unexpectedness of the visit,—the sombre colour of the visitant,—and their own unmentionable position, gave strength to the superstitious fears of their guilty minds, and they at once concluded that his Satanic majesty had come to claim his own, and bear them away. The lady shrieked with terror, and fainted, while Mr. Ferule falling, or rather, rising upon his knees (for the weight of his unknown pupil had borne him to the earth), prayed earnestly fo pardon and deliverance.

How long Miss Pinwell would have remained a lovely type of inanimate nature, or to what extent Ferule might have lengthened out his orisons, is impossible to say, if a shower of rain had not most opportunely fallen, which speedily roused them from their lethargy.

Miss Pinwell was still seated upon the ground, with her head reclining against Mr. Ferule's bosom, when, opening her languid optics, she looked fearfully round—shuddered, and most piteously exclaimed,—

" Oh Mr. Ferule !"

" Oh Miss Pinwell !" responded the trembling tutor

" What will become of us ?" enquired Miss Pinwell.

" What indeed ?" sighed the quaking gallant.

" Did you see him ?" asked Miss Pinwell.

" Yes, love," answered Ferule, and the teeth chattered in his head as he spoke ;—" I did indeed see him : oh horrible ! and I felt him too," continued the little man; " I fear the blow which I received from his club has broken some of my ribs."

" I fear," observed Miss Pinwell, as Mr. Ferule tenderly raised her from her couchant position,—" I fear I have sadly dirted my gown. If we should be discovered by any of the ill-natured creatures of the house, what would they say ? my character would be lost for ever."

" Yes, sweet," sighed the tutor, mournfully, " we should, dear, be utterly ruined. We had better hasten to our chambers," continued Ferule as he supported the lady towards the door of which they had secured the key. " There," said he, as they stepped in, " that's right. Let not a word escape you, dearest, of this unfortunate adventure. You will be able to manage some excuse concerning your gown, and I'll take care to have the lumbago, or the rheumatics, or contrive to fall from a chair to account for my limping gait, and if *nothing else* makes it known, love, no one will learn our secret."

A fond embrace, and a delicious kiss, closed the eventful interview, and groping their way on their tip-toes,— having taken off their shoes,—they retired to their separate beds.

In the mean time, Claudius, who had recovered his breath, which he had nearly lost by his recent extraordinary exertions, wellnigh lost it entirely by fright. He had occupied his seat only a few minutes when the wind ceased, and he heard, at no great distance from him, the sound of human voices. Not doubting that his escape had been discovered, and that the servants were in pursuit of him, he rose in haste like started game, and ran towards the river, determining rather to plunge into the rapid stream than suffer himself to

be captured. As he approached the margin, he stood a moment to listen;—all was silent again : but as he turned his eyes towards the point whence the sounds had proceeded, he beheld a blazing fire in the distance, and perceived several strange-looking figures seated around it smoking ; while two or three others were exhibiting some singular contortions of body, as if for the amusement of their fellows. The sight—although unable fully to comprehend its meaning—relieved him from a crushing weight of anxiety, while an indefinable sensation took possession of him, like the fluttering of hope, combated by fear ; but in which hope maintained the pre-eminence,—that among this singular body of people he might find an asylum and escape detection.

Influenced by such emotions, he stole, with the caution of a grimalkin when about to spring upon its devoted prey, towards the group, and in a little time perceived it was a camp of gypsies, who were merrily regaling themselves, after the toils of the day, upon what they had levied either from the credulity or carelessness of the villagers around them.

"Hist, hist," said an old wrinkled-faced female, raising herself in a listening attitude, and placing her bony finger upon her skinny lips, while nstantly, as she spoke, the revellers ceased :—"I hear footsieps approaching ; who of our camp is yet absent ?" and as she made the enquiry, she threw her sharp, deep-sunken eyes round the circle.—"Oh, I see," she added, "Cribb has not yet reached our quarters ; he is late to-night ; it is he, I suppose, who is coming."

Scarcely had the wild hag ceased speaking, when a fierce-looking fellow, habited like a tinker, and bearing his kit upon his back, appeared before her.

"May a thousand curses, and a thousand blisters with every curse, seize that old rascal of the rectory yonder," growled out Cribb, as he disengaged his arms from the straps which confined his box to his back, and threw it to the ground.

"What now, Jem ?" enquired the sibyl-looking being who had first spoken,—"has he been crossing us in our business again ?"

"Why yes he has," mutered Jem sulkily, "I had just grabbed as fine a young poker as you ever seed with your eyes, calculating to be sure s how we'd have a rale treat to-night, when up rides the fatblack cove what lives by plunder ;—'Hullo, you feller,' says he, 'what's you arter ?' 'Nothing at all, your honour,' says I.

" ' What is that are, what's your got under that are black apron of yourn there ?' says he, ' I demands to know that.'

" ' Nothing at all,' says I, ' but what I *honestly* calls my own, what I'ze bought and paid for. I'm a reglar onest feller, what does the thing what's right. I never takes nothing of nobody's what a'nt mine. I can seduce a dozen vitnesses to swear as how it's all right.' " I pitched him the gammon hexcellently," continued Jem, " but it was no go; I'm blest if that ere feller ant a knowing cove, for, says he, ' It won't do, I apprehends you,' says he, ' for a waggabond and a thief.' "

" ' Do you ?' says I, ' then I'm blest if I stays ;' and with that, as I thought as how hargument woudn't do no good, I drops the porker and bolts, and clears a wall which Black Coat could not cross with his spavined knacker, and away I scampers as if hunted by a posse of devils; the parson bawling with all his lungs arter me, ' Stop thief.' May I be hung for a thief if I do, thinks I; so what with the darkness which came on, and running hard, I diddled the old scoundrel ; but I was led so confoundedly out of my way, and then was obligated to go so far round to get here for fear of being grabb'd, that it has made me something late."

" Well, well," said one of the party, " misfortunes will happen to the best of men. I have been more fortunate, you see," and he pointed to a large pot which was slung over a good fire. " There," he added, " is mutton enough to last us a couple of days at least, and by that time fortune will send us more—here, drink, my fine fellow ; that's as good a drop of the cratur as if the rascally taxers had been paid duty for it."

" We must shift our quarters," interrupted the sibyl, who had been listening to Jem's harangue, " or may be we shall be moved to quarters we shan't well like. Our course must be towards Ringwood, and to-morrow night we'll meet on the borders of the Forest—now let's to supper, and in the morning at day break we'll strike our tents and away."

In a few minutes two or three large dishes were produced, and a fine quantity of mutton, garnished with various kinds of vegetables of the most seasonable description, sent forth a fragrance which reached Claudius' distended olfactory organs; and as he ad not for several hours past luxuriated upon any thing half so agreeable, his yearning bowels determined him to make friends with the social fraternity before him; and, if they would allow him the honour of membership, become one of their order.

Full of this hastily formed determination, he presented himself to the assembly, and in a few minutes gave them an account of his circumstances and wishes, and was hailed as a lad fit for their community. In a little time he was disencumbered of the dress which he wore, and supplied with one more suitable to the profession he had adopted, and the character he was about to sustain.

Master Bolio had now fairly started into public life. If at the end of one hour his tutor, or even his mother, had met him, the transformed youth could not have been recognised, so completely had he been metamorphosed. His hands and face bore as comely a tawny hue, produced by a decoction of walnut shells, as if the blood of the gypsy race ran in his veins. A straight-haired, matted, carrotty-coloured wig, which was surmounted by a hat minus the greater portion of the brim, the crown of which was fastened in with packthread; his tattered and patched garments fluttered in the breeze, while the apology for shoes which adorned his stocking-less feet, fully came up to the recommendation of a profound Scotch M. D., viz., that shoes worn by children should always be such as would allow the free ingress of water. Thus, equipped with a bellyfull of victuals and the prospect of liberty and novelty before him, he congratulated himself upon his fortunate escape, and on the following morning commenced his peregrinations with his new associates.

CHAPTER III.

" My muse by no means deals in fiction;
She gathers a repertory of facts;
Of course, with some reserve and slight restriction,
But mostly treats of human things and acts :—
        *   *   *   *
Love, intrigue, and fainting—sure there's variety;
Also a seasoning slight of lucubration,
A bird's-eye view, too, of that wild society,
A slight glance thrown on men of every station."
                                DON JUAN.

" THE heart of a woman," says one, " is a sea of kindness, a rich and vast confluence of all that can delight and bless." It would ill accord with the spirit of gratitude for one who has revelled so long and so luxuriously in such a sea to do

other than approve and applaud the declaration. I rather
feel disposed to add, the heart of a *mother* is such a sea,
without soundings or limit; the acts of folly or of crime
which her offspring may perpetrate, appear to open wider
the sluices of affection towards such; while the discipline
which propriety compels her to resort to, wrings from her
heart a pang at every lash.

Such were the feelings of Lady Bolio towards her dear
Claudius. Had the indignity which Mr. Ferule experienced
from him been endured by any other person, it is possible,
nay, 'tis probable the crime would have been passed by with
some slight reprimand; but then there was, or it was believed there was, some womanish feeling, some certain degree
of *penchant* towards the gentlemanly and well-proportioned
little tutor felt by her ladyship; and *therefore* perhaps it
was, rather than a decided wish to punish Claudius, she consented to the execution of the sentence which had been
passed upon him. Gladly would she have remitted the punishment and pardoned the culprit; and hence, in the hope
that matters might have been made up, she requested, as we
have seen, that Mr. Ferule would have the kindness to visit
and make certain overtures to him, the termination of which
treaty proved so disastrous to the tutor.

During the whole of the night her ladyship's rest was disturbed by painful dreams respecting her son and the tutor.
Little did she imagine that her prim waiting-maid had stolen
the warm heart of the little man, neither did she once dream
of the scenes which were transpiring in the vicinity of her
chamber.

At an earlier hour than usual Lady Bolio rang for her attendant. Miss Pinwell at the moment was in a profound
sleep, dreaming over again the circumstances of the past
night, with a few horrible additions, or addendas,—such as
being clasped in the arms of the black gentleman—being
carried through the air by a flaming monster—and seeing
Mr. Ferule desert her at a time when nature seemed to press
her claims upon him.

A second, and much more violent pull of the noisy dis-
turber, roused her in confusion; and imagining she was pursuing the faithless Ferule, she leaped from her bed, and
coming in sudden contact with a large swing looking-glass,
she ran her head completely through it, forcing the back
from the frame; and then, while in the act of retreating from

the ruins she had made, overturned a handsome wash-hand-stand; in a moment the room was deluged with water, and covered with the fragments of a rich hand-bason and ewer, together with a variety of *et-ceteras* usually appended to a toilet for female embellishment.

The loud crash, and the cold water in which she stood, completely waked her. The first thing which met her extended vision was the gown which she had worn on the preceding night. Instantly she resolved to make some advantage of the disaster which had befallen her; and therefore, taking the wet and soiled garment in her hand, she saturated it perfectly in the stream which flowed around her, so as to make it appear that the accident which had just occurred had reduced it to its dirty condition.

Miss Pinwell had scarcely completed her task, although but the work of a minute, before two or three servants were at her door enquiring the cause of the unusual noise they had heard; while Lady Bolio, who slept in an adjoining chamber, almost fainted with alarm. The unfortunate waiting-woman, having thrown a dressing-gown round her person, opened the door of her room, and exhibited such a scene to the crowding servants as the genius of destruction might have gloried at the sight of.

"Dear me, Miss Pinwell," cried the housemaid, "whoever has you had with you in your bed-room, to make all this *defusion* and *construction?* I declares I never seed such dreadful ruination in all my born days!"

"Ruination indeed," echoed the cook, "the fat is all in the fire, sure enough, somebody must have done it, that's certain,"—and she peered round the bed-curtains as she spoke, and stooped to examine if any one had been secreted under the bed.

Miss Pinwell bore the gibes of the servants with considerable temper for some time; at length insinuations of some one being in her room, roused her to self-defence :—injured *innocence* demanded a reply, and she exclaimed—

"Your cruel and wicked hints I can bear no longer. I tell you a mere accident of my own has occasioned the disaster. What part of my conduct has given you license to attack my reputation? My lady shall be informed of it, I assure you, and either you or myself shall leave the house."

"Oh, as for that," replied the housemaid, "I am *sartin* no one has *detected* your reputation. I know who will have to clear away messes; and I will say that all these 'ere things couldn't have ruinated themselves."

"Bless me," cried the cook, in mock sympathy, as she caught up Miss Pinwell's gown, "how sorry I am to see this sweet gown in such a condition; why positively it is quite spoil'd."

Miss Pinwell, as the garment was exhibited, looked like a murderer gazing on the blood-stained dress of his victim,— "very pale." The female inquisitors, mistaking her confusion for vexation at the loss of her gown, changed their tone to those of real condolence.

"It is a sad accident," observed the cook, "but grieving won't make it better, that's quite clear."

"To be sure it won't," echoed the housemaid, "I dare say, if it is well got up, it will not look much the worse. If you will allow me, Miss Pinwell, I will wash it out with a few of my things this morning, and soon make all right."

Miss Pinwell felt happy at the offer, promised some remuneration, and, as the servants retired, hasted to assist her lady to dress.

A few words of explanation satisfied Lady Bolio concerning the accident, while her vivid imagination depicted so plainly the ludicrous position in which Miss Pinwell must have stood, amidst the ruin she had made, that her alarm was succeeded by titillation, and she presently became convulsed with laughter. Miss Pinwell felt no objection to the affair so terminating, and in a short time she recovered her usual equanimity of spirits, and finished her attiring task with adroitness.

Lady Bolio descended to the breakfast-parlour, and felt increasing anxiety to know how Claudius had passed the night. She had not finished her first cup of coffee, when she gave orders that Mr. Ferule might be requested to attend her. In a few minutes the servant returned with the woeful intelligence that Mr. Ferule had not yet risen.

"Not yet risen!" exclaimed Lady Boho, in evident alarm, "how is that?" she enquired, "it is much past his usual hour of rising, is it not?"

"Yes, my lady, two or three hours at least," replied the servant, "but John, my lady, who has been up to him with your ladyship's message, says he was roaring like a bull with pain; he 'as got the, the,—I forgets what John called it, my lady, it was something like *tobago*."

"Lumbago, I suppose you mean," observed Lady Bolio pettishly.

"Yes, my lady, that is it, sure enough; but he said as your ladyship wanted him, he would be down directly."

"By no means," replied her ladyship, "poor dear man; run, Betty, run instantly, and tell him not to disturb himself, tell him I'll despatch a messenger for Doctor Leachum immediately. So worthy a man shall have all the attention he deserves." Betty curtseyed and flew to do her mistress' bidding, while the lady herself soliloquised most pathetically.

"Dear man,—surely such devoted, disinterested, and indefatigable services as Mr. Ferule has lavished upon my family, demand all the attention I can give to him. If it were not that a *few* years of difference existed in our ages I should be jealous of myself, and fancy my warm feelings towards that worthy man were of too tender a nature. But no, no, that is impossible; my own respectability and title forbid,— and yet he is highly respectable too; and as for ages, why a *few* years,—some fifteen or twenty, or so,—but what am I thinking of,—poor dear man, mine is pure Platonic regard, I feel it is—nothing beyond that, I am certain. Bless me, how long the servants are; I fear he is worse,—surely nothing serious, *very* serious, has happened. Where can they stay?"

Her ladyship's feelings were something more than platonically excited. She rose from her chair, walked across the room, and looked out of the window without seeing any thing; and, as the servant opened the door, enquired—"Well, Betty, have you delivered my message?—Is he better?— Does he wish to have the doctor sent for?—You desired him not to get up, did you?"

"Yes, my lady,—No, my lady,—Yes,—No,"—issued from Betty's lips in reply to the several questions proposed by her ladyship.

"Well," said the lady, "what am I to understand?—Is he better?—will he have medical advice?—Is he still in pain? —Will he continue in bed? Answer me distinctly and directly. How long am I to wait for an answer?"

"Yes,—No,—Yes,—No,"—reiterated Betty, again replying to the several questions categorically. "He will be here directly, my lady; he was half dressed when I went to him— that is, when I carried your last message. Nothing, he said, should confine him when your ladyship desired his attendance."

The latter part of Betty's speech was like pouring oil upon a flame, or placing a lighted match to a train. The Platonic passion of her ladyship felt its influence, and she almost unconsciously exclaimed, " Dear, kind man!" and then, after a moment's pause, a significant motion of the head was a signal for Betty to make herself scarce, and she, upon the token being given, vanished.

" Heigho!" sighed her ladyship, as she threw herself upon the sofa, " it is surely a great misfortune to be so excessively sympathetic as I am; and yet it would be the climax of insensibility not to feel for one so devoted to the interests of my family as Mr. Ferule is." She rose, stood before a huge mirror which covered the chimney-front, and, quite unconscious of what she was doing, arranged her head-dress, adjusted a straggling curl, and surveyed with something like complacency her face, and exclaimed pathetically—" Can it indeed be true that I am turned of sixty years of age?"

Once more she threw herself upon the sofa, as if entangled in a labyrinth of thought, from which she half wished, half feared, to be extricated.

" Oh, the bliss, the pain of feeling!" had scarce been uttered by her, when a gentle tap, tap, tap, at the door suffused her face with a crimson hue, and scarcely left her power to articulate, " Come in."

The door was opened, and in came,—not, as Lady Bolio had expected and desired, Mr. Ferule, but John the footman.

" Well, Sir," said her ladyship sharply, " what may your business be?"

" Mr. Ferule, your ladyship, sends his respects," replied John, " and wishes to know when he shall wait upon your ladyship."

" Oh, tell him, John," replied the lady in a softer tone, " I am waiting for him."

John bowed, the lady eased her labouring bosom by a profound sigh, and Mr. Ferule, limping most admirably, and holding his left hand to his back, entered the room. Lady Bolio rose to receive him, and so much was she carried away by excessive sympathy and Platonic regard, as scarcely to know what she did. With astounding tenderness both of look and action, which her high esteem for him prompted, she led him to the sofa, and begged he would be seated. Mr. Ferule felt it his duty to obey, and, uttering a well-expressed and lengthened sigh, accompanied by the exclamation of "Oh, my back," he took his seat accordingly.

All the agitation which the Tutor displayed was not assumed, he really did tremble from head to foot, fearing, as he had some reason to do, that thé unusually early summons which he had received, was only the prelude to something much more unpleasant in reference. to the preceding night. He knew himself guilty, and believed that every person who looked at him knew him to be so too, and therefore he expected a severe lecture, and an instant dismissal from her ladyship's service.

After a moment's pause, and one or two well-managed contortions of the face, he observed, "Your ladyship has some commands for me, I believe."

"Yes," replied Lady Bolio, "I wished to see you particularly"—Ferule trembled. " I have been disturbed the whole of the past night by distracting feelings."

" I assure your ladyship," interrupted Ferule, " I am sorry to hear it, and feel ashamed beyond what I can express that—"

"I know, Mr. Ferule," observed her ladyship soothingly, "your willingness to form excuses for every one; I do not blame you."

"Madam," interrupted the excited Tutor, "allow me to offer an apology, at least by way of extenuation of the circumstance."

"No, no," rejoined Lady Bolio, "none, I am sure, is required. My son's disobedience required harsh treatment."

"Your son, my lady," exclaimed Ferule, forgetting at the moment his pupil's imprisonment, his whole thought running upon his *liaison* with Miss Pinwell; instantly however he hit the right scent, and, in the deliverance which his agitated mind experienced, almost forgot his attack of lumbago.

"You are very, very kind, Mr. Ferule," observed her ladyship, who laboured under another kind of mistake, " to make excuses for him."

"Why, you know, my lady," rejoined Ferule, with inward exultation, "that my high regard for Master Claudius will not allow me to do otherwise; although I fear I have received my present pain in consequence of the severe wetting which he gave me."

"No doubt," said her ladyship, "you have. Let me send

for the doctor, I insist upon it. The consequences may otherwise be serious, and I should never forgive myself."

Ferule trembled more than ever, lest, if the doctor should come, the part he complained of might be examined, and the bruise which he bore upon his side and back might lead to some unwelcome enquiries and awkward exposé.

"I assure your ladyship," replied the little man, "I find myself better even already, and make no doubt another *good* night's rest will perfectly restore me. I feel your kindness, my lady, and hope to be grateful for it."

Lady Bolio expressed her warm wishes that his expectations might be realized, and then enquired if he felt himself equal to the task of visiting her son, concerning whom she declared she felt unusually anxious. As the Tutor was now considerably recovered, and improved every minute, he expressed his readiness t) repair instantly to the place of incarceration.

"If," said Lady Bolio, "you do not think it will be too much for you, I shall feel obliged beyond expression if you will once more attempt to convince Claudius of the impropriety of his conduct."

Mr. Ferule assured her ladyship he would attend to her wishes with the greatest pleasure, and making a profounder bow than usual to the sympathetic lady, he left the room.

With more agility than could have reasonably been expected, the Tutor ascended to the apartment which had been made Master Bolio's prison. The good favour in which he felt assured he now stood with the mother determined him to display his authority with the son; and making one or two loud "hems" as he approached the room,—with the double purpose of raising his own spirit and preparing his pupil for a respectful reception,—he knocked gently, and then louder, at the door, but receiving no reply to his announcement, he threw a little more physical energy into his exertions to obtain a hearing, but with no better success. Supposing Claudius to be fast asleep, he turned the key, and the handle of the lock, for the purpose of opening the door, but felt increasing surprise that entrance was prohibited. He applied his eye to the key-hole, but could not see any thing. "Master Claudius!" he shouted through the same aperture, but neither echo nor reply met his listening ear.

After spending nearly a quarter of an hour in unsuccess-

ful attempts to obtain entrance, he returned to Lady Bolio
to report progress.

"I fear, Madam," said Ferule as he re-entered the parlour,
"Master Claudius is as stubborn as ever; he will neither
open the door to me, nor condescend to reply to my
calls."

"Indeed!" ejaculated Lady Bolio with surprise and alarm,
"It is very strange!" and after a moment's pause she added,
"Then take my authority, Mr. Ferule, and employ such
means as your good sense will suggest to obtain an entrance.
This renewed act of disrespect towards you, sir, shall meet
its reward;—the ungrateful boy!"

The coachman, groom, and gardener, were immediately
summoned; and, headed by the gallant Tutor as commander
in chief of the "*force*," they entered the garden, and raising
a ladder to the window of the prison room, Mr. Ferule ascended half a dozen rounds for the purpose of examining the
apartment, or gaining an entrance that way; but his head
turned giddy, and he was obliged, although unwillingly, to
descend, and allow the gardener to take his place.

"Well, Robert, do you see Master Claudius?" cried Ferule, as the gardener peeped through the window.

"No, Sir; nothing like him," replied Robert.

"Open the sash, then," said the Tutor, "and get into the
room."

"I can't, Sir," rejoined the gardener, "the window is fast
enough inside, and, if it wasn't, I should not be able to
squeeze myself between the bars."

"Come down, then," directed Mr. Ferule, "we must contrive to force an entrance at some other point."

Robert accordingly descended, and having provided themselves with sufficient apparatus, they approached the door of
the chamber, and Mr. Ferule, in the name of Lady Bolio,
called upon Master Claudius to surrender, with a promise of
a full pardon upon so doing. Three distinct proclamations
were made, but no answer being returned, the Tutor declared
he could hold out capitulations no longer, and gave orders
to his "*force*" to lay siege to the place.

After considerably more labour than was expected, the as-
sallants succeeded in forcing the door from its hinges, and
forcing their bodies into the room. Ferule was the last who
entered, fearing as he did the discharge of some deadly missile at his head. But who may presume to describe the con-

sternation of the party, when, after the most diligent search, no traces of the sought-for person could be found?

It was evident that he could not have made his exit by the way of the door or window, and as the chimney was the only remaining opening from the prison to liberty, it was unanimously agreed that by it he had managed to escape. The *"force"* instantly adjourned to the garden, when from the place on which Mr. Ferule and Miss Pinwell had been so supernaturally visited, the remaining portion of the sacking cord was seen dangling from the chimney round which Claudius had placed it, and

> " Confirmation, clear as holy writ,"

was afforded of the fact, that by that way he had managed to elude the vigilance of his gaoler.

The sight of the cord occasioned an instant recussitation of hurried thoughts in the mind of Ferule, and the conviction flashed like lightning through him, of the character of the fiend by whom he had been so terribly alarmed. Cheering himself with the hope that he had not been discovered by the flying imp, he determined to keep his own secret, and not to discover himself.

The mournful intelligence was instantly carried by the Tutor to Lady Bolio, who scarcely heard the tidings out before she fell into the arms of Mr. Ferule, deprived of all consciousness. Whether in his confusion he forgot to ring the bell for help, or whether the agitated state of his nerves deprived him of the power, is immaterial—ring he did not, but staggered with his heavy burden to the sofa, upon which he carefully deposited it, and then resorted to such means as were within his reach, or that appeared likely to restore her.

He was leaning over her ladyship with considerable solicitude, and tenderly chafing her temples, when, opening her eyes and seizing his hand in the excitement of the moment, she exclaimed, " O Mr. Ferule, what will become of me ? my peace and happiness are destroyed for ever !"

Whether the fates were envious of the Tutor's situation, or it was decreed in his horoscope that he should be crossed in love, I know not; but just at the highly dramatic instant referred to, Miss Pinwell, who was yet ignorant of Claudius's escape, entered the apartment ; and seeing Mr. Ferule in such an attitude, and hearing Lady Bolio express herself in such ambiguous terms, her own condition of the preceding night was remembered; and the dark suspicion entered her mind that a similar scene had just been exhibited between Ferule and her ladyship.

The terrible rage of woman's jealousy instantly took possession of her, and flashed with fire from her eye, and burst in passion from her lips.

" So! Mr. Ferule," she exclaimed, grasping hold of the neck of the little man as she spoke, " thus it is you fulfil your vows of constancy to me; thus it is you reward me for the favour I granted you last night; but I'll be revenged on you for it, cost me what it may."

" Miss Pin—well," squeeked out the Tutor, " let go my throat, and I'll satisfy you."

" Don't *Miss* me !" cried the enraged girl ; " I have caught you in the fact."

" What does all this mean, Mr. Ferule?" enquired Lady Bolio, raising herself up. Mr. Ferule was waxing black in the face, for Miss Pinwell had pinned him as fast as if he had been held in a vice; and, therefore, instead of attending to her ladyship's interrogation, he was twisting and kicking to extricate himself from the placid Miss Pinwell's hold. Having succeeded, he seated himself, or rather sunk down, upon the sofa; while Miss Pinwell turned, in true virago style, upon her ladyship.

Now Lady Bolio felt conscious that her Platonic regard for Mr. Ferule was of rather a violent kind ; and fearing that she had unconsciously committed herself, she hesitated to call for help lest some disclosure should take place, so that Miss Pinwell kept almost undisputed possession of the field.

" I heard the whole of it," screamed the waiting-maid, addressing her ladyship ; " What will become of you indeed?—a lady at *your time* of life talking to a *young* man like Mr. Ferule,—monstrous! But he has engaged himself to me; I hold his vows and promises in his own hand-writing ; he knows I do."

" Miss Pinwell," cried poor Ferule, once more gaining his breath, and hoping to soothe his fair inamorato to calmness.

" Oh! you faithless seducer," shouted Miss Pinwell; " you vile, false deceiver ! is it not sufficient you have ruined me, but you will now desert me too ?"

" Dear Mr. Ferule," said her ladyship, turning to him for an explanation,—" what do I hear ? Do, I entreat you, give me an instant explanation."

" Yes; *dear* indeed!" reiterated Miss Pinwell.

" I will explain all to your ladyship," replied Mr. Ferule.
" Be calm," he added : "Miss Pinwell you do me wrong—
upon my honour you do, and mistake me."

" I have indeed *mistaken* you," rejoined Miss Pinwell;
" but I do you no wrong—think of my reputation and then
talk of wrong—and now thus basely to desert me!—oh!
oh! oh!" sobbed out Miss Pinwell, and sunk upon the floor
in a fainting fit.

All the burning love of Ferule rose up instantly to the
highest pressure; and regardless of the presence of Lady
Bolio, forgetful of his lumbago, and fearless of all discovery,
he ran to the assistance of his prostrate lady-love.

" Mr. Ferule, Mr. Ferule," shouted Lady Bolio, " what
are you doing?" The agitated Tutor appeared not to hear
her ladyship's address, so intent was he upon the condition
of the fainting fair one.

" My dear Miss Pinwell," cried Ferule, in the tenderest
tones, " be composed; I swear never to desert you."

" Heyday! Sir," cried Lady Bolio, " these are fine expressions truly; surely it is not *all* true that the girl has said
—you surely cannot love a *waiting-maid.*"

By this time Mr. Ferule had raised Miss Pinwell from the
floor, and was supporting her on one knee. He turned his
eye upon her ladyship as she addressed him; and although he
uttered not a word, he looked to the life the sentimental stanza
of Hudibras :—

> " Lady, to bid me not to love,
> Is to forbid my pulse to move ;
> My beard to grow, my ears to prick up,
> Or when I'm in the fit, to hiccup."

Her ladyship seemed to understand the look; for her strong
Platonic affection veered round instantly to stoical antipathy;
and in the sublimity of her spleen she acquainted Ferule, with
all befitting dignity of tone and action, she should not any
longer require his services in her family; and then turning
to the reviving Miss Pinwell, observed, " I cannot retain in
my establishment a person who, by her own confession, has
disgraced it." These small matters being settled, all the
strength of her affection rushed towards her dear lost Claudius, and she directed immediately that the servants should
take horses and ride in different directions in search of the
fugitive.

CHAPTER IV.

"And thrice the Sibyl cross'd her hand,
And utter'd thrice a groan;
And thrice with speech of foreign land
Invok'd some power unknown."

SCOTT.

WHILE these important events were transpiring at the Hall, Claudius was receiving lessons from learned masters in the art and mystery of fortune-telling, and other slight embellishments connected with the craft. After a fortnight's drilling he was considered sufficiently instructed to undertake a tour, in company with an elder of the fraternity.

It is worthy an observation, *en passant*, as illustrative of this part of our history, that the whole gypsy community moves as regularly as the planetary system. Each company has its given limits and engagements, while an established and effective correspondence is carried on by the agency of individuals 'ycleped "modern mercuries," or swift-footed messengers; so that a work which requires the assistance of numbers, or any information which will facilitate enterprise, is supplied with a promptitude which nothing but systematic order could possibly accomplish. With the view of escaping discovery, or prevent, in general, detection, they assume every kind of garb, and take up with almost every profession. By this means, too, they become possessed of such extensive information as empowers them to exercise their arts upon the superstitious, and enables them to defraud the unwary. None, in fact, but those who have been regularly initiated, can fully comprehend their *manœuvres,* or understand the cabalistic jargon they adopt.

During the expedition upon which Claudius and his gypsy companion were despatched, comprehending the western division of Hampshire, an opportunity was furnished for our hero to display his precocious talents.

The fair complexion of Claudius gave to his dyed skin the appearance of a good-looking brunette, and enabled him, without fear of detection, to don the female garb. A chip hat hanging carelessly on one side of his head, beneath which hung raven-coloured hair in rich profusion, gave an archness to his appearance which could scarce fail to attract attention. His figure, which was tall and slender, was enveloped in a

c 2

faded plaid cloak, while upon his arm dangled a basket of light manufacture, containing threads, tapes, stay-laces, and numerous other *et-ceteras.*

He had not proceeded far into Andover,—his female companion having arranged to meet him on the opposite side,—before he attracted the notice of a fashionably dressed female. In a moment Claudius's quick eye met those of the young lady's—a significant glance, well understood by the assumed gypsy girl, drew him from the public street into a lane on the back side of the town.

" Can you," enquired the female, " satisfy my enquiring mind respecting an engagement into which I wish to enter ? if so, I will reward you for your pains."

Claudius, in strict accordance with the mystery of his profession, gazed for a few seconds in speechless attention upon her, as if his penetrating glance would pierce the fleshly substance which appeared before him, and read the wishes of her soul : and then replied with measured emphasis,—

" Lady, I can."   By the trepidation she manifested he at once perceived she was either in fear of being discovered, or in excessive haste ; the former he considered the most probable, and with provoking deliberation added :—" Our present place of meeting, Lady, at this hour, is not convenient. You judge rightly that we may be surprised. You have watchers about you—meet me here to-morrow, one hour after sun-set ; I will then inform you concerning him you wish to know, and of the fate which awaits you respecting another. Be punctual and be silent ; much that regards yourself in the future depends on it."

" I will," replied the female, awed by the solemnity of tone which Claudius assumed. " Take this," she added, putting a broad piece of silver into his hand, " as an earnest of what you may expect."

Claudius dropped a well-managed curtsey to the fair donor, and then, dropping the coin into his pocket, bade her " good night ;" and, at the same time, assuming the appearance of careless indifference, sauntered slowly away. He took good care, however, not to allow the maiden to escape his concealed leer, but followed her retreating steps until he saw her enter a well-built house at the upper end of the town. Having so done, he hasted to join his companion, and weave a web in which to catch the fluttering moth which had now thrown herself in his way.

" Follow me, Prycat," whispered Claudius to his associate the moment he met her; " I have tidings to communicate, and want your assistance."

Having drawn her from observation, he informed the practised hag in a few words of his interview with the female, and the engagement he had made.

" And what," enquired Prycat, " do you intend to make of this ?"

" All I can," replied Claudius.

"And that *all*," retorted the gypsy, " will make a slender supper for a hungry man, I judge. Why did you delay your business until to-morrow? no time is like the present; she may change her mind."

" I have no fear of that," answered Claudius; " and why I delayed the business was because I wished to obtain information."

"Pshaw !" exclaimed Prycat, wishful to exercise our hero in his business, "how is that to be got at here, where we are entire strangers ?"

"So much the better that we are strangers," answered Claudius, "we shall be the less suspected. I must for a few hours change my dress, and to-night, while I entertain the company of a public-house, which I perceived was only a few doors from the lady's residence, I will obtain such news of herself and family as will serve my purpose."

"Good !" said the sibyl, "well spoken and better planned. In the mean time I will take care to glean up such matters, from the servants and others, as shall secure you success; manage this affair well, and your character will be established."

In less than five minutes, the lady Claudius had just left would not have known him. Beneath his female attire he wore his own masculine habit; his black wig was superseded by a red one, and an old black hat, which was concealed by the article which he carried in his basket, crowned the whole of his dress. Part of his thrown-off garments were added to those his companion wore, while the remainder were stowed away in the basket, which was now taken charge of by the old gipsy.

Thus equipped, as the day closed in, Claudius entered the tap-room of the public-house, and after performing a number of tricks for the amusement of those who were present, he accepted the invitation of a half-intoxicated loquacious barber, to share his pint with him; to this he good-naturedly consented, and soon engaged him in a conversation which reached the top of his expectation.

"I judge," observed Claudius, "your trade flourishes in Andover, or else you are a master at your business."

"Why, as to trade," replied the Barber, "we need not complain; hair you know will grow, and beards will thrive; and as to my abilities, why, though I, Jem Frizzle, says it, I can turn a *raser*, handle a pair of *sissers*, and dress a lady's front with any chap in the trade. Why it was only an hour ago I was sent for to dress the hair of the first lady in our town, the beautiful Miss Winkle, the daughter of a retired Banker, at the large house just above us, with the large lamp before the door."

"Indeed!" said Claudius, gratified with the information, and hoping to obtain more as this was the very house into which he had seen his applicant enter,—"a little girl of the Banker's, I suppose?" he added.

"No such thing, I suppose," rejoined Frizzle, "a fine young lady, I assures you, and on the *pint* of marriage,—no, there I am wrong, they wishes her, that is, her old mother does, to marry an old *feller* with scarce a smasher in his head, a Mr. ——, I forgets his name just now, he keeps one of these here *notorious* gaming-houses in *Lunnun*, where the flats are cotched by the sharps—Mr.——"

"No matter what his name is," said Claudius with apparent carelessness, although at the same time wishing most fervently that he might remember it, "all names are alike to me you know, as I am a stranger here."

"I have it," said the Barber, slapping the table, "by gosh I have,—Raggett,—aye, that is it; well, as I was a saying, because he has got plenty of blunt the old woman wishes Miss Maria, who is a very angel of sixteen or so, to marry him; but as I hears she is desperately in love with her cousin Charley Mansfield, a substantial young farmer, and determines, that is, if she can, to marry him; how the affair will end, I can't tell of course,—but our pot is out, shall we fill it again, my fine chap, eh?"

Our hero was so full of the information he had received, which was so directly to his purpose, that he declined drinking any longer with the Barber, and making an excuse that he had another call to make, he wished Frizzle good-night, and went to the meeting place of his companion.

As soon as Prycat was informed by Claudius of his success, she protested most solemnly, that if he continued thus
to display ability in his business, he would soon be placed at
the top of his profession.

"Let me give you one word of advice," observed the wily
beldame, "before you finish the young lady's fortune, let her
cross your hand with the king's picture; you understand?"

"Let me alone for that," interrupted Claudius, "a prime
minister, even, will not perform an act of duty without his
fee, nor a lawyer advise his client without a tip; I'll see to it,
that the important information I am to communicate shall be
paid for."

True as music, Claudius, habited in his female toggery,
attended at the place of assignation on the following evening,
at the time appointed; but the lady, who was a great reader
of Walter Scott, borne away by the excitement of his fascinating tales, and her own anxieties, felt all the magnanimity
of the heroine glowing in her bosom, and, wishful to know
the hidden will of fate, had preceded the being from whose
lips she was in expectation of learning her future destiny.

"So, lady," observed Claudius as he approached her, "you
are anxious, it would appear, to know what awaits you in the
future, and well you may; another, placed in Miss Winkle's
condition, would not feel less."

"Miss Winkle!" exclaimed the lady in a suppressed tone,
but under strong excitement, "am I then known by you?"

"Known!" rejoined Claudius, "ah, ah! if I could not
tell your name, lady, how would it be possible, suppose you,
I should inform you of the names of other persons?"

"Others!" echoed Miss Winkle. The moon at this moment broke in brightness from behind a cloud, and its clear
light fell upon the lady, discovering to Claudius the agitation under which she laboured.

"You wish to consult me," observed the fortune-teller.

"I do," answered the maiden faintly.

"Give me your right hand, lady," said he.

Trembling with excitement, but without hesitating, she
drew off her glove at his bidding and presented her palm.

"I perceive," observed Claudius, after examining most
carefully the soft white hand which he held, "I perceive
various configurations here, which assure me your mind is
disturbed by certain matters of a momentous kind, involving
your future happiness and prosperity. Here are lines which

point to age and riches, by the side of which I behold the letter R, faintly developed."

"Gracious heavens!" exclaimed the trembling girl, "what will become of me?"

"Be calm, lady, be calm," observed Claudius solemnly, "or I cannot proceed."

"I will, I will," said Miss Winkle, "let me know all."

"You have a mother living, I perceive, and if I understand the occult sciences," said the assumed gipsy girl, "she is no idle spectator in an affair of love, and the Fates decree that you should marry."

"Do they indeed?" sighed Miss Winkle most piteously.

"They do," replied Claudius, "but is there in marriage any thing so very objectionable as to alarm you?"

"Oh, no—no," replied the maiden, "not in marriage,—no, no, but—"

"Take courage, lady, take courage," said Claudius soothingly, "cross my hand with a piece of money; I perceive I have good news yet for you."

With as much cheerfulness and haste as if the purchase of a full remission of the sentence of death was about to be made, Miss Winkle drew her purse string, and a shining half-sovereign was placed in the palm of the fortune-teller's hand. The lady's confidence in the art of palmistry was hereby fully proved, and Claudius felt bound and encouraged to proceed.

"These concave lines," said he, "denote sorrow and conflict,—a crooked path, but safe termination; sorrow at the commencement, but joy in the sequel. You are beloved, fair lady, by one who is equally attached to you,—bound too, as I see, by ties of blood,—vows have been interchanged, lady—tokens have been given and received—have you not a liking for agriculture?"

"Why do you ask me *such* a question?" enquired the blushing, trembling girl.

"Because I perceive," replied Claudius, "by these blue veins, crossed at the top by lines which intersect at right-angles, ploughs, harrows, reap-hooks. Here too is a fine young man of fair complexion and manly figure; the letter M is clear and bold, half-concealing, and yet firmly uniting with W; you are to be a happy bride soon, the mother of many children, and to be united to the man of your heart."

Nothing in the world could be plainer than that the fortune-teller knew all about it, and no predictions could have been half so pleasing to Miss Maria Winkle as those to which she had just listened. She could ill conceal the extacy of her heart, and nearly fainted with rapture. Putting another half-sovereign into the learned woman's hand, she wished her " good night," and with the lightness of a sylph, and the fleetness of a fawn, she bounded to her home, determining, mentally, that, as it was ordained by fate she should be wed to her cousin Mansfield, no promises, persuasions, or persecutions, should induce her to become the wife of an old, decrepit, toothless gambler.

The uncommon success of our hero in this his first essay, raised him considerably in the estimation of the fraternity, so that when next they met, which was at the end of another week on the borders of the forest, to render an account of their several exploits to their head or captain, he received the most flattering encomiums that functionary could bestow.

Jealousy is not confined to the cabinets of princes or the drawing-rooms of dowagers. It rages with equal violence, and proceeds from the same source,—pride, or self-esteem,— among all ranks and in all societies. Even here, in the Gipsy camp, it had obtained a footing, and issued in consequences which none could foresee.

The high estimation to which Claudius had risen in so short a time offended one of the party, who considered that his deeds had been overlooked or underrated, and judging that the growing popularity of his young rival would continue to throw him deeper into shade, he determined to devise some plan, by which, either to remove him from the camp, or sink him in the estimation of the community. An occasion soon occurred which enabled him to put into execution his dastardly design.

At a distance of something more than three miles from the encampment was an extensive farm, the occupier of which had, on more than one occasion, set some of the body right in reference to trifling mistakes they had made respecting certain property, such as a strayed sheep, a little poultry, or provender for a horse, by calling in the eloquence of an official of the law to convince them that the inclosures they had entered were parts and parcels of the farm which he rented.

A few nights only had passed since Philip M'Sheen, alias Slipgibbet Phil, had been most unceremoniously ejected from the said farm-yard, after being well soused in the horse-pond, simply for attempting to stop the quacking of a duck which had by some accident fallen into one of the pockets of his coat, and then, poking his head therefrom, sent forth such discordant sounds as greatly to disturb the taste of his musical ear.

It 'now occurred to Slipgibbet, that this indignity would furnish a fine opportunity to him, to accomplish a two-fold object, namely, to avenge himself upon the farmer and ruin his rival. He was as crafty as he was depraved, and had already learned, that while Claudius felt no objection to such freaks as fortune-telling involved, he felt less complaisance in deeds where injury of person or property were associated. It was therefore a settled point in his depraved mind, that should he propose that Claudius should accompany him in his enterprise to the farm, he would object to do so, and by that means he might be able to charge him with cowardice, and so sink him in the estimation of his fellows, or, should he consent to become his partner, he might so arrange it as to involve him in disaster and then leave him to his fate.

Having thus resolved in his mind, and partly matured his plan, he embraced the fittest opportunity to broach his design; that is, when the influence of drink had so far prevailed as to render some of the most ferocious of the party prepared for any act, and more especially a deed of revenge.

" I say," observed Slipgibbet, without addressing himself to any particular person, " are we to pay off the score we owes the gentleman at the farm yonder; or shall we quietly pocket the affront, and suffer him to insult us in our calling with *compunity?* You know," he continued, " it is always a maxim in a good government, that if any foreign power, whatsomever, dares to *moslest* any of its members, instantly to declair war against them, right or wrong. Well now, what I thinks is just this : we is a government; one of your worthy members,—that is myself by course,—has been insulted, and we ought to *taliate*."

Two or three voices roared out at the same time, as the " worthy member" sat down, " Bravo! Slipgibbet, you deserve to be placed at the head of the government for that ere speech."

· "And depend upon it he will be raised," observed a facetious little fellow, " either by having a garter buckled round his leg, or a cord tied round his neck."

" Chafing aside !" growled Slipgibbet. " What say you to my observation ?"

" What do you propose ?" asked an old wrinkled female form.

" What ?" replied Slipgibbet, " why I propose to give fire for water to be sure—they boiled me, and I'd roast them."

As Claudius heard the proposition, he shuddered ;—at the thought of bloodshed and destruction his soul sickened, and for the first time he wished himself away from his companions ; and drew a hasty comparison between the Gypsy camp and his mother's hall. Very slight opposition to the proposal existed among the band; or rather, to the act itself none offered any objection.

" How is it to be accomplished?" enquired one.

" How ?" shouted Slipgibbet; " easy enough I assure you."

" But if we should be discovered," said another.

" Discovered !" roared Phil, " Ah, ah, ah ; have you forgot Sussex, Wiltshire, and Kent?—discovered ! what, after at least a score of illuminations, are we not able to keep our own secret ?—I wouldn't give that," said he, snapping his finger and thumb, " for a coward. Will you," he continued, " leave it to me to do the job ? I only wishes one to assist me in the affair, and by this time to-morrow night the business shall be done."

" It can't be left in better hands," said one who appeared the priestess of the orgie. " Make your selection, Phil, of a companion."

" Are ye all agreed then ?" enquired Slipgibbet.

" All," shouted the clan.

" Then I shall have this chap to go with me," said he, slapping Claudius on the shoulder; " this bout will prove what sort of stuff the young feller is made of, as well as teach him a trick or two more than he knows."

Claudius felt a cold sweat ooze from his forehead as the hand of the Gypsy fell upon him—all power of objection appeared taken from him ;—he determined, however, not to participate in the murderous design which was contemplated, but at any risk to warn the family of its danger, and, if possible, save it and the property from destruction.

The plan proposed by Slipgibbet was to dress himself in the character of a rat-catcher, while Claudius was to act as his servant ; and in that disguise he felt fully confident he should obtain an entrance into some of the barns, and

effect his purpose. Accordingly, on the following day, they
sallied forth from the encampment about two in the afternoon, habited as became their assumed profession; having the
badge of their calling slung round their shoulders, and a
plentiful supply of ferrets confined in a bag, while in one of
similar size they concealed two or three full grown rats, in
order to make sure of catching some at the farm.

Between three and four they reached the devoted place;
and Slipgibbet, in a well assumed Yorkshire dialect, enquired
for the "measter." His unsuspecting victim appeared in a
few minutes; and after the rat-catcher had assured him he
had some of the best ferrets in the country, and offered to
wager the coat on his back that in less than a quarter of an
hour he would produce some "varmint" from any of the barns
he chose to select, an agreement was made, and they entered
one to pursue their work.

Within the time that had been specified, two rats of mon
strous growth were caught in the bags which they carried,
and with these Claudius was despatched to exhibit them to
the farmer as a proof of the skill of his master. This appeared a favourable opportunity for Claudius to put his benevolent design into execution, and he whispered the farmer,
" Sir, you are in danger; the rat-catcher is a Gypsy who
seeks your destruction—I will tell you more presently."

He feared lest if he held long conversation with the farmer,
Slipgibbet might suspect him; he therefore hasted back to
inform him of the farmer's satisfaction; who promised that if
in half an hour's time two more rats as fine as those just
taken were shown to him, a good lunch should be given to
them. This delay answered a double purpose: it gave Slipgibbet time to look about him for a proper place in which to
deposit his combustible matter, as well as afforded the farmer
an opportunity to secure assistance, if necessary, without exciting alarm.

The barn in which they were was so situated, that in consequence of its contiguity to several other buildings, and a
strong current of wind which blew in a favourable direction,
a few seconds only could elapse, after ignition had taken
place, before the whole premises must of necessity be in
flames.

Slipgibbet had already deposited a considerable portion of
phosphorus among a heap of dry straw, beside a large quantity of unthrashed corn, to which was attached a slow match,

of such a length as that several hours would elapse before it was consumed, which he intended to light as he left the place in the evening.

That a man with such terrible purposes in hand should have been sufficiently collected to allow his thoughts to turn to any other subject, demonstrates that he must have possessed nerves of iron stubbornness. Yet so it was; his animal appetite was as strong as his moral propensities were depraved and vicious. Hence the expected supply of strong beer and bread and bacon, which his unsuspecting victim had promised, on the condition that by a certain hour two more rats should be produced, was kept in mind, and at the time appointed his assistant was despatched with the fullgrown vermin which had been caught, not among the farmer's grain, but in the bag that he had brought with him.

With a tremor which our hero's caution could but ill conceal, he retreated from the barn in search of its owner.

"All is prepared, sir," said Claudius, as he presented the rats to the farmer.

"What is prepared?" asked the honest husbandman.

"That, sir," replied Claudius, "which, if allowed to take the intended effect, will, before to-morrow's sun is up, reduce the whole of these premises, and it may be those who inhabit them, to ashes.

"Merciful Providence!" exclaimed the farmer, astounded by the intelligence to which he listened, "what mean you? Speak out instantly, or—"

"Softly, Sir, softly," rejoined Claudius with all the composure he could muster. "If you raise your voice greatly above a whisper all may be discovered, and I shall pay dear for my wish to serve you. Suspicion, Sir, has sharp ears. I tell you," continued the youth, "that unless proper means are employed to prevent it, your house and barns are devoted to fire!"

The announcement seemed to act electrically upon both the body and mind of the farmer. He started, as if a gaping chasm had yawned beneath his feet, and staggering a few paces, saved himself from falling by seizing hold of the wheel of a cart which stood near him.

"How have I deserved this?" he enquired, "what fiend in human form has planned the diabolical scheme? As I hope for mercy, I know not any fellow-being whom I have intentionally wronged, or wantonly injured."

"Do you not remember," enquired Claudius, "a Gypsy,who some few nights since was thrown into your horse-pond?"

"Ah," exclaimed the farmer, as the fact was suddenly brought to his recollection, "I do; and has he determined upon such bloody revenge for the punishment his crimes called for?"

"He has," answered Claudius, "but I have determined to save you. Hush!" he added, laying his hand upon the farmer's arm, as he was about to give utterance to his excited feelings, and leave the place, "remember my caution. I must leave you a while, or he will take alarm and escape, and then some future opportunity will be found to execute his purpose, while some willing associate will further his design. My presence with him will lull all suspicion, and, until we leave, all will be well. You may depend upon me. Have some men ready to assist you, and, when I give you a signal, seize him."

So saying, Claudius hasted with the supply of provision he had received to join the assumed rat-catcher.

"Well done!" shouted Slipgibbet to Claudius as he entered the barn with a can of beer and a good supply of eatables, "but you have been somewhat longer than I expected;" he added, "they were unwilling, I suppose, to part with what they had promised, the greedy curs,—Eh?"

"Not so," replied Claudius, fearing lest his jealous suspicion should take alarm, "but the rats were an object of curiosity. Such handsome grown ones they had never before seen on the premises, and they account you a good hand at your business."

"Ah, ah, ah!" roared Slipgibbet, "do they so? that's right, my boy, and they shall find presently I do understand my business well; and I'll do it properly, I promise them. But let us try the strength of their home-brewed," he added as he seized the can, and, applying it to his mouth, drew a long and deep draught from it. "Why that's not so bad," he observed, slapping his lips; "much better than the muddy water of the horse-pond," he whispered, "but I'll be quits with them, or may a neckcloth of hemp keep my neck warm; fire for water they shall have, with full interest."

Once more he raised the vessel to his lips, and, before he drank, whispered, "Here's success to our plan, and may every man be rewarded as he deserves."

"I am sure it will be no fault of mine if it is not so," observed Claudius; "at least I'll do all I can in the business; and I think the farmer here deserves all he is likely to meet with."

"That's well said," rejoined Slipgibbet, "I like you, my lad, for that; you have more spirit than I ever supposed you had. But a thought has struck me since you left the barn. We had as well I think share in the spoil as let the fire have all: while you amuse yourself with the ferrets in the large barn yonder, I'll run back to the camp, and bring with me a few of our comrades. Say nothing of my absence, and no suspicion will be entertained of my leaving; in an hour's time I will return."

During the time that Claudius had been in conversation with the farmer the fiend-like Gypsy had set light to the slow match, and, by the artful manœuvre which he now proposed, he intended to accomplish two objects. The first was, to draw away his companion from the fire, lest when left alone he should be tempted to extinguish it, and so frustrate his purpose of destruction; and secondly, supposing the fire should not spread to the extent of his wishes, that the whole of the blame might be thrown upon the youth, while himself and his fellows, to whom he purposed offering some excuse for Claudius' absence, might effect their escape.

Bad as our hero's opinion was of Slipgibbet, it was fair and bright as an angel's, compared with his actual character. Still, the proposal he had just made of leaving him for a while occasioned some misgiving in his mind as to his real intention. To allow his suspicions to be perceived by the incendiary, he was aware would destroy his merciful project of saving the farmer and his family, and therefore he pretended eagerly to fall in with the proposed plan; secretly determining, at the same time, to give information to the farmer of the Gypsy's departure.

Having consumed as much of the provision as they felt disposed to eat, they collected their rat-catching paraphernalia together, and walked with it into another barn, from whence, after making some pretended arrangements for future operations, and cautioning Claudius once more against allowing his absence to be known, the artful villain cautiously stole forth, leaving, in intention, his young companion, as a devoted victim to sanguinary jealousy!

CHAPTER V.

"Dost see those fellows ?—Note them well, sweet Coz—
'Tis but in finance, and in paltry garb
That slender disagreement may be trac'd.
In all that forms the *man*, they closely pair.
One robs by legal license, and is hail'd
A holy, just, and honourable man ;
The other has no law to gild his deeds,
But with a blushless front pursues his course,
And bears the public odium of Rogue !"

BEAUMONT.

A FEW minutes only had elapsed after the Gypsy's departure,
which brief period Claudius had employed in deliberating
upon the course he had best pursue, when the conviction
suddenly flashed upon his mind, with all the crushing influence of positive assurance, that his companion had outwitted and intended to betray him—his remaining there
alone would be proof against him of criminality, and by the
loss of his fellow he had lost every evidence which he might
have adduced of his innocency ; so, in the perplexity of his
mind, he reasoned. That the fire was already burning slowly
which was to lay the entire premises in ashes, never occurred
to him, or he would have conceived his own destruction cer-
.tain ; all his thought rested upon Slipgibbet's departure alone,
and of that he hastened to give the necessary information.

Never did the beat of drum, the loud blast of the trumpet,
or the cry of " To arms ! to arms !" shouted through a camp
or a city, produce greater effect than the tidings which Claudius communicated. In a moment the farm-yard became a
scene of ludicrous bustle and confusion, as if an armed body
was preparing to charge the alarmed bumpkins at the point
of the bayonet. Pitchforks, spades, reaping-hooks, hedge-
stakes, and a variety of *etcetera*, were instantly in requisition,
and a regular troop of *heavy* brigade stood marshalled before
Claudius—

" Who languish'd for the fight, and beat the air
With brandish'd weapons;"

to whom they looked for the word of command, by directing
them in the most likely way of pursuit. The farmer, with a
portion of his men, sallied forth in one direction, while the
remainder, headed by a spirited volunteer, took another, each
party beating with a strong desire to capture the fugitive.

Meanwhile the sharp-witted Gypsy, anticipating the con-

sequences which would result from his departure being discovered, and in order to secure, as far as possible, a good and
safe retreat, had taken a contrary direction to the one which
Claudius had expected, and clearing, with the agility of a
greyhound, every impediment to his course, soon found himself at a good distance from the farm-yard.

After an hour's fruitless search, and fatigued with scaling
gates, leaping ditches, and forcing their way through quick-
set hedges, one party returned just in time to prevent a general conflagration taking place. The slow-match had fallen
from the position in which Slipgibbet had placed it, which
coming in contact with a quantity of wet straw at the bottom
of the barn, a thick volume of smoke arose from the smoul-
dering heap, filling all the place, and issuing in alarming
quantities from every aperture at which it could escape.

The fearful discovery was first made by Claudius, who was
at no loss for a moment to conceive of the cause. Giving on
the instant the alarm of " Fire !" he rushed, with a daring intrepidity through the suffocating cloud of smoke, to where
the combustible matter had been laid by Slipgibbet, which
having secured, his worst fears were considerably allayed,
and by the application of a plentiful supply of water, the few
sparks which had appeared were soon extinguished, without
any further loss being sustained than the destruction of a few
trusses of straw.

As soon as the complete safety of the barns and their contents was ascertained, the attention of the inmates of the
farm-house was directed to the young Gypsy, whose generous
conduct had been the means of their preservation.

Nothing short of Claudius' being introduced into the best
parlour would satisfy the feelings of the grateful Mrs. Primrose, the farmer's wife, and therefore, partly to gratify the
curiosity of her four daughters with the sight of a Gypsy
boy, and partly to acknowledge their obligations to him, he
was, with as much form almost as would accompany the introduction of an ex-mayor, or the ruling steward of a Lord,
ushered into the apartment.

" Bless me !" cried Miss Kate, in a rather loud whisper to
her sister, as Claudius entered the room, " what a nice looking lad he is for a Gypsy boy. Well, really I always conceived those people were a coarse, smoke-dyed, withered set
of creatures, enough to shake one's nerves to look upon."

" Hush, Kate," said her sympathising sister Patty, " the

poor wretches are flesh and blood as we are, and I dare say, if some of them were possessed of advantages such as we possess, they would not be very much our inferiors."

The other two girls were more timid than their elder sister, and therefore, to escape from the Gypsy boy, whose very name terrified them, they had taken their places behind their mamma's old fashioned high-backed chair, from whence they stole occasionally some sly and fearful glances at the stranger.

"My dear," said Mrs. Primrose, addressing herself to Claudius as he entered, "I feel I am greatly indebted to you for the kindness you have displayed in rescuing myself and family from the cruel designs of that unprincipled man with whom you came hither. But, surely you are not one of their company. I fear you have been the victim of their base designs, and that some fond parent has been made to mourn your loss."

Claudius felt himself placed in awkward circumstances, and had not his pride opposed, the touching observation which the farmer's wife had made would have drawn from him a full disclosure of the truth. This, however, he determined not to do; and yet to continue longer on the present topic would almost compel him to break his resolve; he therefore contrived naturally to shift the conversation, by replying that he had done no more than his duty in the course which he had pursued, and, therefore, no thanks were due to him.

"I dare say, now," whispered Kate to her sister, "he could tell us our fortunes; la, how I do wish mamma would leave the room. I am determined to ask him."

"Why, yes," responded Patty, "no doubt he could. I should like it above all things. How can we manage it? No doubt we should learn how long we are to wait before we have houses of our own. At least we might learn whether the gentlemen ever intend to propose or not. What shall we do to accomplish it? Cannot you think of something Kate?"

"Why, I am thinking," replied Kate, "it would be a great pity to lose so fair an opportunity as may never again occur."

While the elder misses were thus conversing aside on a subject in which they felt beyond expression interested, the little ladies had crept from their hiding-place, and were examining, with a mixture of surprise and curiosity, the dress and appearance of the Gypsy boy.

"I am sure," said the youngest, "I should not like to be a Gypsy man.   Should you Ann ?"

"No, that I should not, nor a Gypsy *girl* either," answered the little one.   "How long have you been a Gypsy boy ?" inquired the artless girl.

Claudius felt uneasy.   The question was much more direct than he wished or expected, and while attempting to stammer out some evasion, he was relieved from his trepidation by the return of Mr. Primrose and his party.

"Well, my dear Mr. Primrose," exclaimed his wife, as he entered the parlour, "Have you succeeded in securing the miscreant ?"

"I have not, my love," returned her husband; "he has fairly escaped us this time.   I have, however, given information of the encampment of the party in the wood, so that the nest will be broken up; and unless they make a very sudden retreat some of them will be secured."

A few words of explanation followed, touching the fire which had just been extinguished; interlarded with which, were encomiums of the warmest character upon the conduct which Claudius had displayed upon the occasion, which flowed from the kind-hearted Mrs. Primrose with the smoothness of oil and the richness of nectar.

"You are a worthy lad," observed the farmer, turning to Claudius, "and if you are disposed to leave your old life and reside with me, I'll engage to take care and put you in a way to obtain an honest living.   What say you ?—are you willing to have me for a master ?   I promise you not to forget the service you have already rendered me, and such treatment as such service merits you may depend upon receiving."

The bargain was soon struck between them; and, as Mr. Primrose had no son, he jocosely observed to his wife, "I think we may as well adopt the Gypsy lad at once;—what say you, wife ?   Perhaps one of our girls may take a fancy to him when he is smarted up a matter.   Which of you," he continued, addressing himself to his daughters, while a smile such as could only have come fresh from the warm heart of a fond father lighted up his manly countenance,—. "Which of you will have the poor Gypsy boy for a brother ?"

"I dare say, papa," replied Kate, "we shall all feel a pleasure in making the stranger happy.   That which a sense of duty inculcates, inclination will prompt us cheerfully to perform."

The sound of a carriage driving up to the door terminated the colloquy; and while considerable speculation was in ex--ercise among the young ladies who the visitor might be, the Rev. Dr. Titheum was announced, and in the next minute his dumpty Reverence was received at the parlour door by the worthy farmer and his wife.

"Well, Farmer Primrose," said the doctor, "I hope you are well;" making a slight inclination of his head as he spoke. "Mrs. Primrose," he added, bowing gracefully, " my respects to you, madam. Ah! ladies," he continued, addressing himself to the daughters, and bowing still more profoundly, "your servant; glad to see you,—quite well? Eh?" he exclaimed, abruptly, "Who have we here?" eyeing, as he spoke, the Gypsy boy with a suspicious and searching look, " I hope," said the anti-Samaritan doctor, turning to Mr. Primrose, " you give no countenance to these miscreants. Why, the parish, Mr. Primrose,—nay, I might say, the county is likely to be ruined by them. It was no longer ago than yesterday that I detected one of the rascals myself bearing off a fine sucking pig of mine;—it was well for him that a wall of six feet high prevented my following him, or I am not in the commission of the peace for the county, but I would have given him a lodging in the county jail for a few months, or have sent him on a voyage across the water."

It was a happy circumstance for all with whom the doctor had to do that he never stood to his text, or continued long on any one subject—excepting only and always that which was the sun-light of his existence, the *summum bonum* of his happiness—*the rights of the church!* in which, as distinguished items, he, of course, included tithes and Easter dues. On these moving topics the doctor was always verbose, although not always logical or eloquent. He could prove, indeed,—at least he could, and frequently did, *attempt* to prove to the people of his charge, that in the whole circle of invaluable blessings with which they were surrounded, *tithes* were the most invaluable;—a sort of constellation of good in themselves, amidst a constellation of goods. Acting up to his system in this particular, and that none of those over whom he held spiritual jurisdiction should lose their share of benefit through his laxity, he exacted most rigorously—if not most righteously,—the full tithing of all they possessed. During the twenty years and upwards, that he had held the living of the parish, he had never been known in any more distinguished character than as a money-loving, griping, gluttonous parson; and holding, as he did, a magisterial commission, he possessed peculiar facilities to exercise the ruling passion of his soul. So long had he used his authority with unrelenting rigour as to cause the doggrel rhyme of a poetaster to become a sort of proverb in the lips of all people.

"For twenty years the people said,
Their parson was a wood un;
He punished many an action bad,
But never did a good un."

At every marriage feast or christening treat, when an invitation was given, the worthy doctor set an example of courtesy to his parish, by attending; without making any dis. tinction as to the rank or character of the persons from whom the invitation came. On such occasions, he was aware that a plentiful supply of the good things of this life would be furnished, and that consideration always settled in his mind any doubt which might arise as to propriety or otherwise—and he accordingly went.

The object of the doctor's present visit to Mr. Primrose's was of no ghostly or spiritual nature, but to settle a little matter relative to the amount of value of a few acres of pasture land which the farmer had recently added to his farm. As, up to this period, Mr. Primrose had compounded with the rector for his portion of tithes, it now became necessary that a few extra shillings per annum should be added to the previous amount.

As has been said, the doctor's forté lay not in categorical order; hence the question which he started at the head of this digression, when his eye fell upon Claudius in his Gypsy guise, was swallowed up by his reference to the person he had detected in the act of running off with one of his own sucking pigs; and that again was lost in the all-absorbing theme of *tithes:* and to that subject, therefore, he directed the attention of Mr. Primrose, without allowing him time to reply to the questions he had himself proposed.

English hospitality has been long and loudly lauded; poets have sung its praise, and moralists have eulogised its character. Did I possess the power to transport my reader to the dwelling of the honest farmer in question, he would at once be furnished with a tangible evidence, as well as ocular demonstration, that in so far as *he* was concerned this estimable trait in the British character, while it was no Utopian fable, had not been too highly rated. His house, and all it contained, was as free as his speech; he never expressed a pleasure which he did not feel, nor professed to be gratified by the visit of one whose person he hated. He shook no man by the hand, and called him "friend," to whom his friendly professions were not sincere. He had already given Dr. Titheum a hearty welcome; because, although the esti- mation in which he held him as a divine rose not very high, he enjoyed his company as a table companion. He well knew the doctor's love of *justice*, so far as tithes were concerned, as also his strong *penchant* for a few glasses of good wine, when drawn by Freeman's key, and, therefore, felt neither surprise or displeasure at the cause of the present visit.

In order to enjoy the doctor's company for an hour or two, he proposed settling the tithe affair over the tithe bottle. No objection being urged by the divine to the proposal, the wine was placed upon the table, and with as much pleasure as Sir Walter's Michael Lambourne swallowed Rhenish, they pro- ceeded to discuss in free potations the merits of the farmer's excellent port.

Having easily disposed of the little tithe question, to the entire satisfaction of the rector, and filled his glass twice or thrice, he listened with the attentive gravity of an official to his host's statement of the recent attempt that had been made to destroy his premises, the escape of the culprit, and the dis- tinguished and honourable part which Claudius had taken in the affair. By the time the brief account was finished the glass had been put into requisition at least half a score times, and his reverence began to wax warm beneath its potent influence. His plump cheeks, which hung in large rolls over his tightly tied cravat, looked like two well-filled, illu- minated bladders; a profusion of large pimples, which adorned his face, like unstoned plumbs in a Christmas pud- ding, now glowed with the radiancy of burning coal, while his little sharp eyes sparkled from beneath long dark lashes with unusual brightness, from whence the indignation of his soul flashed forth as he listened to the statement of his host.

"You did right—perfectly right, Mr. Primrose," said the doctor, "in forwarding information to the authorities con- cerning the rogues' encampment in the wood. I have no doubt," he added, elongating and bridling up his person to the utmost extent his rotundity would allow, " I have no doubt, if I had been present to head you in the pursuit of the

incendiary, we should have secured him. *We* understand
these matters, Mr. Primrose; it is our profession—I mean
those of us who are in the commission of the peace."

"Why, I have heard, doctor," observed Mr. Primrose
jocosely, "set a thief to catch a thief, and you are sure to
succeed."

"Ha! ha! ha!" laughed the doctor. "Not exactly so,
Mr. Primrose, not exactly so; but we know their tricks. If
one of the villains is taken, I am not in the commission of
the peace for the county if he shall not swing for it. I see
no way of ridding the country of such pests, but by positive
extermination. Your wine is excellent, Mr. Primrose! never
drank better! To have destroyed this, would in itself have
been an act richly deserving of death."

"Your judgment, doctor, on such a subject," replied Mr.
Primrose, "is undoubted."

"Why, I am allowed to have some taste in such matters,"
rejoined the divine, emptying his glass; "indeed, my neighbour, Lord Dashwood, invariably takes my opinion in the
choice of his wine."

"Mentioning his lordship," observed the farmer, "Is it
correct that he dislocated his shoulder in last Saturday's
hunt?"

"Oh, yes; that is quite correct, I can assure you," returned the doctor, "I was within a yard of his lordship when
his horse stumbled. My Nimrod, although one of the best
hunters in the county, shyed as my lord went over his horse's
head; in consequence of which I lost the brush, and barely
escaped being smothered in a deep ditch of black mud. That
was a day of exciting sport," continued his Reverence, rubbing his hands, as if in extacy at the recollection. "It was
rather late, by the bye, before we separated on Sunday morning, and my head ached so confoundedly that I was scarcely
able to get through my duty. Mrs. Primrose," he added,
"allow me to pledge you?" and he again filled his glass; but
either his hand had become somewhat unsteady, or his eye
failed to measure correctly the diameter of the glass, for before he had completed the task he had emptied a larger portion
of the sparkling juice upon the table than into the vessel.

"Bless me!" exclaimed the dumpty black coat, "I have
certainly committed a blunder—how could it possibly have
occurred?"

"A mere accident, doctor," observed the farmer, "the

most expert hands you know will sometimes err ; and, when
excited, the nerves shake a little."

"True, true," said the divine, "Ha! ha! ha! you are
right, Mr. Primrose, perfectly right—correct in judgment—
really you ought to have been in the commission of the peace
before now. There," he observed, as he took his handkerchief from his pocket, and soaked up the wine, " that little
affair is soon settled. Miss' Primrose," added the doctor,
"Will you oblige an old friend ?"

"I shall feel much pleasure," replied the lady, "in doing
any thing in my power, Sir."

"Why, that's kind (hiccup), Miss Primrose," said the
rector ; " beg pardon—you are very obliging. How old are
you, my dear ?"

"How old, Sir ?" rejoined Miss Primrose, " A lady's age,
Sir, you know is—"

"True, true ; very true," interrupted Dr. Titheum (hiccup),
" I beg pardon. I suppose, however, we shall soon have to
pronounce our blessing (hiccup)—I beg pardon—upon you
at the altar. Eh, Miss Kate, am I not correct ?"

" Really, Sir, I cannot inform you," replied the blushing
girl.

"True, true," hiccuped out the rector. " I shall at any
time be glad to wait upon you ; but I had forgotten, you
promised me a favour. You know I am passionately fond of
music. Come, now, oblige me with your last new waltz or
quadrille ; or, let me see, have you that exciting thing which
has just come out ?   It begins thus :—

> "Hark! hark, to the sound of the horn,
>   As it echoes through dingle and grove ;
>   When, uprising at day's early dawn,
>   We join in the sport that we love.
>   'As tantivy, tantivy, we sing, and away."

This stanza the doctor chaunted as well as the loss of a
front masticator would allow him ; and, whatever deficiency
there might be in point of harmony, he more than supplied
by spirit and action. He entered, as every man who *feels*
his subject does, heart and soul into it, to the evident and
high mirth of all present.

"Bravo! bravo!" shouted the farmer, causing at the
same time his knuckles to come into strong contact with the
table. " I always feel pleasure in supporting native talent,
and yours, doctor, is of no common kind. I'd wager a dozen

of the best Sherry in my cellar against as many quarts of spring water— and *you* know I have some excellent."

" True, true," interrupted the doctor, smacking his lips, "it is excellent, very excellent."

" I'd wager a dozen of it upon your head against any squeaking, bawling foreigner that ever gulled a public assembly," continued Mr. Primrose.

" I value your judgment, Mr. Primrose," returned the divine, bowing low, "and thank you for your approbation and high opinion. I fancy I have some talent that way. I sometimes wish I had been sent to Italy rather than to Oxford; a *leetle* improvement might have been a fortune to me."

" Certainly it would," replied the farmer. " It was a thousand pities you were sent to Oxford; we lost a first-rate singer, merely to obtain—I mean no disparagement to yourself, doctor—one of which the country is overstocked." The farmer winked as he uttered his compliment, and a convulsive titter went round the family circle. As soon as Miss Kate had screwed up her face to something like seriousness, and an opening in her papa's and the doctor's colloquy allowed it, she expressed her regret to his reverence that she had not yet met with the ballad of which he had favoured them with a stanza.

" Well, well, my dear," said the rector, " you have some other, I dare say, equally good; oblige me with one of your last new ones ?"

Miss Primrose drew the music-stool from under her cabinet, and ran her fingers over the keys of the instrument.

" With your leave, Madam," said the doctor, addressing himself to Mrs. Primrose, " I must crave one other small indulgence while Miss Kate obliges me with her song, and then I shall feel quite at home."

" Certainly, doctor," returned Mrs. Primrose, "you have only to express your wishes here, to have them—so far as our abilities go—promptly met."

" Thank you, madam," said the rector, "you are kind, very kind. I shall relish the wine and song better, I think, although I enjoy the wine very much already, if I can be favoured with a pipe."

" I beg pardon, doctor," responded Mrs. Primrose, "it was not thought of before. I remember now your devotion to that innocent indulgence. It shall be brought immediately."

D

"Thank you, madam,—in good time," returned Dr. Titheum, and emptied his glass.

The *leetle* indulgence was soon supplied, and after lighting it, and puffing two or three clouds, as dark and powerful almost as if issuing from the funnel of a steam-engine, maugre all the sage and satiric observations which the immortal COWPER has made upon its use in female company especially, the doctor observed,—

"Now, Miss, I think I shall be able to assist you in the vocal department."

Again he puffed, and again filled his glass; and then, rising from his seat, and reaching across the table, "Allow me," he said, "Mr. Primrose, to assist you?" charging as he spoke, with a little difficulty, the farmer's glass. This done, he proceeded to resume his sitting; but, by some unfortunate circumstance, he completely missed his chair, and his *finale*, with no very gentle action, came in contact with the floor, on which the short, fat doctor rolled, like a black-pudding, or a hedge-hog, to the infinite diversion of the junior members of the family. Mr. and Mrs. Primrose ran to his assistance, and soon placed him in a perpendicular positiou.

"The devil take the chair!" said the doctor, as soon as he had recovered his feet. "I beg pardon. How, in the name of wonder, did it happen? As true as I am in the commission of the peace, I never met with such an occurrence in my life before. Bless me! I have broken my pipe too, I perceive," he observed, as he looked at the scattered fragments upon the carpet.

"You have not hurt yourself, I hope, doctor?" said Mrs. Primrose.

"Oh, no, madam; no, I assure you," replied the rector, rubbing his posteriors, "not in the least, I think. I'll be more careful now," he added, and feeling for the chair's bottom, he succeeded to fix himself firmly upon it. "I regret that I have, by my accident, caused some confusion. Your kindness, madam, will, I hope, excuse it."

"Don't trouble yourself, my dear sir," replied the farmer. "Had it not been at your expense, we should have enjoyed it as a variation given to the monotony of order. But, come, sir, shall I give you a toast?"

"With all my heart," responded the doctor, and he filled to the brim.

"*May those who fall, never want a friend to assist them to rise again,*" drank the farmer.

"Good! good!" shouted the rector. "Ha! ha! ha! ready wit, by all the saints in the calendar. I should feel no objection to drink such a toast in three times three. May those who fall—fall—how was it? Oh!—never rise again."

"Not exactly so, doctor," cried Mr. Primrose, "you have misquoted your text."

"Good, again!" said the divine. "Ha! ha! ha! I stand corrected. How went it?"

"May those who fall, never want a friend to assist them to rise again," repeated Mr. Primrose, as the doctor fixed a look of deep attention on his face.

".Aye, to be sure," said Titheum, "how sieve-like my memory has become. I'll fill again, to do.credit to so good a toast," and he suited the action to the word. "Now for it," he continued, "May those who fall, never want a—a friend to assist them to rise."

By the time the doctor had managed to give the toast and swallow his wine, a fresh pipe was placed before him; after lighting which, he requested Miss Primrose would proceed with her expected entertainment. A few leaves of a music book were turned over, and then, having made her selection, she threw out a fine bold symphony, at the close of which she sung the following stanzas, the doctor, the mean while, beating time with the flourish of his pipe, and joining with his voice as well as he was able.

> "Ye shepherds who stray with my swain,
>   Companions in sport and in youth;
> Oh! tell him how great is my pain,
>   How I grieve for the loss of his truth.
> Oh! tell him how oft he has swore
>   He never would cease to be mine;
> Or leave me, his faith to deplore,
>   Or with heart-breaking anguish repine.

> "Remind him, how oft in the grove,
>   At my feet he in rapture would kneel;
> And implore me to pity his love,
>   Till he taught me, fond fool! how to feel.
> Oh! tell him, 'tis now he must come,
>   For more my poor heart cannot bear;
> Or the maidens will carry me home
>   The victim of love and despair."

Before time was allowed the learned doctor to pour forth a long string of compliments,which his gallantry had concocted, in favour of Miss Primrose's performance, and even before the last notes of the instrument had died away, a piece of unexpected intelligence gave an entire change to the thoughts and engagements of the company.

A female servant entered the room, and informed Mr. Primrose that Murphy Doyle wished to speak to him on something of importance.

"Well, tell Murphy," said Mr. Primrose, "if he'll promise to be brief and clear in his communication, as I am engaged just now, he may come to me ; but if he cannot pledge himself to these particulars, I cannot attend to him."

The servant dropped a curtsey, and departed with her master's answer; and, in the twinkling of an eye, a tall, knock-kneed, ragged-headed, and raggedly-dressed personage made his appearance at the door, twirling about a half brimless hat, the crown of which swung backwards and forwards, like the creaking sign of a country ale-house in a high wind.

"Well, Murphy," said Mr. Primrose, "what are your wishes ? Is it something short and sweet you are about to communicate ?"

"Plase your honour," replied Murphy, "it is short enough for that matter ; but as to sweet, that's as it may be, yer honour ; barrin' the things that don't belong to it, sure enough it's all about your own affairs I'd afther spakin' to ye."

"About my affairs, Murphy!" observed Mr. Primrose, "which part of them, pray ?"

"Faith, now," answered Murphy, "it's a hard question yer puttin' to me ; barrin' the larnin' o' the pathernosther, I niver was more bothered since the first time I was born. What part o' them ? Och, sure now I'm not lyin' if I jist say every part of them ; bekase, if I hadn't fought the murderin' thief wid the courage of a devil,—savin' the ladies' pardon for usin' sich a word—ye had, by to-morrow night it may be, been burnt to dith in your beds, without livin' to make your wills in the mornin'."

"I do not understand you, Murphy," said Mr. Primrose, "Who is the person you refer to ?"

"Who, now ?" shouted Murphy, with as much expression of surprise in his countenance and tone, as if he had seen his master swallow the old hat which he still held in his hand. "Och! by my sowl, is'nt it the ill-fatured, mallet-headed, bog-throtter, who was jist thinkin' to divart himself by lookin' at the fire of your premises to-night, as they were blazin' as merry as a Saint Bartlemy bonfire?"

"Do you mean the Gypsy?" inquired Mr. Primrose eagerly.

"Who else should I mane, you honour?" rejoined Murphy.

"And what of him?" continued the farmer, "Have you seen him?"

"Have I seen him?" responded Murphy. "Sure but I have seen him; and, by faith, he would not deny it himself, blackguard as he is. The basthin' I have given him is as honest a one as ever a mortal baste would need or desire. I'll jist tell ye, jintlemen, how it happened. I was returning from the market, to which I had been sent in the mornin', when, jist as I was thinkin' o' nothin' at all, but only settlin' the day's account wid myself, who should fall plump in my road but Squire Wheeler's footman. 'Well, Murphy,' says he, 'so your master's barns are going to be burned down wid combustible fire, and the family destroyed into the bargain.' 'Are they?' says I. 'But let the spalpeen stand out o' my way that would do it.' 'It is true,' says he, 'upon my bible oath; but the Gypsy blackguard had another call to make, I suppose, and so didn't stay long enough to do it. All the servants are in search of him; but the baste is as cunnin' as a fox, for he has taken earth, and they cannot meet with him.' 'Och, my darlin'!' said I, 'Only let him stand clear of my little switch here, for if I mate him I'll jist be afther breakin' every bone in his impident skin.' With that, I hastens homewards, without matin' a sowl by the way, beside myself, when, jist as I reached the little wood on the other side the five-acre field, what should I fix my ogles upon, but a bundle o' rags, hid away in a bush. Well, your honour, what would your honour think came into my head?"

"I care not what came into your head," answered Mr. Primrose, "come as soon as you can to the end of your story."

"Sirrah!" said the doctor, with magisterial action and accent, "you trifle; speak out at once what you have to say."

"Sure, your honour, it was no trifle either," replied Murphy; "and as to saying all at once what I have to say, it is what my mouth never could do since it belonged to Murphy Doyle. But, as I was saying, your honour, thinks I that bundle of clothes yonder will serve to patch my dress; so at it I pulls wid all might, for it stuck fast in the bushes, when presintly up starts the divil's couzen of a Gypsy. He seemed sinsible it couldn't be good for his health to stay any longer couched upon his hams like a hunted hare; so off he set, like a flash o' lightnin'. 'Oh, oh, that's your gave to be sure,' says I, 'is it;' so afther him I bolts, and before he could say hot-codlings, I was at his heels, and with one touch of my shilelah I made him stand flat on his back at my feet; and then, while he roared like a bathed bull, I bate him for fallin'; afther he had bawled for mercy as long as I could spare time to hear him, I tied his hands behind his back, and fastened the cord to one leg; and then, afther the fashion we drive pigs from Donnybrook fair, I made the brute hobble before me home, and he is now waitin' to see your honour in the stable, where I have tied him fast, like a baste as he is, to the manger."

"Murphy," cried Mr. Primrose, as he finished his some-what prolix tale, " you are a brave fellow, and shall not lose your reward for thus doing your duty."

"Reward, your honour!" returned Murphy, " and sure what reward does a man desarve for only knockin' out the brains of a villain? Sure no Irishman that wasn't born in England would ever think of reward for doing his duty."

" Well, well, my honest fellow," observed the farmer, " as you please; but I never enquire of what country a man is who has done nobly and well, before I admire the action he has performed; the bond of our common nature binds me to him, and I love him as a man and a brother. But here, Murph y," he continued, " drink this glass of wine, and hasten back to your prisoner, and guard him well until I send for you. See to it that he does not escape you."

" Thank y our honour!" said Murphy, as he returned the glass, " Sure I'll break every bone in his skin before he shall live to run away again; never fear but Murphy Doyle will hould him fast. Faith, but it would be a disgrace to the name of an Irishman to let any thing slip through his fingers."

As soon as Murphy had left the room, a consultation was held as to the best method of proceeding with the Gypsy. The reverend magistrate determined to examine the culprit himself; and if he found, as he felt quite certain he should, that he had with malice propense sought to fire, and thereby to injure or destroy the premises of Mr. Jeremiah Primrose, of the county of Hants, he should then feel it his duty forth-with to commit him to the county jail, in order to his taking his trial for the capital offence of arson, as with him it was a principle from which he never swerved—*festinatio justitiæ est novera infortunii.*

As a preliminary step to the proceedings about to be instituted, it was determined that Claudius should leave the court—into which the farmer's parlour was about to be transformed—and hold himself in readiness when called upon to give such evidence touching the prisoner as he upon his oath could feel justified in advancing.

"I shall be ready and willing, Sir," said Claudius, "whenever I may be called upon, to state the whole truth, upon whomsoever the consequences may fall. I detest the crime which I have been the instrument of preventing, and, therefore, I discovered the plot."

"You did your duty, my lad," answered the Doctor, who had listened with distended eyes and ears to the Gypsy boy. "I shall do you justice, and shall not punish you if I find you have not been actually engaged in the affair. You may retire."

Claudius bowed respectfully, although with an assumed awkwardness, fearing that a discovery, which he wished to avoid, might take place, and attended to the law of the court.

This appeared as fair an opportunity as the young ladies could have desired, and they, therefore, cheerfully accompanied the Gypsy boy to another apartment, in high expectation of having their fortunes told, while Mrs. Primrose busied herself in making such preparations for the approaching trial as appeared necessary.

CHAPTER VI.

"And there sat the priest in the judge's chair,
Who a text from Blackstone quoted;—
While he sagely sat, the case to hear,
And points of evidence noted.

   *   *   *   *

"The rogue, with a leer of ludicrous grace,
Which proved his heart no trembler,
Cried, 'How much, Sir, is mine like the Saviour's case,
And yours, how very dissim'lar.'"

OLD BALLAD.

IN a brief space of time, paper, ink, and pens, were placed

before the doctor, who, after taking another glass of wine, consented, with very evident reluctance, that both it and his pipe should be removed.

"Hem!" cried the magistrate, with official cadence, as he settled himself in his chair with the same pompous air of dignified authority as is generally displayed by such worthy functionaries in their own little legal empires. "We must," he added, with befitting emphasis, "have a messenger dispatched immediately to my trusty servant, Moses Grabum, the constable, desiring his attendance here without delay; and, Mr. Primrose," continued the justice, "let me see,—you havn't, perhaps, such a piece of legal furniture in your house as a pair of hand-cuffs?"

"Oh, no, doctor," replied the farmer, "we need no such things here. I pay my men well, and treat them kindly, and while they require no confinement put on their limbs, I know not a man among them who would not risk his own person to defend mine, or to protect my family and property from harm; hence I sleep without fear, and my commands are executed with promptitude."

"Well, well," said the doctor, "I merely inquired. "We who are in the commission of the peace are obliged to have regard to those things, and to employ them frequently. If, indeed, we did not, it is a hundred to one but ninety-nine out of a hundred of us would have our brains knocked out by the scoundrels we are obliged to commit. We shall need them now, I am certain."

"Do you imagine so?" asked the farmer.

"No, Sir," returned the justice, "I do not imagine so, I am quite confident of it. Bless you! I would not sit here to examine such a desperado as is this Gypsy villain without his hands being confined for the value of a king's ransom! I have no doubt that the law is frequently improperly administered; not so much from the misapprehension of it on the part of our magistrates, for, generally speaking—I might have said universally—they are well read in the jurisprudence of our country; but, from a sense of danger, to which their office exposes them. I know what those feelings are, Mr. Primrose, having often felt them since I have been in the commission of the peace. There," continued the doctor, sealing, and handing him a note which he had just written, "let that be conveyed with all possible speed to Moses Grabum. I have therein desired him to attend me here forthwith,

and that he is to come with his conveyance—as I fully intend
to commit—in which to convey the prisoner to the place of
confinement; and, by all means, not to forget a brace of
pistols, for I have no doubt they will be required, and a pair
of strong hand-cuffs. Now, let one of your most active
men set off; and, as some time will be occupied in that part
of the business, I think I shall have sufficient leisure to take
one more pipe, and another glass, or so, of your excellent
wine. Really, I somehow quite enjoy it—it must be *very*
excellent. *We*, Mr. Primrose, who are in the commission of
the peace, very often require some stimulant, I assure you—
ours is no easy duty; and were it not that we feel the importance of the office requires men of more than ordinary
judgment and probity, I am sure, I can speak for myself, I
should give up. But, you know, Sir, 'England expects every
man to do his duty,' as the immortal Nelson said, and conscience compels—"

"Very true, doctor," rejoined the farmer, scarcely able to
restrain his feelings at the boasting of the reverend gentleman,
"We *do need* that men of judgment and probity should fill
the office."

The wine was by this time replaced on the table, and again
the doctor filled and lighted his pipe; and, after puffing
hard at it for a minute or two, he observed, "The way to be
able to do justice to others, Mr. Primrose—(puff—puff)—is
to—(puff)—do justice to—(puff—puff)—ourselves first—
(puff—puff). Now, as to this fellow, Mr. Primrose, you
can, of course, swear to him; you have a perfect recollection
of—(puff—puff)—his person?"

"I have no doubt on the subject, doctor," replied the
farmer, "and if the man who has been taken by my servant
is the same as assumed the profession of a rat-catcher this
morning, I should know him among a thousand; and if any
doubt could arise in my mind as to the identity of his person, there will be the evidence of the boy, you know, which
must be conclusive."

"Ah! true, true," said the learned functionary, "that is
a fortunate circumstance—(puff, puff, puff),—such evidence
must indeed render the case plain—(puff, puff). We, who are
in the commission of the peace, always wish to have things
plain before us, Mr. Primrose—(puff, puff). Ah! well thought
of," continued the doctor. "See the advantage resulting from
a soothing pipe, but for it I should have forgotten an im-

portant matter.   Have you a copy of Blackstone, or Coke
upon Lyttleton?   There may arise some points of special
character in the case I am about to investigate; and although
I am—I speak it without egotism I assure you, Mr. Primrose—as familiar with the science of law as any lawyer, perhaps, that ever undertook a brief; still, since I have been in
the commission of the peace, I like, in all my decisions, to be
able to put my finger upon the page and declare—'Thus
saith an authority upon the subject.'   It will somtimes happen, from the perplexity and cumbrous nature of the law,
and, unless I am particularly excited, my memory fails of
being so tenacious as I could wish it."

  " Why, very fortunately, doctor," replied the farmer, " a
trifling dispute which I had recently with my neighbour,
Lord Dashwood, respecting his right to injure my property,
by coursing over and destroying no small quantity of wheat
every year, led me to purchase two works on law affairs—by
reading which, I believe I am more perplexed than I was before—the one is ' Every Man his own Lawyer,' the other
' Burn's Justice ;' these are all the works I possess on such
subjects, if they will serve your purpose, you shall have them
in a few seconds."

  " Why, they are not just the thing, Mr. Primrose," answered the sapient justice; we of the bench always patronize
the best authorities,—however, if you will oblige me, I will
make shift with them."

  The farmer slipped to his book-case, and, from two or
three dozen tomes of small literature, selected the legal de-
sideratums and placed them before the reverend magistrate.

  " That will do, Mr. Primrose," said the doctor, " that will
do.   Now I think of it, I will take the depositions of the
Gypsy boy, which I shall be able to do before the constable
arrives.   I fear I shall have to commit them both ; we, who
are in the commission of the peace, are frequently obliged to
do violence to personal feelings—' *Agentes et consentientes
pari pœna plectentur*'—that is, ' the parties acting, and the
parties consenting, are liable to the same punishment.' "

  " Doctor Titheum !" exclaimed the honest farmer, " to
that youth, myself and family are, in all probability, indebted
for our lives ; my property, it is most certain, has been
preserved from destruction in consequence of his noble conduct: and now to commit him to prison, would, I think, be

an ill requital for services the most invaluable. His action has evidently been the result of constraint and not of cheerful consent."

"Well, well," rejoined the justice, "I shall see. If what you state is proved to be correct, Mr. Primrose, the case will be changed in a material point; it will amount to what we in the commission of the peace call a ' *non est factum ;*' but I'll take care the lad shall have '*jus in re*'—complete and full right. However, it is necessary that I should—(puff puff, puff)—interrogate him closely."

Mr. Primrose rang the bell and a servant entered, to whom he gave directions that the Gypsy boy should be brought in. As Claudius appeared at the door, the doctor put himself into an official attitude, and then, as a prelude to the important business in which he was about to engage, he drew forth his pocket-handkerchief, the same with which he had wiped up the wine from the table, and employed it now in wiping away the thick perspiration which oozed from his pimpled and bloated face; this done, he proceeded to the examination.

"Hem! Sirrah—So sir, you have been found in company with a person who has made an attempt to fire and destroy the property of Mr. Primrose; what account have you to give of yourself?"

Claudius turned his look full upon the reverend magistrate's face, when delicate and perilous as his present situation was, his sides shook with suppressed laughter. He attempted to reply to the interrogation which had been sternly put to him, but found it impossible to do so. He bit his lips, held in his breath, swallowed his spittle, and, in fact, did every other thing that he could do to stifle his unseasonable and indecorous inclination to cachinnation, but in vain. Fortunately for Claudius, the doctor had taken so many glasses of wine as to disqualify him to judge correctly of the character of the affection under which the prisoner laboured; the most distant thought, however, never occurred to him, that the Gypsy boy was guilty of what he would have pronounced —' contempt of court;' but supposing from the tit, tit, tit, which, in spite of every effort, issued from his lips, together with his silence in reference to the question which had been put to him, that he was affected and confused by his situation, again addressed him, but in gentler terms than before.

"Speak up, my lad," said his reverence—(hiccup)—"you

have nothing to fear, if you have not willingly engaged in this wicked design. Tell me—(hiccup)—bless me, what ails me now?—tell me, did you, with your own free and uninfluenced consent, enter upon—(hiccup)—this business?"

Claudius turned away his eye from the interrogator, that the cause of his distressing titillation might no further affect him, and replied—

" No, Sir, I did all in my power to prevent it; the gentleman there," pointing to Mr. Primrose, " knows that I gave him information, before any thing had happened, to put him on his guard."

" That is correct," said the farmer.

"How then came you to be in company with the perpetrator of the deed?" enquired the justice. "Did you come willingly?"

" I was appointed to the purpose," answered Claudius; " and I felt convinced it would be dangerous for me to refuse; beside, Sir, I knew the evil which had been determined upon, and I was resolved, if possible, to prevent it, and therefore I came the more cheerfully."

"Hem!" said the doctor, " Did you ever learn—(hiccup)—bless me, how troublesome these hic—(hiccup)—hiccups are!—did you ever learn your catechism?"

" Yes, Sir," replied Claudius, wondering at the strange question.

" Good," said the doctor. " Do you know what your godfathers and god-mothers promised and vowed for you?"

" Yes, Sir," returned our hero.

" Good," repeated the magistrate; " then you know—(hiccup)—you are aware of the consequences of telling a lie, or taking a false oath."

" Yes, Sir," answered Claudius.

" Well, then," said the doctor, " knowing as you do these things, are you prepared to state before me (hiccup), in the presence of your late companion, all you know of this serions affair?

" Yes, Sir," answered Claudius, "whenever you please."

" Good," said the divine. " How came the premises on fire, and by what means, and by whom was it lighted?"

With as much distinctness as he was able, he related all the circumstances connected with the affair; of which the doctor, as well as he was able, took notes, and at the end of the hearing, was pleased to applaud the line of conduct he had pursued, and then dismissed him.

For the information and satisfaction of the reader, it is necessary that the cause of Claudius's strange conduct previous to his examination should be explained. It happened
that when the doctor soaked up the wine with his handkerchief, a quantity of candle-snuff had by some accident fallen
from the snuffers upon the table; this the doctor did not
observe, and had therefore wiped it up with the wine, and,
by so doing, soiled his handkerchief not a little. As has
been stated, at the moment that Claudius entered the room,
he used this handy three-quarters of a yard of figured silk,
in doing which he had so admirably tattood his face on one
side, as to render himself an excellent personification of a
Tattoorowan chief. As, however, the farmer sat on one
side of the doctor, he did not perceive it. The ludicrous
figure which the fat, red, and black faced justice exhibited,
met the eye of Claudius as he stood full before

" The learned member of the legal art,"

and occasioned the feeling which has been noticed.

A short period only had elapsed after this novel and brief
hearing before the rambling of the constable's cart announced the arrival of that important personage, and presently afterwards Mr. Moses Grabum, beadle and constable
of the parish of Christchurch, made his low bow before his
magisterial master.

There was in the person and deportment of Moses, something so perfectly original, and withal so highly characteristic, that he would have made no despicable study for the
chisel of Chantry, the pencil of Cruikshank, or the pen of
Smollet. In some respects he might have been styled a
lump of deformity. So long and disproportionate was his
body, that he had for years been known by the familiar cognomen of Moses Long-body. From his broad round shoulders swung a pair of arms, well suited, in point of length,
to a figure half a cubit higher than his own. His neck,
which was exceedingly short, appeared shorter than it actually was, from the circumstance of his being somewhat
hump-backed; so that his head appeared none other than
a prodigious sarcoma growing out of an unsightly trunk like
that of a turtle's when just protruded from its shell; his
face, which was uncommonly broad, and as flat as a full
moon painted on the sign-board of a country ale-house, was
ornamented with a mouth, at least, one-third wider than the

dimensions of what was generally allowed to be a very large one ; and a pair of eyes, which nearly appeared as if about to make a sudden exit from their sockets; his legs were short and thick, and so finely bowed, that a China-bred pig, not exceeding twelve stone, might have run with convenience between them, without in the least disturbing the perpendicular position of their owner.

Moses had, in his time, served in most of the public offices of the parish ; but had, for the few last years, settled down, with a kind of respectable permanency, into the two posts which he now filled to admiration. Among the country people with whom he had to do, and especially by old women and young children, he was considered a species of " *locum tenens*" of the parson-justice. Among a variety of excellent qualities with which he was gifted, was a ready knack which he possessed of accommodating himself to the whims, tastes, and prejudices of his superiors. He felt it no degradation, either to his manhood or to his office, to be what, in improved modern phraseology, is called *a toad-eater*, to any man in power. If any scrupulous person ventured to offer an observation in his hearing, touching the trivial matter of contradicting his own declarations, or abandoning his professed principles, he with an indifference which would have done credit to the school of Plato, when that placid gentleman presided over his own college, amidst the grove of Academus, invariably offered as an apology, or sufficient reason, for his conduct,—" My betters do so every day,"—none ever disputed the truth of his statement, and there the matter ended.

The moment Mr. Moses, in all the paraphernalia of his office, entered the newly formed justice-room, he perceived at a single glance,—for be was a shrewd observer,—that the reverend magistrate had been, as he *sometimes* was in the habit of doing, sacrificing freely to the god of the luscious grape.

" Oh! you have arrived, have you, Mr. Grabum?" observed the doctor.

" Yes, your honour," replied the official, " I have made all the despatch it was possible for a person to make, to attend upon your worship."

" Good!" said the doctor. " You are a trusty servant, Moses : have you brought with you the little matters which I mentioned in my note ?"

" O yes, your honour," replied Grabum, " here is as pretty

a pair of bracelets as a man could wish to put on," exhibiting a pair of strong bright hand-cuffs; " and here, Sir," he added, as he drew from his pocket a brace of horse-pistols, " is as nice a pair of pop-guns as ever kept a rogue in subjection."

" Good, Mr. Grabum !" rejoined the divine. " You may now retire for the present ; and as soon as you have properly secured the prisoner, bring him up for examination—observe me ;—properly secured I say."

" It shall be done, your worship, according to your wishes, ' replied the constable, as he again bowed low and left the presence.

Arrangements were a second time made for hearing the case. The doctor finished his last glass of wine, took two or three long whiffs at his pipe, and laid, with due care, " Burn's Justice," and " Every Man His Own Lawyer," like right-and-left-hand supporters, before him, one on either side, while Mrs. Primrose, in order to witness the proceedings in perfect safety from the violence of the monster-man, placed herself by the side of her husband.

The sound of several feet in the hall announced the approach of the culprit. Mrs. Primrose cringed closer to the farmer, while the doctor, placing his arms a kimbo, made the most of himself for the occasion.

After a few seconds of agitating delay, the prisoner, safely hand-cuffed, and attended by the constable, entered, while Murphy Doyle, as if to secure and keep in order the captive he had made, followed close at his heels. Slipgibbet, as he advanced into the apartment, threw a sly sharp leer around its circumference as if looking for some person ; in a moment his countenance underwent a striking change ; from the fierce and sullen scowl which sat upon his brow his looks brightened up to an appearance which indicated impudent assurance. Without doubt he expected to have met Claudius, but finding he was not present, he at once calculated that he had fled, and that therefore no positive evidence, in his absence, could be produced against him, he determined to brave the case impudently, or charge the lad with the crime of which himself alone was guilty.

" What is your name, prisoner," demanded the justice.

" Harry Williams," answered the Gypsy, saucily.

" Harry Williams," repeated the doctor. "Hem! note that,"

he added to Mr. Primrose, who had volunteered his services as clerk of the court upon the occasion.

"Aye, note it if you please," said Slipgibbet, "that's the name of an honest man."

"Silence," shouted the judge in his own little court, "you are here to answer *my* questions, and to do nothing else."

"I know it," returned the Gypsy, in a saucy tone.

"What is your profession?" enquired the doctor.

"Why, I'se a rat-catcher," replied Slipgibbet, in the same tone.

"Where do you reside?" interrogated the justice.

"Why, I travels the country for an honest living," returned the prisoner, "and I lives sometimes here, and sometimes there, just as trade goes."

"You came here, I suppose, this morning," continued the doctor, "in the way of trade, then?"

"Sartainly I did," said the Gypsy, "and that ere gentleman," pointing to Mr. Primrose, "knows as how I cotched as fine rats in his barn as ever a man looked on with his eyes; and I has no doubts whatsomever as how I should have destroyed all the varmint if the young villin what come with me hadn't run'd away. I was just a seeking of him when I was stopped and mistreated by this ere feller, who I demand should be taken into custody for the assault."

"Och! the lyin' wagabond!" shouted Murphy, "wos'nt it myself, now, that stopped your runnin' away?"

The Gypsy directed a fierce withering look at Murphy, and was about to reply, when the doctor prevented him by enquiring,

"Do you know any thing respecting the fire in the barn?"

"The fire, your worship," responded Slipgibbet,--"I solemnly protest I knows no more about it than the child what's not born'd into the world."

"Indeed!" exclaimed the justice; "Why, then you are a perfectly innocent man."

"Oh, intirely so. I assures your worship," said the Gypsy, "not even your worship's self is more innocent than what I am."

"Then you can give me no information, I suppose," continued the learned man, "respecting a certain quantity of combustible matter, and a slow-match, which was placed among the wheat in the barn when you were seeking rats?"

" Me inform your honour ?" said Slipgibbet. " Why no, I says I knows nothing at all of the affair—I'm blow'd if I do ; and it would be no sarvice for a chap to say so to a lie ; would it, your worship ?"

" I can't conceive it would," replied the doctor.

" Well then, blow me tight if I do," continued the Gypsy, " and that's more, all I know's about it—that is, all what I supposes consarning it is, that that ere young rogue what was with me wanted to play off a game upon me for an old grudge, and so he 'tended to set light to this ere place, and leave me to settle the reckoning."

" It will be a heavy reckoning," said the doctor, " whoever may have to pay it."

" Well, your worship," rejoined the prisoner, " I was a thinking so ; but if your worship will oblige me by taking off these ere things from my wrists, and allow me to go, I'll be bound, on the word of an honest man, to come back with him in safe custody in less than a couple of hours."

" Why, that is fairly promised," said the doctor, " but I fancy we can save you the trouble. Desire the lad who is waiting without to attend directly."

As the order was given the Gypsy started, and a convulsive shudder shook his frame. The effect, however, was only of transient duration. A look of fierce defiance glared upon his dark visage, and, as if reckless of consequences, he appeared to stand prepared for the worst.

At the moment that Claudius entered the room, Slipgibbet stood with his back towards the door, and therefore did not perceive him ; but as he attended the beck of the doctor, and advanced towards his side to give his evidence, the eye of the Gypsy caught sight of him. With a degree of rage, which, with all his art at disguise, he knew not how to conceal, he gnashed his teeth, and bit his nether lip, and, but for the pistol which Grabum held pointed at his head, would, in all probability, have discharged his Satanic fury upon the youth.

" Do you know that man ?" enquired the justice of Claudins, pointing to the Gypsy.

" I do, Sir," he replied, without hesitation.

" Where did you last see him ?" asked the magistrate.

" In the barn, Sir, in the middle of the farm-yard yonder," answered Claudius.

" Are you acquainted with his name and profession ?" continued the doctor.

"His name, Sir, is Slipgibbet Phil," said Claudius.

"Slipgibbet!" exclaimed the justice, opening his heavy eyes wider than he had done during the previous half-hour, —"Slipgibbet! an ominous name truly, but it will, I think, be falsified soon—' the pitcher may come to the well once too often,' as the saying is. Umph, Slipgibbet! Well, since I have been in the commission of the peace it is the first time I have heard so offensive a name. 'What's in a name?' Much, Mister Shakspeare;—by implication, very much. I am called Justice,—and that implies truth and power;—and Slipgibbet, by logical deduction, proves that a man has escaped that which he has deserved—hanging! Now, my lad, give me such an account of the circumstances connected with the fire in the barn as comes within your knowledge."

"I will, Sir," replied Claudius, and he at once proceeded to narrate the same facts as he had a short time before communicated. At the conclusion of his evidence, in which there was neither contradiction nor confusion, the justice addressed himself to the Gypsy, and enquired—

"Have you any thing to reply to the statements which have just been made in your hearing? if so, you are at full liberty to make it."

The prisoner stood convicted and confounded, the fury of his passions appeared in the alternating colours of his countenance—"from crimson red to ashy pale"—and the distension of the veins in his forehead, which looked as if ready to burst. He seemed convinced that any attempt he might make at recrimination or justification would not avail to exonerate himself, and he therefore maintained a sullen and unbroken silence.

"Have you any observation to make prisoner?" again asked the justice.

"No," he replied surlily; " and I s'pose 'twou'dn't be of no sarvice if I had."

The doctor proceeded most gravely to comment upon the enormity of the crime of which he stood charged, and the eminent peril in which he was consequently placed; and then, having made out his *mittimus*, he committed him to the tender mercies of Grabum, with strict orders to see him well bestowed in the county jail until the time came for him to take his trial at the assizes. The parties having left the room in the same order as they entered, the doctor resumed his pipe, consenting, at the invitation of the warm-hearted

farmer, to take a glass or two more wine, in order to refresh himself after the fatigue of the examination.

"Was it not a fortunate circumstance," observed the doctor, "that I made my call upon you at this particular time, Mr. Primrose? You see I have despatched the business without any vexatious delay. It doesn't always happen, that we, who are in the commission of the peace, do things in this way; but I—*I*, Mr. Primrose, feel it a duty which I owe society always to use despatch." Here the doctor swallowed his glass of wine, and sent forth two or three heavy clouds from his earthern tube, and then added—"It is *my* custom, Mr. Primrose, always to use despatch."

"Your custom, Sir, is a good one," returned the farmer; and it would be well if all who are engaged in the law would copy so excellent an example: then *justice* would be experienced where *law* alone is felt, then so many injured families would not be ruined, so many hearts would not be broken, so much wretchedness from the law's delay, or from legal iniquity, would not be witnessed, so much—"

"Hush, hush, Mr. Primrose," exclaimed the doctor, interrupting him, "I cannot sit quietly by and hear the profession of the law traduced. All men, you know, must live by their profession, and the *little* delays which take place are undoubtedly made to do so professionally; the number of legal advisers in fact require it, otherwise half in the profession would starve for want of engagement. I admire the profession, Sir,—(puff, puff)—and regret that I did not study—(puff, puff)—law, rather than divinity."

"Well, well, doctor," added the good-natured farmer, "we will not quarrel on the point. Let us charge our glasses, and I'll give a toast."

"Good, good," said the doctor, "let us have it."

"A speedy reformation to the abuses of the law," said the farmer, as he drank off his glass.

"Well, Mr. Primrose," rejoined the justice, "as I wish as much as any man, whether in the commission of the peace or not, to see all *abuses* reformed, I feel no objection to your toast.—A speedy reformation—(hiccup)—to the abuses of the law."

Another and another glass of wine was taken, during which time Claudius became the subject of conversation. The proposal which the farmer had made to engage him in his service was stated, as well as the youth's willing acceptance of the offer; all which met the entire approbation of the doctor. So far, however, had the open and intelligent manner in which Claudius had acquitted himself in the presence secured for him the notice and good will of the justice, that he felt desirous to engage him in his own service, and especially so, as he was in want of a shrewd and intelligent lad as a livery servant.

"I have been—(puff, puff)—thinking, Mr. Primrose," said the doctor, "that I should like to take the boy under my own care, for—(puff, puff)—it appears to me that he is just such a lad as would suit my present purpose ;—(puff, puff)—and if I find him, what I feel inclined to believe I shall—intelligent, honest, and active—(puff, puff, puff)—I will take care his future prospects shall not be neglected. Are you disposed to let me have him?"

"Why, to tell the truth, doctor," replied the farmer, "I do not stand in need of a boy at present, although I could employ one; but the service which this lad has rendered me and mine, has laid, I feel, an obligation upon me to do for him all that lays in my power, and such is my determination. If, however, he is perfectly willing to enter your service, I shall feel happy to see him well settled with so good a master."

The arrangements were, in a little time, made; and as to Claudius, all places appeared equal, excepting that the prospect seemed fairer that he should, if engaged by the doctor, see more of public life than in the secluded situation which the farmer occupied—he consented to change masters before he had served either, and on the same evening accompanied the justice to his residence.

CHAP. VI.

"*Romeo.* Is love a tender thing? it is too rough,
            Too rude, too boist'rous; and it pricks like thorn.
 Mer.   If love be rough with you, be rough with love.
            Prick love for pricking, and you beat him down."

DURING the busy scenes already narrated, in which Claudius had been engaged, others of a no less exciting character had passed in rapid succession in the mansion of Lady Bolio, and as they may have some connexion with the subsequent history of our hero himself, it is proper that a brief reference should be made to them.

The first burst of feeling had scarcely escaped the lips of Lady Bolio, by which she informed the ill-starred Ferule and Miss Pinwell, that their services would no longer be required in her establishment, than, as the reader has been informed, she despatched her servants in various directions in search of the run-away; that they did not however, after the whole day's search, succeed, the new station in which Claudins has just been left fully proves. As soon as the orders above referred to had been given, she retired to her room in as sad and pitiable a state of feeling as can possibly be imagined. On the one hand, she felt as a fond mother naturally would feel for her lost son, concerning whose fate she experienced almost distracting anxiety. On the other, the green-eyed monster Jealousy—as some of the wise ones call the, thing—had enfolded her, although rather of bulky dimensions, in his maddening embrace. With phrensied emotion she paced the apartment, and then threw herself upon the sofa; but, as if the horse-hair couch had suddenly lost its elastic qualities, she turned and twisted as if placed upon the sharp points of an harrow to do penance for the sins of her youth, as a meritorious act decreed by some inquisitorial sage, or saintly sprig of holy mother church. Then, again, she rose and walked in a soliloquising mood. Every ten minutes she rang the bell, and, in an agitated tone, enquired if any tidings had yet been obtained concerning her son? To which question, the soul-sickening "No"—like an unchanging echo—was the unwelcome and heart-distracting reply.

"Was ever woman," exclaimed her ladyship in a tempest of feeling, in which every destructive passion of human nature appeared contending for the mastery, " was ever woman in so wretched a condition as I am? My almost idolizing affection for my son has only met with disrespect an'd unfeeling desertion. The esteem in which I held his tutor has received the most cold and cruel return; while my waiting-maid—she in whose integrity and prudence I confided with unqualified assurance—has committed herself, stolen the affections—but whither am I wandering?" enquired the lady of herself—" I mean has sought to entangle the affections— that is, mean, expected—that is, desired—I know not what I mean, or why I refer to the subject at all; to *me* it can be of no consequence—I am, I fear, about to be bereaved of my senses;—was ever woman circumstanced as I am?"

At the end of two hours her emotions had mounted to such a height, and acquired such fearful power, as to render it impossible she could sustain them, and therefore she again rang the bell with more than usual violence, and desired the servant who entered to inform Mr. Ferule she wished to see him directly.

At the moment the message reached the tutor, he was employing his eloquence in striving to sooth the disconsolate Miss Pinwell—who was making arrangements to leave the house—with declarations of inviolable affection.

"I will wait upon her ladyship immediately," said Mr. Ferule to the servant.

"You surely are not serious in what you say, Mr. Ferule?" observed Miss Pinwell as the messenger left the room.

"Not serious?" rejoined the tutor.   "In what, Miss Pinwell, do you imagine I am otherwise than serious?"

"In what?" returned the waiting-maid, with emphasis, "in waiting upon Lady Bolio, certainly."

"Why should I not?" enquired Ferule.

"Because," said Miss Pinwell, "I fear lest something should occur, which might have the tendency to cause a repetition of the distressing scene we so recently witnessed."

"No danger of that exists," rejoined the tutor.   "Lady Bolio is fully acquainted with the fact of our mutual attachment; and, besides which, we cannot now be considered as parts of her establishment.   Doubtless her object in requiring my attendance is, that she may confirm her expressed determination, and settle the pecuniary account which exists between us.   Of the particulars of which I will hasten back to inform you and complete such arrangements as circumstances may require; 'till then, dear Miss Pinwell, farewell, and believe me when I say that, in the fullest sense, I can employ the poet's language as my own,—

> "To thee will ever turn my faithful soul,
> As turns the needle constant to the pole ;
> No time will change, nor circumstances sever,
> My heart from thee, which loves, and must love ever!"

Such a string of heroics, delivered with all due regard to intonation, emphasis, and action, could have scarced failed to convince any young lady, similarly circumstanced, of the ardour and undying affection of the person who delivered them. To Miss Pinwell they were perfectly satisfactory, at least at the moment she thought they were, and hence she heard the retreating steps of Mr. Ferule without swooning or falling into hysterics.

From the time that Lady Bolio had despatched the servant for Mr. Ferule, up to the moment that he entered the apartment, in which her ladyship still paced with hurried steps, she had been striving to screw up her feelings to such a state of tension as that not even the presence of the favoured tutor himself should be able to move her.

"So, Mr. Ferule," said Lady Bolio, as he appeared before her, "I have sent for you—that is, I desired your attendance in order—"

Whether her ladyship laboured for thought, or for language to express her thoughts, or for breath to give utterance to language, is immaterial; before she could finish the above sentence she "stuck fast." Mr. Ferule, in order to deliver himself, as well as Lady Bolio, from the awkward dilemma in which he felt himself placed, observed,—

"I have attended your summons, Lady Bolio, and wait to receive your commands."

"It is well," rejoined her ladyship with considerable emotion.

"If I have offended you, Madam," said Ferule, "I—"

"*If* you have, Mr. Ferule," interrupted the lady—"*if*—surely, Sir, you do not feel disposed to plead ignorance on a subject with which you must be well acquainted?"

"I assure your ladyship," replied the tutor, "any offence I may have given has been perfectly unintentional, and—"

"Oh! certainly, certainly," exclaimed Lady Bolio, "unintentional of course; yes, that was *perfectly* unintentional, I dare say, with which that young woman charged you; it was *perfectly* unintentional, without doubt, that you paid her such delicate attentions scarcely two hours ago in my presence."

"I regret most sincerely, Lady Bolio," replied Mr. Ferule, "that I have given you offence, and I beg leave again to declare it was unintentional. But may I enquire your ladyship's present commands?"

"Oh! then, I suppose, you cannot spare time to wait my pleasure," replied Lady Bolio, somewhat piqued at the manner of Ferule, as well as vexed with herself for displaying emotions she would fain have concealed.

" Madam," returned Ferule, "you mistake me; I merely wished to enquire your ladyship's pleasure, that I might, if possible, attend to it before my departure."

" Before your departure !" exclaimed Lady Bolio, scarcely aware of the expression to which she gave utterance, until the expression had entered into the tutor's tympanium, from whence she could not extract it.

" Yes, Madam," returned Mr. Ferule, " before I leave your house as well as your service."

" Do you fully intend to leave then?" enquire her ladyship in softened tone. " Perhaps I was rather too hasty ;" and then, as her mind glared back upon the scene with Miss Pinwell, and the expressions of attachment which he had uttered towards her revived in her recollection, she added with fresh warmth, " It was the degrading position in which you placed yourself with that young person which put me beside myself." Again she softened, and showed all the woman in her excited feeling.—" You could not possibly mean what you expressed, Mr. Ferule?" she continued ; " mere sympathy for our weak sex, under peculiar circumstances, must have been the cause. Well, as you have repeated your professions of *regret* at having given offence, I must, of course, believe it was as I have supposed, and shall therefore pass over the affair without further notice. Be seated, Mr. Ferule," added her ladyship, pleased with the conclusion to which she had brought her own premises, " I wish to consult with you respecting my dear lost Claudius."

The desire, which was expressed in the kindest manner by Lady Bolio, that Mr. Ferule would be seated, was cheerfully attended to by him.

" No tidings have yet been received concerning him," subjoined the lady, drawing her chair towards the one occupied by the tutor.

" None that I am aware of, Madam," said Mr. Ferule.

" Heigho !" said the lady, " how had I better act, Mr. Ferule ?—You surely are not disposed to leave me under such peculiarly distressing circumstances ?"

" I know not, my lady, how you can act in reference to Master Bolio," replied the tutor, " with more propriety, or indeed otherwise than you have done ;—but as to my leaving you, Madam, I only obey, in so doing, your ladyship's will."

" My dear Mr. Ferule," returned Lady Bolio, drawing close to his side, " I own I was somewhat too hasty in my expression to *you*, but that has passed away; I need your services more than ever, indeed I cannot do without them; my own mind is too much excited and disturbed to attend to the affairs of my household. I feel more and more that I am a lonely woman and require the assistance which you can render me. If the salary you have received as my son's tutor is considered insufficient, make your *own* stipulation, and I will, whatever it may be, agree to it."

"I feel the obligation under which your ladyship is laying me," returned Mr. Ferule, "and as I never *have* been willingly, so I never *will* be,—ungrateful for your favour. In whatever way, therefore, I *can* render you service, it will be my constant pleasure and study to do so."

"Why, that is speaking like yourself again, Mr. Ferule," said the lady, while the internal gratification she experienced beamed forth from her sparkling eyes. "Your first piece of service then shall be to assure me you will not leave my house; for, as I have said, your assistance is indispensable."

"As your ladyship appears to wish I should remain," replied the tutor, "I shall not, I am sure, feel desirous to leave. Have you any further commands, Madam?" he added, rising from his chair.

"Not at present, Mr. Ferule," said her ladyship, following his example, and following him to the door of the apartment, at which he bowed, and withdrew.

For some minutes Lady Bolio felt as if the heat and weight of Mount Stromboli had been taken from her oppressed frame. She walked with as much buoyancy as if forty years had been struck out of the record of her past existence, and seemed actually to forget that she was a mother. But this Elysial feeling, this heaven of bliss, however, was of brief duration,—as evanescent as it was delicious and exciting. The scathing recollection rushed like lightning through her brain of *dear* Mr. Ferule's declaration of constant affection to her waiting-maid. Oh! the pangs and penalties, the unutterable and inconceivable torment of despised love, albeit that love be merely Platonic in its nature. Lady Bolio seemed to feel what Young has so powerfully described when making his Moor descant on jealousy:—

> "I have turn'd o'er the catalogue of woes
> Which sting the heart of man, and find none equal.
> It is the hydra of calamities,
> The seven-fold death; the jealous are the damn'd!

E

O, Jealousy! each other passion's calm
To thee, thou conflagration of the soul!
Thou king of torments! the grand counterpoise
For all the transports beauty can inspire!"

Like another Roxana, she could bear—

" No favour'd rival near her throne."

Nothing, surely, is half so ridiculous as an old man or woman in love. Too well skilled in the deceptions by which they were entrapped in the heyday of youth to enter fully into the magic circle, and strive to fill themselves with that which never satisfies, and yet too powerfully allured by the glare which promised enjoyment presents, they seem circumstanced like him of fabled memory—who, suspended betwixt heaven and hell, partook fully of neither, yet dreaded the one, and feared the loss of the other. In such pitiable condition Lady Bolio now felt herself. Her moment of enjoyment lately tasted had passed away, and all the misery which such loss occasioned festered upon the core of her being.

One only way presented itself by which she could hope even for deliverance from the torture of doubt and the enjoyment of hope, and that was by issuing a positive order for Miss Pinwell to leave the house immediately. Her hand was already on the bell-pull, when she bethought herself that the better way to proceed would be to have the assurance from Mr. Ferule himself, that he really did not mean what he had said as he raised the fainting lady from her fainting fit. Yet, how to obtain this was a question she could not directly answer. At a time like the present, thought rather inflames than cools ; yet Lady Bolio attempted to think. Fortunately, she recollected the kind statement which the tutor had just made to herself, " that in *whatever* way he could serve her, it would be his happiness and study to do it." She had, indeed, by laying the emphasis upon a different word than that on which Mr. Ferule had placed it, in no small degree changed the meaning of the sentence ; but she perceived it not—she read it as her own feelings dictated ; and now, half hoping, half fearing, rang the bell, determining to call upon Mr. Ferule to fulfil his promise, by serving her as she *wished* to be served, whether he *could* so serve her or not.

" Oh, Janet," said her ladyship, with assumed *nonchalance,* as the servant entered, " say to Mr. Ferule, I shall be glad to see him for a moment if he is not too greatly engaged."

" Yes, Ma'am," said Janet, and, curtseying, withdrew.

The brief period which elapsed between her orders being given and Mr. Ferule's appearance was actively employed by Lady Bolio in arranging her head-dress and putting in order some straggling ringlets which had that morning been sent from her hair-dresser's, and which now sported luxuriantly to the no small embellishment of her ladyship's physiognomy on each side of her temples, concealing most effectively

> "The silver locks which age had given,
> As suited to her wrinkled brow."

" I am sorry, Mr. Ferule," said Lady Bolio, as he entered, " to trouble you again; but as you have so kindly promised to serve me—" she hesitated—

" In all I *can*, Madam," replied Ferule, " I shall feel most happy to do so."

"Thank you, Mr. Ferule," returned her ladyship, "you are very kind. I have ever found you ready to seek the interest of myself and son. I regret that you have not hitherto met with the reward which such exemplary services have a claim to."

" A consciousness, Madam," returned the tutor, " of having performed to the extent of our abilities the duties which providence has imposed upon us, is ever found to be a high and rich reward to the conscience of an honest man, although every other should be withheld."

" Oh! Mr. Ferule," sighed Lady Bolio, almost overcome by the lofty sentiments of the dapper pedagogue, " how much do I admire your noble spirit! but," she added, " if a compensation, as far equal to your deservings as *I* can render is not enjoyed by you, it will be no fault of mine, I assure you. I shall be most happy, to the extent of my poor abilities, to make you the happiest of men. If *all* I possess can do it—"

" Madam!" exclaimed Ferule, starting, as if stung by a dragon-fly, " What mean you? I do not understand."

. " What do I mean, Mr. Ferule?" interrupted her ladyship, half confused, half confounded," I—I mean—nothing. What could you suppose I meant? That is, I mean I shall feel proud to evince my high regard of your worth and character by making you every return in my power. Now, do be seated,

Mr. Ferule, and attend to what I wish you would have the kindness to perform for me."

"With pleasure, Madam," replied the tutor, taking the offered chair, "I am bound to do *all* I *can* do, and, as I have repeated, I shall feel most happy in the performance of it."

"Well, then, there is one little point I must trouble you to settle for me directly—my nerves are too much affected at present to attend to any arrangement in my establishment. I never take pleasure, my dear Mr. Ferule, in dismissing a servant; indeed, it is always a painful task to me, although sometimes a necessary duty. You understand me, Mr. Ferule?"

"Perfectly, Madam," replied the tutor.

"Well, then," said Lady Bolio, "I wish you would, without delay, settle my account with Miss Pinwell."

"With Miss Pinwell, Madam !" exclaimed the astounded Ferule, starting from his seat, and gazing upon her ladyship with distended organs.

"Ye—ye—yes;" stammered out the lady. "You do not object, I hope, Mr. Ferule ?"

"Object, Madam ?" replied the little man, "Oh, no, no, Madam, certainly not. If it is *your* wish, why—"

"That is kind now, *very* kind," observed Lady Bolio, brightening up again. "I am indebted to her one half-year's salary. There are fifteen pounds, ten shillings; and, in consideration of her past services, and the obligation I am under to dismiss her thus suddenly, there are ten pounds in addition, which I intend making a present to her;" and she spread the notes upon the table as she spoke. "Now, you will oblige me by paying that sum into her hands, and seeing that she leaves this house this evening."

"I promised you, Madam," replied Ferule, in the utmost amazement, "that all I *could* do, I would cheerfully perform; but, as I feel no obligation from the office I have filled in your establishment, so neither have I the inclination to perform this work. However, Madam," he continued, "I have no doubt that Miss Pinwell, as well as myself, will be willing to attend to your ladyship's wish in this respect."

"What do you mean, Mr. Ferule ?" exclaimed her ladyship, almost fainting with alarm.

"I mean, Madam," replied the tutor, with calm emphasis, "to prove, that although I may not retain your ladyship's favour, I will deserve it !"

"Yes, dear Mr. Ferule," returned Lady Bolio—"You *do* deserve it; and I am convinced you *always* will deserve."

" I should not, Madam," rejoined Ferule, " were I to desert a woman who has given me her heart, and to whom I have pledged myself. In such case I should be a very rogue, an execrable villain, deserving only universal scorn."

"True, true, Mr. Ferule," exclaimed Lady Bolio, who, by some unaccountable obliquity of conception, applied his ardent declaration to herself instead of Miss Pinwell.—"Then you do accept the offer, which I blush to tender ? Oh! my dear Mr. Ferule, from what a load of misery have you relieved me!"

The surprise and confusion of Ferule at this singular declaration, and the palpable mistake under which Lady Bolio laboured were so great, that for several moments he could neither oppose the endearing actions, nor undeceive the infatuated mind of the doating lady,—at length he exclaimed:—

" Madam, you are labouring under an error, from which, as a man of honour, I am bound to relieve you.—It is to Miss Pinwell I stand engaged !"

Had a lighted bomb-shell suddenly fallen into the centre of the room, and by its loud hissing announced impending destruction, the excited countenance of Lady Bolio could scarcely have displayed the working of more powerful passion,—the effect produced was crushing as it was sudden and unexpected.

" To Miss Pinwell !" shrieked Lady Bolio, and, staggering to the sofa, almost fainted as she fell upon it.—" Oh, you ungrateful man !" she continued—as soon as she could find sufficient breath to do so—" Is it thus you return the high regard in which I have held you ? Is it thus I am treated in return for the sacrifice I was ready to make ? But, no matter, Sir," she added, raising herself from the recumbent position she had assumed,—" I will let you see that a woman can scorn and hate as strongly as she can—respect."

" I have not merited your scorn or hatred, Madam," replied Ferule ; " nor am I conscious of having done aught to forfeit the respect in which you were pleased to hold me. But, now, Madam," he added, retreating towards the door as he spoke, " since this explanation has taken place, propriety dictates that Miss Pinwell and myself should immediately leave your residence. We shall only wait your ladyship's pleasure to close our accounts with us, and then withdraw."

"Mr. Ferule,— dear Mr. Ferule!" cried her ladyship, roused and softened by his motion towards the door,—"stay but one moment, and consider before you determine."

"I have considered, Madam," returned Ferule, "and upon that consideration my determination is formed,—your servant." So saying, be bowed respectfully and retired.

*   *   *   *   *   *

The clock in the hall had struck three, just as a party re-turned from an unsuccessful search after Claudius; in order to communicate which intelligence to Lady Bolio, a servant entered her apartment. A loud shriek burst from the lips of the affrighted girl as she run from the room screaming with terror—and "Help, help, help—my lady is dead,—is mur-dered!"—sounded through the mansion.

The cries of the terrified girl soon collected a posse of at-tendants, who, hastening to the room from which the servant had fled as if followed by a blood-dripping dagger, found Lady Bolio lying senseless upon the carpet drenched in blood. With care and despatch they raised and placed her cold form upon the sofa, while a messenger was despatched, post haste, for Doctor Leachum. In a short time the skilful leech arrived, and proceeded to examine the injury which her ladyship had received. As soon as the blood was washed from her face, it was discovered that, in addition to two or three bruises, a wound had been inflicted on her right tem-ple, which, as Mercutio would have said, was "not so deep as a well, nor so wide as a church door." Several layers of strapping were soon applied to the incision, and a bandage wound round the lady's head, when, upon the use of some powerful remedies, signs were given of returning conscious-ness.

Immediately, upon opening her eyes, she looked wildly round, with the astonishment of one suddenly roused from a confused dream.

"What does all this mean?" enquired her ladyship.

"Be composed, Madam," replied Leachum, "your lady-ship has met with a slight accident, but with quietness, and such attention as I shall give, no serious consequences need be apprehended; and soon, I hope, you will be perfectly restored."

"Where is Mr. Ferule?" resumed her ladyship, looking

round the group,—and then, as if a sudden but confused recollection of past circumstances was possessed by her, she added,—" I have something particular to say to Mr. Ferule, desire him to attend upon me directly."

" Mr. Ferule, my lady," answered a servant, " has left the house more than an hour ago in company with Miss Pinwell."

" Left the house!" shouted Lady Bolio—" with Miss Pinwell too ?—Oh! oh,.oh," and again she fainted.

There was a degree of mystery about this part of the business, which even the occult skill of the disciple of Esculapius could not unravel. He directed, however, that her ladyship should immediately be conveyed to her chamber, which order, after some considerable trouble in consequence of the rotundity of Lady Bolio's person, was attended to, and the languid patient, by the active exertion of half a dozen female servants, was placed in bed.

That a variety of suspicions and dark surmises should be entertained by the different members of Lady Bolio's establishment, concerning the condition in which she had been found, was perfectly natural; connected too, as it appeared to be, with the flight of Mr. Ferule and Miss Pinwell. Now the fact of the case is simply this,—the high Platonic feeling of Lady Bolio received so powerful a shock on hearing Mr. Ferule's plain declaration of his engagement with Miss Pinwell, that immediately on his leaving her apartment, shame and disappointed love acted so powerfully upon her sensitive nature that all consciousness of the trouble of this naughty world faded from her

" Like the baseless fabric of a vision;"

and, falling in a fainting fit from the sofa on which she had reclined, her temple came in violent contact with the corner of her footstool, by which means she received the wound referred to, and in that condition,—" bleeding at this new made pore"—she had lain until the entry of the servant led to the discovery.

During the first night of Lady Bolio's confinement, her mind wandered continually to the object of her soul's affection, and, in accents corresponding with such feeling, she repeatedly called for Mr. Ferule: sometimes, the partner of his travels,—Miss Pinwell, was named, and then a wild incoherent string of complaints, gratulations, and criminations, was uttered by her.

"For shame, Mr. Ferule!" exclaimed her ladyship,—"consider what you are doing,—ah! how degrading,—well, well, mighty fine 'pon my word,—what, with a waiting maid ?— now that is kind—very, *very* kind,—bear her away,—put her from the room.—Yes, yes, every thing,—all I possess shall be yours,—there, there is my signature:—now you will not leave me, will you dear ?—no, no ; I do, indeed, I do believe you."

In this way the lady continued to rave the whole night, while those who attended upon her, supposing that her expressions of regret and of fond endearment referred to the lost Claudius, sympathised with their afflicted mistress, and regretted their want of ability to minister to her wants or relieve her from her sufferings.

Week after week passed away, and no tidings could be obtained of Master Bolio; during all which time the lady was confined entirely to her room, and almost to her bed. Once, and only once, Mr. Ferule had called at the mansion since his departure, on which occasion he was favoured with a *tête à tête* with Lady Bolio solus. What the nature of the interview might have been has not transpired; all that is known is that the tutor, having brought with him Miss Pinwell's authority to receive her salary, had done so, together with his own, and that shortly after his departure, the invalid experienced a serious relapse, which threatened serious consequences. The attendants sagely enough concluded that the fresh attack had been the result of a renewed recollection of Claudius occasioned by the sight of his tutor.

The assiduities of Doctor Leachum, like the surgeon of Seville, were incessant; and if, like that renowned personage, he had not recourse to bleeding and hot water as an exclusive and infallible panacea, he at least did not spare the lancet, omit draughts, or furnish a niggard supply of pills and boluses. By these wholesome means, and spare diet, he succeeded effectually in suppressing fever, by draining almost every drop of blood from her system, and reducing her " too solid flesh," if not " into a dew," to little less than the "unsubstantial shadow of what it was."

Having thus practised his art successfully upon Lady Bolio's frame, so that if any spark of Platonic, or any other kind of affection almost, had hitherto lurked in any portion of her body, it must, without doubt, have been "bled and purged away," he had recourse to a more generous mode or

treatment to bring her into flesh again. He ordered that rich jellies, nourishing soups, cheering cordials, and invigorating wine, should be taken as often, and in as large quantities, as the stomach would receive without loathing.

The reduction of Lady Bolio had been the work of only a few weeks, so perfectly did Leechum understand, and so successfully practise, the depletive part of his profession; but to re-invigorate debilitated nature was a task of much more difficult character, and hence, after months had elapsed, she was merely able to rise from her bed and stagger from one end of the apartment to the other.

"Do you really think I am better?" enquired her ladyship of Dr. Leechum, during one of his visits.

"Better, my lady!" replied Leechum, "beyond a doubt. Your pulse, madam," he observed, taking her wrist gently between his thumb and finger, "your pulse, madam, is regular and placid as an infant's; a *leetle* more action, perhaps, is desirable. You sleep well, do you not?"

"Only middling, doctor," answered the lady; "scarcely nine hours the whole night long, and not above two-thirds that time in the day."

"Well, well," said the leech; "that is but middling, still it is better than to sleep too soundly all at once. Your appetite is improving?"

"Not exactly so," replied her ladyship.

"Ah, well, that's of no great consequence," returned the doctor, "the digestive organs have not as yet quite recovered their usual tone of action. A little bark will soon set that right. Your tongue, madam,—allow me, if you please?— Umph!" said the man of the pestle and mortar, as he looked professionally upon the unruly member which hung out of Lady Bolio's mouth; "that's good—decidedly so—no disease, that is certain. Fever has entirely disappeared; a small portion of languor merely, proceeding from weakness. You, of course, took the draught which I sent you last night?"

"The draught, doctor?" said Lady Bolio, "no; surely my servant did not omit it."

The doctor turned over the leaves of his visiting memorandum, and added, "Oh! I see, it was my mistake—none was sent—it was unnecessary; however, we will take care and supply you this evening, and as soon as the season will permit I should recommend a visit to Bath or Clifton; the salubrity and bracing qualities of those charming spots, and the fashionable company that resorts thither, will, I have no doubt, with a little care, and some attention from myself to your system, completely restore you."

"Your kind attentions, doctor," rejoined Lady Bolio, "will, I fear, never be repaid by me."

"Why, in truth, madam," said the leech, "yours was a case which required all the skill and attention that could be obtained, and I am proud to have been the means of accomplishing so much as has already been done. But my time is gone," he continued, looking at his repeater. "Good morning!" he added, as he bowed, and withdrew.

It should be observed, that in one particular, at least, Dr. Leechum was unquestionably skilful—in the slang of his profession. He could produce a reason for any failure, and lay claim, without blushing, to having performed a miraculous cure, although by his treatment he had reduced his patient to the borders of the grave; and then, if by some extraordinary effort of nature, or a successful experiment, the half-murdered invalid rallied, and so baulked the *grave* man and the physician, the whole circle of his connexions were informed of it by his agents, and, instead of receiving a well-deserved bastinado upon his breech, a handsome douceur is thrust into his purse, and the loud voice of ignorance trumpets forth his fame.

In the experience of Lady Bolio the case was precisely as has been stated; and, when at length she had so far recovered as to direct arrangements should be made for spending a season at the places recommended, she insisted that the doctor—to whom she was under such lasting obligations, and without whose presence she dared not venture forth—should, in company with his lady, spend as much of the season with her, at the mansion she had engaged, as his professional duties would allow

CHAPTER VII.

"Aye,—by a holy Palmer's faith, I swear
The metamorphis suits the youngster well.
Had madam Nature, in a merry mood,
Design'd him for the office that he fills,
Her art could scarce have made a better fit.
At every point he is the thing he apes.
From the gold lace he on his bonnet wears,
E'en to the well-gloss'd shoe his livery fits ;
While he in spirit suits the dress he wears."

J. YOUNG.

THE Reverend Winchester Titheum, D.D., to a slight acquaintance with whom the reader has been already introduced, and of whom something more remains to be stated,
from his present connexion with the history of our hero,
felt proud to be able to boast of himself as a sprig of nobility.
If, indeed, he had been influenced by nobility of spirit, he
would have allowed that circumstance to pass without notice,
from the consideration that even *royal* descent could add
nothing to deserved reputation, nor of itself communicate
honour, while that which constitutes true dignity is not possessed ;—dignity of mind, and nobility of principle. But,
what will not a man do in such degenerate times to be gaped
upon by his fellow-men as a descendant of a noble line ? It
is true there is no more credit in such circumstance than
there is discredit in being the offspring of a felon, neither of
the descendants having any hand in the matter. Such, however, was Dr. Titheum ; and to that circumstance, in all probability, rather than to any natural or acquired recommendation, he was indebted for clerical honours and preferment, as
well as the seat which he filled upon the magisterial bench.
Once he had entered the delectable state of matrimony ;
but, at the time that he engaged Claudius professionally as a
livery servant—but really as his factotum—his lad of all-
work—he had worn the symbols of widowhood nearly eight
months : but time, that softener of the acutest sorrow, had
considerably mellowed his, so that, as has been seen, his
great loss (Mrs. Titheum had nearly doubled the doctor's
weight) interfered not with that hilarity of spirit which it be-
hoved him to display at all convivial meetings.
The fruit of the divine's matrimonial connexion was one
daughter, who the same day that the mother ceased to live

entered her sixteenth year. If the heated and half-crazed imagination of a poet had been allowed to descant on the personal charms of the lovely girl, he would have spoken of her as Byron did of his first lady-love, as being formed out of a rainbow—all beauty and spirit; but a mere matter-of-fact man would have described her as she really was—a very beautiful creature, but withal, a very daughter of Eve.

In person she was tall and slender. Her countenance would have led any physiognomist to pronounce her a satirist of no mean power; and in forming such judgment he would not have erred. Her swan-like neck, and finely moulded shoulders, which were fair as Parian marble, and beautifully tinted with the warm glow of life, were partly concealed by clustering locks of glossy chestnut-coloured hair, which the maiden allowed to fall in natural and unconfined curls.

It is not too much to say, that the doctor was justly proud of his beloved Georgiana; and what fond parent would not have been proud of such a gem of human nature? He had been lavish in his expenditure to procure all the advantages and embellishments which a finished education could afford her. In pursuing this object, however, he had committed one cardinal blunder; but which, having become fashionable, is, like all other fashionable absurdities, as fairly considered an act of propriety as if truth and advantage supported the notion :—that is, he had transported his daughter for some years to a celebrated boarding-school in the vicinity of Paris; and, as a necessary,—or at least, general consequence, she had returned learned in frothy literature, and an adept in Parisian artifice and intrigue.

Of the doctor himself little more need be stated to render the reader sufficiently familiar with his character and habits. It is admitted, that he did indeed lack the power, and, perhaps, would have blushed (although of that act of disgrace to a plump, ruddy phiz, he was not very frequently guilty) to have laid claim to an art equal to that possessed by the Athenian orator, Antipion, to drive away sadness; nevertheless, he *was*,—as it is reported to have been the case with that poet and orator,—fond of selling his orations at a very high rate; hence, although his living —without including all he could legally insist upon,—and all he *could* he *did*,—amounted to the no very despicable sum of upwards of eighteen hundred pounds a year—he felt no compunctious throes of conscience, —notwithstanding having been *moved* by the Holy Ghost to enter into *holy* orders,—at refusing to preach any oftener than the authority of his diocesan rendered obligatory ; and even such obligation his ghostly (query, fleshly) reverence contrived to evade the personal endurance of by engaging a proxy to perform this part, as well as the general fag of his other duties.

The gentleman whom Dr. Titheum had engaged as his curate was a needy, unpatronised son of the church—" a brother beloved," who had recently graduated at Oxford, and who, for the liberal consideration of seventy pounds a year, and an occasional feed with his rector, undertook to do the thing for him.

Pshaw ! Gentle Sir, we anticipate your grave look while you pause or re-read the statement just made—but of its verity we pledge our fair fame and undying honours in the republic of literature. But who in all this matter can cry *shame*, while the well-known adage is practically, or in spirit, observed by all ?—" Fresh violets, when cheap, send forth an unsavoury odour."

Mr. Milksop, the doctor's lecturer, possessed a kindred spirit with his own, although in personal appearance he was strikingly dissimilar. He was a tall, lank personage, somewhat about two yards long ; his cadaverous aspect and thin body formed as fine a contrast with the rector's plump cheeks and " fair round form," as one seeking the complete opposite of mortal things could possibly have found. The doctor, indeed, was the wiser man of the two ; for he let the world wag as it would, without perplexing himself about its busy workings any further than immediately concerned his own interests and enjoyments ; while Mr. Milksop was a politician of the first class,—a complete out-and-outer, so that rather than have possessed the mitre of a bishop without blending the political with the priestly character, he would, had the offer been made him, have thrown up the dazzling order to have filled a seat in the lower house.

It is scarcely necessary to mention to the reader what he must already have observed, namely, that the rector was fond,—*very* fond of a pipe. Like the learned professor, Box-hornius, of Leyden, he was almost an incessant smoker. Of the professor it is stated, that he wore a large-brimmed hat, with a hole in front of it, through which he dexterously thrust his pipe, by which clever contrivance he obtained an excellent support for the earthen tube while he studied and wrote. Now to this extent there was no parallel between those dignitaries, inasmuch as Doctor Titheum did not wear a hat when smoking in the house, as he required no support for his pipe of the description used by the learned professor, and simply, because he was not, like him, in the habit of studying.

The members of the rector's establishment consisted of a lusty cook, who had ministered to his appetite for some two or three years with credit,—a housemaid, and a man who filled the opposite and responsible offices of butler, gardener, and coachman—for the doctor maintained it as firmly as he believed in the thirty-nine articles, that no sinecurist was worth the salt he ate, whether found in a state or a family, and, therefore, he determined that no one should hold a sine-cure under his roof.

On the next morning after the doctor's return from Farmer Primrose's, a messenger was despatched to Mr. Jacob Buckram's, the family tailor, desiring his immediate attendance at the rectory, to which order the *sheer* man paid prompt attention. Immediately upon Snip's arrival, he was ushered into the august presence of the doctor.

"So, Mr. Buckram," said his reverence, "have you brought a measure with you?"

"Yes, please you," replied Buckram, making a salaam of modern cut, well suited for a high day salute to any three-tailed bashaw. "What garment shall I take measure of your reverence for?" he enquired.

"I do not want any thing for my own person, Master Jacob," returned the doctor, "but I have taken a fancy to a poor lad, whom I met with yesterday, and for him I wish you to make, with all possible haste, two suits of clothes; one of such a sort as he will require to perform his task about the house and garden in, and the other I wish to be a good livery, fit for him to appear before company in, and to attend myself or my daughter when we pay any visits. You understand me, Mr. Buckram?"

"O yes, Sir," replied Snip; "your reverence's orders shall be attended to."

"I expect company the day after to-morrow," added the doctor, "by that time the best suit must be brought home."

"It shall be here, without fail," replied Buckram. "Does your reverence wish that any change should be made in the

quality or colour of the cloth from those I made before for
your servant ?"

"No," answered the doctor, "in neither ;—but take care
you are punctual, Master Jacob. We who are in the commission of the peace love punctuality. You will find the
lad in the kitchen. Good morning, Mr, Buckram."

"Good morning, Sir," replied Buckram. "You may depend upon me, Sir. I never disappoint a customer who
can afford to pay," he added, in an under tone, as he backed
and bowed out of the room, and hastened to seek Claudius.

In a few minutes his measuring tape was wound round and
stretched in perpendicular position on the person of the
Gypsy boy. Having taken his dimensions, he re-measured
the foot of Betty, the cook, who, with native kindness, un-
locked her private store, and supplied the man of tape and
bobbin with a large thimble-full of excellent Sherry, which
she had carefully preserved among a few other bottles as
some of the perquisites of her office.

At the appointed time Claudius stood before the rector in
his span new livery, his camp equipage having been, with due
form and ceremony, consigned to the flames, as a purifying
process it was considered indispensable it should undergo.
So greatly had a change of dress improved the personal appearance of Claudius, that even the doctor expressed his gratification as he appeared before him. The suit was of dark
green, with metal buttons, neatly adorned with yellow braid-
ing, and turned up with facings of the same colour. Instead
of a hat he held in his hand a species of jockey cap, from the
centre of the crown of which a yellow silk tassel depended,
while the edges of the cap were bound with cord of the same
bright character.

"Umph!" said the doctor, as Claudius appeared in his
presence ; "dress has certainly improved your appearance. I
hope we shall be able to improve your habits and morals as
greatly. It will be your own fault if you do not become
respectable."

Claudius, while under the instruction of Mr. Ferule, had
been so far tutored into the art and mystery of elocution as
to have cut no despicable figure among a group of juveniles,
who at a Christmas party had enacted some scenes from
Home's "Douglas"—and now, half forgetting himself, or
conceiving that some of the lines he had then repeated, per-
tinently applicable to the doctor's kind address, replied,

" Rude I am
In speech and manners ; never till this hour
Stood I in such presence ; yet, kind Sir,
There's something in my breast, which makes me bold
To say, that I will never shame your favour,"

" Heighday! heighday!" shouted the doctor, looking at
Claudius, as if incredulous whether his eyes, or his ears, de-
ceived him, or if his new livery servant, or some more distinguished personage, stood before him,—" a very Garrick I
declare!"—he at length exclaimed ; "where learned you this
my lad?" enquired the Divine; but before he permitted
Claudius to reply, he continued,—" How do your clothes
fit boy, eh? turn about, turn about."

" Very nicely, Sir," replied Claudius, at the same time
performing the rotary movement required of him.

" Good," said his reverence, closely inspecting the fit,
' you are quite willing, faithfully and truly to serve me, are
you?"

" I shall feel proud to do my best, Sir," answered Claudius.

" Well, and fairly spoken," rejoined the doctor,—" but
remember I am in the commission of the peace, and while
I reward liberally all who serve me well, I never fail to punish,
with the utmost rigour, such as deserve it; therefore, being
forewarned, you will, I hope, take care."

" I shall not willingly incur your displeasure, Sir," replied
Claudius.

" Well, well, we shall make something of you I dare say,"
said the rector, " I will just inform you of the few matters
you will have to attend to. Do you understand waiting at
table?"

" Yes, Sir," answered the livery servant, " I can serve."

" Oh! ah! certainly," interrupted the doctor, "you were
head waiter in the camp, I suppose. Ah! ah! ah! well well,
we shall see; a little instruction will qualify you for higher
service. Now I expect company this evening, when it will
be your duty to attend, some hours will elapse before then ;
in the mean time Betty, the cook, will give you a lesson or
two; attend punctually to her directions, and I shall expect
to find you a clever lad."

" I will be sure to do so, Sir," answered Claudius.

" Good," said the doctor,—"let me see," he continued,
" you will have to clean boots and shoes, attend to the poultry
and two or three cows, to clean the harness, and other little

matters; when I go out, you will accompany me, and if Miss Georgiana requires you on any particular business, you must obey her instantly; in short, you must make yourself handy and useful. For the first year's service, I shall give you four guineas, with two suits of clothes, and all the perquisites you get you may consider your own. If you are a good lad and steady, always speak the truth, seek to oblige every body, and are ready to perform whatever you are told to do, why your fortune will be made, and you may be as happy as the days are long, and I will take care, on the first opportunity, to advance you both in service and salary."

To the several parts of this highly interesting address Claudius bowed, and half wished a memorandum had been furnished him of the various items of duty which he would be expected to attend to, fearing as he did, that, amidst their diversified and multiplied character, some might run through the sieve holes in his memory.

The doctor having come to the end of his string of instructions, Claudius was dismissed to the kitchen, there to receive a few fresh lessons, and some further directions, from the cook. With this important personage he succeeded, in a short time, to become a decided favourite, and was advantaged not a little by her good graces.

"Now," observed Mistress Fatpan, addressing herself to Claudius, "as I am to *instillate* some information into you, I must, in course, know if you are quite willing to learn."

"Oh! quite so, I assure you," replied Claudius, "any body, I am sure, would be quite willing to learn from *you.*"

"Well now, that is very sensible said," observed the cook, flattered by the high opinion which Claudius appeared to entertain of her. "Well then, above all things in the world, I like to teach them as is willing to be *constructed*; now observe the first things you must do is to do *nothing.*"

"Indeed!" said Claudius, "I shall soon learn that, I dare say."

"Well then," continued Mistress Fatpan, "you must be blind, deaf, and dumb."

"Oh! I can't be blind, I can't indeed," said Claudius, rubbing his eyes, "I'd give up the best place in the world before I'd part with my eyes."

"Ha, ha, ha," roared the cook in the most hearty style, "hexcellent, hexcellent upon my word; ha, ha, ha, well now, this ere shows how much need there is that I should *edecate* you. Now I tell you, Claudo,—that is your name I think."

"Claudius, Mrs. Fatpan," answered our hero.

"Oh! well, that's too long for a sarvant, Claudo will do; now listen to me with intention Claudo," continued the cook, "and your fortin will soon be made. I say, in the first place, you must be blind, deaf, and dumb, as all good sarvants is. You must be blind to all you see in the kitchen, deaf to all you hear, and dumb to tell what you know. You compre-stand me now, don't you?"

"Why ye—s," stammered out Claudius not more than half liking the first lesson for fear of unpleasant consequences which might ensue, "I think I do."

"If you wish to succeed in a gentleman's family," continued Mistress Fatpan, you must be on good terms with the *upper* sarvants : you had better offend the whole of the family than one of us."

"I'll take good care not to offend *you*," said Claudius, "I shall always feel happy to return your kindness in instructing me."

"There's a good lad," rejoined the cook, chucking him under the chin significantly, "now if you *should* see any thing this evening, which you are not quite acquainted with, you are *not* to see it,—do you see?"

"Why, yes," said Claudius, "I think I do."

"We intends enjoying ourselves in the kitchen," observed the cook, "while the gentle folks enjoys themselves in the drawing room,—do you see?"

"I think I do," again replied Claudius.

"Well, but you are *not* to see," rejoined Mrs. Fatpan.

"Oh, I understand," said Claudius,—"Eh? eh? eh?" what can she mean thought he to himself,—"yes, I understand,—I don't see when I see."

"That's right, that's right," cried the cook; "we shall have a few of the parson's bottles, which Mister Joseph, the coachman and butler, has promised us; and I'll take care of the eatables,—but you are blind you know?"

"Stone blind," cried Claudius.

"Ah, ah, ah," roared the cook, — "and you must be deaf too."

"As a post," returned Claudius.

"And dumb," added Mistress Fatpan.

"As an Egyptian mummy," cried Claudius.

"An Egypt what?" said the cook.

" An Egyptian mummy, "—returned the livery lad.

" What in the world kind of a person is that ?" enquired the cook in surprise, " Is it somewhat that you Gypsies uses in telling fortins ?"

" Not exactly, " returned our hero,—" it is a person that has neither eyes, ears, nor tongue."

" Ah ! well, that is just what you are to be," replied Mrs. Fatpan. " Hexcellent ! now, I think you understand all about it.—the other things you will get hold of by practice. Hush !" she continued, " I have a little cordial which I am obliged to take sometimes, my duties obligate me ; you, of course, see nothing."

" Oh, not I," said Claudius, " nothing I assure you Mistress Fatpan. "

" Well then, you shall just taste it," said the cook, and going to a small cupboard of which she held the key, she took from it a stone bottle, and having poured out a brimmer, she swallowed it, without changing a single muscle of her full moon face, and then refilling the glass, presented it to Claudius, who, after a considerable time spent in ridiculing his squeamishness, and highly recommending the thing as an *hexcellent preservetment* against lowness of spirits, he put to his mouth and drank a portion of, persisting against taking the whole.

· " Well, I will not be rude and force it," observed the cook, " but it must be drunk, " and so saying, she good-naturedly made up Claudius' deficiency, by causing it to follow what she had before poured down her throat. Whether the spirit she had drunk operated upon her animal spirits, or whether the new dress in which Claudius was arrayed made him appear older than he really was, and therefore a fitter object of female regard, than he otherwise would have been, is a question which, like that of perpetual motion, has not been settled ; all that can with assurance be affirmed is, that Mistress Fatpan, like another Donna Innez, semed wishful to metamorphose Claudius into another Don Juan,—and with that point fully made up in her mind, she threw her brawny arms round the neck of our hero in the most gallant style, and before a thought of her intention had occurred to Claudius, would have accomplished her purpose fully, had not an incident, which threatened to prove fatal to her reputation, unexpectedly happened.

" There is many a slip between the cup and the lip, " is so musty a proverb, that did not its metaphorical import apply most aptly to the case in hand, we should fear to employ it.

But whether some malignant influence, either planetary or
diabolic, resolved, by an illnatured freak, to mar the pleasure
which Mistress Fatpan had calculated upon, or whether
natural causes produced the effect referred to, we cannot de-
monstrate; but just as the cook's rosy lips were coming in
contact with Claudius', who should drop into the kitchen
but Mister Joseph, the butler, &c. betwixt whom and the
cook a tender engagement existed: so intent was the amorous Mistress Fatpan upon enjoying the luscious kiss, that, in
all probability, she would not have observed the presence of
a third person, if a loud crash had not suddenly aroused her
from the waking dream into which she had fallen.

Mister Joseph had contrived to abstract, from the doctor's
store, a bottle of his best Sherry, for the enjoyment of the
kitchen party in the evening. In order to prevent detection,
he had concealed the brittle vessel beneath his coat under his
arm, when, as he opened the door of the kitchen, and beheld
the loving attitude in which his defianced stood with Claudius; every thing beside was forgotten; his arms, with unconscious action, flew up, and the same instant the bottle
dropped *down* and was smashed into pieces upon the stone
floor, over which the precious juice flowed most provokingly.

"Bless me, Joseph!" exclaimed the cook, starting from
her position, as she uttered a loud shriek, "how you have
alarmed one!—why what in the name of goodness have you
done?"

"What have I done?" replied the butler, "Umph, I
think Mistress Fatpan, you had as well ask what you were
doing!"

"Doing Joseph!" rejoined the cook, "why, what should
I be doing?—nothing, nothing, I *protestify*,—upon my
word and *honour*, and that is saying very much Joseph."

"Why, I rather think it *is*," returned Joseph drily,
"your pledge is a high one."

"Well, at least," rejoined the cook, "there was no
harm in what I was doing."

"No harm!" exclaimed the butler, trembling with excited
feeling, "Oh no, certainly not,—but it looked very suspicious."

"No dear Joseph," continued the lady,—"it is yourself
what is so *perticularly* suspicious. I am sartain sure there was
no suspiciousness in what I was a doing, was there Claudo?"

In all such matters as the present, Claudius having only

just entered upon his noviciate, could not be supposed to possess the same acute understanding as was enjoyed by his erudite instructress. For a moment or two he stood

" Lost within a wilderness of thought
While thinking but increased the labyrinth, "

perfectly unresolved which side to take, when fortunately the thought suddenly entered his head, that he might profit by the lesson which but a short time before he had received from the cook; accordingly he commenced by being blind and dumb.

" Why don't you answer my question ?" enquired the cook, in somewhat of an acid tone.

" Because," answered Claudius, " I can't see."

" Can't see !" shouted the cook. " Don't you see that I am conglomerated all over with fright, and that I am likely to be ruinated by false suspicionings ?"

" No," replied Claudius, with provoking calm indifference, " I don't see; and if I did, I am dumb."

A happy thought struck the cook's ready imagination, and, bursting into a hearty laugh, she turned to Joseph, and observed, " Well, now, I declare, the uproar you made at coming in drove all thought out of my head until this moment. I can now tell you what I was doing. I was whispering a lesson into the new servant's ear—giving him some construction how he is to behave himself in this here place. Did n't you hear him this instant repeating it ? I was telling him, he must be blind, deaf, and dumb."

" Ha ! ha ! ha !" roared Joseph, in a forced laugh. " Was it so, indeed ? I dare say," he added, to himself, " you imagine that *I* am blind. I must bear it now, I suppose, but after the wedding is over I'll *see* more clearly, and shan't then be quite so *dumb*."

Before this splendid scene was brought to a close, a loud ring of the doctor's bell summoned Claudius to his presence, to which noisy notice he had already been given to understand it would be his duty to attend.

" What, in the name of propriety and quiet, has happened in the kitchen ?" demanded the rector, as Claudius entered the room in which he was sitting.

" Whe—re, Sir ?" stammered Claudius, in the utmost alarm, remembering the circumstance which had just taken place, and the lesson he had received.

"In the kitchen—the kitchen I say! Did you not hear the cook's loud scream a moment or two since? Something serious must have happened, I fear. Run directly, and enquire the cause."

Claudius waited not for a second bidding, but, happy to escape from such a perplexing condition, he moved, with double quick time, back to the kitchen.

"Here's a pretty kettle of fish!" said he, as he encountered the cook, who was busily engaged collecting the fragments of the wine bottle, while Joseph mopped up the liquor.

"Why, what's a-miss?" enquired the cook.

"Why, a *miss* is not a *hit*," replied Claudius; "but this is a decided *hit*, I assure you, and we shall know it soon, I warrant you, though we are all blind, deaf, and dumb,—ay, and I was going to say, dead into the bargain."

"Now, if you please, Master Claudo," said the cook, snappishly, "be so kind as to let us into the information. What's the matter? I wants to know."

"Oh, nothing,—nothing at all," replied Claudius, "more than you already know; only master heard your shriek, that's all, and desires to be informed of the cause of it."

"Whew! Is that all?" said Mistress Fatpan, having finished her job. "Make my compliments—my respects I should have said, and tell the doctor that I have scalded my foot."

"Wouldn't it be as well," enquired Joseph, laughing, "to say that you have scalded your tongue? Ha! ha! ha! It will never do to say you have scalded your foot, for the apothecary will be sent for to examine and dress it, and then, perhaps, all will come out. Say,—say,—What had he better say, Mistress Fatpan? You are a better hand at these sort of things than I shall ever be."

"Well, then, you must say," observed the cook, "that a large mouse ruun'd over my foot, and alarmed me almost into a jelly. That will do, won't it?"

"Capital!" shouted Joseph. "You women are famous hands at backing out of a scrape."

"You understand, Claudo?" said the cook, placing her finger significantly upon her lips, "A mouse—eh?—"

"I am dumb," replied Claudius, as he vanished from the kitchen, and ran to the doctor, to whom he made his report; who, upon hearing it, almost cracked his sides with laughter at what he supposed the foolish fears of his cook. Could he have known that the cracking of one of his bottles of fine Sherry had been the cause, it is highly probable that his fevered brains, or his protuberant body, would have well nigh cracked with anger. As it was, however, the affair passed over without further notice, while active preparations were prosecuted for the entertainment of the expected guests.

CHAPTER VIII.

" And wherefore play we ? Why for very sport.
And if perchance we quarrel in that sport,
Why still '*tis* sport. Aye, though the tongue should wag,
Out chasing in its speed the courier's pace,
While ranting passion leads to clenched fists,
Why still 'tis sport,—for still for sport we play."

A GAMBLER'S REASONS.

ONE of Dr. Titheum's near neighbours, and intimate friends, was Sir Marmaduke Varney; who, in addition to a handsome fortune of his own, had expectations to a considerable extent in consequence of his connexion with some of the most wealthy and influential families in the country. Sir Marmaduke had long been known as a distinguished patron of the turf, and, if report was to be credited, had on several occasions been made the dupe of a gang of sharpers, by whose well-practised artifice he had been drawn into engagements of *honour*, from which he felt neither the ability nor disposition to free himself until he had been fleeced to a fearful extent.

The passion which this gentleman had imbibed for play appeared to have become a fixed and enthusiastic principle of his nature. It exceeded the broad bounds of mere habit, and seemed to form a part and parcel of his very self, so as, apparently, to be as necessary to his enjoyment of life as were the pulsations of his heart to the continuation of that life.

As a sportsman, or lover of the sports of the field, he was well known for at least fifty miles round. His fearless, madbrain riding, had gained for him the familiar cognomen of Sir Neck-or-nothing ; and never were the hounds unkennelled, or a fox unearthed, or a puss got scent of in his own or an adjoining county, but he was sure to be found joining in the jocund halloo !

Our reverend doctor, it should be remembered, was, from family connexion, powerfully attached to rank and fortune; so strongly had this passion taken possession of him as to admit of no rival, except indeed his love to a good treat, free of all charges, might be admitted to the contest; hence it was that the trifling circumstance of twenty years or so in Sir Marmaduke's age above his daughters, together with his well known habits, as above recorded, weighed not a hair's weight with him against his wish to see his beautiful Georgiana the admired lady of the sporting knight. To promote, if possible, this ardently desired (on his part) consummation, was one grand object of the expected party. The lady, it is true, was ignorant of the offer, neither had the subject been as yet, broached to, or by, Sir Marmaduke himself.

Among the guests invited on this occasion, besides the knight, was a gentleman of years and substance, who lived upon his own estate, a portion of which he farmed to considerable advantage, both to himself and the doctor as the tithe taker. He had acquired the familiar name of Billy Gripes,—alias Mr. William Gripeall; and, by the shorter title, was generally known, by his servants and neigbours. There was also a retired tradesman of large property, who once had large expectations of ascending the civic throne, but, being disappointed in his hopes and wishes, he suddenly became disgusted with London and its vulgar inhabitants; and having with all possible despatch,—keeping as usual a sharp eye on the main chance,—disposed, to his own advantage, of his stock in trade to a young man, of great fortune but with little brains, he retreated with his capsicum-tempered wife into the country, purchased a snug family residence, and dubbed himself—Esquire. This same Jacob Threadlace, Esq., and his lady, with some half dozen others of either gender, made up a *cortège* of no despicable order.

As the clock in the tower of the church proclaimed the hour of seven, Mr. Gripeall was announced; and, in less than twenty minutes after, the whole party met in the doctor's drawing-room. After a few common-place compliments had been banded backwards and forwards, like some disfigured bantling whom no one cared to retain, and flattering expressions of happiness at meeting, high regard, &c., which scarcely a heart present felt, had passed, a few glasses of the rector's sparkling Sherry and crusted Port were handed round, and then two or three parties sat down to the anti-intellectual temper-souring amusement of cards, while the doctor, with Esquire Threadlace, and Mr. Gripeall, adjourned to a tastefully fitted up smoking-room, for the purpose of enjoying themselves with what the rector called, some rational conversation, and a friendly pipe.

Esquire Threadlace, having been a common-councilman when in London, had very naturally acquired an excellent taste for any thing that was good both in liquids and solids, while Mr. Gripeall was a bacchanalian of the first order— albeit, he had in his constitution a considerable quantum of Elvish parsimony. As, however, his constitutional defect-ability was only known to operate when the expenses of a treat caused his own purse-strings to be drawn, he revelled with manifest delight amidst the viands of his friends, mak-ing it a point of etiquette always to honour their hospitality by filling his skin full of all kinds of delicious and strong things. Hence, the doctor and his two friends formed a trio of un-rivalled excellence ; and, while the card-players were disput-ing about shuffling, cutting, and trumps,—the ladies so far forgetting themselves, in their devotion to the game, as to use harsh expressions, and look daggers ; and the gentlemen, maugre their proud claim to gallantry and good breeding, charged their *fair* opponents with *un*fair dealings, and re-signed to them the bank with consummate ill-nature. The smokers were unravelling the Gordian knot of both church and state, and concocting with matchless skill a new and liberal system—to meet exactly their own wishes, and satisfy their own desires.

" 'Pon my honour, madam," said Sir Marmaduke, address-ing himself to Mrs. Threadlace, " you shuffled the last hand. You did, 'pon my honour."

" Sir Marmaduke," shouted the lady, " I am positively sure you are wrong."

" Indeed I am not, madam," repeated the knight ; " 'pon my honour."

" Your honour, Sir, indeed !" added Mrs. Threadlace, sar-castically. " I blush to hear such unblushing statements. You are so much in the habit of *shuffling*, that you appear to think you have a privilege to shuffle, even when you do not deal. I think it is time for us to *cut*."

" I beg your pardon, madam," continued Sir Marmaduke, in high dudgeon, " I am not used to such *equivoque*—'pon my honour; and if you were any other than a lady, I should require satisfaction—'pon my honour."

"And have it you shall, Sir, if you please," retorted the lady. "I know nothing about your *equivokes*,—but I do know too well for my patience—which is not easily moved, and for my partner, who for himself appears afraid to speak his mind,—but I never saw the man yet that I feared,—and I will have a woman's privilege, to speak when I feel occasion —I do know, Sir, that I am determined not to submit calmly to your doing me."

"*Doing* you, madam !" exclaimed the knight, with emphasis, stung to the quick by having his fair fame soiled by a woman's tongue. "Doing you, madam ! I know not what application you intend should be given to your own expression. If by it I am to understand cheating you, 'pon my honour no thought of the kind ever occurred to me. Still I must insist upon my right to shuffle."

"Oh, no doubt, Sir !" returned the sarcastic lady. "I said as much ! But I'll take care you shall not· *shuffle* me. There," she added, as she threw the cards in confusion across the room, "I have *cut*, you see."

"'Pon my honour," exclaimed the knight, as he gazed with surprise at the printed pieces of pasteboard—but the reverie into which he seemed about to fall was suddenly broken up by a strong rush being made by the party at the bank, headed by Mrs. Threadlace. In the struggle which ensued, the table was unfortunately overturned, and the lights were extinguished, while Sir Marmaduke was brought to the ground. Confusion climaxed followed. The ladies shrieked, and, while endeavouring to extricate themselves, tumbled over the prostrate knight.

The smokers, at the moment the noise reached them, were elevated above themselves by a lofty subject they were discussing, and the wine they had swallowed. Judging from their own convivial feelings, they supposed their friends in the drawing-room were enjoying themselves in some innocent gambol; and feeling a desire to be participators in the sport, they started up, and ran with as much speed as their lusty bodies and free potations would allow them, to the apartment. Without waiting for ceremony they rushed into the room to share in the hilarity. The doctor led the van, and was followed so closely by the esquire and Gripeall, that

in a moment the three worthies were rolling with their prostrate friends upon the floor.

"Georgiana! Georgiana, my dear!" shouted the doctor,
"What does all this mean? What new piece of entertainment may this be called?"

Now, fortunately for Georgiana, she was the only person
in the room who had not played at *all-fours;* she stood in a
corner of the apartment, almost bursting her sides with
laughter, and continued so convulsed as to be unable either
to ring the bell or call for lights. In answer to the doctor's
question, she replied, " I fancy it is called trumps, papa ;—
at least, if clubs are trumps, it is so, for here has been club-
bing with a witness."

"Mr. Threadlace!" shouted his good lady. "Mr. Threadlace!"

"Yes, my dear!" answered her swain. "Here I am,
love!"

"And what are you doing there?" returned his rib.
"Why don't you come and help me up?"

"Where are you?" enquired Mr. Threadlace, groping on
his hands and knees.

"Why here I am!" returned his wife, "under the table ;
do help me up, or I shall be strangled."

Georgiana at length rang the bell, and ordered Claudius to
bring in fresh candles. With the speed of an antelope he ran
back to the kitchen to perform his young mistress's bidding,
exclaiming, as he entered, "Oh! there's a pretty game playing in the parlour!—hunt the slipper, I should think, for all
the lights are out, and all the company are on the floor.
They want fresh lights directly."

"Here, Juno!" exclaimed the Cook to Sir Marmaduke's
black servant, who was one of the finest specimens of West
India produce, both in bulk and good-humour, "here! take
this light, and follow Claudo into the drawing-room—make
haste!"

"Oh, yes, Missy Fat-in-de-pan ; I like veddy much to run
when good-natured woman say—Run Juno ; especially when
dey say—Run to *me*, Juno. Ha! ha! ha!"

"Hold your prating just now," exclaimed the Cook ; "and
run back as fast as you can."

"Oh, yes, yes, Missy, I run now," said Juno, "like dem
English slave-dribers what crack! crack! crack! de whip

over de black nigger's back!" and away he hasted after Clau‑
dius, who had preceded him with a light.

Oh! what a delicious banquet for Momus was presented
as the re-kindled tapers threw light upon the ludicrous
subjects.

> There lay the knight, unfell'd by a blow,
>   Held down by the weight of a lady ;
> Who utter'd her griefs in moanings low,
>   As harmonious as Tate and Brady.
>
> And there too, the squire's mild-temper'd wife,
>   Confin'd by the leg of a table,
> Groan'd, struggled, and kick'd, as if for life;
>   And bellow'd as she was able.

"Oh, you cruel man!" exclaimed Mrs. Threadlace to her
husband, as soon as she found herself freed from the confine‑
ment of the table's leg. "Why did you not come earlier to
my rescue? I might have been shuffled, and murdered into
the bargain for any concern you would have felt."

However correct Mrs. Threadlace might have been in her
statements, Mr. Threadlace well knew it was as much as his
two eyes were worth to state so much. If a single muscle of
his face had afforded the slightest intimation of it, in all pro‑
bability his good-tempered, plump face, would have changed
its complexion; and he therefore replied, in the mildest tones,
"I assure you, my dear Mrs. Threadlace, we came as soon
as we heard our company was required. Did we not, gen‑
tlemen?" he added, appealing to the doctor and Mr. Gripeall.

"Most assuredly we did," replied the rector. "But what
am I to understand by what I see and hear?" he inquired.
"How came such a scene of confusion to pass?"

"'Pon my honour, doctar," answered Sir Marmaduke, "I
scarcely know myself; the overturn was so unlooked for a
calamity, as almost to have deprived me of my senses—'pon
my honour."

"Oh! a little mistake, Sir, in the matter of shuffling,"
said the knight's partner, "that's all;—a mere trifle, I assure
you,—and one of very, very common occurrence at our even‑
ing parties where success has happened to be all on one side.
Why, I felt, I confess, half surprised that so much ado is
made about nothing. Come! come!" she added, address‑
ing herself to the offended lady, "shall we draw stakes, and
settle the matter? You may rely upon it the mistake was
yours."

"My mistake! Impossible!" interrupted the esquire's lady, with a bounce like a pea in a hot pan. "No, no; I never make mistakes—do I Mr. Threadlace?" she continued, appealing to her placid husband.

"Never, my dear," answered the esquire, fearing to make any other answer. "That is, *very* seldom."

"Seldom!" she exclaimed, as she threw an affectionate glance at him that made him tremble, "I say that I *never* do;—and I never will be *done*, without making some resistance. No, not even by Mr. Threadlace himself."

"Miss Georgiana," said Sir Marmaduke, "you can, perhaps, explain the matter. It is very unfortunate, 'pon my honour."

The eye of the doctor glistened with delight as he heard the knight appeal to his daughter, not doubting it was ominous of the future accomplishment of his wishes, and internally he rejoiced that the present affair, whatever might have been the cause of it, or however it might terminate, had happened, by which the attention of Sir Marmaduke had been directed to his daughter.

"Ah! very true; tell us, Georgiana, all about it," said the doctor. "That is, as Sir Marmaduke has very properly observed,—*explain* the matter."

"Why, truly, papa," replied the laughing girl, "the affair has been so highly dramatic, that I think I have the most cause of complaint; for I do think I shall have a pain in my side for the next four-and-twenty hours, from laughing so heartily. Ha! ha! ha! But, as to explaining—I don't know about that; for I fancy, in the present case, as in many others between ladies and gentlemen,—the least said is the soonest mended. If, however, I must give evidence, I feel obliged for once to take side with the rude opposers of my sex, and say that my dear Mrs. Threadlace did make a little mistake.

"Well, if *you* say so, Miss Titheum," answered Mrs. Threadlace, "I will admit I *may* have done so;—but, really I do not see it. However, *if* it was I who made the mistake, I feel bound to offer an apology to Sir Marmaduke, and—"

"'Pon my honour, madam," interrupted the gallant knight, "I cannot allow a lady to do any thing of the kind to me,—'pon my honour. I have only one request to make, and, if you will condescend to grant me that favour, we shall, I fancy, be better friends than ever, and I shall consider it a gratifying apology."

"Oh, certainly Sir," returned the lady, "if I can *prudently* comply, I shall feel gratified in doing so, believe me."

"'Pon my honour," returned Sir Marmaduke, "you are very kind. The favour I solicit, fair lady, is that you will become my partner this evening in a quadrille,—and I pledge my honour that I will not shuffle you on that occasion."

"Well, Sir Marmaduke," replied Mrs. Threadlace, flattered by the way in which the *favour* had been solicited, "I will promise that, with the proviso, that you will not make either Mr. Threadlace or any young lady in the room jealous."

The whole party declared their approval of the amicable arrangement, and none *felt* otherwise than pleased, excepting the doctor, who would much rather Mrs. Threadlace should have continued offended, than that his daughter should have lost the hand of Sir Marmaduke for the evening.

Harmony and order were once more restored; the ladies took a glass of wine, and the gentlemen two or three; while the pleasure of a card-party, a steeple-chase, and a pipe, furnished matter for conversation until the announcement was made that supper was on the table, when Mrs. Threadlace, hanging on the arm of Sir Marmaduke, as an evidence of perfect reconciliation, and followed by the rest of the company in pairs, walked to the dining-room, and took their places round a table which groaned beneath the substantials and delicacies of the season.

"'Pon my honour, doc*tar*," observed Sir Marmaduke, "your poultry is admirable—never get any equal to it any where, *positively*. Can you let us into the secret, doc*tor*?"

"Happy to hear you enjoy it, Sir Marmaduke," replied the rector. "The whole secret is with my daughter, I assure you. It is to her," he added, wishful to turn the knight's attention to Georgiana, ",you are indebted, if to any one, for the excellent poultry."

"To me, papa?" exclaimed Georgiana. "I beg you will excuse me on this occasion if—"

"Ah, indeed!" observed Sir Marmaduke. "'Pon my honour—no wonder it is *par excellence* under *such* management."

Georgiana bowed, and observed good-humouredly,—"I know not, Sir, in what way I merit the compliment your politeness has paid me, but I feel bound to assure you papa has made a mistake."

"'Pon my honour," exclaimed Sir Marmaduke, "has he indeed? Do have the kindness, doc*tar*, to inform us in what way our obligations belong to the lady who rejects our acknowledgments."

"Oh, with pleasure, Sir Marmaduke," replied the doctor. "My daughter superintends the poultry in our little domestic farm-yard, and—"

"Now, indeed, papa," interrupted the blushing girl, "you are giving me credit for what I never perform. It would be as parallel a case to say that I preach your sermons, because I sit to hear you."

"Indeed!" replied the doctor, somewhat disconcerted, "I should have said, perhaps," he added, "the cooking was performed according to her directions."

"Worse, and worse," replied the young lady. "Ha! ha! ha! Now, why papa, don't you inform Sir Marmaduke," she continued, with archness of look and expression, "that the flavour of the tarts, of which we hope he will presently partake, results from my having looked at the jars in which the preserves were kept?"

"Ha! ha! ha!" laughed Mrs. Threadlace. "That is clever, indeed, Miss Titheum. You would make an excellent hand in a large retail draper's shop; such ready wit would please the customers surprisingly."

A suppressed titter went round the room at the simple but well-meant remark of the ex-common-councilman's wife. Georgiana bowed, and observed,—"The honour you have done me, madam, exceeds my poor abilities properly to acknowledge. Let, then, expressive silence be my reply."

"Hush, my dear!" said the 'Squire, aside, to his rib, although without being able to stop her until she had finished her observation. "Hush, my dear! You will let out the secret of our former profession before the whole company. Recollect, some are strangers here to our early calling in life."

"And if I do?" returned Mrs. Threadlace, who never delighted in being dictated to, and especially by her husband. "I am not ashamed," she continued, "to acknowledge *how* we obtained our present handsome property; and the man who blushes to own the honest means by which he became wealthy, deserves to lose that which he possesses; that's my opinion on the subject, Mr. Threadlace."

The latter part of this magnanimous reply was given in an

upper key, and received, for the correctness of the principle
it contained, due applause from the company.

"I shall be happy, madam," said Sir Marmaduke to Mrs.
Threadlace, "to take a glass of wine with you."

The challenge was cheerfully accepted, and Port and Sherry
went round the table. Good temper and hilarity prevailed,
and smiling faces alone surrounded the board. The doctor's
wine was praised as heartily as he had before praised Farmer
Primrose's, and drank by the male part of his company as
freely as he drank it; when a messenger entered the room,
and whispered in the doctor's ear something that appeared
to move him greatly.

"Direct that he is kept fast until supper is over," said the
rector, "and then we will see to the matter."

As the servant left the room the doctor continued,—for the
benefit of the company,—"I am informed that an escaped
prisoner has been re-taken, whose appearance, as the messenger states, is of the most ferocious character. They hold
him in confinement, I am told, in one of my out-houses. We
who are in the commission of the peace," he continued, addressing himself to Sir Marmaduke, who was a brother law-
dispenser, "feel the importance of attending to such matters
without delay; and as it would, perhaps, be a novel ceremony
to some of my friends to hear a prisoner examined, I think
we may as well, if you approve it, Sir Marmaduke, give him
a hearing in the drawing-room after supper."

"'Pon my honour," replied the knight, "you are an excellent man of business, doctar; I of course can offer no objection,—'pon my honour—"

"Oh! I should like it above all things in the world," said
Mrs. Threadlace.

"But are you certain he is well secured?" enquired Mr.
Gripeall; "I am extremely nervous; and such desperadoes
you know, doctor, are not nice in what they do."

"I'll take care of that," replied his reverence; "for although I fear no man, yet such hard-faced villains as we
have to do with, who are in the commission of the peace,
make one shy."

"'Pon my honour," observed Sir Marmaduke, "you say
right, doctar; but let it be as you have said: after supper we
will examine him, leaving it with you to see that he is properly secured; an accident may soon occur, 'pon my honour."

It is exceedingly probable that a considerable portion of the doctor's pastry escaped destruction by this little circumstance, as each appeared eager to gratify their sight by gazing on a fellow-creature, whose supposed crimes had placed him in the iron grasp of justice, and who, in consequence, was deprived of the benefit of female sympathy even! Thus, as by *ex-parte* evidence in whatever way given, or in whatever form received,- the prisoner is found guilty in the minds of a prejudiced jury even before his case has been heard.

In a short time after the announcement referred to had been made, the whole party had taken their seats in the drawing-room, with the two sage administrators of justice, when a large figure was ushered into the room, muffled up in a ragged great-coat, having a large tattered hat slouched over his eyes, so as effectually to disguise his countenance. His legs were confined together by a strong cord, which merely allowed him to step somewhat less than half a yard at a time, while his hands were safely secured by hand-cuffs.

It was very evident from the unsteadiness of the prisoner's motion, that he was what a sailor would have pronounced "half-seas-over;" and hence his present rather unpleasant condition gave him little or no concern.

"Well," he grumbled out, "how much further are you going to drag me? If I don't punish you all for this one day, I an't a constable."

"'Pon my honour," exclaimed Sir Marmaduke, "the fellow is surely mad, doc*tar*."

"Well, prisoner," said the divine, "what account have you to give of yourself—eh?"

"Why a good one I hope," replied he with the bracelets; "although I grant you, rather queer-looking like;—sartainly for a person like me to be so sarved is very ridiculous."

"Well, Sir," continued the doctor sharply, "what is your name?"

"My name?" rejoined the man; "why what can the odds of my name be,—howsomever, it is the name of a honest man, as I'll make you all know one day."

"'Pon my honour!" shouted the knight—"What may your name be, fellow?—who and what are you?"

"I am constable and beadle of the parish of Christ-church," replied the prisoner, "and my name, it is well known, is Jacob Grabum."

"Jacob Grabum!" exclaimed the doctor—"Impossible!"

"Is it though?" returned the man; "but it arn't impossible though: and if," he added, hiccuping, "I am not Jacob Grabum, have the goodness to inform me who I am."

"Take off his hat," said the doctor; which, in contempt of court, had very strangely been permitted to continue to cover half his face as well as his head. The moment the order was obeyed, all doubt of his identity vanished; the large flat full-moon-looking face of the constable was instantly recognised.

"'Pon my honour," exclaimed Sir Marmaduke, "it is Jacob indeed!"

Jacob turned his heavy eyes in a semi-maniacal stare upon the court—a sudden ray of illumination appeared to dart athwart his obscured understanding; and perceiving the doctor, he addressed himself to him, nearly sobered on the instant.

"Please your reverence, I am glad I am here and alive— I never expected to see your worship again—I have been unmercifully used."

"Where is your prisoner?" enquired the doctor with eagerness.

"That I cannot tell," replied Grabum.

"Not tell!" responded the justice; "why you surely have not allowed him to escape?"

"No, your worship," answered the constable, "I did not allow him, as one may say; but he would go, and I was left in his place."

"Explain yourself," said the doctor,—"what are we to understand from all this?"

"I will, your honour," said the beadle, "as well as I am able. Your honour knows I secured my man properly before I set off with him; and as soon as ever I got clear of Farmer Primrose's farm-yard, I drove at a good round rate towards the prison. As, however, the distance was rather long, I stopped at the Green Dragon to bait; and as my prisoner was very quiet and civil, and begged hard to have a drop to keep the cold out, I allowed it—only one glass, I assures your worship;—well, on we went again as if the old mare had turpentine under her tail; and presently we overtakes a man what I had seen talking with the Gypsy, at the door of the Green Dragon. Now as I has room for three or four in my *wheicle*, I allowed him, as a decent-looking person, to ride a few miles with us without thinking no harm; when, just as we reached within half a mile of the forest, the feller what I had accommodated with a ride, offered me half-a-crown to change for him, desiring I would accept a tanner for my kindness, as he said. I never refuses a trifle, your worship—so thinking no harm, I lays down my pistol in my lap, ready cocked, for to take out my purse to give the change—when before I could say 'turnips,' up the feller grabs the popper, and holding it to my head, swore as how he'd blow out my brains if I offered the least resistance, or gave the least alarm. Now what could I do, your worship, but be quiet?—for I knew if he blew out my brains I could not give any alarm ; and, therefore, I did just as he wished me, and sat as mute and as still as a man what is going to be buried. With that he takes the other pistol out of my pocket, and the reins from my hands, to save me, as he said, the trouble of driving any further,—and off he turned the mare in a contrary direction. I soon found that I had helped one of the Gypsy gang to a ride ; for in less than half an hour, with hard flogging the poor beast, we reached their camp. I was instantly compelled to dismount, and the keys were taken from me, my prisoner was set at liberty, and I was confined. After keeping me in that state until this morning, at day-break, they took from me the excellent great-coat which I wore, and made me put on this heap of rags, which they buttoned tight round me ; they then fastened my legs in this way, and hand-cuffed me as you may see. Having so done, without my daring to say 'no', they poured down my throat almost a pint of raw gin, and, driving off with the horse and cart, left me to my fate. I hobbled on some distance, until the trees seemed to dance round me, and the earth was unsteady. Being unable to stand, I laid myself down and slept, until I was found by those who brought me here."

"'Pon my honour," exclaimed Sir Marmaduke, "this is a most singular affair—quite a romance of real life,—ha! ha! ha! —perfectly ludicrous ! I am vastly amused by an adventure of this kind—'pon my honour."

"Indeed, your honour, it was very amusing, I assure you," observed Jacob, with a forced laugh,—" I wish," he added in an under tone, "the pistol had been held to your head instead of mine, the amusement would then have been rather serious to you, I have no doubt."

"It is, indeed, a strange piece of business," observed the doctor.—"Ha! ha! ha!—I suppose we had better let Jacob join the party in the kitchen, while we amuse ourselves and forget for a while the troubles which we, who are in the commission of the peace, have to contend with."

The reverend doctor's head was a little clearer at the present moment than when he committed the Gypsy; and having a shrewd guess that he had on that occasion gone a step beyond his authority, he felt willing to allow the case to pass unnoticed, for fear his own conduct might undergo a trifling degree of scrutiny beyond what might reflect credit or advantage on himself: he therefore cheerfully proposed that the constable should forthwith be liberated and conducted into the kitchen, to share with the servants in what Mrs. Fatpan might furnish to them—as it was considered that his long abstinence might render a fresh meal desirable and necessary · before he reached home; besides which, as an under functionary of the law, it was held proper that all convenient attention should be paid to him for his office' sake.

Having thus summarily disposed of this grave matter, the gallant Sir Marmaduke, throwing off that portion of legal gravity which, as a magistrate, he felt bound to assume, declared—" 'Pon my honour I feel particularly happy that confoundedly troublesome business is over ;" and then claimi   the promised hand of Mrs. Threadlace, they led off the dance.

CHAP. IX.

" There's merry-making at the hall,
    The men with the music are there ; .
And age looks young at the splendid ball,
    And trips with the blushing fair.

" There's life above, and there's life below,
    As if Bedlam's self were broke :
The Parson's guests make grape-juice flow,
    While the servants each crack a joke."

RECORDS OF OUR PARISH.

EVERY earthly enjoyment has its drawback ; and, the more full the cup of human felicity, the more likely it is to be spilled.   So it fell out on the present occasion.

" Music," says the immortal bard of Avon, " has charms to soothe the savage breast."   It now appeared to have power to *move* the breast of a snarling little pet, in the shape of a poodle lap-dog, which belonged to Miss Fidget, a *young* lady, whose age might not be mentioned, but concerning which delicate subject ill-natured and gossip-loving persons would speculate. Some such, who professed to have known her forty years, declared that at *that* time she was a full-grown woman; however that might be, her hair was yet a bright auburn, and her cheeks glowed with as much colour as a milk-maid's on a bracing spring morning. It was hinted, however, that the hair which she wore was not *false* hair, but real human hair, purchased at a fashionable depôt for such material, somewhere in Bond Street; while those who had frequently seen Miss Fidget early in the morning, protested that her face was of the colour of pipe-clay, and they therefore concluded that the blooming glow upon her cheeks was of rouge origin, and therefore not "*nateral.*" Whether such was really the case or not, is not greatly material; she looked, when splendidly dressed in the attirements of youth, and when beheld by candle-light, remarkably well, and might have passed (as she felt anxious to do), in the judgment of a stranger, for a miss in her teens, excepting, indeed, when she was approached within a certain number of yards—say half a dozen—or when she opened her mouth; for then wrinkles would most provokingly obtrude themselves,—and the loss of a few teeth,—or rather the possession of *but* few,—told a tale which neither rouge, curls, nor youthful array, could give the lie to.

Now, the only living creature in this terrene state of which Miss Fidget appeared to be *really* fond,—of course excepting herself,—was the above-named poodle dog—he (for it was of the masculine gender) was her idol. She watched over him with the tender care of a fond parent, and attended to his wants with the solicitude of a devoted lover. Fond as Miss Fidget was of parties, routs, and balls,—and among these she lived, moved, and had her being,—she would have sacrificed her own delight in such particulars, and have sent back a card of invitation, if her "*dear Dido*" had not been invited with her.

Fortunately—(query)—for Miss Fidget, she was a lady of large fortune, and a considerable benefactress to the parish. She had for years undertaken to find all the wine used in the church, as well as provided surplices, and kept them clean too—no unimportant item in parish affairs,—with gowns and bands for the doctor; although her attendance was not quite so regular or frequent as at other and more fashionable places. From considerations so weighty as those just detailed, an invitation had, of course, been sent to Miss Fidget, craving the favour of her own and Dido's company, &c. As, however, the *dear* little creature was not quite well in the early part of the day, Miss Fidget had ordered that her carriage should not be prepared for her until she felt certain that some improvement had taken place in his health. The consequence was, that her arrival was announced only a short time before the party commenced dancing.

The fair hand of this blooming spinster was craved by Esquire Threadlace, but with a *leetle* more softness of note, and Adonis-like action, than Mrs. Threadlace thought quite proper for *her* husband to employ, and she managed to shoot one or two of her most delectable glances so adroitly as to meet the eye of her lord. The effect which those connubial *doux yeux* upon the nerves of the retired draper was as if one of the Whitechapel blunts he had been in the habit of retailing had been thrust red-hot into his ultimatum ; and when the smiling Miss Fidget put her taper fingers into his hand, as she rose to the dance, a dizziness shot through his brain, which caused him to stagger as if he had taken a few too many glasses of the doctor's sparkling wine.

The flashing fire of a jealous woman's eye is dreadful ; it is as withering to joy or peace, to delight or comfort, as is the sirocco of the desert to health and life. Like the Upas tree, it spreads pestilence and death around the circumference to which it extends. To be favoured with such a sight *once,* is to behold what never will again be forgotten ; one's teeth chatter at the thought of it, the very flesh crawls upon the bones—"'tis horrible, horrible, most horrible !"

Poor Threadlace felt all this. The eye of his *dear* Mrs. Threadlace enchained his vision, and bound up his thoughts. His blunders were so frequent and flagrant as almost entirely to break up "the merry skipping on the light fantastic toe." More than once he trod upon Miss Fidget's tender toes, so that she felt it indispensably necessary, to prevent being crippled for life, to keep at a respectable distance from him.

At the commencement of the Esquire's *gallop-hard* Miss Fidget had tenderly laid her dear Dido on her own chair, covering his lips with kisses, and his body with a rich crape;

shawl. Either, however, the music *moved* him, or his love
for his mistress,

> " Like that her own soft bosom felt,
> Reason did not control,"

for he raised his shaggy head from under his gay coverlid,
looked a few moments at the dancers, and then leaped from
his place to mingle with them.

Now, as the eyes of Mr. Threadlace were still fixed upon
his wife's angry glare, he perceived not the approach of
" Dido," until, by an unlucky step, he trod more violently
than he had before done upon his partner's toes, upon the
fore paw of her favourite. Not being used to, and especially
not being pleased with, such treatment, the revengeful poodle
yelped loudly, and snapping fiercely at his tormentor's leg,
tore his silk stocking from the calf to the ankle.

At the sound of Dido's wailing note Miss Fidget screamed,
and nearly fainted.

" Oh! my dear, my precious Dido!" she exclaimed, "who
has been inhuman enough to injure you?"

At the moment that the Esquire felt the application of
Dido's teeth to the calf of his leg, a sudden and involuntary
movement, like the action of an automaton, took place in the
member, and then, with the same unconsciousness, he sent
the yelping pet to the other end of the room, by the application of his toe to his closely shorn body.

All was confusion in a moment—the plaintive cries of
Dido drowned the music, and nothing was in unison with
the deafening noise, save the dolorous lamentations of the
afflicted Miss Fidget.

" My dear love!" ejaculated the lady, after an hysteric
pause, as she enfolded the poodle in her arms, and pressed
him affectionately to her heaving bosom, " where are you
hurt? tell your own mistress. How could you be so foolish
as to leave the place where I left you? couldn't you spare me
a little while, dear?"

Dido looked sagely in his mistress' face, licked her cheek,
—and thereby caused the colour of one of them to fade,—
and wagged his tail,—but made no oracular reply.

" There," Mr. Threadlace," said his sympathising wife,
looking at his rent hose, " that is what comes of being *over*
polite;—it would not have been of great consequence if

your leg had been torn instead of your stocking," she added aside to him.

"'Pon my honour," observed Sir Marmaduke, as he applied his scented handkerchief to his nasal protuberance, "I wish the confounded beast had been converted into mock turtle soup for an alderman's' feast, before his yelping had disarranged our delightful entertainment; we were just entering into the spirit of it, my dear Mrs. Threadlace."

"Do you indeed, Sir?" observed Miss Fidget, referring to the Knight's kind wish, "Do you really wish my beautiful Dido devoted to such vile purposes?" She evidently *felt* the familiar adage—"hurt my dog, hurt me,"—as she added, "Such monstrous barbarity absolutely shocks me! Look at him, Sir Marmaduke," she continued, holding the creature full in his face,—"look at him, and say if his sorrowful countenance is not sufficient to make any *feeling* heart ache?"

"'Pon my honour, Madam," rejoined Sir Marmaduke, "I intended no offence—none, 'pon my honour! I hope the sweet creature has not received any serious injury—'pon my honour, Madam."

"Not *so* much, at least,"—observed Georgiana, with a slight dash of sarcasm in her manner—"as Mr. Threadlace's stockings."

"Mr. Threadlace's stockings!" echoed Miss Fidget, turning her eyes towards her partner's leg—"well, I declare it is damaged a trifle; but that is soon remedied, while Dido's hurt might have been of serious consequences."

"Very true," observed the doctor,—"very true; and if you, Sir," he added, addressing himself to Mr. Threadlace, "do not object to case your legs in canonical hose, there is no need we should be put out long by this accident. Walk with me into my dressing-room, and I will supply you."

"Ah! you are very kind, doctor," observed Mrs. Threadlace, replying for her husband,—"you are very kind; but you know, Sir, if persons *will* become too intimate with *young* ladies, they need feel no surprise if they soon want—a more important part of dress than stockings."

Mr. Threadlace felt disposed to reply; but the words stuck in his throat, and he could only mutter, not speak out—"Accidents, my dear, will—"

"Accidents!—fiddlesticks! I say," roared his wife,—"accidents indeed! a man may by *accident* put his foot into a man-trap while walking along the king's high-road—it is not very likely, however; but if he steps over his neighbour's fence, why—eh?—*accident*,—oh! Mr. Threadlace, Mr. Thread-lace—you know what I know,—at your old tricks again;—you have not forgotten the 'Goose and Gridiron' I suppose?"

Mr. Threadlace groaned in spirit, and trembled in his pumps; while the doctor, in order to put an end to the interesting matrimonial *tête-à-tête*, enquired—"Well, Mr. Threadlace, shall it be as I have said—will you accompany me to my dressing-room, and—

> ——" By a change of stockings end
> The calf-ache, and a thousand other things
> The naked leg is liable to ?"

The pleasant turn which the doctor's wit in corrupting Shakspeare's language had given to the serious cast the conversation had assumed, acted electrically; and a loud laugh rung the room—in which even Miss Fidget with her partner and his wife heartily joined.

"Come along," said the doctor, taking Threadlace's arm, "and, in the mean time, Georgie," he added, speaking to his daughter, "see that our friends take some refreshment, and in a little time we shall be ready to rejoin you." So saying, the rector and his guest retired, while Georgiana rang the bell, and Claudius, entering, handed round wine and fancy biscuits.

While the party above stairs were enjoying themselves with music and dancing, those in the kitchen were not less cheerful. Mistress Fatpan had already drawn forth from her private still, two or three bottles of generous wine, which the butler had committed to her custody for the entertainment ot their party, and likewise a case-bottle, half filled with brandy, which the thrifty cook had saved at different times, by bestowing a less portion of the intoxicating fluid on the sauces she had manufactured. Of these, the kitchen guests had taken some large libations, and a hearty laugh continued to shake the sides of all present, provoked by a tale which Claudins had just been reciting, when Jacob Grabum, alias Long-body, entered, to the no small surprise of those who were present

"Whew!" whistled Juno. "Here come de man what dribes de English niggers out of de town wid him long pole ın de place of de whip—whack! Ha! ha! ha! He no dribe us out of de kitchen while de strong drink be plenty."

"Hollo, my lads!" shouted Grabum, in a half authoritative, half canting tone, "you are all as merry here as crickets in a bake-house, and as busy as gad-flys on a hot summer's day upon horse-flesh. Why, what are you all about?" he continued, clipping the last word with a strong hiccup.

"Ha! ha! ha! That's good, however," replied Mr. Joseph. "What are *we* about?—why, have n't you told us that we are merry and busy? But what have *you* been about? I should like to know. Why, I declare, if you arn't half groggy, Mr. Grabum!"

"What's that you say, Mister Joseph?" roared the man of authority. "I half groggy! I'd have you bridle your tongue when you give vent to your thoughts, and presume to speak of an officer of the parish. *We*, Mister Joseph, recommend this in friendship;—or it may be *we* shall,—you understand me," he added, winking significantly—"Eh?"

"No, indeed, we don't understand your short-hand talk, Mister Beadle," replied the cook. "*I* says that you are half *'toxicated*."

"Yes, Massa Cock-hat," chimed in the negro, showing his ivories by a good-natured grin, "we all say de same ting.

> Little drink got in your noddle,
>   Fal! lal, la!
> And it make you widdle, waddle,
>   Fal! lal, la!
>
> All de tings go round and round,
> While de drink be in your noddle;
> And you feel upon de ground
> For de sky, and widdle, waddle,
>   Ha! ha! ha!
>   Fal! lal, la!
> While de drink be in your noddle,"

So chaunted Juno, dancing at the same time round and round Mr. Grabum, until he actually became giddy by turning about after the whimsical black.

"Indeed!" hiccupped the beadle, as Juno closed his chaunt, and the whole party joined the chorus of Ha! ha! ha! "Well, then," he continued, with philosophical coolness, "I suppose it must be so;—that is, I may be somewhat fresh. Howsomever, I arn't come here for to quarrel with nobody, and I hopes nobody intends to quarrel with me."

"Ha! ha! ha!" resumed Juno. "Come to quarrel—no, no, Massa Grabum, we shall neber quarrel while we in company of de lady,—that is, of Missus Fat-in-de-pan."

"Thank you for your compliment, Juno," said the cook, "You are the *politestest* gentleman in the company; and I don't know why we shouldn't have good manners in the kitchen as well as in the parlour."

"That's right, cook!" shouted the beadle. "But as you have n't been so polite as to *ax* me to take a chair all this time, why, I shall show good manners to myself, and take one. There," he soliloquised,—"be quiet, Jacob Grabum, and enjoy yourself for an hour, and then hie home, and to bed."

"Well, to show that we are not all quite without *manners*," said Joseph, "allow me to hand the glass to you, Master Grabum,—you will, of course, drink with us?" and he presented a glass of almost boiling-hot brandy-and-water.

"With all my heart," replied the functionary; and, seizing the offered liquor, he took a hearty mouthful, and in a moment spirted it out again, while he jumped and plunged about the kitchen like a maniac, from the effects of a scalded mouth.

At this moment Claudius returned from serving the refreshments in the drawing-room; and, seeing the beadle cutting such grotesque figures, while streams flowed from his eyes so as completely to deprive him of sight, determined to retaliate a little insult which he had received from the officer of the parish, in the shape of a painful gripe on the arm, and a surly push, during the time that he wore his Gypsy guise.

He was well aware that scarcely any noise which might be made in the kitchen would be heard by the party in the dancing-room, because of the distance of its situation. He therefore attempted, and succeeded most dexterously, in attaching a cracker to the tail of Grabum's coat, and then, setting fire to it, the terrified beadle, almost forgetting the pain of his mouth, ran and curvetted round the kitchen, striving to avoid the hissing and explosion which continued to follow him, half imagining for the moment that some perturbed spirits, towards whom he had exercised his power with unmitigated severity in the days of their flesh, were now hunting him

"To dark Cimmerian vales,
Where brooding misery hatches pain,"

" Mercy! Pity! Mercy!" he exclaimed, panting for breath. " Will no one pity? Will no one help me?"

Overcome by the feelings of his excited imagination, he fell senseless upon the floor, a pitiable lump of clay-cold matter. The application of some cold water from the pump, which, with unsparing hand, the cook threw into his face, soon restored the terrified official to consciousness, who, on opening his eyes, stared round the place with a wild and haggard look, like one just awakened from a horrible vision.

" Where am I?" he enquired, in piteous tones. " Have mercy on me!"

" Where are you?" replied Claudius, " why, where should you be but among friends? You have slept soundly, I fancy, for some time."

" Have I though?" returned the beadle, with evident astonishment.

" I fancy you have," replied the cook; " we almost doubted whether you would wake again."

"Indeed!" responded Mr. Grabum,—" how very singular!"

" Aye, it is singular enough, as one may say," observed the cook, " that one who boasted so much of good manners should forget his own, and snore before company."

" Well, really," said the beadle, rubbing his eyes, which were yet but half open, " it was, I own, not quite *mannerly* of me."

" Are you subject to the night-mare?" asked Mistress Fatpan.

" The night who?" enquired the beadle.

" The night-*mare*," returned the cook; " what people has who doesn't sleep well."

" Oh! aye,—I understand you," answered Mr. Grabum, " I fancy I may be on odd occasions; but why do you ask such a question? Have I misbehaved myself greatly in any *perticular* way?—I did'nt kick, or so, did I?"

" Kick!" shouted Joseph,—" Ha! ha! ha!" in which hearty laugh all in the room were joining, but in a suppressed way.—" I believe you did kick, man, and not a little neither; the kicking of a horse when being burned for the spavins is a fool to it; and as to hallooing,—my eyes! if I didn't think we should have had all the company from above coming to enquire what was the matter."

" Why, did I now?" replied the beadle, astonished at his own conduct.

"Did you now?" rejoined Joseph; "why *ax* Betty, and Claudo, and Juno, and the rest there."

"Indeed you did, Master Grabum," said the cook,—"we were *obligated* to sprinkle you well before we could rouse you."

"Ha! ha! ha!" laughed Grabum, rising,—"Well, that is strange enough, howsomever. I have had a plaguy ugly dream, I fancy."

"Well, never mind dreams now," said Joseph; "here's to your health, Master Grabum; and when next you *dream* may your dreams be pleasant."

"Thank ye, Joseph; thank ye," responded the beadle, seizing him by the hand, and shaking it heartily.—"But how goes time?" he added, turning his eye towards the kitchen clock: "I suppose I must see about moving, or I shan't get home to-night."

"Oh! 'tis early yet," replied Claudius, "they have only just commenced dancing above stairs—I am fond of dancing, and hope we shall be able to amuse ourselves in the same way. What do you say, Mrs. Fatpan? shall you and I lead off?"

"With all my heart," replied the cook; "but who is to be the fiddler?"

"Oh!" exclaimed Juno, "I be de fiddler! I can fiddle wid my mouth—what tune you like, Missus Fat-in-de-pan."

"Can you give us 'The Wedding Day'?" asked the cook.

"Oh, yes," returned Juno; who, after whistling a few notes, enquired,—"How you like my fiddle, Mrs. Fat-in-de-pan,—eh?"

"That will do *hexellently*," returned the cook.

"Which you like best," asked Juno, "de tune, or the day, eh?—but nebber mind em day, de wedding day and de wedding nights come soon, and den Juno play de fiddle for you, Missus Fat-in-de-pan,—eh?"

"Well, I don't know *hexactly*, Juno," replied Mistress Betty; "I suppose you must ask some one else," and she leered out of the corner of her eye, as she spoke, towards Joseph.

"At all events," said Joseph, "if I am of the party on that occasion, you will not play the first fiddle, Mister Juno."

"Why, what a fuss you are making now about your wedding days," observed Sally, the house-maid, who as yet had not a glimpse even of enjoying such a delightful day, but

who was now "all agog" as grandmama used to say, for a
dance.—" Let us have 'The Wedding Day' *now*, and talk
about the other afterwards."

" Oh! to be sure, Missus Sally," returned Juno, " you
are all in de great hurry, like all de ladies, for de wedding
day ;—which you have first, husband or wedding day, eh ?—
ha! ha! ha!—tell me dat now ?"

Sally frowned, and looked at Juno almost as black as Juno
himself—the jesting negro took the hint, and, to save himself from her wrathful displeasure, commenced whistling "The
Wedding Day ;" while the cook, taking the hand of Claudius, performed something between a reel and fandango.

If the looks of Joseph had been regarded, it might have
been supposed that he did not *quite* approve of the partner
which Betty had taken ; or otherwise that he *dis*approved in
toto Betty's accepting him—nevertheless she said nothing, determining *after* the wedding day to alter the method of doing
things, by proving himself a lord of creation. As his
affianced had engaged herself, he mated himself with Sally,
while two other pairs,—servants of the doctor's guests,—
completed a double set.

This important preliminary step to the *ballet l'divertisment*
having been taken, Juno inflated his ebony-coloured cheeks,
and then again emptying them, poured forth the enlivening
tune most gloriously ; and, at the same time, capered round
the spacious kitchen to his own music, throwing his arms
about like the sails of a wind-mill, or as if exhibiting the
effects of a powerful dose of gas upon his system.

Unmoved by the dulcet notes of Juno, any more than he
would have been by the blowing of the bellows in the forge
of Vulcan, Mr. Grabum sat enjoying himself over the brandy-
and-water, using but a small quantity of the *latter*, as he was
subject to the gravel, and feared lest the fluid might not
have passed through a drip-stone, and so might irritate his
disorder. There he sat, like the son of Jupiter Ammon, at
his royal banquet, quaffing long and deep draughts of the
thing he loved, like a lady in her *boudoir*, and not sipping it
as a female lover of it does before company.

Twenty minutes and upwards had elapsed before the clap-
per of his leaden head began to play ; and when it did, the
sounds it sent forth were harsh and inharmonious.

" Go it, go it," he shouted, as the spirits mounted to his
brain,—" that's bravely done ! I say, Mister Joseph, have a

care boy, have a care, you rogue—(hiccup)—that Mistress Fatpan don't see you getting so close to Sally there, or you'll get a *basting*, I warrant you ; such as you won't much relish. Here, Fiddler, drink,—drink, I say—(hiccup)—your whistle must be dry, I'm certain.—Oh, oh ! I beg pardon—(hiccup) —yes, I beg pardon ; if you drink your fiddling will stop, and then the dance will stop—and then, perhaps, my brandy-and-water will stop ; and then this glorious treat will stop— dance, dance away, by all manner of means!—you may fiddle 'till doom's day for any thing that Moses Grahum cares about the matter, so that these ere supplies ain't stopped."

The loud ringing of the drawing-room bell summoned Claudius from the dance, to wait upon the dancers. As, however, Mistress Fatpan felt no inclination to allow herself to remain destitute of a partner, the beadle was obliged, by a *tangible* invitation, to stand up ! Fortunately for himself and others, he was not expected to stand steady or erect ; that, in-deed, would have been as difficult a task for him to perform, as it would for a landsman to maintain a perpendicular position on the deck of a cutter in a furious storm. Once or twice he performed the evolutions of the merry dance ; but the twisting and twirling about, chasing and being chased, so mazed his head and curdled the wine and brandy-and-water he had swallowed, as to render him incapable of distinguish-ing his own partner, the jolly skipping cook, from the sta-tionary kitchen clock before which he stood curvetting, with his head lolling from left to right, like a weaver's shuttle ; or backwards and forwards after the fashion of a carved Man-darin's.

" Master Grabum," shouted Mistress Fatpan, as she waited for her partner at the bottom of the room, " what in the name of goodness are you doing there, man ? why don't you come down ?—how long is one to be kept waiting ?—what are you whirlygiging there about ?"

" Come down ?" replied Grabum, as he turned his head in the direction whence the sound proceeded,—" Come down— (hiccup)—is it, eh ?—that's easy enough said, arn't it now ? —come down !—very pretty, indeed ! my pretty partner— ha ! ha ! ha !—(hiccup)—why don't you come *up* I should like to know ?—(hiccup)—I think I soon shall come down, or *go* down if I arn't careful."

So saying, he turned his long body with the intention of following the inviting voice ; but unfortunately the turn was too much for him; he reeled and cut a *new* figure—staggered —and cut *himself* by pushing his hand through a pane of glass, and then fell, to the entire discomfiture of the dancers, the amusement of Juno, and the destruction of *all* the figures that *were*, or that were contemplated.

" There now !" roared the prototype of an overgrown turtle, as he sprawled upon his hands and knees, endeavouring, but in vain, to place himself upon his own good *understandings* again,—" I told you I should soon attend to your wishes and come down—(hiccup);—but where are you, Mistress Fatpan? I don't perceive you,—are you down too?—your confounded twirling about has completely turned my head."

Just at the moment that the beadle was in the position referred to, with his posteriors turned towards the kitchen door, Claudius returned ; and supposing that Master Grabum was performing some novel exhibition for the amusement of the company, who all stood holding their sides with laughter, the thought entered his mind that he could give some little colouring to the feat, and so heighten its effect. The thought no sooner entered his cranium than he hasted to put it into practice ; and, therefore, with one spring he vaulted upon the back of the fallen official, like a grinning champhenzie on the shoulders of a dancing bear. The action, however, being unexpected, and the beadle's head inclining towards the centre of gravity, he again returned to his position of all-fours, while Claudius, curled up like a hedge-hog, was rolled at the velocity of sixty miles an hour against the perpendiculars of Mistress Sally ; by which concussion, like the effect of a well-aimed ball at a pair of nine-pins, she was reduced to a level with, and placed by the side of, the sprawling Master Grabum.

Without waiting to enquire how she had been so reduced, Sally leaped up again in the twinkling of an eye, and apparently entered into the sport with as much delight as any one of the delighted party; while even Grabum felt amused by the circumstance, and, forgetting his own ignoble position, laughed heartily in concert with the other members of the kitchen.

As soon as order was restored, Claudius performed the duties of his office, by handing a glass of wine to each of the *ladies*, while a fresh supply of hot water, with which a good quantity of the doctor's cognac was associated, was furnished the *gentlemen* with unsparing freedom, for—

" None grudg'd his fellow that which cost him nought."

CHAPTER X.

"*Nina.* 'Tis said that marriages are made in heaven;
         Dost think so, Eustace?
  Eus. I never yet have climb'd so high, fair Lady,
         And therefore cannot speak to't.
Nina. Pshaw! Eustace, I ask your thoughts merely.
  Eus. Well, then, thus they run:—I do believe
         That far the greater number here made up
         Heav'n disapproves.—Ergo,—they were not made in heav'n."

"COURTSHIP A LA MODE."

"PAST twelve o'clock, and a rainy night," had just been
bawled by one of the guardians of the right, and Claudius
was amusing the company in the kitchen by spouting the oft
recited description which Norval gives of the means by which
he acquired a knowledge of the art of war, commencing
with,—

"Beneath a mountain's brow, the most remote,
And inaccessible, by shepherds trod;
In a deep cave, dug by no mortal hand,
A hermit lived, a melancholy man.—

He had proceeded so far as—

"Pleas'd with my admiration, and the fire,
His speech struck from me,"—

when Grahum, who had fallen fast asleep over the glass
which he had emptied half-a-dozen different times, tumbled
from his chair, completely overcome by the potent influence
of Morpheus and the sincere devotion he had paid to Bacchus.

It now became an important question how, or in what way,
this fag-end piece of the law should be disposed of. His return home until

"Bright Phœbus had mounted his car in the east

was out of all question;—with as much ease might the stone
figure of Ganymede, which adorned the lawn at the back of
the parsonage, have stepped down from the pedestal on which
she stood, and have waited on the inferior deities who were
enjoying themselves in the doctor's drawing-room, as Grahum
could have walked a yard.

After a short time spent in deliberation over the prostrate
hero, it was proposed by Claudius, and carried with acclama-

tion, that he snould be conveyed forthwith to his (Claudius's) bed. In pursuance of this resolution the cumbrous body of the constable of Christchurch was, with no little difficulty, raised upon three or four shoulders, Juno having placed himself behind to push up the fleshly load; while Claudius, taking a candle, went before to light the bearers to Grabum's intended resting-place.

The great difficulty which existed in raising the beadle from the floor operated partially to rouse him from his heavy stupor; who, dreaming, it would appear, that he had been a successful candidate at a contested election, and was just returned as the representative of a rotten borough, supposed that the act of chairing was taking place. So powerful was the effect of the phantasmagorial illusion upon his distempered brain, that he acted to the life some of the highly characteristic scenes played off by not a few newly created legislators of the nation, and roared out, with understanding about upon a par with theirs, in half articulated sounds:

"The consti—(hiccup)—tution for—(hiccup)—ever!—The church—(hiccup)—and con—(hiccup)—stitution !—Gentlemen, I promise—(hiccup)—I promise to ,exert—(hiccup)—myself, and to employ my—(hiccup)—influence for the—(hiccup)—repeal of all taxes ;—huzza !—(hiccup)—huzza !—liberty and plenty—and no tax—es!"

Thus he continued to roar in excellent style, until his head again sunk upon his breast, and in that condition he was borne from the scene of his debauch, while the cook and the housemaid were left to their own cogitations.

The parsonage-house was one of those large old-fashioned rambling edifices, which during the reign of Elizabeth were erected, as if for the double purpose of supplying comfort and defence,—half castle, half dwelling-house. A wealthy Romanist, to whom it originally belonged, had, at his decease, left it, together with other property, to the church, in order that a certain number of masses might be said for his soul annually,

> " 'Till the foul crimes, done in his days of nature,
>   Were purged away."

At the time of the Reformation, when a bill was passed for the suppression of the newly erected monasteries, the abolition of the mass, and the re-establishment of the liturgy adopted in the reign of Edward, the property of the church

passed into other hands; so that the Catholic clergy were not only by solemn and public disputation beaten at all points, and silenced by act of Parliament, and thereby stopped by the imposition of pains and penalties from pursuing their religious functions; but at the same time were ousted from the possessions which were their *bonâ fide* right, by being made over to them voluntarily by their friends and benefactors.

The house in question, which was now occupied by Dr. Titheum, was among such transferred property; and here, where once a studious Romish Priest dwelt, a revelling Protestant Divine resided.

As has been stated, the house was a large old-fashioned one. The turnings and windings in this many chambered building were sufficient to puzzle any one who possessed not a clue something like that by which the hero of ancient story traversed the labyrinth of Crete.

Now as Claudius had only very recently become a tenant of this said mystically constructed mansion, it would not have been very surprising if, in the present excited state of his feelings, he had missed his way;—whether such really was the case, or whether a freak of fancy, the mere out-breaking of his inherent propensities, moved him to the act, is not material to our subject: it is sufficient to state for the information of the reader, that either he did *mistake* his way, or by a wilful piece of waggery, he entered the bed-chamber of the cook instead of his own, and into it the party followed, bearing with them their heavy and unconscious burden. Having placed the beadle on the floor, they proceeded to unclothe him, which task having been performed with all possible despatch, they laid him quietly between the sheets, and then returning to the kitchen they

" Left him alone in his glory."

During the whole of this period the spirit-stirring sounds of music, and the doctor's generous wine, kept the guests in the drawing-room in the best and most happy humour. Dance after dance was performed with taste and spirit; after which Georgiana, at the request of the company, sat down to her instrument, and played several tunes, accompanying its sweet tones with,—as Sir Marmaduke declared, 'pon his honour,—" her own sweeter voice."

The compliment paid to the young lady by the man whom the doctor longed to call " son-in-law," delighted the fond

father beyond expression, and inspirited him to make an attempt to bring the matter about.

"I fear, Sir Marmaduke," observed the rector, "you are
at your old tricks again—employing flattery for sinister purposes."

"No! 'pon my honour," replied Sir Marmaduke,—"say
sincere, if you please, my dear Sir;—I never was more so in
all my life, I assure you. Miss Georgiana's voice is positively enchanting!—'tis, 'pon my honour. Whether her strains
are allegro or pensoroso, they equally delight by their full
flowing melody!—they do, 'pon my honour—"

"Now, Sir Marmaduke," interrupted Georgiana, "I really
feel surprised that one so skilled in the rules of etiquette
should so far forget what is due to the lady who has honoured
you with her hand for the evening, as to turn the full tide of
your eloquent flattery upon another. Now, ladies," she
added, turning to the softer sex, "I do think that we have
a right to take some revenge upon Sir Marmaduke for his
treatment of Mrs. Threadlace; as an offence committed
against *one* should be considered an insult done to the *whole*
of the sex. What say you, ladies?"

"Allow me, Miss Georgiana," interrupted the knight, "to
say,—'pon my honour—"

"Oh, yes,—you may *say* so much," resumed Miss Titheum,
with provoking satire in her tone and look; "but you know,
Sir, that *honour* and courtesy should always be associated."

"'Pon my honour," rejoined Sir Marmaduke, "you are
very severe,—I beg pardon,—you are indeed—very—'pon
my honour." His confusion caused his thoughts so to jos-
tle against each other, that he committed a blunder every
time he opened his mouth, or gave utterance to expressions
he intended not to employ; and then again, while striving to
correct one mistake, made another and more palpable one.
The knight's embarrassment afforded more real sport to the
arch satirist than she had derived from all the entertainments of the evening.

"Ha! ha! ha!" laughed Georgiana,—"Do you, indeed,
believe so of me, Sir Marmaduke?—I am not *cruelly* so, I
hope; bear witness, ladies, is my severity beyond—?"

"Excuse me, Miss Titheum," interrupted the knight; "I
bow to your decision; but really, Miss Titheum, you are—
'pon my honour."

"Am I *upon* your honour, Sir Marmaduke?" shouted the

lady, playing upon his expression. "Ha! ha! ha! Indeed! —well then, I shouldn't wonder, if, like some fiery Pegasus, I am run away with; I do hope, however, it will bear me softly and safely."

"Of that there can be no doubt," interposed the doctor. "The honour of Sir Marmaduke is a fortress of defence; and happy must that lady be who may live beneath its protection."

"'Pon my honour," replied the knight, "I feel proud of possessing such an opinion from one so capable of judging correctly, and giving an unbiassed verdict, as Dr. Titheum."

"I have for some time, Sir Marmaduke," resumed the doctor, "felt beyond measure astonished, that you, with all the recommendations you possess, and the evident good grace in which you stand with the fair sex, should so long remain in the unsocial and unnatural state of celibacy, as if you had taken orders as a Jesuit. I had hoped to have had the pleasure, long before now, of presenting you with one of the best gifts that Heaven has bestowed upon man in this world."

"'Pon my honour," replied Sir Marmaduke, "What do you mean, doc*tar*—eh? I confess I do not clearly construe your meaning. I am certain your gifts to-night, in the shape of an excellent supper, choice wines, and, may I add, delightful company," bowing to the ladies, "have been most excellent; indeed, I can't conceive how any man could desire better,—'pon my honour, doc*tar*."

"Why, of the *kind*, Sir Marmaduke," rejoined the doctor, "they are, I am happy to say, good; but what are these, compared with a *good wife?*"

"A *good wife!*" exclaimed the knight. "Whew!—'pon my honour—"

"Aye," said the doctor, "*that* is the gift I refer to. I am sure Mr. Threadlace will join with me in opinion, that a good *wife* is of all good things the very best."

"Oh, certainly, doctor," replied 'Squire Threadlace, while the words almost stuck in his throat; and then, as if recollecting himself, he added, with emphasis and vivacity, "A *good* wife is beyond the price of rubies!"

"Ah, Mr. Threadlace," interposed his *dear* wife, "you, of all men, have reason to say so."

"Indeed I have, *love*," rejoined her lord, although not with such a response as a full conviction of the benefit to which Mrs. Threadlace referred would have sent forth. "Matrimony, doctor," he continued, as if inspired by the mere mention of the subject, "is a blessed thing ; it is the *making* of one for life,—and has," he added aside, "made me miser-able for that period."

"'Pon my honour," said Sir Marmaduke, "such flattering recommendations are almost irresistible ;—they seem something like lime-twigs set to catch young birds on. But, tell me, doc*tar*, is it not, think you, a greater game of hazard than the state lottery presents of obtaining a prize, whether a *good* wife may be obtained or not? And, if a *bad* one should come out of the wheel,—how then? 'Pon my honour! I think, doc*tar*, you say it is 'for better for worse, for richer for poorer, in sickness and health, to love and to cherish till death us do part'—does it not so run, doc*tar* ?"

" Exactly," replied the rector. " You are already perfect in an important part of the ceremony."

"'Pon my honour," rejoined Sir Marmaduke, "I think then, doc*tar*, it is a fearful experiment. Perchance it may turn out all *worse* and no *better*,—and then where are we to look for redress—eh ? Now, it is my opinion,—posi*tively* it is,—that where no trial is permitted before the bargain is finally and for ever made—a man should look well be-fore he leaps,—'pon my honour. I recollect, doc*tar*, having read a stanza to the point, from, as I opine, the pen of some unfortunate wight in this respect. Something in this way—Um!—Oh!—Ah!—I have it!—

> Maids, while you court, and talk of love,
> Will smile, be pleased, good-natured, civil;
> The maid, once made a *wife*, will prove
> A very angel or a ——.

Save your presence, ladies, I cannot repeat what the author says she may become. You, doc*tar*, know what will make a rhyme,—and understand,—'pon my honour."

" Ee! ee! ee!" giggled the doctor, in an abashed way. " You are satirical, Sir Marmaduke."

" No,—'pon my honour," replied the knight ; " positively serious,—never more so in all my life."

" Well, well," added the rector, " you say true about look-ing and leaping ;—nevertheless, the figure is rather an un-gallant one. Is it not, Sir?"

"'Pon my honour I meant no offence," answered the knight. " It was a saying, doc*tar*, which, as I may say, was at hand ; and, without fatiguing one's mind for something.

fresh, I judged it would answer all the purposes I intended. I merely mean, we should leap cautiously, as we say when on the scent."

" But, Sir Marmaduke," replied Dr. Titheum, " if a lady could be recommended, of whose character, spirit, accomplishments, and *property*,—every thing excellent and desirable could be said,—what would your opinion be ?"

" Why, then, doc*tar*," answered Sir Marmaduke, " I should fear the recommendation was either an imposture by design, or an error through ignorance."

" Oh, the Vandal !—the Goth !—the monster in human form !—the unnatural brute !" whispered Mrs. Threadlace to Miss Fidget, scarcely able to hold within any thing like moderate bounds the boiling passion of her soul. " Why don't you speak to him, Miss ? Oh, that I were a *young* lady, for his sake !"

" Me speak to him ! *Me*, Mrs. Threadlace !" exclaimed the poodle-loving lady, " Oh, no, no, no,—not I, indeed ; he would, in that case, be vain enough to believe that I would condescend to receive his addresses."

" Then," resumed the doctor, " I presume, Sir Marmaduke, you have entered your unchangeable protest against the holy estate ?"

" Why, not exactly,—'pon my honour," replied the knight, " but I feel so excessively awkward at the business, when I turn my attention to that point, that I fear unless some young lady, in the condescension and angel-like kindness of her nature, meets me more than half-way, I shall be consigned to perpetual celibacy,—'pon my honour. This, doc*tar*, more than any fear of the consequences, keeps me, I think, from holy matrimony."

" Ha! ha! ha!" roared the doctor, revived in his hopes by the knight's confession and declaration. " There is yet hope of you then, Sir Marmaduke, and a chance for the ladies present. Come, Miss Fidget," he continued, in a tone of jest, and really without any expectation or desire that his observation would be responded to by her, " come now, what say you to this bashful penitent ?"

" *Me*, Sir ?" replied Miss Fidget.

" Aye, *you*, my dear Miss," replied the doctor. He would have proposed the question to Georgiana, but supposing that the *certain* age of Miss Fidget would at once settle the matter and furnish him with an opportunity of proposing seriously his daughter afterwards, he named the senior lady first.

"'Pon my honour, doc*tar*," observed Sir Marmaduke, ' your indefatigable labour in my behalf lays me under a mountain of obligation;—it does, 'pon my honour. If I could dare entertain one encouraging hope concerning Miss Fidget, all my objections,—that is, my fears on the momentous question in hand would, like the thin mist of morning before the glance of the solar ray, recede and disappear, nor leave a trace behind;—they would, 'pon my honour."

"Oh, Sir Marmaduke!" simpered out the affected *young* lady, with maidenly shyness, " you surely cannot be serious in the statements you make."

"'Pon my honour, madam," replied the knight, throwing the back of his right hand into the palm of his left, " I not only *can* be, but *am.*"

The doctor looked as awkward as a young spendthrift on the first day of term, when tapped on the shoulder by one of those ubiquitous—every where present things—called a sheriff's officer. He had drawn his arrow to the head, and, as he had cause to fear, shot it too far; while the *young* lady half hung her head, but not

"Like Niobe, all tears."

Oh, no; neither did the colour go from her face,—that was *stationary;* but she felt—oh, what did she not feel!—her emotions were unutterable—almost unbearable. The sun of her fortunes appeared to shine; it seemed not merely to stand still, but, like the shadows upon the dial of Ahaz, to retrograde, for the purpose of smiling upon her. The cloudy winter of discontent was gathering fast about her, threatening to consign her to perpetual vestality, when suddenly the spring of hope blossomed forth promisingly,—if rightly she augured,—a joyful harvest of matrimonial felicity. The truth is, Miss Fidget had all her life answered to her name. In the days of her teens, lovers, like fluttering insects in a summer's sun, crowded about her path, each one seeking to live in her smile. Three-and-twenty came, and still she had lovers in plenty. Thirty arrived,— and even *then* she might have made her own selection; but no, she allowed *ten* years more —a fatal number when love and beauty are thought on— like other buried years to pass,—and then her suitors became

"Like angel visits, few, and far between."

Now her eyes were opened to behold her folly, and her heart sickened as she looked upon the figure of herself displayed by her mirror :—hair grey, flesh shrivelled,. face pale, teeth —but why need we proceed ? She feared, and not without cause, that her day was over. 'Tis true, her wealth was con. siderable, and in that lay her only chance,—when suddenly and unexpectedly, as has been seen, one bearing a title crossed her path, and bade her hope.

" Sir Marmaduke," said Miss Fidget, as well as the flutter of her bosom would allow her, "I should think that any *young* lady would feel flattered by such compliments, and— although I ought not, perhaps, so freely to confess myself, —but I detest hollow prudishness. Yet, if I were inclined to listen to the advances of *any* gentleman, I should feel half disposed to say to you, as Desdemona did to the brave Moor,

> 'If you have a friend that loves me,
> And could but teach him how to tell your story,
> Why that should win me.' "

" Umph !" said the doctor. " Why that is speaking fairly at all events. How think you, Georgie ?"

" Indeed, papa," returned his daughter, " on such matters I feel scarcely allowed to think ; but if I did think, and were allowed to give utterance to my thoughts, making them vocal, perhaps I might feel *disposed* to say, as Miss Fidget says Desdemona did, that Sir Marmaduke ought to do as Othello said he did upon his lady-love's *hint*,—he ought to speak out,—

> 'And, while she loves him for what he has said,
> He should love her because she listen'd to him.' "

" 'Pon my honour, Miss Georgiana, you are an excellent adviser," said Sir Marmaduke, " and, with such an instruc- tress, I may hope to succeed."

" Miss Titheum !" exclaimed Miss Fidget. " Miss Tithe- um ! do, for mercy's sake, have some respect for my feelings."

" Why, really now, my dear Miss Fidget," replied Georgiana, in the same provoking tone of raillery, " one would imagine, to hear you, that I had been *looking* nameless things at Sir Marmaduke ; now, I am very sure I do respect your feelings, and promise I will neither by word or deed, by wink, nod, or whisper, mar the splendid conquest you have just made.

Ha! ha! ha!   May all your well-earned laurels flourish for ever upon your deserving head."

"Miss Titheum! Miss Titheum!" cried the *young* lady.

"And I further promise," continued the satirist, turning to the rest of the company, "I do further promise, in the presence of this goodly assembly, that I will cheerfully, at an hour's notice, attend your summons,—should it please you to honour me so far,—and become your maid of honour at your nuptials."

A loud and hearty laugh, which had long been suppressed, broke forth as Georgiana closed her address, while Mrs. Threadlace protested she never heard *nothing* more handsomely offered in all her life,—adding, "I have no question, Miss Fidget and Sir Marmaduke, that all present will, with much sincerity and pleasure, wish you every blessing,—and as much happiness as Mr. Threadlace and myself have enjoyed."

"And if," said the 'squire to himself, "it is only as *much,* you will not be surfeited."

"'Pon my honour," returned Sir Marmaduke, "you are suffocatingly kind; and I promise, Miss Titheum, if I have any influence on the occasion, you shall perform the honourable duties your friendship has offered;—'pon my honour."

The doctor felt chagrined, almost beyond endurance, at the abortion of his plan and the failure of his hopes, and, therefore, with less regret than otherwise he would have done, he heard orders issued for the preparation of the carriages, and, as his guests departed, pair after pair, he endeavoured to console himself with the hope that some other alliance, equally desirable, in reference to property and family connexions, might at no very distant period be effected for his lovely daughter.

CHAPTER XI.

"Hist! hist! hist!
The reveller's fete is o'er.
List! list! list!
To a tale never heard before;
Of alarm—
Not of dread;
Of one who was found
In a lady's bed!"

SALLY MAGGS.

DISAPPOINTMENTS experienced, and hopes destroyed, form a species of mental gangrene—a blight and mildew—to all the enjoyments with which a kind Providence may have favoured us. Like the canker and palmer worms, the locusts, and the caterpillars of old, they devour the health of the spirits, and turn to barrenness the most fair and fruitful spots in the soul. " What availeth me all these, " is the language of such a disappointed one as he turns a cold and hasty glance over the good which yet remains to him, " while that upon which my heart's strongest wishes and warmest desires was fixed, is not,—cannot be enjoyed?"

All this was now felt by the doctor, with a degree of severity which acquired strength fron the circumstance of his expectations, which were sanguine, having been so suddenly and unexpectedly cut off : neither reason nor philosophy were sufficient to relieve his mind from the gnawings which it endured. His experience formed but too close a parallel to that of the jealous Haman's of old.

Georgiana perceived the cloud which hung upon her parent's brow, and by some innocent and playful raillery strove to dissipate it; but her efforts were unsuccessful. She knew not how to meet the gloom, being unacquainted with its cause—she imputed it to the change which had followed the departure of the guests, little imagining that herself and Sir Marmaduke

> " Had hung around his manly brow
> The marks of scathing care."

Feeling herself heavy with sleep and fatigued with dancing, she rang for bed candles ; and then having, as was her wont, kissed her father affectionately, and recommended his retiring to rest, she wended her way to her chamber. Left to himself, the doctor determined to try the narcotic influence of a pipe ; and accordingly, he rang the bell, and upon Claudius's appearing, desired him to bring his dressing-gown and slippers ; which done, he repaired to his smoking-room, mixed himself a stiff glass of brandy-and-water, and then sat him down before a cheerful fire to luxuriate amidst the double fumes of tobacco-smoke and strong spirits.

Some faint glimmerings of approaching day appeared in the east, when Sir Marmaduke Varney's carriage, the last of the party, drove from Dr. Titheum's door. In a short time all within the mansion was silent as the grave, where one short hour before all was life and revelry. The servants, one

by one, had retired to their beds ; Betty, the cook, alone remained in the kitchen, and she was preparing to follow the
example of her fellows, by pouring out one more glass of
cordial in order to compose her to sleep during the few hours
she had to lie.   Having taken this final dose, she hasted to
her bedroom, more asleep than awake.

" How very *dreadful* sleepy I am, to be sure !" she yawned
out; "I declare I can hardly hold my head up !—Oh, dear !—
I don't know how I shall undress,—I can't curl my hair to-
night, or this morning I might say for that matter—no, that
I can't. Well, it isn't no great *consequence*, that I knows of."
And again she yawned.   Piece by piece her garments fell
from her as she unpinned or untied them ; and as they fell, so
they lay, for she was too much overpowered with sleep to
place them in order.

" Well, I do wish I was married—that I really do," she
soliloquized; "then I might, possibly, get some rest, if it
was but little ; for *little* rest, as the boy said, would be better
than none at all; and I'm sartin sure I shall never get any
in this ere place." Her tongue refused sending forth any
more sweet sounds ; and, as she proceeded to undress, her
eyelids fell, and it was with the utmost difficulty she could
perform the office of waiting-woman to herself.   At length
the really difficult business was accomplished, the light was
extinguished, and Mistress Betty rolled into bed.

" Oh !" yawned the fatigued cook, as she stretched her
limbs to their full extent,—" how refreshing this is !"

Scarcely had the sleepy sounds issued from Betty's lips
before her feet came in contact with a warm body, while a
rough uncourteous voice exclaimed—" I say, what are you
arter ?—Be quiet, wilt ?"

Betty heard no more,—her ears and eyes were wide open ;
—with a loud shriek she bounded from the bed, and fell
fainting on the floor.

The time that Grabum had slept,—for he it was who still
occupied the cook's bed,—together with the loud cry that
had just sounded in his ear, operated partially to restore him
to his senses.   Still, the remaining stupor of intoxication so
much confused as to disqualify him to comprehend distinctly the meaning of what he had heard.   Some indistinct
recollection floated across his brain of the scene he had played
with the Gypsies, as well as of the last night's carousal;—
these, however, were so entangled as to darken rather than
illumine his mind.

Raising himself up in the bed, he endeavoured, by rubbing his eyes, to brush away the chaos of perplexity by which he appeared to be surrounded—the mist and confusion of contending thoughts by which he was harassed.

In order to ascertain the exact position, if possible, in which he was placed, he felt for the edge of, and then stepped from, the bed. He had not, however, proceeded two paces before he came in contact with the prostrate body of the unconscious cook, over which he stumbled and fell headlong upon the floor.

> " Was ever scene like that which followed,
> Since a large fish the prophet swallowed ?"

The huge head of the falling man of authority came into sudden and violent contact with a certain chamber requisite, and shivered it into pieces ;—if, indeed, it had been composed of less fragile material than it was, the *hard* head which now, like an ancient battering-ram, came against it, must have caused its demolition. Instantly, a fragrant stream flowed round his perturbed cranium, and saturated every thread of his linen.

If Spleen, with her wrinkled brow and scowling eye—or Passion, with distorted countenance and swollen veins—or Melancholy, with her languid look and morbid feeling,—had been present to view the ludicrous scene which was exhibited, the fearful character of their several forms would have undergone an instant change,—or

> " Laughter, holding both his sides,"

would have driven the acrid-tempered spirits from the spot, and claimed it for his own.

Claudius had long been listening in anxious expectation for the commencement of this *anti-*musical farce, and therefore had not entirely unclothed himself. No sooner was the first note sounded in the shriek of the cook, than, leaping from the bed, he ran to her bedroom door, which being much more contiguous to his own than any other, he soon reached—as, also, from that circumstance he was acquainted with its exact position, of which the other male servant was ignorant.

" What is amiss, Mistress Fatpan ?" enquired Claudius.

" Mistress who ?" groaned the half-stunned Grabum, raising his dripping head,—" For heaven's sake," he continued, "tell me where I am ?"

"Why, who are you?" enquired Claudius, half choked with laughter at his own mischievous trick.

"Who am I?" replied the beadle, "Why I took myself to be Moses Grabum, beadle of Christchurch, but I fancy I am mistaken."

"I am greatly mistaken if you are," observed Claudius in an under tone; "but how come you in that room?"

"Oh! I know not,—no more than a child unborn, as we say, how I came here, or, indeed, where I am!—Can you inform me?—I am in a sad state, howsomever."

"Oh! oh!" cried Claudius,—"Is that what you mean? You have broken into the house, and now you pretend ignorance, do you? We'll let you know presently where you are, I promise you. Here, Joseph!" shouted Claudius, as he ran to his chamber-door, "make haste; bring your pistol with you—here is a robber in Mistress Fatpan's chamber!—Be quick!—fly!—or he'll murder her perhaps!"

The first ungentle knocking of Claudius at the butler's chamber-door, roused him from a sound sleep, in which he was dreaming of his beloved Mistress Fatpan, and the identical person who had now so unceremoniously called him back from the regions of ideality to the world of actual existence. At once he obeyed the call, without exactly knowing for what purpose, or by whom it had been given. Drawing on his leathern unmentionables, and seizing a pistol which fortunately was unloaded, he followed the sound and rushed towards the cook's sleeping-room; when who should he encounter but Claudius himself with a light in his hand, who, having placed his mouth to the key-hole, was enquiring how Mistress Fatpan found herself.

Mistaking the dream, from which he had just been so suddenly awakened, for a painful reality, the confused butler was almost strangled with rage. "You audacious fellow!" he exclaimed, "have I then caught you at her door?"—Without interrogating further, or waiting, as good manners would have dictated, for an answer to his question, he aimed a fearful blow with the butt-end of his pistol at the head of our hero, who parrying the stroke most adroitly with the candlestick, the taper received the fracture which was intended for Claudius's pate, and in a moment they were in total darkness, wrestling for the mastery.

"Are you mad, Joseph?" enquired Claudius, getting breath, "and if you are not, why do you treat me thus?"

. If any of my readers have at any time laboured under the influence of the insanity of jealousy, they will at once be able to account for the singular conduct of the coachman on the present occasion; and if they have *not*, no description which by

"That mighty instrument of little men,"

as Byron calls a pen, can be furnished, can he be made to understand it. The attitude and action in which he had seen the cook with Claudius, when he suddenly entered the kitchen, had haunted him from that hour;—he had dreamed about it,—and now the first thing that salutes his ears, and that greets his eyes, is Claudius seeking, as he imagined, an entrance to the chamber of his fair *inamorata*. The very question which Claudius proposed, and the conciliatory tone in which that question was proposed, appeared only like placing a lighted match to a train of gunpowder. He foamed with rage, and gnashed upon the livery lad with his teeth.

"I'll make *you* mad before I've done with you!" roared Joseph; "or I'll stop your wizzen altogether."

Perhaps he would have effected his purpose, so tightly had he grasped the throat of Claudius, and by so doing have terminated the freaks of the mischief-loving youth, if at that moment the voice of Betty, who was just awaking from her swoon, had not been heard.

"Help! help! help!" she exclaimed. "Joseph," she added, "here is a man in my room !—Make haste, or I shall be murdered !"

"Where am I?" again enquired the almost fainting Grabum, his teeth chattering in his head as the effect of his recent ablution and the terrible alarm which began to creep over him.

The doctor, who, as we stated, had retired to his smoking room to enjoy his pipe, &c., having been roused from a reverie into which he had fallen while meditating upon tithes, pluralities, and a see, by the noise he heard, and feeling himself doubly bold from the effects of the grog he had taken, waited not to ring the bell and make enquiries, but ran, or rather staggered, on the instant to the scene of confusion, with his lighted candle in his hand.

Joseph still held Claudius fast, after the fashion that a rapacious falcon holds in his talons a harmless wren.

"Heighday! heighday!" exclaimed the doctor,—"What, not yet in bed—(hiccup)—Joseph—eh? and Claudius too!"

he added, holding up his light with as steady a hand as he could command. " What is the matter here ?" he enquired; " are you drunk, you rogues, you ? and here in my quiet house, at this unseasonable hour, making brawls which would shame a pot-house ?"

" Sir ! Sir !" stammered out Joseph, " I ax your pardon, but this ere Master Claudo has been making too free with Mistress Fatpan."

" Pooh ! pooh !" rejoined the doctor,—" This is both an idle and silly excuse ;—think you that I—(hiccup)—am so to be imposed upon—eh ? Now I am sure that you are drunk, and you know I am constantly warning you against that. I hate above all things a drunken servant, and am de- termined never to keep one ;—neither property, nor life in fact, are safe in the hands of such !" and then, in the true spirit of Brabantio, he added—

> " Thou must needs be sure ;
> My spirit and my place have in their power
> To make this bitter to thee."

" If you will hear me, Sir," said Claudius, as the relaxing grasp of the butler afforded him the power of speech, " I am confident you will acquit me, Sir, of all blame."

" Well, speak out, and be brief," answered the doctor.

" Help ! help ! help !" again shrieked out the cook.

" What does all this mean ?" enquired the doctor, staring with amazement, as if he would have pierced the pannels of the door with his optics. " Is the house beset with thieves?"

" Sir," replied Claudius, " I heard the cook scream some time since, and, thinking all was not right, I called up Joseph to assist me in making examination, and the moment he came to this place he ran upon me as if he intended to kill me on the spot; at the same time calling me ugly names, and charging me with being intimate with the cook. Why he has so used me I am sure I cannot tell."

" Well, well," said the doctor, " of that we will enquire hereafter; other matters appear to demand our attention now. Why has the cook roared out for help so—is she dreaming, think you ?"

" Oh ! that I should be placed in this miserable condition!" sighed out Grabum.

" Hark !" exclaimed the doctor, half petrified with alarm, " as I am in the commission of the peace, there is a man within! Open the door immediately," he added, addressing Joseph, " and ascertain who it is."

Joseph made the attempt, but found it fast on the inside : when, applying his mouth to the key-hole in the way his supposed rival had done, he called out to the cook, " What is amiss, Mistress Fatpan ; is any one in your room ?"

" Oh, Joseph! *dear* Joseph!" replied the cook; " is that you ? Do come in and help me, or I shall be murdered, I fear!—Here is somebody in my bed, I am sartin ; at least there was, for I felt them. Oh, do come and help me !" she added, with a scream of terror.

" Somebody in her bed!" observed the doctor,—"Pooh! pooh! pooh! pooh! I see how it is: she has been dreaming. In her bed! Why, to be sure, there was when she was in it. I have been mistaken in the voice I fancied to be a man's."

" Oh, Betty!" roared Grabum, as if he had just recovered his senses sufficiently to understand something of his position, " is it *you* who are here ? What a trick you have played me !"

" Get out, you monster!" cried Mrs. Fatpan.—"Joseph! Joseph !" she shrieked again, " I shall be turned into a *hactual* jelly if you don't come and help me."

" Open the door," replied the butler ; " you know as how I can't get through the key-hole."

During the whole of this time, Claudius was standing behind, almost bursting with laughter at the effects of his own waggery, and expecting to be gratified with a still more delicious treat in the sequel.

" Then it really is a fact that there is a man in the room, is it ? Force the door instantly !" exclaimed the doctor. " As I am in the commission of the peace, I'll punish the intruder! But stay,—stay a moment or two ;—here, run Claudius to my room and bring my blunderbuss before the door is broken ; it may be we shall require some defence."

The command was performed by Claudius in the twinkling of an eye ; and had he been as ignorant of the whole affair as the doctor himself, he could not have put on a more heroic and intrepid bearing than now he did.

" Allow me, Sir," said the hero, stepping forward, " to take the lead here ; I am not afraid to meet any man ; and I would rather receive any injury myself than you should be harmed, Sir."

As no contention on this point arose among the assembled

brave spirits, neither the doctor nor Joseph having any particular desire to run the hazard of having their heads broke,
or their brains blown out, the daring champion, Claudius,
was permitted to enjoy the honour to which he had aspired.
The command which the doctor had before given not having
been countermanded, Claudius applied the butt-end of the
blunderbuss to the lock of the door, and it flew wide open in
an instant.   A sight was presented immediately of the most
ludicrous character.   There stood the beadle, not merely
shorn of his official habiliments, but almost in a state of nu-
dity, dripping like a sop just taken from the pan; fragments of the demolished vessel lay scattered about the room
in glorious confusion: while the floor was still flooded, notwithstanding the quantity which Mr. Grabum had soaked
up.
   The instant that the door was burst open, and the glancing
ray of the candle, which the doctor still carried, made visible
the objects in the room, Betty concealed herself behind the
curtains of the bed, to which point Joseph kindly threw her
garments; while the constable of Christchurch, falling upon
his knees before the rector, prayed earnestly for forgiveness.
   It was a happy circumstance that Claudius retained possession of the blunderbuss, for in all probability, if it had
been in the hands of the doctor, its contents would have
riddled the long body of the unfortunate official; if indeed
the magistrate's trepidation had suffered him to distinguish
the stock from the barrel, or to have pulled the trigger.
   "Who are you?" asked Claudius, running up to the hu-
miliated beadle, and seizing him by the hair of his head.
   "Who are you, and what is your business here?" interrupted the doctor.
   "O S—i—r! S—i—r!" stammered out the trembling
culprit.
   "Speak out at once, and plainly answer my question," continued the now courageous doctor:—"Who are you?"
   "Who am I?" replied Jacob, trembling from head to foot;
"why, don't you really know me?"
   "Know you?" rejoined the doctor;—"why the fellow's
impudence is only equalled by his shameless disregard to de-
cency!—I am not in the commission of the peace if I don't
soon make you know who I am."
   "Oh, Sir!" groaned Grabum, "I do know who you are; I
cannot deny that."

"Ah, I thought as much!" exclaimed the doctor, " and you shall have better cause of knowledge soon. But answer my question," he continued—"How came you here ? was it by, or with, the consent, understanding, knowledge, or connivance, of the young woman who has called for help ?"

" No, your worship," replied Grabum, with increasing alarm.

" Thou art an impudent scoundrel, then," replied his worship, " and I am not in the commission of the peace if punishment equal to your crime of house-breaking, and other criminal acts, shall not be suffered by you."

" Punishment! house-breaking!" groaned out Grabum.— " Oh, have mercy, your worship! have mercy!" he continued, falling again upon his knees, from which he had risen a moment before,—" I am as innocent of house-breaking, your worship, as a sucking lamb."

" You are as guilty as a cunning *calf*," replied the justice. " How came you hither ?"

" Indeed, your worship, I cannot tell," returned the beadle.

" Oh, oh!" rejoined Titheum,—"You *cannot* tell, can't you ? Oh, that is not quite *convenient*, I suppose. Well, well, we shall find means to *make* you tell."

" Indeed, Sir," replied Grabum, " I do not know."

" You do not know!" ejaculated the doctor,—" Oh, oh! worse and worse;—never since I have been in the commission of the peace, until this hour, have I met with so barefaced and incorrigible a rogue. Not know!—Do you then determine to brave and lie it out ?—I suppose your next step will be to declare you are not here! Oh, monstrous !"

" As true as I am a sinner, your reverence," replied Grabum, in accents of so pitiful a kind as would have melted the heart of a stone, could it have felt ;—" as I hope for your pardon, I speak the truth—I know not how I came here."

" Who are you ? what is your business ?" cried the reverend magistrate; for never having seen Grabum in his. undress, or rather *without* dress, before, and especially in so ludicrous a position as now he was, he had not yet recognised his person.

" Oh, Sir !" sighed out the beadle, " is it then true that you do not know me ?—I am Moses Grabum, Sir," he continued, " constable and beadle of the parish of Christchurch."

"Moses Grabum again !" exclaimed the doctor. "Why, let me see," and he pushed the light close to his face,— "What say you," he added, appealing to Joseph and Claudius, "is this Moses Graham ?"

"Why yes, please your reverence," replied Joseph, "I think as how it is."

By this time the wrath of the butler had considerably abated; beside which, "a horrible light" broke in upon him, touching the part which he had taken in placing the beadle in the chamber of his affianced. It was true that he had done so in ignorance; but to set up such a plea he feared would avail him nothing, either with the doctor or Mistress Fatpan.

"Ha! ha! ha!" roared the doctor, all his fears suddenly passing away, and tickled by the singular figure and circumstance of the constable. "Please to take up your clothes, Master Moses," he added, "and walk into another room. I must enquire further into this affair."

Gathering up his scattered garments upon the rector's bidding, the trembling culprit followed his reverence into another apartment, escorted by Claudius and Joseph as a sort of body guard, or guard of honour. With all possible despatch he jumped into his toggery; after which the doctor proceeded to examine him upon the singular circumstance of his having been found in the cook's bedroom, and, as he stoutly maintained, without his knowledge or privity.

After a considerable time had been spent in the business, without any thing elucidatory being obtained from him, for he continued to insist (notwithstanding the cross-questioning he underwent by the subtle justice) that he was ignorant of the means by which he had entered the place in which he was found, Claudius ventured to suggest to his reverence, that he thought some mistake had taken place, which he believed, if his reverence would permit, he could explain.

"So, so, Mister Wiseman !" observed the doctor,—" you fancy then, that you have wisdom in this dark affair beyond what I,—I who am in the commission of the peace, possess—eh ?

"I beg your pardon, doctor!" replied Claudius, modestly; "I only ventured to say, that I thought some mistake, which I could explain, had taken place."

"Umph !" said his worship,—" you think so, do you ?"

"I do, your worship," answered Claudius.

"Well, then, let us hear it," rejoined the rector, "in as few words as may be."

"I will, Sir," replied Claudius, and he proceeded in as delicate a way as possible to state the case, by referring to the last evening's revel; the entrance of Master Grabum into the kitchen, fatigued and cold; the supply afforded him (a small quantity of *cordial* which the cook possessed for her own private purpose); and the effects it had upon him in consequence of his long abstinence.

"Why, surely, he was not intoxicated!" exclaimed the doctor, as if horrified at the bare thought.

"Intoxicated, Sir!" replied Claudius; "oh no, Sir; a little *cordial* could not intoxicate—he was taken unwell, Sir, as Joseph well knows."

"Yes, Sir," said Joseph, "very unwell."

"I was, indeed, Sir," added Grabum.

"Well, well," observed the doctor, "what then?"

"Why, Sir," continued Claudius, "I proposed he should be placed in my bed for a short time, in order to refresh him."

"Well, that was kind," said the doctor; "that was kind and proper;—what then?"

"Why, Sir," replied our hero, "amidst the bustle of the evening he was somehow forgotten, and when I went to bed, not finding Mr. Grabum there, what could I conclude, Sir, but that, as I knew he was anxious to return home, he had arisen and left the house while I was busy serving in the drawing-room? But, Sir, I fancy that by mistake, in our hurry, he was placed in the cook's bed instead of mine, where, falling asleep, he did not wake until the loud scream of Mistress Fatpan, on finding a man in her room, aroused him."

"Ha! ha! ha!" shouted the doctor.—"Well, well, that is a strange circumstance, truly I see how it happened perfectly well;—I see, I see!—ha! ha! ha!—The kindness of your friends, Master Moses, had nearly proved fatal to you —eh?—ha! ha! ha!"

"Yes, your reverence," replied Grabum, his teeth still chattering from cold.

"Well now, Claudius," continued his worship, "as you have in some measure been the cause of Mr. Grabum's alarm, and the unpleasant condition in which he has been placed, it will be but fair that you should accommodate him with part of your bed for a few hours, without making another mistake."

" Most willingly, Sir," replied Claudius.

" And you, Mr. Joseph, are bound, I think," added the doctor, " to make some apology to Claudius for the fierce attack which you made upon his person, and the unworthy act with which your false suspicion charged him."

" I am obliged to your reverence," interrupted Grabum ; " but as the morning is breaking, I will, with your leave, make the best of my way home. I fear my long absence will have caused considerable alarm already."

" Well, well," replied the magistrate, " as you please. I release you from the present charge, and hope you may never again be taken up upon suspicion ; for a second committal, however innocent you may be, will go hard with you. Now be careful, and when *cordials* are given to you, take care they are not too strong."

" Thank your reverence," said Grabum, bowing, " I will attend to your worship's good advice."

" Joseph," said the doctor, " see him safe out, and then secure the house, and see yourself safe to bed without making any further disturbance." So saying, his worship toddled to his chamber. Joseph, in company with Claudius, having performed their master's bidding, followed his example ; while Master Grabum, thankful for having escaped so well, bent his course towards his own habitation.

CHAPTER XII.

" Stand you there awhile,
And, with your fingers thus upon your lips,
Note with what gallant grace I'll hoax him :
Aye, to the full bent of his own desire,
I'll do it, and work a double purpose ;—
Serve my own ends, and flatter his vanity."

CYCLOPS.

IT may possibly have been supposed by some who have perused these veritable records, that the concern which Lady Bolio experienced for the loss of her son, of whom it was before stated she was passionately fond, did not partake of those striking features of poignant sorrow which the ardent temperament of the lady might have led them to expect. Such conception, however, is founded in error ; her feelings were as powerful and enduring as, perhaps, her nature could have sustained. That a mitigation of what she would otherwise have endured was experienced by her, through the singular and unaccountable regard she had imbibed for Mr. Ferule, is beyond a doubt ; the one passion for a while coming in contact with, and combating, as it were, the other, and so, to a certain extent, neutralising or weakening the power of both.

We have called her passion for Mr. Ferule *singular* and *unaccountable*,—and so, indeed, it was ; and yet there is nothing exceedingly wonderful or singular in its being singular and unaccountable. If the history of a hundred attachments which exist betwixt almost any fifty couples were rendered public, it is highly probable, that of ninety-nine out of the hundred it might be said, they are singular and unaccountable ; either in reference to the parties themselves, or in connexion with the circumstances and means by which such attachments were brought about. Nay, perhaps, no less degree of mystery hangs around the experience of the very persons themselves who have occasioned this brief digression, although their circumstances and ages may differ from those of Lady Bolio's and Mr. Ferule's. That, however, which is merely speculation, not admitting of proof, can, by no mode of reasoning, be brought within the power of demonstration. Thus it is with the parties we have been supposing ; but, however the case may be with them, it is not so with Lady Bolio ;—all that a mother could feel she felt, and

" Who like a MOTHER can LOVE !
Ah ! who like a mother can FEEL !"

As soon as the object of the rival passion was removed from the lady's mansion, by the withdrawal of Mr. Ferule, the full force and current of her heart's undivided affection turned towards the absent Claudius ;—it troubled her waking and engaged her sleeping hours, and, when every means had been resorted to by which to recover him had failed, and every clue to his place of residence, if he still existed, was cut off, the conviction fastened with lacerating effect upon her mind, that he was dead, and she mourned for him accordingly ; " bereft at once of peace and hope."

It was in consequence of a relapse which Lady Bolio experienced, produced by the circumstances referred to, that Dr. Leechum's prescribed visit to Bath was necessarily delayed a few months longer than was intended ; during all which time Claudius continued to reside with Dr. Titheum, performing the duties connected with his office to the entire satisfaction of his master, and the pleasure of his fellow-servants, while in his own person he was, as the doctor said he would be, " happy as the days were long."

Not a few, however, were the tricks which his constitutional eccentricity led him to play off upon every member of the family, from the doctor himself, down to Mistress Fatpan, the cook. As, however, we feel a sort of obligation resting upon us to accompany Lady Bolio in her projected excursion to Bath and Clifton, it will only be possible at this period to furnish a hasty sketch of the hoax which he played upon the reverend justice, and the unexpected consequences to which it led.

It may here be premised, that as the shadow of a shade even of suspicion had never entered the mind either of the doctor, or any one of the family, of Claudius being any other than the offspring of some one of the wandering Gypsy tribe, so neither was any thought entertained that he possessed the capabilities which in reality he had acquired by a good education, and hence his diction and handwriting were of so superior a character as easily to pass for the production of a person in respectable life ; unless, indeed, he wished to put on disguise, and then no clod-pole would have expressed himself in more barbarous terms, or have produced a more detestable scrawl, unless he had employed a ploughshare with which to form the characters in the place of a pen.

Some months had passed since Claudius entered the service of Dr. Titheum, during which period he had not seen so much of the country as he wished and expected. He could not *command* his master to travel, and he therefore determined to put his wit to the stretch, and, if possible, devise some means by which to *induce* the doctor to journey, and in such a direction as would gratify his own inclination.

Perhaps that wily politician, that prince of diplomatists, the celebrated Talleyrand, never conceived a more daring design, or one more difficult to accomplish, during the whole period that he managed the alternating governments of France, and made princes and monarchs his tools and play things, than this which had now been hit upon by Claudius, —not merely to make the master travel for the servant's pleasure, but to take *such* a direction as that servant's will should dictate.

The mere concoction of a scheme, however, is not so mighty a work, laboured and complicated as it may actually be;—a vivid imagination can accomplish this;—but to work out the scheme, and give the creature of the brain life and being, is a task which requires something superior to imagination to accomplish,—it requires *genius ;* and in this lofty attribute of human nature Claudius was not deficient.

Our hero was fully aware of what constituted the doctor's "weak side," and he also knew that to touch upon any subject by which his vanity, as one in the commission of the peace, could be flattered, would work wonders in the perfection of his scheme : on this point, therefore, he determined to found his plot.

In a short time he had drawn out the plan in his mind; and, having procured a finely glazed and gilt-edged sheet of writing-paper, with pen and ink, he sat him down in his bedroom, after the family had retired to rest, and wrote the following polite epistle :—

"*To the Rev. Dr. Titheum, Magistrate of the County of Hants.*

"Reverend and Worshipful Sir,

"An affair of more than ordinary importance has lately taken place in the vicinity of Chichester, in the county of Sussex; to deliberate upon which, a full bench of magistrates has been summoned. Your long standing in the commission of the peace, great learning, and legal acumen, have induced the members of a preparatory meeting to solicit your valuable assistance on the occasion, in order that your matured judgment and extensive information may in some measure guide them in their proceedings. The meeting will be held in the Council Chamber, North Street, Chichester, on Thursday next, the 16th instant.

"I have the honour to be, Rev. and Worshipful Sir,

"Your very obedient, humble servant,

"GEORGE HIGHMANS."

"P. S. As the meeting is to be a *profound* secret, you will oblige by not mentioning it to any individual."

Having folded, wafered, and directed this delicious morceau, his next difficulty was how to get it delivered so that it might appear to come from the place referred to. Here he was at fault for a moment or two.

"If," thought Claudius, "I could transport it to the post-

H

office in Chichester, all would be well, for then it would come safe and direct; but that I cannot do,—and to put it into a post nearer home would infallibly lead to detection, as in that case the post mark would blab out, and I might be discovered. What is to be done? Let me see,—hem! I have it!" he exclaimed, after a short pause, rising, and clapping his hands, as expressive of high gratification at the discovery, —" I have it—suspicion, I defy thee! On such an important occasion a courier surely cannot be considered out of place;—no, and one shall be had;—it will appear respectable, and as the doctor loves that honour should be given to whom honour is due, never questioning at the same time that he has as good a claim to it as any man living, it shall be brought express. But then, how am I to receive it? Let me see ;—I have it again! To-morrow will be Tuesday. I have then to go on an errand to Farmer Primrose's ; it will not be very difficult to fall in with the hasty messenger,—for in haste he must be,—of whom I can receive the letter, and, on my return home, deliver it, of course, to my master. It shall be so; and whether the doctor consents to go, or determines otherwise, I, at least, shall escape detection."

Whatever applause the wit of Claudius may command, the falsehoods which he had deliberately planned, and the artful deception to which he voluntarily consented to submit, merit nothing short of execration and abhorrence. Our object in recording such cases is, not to recommend their imitation to the young, the middle aged, or the old ; but to hold " as 'twere the mirror up to nature, to show virtue her own feature, scorn her own image, and the very age and body of the time, his form and pressure," and thus exhibit character perfect and entire, without omitting ought, or setting down any thing from a feeling of anger or favour.

Claudius, having *fully* concocted and carefully arranged his plan, retired to bed to think it over again, or, perhaps, to dream of its successful accomplishment.

On the following day he was the bearer of a note to the farmer's; and at the same time he carried, safely lodged in his pocket, the letter which he intended for the doctor.

There was in the breasts of the Primroses a well-spring of gratitude. The services they had received at the hands of any one,—without regarding their standing in society,—were never forgotten by them. They did not, like too many, make it appear by their conduct that they imagined those

beneath them in circumstances deserved no kind returns for
faithful and serviceable duties performed, or that those who
enjoyed the comforts and luxuries of life possessed in *them*
a title to every service a poor man could perform, as if some
irrational beast of burden had wrought the action. Oh, no;
they estimated the service done according to its own merits,
and never forgot the *person*, any more than the *act*. Hence,
when Claudius reached their dwelling on the morning in
question, he received at the hands of Farmer Primrose, as
well as from every other member of the family, the most
friendly and warm salute, and while he remained, each vied
with the other in their exertions to express their gratitude
for one who, in the fulness of their hearts, they hailed as
their preserver. The little ones, who, when first they saw the
Gypsy boy, slunk from him behind their mother's chair, now
ran to him, and played with his fine clothes, while even Miss
Kate looked upon his change of appearance with pleasure in
her eye, and more than half fancied he was a *very* fine-look-
ing *young* man.

Having performed his master's business at Mr. Primrose's,
Claudius returned to the rectory, and after delivering a
message, of which he was the bearer from the farmer to the
doctor, who was seated in his library, he made a low bow, and
retreated a step or two towards the door, when, as if suddenly
recollecting something, he turned back, and observed, as he
took from his pocket the letter of invitation he had written,
"I beg pardon, Sir, I had wellnigh forgotten this note,
which I received from a person on horseback;" and he laid
the billet on the table.

"Umph!" said the doctor, as he took up the epistle,
"some important matter, I dare say, from some troublesome
personage or other, making very humble and very earnest
request that I would render them assistance. I am so pes-
tered with these things, that I have, more than once, determined to receive no more communications unless I have some
notion of the quarter whence they may come. Let me see," he
added, taking up the letter and surveying it, "this may be
of some consequence; the superscription speaks well for it;
the hand is evidently that of a gentleman's. Umph! that alters
the case;—it is undoubtedly the writing of a *respectable*
person."

"I think so, Sir," observed Claudius, encouraged to speak
by the manner of the doctor; "it looks like some great man's
H 2

writing, I fancy, Sir, if I may be allowed to say so much, and it was for that reason I took it. The messenger, Sir, appeared in a wondrous hurry; his horse looked uncommonly distressed, and the moment he had delivered the letter into my hand,—about one hundred yards from the house, Sir,—he turned tail, and galloped out of sight in an instant almost, merely saying he had to go twenty miles in another direction, and, as he was pressed for time, he was glad he had hit upon one of his worship's servants."

"Indeed!" responded the doctor, who had listened with more than ordinary patience to Claudius; "'tis very singular. Let us see,—let us see," he continued, as he tore the letter open, and read, half audibly, "'To the Rev. Dr. Titheum, Magistrate of the County of Hants.'—Ah! What can this mean? Some business of importance, no doubt! You may go," he observed to Claudius; "but, no, no," he added, in the same breath, as Claudius moved towards the door, "stay, stay, child;" and again he commenced reading. "'Reverend and Worshipful Sir.'—Um! How was the messenger dressed?" he enquired. "Did he wear livery?"

"I think he did, Sir," replied Claudius.

"You *think*," responded the doctor. "Do you *only* think? Cannot you be certain?"

"Yes, Sir," said Claudius; "that is, I am sure he did."

"He did wear livery,—eh?" repeated his reverence.

"O yes, Sir, I am quite positive of it now," rejoined Claudius; "a handsome one, now I remember. It was a good deal like the one which I wear, Sir."

"Was it so?" said the doctor, swallowing the double compliment, for he felt it a compliment to have a handsomely dressed livery servant despatched to him with a letter; and to hear that which his own servant wore so called,—although by the servant himself,—was not less so.

Of all the evidences of a little or degraded mind that men display, few, if any, exceed the greediness with which flattery is received. From whatever quarter it may proceed, in whatever measure or "questionable shape" bestowed, it is equally swallowed, and never appears indigestible; nay, even when the opinion of the person who may "pour it on" would on all other subjects be held as mean and despicable, on this he is not merely tolerated, but held as an oracle. Like intoxicating fluids, the more it is received the more it fires the receiver for a fresh supply. Like the grave, the soul of the lover of flattery is never satisfied with its grabage-like food, for, with the thirsty horse-leech, it continues to cry—*Give.*

How true, and yet how humiliating are the well-known lines of the venerable Home:—

" Flattery direct
Seldom disgusts. They little know mankind
Who doubt its operation. 'Tis the key
That opes the wicket of the human heart."

The doctor drank of the fetid stream with uncommon zest and relish ; and, having smiled his gracious approval of Claudius's reply, proceeded to finish the reading of the letter.

" So, so," he observed, having concluded it, his eyes the meanwhile sparkling with unwonted fire, and his breast swelling with elation, " this must be seen to. An affair of more than ordinary importance,—Umph! ' Long standing, —great learning,—legal acumen,'—good, good," he half muttered to himself, still looking over the letter. " I shall want the carriage early in the morning, Claudius," observed the doctor, " and you must—"

" The carriage, Sir ?" interrupted Claudius.

" Yes, the carriage," rejoined his reverence. " Speak I not plain ?"

" Your worship forgets," replied Claudius, " it was taken to be fresh painted some days since."

" Oh, ah !—right, right. I had forgotten that, indeed," returned the doctor. " Well, no matter,—the roads are good, and the business is important; the journey can be performed in the saddle. Let my horse be ready by six o'clock in the morning at the latest, and be you in attendance in your best livery; you must ride with me. Hasten to Joseph immediately, and desire him to see the horse's shoes are all in good order; give my top boots an extra polish,—and let Sally see that a change of linen is in readiness and well aired ; and,—there, see all is done as I have ordered."

" I will, Sir," replied Claudius; and with as much pleasure and gratification at the success of his scheme as a minister would feel who had succeeded in some diplomatic arrangement on which the peace of nations and the lives of thousands depended, he ran to perform the commands of his master, and prepare for the delightful excursion he was about to take.

All in and about the parsonage became instant bustle, as
if its inhabitants were making preparations to defend the
venerable edifice from the assaults of a foe, or to preserve to
themselves its possession from the grasp of its original owners, who had returned from their disturbed quiet in the grave
to give it back again to those to whom it righteously belonged by right of bequest.

It was six o'clock when the doctor read the letter, and
therefore, as he determined to start at six the next morning,
and wished to attend the convocation of his brethren in the
commission of the peace in such style of appearance as should
bring no reflection on his present distinguished popularity,
it was indispensable that all engaged in his establishment
should be on the alert.

As soon as Claudius had gone to attend to his orders, the
doctor sought Georgiana, and informed her that business of
the utmost consequence required his attendance at Chichester
on the following day, where it was possible he might be detained a day or two ; she would therefore not feel uneasy respecting him, although his absence should be extended even
to three days.

Georgiana, in the true spirit of her sex, felt a sudden irrepressible degree of curiosity possess her to know what could possibly call her papa so suddenly from home.

" Your departure is *very* sudden, papa," she observed.

" Why, it is *rather* so, my dear," returned the doctor ;
" but *we* who are in the commission of the peace never feel
surprised by such things. We hold ourselves in preparation
for a moment's call."

" Is it *very* important business, papa ? " enquired his
daughter.

" *Very* important, my love," returned the rector ; " every
thing connected with the—that is—it is—as I said, dear—it
is *very* particular business."

" I wish I could ride with you," observed Georgiana, coaxingly, " I should so much enjoy it."

" That is impossible, love," returned the doctor.

" Impossible, papa ! " reiterated Georgiana.

" Yes, it is *quite* impossible, I assure you," rejoined her
father.

" And why is it so *very* impossible ? " asked the daughter.

" Because the business, love, is to be kept a perfect secret—
that is—," said the doctor, checking himself, and stammer-
ing for a reply,—"because, my dear, for certain reasons —"

The confused and hesitating manner of the rector gave a deeper tinge of mystery to the subject in the romantic mind of Georgiana, and she felt the keen edge of her curiosity sharpened to become acquainted with the secret, in proportion as concealment appeared to hang about it.

"Well really, now, papa," she continued, "you have promised me an excursion for several months, and this is just such a one as I should like to take."

"Well, but I tell you," replied the doctor, "it is impossible at this time. You know, my dear, the carriage is not at home."

"I know that, papa," continued the unbending girl, winningly; "but I can ride in the saddle, you know. Is the business of an ecclesiastical or legal nature?—Oh, I guess it, now," she added. "Ah, it must be a great. *secret ;* but it will soon be known. I suppose you are going to marry Sir Marmaduke and Miss Fidget?"

"Marry who?" ejaculated the doctor, starting.

"Sir Marmaduke Varney and Miss Fidget," returned Georgiana;—"Now is not that it?"

"No, love; I assure you, you are entirely wrong in your conjecture," said her papa,—"I am not going on any business of the kind;—indeed I am not, Georgie," continued the doctor, as he patted her playfully and fondly on the cheek; "it is an affair of much more importance."

"What! of more importance than *marriage*, papa?" exclaimed Georgiana; "why, I always understood that was the *most* important thing in the world."

"So it is, my dear," returned the rector; "I did not mean exactly so; but *we* who are in the commission of the peace have good reasons for being secret sometimes—all we do, love, it would not be proper to make known; my long standing in the commission of the peace, and extensive legal knowledge, render my presence essential on important occasions, such as,—but don't cherish a spirit of curiosity, my dear," added the doctor gravely, again checking himself, "it is not becoming in a young lady."

"I am sure, papa," returned Miss Georgiana, "you cannot say that *I* am particularly curious; I merely asked for the purpose of—of knowing, that was all."

"Your method of freeing yourself from the charge of curiosity," returned the doctor, "is, certainly, any thing but conclusive, Georgie ;—well, well, I will accept it; and I now promise that, on my return from Chichester, you shall have the long-promised excursion to Brighton, or Bath, or some other fashionable resort. Now be sure, Georgie," he continued, " while I am away, you look well to the concerns of my establishment—keep the servants all at their posts,—if any visitor should call,—not at home, remember,—if any tithes are brought (and I hope some will be paid), receive them, and say I will send receipts when I return ;—and, do you mind me, Georgie, if Sir Marmaduke should call, why —be yourself ;—if he wishes you to touch your instrument, do so ; or to sing the last new vaudeville you received from London, meet his wishes, and be agreeable. I need not say, remember you are my daughter—

" Sole heiress of my house and heart."

" I shall not forget it," replied Georgiana, half vexed that, with all her pressing, she could not dive into the mystery which appeared connected with her father's visit to Chichester.

" I hope you never will," returned the fond father to his daughter's reply ; " and let the recollection," he added, as he kissed her affectionately, with rising dignity of feeling, " of the high character of those from whom you sprung, act as an amulet to you on all important occasions. Go now and see all is got in readiness, and properly arranged, for my departure."

Georgiana returned her father's fond salute, and withdrew.

CHAPTER XIII.

" Now fairly in saddle, away they ride,
    Like the Knight and his 'squire of old ;
Whose marvellous deeds and mishaps beside
    Don Cervantes has bravely told.

Right onwards they press'd with hearty good will ;
    Now fast,—and now more at leisure :
The master rode after a phantom still,
    The servant he follow'd for pleasure."

METRICAL RECORDS.

THE beautiful and glowing month of June was hasting fast to its close ; and hence the *summer solstice* had fully set in, when Dr. Titheum's hasty visit to Chichester was to be undertaken. The hours of day were extended to their utmost space; night could scarcely be said to exist, for the *crepusculum*, or twilight, continued from the setting of the sun until the glorious regent of day arose like a strong man to resume his bright and beneficial race. All nature seemed redolent with sweets and beauty, while every sense of man was regaled. The very air which was breathed through the valleys, and kissed the mountain tops, was pregnant with salubrity, as if scented with the delicious odours which arose from thousands of wild flowers, and hedgerow fragrance; or from rich and beautiful parterres that adorned the useful plots attached to the cottages of the peasantry, or ornamented the more stately mansions of the wealthy.

In every direction the eye was gratified with scenes of transcendent loveliness. The ear was regaled by sounds of almost unearthly cadence, while the sense of smell was met by sweets which contained invigorative properties. The entire man *felt* the unutterable and almost magic power which such sights and sounds contained, and in which his whole nature revelled in high delight.

Such was the season of the year, and such the glowing loveliness of the day referred to. The sun was already gilding with its radiant brightness the heavens above and the earth beneath: all nature seemed attuned to harmony and praise, and with inarticulate expressiveness called upon the most noble and most favoured, but most ungrateful of God's creation,—Man! to join in the universal anthem which was ascending from every grade of being to the uncreated throne of HIM whose name is excellent in all the earth.

As six o'clock tolled in the tower of the church, the horses which were to convey the doctor and Claudius to the expected scene of *more than ordinary importance*, were led to the front of the parsonage by Joseph and our hero; and in two minutes after the reverend magistrate appeared, equipped at all points for his journey.

" Is all right?" enquired the doctor.

" Yes, Sir," replied Claudius.

" You have looked at the mare's shoes, have you, Joseph?" asked his worship.

" Yes, yes," responded the coachman. " Will Horsenail was here last night and examined both on'em. Your mare, Sir, wanted a near fore shoe; and Mayflower, what Claudo is

H 5

going to cross, had cast both hind'uns; but Will did the business, and see'd all the others was right."

" Very well," observed the doctor, " and you gave them
a good feed this morning by five, did you ?"

" At half-past four, Sir," replied Joseph, " they had it ;
and I'll warrant they'll do now for some hours. A month-
ful of hay and a wash would carry them half through, at
least."

" I shall see, I shall see," rejoined the doctor ; and added,
to Claudius, " We have a long ride before us, and must
push hard to accomplish it in time for my business this evening. Where is my whip, Joseph ?"

" Here, Sir," replied Coachee, handing the instrument of
punishment.

The doctor mounted the horse-block which stood at the
side of the gate, and from thence seated himself in the saddle ;
while Claudius vaulted into his with the agility of a horse-
dragoon. At this moment Georgiana appeared at her window, from which she waved her handkerchief to the doctor
as he put his horse on a canter ; while the cook, peeping out
at the door, saluted our hero.

" A pleasant day to you !" observed Joseph to Claudius.

" Thank you," returned the delighted livery servant,—
" Be sure you take care of yourselves. I don't doubt I
shall be all right ;" and kissing his hand right gallantly to
the cook, he gave the reins to Mayflower, and followed his
master.

The doctor had determined to push on as far as Titchfield,
and there take breakfast, in order that he might be able to
refresh himself and horse an hour or two at that place, and
travel leisurely during the heat of the day. Keeping this
purpose in view, he passed over the ground at as rapid a rate
as if he had been the plenipotentiary of some mighty one of
the earth. The travellers had not proceeded more than ten
miles through the forest, before an unexpected circumstance
occurred which had wellnigh changed their route, and stopped the doctor's progress altogether.

It has already been noticed that the doctor was a lover of
the sports of the field ;—*he* knew *no* reason, and frequently
exercised his logical powers to prove there was *none*,—why a
gentleman, whose profession happened to be of clerical character, should not enjoy himself in a cheerful hunt as well as
a lawyer, physician, or statesman. The horse which the doc-

tor rode was as great a lover of a day's good run as his master—the sound of the horn, or the echoing "halloo!" was as
inspiring to the noble beast as the martial drum and the rat-
tling of the spear were to Job's inimitably described war-
horse.

The equestrians were pursuing the even tenour of their
way— the doctor dreaming over the glory he should on that
day acquire, and the loud plaudits which would be poured
upon him by his compeers in the commission of the peace;
and Claudius felicitating himself upon the success of his
stratagem, and laughing in his sleeve at the singular disap-
pointment his master would meet with on his arrival at Chichester, when suddenly, "Halloo, halloo!" rang through the
forest, and in the next instant, the scarlet livery of the god-
dess of the chase blazed in the distance, and half a score
huntsmen, surrounded by a pack of hounds, dashed across
the road in full cry, after a hard pressed fox. The high blood
of the animal which the doctor bestrode, appeared to course
its veins with increased rapidity;—he snorted significantly,
pricked up his ears, and, despite of bit or bridle, turned suddenly aside to mingle with his fellows in the sport.

A hedge of some six feet high, which surrounded an inclosed spot from the forest, interposed betwixt the doctor and
the hunters; but this barrier availed nothing to stay the im-
petuous career of this high-mettled courser—he cleared it
with as much ease as the hunted chamois leaps the craggy
projections of their own native wilds.

The doctor, although entirely unprepared for such a sudden elevation, maintained his seat like a good horseman—
neither did his head turn giddy, as some persons' have done
by an unlooked for rise;—no, steady and calm as when on
even ground, the practised sportsman passed the prickly
barrier.

"Let not those who are leaping boast like those who have
taken the leap," is sage advice; applying, however, not only
to a sporting leap, but to leaps of a more serious and important kind. But as this fly of the doctor's was *bona fide* of the
nolens order, he cannot bear blame for not taking and acting
upon the above counsel.

On the opposite side of the hedge from that on which his
reverence was just before riding quietly, was an excavation of
nearly three feet deep, into which the land-springs from a
large tract of ground drained during the wet season, and

which still contained a few inches in depth of water. No calculation having been made for such a descent, the shock was tremendous; and before Ithurea had obtained firm foot-ing, the doctor was shot over her head, and lay as if taking a few minutes' rest in the soft clay and water.

At the moment this unexpected leap was performed, the doctor was about twenty yards in the advance of Claudius; and having turned an abrupt angle of the road, his flight over the hedge was not perceived by our hero; so that when he reached the angle referred to, his astonishment exceeded all expression, as no trace of his master existed. He reined in his horse as quickly as possible, without knowing how to act. To return home without the doctor, and especially without being able to give *any* account of what had become of him, was an awkward thing. To make a simple statement of the affair as it stood, would subject him to be laughed at for a fool, or expose him to the dark suspicion of having murdered and buried his master.

He began to reason on the possibility of his master's hav-ing returned; but that idea was soon abandoned, as in that case he must have seen him. That he could have passed over the long and straight piece of road which now lay before him, was impossible—had the earth taken him *in,* or had some attractive influence taken him *up,*—neither thought came within the range of probability.

After a short period of perplexing rumination, he heard, or imagined he heard, a voice like the doctor's, calling him by name,—"Here, Claudius, Claudius, I say!—Make haste and assist me, or I shall be drowned, or smothered in this mud and water!"

Claudius might almost have supposed himself the play-thing and sport of some wicked necromancer;—he rubbed his eyes and pinched his cheeks, to ascertain fully if he was really awake, and whether the whole might not be a freak of Queen Mab.

"Claudius, Claudius!" was again shouted lustily by the doctor.

"Where are you, Sir?" enquired the called one.

"I am here," returned his reverence,—"here in the clay-pit, over the hedge."

"Over the hedge," thought Claudius, "and in the clay-pit!—why, how in the name of wonder came you there?"

As this thought ran through his head, Claudius walked his

s.page 157.

horse in the direction the voice came from, and approached as near the hedge as possible. He presently beheld part of the doctor's person, and at a short distance saw his canonical castor floating like a pitch-kettle upon the pool. At the distance of a few yards he discovered a gate, and making to it, he soon gained an entrance into the enclosed ground; and in five minutes' time, with the assistance of a gentleman of the hunt, who had seen the accident and turned back to afford his aid, succeeded in pulling the doctor from his place of repose, and regaining the hat from its aquatic excursion.

The bedizened figure of the reverend gentleman provoked the laughter both of Claudius and the huntsman; while the doctor himself, finding that the only injury he had sustained consisted in his being soused in the water, and imbedded in the mud, joined with them in a good-tempered "ha! ha! ha!"

Ithurea had behaved in the most uncourteous and unladylike manner; for instead of staying to enquire if her master felt comfortable in his situation, or was disposed to follow the fox, she pushed on in pursuit of the baying pack. Her singular appearance, however, soon attracted the notice of one of the hunters, who, supposing some one had been unhorsed by accident, directed his servant to arrest the fugitive; which, on being so effected, she was led back to the point from whence she had been seen to come, as it was considered highly probable her owner might be in that direction.

Claudius proceeded to scrape some of the mud from the doctor's dress, and by the time he had accomplished his task Ithurea came in sight; and at the end of almost twenty minutes from the time of her forsaking her master, she was again bearing him onwards; and with as much speed as they could command the rector and his servant pushed towards a road-side inn near Brockenhurst.

In all circumstances of calamity or mishap, every disposed person may find certain points of alleviation by which to solace himself, and escape the unalloyed severity of the event; and where none other can be discovered, the commonplace one, at least, may be found, namely, "it might have been worse;" and even this, simple as it may seem, and however much the derision of the fastidious may be poured upon it, savours not a little of philosophic wisdom: for it may be maintained as sound philosophy, that whatever innocent means can be resorted to, to ease or allay the sufferings of the body, or the pangs of the mind, have claims upon

the attention of the wise, while only such as are destitute of
the wisdom of which they proudly boast, would treat them
with contumely, or reject them with disdain.   The stanza of
One of the olden times" is true :—

> " However brave and wise the man may be
> Who bears, unmurmuring, sickness, bondage, pain!
> He lays just claim to sound philosophy
> Who uses means deliverance to obtain."

Our reverend hero's case did unquestionably admit of all
the benefit which could arise from the consideration that,
"bad as his condition was, it *might* have been worse."   It
would certainly have been considerably more unpleasant if a
leg, or an arm, or the neck of his worship had been broken ;
or had the somerset been taken during the period when—

> " *Winter*
> Chills the pale morn, and bids his driving sleets
> Deform the day delightless."

It would have been much more uncomfortable to his person,
and less good for his health ; but beside these considerations,
one other, not less important, so far as feeling was concerned,
existed in the circumstance that the road over which the doctor had to pass before he reached the inn was less frequented
than either Cheapside or the Strand ; indeed, it was a chance
if any thing, excepting a stage coach, a common cart, or a
waggon, was met with ; had it been otherwise, the appearance of the plump, bedaubed rector, would have supplied
matter for jest, jibe, and merriment, little less than that
which is placed to the account of the celebrated Johnny Gilpin, when he rode against time, to and from Edmonton.
Every inn has its wag, either in host or waiter, and it is
only necessary to ascertain in what channel the vein of their
humour runs, to be furnished with as fair a specimen of racy
wit, although in humble life, as ever Sheridan or Foote displayed.   Two such souls resided at the " house of entertainment for man and horse" at which the doctor and his servant
put up, alias, where they got *down*.
The moment our travellers appeared before the door of the
said inn, Timothy Trump, waiter, hostler, boots, &c., with a
species of instinct peculiar to his calling, ran from the stable
yard to wait upon the visitors.   Tim's long matted hair,
which looked like an uncoiled ball of red oakum, was stroked
on one side of his pimpled forehead, and terminated in what

was meant to represent a curl; but, unfortunately, the curry-comb, which he had employed as a substitute for an appendage to the toilette, had performed its office so vilely as to give to Timothy's carroty-coloured wig the appearance of a basilisk twining about his temples. Putting his hand to the place which was intended as the resting place for a hat, but which was seldom so much honoured as to bear one, he inquired, "What may ye plase to *vant*, gemmen?"

"I want the hostler," replied the doctor. "Are you he?"

"Yes, Zur, I be's the orsler," replied the waiting man, "at your sarvice, Zur."

"Take my horse then, my lad," said the doctor, dismounting, as Claudius, who had vacated his saddle, held Ithurea's head; "take my horse, and mind you put her into a warm stable."

"Yes, Zur," returned the hostler. "You may rely upon Tim Trump for any thing as consarns orses; and if you should want rubbing down arter I'ze done the orses, I'm your sarvant, Zur," added Mr. Trump, looking at the doctor's soiled dress, and winking archly at Claudius as he led the horses into the stable yard.

As the doctor entered the inn door, he was met by the happy-faced hostess, who, eyeing his canonical covering, without perceiving his bespattered condition, dropped a low curtsy, and shrewdly guessing that he was in the commission of the peace, as several of the *respectable*, alias consequential reverends in the neighbourhood were, and fearing too that a screw might be loose in the healthy existence of her establishment, she put her mouth into the best possible position, and enquired, "Will your reverence please to walk into the parlour?"

"Yes, my good woman," replied the doctor; and as he so said, followed her guidance.

"Mercy on me!" exclaimed the hostess, as she looked upon the doctor when he entered the room, "Why, I declare Sir, you are nothing but a lump of dirt,—and dripping wet too, as I live!"

"You are nearly right," rejoined his reverence; "but where is your husband?" he added.

"My husband, your reverence?" reiterated the landlady.

"Yes, woman!" said the doctor, rather warmly. "Your husband! You have a husband,—have you not?"

" Yes, Sir," answered the alarmed hostess, "I have a husband."

" Well, I wish to see him," returned the doctor. " Go, and send him to me."

" Why, what has he done now, Sir?" enquired the woman, without attending to the rector's bidding, and in increasing alarm.

" What has he done!" responded the doctor, pettishly; " why—"

"Has he been poaching again, your worship?" asked the landlady.

" Poaching!" repeated the magistrate. "Why, does he then follow such illicit practices—eh? is he then a poacher?"

" Oh, no, no, no, Sir!" replied Mistress Boniface, brightening up, as she perceived her fears were groundless, and that she was enlightening the mind of the ignorant on a subject on which she wished ignorance should remain. "No, Sir, I assure you, nothing of the kind; my husband, Sir, has too much respect for his *superiors* to attempt in any way to spoil *their* amusement by gratifying himself, and honours the *laws*,—I should have said the *equitable* and *righteous* laws of his country, to do any thing of the kind."

" You speak like a sensible woman," replied the learned functionary. " It is right and good *always*, and in *all* things, to yield *implicit* obedience to the powers that be. *We* who are in the commission of the peace always enforce these things;—but I thought, by your observations," continued the doctor, " that he had been one of those who defy *all* laws, and that he poached."

" Oh, no, Sir," continued the hostess, " he does no such thing, as one may say, your reverence. Oh, no, your worship; you may depend upon my word and honour,—and that, as your reverence knows, is not a little to say. You may, I say, depend upon my word and *honour* that we are honest people, what gets our living by working hard; only Sir, I did fear as how it was *possible* he might have been led astray."

" Well, well, my good woman," observed the doctor, who began to lose his patience, " I wish you would be so kind as to *lead* or *send* him to me; I want him particularly and immediately."

" Oh yes, Sir," exclaimed the hostess, all fear of a *committal* being taken from her mind, " I'll send him *momently*," and, making another low curtsy, she disappeared.

"Claudius," said the doctor, "where is my change of linen?"

"Here it is, your worship," answered Claudius, handing him a neat leathern case, in which cravats, hose, a night-cap, &c., &c., were neatly packed.

"Very good," replied the doctor, "that will do. Now, while I dress, go you to the stable, and see how the horses are disposed of, and take care they are rubbed down dry, so as to be ready in about an hour's time."

Claudius made his obeisance, and did as directed.

"I have met with an accident," observed the rector, as Boniface entered the room.

"I am sorry to hear it, Sir," replied the landlord, with the politeness and suavity of his craft, when one who appears able to pay demands their attention. "Can we serve you here in any way?—shall feel most *happy* and *proud* to wait upon you."

As all hopes of getting to Titchfield to breakfast had faded from the doctor's mind, like the bright gloss from his silken hose, from one and the same cause, he considered it would best comport with propriety to yield unobjectively to unavoidable necessity, and take his first repast where he was. Having so determined, he replied to the landlord's courteous interrogatory and polite declaration, "Can you oblige me with the loan of a suit of your clothes, while my own are being dried and brushed?"

"Why, if your reverence wouldn't object to my corduroys and Sunday frock," replied the landlord, "they are at your service. A whiter, or a better frock, is not worn by any yeoman in the county."

"Havn't you a coat, my friend?" enquired the doctor.

"Why, no, your reverence," returned Boniface, "that is a piece of finery I never aspired to; and I rather fancy I should feel as awkward in such a thing as I should in your reverence's gown. Frocks are much more handy for *our* profession."

"Well, well," replied the doctor, "your offer is a kind one, and I will accept it. Show me to a chamber, where I can make the change, and, while I am dressing, you can prepare me a good breakfast."

"I'll see it shall be done, Sir," replied the landlord; and, leading the way to an attiring room, the offered dress was soon furnished, and, after a little puffing and blowing, the doctor succeeded in getting fairly into the homely costume of the tapster of the inn. The metamorphosis of the rector was singular as it was sudden; while the transformation was so unique, that a stranger to mine host might have been forgiven the offence of mistaking the ordained minister for a licensed victualler. There was only one particular in which his newly donned habit challenged remark, and that was,—as the Welshman said of the marine's jacket,—" it fitted him too much ;" in plain English, it was too large for him. The landlord was about six inches taller than the divine, and bore " a fair round paunch," which was not unfrequently " with venison lined," equal in girth to his Patagonian stature.

As soon as the doctor had completed his change of dress, his own clothes were given into the charge of the landlady, by whom they were in a short time placed before a blazing kitchen fire, and his reverence took possession of the parlour.

" I say," observed Timothy Trump to Claudius, as he entered the stable, " beant your measter a rum old codger ?"

" Why do you ask such a question ?" enquired Claudius.

" Oh, as to the matter o' that," replied Tim, " I does many things, like my betters, without *ony* reason, as the saying is."

" Well then," returned Claudius, " I, like many others, have *no* reason if I don't answer your question."

" Be you that sort o' chap ?" enquired Tim, suddenly turning from the horse he was rubbing down, and staring openmouthed at Claudius, " Why, I'm blowed if you arn't a pair o' rum un's !"

" Why so ?" demanded Claudius.

"Vy so?" shouted Tim. "Ha! ha! ha! Vy, *bekause* as how, d'ye see, I never yet in all my bornd days knowed any sarvants what comed here what didn't feel mortally pleased to speak a bit o' their minds consarning their measters. Vy, bless you, I knows the characters of all the rich uns as ever called here ever since I became *orsler ;* you are the only *conception* to this ere rule. Now, it *decurs* to me that I guess the reason o' the cause of this."

" Do you ?" replied Claudius. "Perhaps you will favour me with your *guess ?* I shall be better able than yourself to judge if it be correct or not."

" To be sure I will," replied Tim. " I never cares the *vally* of the jingle of a tanner on a tombstone who knows what I thinks. I thinks then, as how you thinks as how I does n't know how to keep a secret.—Whew ! Arn't I right now,—eh, young man ?"

"Not exactly so," returned Claudius.

"Well, now that is *perticilarly* odd," continued Tim ; " I never was wrong afore. And so, I 'spose you think as how I can't tell then. Ha! ha! ha! Bless your heart, *I* knows what you thinks."

"Indeed!" returned Claudius. "I feel certain you don't."

" I'll wage you a quart on't, and down with the browns. There," continued the hostler, "one, two, three, and a mag," as he counted out the money, and laid it on the window sill. "That's for a quart o' the best. Dares' take me?"

" Yes, answered Claudius, "I do dare;" and counting out an equal sum, he placed it by the side of Tim's.

"Well then," said the knight of the stable, "you *thinks* as how I can't tell you *what* you *thinks.* Arn't I right, my lad, —eh? Ha! ha! ha!"

Claudius felt himself outwitted, and at once replied, "You have won the wager, although rather craftily. Let us have the beer."

" I'll fetch the heavy in a moment," said Tim ; and off he ran with Claudius's pence, and soon returned with a pot of home-brewed.

"There's a head for you," observed Tim. "Arn't it a complete *kollyflower ?* Here's to our better acquaintance," he added, as he blew the froth aside, and put the earthen jug to his mouth, and having swallowed half the quart, he handed it to Claudius, observing, as he smacked his lips, "That's fine stuff!—never tasted mother's milk half so good! I could drink that ere stuff until all's blue, and never say I was tired."

A loud ringing of the bell cut short Timothy's loquacity, and he ran to attend it. " I'll be back in a pig's whistle," he observed," as he left the door; "you enjoy yourself."

The doctor had seated himself in a roomy arm-chair in the best parlour, and was busily engaged reading the morning paper, when Timothy entered with the breakfast tray, for the purpose of making arrangements for the rector's first meal.

Mistaking the divine for his master, from the dress which he wore, he started with surprise at seeing him so seated, and in his Sunday clothes. " I zay, measter," he observed, " that old chap's a rum un which has comed here this morning ; and so for that ere matter is his livery sarvant in the stable there. I'm blowed if I can pump any *think* out o' him, he's as close as an *oshter*; I'm blowed if he an't."

This eloquent and elegant address was delivered by Timothy while engaged in the adjustment of the breakfast service; but as the doctor was busily engaged with a paragraph in which the extent of the power of the magistracy was laid down, with certain illustrations and exposés of magisterial ignorance and misrule, he paid no more attention to Tim's harangue than he would have done to the sneezing of a cat, until the stable was mentioned, and the term "*blowed*" grated upon his ear; when, supposing that something had happened to his favourite horse, Ithurea, he started from behind the large dotted screen he had been perusing. "Eh! what is that you say?" exclaimed his reverence. "My horse blowed! Did you say so? Then you have given her too much water; and I am not in the commission of the peace if I don't punish you for the act."

"Who are you?" enquired Tim, putting himself into a pugilistic attitude, as he supposed the threat he had just listened to implied a contemplated attack. "Let me tell you, my codger, that Timothy Trump has had too many brushes of that ere sort with some rum uns to be frightened by you."

"What have you done to my horse?" exclaimed the doctor.

"*Your* orse!" echoed Tim. "I knows nothing consarning your orse; did n't know you had one,—I am blowed if I did."

"You impertinent scoundrel!" roared the doctor, waxing wrath at what he supposed to be the hostler's insolence."

"No, I arn't nothing o' the sort," retorted Tim, placing his arms a-kimbo.

"Did I not direct you, scarcely ten minutes since," continued the rector, "to be sure and put my horse into a warm stable?"

"What, *you*?" shouted Tim. "You tell *me*? I'm blowed if you arn't mad,—right down cracked in the knob! Why, I never seed you till this ere blessed moment; and if you don't tramp, you'll soon be pitched out o' the vinder with a dung fork for an *imposterer*, when the gemman comes, he for what this ere breakfast is for,—mind that now."

The doctor had forgotten the change which his masquerade dress had made in his personal appearance; had he at

this moment beheld his own well-known and well-beloved figure in a mirror, it is ten to one that he would have questioned his own identity, or at least have mistaken it as much as Timothy Trump. " Here, landlord! landlord!" shouted his reverence, ringing the bell violently at the same time, and almost frantic with vexation.

" Oh! you may bawl till your lungs burst, and you will," observed Timothy, with the calmness of a stoic; "measter will take my side, I knows. Here, measter!" shouted Tim, at the top of his voice, and with nearly as unpleasant an intonation as an Italian opera singer, " Here, measter, I'ze just been telling this ere feller to *vacanate* this ere place, as the gemman up stairs is a coming to go to breakfast, and I'm blowed if he isn't going to pitch into me for't.".

" Landlord!" cried the doctor, " do you patronize the insolence of your servants in this way towards your customers ?"

" By no means, Sir," replied he of the inn; "but I fancy honest Tim is taking your part against yourself."

" There now," said Tim; " hear that ere,—*onest* Tim!"

" *Taking my part against myself!*" exclaimed the doctor, with emphasis, " Why, what in the world do you mean ?"

" Why, thus it is, your worship," rejoined my host; " he does not recollect you in your change of dress, and supposing *you* are still up stairs, he imagines that *you*, as a *stranger*, are taking possession of a place which another should fill."

Tim's face elongated some inches out of its oval form as he heard his master's explanation, and observed, aside, " I'm blowed now if I arn't put my foot into it preciously."

" Ha! ha! ha!" laughed the doctor, turning to a mirror, which hung behind him. " No doubt it is so."

" Yes, Zur," returned Tim, scratching his head, "it is a Bible truth that I took you for another *parson*, and I don't like to see any one choused out o' their grub."

" Did you so ?" rejoined the divine, mistaking Tim's pronunciation. " Then parsons do visit your house in disguise, do they ?"

Tim's waggishness tempted him to play upon the term which his reverence had mistaken, and he replied, " No, bless your heart, Zur, they never *comes* in disguise, not they; but they gets tarnationly *disguised* before they leaves, I assure you. Why, I has more trouble with them ere parsons,—no offence to you, your reverence,—nor I has with all our *cus-*

tumbers asides; they gets so rumbustical like, when they gets a few bottles o' wine in their skins,—but I, —"

" Well, well," interrupted the doctor, " I wish to hear no more. It is a bad thing to speak ill of any one."

" Nay, Zur," observed Tim, " as for that matter I never speaks no ill o' any one ; all I does is to say what *hexactly* takes place like. If it wor ill, I 'spose them ere gentlemen parsons wouldn't do it."

" I say again," cried the doctor, " I wish to hear no more. Go and attend to my horses ; I shall want them in an hour, and tell my servant to go into the kitchen and get some refreshment."

" I will, Zur," said Tim ; and he hasted to perform the task assigned him ; while the divine set about discussing sundry cups of coffee, a plate-full of toast, three or four eggs, and a *few* slices off a sirloin.

" Ha! ha! ha! " burst forth Tim, as he re-entered the stable, making as many contortions of face and body as if he had swallowed a quantity of laughing gas.

" What's amiss now ?" enquired Claudius.

" What's a—ha! ha! ha!" roared Tim again. " What's amiss—ha! ha! ha! I'm blowed if ever I seed sich a rum feller as that ere measter o' yours in all my born day ; that's for a sartin,—ha! ha! ha! He's a reg'lar rum un; he ort to be dited for making people kill themselves of larfin, —I'm blowed if he don't."

" Why, what has taken place ?" asked Claudius.

" What has taken place !" shouted Tim. " Oh, my eyes ! only jest go and pop your ogles in at the vinder yonder, and if you don't die o' larfin, say my name arn't Timothy Trump, that's all ;" and again he burst into an immoderate and convulsive fit of laughter.

Claudius did as directed by Tim, but unfortunately at the very moment he had raised his head above the blind of the window, which reached half-way up the second pane of glass, the doctor's eyes were turned to the spot, and with a significant motion of the fore-finger of his right-hand, which Claudius could not misunderstand, and dare not disobey, he summoned our hero into his presence.

" Have you seen the hostler, Claudius ?" enquired the rector.

" Yes, Sir," he replied, biting his lips until the blood nearly flowed from them, to suppress a laugh.

"And the horses," continued his reverence, cramming the beef into his mouth all the time he was speaking, "are they taken good care of,—eh?"

"Yes, your worship," returned Claudius.

"And have you had your breakfast yet?" asked the master.

"No, Sir," answered our hero.

"No!" exclaimed the doctor, suspending for a moment a fine slice of the sirloin between his masticators and his plate, upon the point of his fork, "No, did you say?" Claudius repeated the expressive monosyllable.

"And why not?" asked his worship. "Did not that chattering fellow of a hostler deliver my message to you?"

"No, Sir," replied Claudius, "I have not received any."

"In half an hour we leave," continued the divine, "and when I shall require your attendance, you will be taking breakfast, I suppose. What were you doing at the window when I called you in just now?"

"At the window, Sir," repeated Claudius, the recollection of the hostler's description of his master rushing into his head, and provoking, almost beyond endurance, his propensity to laugh. "I was looking, Sir,—that is,—I was passing by, just to let your worship know that I had not been to breakfast."

"Well, then, make haste now into the kitchen," said the doctor, "and when you have satisfied yourself let me see you again."

Claudius felt glad at being so delivered, and hasted to leave the presence, and to pay his respects to the supplies the kitchen might afford.

As he approached the domain of the cook, he heard a loud burst of laughter, which made the place echo, and in a moment distinguished the tongue of the waggish Timothy Trump, who was describing to two or three important personages, with infinite glee, the strange appearance of the doctor. As, however, Claudius felt more interested concerning the horses than Tim's wit, he turned into the stable to take another look at them.

"I'm blow'd," said the Sir Oracle of the kitchen, "if you ever seed his feller; he looks for all the world like one of them ere things which is stuck up in that ere place where they draws for lottery in Lunnun—Mister and Mistress Gogs I think they calls um."

" Ha! ha! ha!" roared the guests, tickled by Tim's graphic description.

" Who is he?" enquired one of the party.

" *Who* is he?" repeated Tim; " why, he's a parson."

" A parson!" echoed two or three voices.

" Aye, that's sartin," said Tim; " and more nor that I can tell, an I *chuse*."

" Why, what more?" asked the first speaker.

" Why, I thinks as how he's a *gistis* o' the peace," replied the ostler.

" Whew—" went round the kitchen.

" A justice!" exclaimed one of them,—" I must cry quits, then, or I may have to say nabs,—you understand?"

" Aye, aye," replied two or three others, " we understand."

" What kind of a chap is this ere servant you speak of?" enquired the first spokesman.

" Why, he's a good-looking young feller, what wears his master's clouts," replied Tim, " and they are bound about with *yaller*."

" Do you know what he is called?" asked the interrogator.

" Not I," replied Timothy; " and yet, now I recollects, I did hear some name as I tooked the orses; it was something like,—I'm blow'd if I arn't clean forgot it."

" Should you know it again, if you heard it?" enquired the man.

" May be I should," replied Tim; " but I can't swear to that."

" Was it Claudius?" asked the questioner.

" Aye, that was it, as sure as a gun," cried Tim.

" Ho! ho!" shouted one or two voices,—" Parson Titheum, by the rood."

" The very same," cried the first speaker; " the feller that was going to commit me for *cotching* rats in a barn; only I doubled the constable—ha! ha! ha! But I must be off—I wouldn't be seen by that young chap for a fist full of bobs. Find out, if you can, where they are going, and, perhaps, I may pay my respects to them for past services."

" Aye, aye," said some mixed voices, " we'll do't."

" Enough!" said Slipgibbet, for he it was—in company with some poachers; and hasted away.

" Hush!" said the cook, as she saw Claudius at the kitchen door; " here comes the servant."

"Well, my fine fellow," said Tim, addressing himself to Claudius, "what thinks you now—ain't your measter a precious rum-looking covey ?"

"Stay until I have got my breakfast," said Claudius," and I may, perhaps, have time then to talk to you ;" and with as little ceremony as a stage-coachman feels when he steps from his box on a cold winter's night, and enters the bar of a house of call, where he is greeted by the smiles of an accommodating landlady, Claudius set too with a good appetite.

While our hero continued to eat in silence, Timothy's love of good things appeared to gain zest by wagging his tongue as he emptied his mouth; or even while that crater-like orifice was well filled.

"I say," observed the hostler, "that was a clever trick what Frank Pullbottle played that ere *bum baily*, the other day,—wasn't it ?"

"What was that ?" asked one of the party.

"*What !*" replied Tim, "why, ain't you heard it ?"

"No," replied the fellow, "I havn't been home for a week, or more ;—I have been engaged, looking which way the wind blowed," and he placed the end of the thumb on his right hand to the top of his nose, and twisted his open fingers about like the vane of a weather-cock. "D'ye nick me ?"

"Yes, yes," replied some of the party, "we smells the scent ; but let's have the story, Tim."

"Ha! ha! ha!" roared the facetious Trump,—" I never heard a better since Cain was a shoe-black. I glories in a chap like that ere Frank, what never allows himself to be *frauded*, without *taliation*, by them ere *rascallous* officers. Because a man ain't got no work, and, by reason of it, no money, why I'm blowed if it ain't à right down highway robbery to go and grab all what little matters he has, and turn his wife and little kids into the street."

"So it is, Tim," replied the company ; "but we want to hear the story."

"Oh! aye," replied Tim—"Well, Frank made Master *Bum Baily* sing 'Bob's a Dying,'—I'm blowed if he didn't, —ha! ha! ha! It makes one die o'laughin to think about it. D'ye see as how, it happened that Frank,—as hard a working feller as ever tooked a shovel in hand,—had been out o'employ for the matter o' two or three weeks, and, by course, didn't get a mag from none. His wife had just brought him

another kid,—and the poor here are as *fortinate* as the rich,—
making in all six, and one had just died, which was seven.
Well, he goes to the parish *hofficer*,—a feller with a *art* as
hard as a smith's *hanvil*,—and axes him for something to
keep his wife and kids from *hactual* starvation; but I'm
blowed if he'd notice him any *furder* than calling him a
skulking feller; and says he, ' Why don't you go to work ?'
—' Why, *acause* I can't get no work to do,' says Frank.
' Well, then,' says this pretty rascal of an *hofficer*, ' if you
don't work you must starve,' and then the infidel backed his
rascally obsarvations by a piece of the Bible. I'm blowed if I
wouldn't transport the whole pack of 'em to *Bottomby* Bay,
for as long as they lived, and a twelvemonth arter. But, as
I was saying, it was of no sarvice to tell Frank to work, for
he wouldn't have gone to ax for charity if he could have got
work to do,—not he. Well, you know, a feller can't see his
wife and pretty little kids starve before his eyes ; so he gets a
little on tick, you see, and so gets behind a trifle—when,
presently, a *Bum Baily* is popped into his crib, to seize his few
traps for the *vally* of a few bobs. If you had seen the distress (and even Tim shed a few tears as he told his unvar-
nished tale),—but no matter," he continued, wiping the
tear from his eye with his shirt sleeve, " Frank sarved the
feller out ;—he was as hard-hearted a cove as *Farer*."

" *Pharaoh !*" said the cook, who was considered by the
other servants as a bit of a *scholard*.

" Well, I said *Farer*," replied Tim, still retaining his own
orthography in the pronunciation of the name; don't put
me out so; if you do, I shall never get to the end of this ere
story. Well, as I was a saying, the neighbours pitied Frank's
family, and took them all into their houses, while Mister *Bum
Baily* takes possession of their room. The next day arter,
Frank comed home from seeking o' work, and hearing how
the cat jumped, he goes to Mister *Bum Baily* and civilly axed
him to quit ;- but I'm blowed if he'd budge a peg. ' Werry
well,' says Frank, ' then stay, and bide *consarquences*, and
I'll put all my property into this ere room, and so you'll have
all on it under your own care ;' so with that he shuts the
door arter him, and goes into his little garden, and there
stands a fine hive o' bees, which he had nursed with the
hopes of making something o' the 'oney. Well, down he
takes um, and brings um to the house, and then, throwing
up the vinder, he throws the hive, bees and all, smack into

the room, and then pops down the vinder close again. My eyes, what a lark! Ha! ha! ha! I'm blowed if the *Bum Baily* didn't roar like a bull what the dogs has pinned, while the bees stuck to him like wax. He didn't want axing to quit any more, for out he bolted, like a cat with her tail afire, kicking, and roaring, and fighting like mad; his eyes were almost sowed up; so, for the want of his *hoptics,* he runned, without knowing where, and presently, in he plunged, neck and crop, into the *'orse* pond at the end o' the lane, where he plunged and spluttered, for all the world like a *man* mer*maid,*—that is, as I have heard, as I never by course seed one of them ere things. His kicking would soon been finished, but for Frank's good *nater,* who ran to his help, as he scorned, he said, to *triump'* over a *wankished henemy,* and lugged him out."

"Ha! ha! ha!" roared all the company. "And may all oppressors of the poor in the county be used in the same way."

" A right good wish," said Tim. "Arn't it, my young un'?" he added, addressing Claudius.

"Capital! capital!" answered our hero. "I detest oppression in all its shapes, and like not to see any one injured, whether *rich* or *poor,*" and he again filled his mouth.

" You seem to enjoy yourself with your breakfast," observed one of the party.

"Oh yes," replied Claudius, " a good appetite is better than rich sauce."

" I 'spose you have rode a long way this morning?" he continued.

" Why, no, not a *long* way," replied Claudius, "but I like to lay in a good supply."

" Right," resumed the man; " that's wisely said. You have a long journey before you, I guess?"

" Tolerably well for that," said Claudius. "A good and pleasant ride, such as I hope to enjoy."

" Ah!" resumed the speaker, " as far as Titchfield perhaps? or, may be, to Porchester?"

" Yes," said Claudius, " and a few miles beyond."

" Indeed!" exclaimed the fellow. " To Cosham or Havant?"

Claudius shook his head, and observed, " not quite right yet."

"Ah!" said the enquirer, " Well, I will e'en guess again, as I have gone so far.   Is it so far as Emsworth ?"

" Still at fault," replied Claudius.

" Chichester!" exclaimed the man, " or I'll give it up."

" You have it at last," said our hero; " and what are you the better for your knowledge ?"

" Why, nothing that I knows of," replied the fellow, with assumed carelessness.   " To *me* it can be of no consequence either which way or how far you are riding ; but you won't return to-night, I can guess *that*, without any mistake."

" No," said Claudius, " nor to-morrow either it may be. We shall at least remain one day."

" Well, if you stay a week," returned the man, " it will make no difference; all will be right, I warrant you."

" All will be *right*," echoed Claudius.   " What do you. mean ?"

" Why I mean," said the fellow, " what I says.   Don't you understand me ?"

" Oh, yes," said Claudius ; " I understand.   " The doctor, my master, pays all bills, and settles all accounts.   Yes, yes, it will be all right ; we shall not starve, I dare say.   But the clothes are dry, I see," he observed, turning towards the fire.

" Aye, and brushed too," said the cook.   " No one would guess now that your master had tumbled into the mud.   He'll pay well, I hope.   How does he bleed ?"

" He'll pay you, no doubt," answered Claudius ; only don't blush to ask, or he *may* forget ;—you understand.   But it is time that I pay my respects to the parlour, for in a little while we must be moving," and away he ran.

The rector had finished his morning repast, and was again amusing himself with a " Chronicle of the times," as Claudius entered the parlour.   " Are my clothes dry ?" enquired the doctor.

" Yes, Sir," answered Claudius ; " they are dry, and well brushed too,—not a single spot so large as a pin's head can be found upon them."

" Very good," rejoined the rector.   " Now, go you and see the horses are prepared while I change my dress again, and then we must on with speed."

Claudius bowed, and hasted to perform the commands of his master, while the divine, having directed that his " customary suit of solemn black" should be taken up stairs, in a brief space followed, and at the end of about a dozen minutes Dr. Titheum was himself again.

The bill of mine host having been discharged,—and he had with ready skill, well known and commonly practised by those of his occupation, made it a tolerably heavy one,—and the cormorant-like claims of the servants being met, our travellers once more crossed their chargers, sounded, " hie for Chichester !" and were speedily out of sight of the dwellers at the inn.

Leaving Claudius and his master to pursue their course, we shall, as in courtesy we are bound to do, turn to the mansion of Lady Bolio.

CHAP. XIV.

"*Alesco.* I tell you, Marco, I have found out that
    For which the world will hold my memory dear.
Marco. Sayest thou ?—why then our fortune's made, that's clear.
    But, now propound, my master, what and how?
Alesco. Well, 'tis to make a woman hold her tongue.
Marco. Good, by the prophet's beard!—But how ?
Alesco.   Why, even thus;
    Suffering the unyoked working of her spleen,
    Till the tir'd member can no longer wag."

TAMING A TARTAR.

IN a preceding chapter we stated that the visit to Bath, which had been proposed to Claudius's mother, had been delayed in consequence of a relapse which Lady Bolio had experienced. At length, however, every thing like disease having passed away, leaving nothing behind except the mere languor resulting from debility, it was determined that immediate preparations should be made for the recommended excursion, and on the very day that Dr. Titheum took his cold bath, as already stated, Lady Bolio, ensconced in her warm carriage, accompanied by Dr. Leechum and his lady, left home, on a trip to Bath.

If woman's weakness is exhibited in one particular more than another, it is, perhaps, in the inordinate attachment she feels for display. In this particular Lady Bolio was not a whit behind any of her sex. On the present occasion she felt anxious to make the "gude folk" of Bath, as well as all others into whose houses she might enter in her way thither, think of and treat her with all befitting respect. In order to secure such homage, her coachman and footman had been supplied with new liveries, her horses with new trappings, and her carriage with new decorations of paint and varnish. All was, therefore, *new*, at least in appearance, and Lady Bolio felt, if not quite *happy*, at least highly gratified at the thought of receiving a harvest of golden opinions from all sorts of people.

The first place at which they halted was Blandford; but here, while the shopkeepers looked inquisitively, and the artizans gaped rudely at the splendid " set out," as they called her ladyship's carriage and equipage, she received not that *sort* of attention at the inn on which she had fondly calculated. She felt,—and who in her circumstances, and with her *feelings* would not?—she felt displeased, because disappointed, and therefore, of course, her stay was of brief duration.

At four, they entered the ancient city of Salisbury, and in a few minutes drew up at the White Hart Hotel, one of the most respectable and well-ordered in the town, and were received with the most marked and polite attention by a smart, curled-haired waiter, who, with as many contortions of face and body as if labouring under the wild pangs of tic-douloureux, or the nerve-exciting influence of St. Vitus's dance, enquired, as he bowed before her, " Will your *leddy*ship allow me to show you *up*?"

" Show her *up*," whispered John to the coachman, as the party vanished into the hotel. " A public exhibition that, I'll warrant you. Who'd a thought it that missus would ha' ta'en all the trouble to a comed to *Sallsbury* to be showed *up*! Ha! ha! ha!—that's a good un, however;—*show her up*, Tom!"

" I'm blessed," rejoined Thomas, " if I shan't be glad to have something showed up to eat. Dash my buttons if I don't think I could hide away a whole porker in my bread cellar,—trotters and all."

" I should have no objection to help you out with it," observed the footman. " Here comes one, I 'spose," he added, perceiving the hostler approach, " to show us *up* into the stable yard."

John was right in his conjecture, and in a short time himself and his fellow-servant were *showed up* into the room provided for the accommodation of the *gentlemen of the whip*.

"Dr. Leechum," said Lady Bolio, as she threw herself upon a rich sofa, " I think the appearance of things here is much better than at that vile place, Bland— What is it called?"

" Blandford, your ladyship," replied the toad-eating son of Esculapius.

"Aye, Blandford," repeated Lady Bolio. "I think we may venture to remain here for two or three hours, doctor?"

"Oh! certainly, my dear lady," replied the doctor's better half,—a lady about half his age, and who, until she became Mrs. Leechum, moved in a sphere upon which her *rise* in life had taught her to look *down*, and whose particular partiality of having her *own* way in all *things*, and urging her opinion on all *occasions*, rendered it necessary that the doctor should cultivate practically the doctrine of passive obedience and non-resistance.

"Your present weak state," continued Mrs. Leechum, "requires you should avoid every thing like fatigue;" and then, with something of the professional slang which she had learned from the learned doctor, she added, " I should advise that three or four hours' rest should be taken here; during which time we can take dinner, and refresh ourselves properly, after having surveyed the beautiful cathedral, and in the cool of the evening continue our *tour*."

" What is your opinion, Dr. Leechum?" enquired her ladyship. " Do you *think* a good dinner would be injurious? if so, I must still practise self-denial. But, I confess, I do not conceive it would do me any harm ;—indeed, I feel my appetite exceedingly improved already by the journey."

Now, it should be known, that Dr. Leechum rejected altogether the hypothesis which some have, in evident ignorance of anatomy, attempted to establish, namely, that poets can live upon the air ;—and if he had not so done, as he was *not* a poet, he would have felt no obligation to have exploded the notion practically,—but the fact is, he did love a good dinner *dearly*, as the immortal Goldsmith used to say when describing to his friend, Dr. Johnson, his attachment to a bottle of Port,—at the same time he felt no inclination to offend either Mrs. Leechum or Lady Bolio. To displease the *first*, was unnecessary and dangerous, as Mrs. Leechum

would have her own way, or otherwise she would *not* let the
doctor have any quiet; while, as Lady Bolio paid a rather
high price to have *her* will, and, if thwarted, might possibly
cut off supplies, by selecting another medical adviser, who
would let her do as she pleased, he, as might be expected,
echoed the proposition of his *gentle* wife, only *gently* hinting,
that if possibly it could be avoided, they had better not pro-
long their stay beyond seven o'clock, as the air across the
Plain after that hour might affect the invalid.

" I have no idea of that," observed Mrs. Leechum, " the
evenings are exceeding fine, and the carriage very warm, so
that no fear of the kind need be entertained. I am sure,"
she continued, with a *leetle* tinge of warmth, " I dare say 1
consider the comfort and health of Lady Bolio as much as
yourself, Dr. Leechum, and would not advise any thing of
which I had not the fullest conviction it would not be injurious."

" I know, my *dear*, you would not," replied the doctor,
mildly, " I merely *hinted* —"

" You are very kind, my dear friends," interrupted Lady
Bolio. " We will have dinner ordered immediately, and
while it is preparing, if *quite* agreeable, we can just saunter
round the cathedral. I have, I think, a degree of superstitious reverence for such venerable edifices."

" I am sure," observed Mrs. Leechum, " I feel so attached
to them, that I could kneel down and kiss the very stones of
the buildings ; and I don't think *any* person can be a good
Christian who does not feel so."

" My dear," Dr. Leechum ventured to observe, " do you
not think you express yourself *rather* strongly ?"

" Rather strongly, Dr. Leechum," exclaimed his lady, as if
alarmed by his observation ; " rather *strongly !* Why, I declare one might half fancy you were a papist, or an infidel, or
what is the same thing,—a *dissenter*, and that you wish to
demolish all the churches in the land, and *so* drive out all religion from our poor country."

" Oh, no, my dear," returned the doctor. " I assure you
I only hinted —"

" Hinted, indeed !" interrupted Mrs. Leechum. " Such
hints, Dr. Leechum, are like the sounding of the tocsin,
ominous of nothing good. *I* say I reverence such sacred
buildings, although, to be sure, my overwhelming engagements do not allow me much time to attend *service* in the

church very often; yet it is out of no disrespect to the holy buildings."

" Well, I really feel with yourself, my dear Mrs. Leechum," observed Lady Bolio; "and I am sure Dr. Leechum is with us in this respect; but at present we will not discuss the matter further. A glass of wine, doctor, will not harm me, I hope ?"

" Oh no, my dear Lady Bolio," cried Mrs. Leechum, "nor two, I'm certain, after our long ride."

"If a little diluted," said the Leech, "otherwise I fear a return of fever."

" Oh, there is no danger of that, *I* am confident," interrupted Mrs. Leechum. " Why, you are as cool as a cucumber, Madam; and your hands are in as nice and healthful a glow as my own. You are so *very* fond of dilution," continued Mrs. Leechum.

" Well, I merely hinted," rejoined the doctor. " I wish," he added to himself, " I could dilute you a little,—and, indeed, a *good deal* would do no harm."

" Well, I am entirely in your hands," observed Lady Bolio, " and must attend to your directions, Dr. Leechum; but I *do* think, as my dear friend Mrs. Leechum says, there is no fear of the return of fever; and I confess I do not enjoy diluted things myself."

" Certainly not," said Mrs. Leechum; "let those who fancy such slops have them,—*I* like such as are genuine and unadulterated, better."

", Well, my dear," returned Leechum, " I merely hinted, and see no harm in your proposal—*none* whatever,—*two* glasses can do no harm."

Wine was poured out, and the doctor handed it gracefully to the ladies. Lady Bolio's appetite was stimulated by the cheering beverage;—two or three sandwiches were despatched, another glass of wine handed round, and then the proposed saunter was taken, and a delightful survey of the *sacred* building, towards which Mrs. Leechum felt so much veneration, followed.

It was exactly half-past five when the hungry trio sat down to a good and plentiful dinner, to supply the requisites for which the air, the earth, and the sea, had been plundered of a portion of their delicacies.

Certainly, no person would have justly merited the charge of being *non compos mentis*, who, having been present during this repast, had ventured to express his firm conviction that Lady Bolio needed the use of the dumb-bells rather than the attendance of a doctor; for of each of the three courses which were served, she consumed what would have been sufficient for a couple of meals for a pauper,—calculating, according to the present scale of allowance made for the supply of the wants of that unfortunate class of human beings,—without the addenda of pastry, fruit, and wine.

At the end of *two* hours the party had succeeded in satisfying, or rather cloying, their appetites; and a gentle *hint* was thrown out by the doctor respecting re-commencing their journey.

The bright yet mellowed beams of summer's eventide, which had given to each surrounding object a distinctness and glory, such as is sometimes seen so powerfully portrayed upon canvass by some of the old masters, had passed away, and, occasionally, heavy clouds hung between the sun and the earth, giving to nature a tinge of pensive sadness.

" I fear," observed Dr. Leechum, as he looked from the window, " the weather is about to change."

" Oh, no such thing, my dear Dr. Leechum," replied his lady; " you are always *fearing* something or other;—I do really think you sometimes *fear* you shall find nothing one day or other to *fear*. I almost wonder you did not *fear* to get married."

" Ha! ha! ha!" laughed Lady Bolio.—" You are determined, by your pleasantry, to preserve your company from that climax of misery—*ennui.*"

" *Pleasantry,*" thought Leechum; and then replying to his *dear* wife, observed, " *Then,* my dear, *all* was fair and bright; or, to employ the language of an old friend and poet,—

> " Not a cloud did arise
> In your gay smiling eyes,
> Or a frown your sweet features deform;
> All was bright *then,* my love,
> As the blue sky above,
> When no prospect appears of a storm."

The doctor, with intention or otherwise, had given a degree of emphasis to the *thens* which had occurred in his reply, which attracted the notice of Lady Bolio, and she playfully observed,—" Now that is really too bad, doctor; you are indeed *very* severe;—I would I were Mrs. Leechum, for your sake."

" I would you were, with all my *heart*," replied the lady.
" This is the way he is continually treating me;—it would
seem that Dr. Leechum does not understand what are the
privileges belonging to our sex;—are we not to *frown* if we
please, sometimes, or to state our own opinion? or,—but I
declare, I give way, as you perceive, in every thing, and am
always as *even* in temper as the mildest infant,—*you* know I
am, Dr. Leechum."

" Yes, my dear," replied Leechum; " I know you are. I
intended nothing—I did not, indeed, love; I merely hinted
that the weather—"

" Pooh! pooh!" exclaimed Mrs. Leechum, "the weather
is very good,—very fine indeed.—I long to enter Bath—do
you not, my dear Lady Bolio?"

" I confess, my dear Mrs. Leechum," replied her ladyship,
" I shall be glad to reach there."

" Well," said the doctor, " I yield me to your wishes;—I
was merely going to hint that it would, perhaps, be advisa-
ble to remain here until the morning, if—"

" Worse, and worse!" shouted his dear lady; " however
could *such* a thought get into your head, Dr. Leechum?—
really, I feel surprised at you!—How very strange you do get
of late."

" I feel a little languid," observed Lady Bolio, as well she
might after the mastication and digestion of so many solids,
and the consumption of so much liquid. "But I think," added
her ladyship, " I shall be able to bear the fatigue, doctor."

" Certainly, Madam," said Mrs. Leechum.

" Very well;—I have no doubt," responded the doctor—
" I merely hinted—"

" *Hinted* again!" observed his lady, with a look which almost electrified her lord.

" Well, well," said the doctor, " be it so."

Orders were immediately given for the carriage to be prepared; and about a quarter of an hour before eight they
drove through the city, directing their course towards the
ancient borough of Devizes.

As they ascended the serpentine road, which rendered
Salisbury Plain visible as far as the eye could reach, the
gloom which had been gathering appeared considerably to
have increased; and on turning their eyes to the right they
perceived a dark lurid cloud hanging over Old Sarum, of por-
tentous aspect; while thick murky vapours were seen sweep-

ing over the plains, although all was hushed and calm, as if
propelled by some powerful yet invisible and unknown influence.

"Well, I do'think we are going to have a storm," observed Mrs. Leechum. "I almost wish now that we had not
started. Would it not be better for us to turn back to Salisbury?"

"I really don't know what to think of it," replied Lady
Bolio, in much less alarm than her excited companion :—
"What is your opinion, doctor?" she added, turning to
Leechum.

"As we have started," replied the doctor, "my opinion
is, we had better push on—the Hut and the Bustard inns are
before us, at either of which, if necessary, we can stop ; but
I don't apprehend we shall have need to do so."

"Well, I think differently of it," rejoined Mrs. Leechum,
as if wishful to be always on the O. P. side of the house. "I
am *sure* we had better return ;—however, I am confident you
will oppose me, Dr. Leechum, if only for opposition's sake,—
it is ever thus."

The Hut was reached and passed, and on they continued
to drive, descending one steep hill, and then climbing the
side of another steeper still. The Bustard appeared in sight ;
yet no immediate cause existed why they should halt.

The heat now became oppressive, and they let down the
carriage windows to catch the little air which the quick motion of the vehicle occasioned. The sultry state of the atmos-
phere, and the death-like stillness which prevailed, appeared
to affect even the lambs who nipped the herbage on the
downs, for they ceased from their gambols ; while the birds,
which were lately on the wing, had fled as if seeking shelter,
and only a solitary rook was seen at distant intervals, cleav-
ing the air with all its might, and pursuing its straight course
towards its resting-place.

They had passed the last inn some time, and were in the
bottom of a deep valley, when a loud and fearful crash broke
like the explosion of a thousand pieces of artillery just over
their heads, and ran echoing in terrible response among the
hills on the plain ; at the same instant a broad sheet of lightning descended, and appeared to envelope the carriage in blue
flame. The darkness became appalling, and peal upon peal
roared above them, or in long continued burstings rolled
around. The war of elements was sublimely awful, which

seemed greatly heightened by the hour and the loneliness of the place. The rain descended, not in ordinary drops, but as if a mighty sluice had been suddenly opened, or a deluging cataract discharged upon them its streams—it came down and flooded the roads.

The horses, alarmed and terrified, shyed as the lightning appeared to fall at their feet. Considerable danger existed, either of the carriage being struck by the electric fluid, or of the horses becoming unmanageable, and overturning it into some of the ravines of that wild, cheerless, and uneven plain.

After a while it was discovered that a circumstance had occurred which added greatly to their previous perplexity, which was, that in consequence of the coachman never having travelled the road before, he had entirely missed his way; for when he had reached the point of road where the road to Devizes inclines to the right, while the other leads to Laving- ton, he had turned to the left. His attention had been so entirely engrossed by the horses that the directing-post was not noticed by him; while the footman was crouching down behind the carriage, to avoid as much as possible the "piti- less pelting of the storm," and, therefore, with his fellow- servant, passed it by unheeded. At length they overtook a market cart, from the driver of which they learned their mis- take; and, turning back, succeeded without difficulty in find- ing and getting into the right road.

The tempest continued to rage with unabated fury *without,* while the tongue of Mrs. Leechum, moved to action by alarm and anger, raged with equal violence *within* the carriage.

"There, Mr. Leechum!" said the lady; "I told you how it would be—I was certain we were going to have a storm; but your superior wisdom rejected my advice, and, of course, opposed my wishes."

"Well, my dear," replied the doctor, "don't be alarmed; I did *hint* to you that the weather was changing."

"You did no such thing, Dr. Leechum," returned his *dear* wife.

"I beg pardon, my love," replied Leechum; "you may remember—"

"I do *remember,*" interrupted his lady, "that I wished we might not undertake the journey; but *you* may *remember,* you opposed me."

Lady Bolio sat viewing the lightning as it played across the wide plain, and appeared so entirely absorbed by the

scene as to be unconscious of the interesting colloquy in
which the doctor and his wife were engaged, until she was
directly appealed to.

" Did I not *hint*, Lady Bolio," said the professor of phy-
sic, " that we had better remain at Salisbury until- the
morning ?"

" Why, I think you did, Dr. Leechum," replied her
ladyship.

" There now, my dear," observed the doctor to his gentle
spouse, " I told you I did so."

" Oh, yes," rejoined Mrs. Leechum, " I am aware you—
did *hint* something about remaining; but you know that I
proposed we should return, when I *knew* there was occasion
for so doing. Oh, what a long dreary road this is, Lady
Bolio !" she continued.

" We have not more than five miles further to go," said
the doctor, " before we—"

" Five miles further !" exclaimed Mrs. Leechum.—Oh, I
am confident I shall never be able to bear it."

" What will the poor coachman and footman do ?" asked
the doctor—" they must be sadly wet."

" Oh, they are used to it," returned the tender-hearted
Mrs. Leechum.—" You appear much more concerned about
a mere servant than respecting my comfort."

" I was merely about to *hint*, my dear," rejoined the Leech,
" that they are men, and have feelings as susceptible as our
own."

" Oh, no doubt," returned Mrs. Leechum.—" Then you
place *them* on a footing with your wife ? Truly you are a gallant courtier.—Oh !" she screamed, as a vivid flash of lightning entered the carriage windows, accompanied with a burst
of thunder so loud as apparently to make the whole plain
tremble.

" Don't be alarmed, my dear Mrs. Leechum," said Lady
Bolio, whose nerves were composed of stronger stuff than
those possessed by her female friend, " the danger is past,
and I hope the storm has spent its violence ;—we may expect
soon to reach Devizes."

Lady Bolio was right in her conjectures,—the lightning
became fainter and less frequent, the thunder roared at a
greater distance, and the rain was less heavy ; until at length
the tempest entirely subsided. The moon, " round as a
shield," shone brightly forth as the parting clouds rolled

noiselessly away; and in a short time the heavens looked as beautiful and serene as if the fair face of nature had never been disturbed from its placid state—all was quiet loveliness and beauty.

The clock was striking ten as Lady Bolio's carriage passed Devizes Green—it had reached within one hundred yards of the Castle Inn; at which comfort-yielding and respectable place it was proposed a halt should take place, when an accident occurred which obliged the travellers to halt a little earlier, and somewhat longer, than they intended.

Any person who has *once* paid a visit to this said borough town, with his eyes open—(and we recommend it to all travellers,—"to prevent mistake,"—never to travel with their eyes shut),— in which, during these modern days of political faction and renegadeism, party spirit has assumed a Gorgon aspect,—need not be informed of the inelegance of the entrance into it at the east end; or of the many dangerous turnings and windings which a vehicle must take before either the market-place, or the inn at which our travellers intended to stop, can be reached;—we know but of one, since the days of Troy town, that can claim equality with it,—the dirty straggling town of Petworth, in Sussex.

The moon, as we have already noticed, was shining brightly, and threw its rays down Market Street; one side of which, however, was thrown into deep shade in consequence of the proximity of the buildings on one side to those on the other. A large heap of rubbish lay piled on the dark side; when, just as the carriage turned the corner, it came in contact with this dangerous obstruction, and in a moment it was thrown out of its equilibrium, and the right hand wheels whirled round and round in empty air. At the instant of the overset, the left side door of the vehicle flew open, and the three insiders were thrown completely outside, and placed in the most ludicrous position, in a bed of soft mud of ample dimensions.

All the aid that activity and sympathy could give was promptly afforded; and it was soon ascertained that no other evils had arisen from the accident than soiled clothes and a few harmless scratches.

It was a very fortunate circumstance for Dr. Leechum that his gentle wife's mouth was so filled with filth as to prevent her employing her glory

"In strains with sympathy or passion fraught."

It would, beyond all question, have afforded her considerable relief, under the unpleasant and mortifying condition in
which she was placed, if she could have lectured the doctor.
A few words, indeed, did escape her ; but they were only like
a limited escape of steam from a surcharged boiler, which is
ready to burst, made up of unconnected and little more than
half articulated expletives, which rather excited than allayed

> " The maddening turmoil of her frenzied brain."

Every thought of leaving Devizes for the night was now
driven out of their minds.   As soon, therefore, as the party
reached the Castle,—to which they were obliged to walk, frequently over their shoes in water,—changes of raiment were
taken from their travelling trunks, beds were ordered, and a
supper was put into a state of preparation.

In half an hour after making their first appearance at this
celebrated inn, our travellers met each other fresh clad, from
" top to toe," in a handsome parlour belonging to the hotel,
without any outward signs of any inward ailment.

The current of Lady Bolio's temper ran, ordinarily, in a
cheerful channel ; and now, having been well assured that no
damage had been sustained which called for fine or deodand,
appertaining to life, limb, or carriage, she found herself in a
right merry mood.

" Well, I declare, my dear Mrs. Leechum," she observed,
as she entered the apartment, " I could almost kill myself
with laughing heartily at our multiplied disasters.   I was
always delighted with something out of the dull monotony
of every-day life ; and my enjoyment of such diversities has
not suffered a particle of diminution.—Ha ! ha ! ha ! How
ludicrous our positions must have been while floundering in
mud and water !—positively, it is as excellent an adventure
as the heroine of a romance ever met with.   I have never yet
tried my hand at novel-writing, or I do fancy I should make
something of this affair.   What would Mrs. Radcliffe, La-
Fontaine the simple, or your own favourite of all favourites,
Scott, have given for such incidents as our journey to-day
would supply !—Ha ! ha ! ha !"

" I can't tell," replied Mrs. Leechum, rather snappishly,
" what *they* would have given ; *I* would rather have given almost any thing than have met with them.   This all comes of
your unkind, I might say *cruel,* opposition to my reasonable
wishes, Dr. Leechum," continued the gentle dame.—" If *my*

desires had been attended to, we should have been safe and comfortable at Salisbury."

" Now, my dear Mrs. Leechum," replied the doctor, soothingly, " I admit we have been somewhat unfortunate—"

" *Somewhat* unfortunate !" exclaimed his *dear* wife,—" Indeed, Sir, I think you might have said ' unfortunate beyond parallel !' and, so saying, you would not have exceeded the truth."

" Well, my dear," returned her kind spouse, " I do admit all you wish ; but, my love, it might have been worse, you know."

" I don't know any thing of the kind," returned the lady.

" Now, only see, my love," said the doctor, " with what good temper Lady Bolio bears the accidents ;—if you, my dear, only—"

" If I,—if I *what*, Dr. Leechum ?" enquired his wife ;—" Tell me,—do I not bear the provoking disasters properly and mildly ?"

" O yes,—certainly, my love," returned Leechum, quaking with alarm at the anticipated consequence which his own unfortunate comparison appeared likely to produce.—" Yes, —you do, dear ;—I was merely going to hint—"

" Oh, Dr. Leechum, I am really astounded at you !" returned the lady.—" Your ceaseless opposition to my wishes, and unconcern about my comfort, are beyond endurance,—I can't—indeed I can't submit to it."

Lady Bolio had made several attempts to give a new tone to Mrs. Leechum's harmony ; but it would not do, her attempts all proved abortive. Happily for the doctor's peace, at the moment the storm of Mrs. Leechum's breath was about to burst forth in fury as fearful as the elemental strife they had just witnessed, a servant entered, and produced the desired change at once which Lady Bolio's efforts had failed to accomplish, by announcing that Mr. Wildolett, the gentleman who had rendered his active assistance in extricating the party from the mud, wished to enquire if they had received any serious injury.

Now, the service this distinguished personage had rendered, was in some sort perfectly in keeping with his character,—that is, he was fond of meddling in *dirty* matters ; and had, by a course of *dirty* tricks, succeeded in freeing himself from certain unpleasant disabilities of a pecuniary nature ; and by the same process, and

" A tace bronzed o'er with impudence,
    On which a blush was never seen ;
And brains cramm'd full of reguish sense,
    Where honest feeling ne'er had been,"

he had managed to raise himself to the *appearance,* at least,
of possessing property.   With as much rhodomontade—(an
expression, by the bye, of which he was remarkably fond, and
which he thrust most unceremoniously into almost every sentence),—with as much of it as would have supplied half a
score bullies in the place of courage, or half a dozen petty-
fogging lawyers in the stead of respectability, he had succeeded in gulling a large circle of *less* wily or *more* honest
tradesmen ; so that from being a bankrupt draper for a few
thousands,—on which he had paid the respectable sum of
one shilling and eightpence, or thereabout, in the pound,—
he had become the possessor of a splendid mansion,—most of
the money being borrowed from simple souls,—and extensive grounds, not a dozen miles from Market Lavington,
where he undertook to cure the *insane,* or to *drive the sane
mad !* This *respectable,*—of whom we shall have several
grave and important matters to relate hereafter,—was, as we
have said, *anxious* to enquire, &c. &c.,—that is—(for the
secret must out),—he loved good feeding, was remarkably
fond of wine, and kept his eye open to business.   These
things being all connected with his present *anxious* enquiry,
he of course felt desirous to know if those whom he had been
so *fortunate* as to assist, might not in some way be made to
assist him.

He had, in less than five minutes after the arrival of our
travellers, succeeded in fishing out the names, titles, destination, and every thing else thereunto belonging, of the party ;
so that when he made his appearance before them, he felt
himself as much at home with each and all of them as impudence and cunning could make a man.

"I hope, ladies," he observed, bending his corpulent
figure with as much address as his aping the character of a
gentleman could command, " you have received no serious
injury from your accident ?"

"None whatever, Sir," replied Lady Bolio ; " and allow
me to assure you, we feel greatly obliged by your kind aid
and polite attention."

"I beg, my lady," returned Wildolett, with a devout
grimace, "that you will not refer to my poor services—I

feel more than repaid for any little assistance I may have rendered, by the gratification I have experienced in being allowed to afford help to such distinguished persons ; and permit me to say, ladies," he continued, " that we are all dependent upon each other; and Providence has ordained, therefore, that we should minister such aid to our fellow-creatures in distress, as, in a change of circumstances, we should ourselves be desirous to receive."

" Very true, Mr. Wildolett," observed Mrs. Leechum ; " and I feel assured, if you had not hasted to my help, I should have been suffocated before Dr. Leechum would have given me any assistance."

" Now, my dear Mrs. Leechum," interrupted the doctor, " consider what—"

" I have well considered," returned his wife—" I am *positive* of it, I say ; and I am not in the habit of speaking so unless I have the clearest proof,—you know I am not. I am indebted to this gentleman for my life, I say."

" Madam," observed Wildolett, as he again bowed in humble attitude before the last gentle speaker, " I feel no inclination to boast of any thing I do—the mere rhodomontade of some people I despise ; yet, I may say, and I do so with conscious unworthiness of all praise,—no one feels more happy than I do to serve ladies."

After acknowledgments and compliments had been cut for, given to, and gorged by Wildolett with as much voracity as a shark would a man's leg, supper was announced as being ready in an adjoining room—an announcement at which the mouth of the *modest* gentleman actually watered ;—his manœuvres had succeeded to the full bent of his desire ; and a pressing invitation was given by Lady Bolio that he would join them at the board. With assurances which could not have been more hearty had they been sincere ; and repeated with a volubility which, for a time, appeared as if they would have no end, he protested that *nothing* but their pressing kindness could have induced him to remain, but, under such circumstances, he *felt* it his duty,—(he might have said *interest*,)—to accompany the party to the supper table ; where he again managed to make himself useful, in a way which assured all present that he felt no inclination to do discredit to the cordial invitation.

" Lady Bolio," said the modest man, " will you allow me the honour of taking a glass of wine with your ladyship ?"

The honour was granted with good humour—an honour of
which even Willdolett himself felt he was greatly unworthy,
—who, smacking his lips as he swallowed the wine, observed
right knowingly :—" That's not amiss ;—they used to have
wretched accommodation, and worse wine here, until *I* and
some of my friends insisted upon a change. In fact," he
proceeded to observe, " I had occasion to dine here once or
twice a week, some years ago ; at which time we paid for our
dinner, took a glass of ale, and dispersed. *I* proposed, however, that we should take wine after dinner, and my suggestion was adopted ; and from that time to the present the
custom has been continued. I mention this merely to show
what a reformation in *low* habits one spirited and *influential*
individual can produce."

" Very true," observed Dr. Leechum. " I could relate as
much when I studied at Saint Luke's."

" At Saint Luke's !" exclaimed Wildolett, getting on the
wrong scent, mistaking Saint Luke's Hospital for a mad-house
of that name.—" Were you ever an inmate of that place ?"

" An inmate !" ejaculated the doctor.—" I studied there,
Sir,—and from that same respectable hospital obtained cer-
tificates which secured my diploma of M. D."

" Oh, oh,—indeed, Sir !" returned the man of the private
asylum, perceiving his mistake ; " that is a noble institution.
I shall feel much pleasure, doctor, in pledging you," and
again he filled, and as quickly *emptied*, his glass.—" All com-
panies," he continued, " know that I am a professor of religion ; yet I can enjoy myself as well as the best of them. I
like a good joke—and good company ;—I can drink my pint of
wine after dinner,—a bottle for that matter ; but I never allow myself to be any thing more than merry with what I
take. My respects," he added, " ladies," pouring out another glass.—" I find I gain the good opinion of all parties
by being free, and accommodating myself to all. I converse
about politics, pass a broad joke, sing a cheerful song, and
enjoy the good things of life, and see nothing opposed to propriety in so doing ;—in fact, the long sanctified faces some of
my acquaintances make, who charge me with going too far,
and their squeamishness about taking this, that, and the
other, is all ragged fustian, and is one of the chief causes, depend upon it, why religion is brought into disrepute—they
absolutely frighten people from that which they seem wishful
to recommend.—Do you not think so, doctor ?"

page 186.

"Why really, Sir," replied Leechum, "I do not understand so much about particular points as Mrs. Leechum—hem!—who is, as I may say, a perfect theologian ;—yet, I do think with you in your observations."

"My respects, Madam!" said Wildolett, drinking to Mrs. Leechum.—" I feel proud to find myself in such company. You have read Milner's ' Church History,' I dare say ?"

Now, unfortunately, Mrs. Leechum, like Madame Talleyrand, was

> "Neither *bas bleu*, nor *femme savante*,
> But rather, as I freely grant,
> Deficient in her general reading."

She would, in all probability, like the lady referred to, have mistaken the adventures of Robinson Crusoe for the history of some distinguished modern traveller, and she therefore responded to Mr. Wildolett's question by replying—" No, Sir, I do not recollect that I ever did read that particular work. I have heard of it."

"Well then, Madam," returned the interminable talker, "allow me to say you have a treat in reserve. I presume you have seen Neal's ' History of the Puritans,' a work of great research—an abridgment, by the bye, would be a benefit conferred upon society—and—"

"No," responded Mrs. Leechum, "I never saw the work."

"I have read a great deal, Madam," continued Wildolett, scarcely regarding Mrs. Leechum's reply, "and understand the controversy in all its bearings between the Church and Dissent, Protestants and Papists ;—I have a pamphlet at home which I should like you to read very much; it refers to the disputed subject of Church Reform. Religion, I fear, is at a very low ebb ;" and again he filled his glass, which brought the bottle, that he had confined almost exclusively to his own purpose, to a very ebbing state; " I do, notwithstanding, fully believe that the number of good and excellent men, who preach the evangelical doctrines of the Church, is increasing in the establishment. Why, I remember the time," he added, branching off to another subject, and swallowing another glass of wine, " I remember the time when here in Devizes, Toryism ran so high, that it would have been as much as a man's fortune was worth to have ventured to hold a contrary opinion :—but things are changing :—I now find that I can maintain my opinion without giving offence,—I am no radical, I assure you, but the fact is, the rhodomontade of some persons won't do.   Some of the wise ones here begin to see that *my* opinion was right when I said some years ago—*It belongs to the people to rule themselves, and they will do it.*"

Having taken breath, and a little more wine, he proceeded to take the lead, or to maintain *exclusively* the right of talking.

"I shall be most proud to see you at F—— House, if you could make it convenient, on your return from Bath :—I have a snug place there, which I contrive to make shift with. We hang on a pot every day, and I always make my friends tie up their stockings when they come to see me."

Wildolett perceived that the ladies looked enquiringly at each other, as he talked about "tying up stockings,"—and he added, to set them right,—"that is, I expect them to enjoy themselves heartily; and if I can manage to make them a little matter *fuddled*, why so much the better."

By this time the talking man's round fleshy face looked as if a hare's foot covered with carmine had been freely applied to it, while his eyes sparkled with wild brilliancy, and his tongue perpetrated sad acts of violence against the rules laid down by Walker in his Dictionary, and by Murray in his Grammar.

"We feel much obliged to you, Sir," replied Lady Bolio, "for your kind attention, and if opportunity should offer, shall feel great pleasure in availing ourselves of your polite invitation."

Mr. Wildolett having managed to drain the bottle, begged, as he had some half-dozen miles to ride, he might be excused for retiring so *early*—it then wanted nearly a quarter of an hour to twelve! His apology was accepted, although credit must be given him for having, by his rhodomontade, kept the party from falling asleep. The servant entered as soon as the bell was rung, who was desired by the modest man to see his gig was instantly prepared :—he had not then, as subsequently, ventured to sport a phaeton,—his orders were soon executed, and as he drove from the front of the Castle Inn, Lady Bolio and her friends retired to their different chambers.

CHAPTER XV.

"·See from the golden East,,in chaste array.
Like a coy maiden, blushing to be seen,
Young Day comes forth, all life and loveliness,
As if to hail her with a courteous greet.
All nature, waking from a sweet repose,
Carols in various strains, a matin song,—
And forth the travellers sped."

YOUNG.

THE restlessness of Mrs. Leechum's erratic temperament was a serious drawback to her own enjoyment, as well as to the comfort of those who happened to be of her party. It is true that, in the presence of strangers, she contrived to put on a cheerful good-tempered-looking countenance, as if unwilling to allow any person to know how well she *could* pout and scold. As, however, such assumed character was a painful constraint upon her nature, it was not tolerated for any considerable extent of time: the least contradiction on the part of her husband, especially, threw her off her guard at once, and she looked and spoke daggers although she used none.

From the circumstance just glanced at, she had no sooner seated herself at the breakfast-table on the following morning after her entering into Devizes, than she expressed her anxious wish to set off for Bath.

"Well, my dear Mrs. Leechum," said Lady Bolio, "how did you rest last night?"

"Oh, exceedingly well, my lady," replied the doctor.

"Exceedingly what!" exclaimed Mrs. Leechum.

"Exceedingly well, my dear," replied her husband.

"Now really this is provoking beyond all patience," said the lady; "I do wish, Dr. Leechum, most particularly that you would not reply to questions of which you *can have* no knowledge. How is it possible you should know how *I* rested when you *always*, the *whole* night long, from the moment you step *into* bed, until the moment you step *out* of it, sleep, and—I was going to say something, but no matter,—you do so provoke one:—you know perfectly well Lady Bolio did not ask *you* the question."

"Well, my dear, I acknowledge," replied her gentle lord, —"I acknowledge I did wrong in replying, but I merely hinted that—"

"My dear Lady Bolio," interrupted Mrs. Leechum, "I assure you I rested horribly, most horribly, or rather, I had no *rest* at all. What with the fatigue and fright of yesterday, the thoughts of going to Bath, and the disagreeable noise which Dr. Leechum made,—although after *six* months' trial you may suppose I had grown familiar to it,—I could not get one wink of sleep until after *one o'clock* this morning."

"Indeed," said Lady Bolio, "that was *very* distressing; but then you know, my dear Mrs. Leechum, we did not retire until nearly *twelve o'clock*, and then by the time the girl had put your hair into paper, and properly arranged your night-dress, it must have been at *least* half-past twelve, so that you had not to lie awake a *very* long while."

"Why, no, my dear Lady Bolio," returned the gentle dame, "I had not for that matter;—but then, it is so very provoking to have it said *for* you that you slept exceedingly well; and I am so restless when I am *going* to any particular place, that a little thing *sometimes* rather annoys, and I feel more than ever anxious to leave this miserably dull place and get to Bath—is it not wretchedly dull? only look now," she continued, turning to the window,—"there is not a soul to be seen from one end of the street to the other,—I cannot endure such monastic-looking places."

The words had scarcely escaped the curled lip of Mrs. Leechum before two or three flourishes of a bugle announced the approach of a stage-coach. In an instant life appeared to spring from every aperture in the street, transforming the monastic-looking place into a *fac-simile* of a Spanish carnival, as men, women, and children, in various habits, and following different occupations,—some attracted by the hopes of gain, and others to satisfy idle curiosity,—drew towards the Castle Inn.

Now the noisy wheels of the coach, as it rattled over the rough paved street, became louder and louder, until the handsome vehicle, drawn by four smoking chestnuts, drew up; and an important personage, with a broad-brimmed hat, great-coat upon great-coat, well pocketed, and a large dashing neck-cloth wound round and round his thorax, after throwing the reins from his hands upon the backs of the horses, and tossing his whip scientifically to the expecting hostler, descended from his straw-stuffed throne and walked into the Inn with as proud step and dignified an air, as though he had been some plenipotentiary extraordinary from a foreign court.

Several dealers in various kinds of fruit, and sweetmeats instantly, as the coach drew up, flocked around it, almost deafening the passengers with recommendations of their commodities and pressing solicitations to induce them to become purchasers. A single shake of the head, which is generally understood to mean "NO," went for nothing, and even a positive declaration of the negative, until repeated several times with a countenance screwed up to a vinegar aspect, was not believed.

Among the host of competitors for public favour on this occasion were two little urchins, who, like quicksilver, slipped from one side of the coach to the other, and appeared, from the agility of their movements, to be at the front and back of the vehicle at the same time; these were not only more expert in their trade, but more incessant in their applications for customers, than others in the same line of profession. By some accident, however, a breach of the peace between them took place by the overthrowing of the basket of one of the traders. Instantly a scene followed, such as,—although of no uncommon occurrence where stage coaches put up at,—had never before been witnessed either by Lady Bolio or her fellow-travellers.

The two juveniles flew upon each other like infuriated tiger cubs.—"Go it, go it;—pitch into him, Bill."—"Well said, Sam, peg him under;"—with various other encouraging and elegant expressions, were shouted by the brutalized hostlers and stable-men as the youngsters buffetted and clawed each other. Even coachee himself appeared to forget his dignity, or as a patron of the ring, came to the door of the Inn with his hand-full of bread and meat, and offered a penny to whichever stood most beating.

The noise which was excited from the shoutings of the men and the bellowing of the boys, was increased considerably by the barking of some dogs, who, as kindred spirits with their owners, enjoyed with them the scene. This increased uproar was again increased by the screaming and imprecations of two or three female friends of the young combatants, who, rushing from their houses, fell upon them pell-mell, each woman taking the side of the boy to which she stood related or attached, and then, falling upon each other, first with their tongues, and then with their fists and finger nails, produced effects both serious and disgusting.

"Ah, you old Cream of Tartar," roared one, as she clenched

K

her fists and struggled, like another Hamlet, to shake off a couple of female acquaintance who held her from the destructive purpose she meditated.

"Unhand me, ladies!"—
she seemed to say;—

"By heaven I'll make a ghost of her that lets me."

And still she struggled furiously to free herself, and as she struggled, continued to pour forth fiery expressions of her wrath.

"I'll teach thee," she screamed, "to maul a child of mine; —I'll tear the eyes out, and twist the pimpled nose off o' the face, thou ould varmint."

"No you wont, Mother Flower O' Brimstone," exclaimed her opponent, tantalizingly, placing her hands upon her hips, and turning up her nose with provoking coolness at her infuriated rival;—"lay your little finger upon me at your peril," she continued, "and I'll sarve you as I sarved your old seconder there, Old Sour Grouts;—I'll black the white o' your eye for thee;—you 're an old impostering thief, that's what you are, and I'll prove it."

"Let me go," still roared the other, almost bursting with rage, "let me go, I say,—I'll tear her eyes out.—Oh you nasty, ugly, belzibubbing creatur;—you call me an impostering thief, what works hard for every bit of bread what I eats, while you knows whose *usband* was *obligationed* to skulk away for a week for fear of being nabbed.—I'll tell you a piece of my mind, Old Cream O' Tartar."

"Tell your mind, Old Flower O' Brimstone, to the feller what you ruun'd away from your husband with," replied Cream of Tartar, with insulting sarcasm in her voice and attitude.

"Oh, you ugly,—you *abominated* old creature!" again exclaimed Flower of Brimstone, gnashing her teeth. "I'll serve you a trick for this, or my name arn't Muggins."

While this was going on the originators of the affray were busily engaged in gathering up their fruit; which, had they done in the first instance, all would have been well;—while, Coachee's time being up, he laughed heartily at the folly of the old women, and then, taking the reins and his whip from the hands of an attendant, he mounted his box adroitly, gave a *click* with his tongue, peculiar to the driver of horses, and which is well understood, and off he went, while the bellige-

page 194

rents, having exhausted their stock of coarse epithets, and almost their breath, retired from the scene of conflict, growling like angry bears at each other as they turned off, until fairly out of sight.

It would be serviceable to the peace of many other places, as well as to Devizes, if an old custom, practised by our forefathers in Montgomery, was to be revived and put into full operation, which was as follows:—

"In order to prevent, as far as possible, the numerous evils that arose in the above-named town, from their strifes, fightings, defamations, &c., and many other disturbances, such as shoutings and bawlings, which they might commit, when they were taken they were immediately adjudged to the goging stool (answering to the cucking, or ducking-stool, resorted to in early times as the punishment of scolds, when they were ducked in the water for their shrewish propensities), there to stand, with naked feet, and their hair hanging dishevelled, for as long a time as would enable them to be seen by persons passing that way, according to the will of the chief bailiffs."

In ten minutes' time no trace remained of the recent cabal. The horsekeepers were busy in the stables, while those who had been drawn together by the arrival of the coach, had, with its departure, retired whence they came, leaving the street as quiet and as free from things having life or motion, as are the desolated walks of Pompeii, or the deserted gardens of Babylon.

"Well, my dear," observed Dr. Leechum, "what do you think now of the monastic-looking place?"

"What can you suppose I think of it?" returned Mrs. Leechum. "Surely you do not imagine for a moment that it has risen *very* high in my estimation from the disgraceful scene which has just been exhibited?"

"Oh, no, no, my dear," replied her husband, "certainly not. What a dreadful thing warmth of temper is, Lady Bolio!" he added.

"Shocking," observed her ladyship.

"Ah! it is so, indeed," said Mrs. Leechum. "I am thankful that, amidst much that I have to regret, *that* is not a besetting sin of mine."

"What, my dear?" enquired the doctor.

"*What?*" echoed his mild lady, rather snappishly. "Why

K 2

what were you speaking about? Surely you have not forgotten your own observation so soon?"

"Oh, no, no, my love," replied her husband, "certainly not. I seldom forget *that* subject, for a *very good reason,*" he added to himself. "I was merely hinting, my dear, what a dreadful thing *want of temper* was."

"Aye, *certainly* you were; and I do hope, Dr. Leechum," said his gentle lady, "you will profit by your own hinting,—it was *that* to which I referred. I say, and *you* know it, Dr. Leechum, that warmth of temper is not my besetting sin; if it was, I am sure I never could put up with what I have to encounter day after day. I should really go crazed."

"Oh, my patience!" said Leechum to himself, turning up the white of his eyes in astonishment, "how awfully are we blinded by prejudice in favour of self to our own imperfections! *Warmth of temper not her besetting sin!*"

"Well, as you say," observed Lady Bolio, "it is a happy thing to enjoy a mild and even temper;—we poor women have need of it, I am sure,—especially those who have husbands. Thank my stars, I am not so plagued now,—and never will I again be so."

"Indeed, my lady!" exclaimed Dr. Leechum, looking, as well as speaking his astonishment.

"Never!" reiterated Lady Bolio, "*unless, indeed,* I could obtain a second Dr. Leechum."

"Oh!" screamed Mrs. Leechum, with something very like horror in her looks. "A second Dr. Leechum!"

"Thank your ladyship for so flattering a compliment," said the doctor. "You see, my love," he added, addressing his *dear* wife, "Lady Bolio can appreciate—"

"Appreciate, indeed!" returned Mrs. Leechum. "If Lady Bolio knew all I know, and had to endure what I have, her *appreciation* would undergo a material change."

"Will you take a little more coffee, my dear?" asked her husband.

"No," returned the lady. "You know I *never* take above four cups in the morning,—five, at the most. How very tormenting you are, Dr. Leechum;—positively one would suppose you wished to deluge one with *coffee.*"

The sun had nearly gained its highest altitude, throwing its broad bright beams over our world, investing in a girdle of burnished gold, cities, towns, and villages, when

Lady Bollo's carriage started from the Castle Inn, and in a few-minutes Devizes, with its beauties and defects, was left behind.

As the vehicle rattled down the dangerously steep hill which then was, but now is not, at the western extremity of Devizes, Mrs. Leechum's spirits mounted to the very precincts of a region which they very rarely entered,—contentment and good humour,—and turning to the doctor with one of those enchanting smiles which on certain occasions she could command, she observed,—"This puts me in mind, my dear Dr. Leechum, of the morning on which I made you happy."

"Indeed!" said the doctor, from the tablet of whose memory the circumstance had been scoured completely out by the friction of a weary *six months* of connubial litigation.— "Pray to what particular do you refer, my love?" he enquired.

"Why, is it possible!" returned the lady;—"Is it possible that you can so *soon* have forgotten a morning on which so important an engagement was entered into; when *I* simply and foolishly, although most unreservedly, sacrificed to you all I possessed, and when *you* promised with your body to *worship me*, and—"

"Oh, yes,—yes," responded the doctor; "I do remember it—you refer to our wedding-day, love,—do you not?"

"Certainly I do," replied Mrs. Leechum : "to what else could I refer ?"

"True, love,—true," continued her husband.—"But did I say, '*worship* you?'"

"*Did* you say worship me, Dr. Leechum ?" returned the lady.

"Yes, my dear," responded the husband ; "did I say so ? for if I did, I said what I never should have said—for I said what I can never perform."

"Not perform!" half screamed Mrs. Leechum.—"Do you *hate* me so soon then ?"

"Oh no, no, I assure you ; nothing of the kind," replied the doctor; "but to *worship* you, love, would be an act of gross idolatry, and in direct opposition to the catechism which I was taught in my childhood, which enjoins that no act of worship should be paid to *any thing* in the heavens above, or on the earth beneath, except to GOD only!"

"Well, I'm sure!" exclaimed Mrs. Leechum.—"Did you

ever hear any thing equal to this, Lady Bolio ?—Here is perjury for you!—Has it then come to this after being six
months married ?"

"Well, my love," said the doctor, " you may recollect you
promised to *obey, serve, love, honour,* and—".

" Dr. Leechum," interrupted his almost petrified rib, "are
you not getting beside yourself? If you are perfectly sane,
what am I to think of the statements you are now making ?—
statements which would be a disgrace to any of my sex to
subscribe to.   I was, I confess, in a sad state of trepidation
on the morning I refer to ; but I am sure, *positive,* as I now
sit here, that I neither did or *could* say any such thing ;—it
is altogether opposite to reason and common sense.   In
short, no such monstrous statements and professions are to
be found in the ceremony, I am *certain !*"

" Well, my dear," returned her husband, "if they are not,
I lay under a very great mistake, I assure you.   I don't profess to be quite familiar with such kind of things."

" I believe you do lay under a mistake, indeed," observed
Mrs. Leechum ; " and you feel anxious, it would seem, to lay
me under a burden which no one can bear.   If I had promised such things, why, of course, I should have performed
my engagement to the letter."

" Oh, fie upon you ! fie upon you both!" observed Lady
Bolio, jocosely.—" What ! married six months only, and forget your promises ! Ha! ha! ha!—So it is with you, *young*
people ; you are not singular here, depend upon it.   I have
known fifty couples besides you, who never knew a word of
what they promised at the altar ;—indeed I question much if
one pair in one hundred think a word about it when they
turn from the communion table."

" Well,—but now, my dear Lady Bolio," returned Mrs.
Leechum, " do answer my question : do the words which
Dr. Leechum has just uttered, occur in the ceremony ?"

" Certainly, my dear Mrs. Leechum, they do," returned
her ladyship ; " at least they did when I resigned my liberty ;
but, perhaps, in the new edition of the Prayer-book, the
changes which were so greatly needed on *that* and *other* important points, have been made.   You know our legislative
governors have the high and mighty power to make the
terms of the contract just what they please ; but it is no matter, for I dare say, whatever the *terms* might be, you *married*
ladies would interpret them just as you please ; while no kind

of terms would prevent *some* from getting wed. But, if I were ever to go to the altar again, which I am *sure* I *never* shall, I'd take care to have an agreement sealed, signed, and delivered, by which I would secure to myself the power of doing just as I pleased, and of obliging the happy gentleman whom I should favour with my hand, to do as I wished."

The vein of pleasant raillery with which Lady Bolio delivered her sage observations, produced the effect she desired, —it restored Mrs. Leechum to the temper she was losing, if not lost; and a mutual determination was entered into between the doctor and his spouse to read the marriage ceremony as soon as *convenient* after reaching Bath.

On they dashed in gallant style, without once alighting, until they entered the city of pleasure, and drove up to the door of the mansion which had already been prepared for their reception.

Here, in almost every street through which our visitors passed, all was business and bustle. Crowds of fortune-hunters and pleasure-seekers, of both sexes, and from sixteen to sixty, paraded the streets, strolled in the delightful public grounds, or lounged in the libraries and music-rooms. Fashion, gallantry, and intrigue, with routs, balls, and masquerades, engaged the attention, and fully occupied the time of the wealthy visitors; while the knowing Bathonians laughed at the ridiculous folly of their dashing lodgers and customers; and for *fashion* rather than for enjoyment or accommodation, made them come down handsomely.

The house which Lady Bolio had engaged was large and airy, and occupied an admirable situation in the Crescent; which, from its elevated site, possessed at once an extensive and commanding view of the best part of the town, together with the surrounding country, with its beautiful intersections of hill and dale, wood and water, which together presented one of the most captivating natural dioramas that a warm imagination could conceive of.

"This is really delightful!" exclaimed Mrs. Leechum, as she stepped from the carriage, and surveyed, with a rapid glance, the scene which, like an extensive and beautifully coloured map, lay before her. "Well, I am sure," she continued, "I shall be as happy in this charming place as it is possible a mortal can be in this world. I never shall get fatigued here, or sigh for home again."

"Well, my dear Mrs. Leechum," observed Lady Bolio,

" I am happy to hear you are so much pleased with the place —a few weeks here, and an occasional ride to Clifton, will, I hope, completely restore me "

" Oh, there can be no doubt of it," replied Mrs. Leechum; " and then the company we shall meet with, and the parties we shall have ;—why, I feel confident, that any one who is not *quite* dead, must be restored to perfect health here."

" And yet," observed the doctor, " people do manage, some how or other, to die here."

" No doubt, my dear," returned the lady; " but that is because there are *doctors* in the town."

The sarcastic jest of the doctor's lady was received in good humour by that distinguished professional ; while Lady Bolio, hanging upon his arm, laughed heartily at it, as, walking after her skipping friend, she entered the house; where leaving the party to make their own arrangements, by sending cards and receiving invitations, we shall return to Dr. Titheum and our hero, whom we left making the best of their way towards Chichester.

CHAPTER XVI.

" A gentleman in figure and address,
Having withal free knowledge of the world,
That you might take the fellow for a lord,
So well his bare-faced impudence was mask'd.
None better knew the mysteries of their trade,
Or managed their profession with more skill."

THE PROFESSIONAL.

THE perpetrators of dark deeds ever seek shade and gloom in which to perform them. Now, it by no means follows that because such observation is made in connexion with a certain opinion held by Dr. Titheum, that, therefore, any insinuation is intended, that himself or his brethren in the commission of the peace were perpetrators of dark deeds.

The opinion referred to was certainly a singular one; and how it could have entered the rector's brain, we could never discover; namely, that because the hour or time at which the expected meeting of importance was to be held, was not specified in the letter of invitation he had received, it must therefore be in the evening Strange as the result of such

logical deduction may appear, yet so it was : he settled it in
his mind that the witching hour,

> " When fell Conspiracy, with all her brood
> Of evil-working imps, creep out, and aim
> To ruin men, and murder rest and peace,"

m s certainly be the period at which the meeting would be
hebdt

This being the case, he felt no uneasiness respecting the
flight of time ; although the point of the hand on the face of
the clock in the tower of Havant Church, pointed at four, as
he passed it.   He felt assured that in a few minutes he should
arrive at the Crown Inn, at Emsworth, and there he proposed to dine, for the purpose of refreshing himself and his
horse ; concluding that one hour would do that needful business, and then one more would take him safe into Chichester ; so that without the aid of Algebra, Cube-root, or Simple Fractions even, he felt certain that he should reach the
place towards which he was riding shortly after six.

As the doctor alighted at the door of the inn, his foot
slipped from under him, in consequence of his treading upon
some orange-peeling which had been thrown on the pave-
ment, and in a moment his head came in contact with the
element out of which man was originally taken—at the same
instant a gust of wind bore away his beaver, and whirled it
through the only drop of water which the eye could detect
from one end of the street to the other.

A gentleman who chanced to be passing at the time, possessing more than ordinary genteel exterior, and of the most
polite address, tendered his aid to raise the fallen supporter
of the church and the bench, and then went in pursuit of his
hat.   These important pieces of service were performed in
the twinkling of an eye ; and the stranger, gracefully tender-
ing his arm, walked with the doctor into the inn ; while
Claudius, as was his wont, took his station among his supposed equals ; observing, with the keen eye of a philosopher,
the tricks and habits of the humble prototypes of a repub-
lican state.

"Pray, Sir," said the doctor, addressing himself to the
gentleman as they entered the parlour of the inn, "may I
enquire to whom I am indebted for the kindness I have just
received ?"

"Oh, don't mention my little services, my dear Sir," returned the gentleman ; " I always feel proud to render any assistance in *my* power to gentlemen of *your* profession."

" Sir," returned the doctor, " I am glad to be thrown into your company, although by an accident which might have proved serious."

" I assure you, Sir," responded the stranger, " the pleasure is mutual. If at any future period I may be able to assist you, believe me, Sir, no person in the three kingdoms would do so more cheerfully than myself. You will, perhaps, favour me with a call at your convenience."—So saying, he handed the doctor, from a splendid case, a richly embossed card, on which was printed, in tasteful style,

" Mr. CHARLES AUGUSTUS MONTROSE,

" Abbey House,

" Emsworth."

—the word " Emsworth" being written in so beautiful a hand as scarcely to be distinguished from the steel engraving.— " Good day, Sir," added the stranger, bowing as he retreated towards the door.

" You will oblige me, Sir," said the doctor, " by taking a glass of wine with me, if your convenience will allow it." The stranger lingered, as if undetermined how to act, while the doctor added—" Allow me to press the favour of your company for half an hour."

" Well, Sir," returned the gentleman, " I am merely going to dine; but I would much rather lose a good dinner than your company."

" I am infinitely obliged, Sir," returned the doctor, " and feel happy that our pursuits at the present are alike. I only regret one thing,—my inability, from want of time, to order such a dinner as I should like to press you to partake with me ;—however, Sir, if you will excuse it,—such as the house affords shall be supplied instanter."

The gentleman bowed with a courteous smile, and no further opposition was urged. A substantial cold collation was set on the table, with as much despatch as would have put to the blush,—provided they could blush at any thing,—the waiters of any hotel at either the centre or west end of the brave city of London.

It is ten to one the Rev. Dr. Titheum had never read " The Earl of Chesterfield's Letters to his Son," Philip Stanhope, Esq., or, if he had, the sage maxims they contain had no influence upon his conduct in the present instance. The

Earl's inimitable advice in the choice of a friend would have been worth half a year's salary to the doctor, or nearly so. Speaking of such, Chesterfield observes :—" Beware of those proffered friendships—receive them with great civility, but with great incredulity too ; and pay them with compliments but not with confidence. Do not let your *vanity* and *self-love* make you suppose that the people become your friends at first sight, or even upon a short acquaintance. Have a real reserve with almost every body ; and have a *seeming* reserve with almost no body."

This short extract from a long and rich letter of advice, given by one who well knew the world, may be serviceable to multitudes, as well as to doctors and magistrates. The doctor, as we have said, had not read it ; or, having so done, did not regard it. To be sure, in *such* company as the doctor now was it might have been ill-timed—the *gentleman* sat upon every shred of his costume, and in every attitude of his body, and in every expression of his lip.

The stranger appeared to have an excellent appetite on this occasion, and, moreover, enjoyed with high relish the wine which the doctor, without any necessity, pressed him to take freely.

"You are a stranger, Sir, I presume, in this part of the country?" observed the gentleman to the rector.

" I am so, Sir," returned the doctor,—" that is, I but seldom journey this way—my duties, indeed, confine me closely. One in the commission of the peace, Sir, has enough to do."

" In the commission of the peace!" responded the gentleman to himself.—" Whew!—Some affair of importance, I presume," he added, " brings you this way?"

" Why yes, Sir," returned his reverence, " something of considerable importance."

" May I hope to see you soon this way again?" enquired the stranger ; " that is, when may I expect the favour of a call ?"

" Why, I shall be detained at Chichester—"

" At Chichester?" echoed the stranger.

"Yes, Sir," observed the doctor ;—" are you acquainted with the affair ?"

" Oh no, Sir,—no," returned the gentleman, " not that I am aware of,—excuse me for the interruption, Sir ;—you were about to observe you should be detained at Chichester."

" Ah,—true, true," said Titheum ; " I shall, in all probability, be detained there the whole of to-morrow; so that it will be the day after, at the earliest, that I shall be able to leave."

" May I then expect you will dine with me on that day?" enquired the gentleman.

" Why, Sir, I think," returned the rector, " I shall be able to do so ;—let me see,—well, I promise to be with you the day after to-morrow, by this hour."

" Thank you," returned the stranger, with warm feeling " Bless me!" he added, as his eye fell upon the doctor's canonical, " your hat has received some injury, I perceive ;—my friend Brush, half a dozen doors down the street, will get one of his men to put it to rights in a few moments,—with your permission I will see it done."

" By no means, my dear Sir," replied the doctor, as the gentleman took the covering from the peg.—" My servant will attend directly, and—"

" Sir," returned the gentleman, " I shall feel honoured by the permission ;—allow me in this instance, Sir,—I shall be able to get it done in less than half the time a servant would." So saying, he felt in his pocket for his handkerchief.—" This is a singular case," he observed, having examined both tails of his coat. " I have not a single handkerchief with me ; perhaps you will oblige me with your's to throw over the hat ?"

" Why, if you are determined, Sir," replied the doctor, " to become so obliging—".

" Such honour," observed the gentleman, " have all thy saints."

This was a closing argument—the doctor handed over the requested handsome silk handkerchief, and the gentleman enveloped the rector's new hat with it ; and then leaving the room, made all possible haste to put it into the hands of the hatter.

In the mean time Claudius had filled his belly, and was filling his eyes by gazing at every object which appeared worthy his notice. His scheme, so far successful, called forth his most warm and sincere gratulations, and he now looked forward to the climax of his plan when the hoax should be discovered, at Chichester. As, however, he could not divine under what circumstances he might be placed at that time, he left it to the spur of the moment to meet whatever difficulties might arise.

Since the departure of the gentleman with the doctor's

hat, his reverence had taken a couple of glasses of wine ; and looking at his watch, he found he had already been about half an hour. He began to feel a little uneasy about the time, and drank a third glass—still the gentleman delayed coming. The doctor's anxiety increased, and he rang the bell.

" I wish," said his worship to the servant who entered, " you would run to Mr. Brush's for me."

" To where, Sir ?" said the servant.

" Mr. Brush's," replied the doctor.

" I don't know sich a name, Sir," returned the man.

" Why, the hatter's, just below," returned the doctor.

" I don't know nobody of that ere name, Sir," replied the waiter.

" Hem !" said the doctor.—" How long have you lived here, my lad ?"

" Why, Sir," answered the servant, " only a matter o' six weeks."

" Oh, then you are not acquainted with your neighbours, I suppose," returned his worship.—" Say I wish to see your master."

" Yes, Sir," said the servant, and withdrew.

" You will oblige me," observed the doctor to the landlord, " by directing your servant to Mr. Brush's, the hatter's, for me. My friend, who dined here, has taken my hat to get it cleaned, and I fear I shall be detained beyond my time."

" Mr. Brush's, Sir, did you say ?" enquired the landlord.

" Yes," returned the doctor; " the hatter's, just below.

" I really don't know any person of that name, Sir," replied the landlord : " you have, perhaps, made a mistake in the name ?"

" Why, I suppose," said the doctor, staring at Boniface with surprise, " I must have done so, if that is the case. Well, I imagine I must wait patiently a little longer. Bring me a pint more wine."

" Directly, Sir," replied mine host, and disappeared to execnte the order.

Another half-hour passed away, and still the gentleman did not return. The doctor continued to solace himself with his wine, which he had almost finished ; when, beginning to grow warm, he rang the bell, and enquired of the landlord as he entered, what distance Abbey House was from his inn.

" I have lived here several years, Sir," said Boniface, " and never before heard the name."

"Not heard of the name!" responded his reverence;—
"why, your acquaintance must be very limited indeed."

"Why, for that matter, Sir," replied the landlord, "I have
as many as here and there one, and I know almost every body
within a dozen miles of the town, in every direction."

"Do you so?" said the doctor: "Look here," he continued, as he presented the embossed card on which the name
of his absent friend was engraved; "you know that gentleman, of course?"

"No, Sir," replied the landlord, "never heard of the name
before."

"Impossible!" exclaimed the doctor, "that you can be so
ignorant."

"I assure you, Sir," replied the host, "I state the truth."

At this instant a gentleman of expressive feature rode up
to the inn door, and, dismounting, gave his horse to the hostler; and then walked into the parlour in which the doctor
and the landlord were holding converse.

"Landlord," said the traveller, "has a gentleman called
here to-day, tall in person, and very gentlemanly in dress and
manners?"

"Did you expect to meet such a gentleman, Sir?" enquired the landlord, instead of answering the question.

"I did," replied the traveller.—"Has he called here to-
day?"

"Yes, Sir," returned mine host, "a gentleman answering
your description has been here."

"Oh, I see," continued the traveller, as he looked at the
card which lay on the table, "that is his card—"

"Indeed!" said the rector, "then I shall be all right.—
You know my friend then, Sir?"

"Why, I have not the pleasure of a personal acquaintance," returned the traveller; "but I hope soon to enjoy it.
You are a friend of Mr. Montrose's, I think you say, Sir?"

"Yes," returned the doctor; "that is, he has dined with
me, and I am now waiting his return from a little service he
is doing for me."

"Really, Sir!" resumed the traveller,—"then I shall succeed better than I hoped;—I suppose you guess my business—eh? You know me?"

"Know you, Sir?" returned the doctor—"never saw you
in all my life."

"Indeed!" said the traveller, as if incredulous respecting

the truth of the doctor's statement.—" Come, come! it won't do;—where has this *friend* of yours gone—eh?"

The landlord began to stare in amazement at what he heard; and, although he was unable to comprehend its precise import, he nevertheless expected some dreadful discovery was about to take place:—while the doctor, feeling the wine operate, became more than usually dignified in his own conception, and, therefore, felt what he conceived to be—the insult offered to his worshipful person by the freedom of the stranger.

" If, Sir," he observed, warmly, " you do not leave this room instantly, I will—"

" Oh oh,—indeed! say you so?—rather too flash, I guess. You see these ere pretty things,—don't you?" he added, taking a pair of handcuffs from his pocket, and dangling them before the doctor's face.—" Come, let's see how they'll fit."

" What do you mean?" exclaimed the doctor; " are you drunk or mad?"

" Oh, neither," replied the traveller, with unmoved calmness.—" And what do I *mean?* ha! ha! ha!—a notable question—that. In the first place, then, I *mean* that I have posted from London after you and your *friend;* and in the next place I *mean* to take you both,—if I can catch your *friend,*—safe back in a coach,—you understand. No noise now; it won't do."

" Villain!" exclaimed the doctor, as the traveller approached him,—" Hands off, or I am not in the commission of the peace if I don't punish you dearly for your frolic."

" Well, now,. that's what I call coming it handsomely,—rather strong, though, old chap; but it won't do, I tell you —you're nabbed, and no mistake."

" What does all this mean?" enquired the landlord.

" *Mean!*" responded the traveller, " why, it means just so much:—that this *gentleman* is my prisoner."

" Prisoner!" exclaimed the doctor and the landlord together.

" Aye,—*prisoner!*" repeated the stranger—" that is not so *very* strange,—is it?"

" On what charge?" enquired mine host.

" Why, Mr. Charles Augustus Montrose,—as this *gentleman's friend* calls himself,—and two or three others (all *gentlemen*, of course), have had a good long run; and we didn't grab them because they weren't fledged; but every dog has his day, as the saying is, and then it ends ; and so has every thief. Now these *gentlemen* have just committed a most daring burglary, attended by circumstances of extraordinary atrocity;—as, however, they were disturbed in their game, they fled without filching much, and I am here from Bow Street after them."

"You insulting scoundrel!" exclaimed the doctor, his passion rising above his reason, "is it in this way that you insult a gentleman in the commission of the peace ?—stand off, I say!" and taking up a decanter by the neck, he aimed a furious blow at the head of the officer ; but, fortunately, he was prepared for the attack, and dexterously avoiding it, the destructive missile flew to the other part of the room, and was only stopped by a large mirror, which it dashed to pieces. With as much calmness as though nothing had taken place, the officer took from his pocket a pistol, and cocking it, very deliberately, observed—"You are a game un, however ; but you are not the first rumbustical *gentleman* I have had to manage.—Now be quiet, or you see I shall be under the necessity of making you so. Here, landlord," he added, "hold you his hands while I put the bracelets on."

All opposition now appeared useless—the sight of a cocked pistol has silenced many a fire-eater, and intimidated many a big-worded hero ; in fact, they are awkward things to play with. So thought the doctor, if his confused mind could be said to think at all ; and he therefore became as passive as a lamb beneath the hand of its shearer. In a few minutes the Rev. Dr. Titheum, Magistrate of the county of Hants, was as handsomely manacled as any fellow that ever took up his lodging within that celebrated public establishment, ycleped Newgate.

"Now I remember," said the landlord, "there is another of them who acts as servant to this gentleman; I suppose they are all alike."

"Exactly so," replied the officer.—"Another!—oh oh! I am more fortunate than I anticipated ;—where may he be?"

"In the kitchen," replied Boniface; "at least he *was* there."

"Very good," returned the officer; "desire him to walk in, if you please: say his *master* wishes to see him."

The landlord fully believing, as many wiser than himself have done, that a member of that respectable establishment, *Bow Street*, cannot do wrong, did as directed, and in marched

Claudius, without dreaming of the singular predicament in which the doctor was placed; and, taking it for granted that he wished to know if every thing was ready for their departure, stood ready to reply to his interrogatives.

"Claudius," said the doctor, as he entered the room.

"Yes, Sir," replied our hero, "the horses are quite ready, and fresh as if they had not travelled half a dozen miles. Will you have them brought round directly, Sir?"

"Are they so?" observed the man of Bow Street; "that's fortunate; but never mind them, they may rest in the stables until their owners claim them, which will not be a long time, I dare say: we'll give you a ride in another way."

Claudius's eye turned towards his master, as if to obtain an explanation of the strange speech to which he had just listened, when the handcuffs upon his wrists attracted his attention. Without understanding the cause, he felt an irresistible disposition towards a hearty laugh. That such conduct was exceedingly ill-timed is admitted; but had all the circumstances connected with the singular case been known by Claudius, it is one hundred to one he would, for the sake of the adventure, have enjoyed it still more fully; as it was, however, he felt he must either *laugh* or *burst;* and preferring the former to the latter, he roared with as good a grace as Sancho Panza ever displayed.

"Oh, I see all about it," observed the official, "this is an old bird, although scarcely fledged. Come," he added, "lend us your flippers, my fine fellow; we'll soon make you merry after another fashion."

"What do you mean?" asked Claudius, suddenly changing from laughter to a serious countenance.

"What do I *mean*, again?" said he of Bow Street,—"Oh, you shall soon learn all about it,—look here," he added, "I have saved a pair for you," and he drew another set of handcuffs from his roomy pockets.

Claudius was soon accommodated as *respectably* as his master, and again looked round for an explanation of this strange affair.

"Have the kindness to send for a constable or two," said the officer, addressing the landlord; "I must leave this pair of birds for a short time, and go in search of the *friend* of these *gentlemen;* he appears to have got scent, and has changed his quarters.

In five minutes' time a couple of constables entered, to

whose custody the reverend magistrate and Claudius were committed, while the official set off in quest of the gentleman at large.

It was in vain that the doctor protested he was "in the commission of the peace," or that Claudius maintained he was his worship's servant. The master had been found in company with one of the most celebrated of the "swell mob," and had acknowledged himself his *friend :* and under the most suspicious appearances both master and man had been apprehended.

At the end of half an hour the officer returned, having visited most of the public places in the town, but without finding the person after whom he had been in pursuit.

"He has fairly given us the slip for this time," he observed; "but we shall meet him on the hop yet, I'll swear. Here, landlord," he continued, "let us have a post-chaise and pair of horses as soon as possible, as I wish to be in London with my prisoners before noon to-morrow."

"To London!" exclaimed the doctor, as if just awaking from a distressing dream, to the actual endurance of some still more dreadful reality. "To London!—Impossible."

"Oh no,—asking your pardon; it isn't, I assure you," replied the officer: "quite possible, and certain too."

"I'll not submit to it," vociferated his reverence.

"Won't you, indeed!" observed the man of Bow Street. "Hem!—not very cheerfully, may be ; but still, submit to it you must," and he presented his pistol significantly.—"I shall ride with you, you know, if that will be any comfort to you."

"I have business of importance to attend to, at Chichester," returned the doctor, "touching some serious legal question."

"No doubt you have," returned the officer, with cool irony, "and so you have in London too, I assure you."

Claudius now discovered that both himself and his master were thrown into a serious dilemma, while the whole had issued from the hoax he had played upon his worship. To become so arrant a knave as to turn evidence against himself, was what his noble mind scorned ;—come what might come, he had made up his mind to abide the consequences, and even to the death hide the secret of his waggery in his bosom.

Amidst the busy reflections of his mind, one cheering circumstance, like a solitary star to a tempest-tossed mariner, buoyed up his spirits, and even afforded him pleasure—and that was the thought of the journey to London; although that journey would be performed under very suspicious appearances. He felt assured that if his master had been guilty of some treasonous act, himself would be set at liberty; if, indeed, he had not experienced the confidence which innocence never fails to induce, he would have scoffed at the thought of danger;—he revelled almost, in the anticipated delight which the expected visit to the metropolis of the land was to afford.

The news had already spread like wild-fire through the little gossiping town of Emsworth, that some notorious characters had been apprehended at the Crown Inn. Rumour, with her hundred tongues, circulated the tale; and Exaggeration, with her elastic lungs, gave as many and varied editions of the case almost as there were hairs upon the supposed criminals' heads : the *two* were multiplied to a *score*, and the officer of Bow Street to a file of soldiers. Some asserted that the villains had been detected in concerting a plan by which to stop the navigation of the river that ran through the town —others stated that their object was to destroy the fishing-boats which sailed out of their harbours, if not to poison all the fish that frequented the coast;—not a few maintained, with all the assurance of dogmatism, that they were plotting against the government,—a species of Guido Fawkes. Some *proved* they were highwaymen—nay, that it was quite certain they had perpetrated numerous murders—each man and woman was positive that their individual statements were true.

As was naturally to be expected, the result of these veritable reports was, that crowds flocked round the inn, anxious to obtain if but a glimpse of such awful characters; so that by the time the post-chaise was provided in the yard, all approaches to the Crown Inn were blocked up.

"Come, Sir," observed the officer to mine host, "we must be moving; time forces us hard, and we shall have enough to do to reach our destination by the time I wish."

"I cannot go yet, at any rate," said the doctor, "I have no hat."

"Haven't you?" replied the Bowstreeter :—"Why, what covered your head when you rode here?"

"He had a hat on when he came, I'll take my *affydavid*," said a servant who had been called in to assist the constables, if any help should be required.

" Why, the gentleman who has skulked away, "observed the landlord, "has taken it to be cleaned ; at least, so I was informed."

" Why, there now !" said the officer.—" Is that true ?"

" Yes ; that is the plain fact," replied the doctor, very reasonably expecting this would be a sufficient proof that he had been taken *in* by, rather than connected *with*, Mr. Charles Augustus Montrose.

" Click !" said the man of Bow Street,—" Proof upon proof—nothing so clear ;—a good trick to treat a younker with ; but *we* are too deep to be so done,—would any one have trusted any but a *friend* with his hat out of his sight ;— no, no, I wouldn't trust any *friend* even that I have, with mine : it's all right, depend on it."

" Why, *sartinly* it is," observed one of the constables. "What knowing chaps these 'ere Lunnun *hofficers* is, to be sure —why, I should never have thought on that,—should you ?" he added, " Mr. Addlebrain," appealing to his fellow of the staff.

" No, sartinly," replied Mr. Addlebrain ; " never ;—but ain't it quite *inclusive*, Mr. Wingleby ?—not a shadow of doubt remains on my mind,—I see thief and villain *excribed* on his *werry phixhonome*. These 'ere Bow Street *hofficers* are *instonishing* men, sure enough."

" Well, we must get you another hat," resumed the clever man from London.—" Let us try the size of your knob," he continued, placing his own hat on the doctor's head ;—" aye, that'll do ; I'll accommodate you with a beaver in a brace of two two's;" and out he went, after charging the town constables to look well to their prisoners.   In as brief a space as his own descriptive phrase might be supposed to imply, he returned, bringing in the place of the handsome superfine canonical, such as the doctor entered Emsworth in, a four- and-sixpenny rough felt one; observing, as he placed it on the reverend magistrate's head :—" There, my fine fellow, now you are capped again ;—aye, and a prince need not wear a better ; at least it will serve your purpose until you are legged : and then you'll be glad to catch so smart a castor."

" Who pays my bill ?" enquired the landlord.

" I do, to be sure," said the doctor, " at least for myself and servant ; and I'm not ' in the commission of the peace' if I don't make some of you pay dearly for this vile conspiracy."

For a few minutes his worship fumbled *at* his pockets, making vigorous attempts to get his hand *into* one of them ;

but, like the Siamese brothers, *one would* not go without the other ; and as both *could* not go in, *both* remained *out.* The officer feeling no objection to mine host of the Crown having his reckoning discharged, and especially so as the prisoner appeared disposed to do it, liberated for a moment his hands ; when upon thrusting one into the recess where his purse *had* been, he found that both *it* and its *contents,* by some sleight-of-hand trick, had been extracted.

"That villain has robbed me !" exclaimed his worship ; " he has not only taken away my hat and handkerchief, but my purse and gold likewise."

"Robbed you ?" observed the officer,—"What, dog bite dog !—ha ! ha ! ha ! But how could he have done that ?"

"How ?" returned the doctor, supposing his veracity was questioned ; "why, I leaned upon his arm as I entered the inn, and then, I suppose, he took my purse."

"Still further evidence of guilt," observed the Bow Street attendant.—"Leaned upon his arm, *certainly;* but to rob you of your purse—eh ! eh ! eh ! Well, well, your plan will be to indict him at the Sessions,—we shall nab him before then, I don't doubt. Come, Sir, your hands again ; and as you and that younker have been so intimate, perhaps you would not like to be far apart—eh ? Well, I'll oblige you so for once." So saying, he fastened the right hand of the doctor to the left hand of Claudius, and then gave orders for the chaise to be brought round directly.

At this important crisis an entire new feature was given to the position in which the doctor and our hero were placed. A splendid carriage, drawn by four handsome horses, drew up before the Crown, the gazing crowd giving way right and left for its approach. The door was opened by a liveried foot-man, and two pinks of fashion of the masculine gender step-ped forth. Boniface met them at the threshold of his house, and led the way to a spacious room on the first floor.

"What the devil is all this uproar about, landlord ?" en-quired one of the guests, who appeared to be well known by Boniface.

"A serious affair, your lordship," returned mine host ; " a band of burglars, I think they say, has been followed from London by a Bow Street officer ; they have been here to-day,—two are in custody below, and one has escaped."

" 'Pon my honour," observed the other visitor, " that is no joke ;—suppose we look at them, my lord ?"

" With all my heart," returned the other : " show us the way, landlord."

".I will, my lord," said mine host, and, preceding his distinguished visitors, he led them to the parlour in which the prisoners were.—" There they.are; my lord," observed the landlord, pointing to the culprits.

The moment the doctor saw them enter, he uttered an exclamation of surprise and gladness ; for he discovered in the visitors the companions of many a freak by day and night, in the field and over the bottle—Lord Dashwood and Sir Marmaduke Varney. The rector made an effort to approach them at double quick time, but the clog attached to his right wrist prevented him ; while Claudius, by the sudden pull, was almost thrown upon his all-fours.

" 'Pon my honour !" exclaimed Sir Marmaduke, not immediately recognising the doctor in his *new* hat and novel position.—" Who are you, fellow ?"

" Who am I !" exclaimed his worship :—" Why, surely some strange change must have passed upon me, or you and my Lord Dashwood would not have forgotten me."

" Why, I should know that voice," observed his lordship, —" eh !" he continued, surveying him attentively.—" Why by all that's good, 'tis Dr. Titheum !—Ha ! ha ! ha ! Gentlemen," he observed, after his cachinnatory explosion had taken place, as he turned to the officer and the landlord, " there is evidently some serious mistake here ;—release this gentleman, and I'll engage all shall be set right."

" 'Pon my honour," said Sir Marmaduke, " but this is confoundedly strange, that a magistrate and a rector should be dealt with like a common hind—this is absolutely outrageous."

The man of Bow Street began to suspect that he had made some *slight* mistake, for it was evident, from the attention and deference paid by mine host of the Crown to the visitors, that they were honourable men, and no impostors ; and he accordingly attended with alacrity to the direction of his lordship, by taking the handcuffs from the prisoner.

The common felt was soon removed from the reverend doctor's head, and in a few seconds an explanation was given of the circumstances which led to the mistake that had occurred.

" I am not in the commission of the peace," observed the rector, as soon as he found himself liberated, " if I don't

punish, to the utmost extent of rigour the law allows, this fellow of an officer and his abettors."

" 'Pon my honour," observed Sir Marmaduke, " to cast such disgrace upon a gentleman and a magistrate!"

" I beg your worship's pardon," said the man of Bow Street. " I intended no insult to an *office* which I *revere :—* your worship will. allow that circumstances were of a suspicious character, and if from my zeal to do my duty I have committed a blunder, I hope your worship will look over it; and I promise never so to offend again. If you will permit me, I will immediately proceed after the rascal who has taken your property, and hope before many hours have passed I shall succeed in securing him."

" Well, I am of opinion, Dr. Titheum," said his lordship, you had better pass this matter by ;—mistakes will occur, you know. *We* sometimes trip a trifle, eh !—haven't forgotten," he whispered, " the man you sent to the tread-wheel for a month, who was proved at the end of a week to be the wrong person."

" Why, true, true," said the doctor, " persons may make mistakes sometimes,—and yet these fellows ought to be punished, if only for the sake of example. *We* who are ' in the commission of the peace' are not to be put on a level with our tools—*our* mistakes and *theirs* are very different—and to send a *mere artizan* to prison for a week by mistake, bears no proportion to *my* being handcuffed,—the *former* is a matter of *trifling* consequence, but the *latter* deserves punishment. However, to show how greatly I respect your lordship, I shall attend to your recommendation. — Go," he added to the officer, " and secure the rascal who has decamped with my hat, purse, and handkerchief, and upon condition that you find and secure him so that I recover my property, I forgive your gross blunder."

The officer bowed his thanks and withdrew, while his assistants in office slunk away after him ; and in a few minutes the crowd dispersed from the front of the Crown Inn, and the doctor, with Lord Dashwood and Sir Marmaduke, sat down to enjoy some wine, and laugh over the affair.

By this time it was past seven o'clock, and for a while the important business which had called the doctor from home, escaped his recollection. Suddenly, however, the thought of it rushed into his mind, and at the very instant he was raising the eighth glass of wine to his lips, the recollection caused him to start as Brutus is said to have done when the ghost of Cæsar entered his tent to remind him of the ides of March.—The untouched glass fell from his enervated fingers, and was dashed to pieces.

"Claudius!" exclaimed the rector.

"Yes, Sir," replied our hero, who had taken his place behind his master's chair, according to his directions, to wait upon the party.

".Go, order our horses to be saddled this moment," said the doctor.

"'Pon my honour!" exclaimed Sir Marmaduke, "are you not well, *doctar?*"

"Shall we call in a medical gentleman?" added Lord Dashwood, supposing the recent circumstances in which his reverence had been placed, and the wine he had taken, had produced some serious effects upon his brain.

"I am perfectly well, I assure you," said the doctor, "and require no medical adviser; the secret is this,—until the present moment I had forgotten the important business on which I am going to Chichester: by this time I should have been there. I have no doubt I shall keep a full bench waiting for me."

"'Pon my honour," observed Sir Marmaduke, that is superlatively singular; haven't heard a word about it; how say you, my lord?",

"Not a whisper," returned Dashwood," but that is not very astonishing; I don't trouble myself much about these matters; things of more importance engage every moment of my time."

"'Pon my honour," exclaimed Sir Marmaduke, "things of *more importance,* ah! ah! ah!—I take you,—wine, pretty girls, and play--eh?--close on the scent, I think. .'Pon my honour—eh."

"Softly, Sir Knight," replied his lordship.—".By the bye, doctor," he added, turning to Titheum, and turning the subject at the same time,—"how long do you purpose remaining at Chichester?"

"It is possible I may return in the course of the week," replied the doctor; "can't positively say, the business *may* detain me longer, but—"

"Oh, in the course of the week," said Dashwood; "well, in that case, what say you to being of a party we are making up for Clifton, some time during the ensuing week?"

·" Why in truth," said the doctor, " I have promised my Georgie a jaunt somewhere, and I suppose Clifton will do as well as elsewhere."

"'Pon my honour," observed Sir Marmaduke, " an admirable thought, *doctar*, the divine Georgiana will give life and fire to any company ;—you will join us then ?"

"Aye, you'll promise it ?" said Dashwood : we want one or two choice spirits,—shall it be so ?"

" It shall," returned the doctor, gratified with the feeling he conceived Sir Marmaduke had displayed as he mentioned his daughter, and pleased with the expectation of again bringing the parties together. " Myself and Georgie will meet you at Clifton by this day week at latest."

"·'Pon my honour," rejoined Sir Marmaduke, " but I'll wager a hogshead of Sherry against a barrel of small-beer, something out of the common way will occur on the occasion. Let me see,—Lady Dashwood, Miss Georgiana, the golden Duchess, and Miss Fidget—"

" Miss Fidget !" exclaimed the doctor.

" Certainly," replied Dashwood ; " you don't suppose Sir Marmaduke would allow her to slip through his fingers. Why she is above half a plum, and that, to my mind, is worth making a *little* sacrifice for.",

" Certainly ;—yes, yes," stammered out the doctor, half confused as his rising hopes were again abruptly struck down, " that's an important consideration."

"' Pon my honour," said Sir Marmaduke, " but I flatter myself, if I am so fortunate as to bear away the prize, I shall be in a proper condition to meet a few pressing matters of an honourable nature, and close the arrangements we have been making to-day for the pretty estate in the neighbourhood, and these affairs concluded, we will have a jubilee that shall last as many days and nights as the feast of Ahasuerus."·

" Bravely spoken," exclaimed his lordship. " You *must* carry off the prize, Here's a speedy consummation to your matrimonial spec. ;" and he filled his glass.

" 'Pon my honour," said Sir Marmaduke, " I am indebted to your lordship."

Claudius had hasted with the agility of a hunted stag to perform the bidding of his master respecting the horses, as he felt fearful lest any thing should come out relative to the hoax he was playing the doctor. and so terminate his journey abruptly, even as his hopes had been destroyed of

going to London, although in the character of a culprit.
"The horses are quite ready, Sir," said Claudius, as he stepped into the room. "Shall they be brought round, your
worship ?"

"Oh, yes, yes, instantly," replied the doctor. "Bless
me ! I had forgotten the important business again. Yet,—
stay, stay," he added, as Claudius was leaving the apartment,
"I cannot go as I am,—I want a hat, and money too. Go
directly and find a hatter, if the town contains one, and desire him to bring a sample of hats directly. I suppose I
must make shift without a canonical until I return home."

"Yes, Sir," said Claudius, before his master had finished
his sentence, and he again disappeared.

"I must become a debtor to one of you," said the doctor
to his two friends.

"Shall be proud to supply you," returned Sir Marmaduke, "'pon my honour. Here's my purse, doctor,—hope
you will find sufficient for your present purpose, although I
regret it is but light."

"You have no need to want supplies," said Dashwood.
"If Sir Marmaduke's purse and my own united will not
meet your demands, I can draw upon our host while his exchequer has a guinea in it."

The doctor's pocket was quickly replenished with a sufficient supply of the needful, and his head furnished with a
new hat, selected from a score which Mr. Beaver had brought ;
and, as the horses were already at the door, he bade a hasty
adieu to his friends, and once again set off at full speed for
Chichester.

―――

CHAPTER XVII.

"Now the Parson look'd big,
    And he righted his wig;
But listen! the raven croaks :
    It foretels some evil ;—
    Yet, who,—save the devil,
Will dare his reverence to hoax?"

CONGREVE.

OF Dr. Titheum it might have been said, as of the immortal
Gilpin,—

"He little thought, when he set out,
  Of running such a rig."

Instead of arriving, as he had calculated, by six o'clock, it was nearly half-past eight when they reached the Cross in the centre of the city.

Judging it more than probable that the learned conclave still maintained their sitting in the council chamber, he turned *up* North Street, instead of turning *into* the inn, in order that he might not delay a moment more time than necessity compelled him. Had it been possible indeed, no doubt can be entertained that his worship would have rode his favourite Ithurea into the presence of his worshipful brethren, so anxious was he to appear in their midst and receive the congratulations which already by imagination rang in his ears. As, however, his horse had never yet performed such a feat, and, moreover, as he found the iron gates closed with befitting care when he reached the place, he directed Claudius to alight and announce him.

Our hero managed to do the first part of the bidding, although nearly suffocated by a suppressed laugh; but the second, as he well knew, was beyond his power. The iron barriers refused to yield to his efforts to open them, and neither his vigorous shaking them, nor his manly shouting, brought any living soul or body from the chamber.

"What can all this mean?" said the doctor.

"Indeed I cannot tell, Sir," replied Claudius.

"I really fear," continued the rector, "the meeting is over, and my long and disastrous journey is, after all, fruitless."

"It appears so, your worship," rejoined Claudius.

The very singular conduct of Claudius in shaking the iron gate, and shouting again and again, to the manifest disturbance of the quiet and the peaceable city of Chichester, connected with the strange appearance of the doctor, who still bestrode his beast, excited the attention of several persons who were passing, and in a little time a dozen or two people were gazing, open-mouthed, at our travellers.

"What do you want?" asked a consequential, pot-bellied personage, who stepped from a spirit shop on the opposite side of the road, as he strutted up to Claudius with the dignity of a dung-hill cock, "What do you want, my fine fellow?"

"I want to get in, to be sure!" replied Claudius. "What else can you suppose I want?"

"There is nothing doing there to-night," returned the dealer in liquor.

"How long has the chamber been closed?" demanded the doctor.

"It has not been opened this evening, Sir," returned the liquor dealer and ex-schoolmaster.

"Not been opened!" said the doctor.

"No, Sir; to-morrow night the lecture will be delivered," he replied.

"Oh! I see," said the doctor, supposing that as the meeting to which he had been summoned was a *profound secret*, the present person was of course ignorant of it. "Pray, can you inform me," continued his reverence, "where Mr. Highmans resides?"

"Directly across the road, Sir," replied the merchant, pointing to a tailor's shop.

"Here, Claudius," said the doctor, as he dismounted, "walk my horse gently a few minutes, while I make some enquiries about this matter." So saying, he crossed the street, and entered Mr. Highmans' shop.

Now, for the information of the reader, it is necessary to observe, that Mr. Highmans' profession was the same as that said to have been followed by the graceless wight who, for his peeping propensity when the Countess of Godiva rode through the city of Coventry, was smitten with blindness, and to which said profession,—or rather to those who adopt it, by almost universal consent no higher station in the scale of human character is allowed than that of the *ninth part of a man*. Many of this craft, however, have often proved by "long, stale, and unpalatable bills," that, if it takes nine tailors to make *one* man, one tailor is sufficient to ruin the fortunes of *nine* men.

But however well and truly this opinion may hold good in reference to tailors generally, yet, as in all general statements exceptions are invariably supposed, here such exception was found, as it certainly did not apply to Mr. Highmans. He was a man,—a *whole* man,—and one to whom Pope's elegant line might have been applied without taking any thing from the sentiment it contains :—

" An honest man's the noblest work of God."

It is true he was a *little* man,—that is, in animal stature,—but if, as Watts observes,

"The *mind's* the standard of the man,"

why then Mr. Highmans was *not* a little man. He was one of those noble-minded beings, although but a tailor, which, like some new planet, are only discovered at distant periods.

He was, as we have noticed, short in stature; but could the quantity of material which was inclosed within the limits of his tightly-buttoned great-coat have been pressed into the spare form of a London Dandy, he would have been as tall as the best of them; as it was, however, he perhaps measured between four feet ten and five feet in height, and nearly an equal number of feet and inches in girth.

Perhaps, from the spirit of English independence which glowed within him, together with a nose of rather prominent character, and as sharp as a bodkin, the first impression which his countenance would have produced upon the mind of a stranger would have been, that he was haughty and morose; but he only needed to be known, to convince the most prejudiced cynic that a kindlier soul, or one possessing more excellent qualities, did never inhabit a frail tabernacle of flesh ;—*excepting only* HIM *who was perfection itself*.

Whether in political principles he was Whig or Tory, or any thing else, was not so easy to determine; perhaps it would have been a posing question even to himself;—but of one thing he was certain in his own mind,—and many others knew it too,—that neither Knox, Luther, nor Melancthon, were more sincere or consistent dissenters from the errors they impugned, than he was from the practices, rather than from the principles, of the church by law established; yet, ardently as he loved, and firmly as he believed (as all men should do), the principles he professed, he did not esteem the less any good man who differed from him. His was not the dissent of bigotry or ignorance, of covetousness or expediency, but of an enlightened conscience, and the controlling conviction of the truth of the doctrines and practices he had embraced.

Such was the man to whom Dr. Titheum was hasting with all the stateliness of ecclesiastical dignity and magisterial importance, which an individual body could possess, to make enquiry respecting the important business which had brought him to Chichester. At the moment his reverence

entered the shop, its owner was snugly seated in his little
back parlour, enjoying a hearty but frugal supper ; for, like,
"a good old English gentleman," he attended to poor Richard's well known aphorism,—

> " Early to bed, and early to rise,
> Make a man *healthy, wealthy*, and *wise* ;"

although it must be acknowledged the *second* benefit mentioned in this preamble had not yet been realized by him.

Through a small window which opened a visual communication between the shop and the sitting-room, Mr. Highmans
beheld his visitor enter ; and supposing the divine—as he at
once shrewdly guessed him to be—was a customer from whom
a good order might be obtained, he laid down his knife and
fork, wiped his mouth hastily, and in a bustle which caused
the blood to mount into, and give a crimson colour to his
bald head, stood as erect as a yard-and-half of pump water
before the magisterial doctor.

"Mr. Highmans, I presume ?" said the rector, making a
slight inclination of the body as he spoke.

"Yes, Sir," returned Mr. Highmans, looking as sharp as
a charity boy who had lost his dinner.

"Hem," said the doctor ; "has not the meeting been held
to-day in the council-chamber ?"

"No, Sir," replied Mr. Highmans, "it will not take place
until to-morrow."

"Indeed," said the doctor ; "then the announcement sent
me, stating it would be held on the 16th inst., was not
correct."

"No, Sir," returned Mr. Highmans, "to-morrow, at seven,
is the time."

"Well, I am glad to hear it," replied his reverence, "as I
shall by that time be refreshed from the fatigues of my journey. Pray," he added, "can you give me any information
as to the nature of the business which is to be transacted ?"

"Why, no, Sir," answered the tailor, who knew no more
about phrenology than he did of the properties of hydragy-
rum, "I am not in the secret ; it is, in fact, out of my lati-
tude."

"Aye," responded the doctor, "above your capacity, I
suppose ?"

"Just so, Sir," answered the maker of garments, conceiving he had to do with a facetious customer, and willing to indulge his sportive disposition for the same reason that a child is plied with sweetmeats,—to win him to his purpose.

" Why, I presume, it must be something of an abstruse or difficult nature, or foreign aid would not be required. I flatter myself," continued the rector, and his fair round proportions appeared to increase as he delivered his observations, " I flatter myself, however, that I shall be able to comprehend the business."

" Oh, there can be no doubt of it, Sir," echoed Mr. Highmans; "you are, of course, learned in most of the sciences."

" Why, I don't boast of my attainments," answered Titheum; "but there are few points of law which, from my long standing 'in the commission of the peace,' I am not familiar with."

" Indeed, Sir !" said the man of tapes and threads, while his small sunken eyes sparkled with surprise as he listened to the doctor's reply; and he began seriously to question the sanity of his visitor.

The reader need scarcely be told that both the rector and the tailor were labouring under mistake; the doctor imagining that Mr. Highmans was secretary to the board of magistrates, and that the meeting to which he referred was that to attend which he had visited Chichester; while the tailor, knowing of no meeting excepting the lecture on phrenology, which was to be delivered on the following evening, referred exclusively to it; so that when the doctor spoke of understanding law, Snip, without outraging propriety, supposed him to be only *semi compos mentis.*

" Well," said the doctor, " I have no wish to have it known that I am in the city; you will, therefore, if you please, Mr. Highmans, keep it, like the business of the meeting, a profound secret."

" There will be little danger of my betraying you," answered Mr. Highmans; "I have not the pleasure, you are aware, Sir, of knowing who it is that has favoured me with this visit."

" Why, true,—true," returned the doctor. " Bless me, how singular it is that I should have forgotten to announce myself,—ha ! ha ! ha ! Well, well," he added, " you have heard of the name of Titheum, I dare say ?"

" Who, Sir ?" asked Mr. Highmans

" Titheum," rejoined the doctor

" Titheum,—Titheum," repeated the tailor;—" why, really, Sir—"

" Aye,—Titheum," interrupted the rector, half surprised and as much offended, that *his* name should be so little known ; and, especially, that it should not be remembered by the servant of the meeting from which he was expecting to receive flattering applause.—" Dr. Titheum," he added, with an elevated voice and shrill tone ;—" Dr. Titheum, of Christchurch, and a *magistrate of the county of Hants.*"

" Oh yes, Sir ; I recollect now," replied Mr. Highmans, starting ; for the name had been rendered familiar to him by a circumstance which did not tend to raise either the divine or the magistrate very high in the estimation of a man like honest Highmans. The fact was simply this :—the man to whom Sir Marmaduke had referred as having been wrong fully committed by the doctor to the tread-wheel, had for merly been a highly respected apprentice of Mr. Highmans ; so that, on hearing the account of the committal from the mouth of the sufferer, the name of the magistrate, at whose pontifical *ipse dixit* he had been vagabondized, was mentioned.

" Why, that's well," observed the doctor,—" that's well ; —I thought *you,* of course, must recollect me. But tell me, Mr. Highmans," continued his reverence, " have you any game hereabouts ?"

" Game, Sir ?" responded Mr. Highmans.

" Aye,—game," replied the doctor,—" your downs are ad- mirably adapted for coursing."

" I do not attend to those things, Sir," returned the tailor, " and I think it would be much more in character if some other persons, who *do* attend to them, did *not.*"

" Very wisely observed," returned the rector ; " you speak like a good and honest man : and, as you say, *tradesmen* should not waste their time, or seek to unite with *gentlemen* in *their* sports."

" *Every* honest tradesman, Sir," replied Mr. Highmans, " *is* a *gentleman !*—at least he merits the name far more than many who bear it proudly. But, Sir," he added, with spirit, " I speak not as a tradesman, *merely.*"

" Oh no, no," returned the doctor, startled at the feeling displayed by the tailor ; and then, with the intention of turn- ing from the subject, he enquired :—" Oh, by the bye, is his lordship at Goodwood at present ?"

" I believe he is, Sir," returned Mr. Highmans.

"Ah—a pleasant spot that,—Goodwood," observed his reverence.—"I haven't been on the course for two seasons. Do you not think it a most excellent situation, and a charming place?"

"So far as the country is concerned, Sir," returned the tailor, "it is, I conceive, without exception, unrivalled; but in reference to the race-course, my judgment must be useless, as I never frequent it, and have no desire to unite with *gentlemen* in *their* sports."

"True, true," responded the divine.—"Yes, it is a lovely place, and—that is,—was the company as numerous and good last year as usual—eh?"

"I have said, Sir," returned Mr. Highmans firmly, "I *never* attend the course."

"Never!" exclaimed the doctor.—"What! live within a stone's throw, as one may say, and not attend!—why, really now, this is carrying the tradesman too far."

"It would be far better, I conceive, Sir," returned Mr. Highmans, "if some other persons, whose professions point out to them other occupations, were not found there. The loud war whoop is raised against dissenters,—and, I admit, not without cause in too many cases;—they are pointed at and hooted as if they deserved not to enjoy the rights of citizenship with their fellow-subjects, and they are branded with almost every offensive epithet which the malice and ingenuity of their enemies can invent; and are treated as schismatics and renegades from the church, and by those, too, who should be her defenders, but who are her foulest enemies,— who by their examples teach, nay, *compel* almost, the conscientious to dissent."

"Eh?" observed the doctor, half confounded by the tailor's eloquence.—"Well, well, Mr. Highmans, I give you credit for sincerity; but it is a *mere* matter of opinion, and we shall not fall out on that point."

"I think it, Sir," replied Mr. Highmans, "something considerably above *mere* opinion, and what enters into the very essence of the faith which the church teaches."

"I am not in the commission of the peace," exclaimed the doctor, starting and staring with surprise, "if I don't more than half suspect that you are a dissenter."

"If you were not in the *commission of the peace*," returned the tailor, "or not in possession of a *gown*, I *more than half* suspect, each office might gain by it."

L 5

" What, Sir !" exclaimed the rector, " do you mean to insinuate—do you mean that the union of the two offices is
improper ?"

No, Sir," replied Mr. Highmans, " I do not mean to *insinuate* any such thing ; but, as you have asked the question,
I feel no hesitation in giving you my opinion on the subject."

" Well, Sir, and what is it ?" asked the doctor.

" It is, Sir," returned the tailor, " that the offices are utterly incompatible with each other ! A reverend magistrate is
a burlesque upon the sacred, and a reproach to the legal
office—"

" Sir, Sir," interrupted the doctor, warmly, " can you prove
your statements ?"

" I can prove, Sir," replied Mr. Highmans, with vigour,
" that one much more qualified than any man that either Oxford or Cambridge *ever* sent forth, exclaimed under the pressure of *one* office,—' Who is sufficient for these things ?'—
and if he, Sir, with his very superior, extraordinary, and su-
pernatural qualifications, so felt, what ought to be the feelings of those who bear the same office now, without the
addition of another of weighty character ?—or how, Sir, is it
possible the duties of both, or either, can be properly discharged by those who strive to unite them, who possess
scarcely a grain of qualification for either ?—Or, if you please,
Sir, look at those whose abilities are of the most superior
order, and you will not for a moment maintain that even there
is a proximity to a shadow of a shade of his to whom I have
referred ; and if not, by what means can such perform the
double duties of magistrate and minister, whose talents for
both are most despicable ?"

" *How*, Sir !" exclaimed his reverence, with less temper
than Moses displayed when he smote the rock at Rephidim,
from which miraculously a supply of water flowed.—" How,
Sir !—Why, cannot a curate be procured if the duties of a
charge are too heavy for the incumbent ?"

" A *curate*," returned Mr. Highmans ; " why yes, Sir, a
curate *can* be procured ; but, Sir, does it comport with honesty,—leaving other and higher considerations out of the
question,—does it comport with *honesty*, Sir, that from eight
to eighteen (or more) hundreds a-year should be received by
a man for the performance of duties which he dislikes to attend to, or is unable to perform ; while a laborious worthy
person, unpatronised by title and driven by necessity, is com-

pelled to submit to become the proxy of such, for the paltry
stipend of from seventy to one hundred pounds a-year? Let
those, Sir, who are unable, from disqualification or disinclination, to fill properly the office of a minister, resign to those
who are able and willing.—HE, Sir, who makes men rulers
and judges now, *never makes the same men ministers and magistrates.* It is time, Sir,—*high* time, that the sacred and the
secular should be *dis*united, whether found to exist in the
lower or higher grades of office."

" Sir!" thundered out the doctor, unable any longer to
listen to the wild declamation of the tailor, " I shall report
your conduct to-morrow to the bench of magistrates ; and if
such a person as you are,—holding as you do, opinions so
subversive of the whole system which the wisdom of our forefathers established,—can be allowed to retain the office of
clerk to such a body—"

" As *what*, Sir ?" interrupted Mr. Highmans.

" Why, as clerk, I say," answered the doctor.

" My dear Sir," returned the tailor, who now fully believed
the doctor was mad, " are you unwell ?"

" Am I unwell?" foamed out the divine.—" What! am I
to be insulted, too ?"

" No, Sir, I mean no insult," replied Mr. Highmans; " I
never intentionally insulted any man, much less gentlemen of
your profession, how much soever they insult themselves ;—
but there is a degree of incoherency in your language and observations which I cannot comprehend."

" Very likely !" exclaimed the doctor,— " Very likely !—
But you *shall* understand me,—I will report you, I say, to
the board."

" I am no clerk to any such board as you name, Sir," replied Mr. Highmans; " I am, indeed, clerk to the congregation with which I worship."

" Not clerk to the board !" thundered the divine.—" Clerk
to a congregation!—What, a dissenter !—Pshaw ! Here,
Claudius, Claudius !" shouted his reverence at the top of his
voice, " bring me my horse immediately;" and he bustled
towards the door of the shop with a degree of trepidation and
speed, as if the dread fangs of some harpy monster were about
to be thrown around him ; and then, as if suddenly recollecting himself, he turned short, and taking the letter from his
pocket which Claudius had written,—to which by accident
he had appended a real, where he purposed to have affixed a

fictitious name,—he presented the scrawl to the tailor, exclaiming as he did so,—"Do you deny writing me this letter, Sir?"

"Certainly I do," replied Mr. Highmans.

"You do, Sir?" roared the doctor.—What, deny your own signature!—oh, monstrous! monstrous!—You are a dissenter with a witness.

"I deny that this is my signature," said the tailor.

At this moment Claudius came up with his master's horse, and seeing the letter exhibited, and the doctor arguing with exceeding excitement, imagined at once that the mystery had come out, and stood prepared for an assault.

"Here is your horse, Sir," said Claudius.

"Very good," said the doctor. "Do you," he added to the tailor—"Do you, I once more ask, deny writing this?"

"Your master is certainly unwell," observed Mr. High- mans to Claudius. "How far have you travelled to-day?"

Before the doctor could reply as he was about to do, a friend of Mr. Highmans appeared at the door of his shop. He was an exact counterpart of the tailor in principle and excellence of character; but his Patagonian stature gave him considerable advantage in point of appearance. He was a shrewd calm thinker, and in a few moments saw through the mistake under which the parties laboured, and perceived the hoax which had been played upon the divine.

"If you will allow me, Sir," observed Mr. Irvingood—"I think I can explain the matter; some mistake has evidently taken place."

"A mistake!" returned the doctor. "Have I not Mr. Highmans' own hand-writing here?"

"No, Sir," replied he of the golden cannister—"you have not indeed—Mr. Highmans is but an indifferent sort of scribe; besides which, he is *not* and never *was* clerk to the body you refer to: and as no person of the same name resides in Chichester, depend upon it that some wag has grossly imposed upon and abused you."

Claudius listened to this explanation, and almost trembled at his own wild freak; but recollecting that no one was connected with him in the plot, the secret of it was his own, and could only be made known by his personal confession, and in the retention of it he felt his security perfect.

"Claudius," again cried the doctor, "bring me my horse;" and once more he moved towards the door; "I am not in the commission of the peace if I don't find out and severely punish the villain who has dared to make me the object of this his unhallowed sport."

The doctor stepped from the step of the door into his stirrup, and from thence into his saddle, in which, having seated himself comfortably, he enquired of Mr. Irvingood. " Where had I better put up at,—which is your best inn?"

" I am going within twenty yards of it," replied Mr. Irvingood, "and if you will allow me, shall feel a pleasure in pointing it out to you."

"The doctor acknowledged the kindness, and walked his horse after his proffered guide to the Cross; and then turning to the left, Mr. Irvingood led him past his own well-stocked shop, to the best inn the city afforded; and as there are several of no mean character in this comfortable see, the one to which his reverence was conducted was of course of superior order; and after wishing the doctor good-night, he left him and our hero to dispose of themselves in the best way they were able.

CHAPTER XVIII.

" Ah, ah, say you so?—a parcel for me ?
Come, hand it here quickly, I'm dying to see
Of what, or how much, its contents may be.
From whom can it come ?—are you certain you're right ?
Read again the address,—come nearer the light;
Yes, yes, you're correct,—I shall die with delight."
THE MOUSETRAP.

It was half-past six on the morning of Friday, when Claudius was roused from a sound sleep by the loud knocking at his bed-room door by the hostler of the inn, who informed him, a box directed to his master had just been left from the Portsmouth coach, on which " to be delivered immediately" was written in large letters.

"The porter," observed Joe the hostler, "has been at half a dozen inns already before he com'd here, and may bee it is something importunate."

Claudius would much rather the hostler had taken the box to his master, although a box on the ear had been the only reward he had met with, than have been disturbed so early. The fatigue of the past day had rendered sleep doubly agreeable to him, and in a half angry tone he enquired of the bearer of the box what the hour was.

" Why it is going fast on to breakfast time," replied Joe.

"And at what time do you take breakfast?" asked Claudius.

" Why, at what time we can get it," returned the hostler.

" Indeed," said Claudius, " do you so? and at what time do you expect to get it this morning?"

" Why, may be, at something like half-past seven," replied Joe.

" Half-past seven!" exclaimed Claudius, "why is it not later than that yet!"

" What, now!" said Joe, " ah! ah! ah!—why be'st awake, lad ?"

" Hardly so," said Claudius.

" Well, I judged as good," said the hostler.—"Look at the sun yonder, and you'll soon tell the time o' the morning, I warrant you: it arn't seven yet, by perhaps half an hour."

" Well then," said Claudius, " the box must wait, for I am certain it is as much as my place is worth to call up the doctor at such an unreasonable hour, except, indeed, the hounds were out, and then—three or four hours earlier would not be too soon.

" Well," replied Joe, as he set down the box, " there is the thing at your door; do as you will with it, only fork me out a bob and a tanner: and then, if you choose, you can pop your head under the blankets again."

" A bob and a tanner!" said Claudius, as he appeared at the door;—" no, no,—we don't do things in that way,—we know what's what in the country as well as you city folks."

" I make no doubt about it whatsomever," returned Joe; "but I'll prove the charge what I makes is no more nor correct."

" Well, let's have the proof," rejoined Claudius.

" Oh, you shall have it in a giffy," cried Joe: " In the first place, then, booking at Portsmouth, two browns; then there's carriage from that 'ere place to this 'ere city, one tanner and two browns."

" Well," said Claudius, " that makes tenpence."

" By course it does," replied the hostler.—" Then again," he continued, " there's booking here, two browns."

" Booking again!" exclaimed Claudius.

" Why, to be sure there is," returned Joe, with calculating coolness ;—" you wouldn't have *walluable* property taken no care about,—would you? and if it is taken care of, why, by course, them what takes that 'ere *consarn* must be paid for it. Well, as I said, booking here, two browns more; then there's the porter from that inn what the coach puts up at, three browns,—and cheap too, considering how he has runn'd about to find your master."

"Well, admitting *all* this," said Claudius, "you only make out one shilling and threepence."

"Well, by course," answered Joe, "I knows all about it; but I ain't done yet."

"Why, what more have you to charge for?" asked Claudius.

"Why there's my *perkesites*, to be sure," returned the hostler; "I never does nothing, no more nor other men in office, without the browns. I charges three browns for my trouble,—and well worth it;—it wouldn't answer my purpose to do it for nothing under that. Why, haven't I to leave off polishing the harness of the Red Rover, and to come up from the stable, and then to knock as if I was going to break the door in afore I could wake you, and all for three browns?— if that ain't cheap, never say labour ain't worth being paid for again. You know you can lay on an extra tanner—that will only make it two bobs,—and cheap too;—why, if I hadn't considered you, I should have had three browns more myself, and no joke; however, as I 'spose you'll stand something short out of your tanner, I leaves you an opportunity to get your own *perkesites*. Come, tip us the ready, and I'll be satisfied."

Claudius's initiation into the mysteries of the *fine* arts,—as those delicate sort of robberies were called,—was as yet but partial;—as, however, he felt anxious to receive information on all subjects and from any professor with whom he might chance to come in contact, he was perfectly willing to do so on the present occasion. He knew sufficient of life already to be assured that no one would supply him with instruction free of all expense. Such reflection having passed through his mind, he made no further objection against paying the fee which the present professor of the *fine* arts demanded. Having, therefore, *tipped* the required sum, Joe became as jocose and loquacious as a long-brief'd barrister on the first day of term, or a candidate for legislative honours when seeking the patronage of his "good friends," chimney-sweeps and scavengers.

"Now, that's handsome," said Joe, as the two pieces of silver jingled in the palm of his horny hand; "and if you'll stand the drop I mentioned, I'll put you up to a thing or two that will put a few bobs in your pocket."

" Will you ?" replied Claudius; "you are a kind soul, I dare say."

" By course," returned Joe, " I wish to do a *sarvice* to any body."

" By instructing them how to cheat and rob, I suppose," said Claudius

" No ; on the honour of a man, and a *gentleman* too," rejoined Joe, "nothing of the kind, but all fair and upright."

" Well, let's hear it," said Claudius, " and I shall then be better able to judge."

" You agree then to the tooth-ful—eh ?" observed the hostler.

" Aye, aye," said Claudius ; "go on with your lesson."

" Well, then, thus it is," commenced the logical Joe :— " Your master pays all bills, by course,—that is, he finds the chink,—and if he pays a *little* more on some odd occasions than just the account, why the *overplush* is your *perkesites* by course. 'Spose now, when you are a travellin', he orders the 'orses to have a quartin o' *hotes*, and half a quartin o' beans ; —now you knows the orse can't eat so much, so you orders the *hotes* and omits the beans, and pockets the browns for your *perkesites* ;—you understands that—eh ?"

" Why, I fancy I do," returned our hero ; " it is not very difficult to understand that I am to rob both master and horse for the sake of filching the price of the beans."

" No sich thing," resumed Joe ; " you robs no *one*—all you does is to save the 'orse from over-eating himself. Well," he continued, "boots charges two browns—you, by course, charges three (one for *perkesites*); and then when you pays the *ostler*, you tips him a wink what he understands, as you slips a tanner and a few browns into his hand, and says, just as your master can hear you, ' There's a *bob* for you, Joe,' and pockets the odd browns for *perkesites*."

" Well, but by such means," said Claudius, " I rob both boots and hostler."

" No sich thing, I tell you," returned Joe ; " we understands it, and hold it fair to go snacks with a fellow-servant."

" But much cannot be gained in this way ?" observed Claudius.

" Say you don't know, if any body axes you," continued Joe, with an arch wink.—" Why, bless you, I knows the time when my master what is now, was nothing but a *sarvint* to a gentleman, as you may be ;—he had got a bit o' *larnin* at the

charity school, and knowed how to talk and count : and, by
taking care of the *perkesites,* he saved a few hundreds soon.
He next married the cook, who had been careful too, and
then took a small house at Porchester—here he took care of
number one: and now, you see, he has got one of the finest
inns in this city, and all through taking care of the *perkesites.*
We *ostlers* haven't no opportunities of that 'ere kind—we
can't make more than twenty bobs a week, do all we can;
except at the Race time, or when the Fairs are held, or some
public occasions : then, to be sure, we makes something
handsome, or it wouldn't do by no manner o'means."

"Yours is clever calculation, indeed," said Claudius.
"Ha! ha! ha! I suppose if I should chance to come this
way in a few years' time, I shall see you a coach-master."

"Aye, my boy!" said Joe, "that'll be when you keep an
inn."

"What can this box contain?" observed Claudius, as he
turned it about, "I should like to know. It looks, by the
way in which it is secured, as if some thief, or otherwise some
very suspicious person, had fastened it. Well, as it may be
something of importance, I'll take it to the doctor, and you
shall have the promised drop sometime in the day." So saying, our hero shouldered the box, and hasted with it to the
rector's chamber door; and, after repeated by knocking
with his knuckles on the pannels of the door, he succeeded
in waking his reverence from a death-like slumber.

"Who's there?" demanded the doctor, not in the very
best temper, or in the mildest tone. "Who's there, I say?"

"Here is a box, Sir," replied Claudius, "which has been
sent for you direct from Portsmouth."

"A box!" exclaimed the doctor. "A box for me!"

"Yes, Sir," returned Claudius. "It is directed for you."

"For me!" continued the rector, "and direct from Portsmouth. Impossible! Not a soul in Portsmouth knows of
my being here. No, no,—some imposture; a new trick intended to be played upon me,—but no, no, it will not
succeed."

"What am I to do with it, Sir?" enquired our hero.

"Take it back," said the doctor; "take it back."

Claudius thought of the one shilling and sixpence he had
paid upon it, and knew that Joe would laugh at the idea of
returning the money; he therefore made a fresh essay to
persuade his master to receive it.

"Will you allow me to open it, Sir?" asked Claudius. "It appears to be something of importance by the way in which it is directed."

"Does it so," returned the doctor. "Well, you may do so. Yes, open it, if you are certain it is directed to me."

"Quite certain, Sir," replied Claudius, who had his knife already open, and before a countermand to his commission to open it could have been given, even if the doctor had wished to have done so, the cords by which it was secured were cut, and in one half-minute out tumbled,—what do you suppose, gentle reader? neither a dead cat, nor a live hare; no, nor an infernal machine, or some combustible matter, which, on the touch of an affixed spring, was to explode, and blow out the brains of the inspector,—no, nothing of the kind,—but a *hat!* Yes, a canonical hat; the identical one which the *friend* of the doctor, the renowned Mr. Charles Augustus Montrose, had kindly taken to get cleaned by Mr. Brush, of Emsworth.

"Ha! ha! ha!" roared Claudius, as the castor lay before him.

"What have you discovered," enquired the doctor, "that you are so delighted?"

"A hat, Sir," replied Claudius.

"A hat!" echoed the divine. "What hat?"

"Your hat, Sir," answered Claudius.

"*My* hat!" rejoined his reverence. "What mean you?"

"Why, Sir, your hat which the gentleman took to be cleaned at Emsworth," replied Claudius.

"Impossible!" said the doctor.

"Indeed it is, Sir," returned our hero, "and here is a letter also, which is directed to your worship."

"*My hat* and a *letter,*" soliloquized the doctor. "Well, come in,—come in. Let me see it."

Thus directed, Claudius opened the doctor's chamber door, and, with the canonical beaver in one hand, and the letter in the other, approached the bed whereon the doctor was already seated in his morning gown, waiting to give audience. With the affection and joy of an old friend, his reverence received his hat; and, after examining it with close scrutiny for some time, to be fully assured of its identity, as being his own *dear* hat, he exclaimed, "This is wonderful! It is indeed my lost hat,—and a letter too,—umph! This, I suppose, will explain all   I dare say the rascal has repented him of his sacrilegious conduct, and while his compunctions are strong upon him, is anxious to make restitution. But have you examined the box particularly?"

"Yes, Sir," replied Claudius, "every corner of it."

"And are you certain there is not a purse in any part of it?" demanded his reverence.

"I am quite sure there is not, Sir," answered Claudius.

"Umph!" returned the doctor, "that looks suspicious. Here, put the hat carefully upon the table, while I see what information is contained in this scrawl. Oh! it is plain," he continued, as he proceeded to break open the epistle, "as clear as demonstration can make it, that the hoax played upon me was the work of this villain. Yes, yes,—I see it all now;—very strange I did not see it before. He met me according to his own preconcerted plan, and I must confess he played his part very adroitly; but I am not in the commission of the peace if I do not punish him for it yet. So! What says he?—umph!

'Sir,—Allow me, in the first place, to thank you for the excellent dinner with which you entertained me at Emsworth. I can assure you, on the word of a gentleman, I never enjoyed wine more, and shall feel most happy to take a glass with you on some future occasion. I have returned your hat, as I suspected any attempt I might have made to exchange it for cash would have set some evil-thinking person upon thinking evil of me. Your handkerchief I will borrow, as it will be useful; and as for the purse, and the good supply it contains, I shall keep it as a token of kindly feeling and high respects for one whom I shall always be happy to serve to the best of my abilities.

'I remain, Worshipful Sir,

'Your steady friend,

'CHARLES AUGUSTUS MONTROSE.'

"The barefaced audacious scoundrel!" exclaimed the doctor as he finished this very polite note—"I am not 'in the commission of the peace' if I do not punish him to the utmost rigour of the law;—here, Claudius."

"Sir," replied our hero, whose gladness of spirit was scarcely controllable as he heard the hoax placed to the account of Mr. Montrose, and thereby having all suspicion removed from himself.

"Go immediately," said the doctor, "and tell the Innkeeper I wish to see him."

"Yes, Sir," said Claudius, and he retreated towards the door.

"Yet stay, stay," added the rector considerately, "I'll take an hour to think the affair over; go and desire breakfast to be prepared for me in half an hour." "I will, Sir," returned our hero, and withdrew.

The doctor instantly left his bed and proceeded to dress, during which engagement his mind was actively employed debating on the course he had better pursue in the present rather unpleasant state of affairs. After a while he wisely concluded that the best way would be to let it alone. To noise the hoax abroad would be, he sagely considered, unwise, as in that case he would become the butt of ridicule for the whole of his parish, and if he touched the subject at all he was convinced it would soon spread far and wide. He at once settled it in his mind that he could return to Christchurch at his leisure, as if he had performed the *important business* upon which account he had visited Chichester. His next determination was to take an early dinner, and then travel as far as he might feel disposed during the remainder of the day, so as to shorten his journey for Saturday sufficiently to secure his arrival at home by the afternoon or evening.

Thus purposing, he descended to the parlour and strove to make himself comfortable amidst a plentiful supply of the good things of this life.

"Claudius," said the doctor, "I intend to leave here by three this afternoon; you will therefore see that the horses are in proper condition to start by that time.

"I will, Sir," replied Claudius, wishing at the same time that something might occur to prevent their leaving Chichester before Saturday morning.

"The business I have to transact," continued his reverence, "will not engage me long,—two or three hours at the utmost; but during that time, if you wish, you may look about the place."

"Thank you, Sir," replied Claudius.

"There is one thing," observed the doctor, "I wish you to observe particularly,—that is, that you take no notice to *any* one, on our return home, of the unpleasant circumstances I have met with on my journey—Miss Georgiana would, I am certain, be terrified beyond bearing if she knew all."

"I will be sure, Sir," said our hero, "to attend to every thing you wish me."

"And the business," added the doctor, "which I am here upon, I wish no one should be informed of."

"You may depend upon it, Sir," returned Claudius, "no one will hear of it from me. You know, Sir," he added, "I am ignorant of what the business is."

Nothing could be more true than this declaration of our hero; and even the doctor himself was ignorant of any business he had at Chichester;—all that *was* known Claudius *did* know: and had his reverence been in possession of as much information of the cause of his travelling so far, as Claudius was, the "commission of the peace" would, without doubt, have been exercised with a vengeance upon the waggish culprit.

After our hero had attended to his master's wishes, and supplied his own wants, he availed himself of the permission granted him, and sallied forth from the inn to feast his eyes with such sights as Chichester and its vicinity afforded.

He had not proceeded one hundred yards before his eccentric mischief-loving propensities were strongly excited, and with all the ardour of a young lover he longed to exercise them.

The place to which our hero had unconsciously strolled, was that airy and beautiful promenade,—and which, with the exercise of *a little public spirit*, might be rendered inimitably beautiful,—the North walls. The thick foliage of the lofty and majestic trees by which it is skirted on one side, threw a refreshing shade over the walk, while open and extensive views embraced enclosed fields, through which numerous heads of cattle ranged at pleasure, and gardens stocked with richly laden fruit-trees and bright-coloured flowers, with habitations of various kinds, from the stately mansions of the wealthy to the lowly picturesque-making cottages of the poor. In the distance, as far as the eye could reach, the grounds belonging to Goodwood,—the seat of his Grace of Richmond,—rose in gentle sweep, or in bold sublimity; while forests of pine, fur, larch, and mountain ash, gave a fine relief to the back ground of this natural picture, which appeared to glow with the warmth and life, as the rays of the bright and cloudless sun fell upon it.

As Claudius sauntered on,

> " Feeding his eye with rich and glowing scenes,
> Which seemed with ecstacy to fill his soul,
> And raise his spirit up from earth to heaven,"

his ear was saluted by the inharmonious notes of an angry

huckster's voice, who was talking with more strength of
lungs than sagacity or understanding to his sole companion
in travel, a long-eared ass, and after the method which some
sapient pedagogues adopt to make their pupils receive instruction, followed up his addresses by heavy and quick
blows.

Referring to the same species of quadruped, over whose
cold remains a distinguished living poet has poured forth

    ,"Some sentimental lines with sorrow rife,"

Byron observes with biting sarcasm,

    "A *fellow* feeling makes us *wondrous kind.*"

In many cases it does so, but in the present instance it
did *not ;* for the stupid ass of a huckster had no more
kindness in his stony heart, towards his fellow ass, than if
the most distant connexion did not exist between them.

Claudius turned to the point whence the sounds proceeded,
and beheld the dumb animal, heavily laden with various
kinds of small wares, over whose head and shoulders the
rational brute continued most unmercifully to deal his blows
from a rough heavy hedge-stake, for the purpose, as it
seemed, of increasing the speed of master Neddy.

"For shame of you," said Claudius to the fellow as he
passed him below the wall. "Who are you ?" enquired the
angry, fierce-looking churl; "mind your own business, or
I'll come and sarve you the same."

"I should think not," replied Claudius; "you wouldn't
dare treat the poor donkey as you do, if it could help itself."

"That's my business," returned the huckster : "the ass
is my own, and I have a right to do what I please with my
own property."

"You have no right to use it so cruelly," rejoined our
hero, "and if you do not desist, I'll see if there is not some
person in the city who will compel you."

"I'll dust your master's jacket for you," returned the
fellow, "and cut those smart things off your shoulders, if
you don't mind your own business, I tell you;" and so say.
ing, he moved on, following his ass.

The insulting way in which the huckster had referred to
his dress, roused the ire of our hero, and he at once deter.
mined to let loose the mischief-loving spirit which he felt

page 289.

growing stronger within, by way of retaliation; he accordingly retraced his steps, and saw the dealer in small wares enter the city, when he commenced bawling out the various commodities he had to dispose of.

Claudius had not followed the huckster more than one-third down North Street before he saw him enter a public-house. This appeared a favourable opportunity for him to put his project into execution, and he embraced it with agility; for, stepping into a chemist's shop, he procured a small quantity of turpentine, and begged a piece of lint, which having well saturated in the liquid gum, he stole up to the ass, and, with subitaneous action, succeeded, without being observed, in placing the wet lint under the animal's tail, and then retired to a distance to notice the result.

In a few seconds the turpentine began to operate, and the hitherto taciturn, steady-paced Neddy began to sound an alarm, and whisk about his tail, and throw up his hind quarters with as much agility as the most freaksome pet-lamb. " Ehaw, ehaw," rang through the street, and drew master huckster from his cups, and a crowd of sage citizens round the ass.

"Why what the dickins be come to you now?" enquired the huckster.

"Ebaw, ehaw, ebaw," replied the ass, striking out his legs most vigorously.

"Why what have you been doing to your donkey, Master Matty?" asked a lean, woe-begone-looking common councilman, the very counterpart of Shakspeare's starved Apothecary; having "famine in his cheeks;" "you have been tormenting your animal again : this must be seen to."

"No, I assures you, Sir," replied Master Matty, " I haven't done nothing to the *hannimal*, I arn't touched him with the weight of my little finger to-day. I *'spose* he has made up his mind to have a lark this morning—I'll give it to him yet," he added in an under-tone.

At the moment the threat dropped from the huckster's lips, as if Master Neddy had not only heard but understood it, he wheeled suddenly round, bringing his hinder parts in a direct line with the shop window of the common councilman, before which the huckster was standing; and then backing suddenly, he threw up his legs, and raising a louder " Ehaw, ehaw," than before, placed his hoofs in his alarmed master's

ultimatum, and sent him flying through the bow window, to
the utter destruction of sundry panes of glass, and the discomfiture of lots of pastry, over which he tumbled and
roared like a baited bull.

" Ehaw, ehaw, ehaw," again shouted the ass, and starting
off at the top of his speed, tossed from the hampers which
were slung across his back, cabbages, potatoes, carrots,
onions, and various other culinary articles, while a host of
boys and men followed the animal with shouts and laughter.

In a few seconds the street was lined with males and
females, who rushed from their shops like bees from their
hives ; to the infinite amusement of whom, unlike most
public performers, Master Neddy continued to execute a
number of ludicrous gymnastic feats without seeking for a
reward.

Claudius felt something like regret that he had caused the
animal pain, but that feeling was soon lost amidst the delight he experienced as he witnessed the punishment the
huckster had received, and the effects which were still
resulting from his roguish trick.

" Ehaw, ebaw, ebaw," continued to resound through the
city, from the loud braying of the ass ; and by the time he
had reached the Cross he had succeeded in completely
emptying his hampers, and then bolting, without asking
leave, into a fruiterer's shop at the corner of South Street,
he capered among oranges, nuts, and raisins, to his own
unvarying and almost unceasing tune of " Ehaw, ebaw,
ehaw."

In the mean time Master Matty was cleaning his face and
head from a quantity of raspberry jam, with which he had
been so completely plastered as to look like a moving mass
of raspberry tart. It was soon ascertained that all the injury
Matty had received was a few slight cuts upon his fingers,
without regarding which, he rushed as quickly as possible
from the scene of destruction and ran down the street in
pursuit of his donkey. Every step he took brought him
into contact with scattered portions of his property, while
the cheers and laughter of the entertained assembly as he
passed them, rendered him for once a popular character.

By the time that Matty reached the fruiterer's shop, his
donkey had attained the zenith of his novel exhibition. Never
were the feats which Neddy performed, surpassed in their

ludicrous and extraordinary character, excepting in a dancing-room, by some aged matron striving to imitate youth,
or by an infirm and gouty beau paying homage at the
shrine of beauty.

"Come out, you confounded brute," exclaimed Matty.

"Ehaw, ehaw ehaw," brayed his ass.

"Take care," cried the honest, good-tempered fruiterer,
whose character and commodities are not surpassed in the
country. "Take care, or he'll send his heels through the
window."

"Touch him up behind," cried some voices in the street.

"I wish you may get it," responded Mr. Matty, who
feared to encounter that part of his beast a second time.

"Why he's only gone to get a fresh load," observed
another voice.

"Ehaw, ehaw, ehaw," returned the Neddy.

"Ain't he a capital dancing master?" enquired a bumpkin;
"only see how cleverly he capers to his own music."

"Ha, ha, ha," roared the mob; "go it, my fine un," and
smash went another package of oranges, while the juice
flowed over the shop floor.

"Ehaw, ehaw, ehaw," again chaunted the capering brute.

After many fruitless attempts, Matty at length succeeded
in getting hold of the halter which was attached to Neddy's
head, at which he pulled with all his might, while the
fruiterer behind attended to the advice of some on the outside of his shop, and "stirred him up with a long pole."

"Ehaw, ehaw, ebaw," again roared Neddy, and out he ran
with more speed than his master, over whom he passed
without doing any injury; and running, kicking, and braying, turned the Cross in a moment, clearing his way of all
obstructors, as cleverly and as gently as a squad of the
police force would have done it.

At the end of half an hour the effects of the turpentine
passed off, and Neddy once more became mild and tractable;
or, as his master declared, "as gentle and quiet as a sucking
lamb, as he always was after his trick was over."

The sympathy of the kind-hearted citizens was excited
towards Matty, and in consideration of the amusement they
had enjoyed, and the loss he had sustained, a subscription
was set on foot for him, by which he realized more profit
than he had sustained injury; while the conviction fastened

M

upon his mind, that the vagaries of his ass were a punishment inflicted for his past cruelty; and he determined, and kept his resolve, never to treat it unkindly in future, so that the short pain it endured through Claudius's frolic, resulted in an entire exemption from all harsh treatment.

However great our hero's wish might have been to remain at Chichester until Saturday morning, his desire underwent a sudden and entire revolution, and he now felt equally anxious to leave the place. The lint which he had placed under Neddy's tail had been discovered and abstracted, and suspicions began to circulate, which excited the fears of Claudius that his trick might be discovered; and he already half imagined that he felt the wrath of the people of Chichester, in every kind of filth that clean city could furnish, poured upon him.

CHAPTER XIX.

" ARNOLD.—Mean you the gentleman
    Whose transformations, like an harlequin's,
    Are multifarious and of novel sort?
RIBOLD.—The same, good Arnold: keep him in your eye—
    A fellow most expert at business,
    Who sword or wallet wears with equal grace.'
                  THE SPANISH BRAVO.

WHEN poor Burns wished one of the *best* wishes he ever did wish, he exclaimed,

" O that some power the gift would gie us
    To see oursels as others see us !"

The sentiment contained in the whole stanza is rich, and the stanza itself is beautiful; the *first* line of it we almost feel tempted to adopt ourselves, and wish " that some power the gift would give us," to write poetry ! as in that case we might describe, in language befitting the occasion and subject, the feelings which possessed Claudius as he retired to the stable of the inn, and might then tell of the " leaden-winged hours," the " lagging periods of time," and a thousand other things, all contained in stock poetic expressions; besides weary, tiresome, and fatiguing moments which appeared to lengthen as they passed away, until the appointed period came at which the doctor had determined to dine. But in this case we feel,

" Wishes would be vain, desires fruitless all."

The divine spirit of poetry has been so long grieved and vexed by the vile imitations of leaden-headed, would-be poets—the indifference with which some of the greatly gifted have treated the "influence divine," and the gross insult and cruel neglect which the struggling genius of others of her favoured, but poor proteges, have received from the ignorant, purse-proud, and the mercenary dealers in the proceeds of other men's brains, that she appears almost to have deserted this part of our world. I am, therefore, obliged to narrate in the plain and unadorned language of simple prose, that which would, in the graceful and adorning dress of poetry, have appeared to so much greater advantage.

The hour, the long wished-for (by Claudius) hour of dinner came. The doctor commenced and finished his meal, then washed his hands, and *then* washed down the solids he had consumed with sundry glasses of wine ; while our hero did the best his fear of detection allowed him, which was but little, and then very cheerfully attended to his master's commands to see the horses were ready for their journey.

As the clattering hoofs of Mayflower struck fire from the rough stones in West Street while following Ithurea, the sounds were more agreeable to the ears of Claudius than were the "full-toned" organ's notes which in lofty swells were now pealing through the long and lofty aisles of the Cathedral on his left; he only wished he could strike the rowels of his master's spurs into the flanks of the horse he rode, that he might thereby have provoked and increased her speed.

The pleasant village of Fishbourn was soon gained and passed; and, as at a smart trot they left the habitations of man behind them, the dull spirit of our hero became more and more buoyant; and at length all fear of detection sub-siding with increasing distance, he had leisure to reflect upon the scenes he had witnessed during the morning ; and while he thought them over, felt himself so convulsed with laugh-ter as to be scarcely able to sit erect in the saddle.

The reflections and feelings of his worship were of a very different character from those of his servant. He had been befooled and, as he judged, robbed by the same audacious villain;—had been soused in dirty water,—hand-cuffed as a felon,—and taken to be an insane person,—and was now returning to his home and his parish with almost unbearable misgivings of mind that by some means the secret of his perils and mishaps might get out, and then, in all probability, the laugh of the ignorant and profane might be raised against the learned and reverend magistrate.

As he drew near Emsworth, the recollection of the ridiculous figure he had cut at the inn on the preceding day, determined him to pass through the town with as much speed as possible without exciting particular notice, while Claudius looked forward with sanguine expectations of making his second appearance there, and laughing over the adventures with the servants in the house.

" Claudius," said the doctor, partially reining in his horse to allow our hero to come up with him,—" I wish to pass through Emsworth without being known ; therefore, when you approach the inn at which we stopped yesterday, I desire you to follow me quickly, and by no means look towards it."

" I will do as your worship wishes," returned Claudius ; " but is it not possible, Sir, that some information may be obtained of the fellow who so greatly abused your reverence if you were to call ?"

" Why, true, true," replied the doctor ; " you are a shrewd lad, Claudius, and if you continue to improve, and are steady, notwithstanding your mean origin, you may, as Whittington did, rise to honour. I should not, indeed," continued his worship, " be surprised if one day you were to be placed in the commission of the peace."

" I hope if I ever should be so honoured," said Claudius to himself, " that I shall not keep a servant to hoax me."

" Well,—as you observe," resumed the rector, after a few moments' consideration, " it is *possible* information may be received, and therefore,—but no, no,—I will not stop there to-day."

" If the rogue should have been taken, Sir," resumed our hero, " he will, in all probability, be retained at the inn a short time."

" Why, that is true," added the doctor,—" that alters the case,—and,—still I think," he observed, musing,—" I think I shall not call."

Claudius felt determined not to be beaten, and therefore, returning to the charge, he observed,—" Perhaps, Sir, the *gentleman from London* may be there, and if so, would it not be desirable, your worship, to give *him* information ?"

"How said you ?" returned the magistrate, "give him *information ?*"

" Respecting the return of your hat, your reverence," replied Claudius, scarcely able to retain the gravity of countenance he had put on.

"Aye, true, true," responded the doctor,—"ha! ha! ha!— that had escaped me,—yes, yes, such information is essentially necessary to be communicated, it may possibly lead to detection,—we *will* stop ;—and yet,—now I think again,—I will *not* stop ;—no, no,—you shall call there and, from me, make the necessary enquiries. Say I have received my hat, with a most insulting note,—but no,—don't mention the note; the insults I have received, so far as known, are quite sufficient; if more is told, I shall be taken for an arrant fool,—do not mention the note. If the officer should be there, desire him, from me, to proceed directly to Portsmouth, and if he apprehends the villain, to acquaint me of it forthwith. I will ride on to Cosham. You will attend to my directions with all possible despatch, and then come to me at the principal inn of the place I have named, where I will wait your coming."

"I will be sure and obey your orders, Sir," returned Claudius.

Just then they crossed the bridge which separates the counties of Sussex and Hampshire, and ascended the hill with which Emsworth commences, at an easy pace, until having reached the point which turns directly on the right, bringing the inn in view at which the farce of yesterday was performed, the doctor pressed the rowels of his spurs against the sides of Ithurea : away she went like the wind, and in less than a minute and a half he descended the street on the opposite side of the town, and stretching along as fine a piece of ground as cattle ever trod, in a short time entered and passed the villages which intervene between Emsworth and Cosham, and at the latter place, according to his appointment, he put up.

In pursuance of the order he had received, our hero halted at the Crown, by the host of which celebrated inn he was immediately recognised; from whom, as well as from the hostler, who came to take away Mayflower, he received a hearty greeting.

"Well, my lad," said Boniface as he entered the house, "I am glad to see you safe back again;—how far is his worship behind?"

"Behind what?" asked Claudius.

"Why, behind his squire," returned mine host; "you have ridden forward, I suppose, to announce him?"

"Not exactly so," replied Claudius; "I always keep my place, and doing so, keep *behind* my master! He has passed through your town, Sir, and by this time, I have no doubt, is half-way on the road to Havant."

"Is he so?" returned the landlord, changing from the warm bland tone with which he had first addressed our hero, to one distant and chilling—"pray what may be your squireship's wishes?"

"I have called by order of my master," returned Claudius, "to inform you that he has received his hat, which was returned him safely by the Portsmouth coach."

"Indeed," observed Boniface, "and what then?"

"Why, *then*," said Claudius, "he wishes to know if any information has yet been received respecting the thief?"

"Oh, is that all?" returned mine host; "'Let every man look well to his own business, and every man will have full employment,' is my motto: now, as that is *no* business of mine, I don't trouble my head about it."

"Well,—but my master supposed you might have heard something about him," returned Claudius.

"Umph!" said my landlord, "I have as much of my own concerns to attend to as I can manage, as indeed every honest man has;—your master must learn to look at his company before he becomes *friends* with them."

Our hero felt astonished at the change both in tone and conduct which the lately cringing and fawning landlord displayed; he had yet to learn that a mercenary, ignoble-minded wretch makes his own interests the centre and circumference of his desires; to compass this he can *become* every thing, and *give up* almost every thing;—he connects himself with the family of man only so far as this all-engrossing object can be promoted. So it was with the landlord of the Crown;—his expectation of obtaining the further and good custom of the doctor, made him wondrous kind to Claudius on his arrival; but on finding that would not be experienced, he gave loose to the ill manners of his greedy nature, and ceased to be civil.

Claudius had purposed to have taken some refreshment, but finding the insulting conduct of the landlord increased as the conversation progressed, determined at once to curtail its quantum by cutting short his visit, and therefore, making as low a bow as the celebrated King Nash was wont to do when, during the palmy days of his sovereignty, he conducted the ceremonies at Bath, he left the selfish host, and hasted to the stable for his horse, and after a halt at the Crown for something less than half an hour, cantered after his master at his leisure,—

> "Now fast, now slow,
> As fancy led him;
> Entranc'd by scenes long fam'd in story,—
> Portsdown and Portsmouth,—Hampshire's glory,"

On reaching Cosham our hero had but little difficulty in finding the doctor, as the best inn, and the best room in the best inn, where the *best*, the *very* best accommodation and provisions could be obtained, was invariably—and without doubt, very properly—selected by his reverence for the enjoyment and gratification of his well-beloved self.

Having well bestowed Mayflower in a warm stable, beside the stall occupied by Ithurea, Claudius proceeded to the parlour in which the doctor was sitting, in order to furnish him with an account of the success of his mission to the Crown Inn.

" Well, Claudius," observed the rector, as our hero entered the room where the jolly magistrate was making every reasonable effort of which he was capable to drive away the unpleasant reflections to which the mischances of his journey had given birth, by liberal potations of some excellent Port and an earthen tube;—" Well, Claudius, have you obtained any information touching the business upon which I sent you to the Crown ?"

" No, Sir," replied Claudius, " not exactly so."

" Umph," returned the doctor. " I suppose, then, no tidings have been received of the villain."

" Not any that I could hear of," said Claudius.

" Umph, repeated the magistrate ;—" What said the landlord ? did he express any hopes of success in the affair ?"

" None whatever, Sir," answered our hero ; indeed, he has no hopes on the subject; it is very evident, Sir, he feels no concern about the matter."

"How!" said the doctor, sharply,—"no hopes,—no concern?"

"None whatever, rejoined Claudius, "nor wishes either, if his conduct and language may be believed."

"Why did he not at once enter heartily into the business?" interrogated his worship;—"Did he not appear to feel anxious the villain might be apprehended?"

"Not in the least, Sir," answered Claudius; all he said was that he had business enough of his own to attend to without troubling himself with that which belonged to other persons."

"I am not in the commission of the peace," exclaimed his worship, "if I do not half suspect there is some collision between the parties:—said he nothing more?"

"Nothing, Sir," replied Claudius.—"O yes, Sir;—I beg pardon;—now I remember he did say something else;—he observed your reverence should learn to look at your company before you becomes *friends* with them."

"The varlet,—the audacious fellow!"—roared the doctor, spluttering with rage;—"What does he mean to insinuate? Well, well, he has lost my custom for ever, and the advantage of my recommendation, by his conduct. If he were within the range of my influence as a magistrate, I'd make him *feel* the impropriety of his freedom of speech at the quarter sessions: the renewal of his license should at least be suspended upon suspicion. Such upstart, prating, low-bred hinds, want putting down; and if some change be not speedily effected, I see most plainly that the influence and respectability which belong to a justice of the peace will be lost.—I'll see to it, however;—a change must and *shall* be brought about. This levelling system we owe to the spirit of radicalism, which is spreading like poisonous leaven through the entire mass of the population. All distinction and order will soon be abolished, that's plain, and no gentleman will be at liberty either to *do* or *say* what he pleases:—monstrous!"

How long the wine and temper-heated divine would have continued his vituperation, or to what broad expressions he would have given utterance in reference to the anticipated *compression of the power and privilege of a gentleman!*—alias, an aristocrat—is impossible to conceive, so glibely did his tongue manage the subject, had he not been cut short in his voluble display by the entrance of a venerable-looking personage, attended by a servant-man in handsome livery.

"Pardon me, Sir," said the apparently infirm stranger, addressing himself to the doctor; "I fear I am intruding,—I will retire."

"By no means, Sir," returned the doctor, as the stranger turned towards the door as if to leave the room,—"I shall feel honoured by your company."

The gentleman bowed politely and courteously.

"John," he observed to his servant, in a weak and tremulous voice, "look well to the horses, and see that every thing is in readiness for my leaving in one hour."

"I will, my lord," replied John, as he bowed and left the apartment.

"My *lord*," said the doctor to himself—for that powerful monosyllable had been pronounced most distinctly, or otherwise there was a certain talismanic influence in it which rendered the most dull and heavy ear and head quick of understanding.

"Aha," yawned his lordship, as, after seating himself in a large arm-chair, he stretched his aged limbs with lordly freedom, and to a lordly extent; "It has been intensely hot to day, Sir."

The doctor replied in the affirmative.

"I feel particularly happy," rejoined his lordship, "at this unexpected meeting with a gentleman of the church, as, if I mistake not, Sir, you are."

".I am an unworthy member of that distinguished body," returned the doctor, with considerable truth.

"Ah," said his lordship, "I conceived I must be right— *we*, Sir, who have to do with courts and kings, have too little intercourse with gentlemen of your calling; they are seldom or never found there—that is, Sir, *in* their sacred character; at court they become in spirit lords and courtiers —each one carousing with the spirit of a Rochester, is a patronage and place-hunter. I love the church, Sir, I may say adore her; I always feel anxious to support and uphold the dignity of the clergy, and by that means I feel confident I uphold my own."

"You are perfectly correct in your judgment, my lord," responded the doctor, flattered, as he felt he was, by the company of a peer, and the compliment he had paid the cloth. "You can furnish no evidence of more conclusive character than the *upholding the dignity of the clergy*, of your being a true member of the church."

" You will excuse me, Sir," rejoined his lordship, " but I feel the pride of an English lord strong within me ; it is, I suppose, hereditary, but I *never* mix in company *freely* without knowing with *whom* I associate. May I be favoured with the name of the gentleman with whom it has been my good fortune to meet ?"

If the doctor had felt any thing like objection to make known *who* and *what* he was, he could not, in the present instance, have indulged in such propensity. The *appearance* of his lordship was prepossessing in the highest degree. His hair, which was of snowy whiteness, hung in natural ringlets about his shoulders, being parted with beautiful exactness down the centre of the front of his head. His face was finely formed, and notwithstanding the venerable and slightly bent form of his person, had still, when closely viewed, all the fire and expressiveness of youth about it ; while in his manners there was a winning suavity, a courtly ease, which, when associated as it was with the title of *lord*, was perfectly irresistible. There is, indeed, little doubt that if he had been as ignorant as a wild Caffre or as rude as an untaught dweller of the Polar regions, that fascinating and transforming sound of *lord* would have changed his ignorance into wisdom, and his barbarian vulgarity into a novel point of fashion. What has *frequently* been, may occur again.

" I feel flattered, my lord," rejoined the doctor, " by your question—I am Doctor Titheum, rector of Christchurch, and have the honour to hold a commission for the peace in the county of Hants."

" Ah! indeed !" exclaimed his lordship. " Doctor Titheum, I am most happy to meet you ; I have heard your name mentioned frequently, with high commendation of your extensive legal, as well as theological knowledge, and your particularly close attention to the duties of your office. Have I not had the pleasure of meeting you before ? my memory is somewhat treacherous now, yet I half fancy I have done so."

" Never, that I am aware of, my lord," returned the doctor ; " indeed, I am certain you never did."

" Well, Sir, I may be in error here," replied his lordship, but of one thing I am quite certain, and that is, that Lord Prigall, of Fillchum manor, in Radnorshire, will always be right glad to meet Doctor Titheum, either there or at his town residence."

"My lord," returned the rector, "I feel flattered by your lordship's very polite invitation: and yet it is exceedingly singular that I have no recollection of ever having heard of a manor in Radnorshire bearing such name as—"

"Why that is very likely," interrupted his lordship; "I have but recently come into the possession of it; and as I feel desirous to honour the memory of the man from whom I inherit it, I have called it by his name."

"Ah, indeed," responded the doctor, "that accounts for my ignorance. Allow me, my lord," continued the doctor, "to pledge you—may your lordship live long to enjoy your possession."

"You are very kind, Doctor Titheum, very kind indeed," returned my lord Prigall, "and I sincerely thank you."

"Your lordship will, I hope, oblige by taking a glass of wine with me at this our *first* interview," said his reverence.

"With great pleasure, my dear doctor," returned his lordship. "I am more happy than I can express to meet you here, doctor," he added, as he raised the glass to his lips and sipped it. "It it rather acid, I fear—I dare not take it; the truth is, I have given over drinking any thing but Champagne, a considerable time past; you will, therefore, I hope, assist *me* in a bottle." So saying, he partly rose to pull the bell, when the doctor, with the agility of a youth, anticipated him, observing, "Do not trouble yourself, my lord; I am your junior, although a little over my teens—ha, ha, ha; allow me to meet your wishes. Bring me a bottle of Champagne," he added, as the landlord appeared.

"No, no, doctor," returned his lordship, "it must be *my* order—nay," he continued, as the doctor was about to remonstrate—"I insist upon it."

"If your lordship will allow me to have it in my power," replied the rector, "to say that your lordship has taken a glass of wine with *me*, I shall feel obliged."

"Well, well," rejoined the easy and good-natured lord, shaking his venerable sides with laughter, "you gentlemen of the church have a privilege of directing us, and we are bound to attend to your directions,—I yield the point."

The wine was placed upon the table, and in a short time the old lord proved that he could keep pace with the wine-loving doctor in swallowing Champagne, so that a second bottle was speedily required.

"You will excuse me, doctor," said his lordship, "but I have just thought of a memorandum I wish to make, for the information of a *friend;* it will not engage me two minutes." So saying, he took a slip of paper from his pocket-book, and with a pencil made the notice he had referred to. Having so done, he folded it up, and placed it in one of his waistcoat pockets.

So greatly did the doctor relish the company of Lord Prigall and the sparkling Champagne, that if the noble lord had been disposed to remain at Cosham the whole of the night, his worship would have neither felt or displayed any disposition to separate from such good company. As, however, his lordship's business required haste, he rose for the purpose of summoning his servants; but such was his age and infirmity that he staggered, and would have fallen on the floor if, fortunately, the doctor had not caught him. He rested himself a moment or two on his lordship's arm, and then reseated himself in his chair, expressing his obligations for the assistance he had received.

A third bottle was placed upon the table; when his lordship, after drinking two glasses more, directed his horse to be brought out immediately; and then, bidding the doctor "good evening and a pleasant ride," seated himself in his saddle, and, followed by his servant, set off in the direction of Portsmouth.

As the doctor felt no inclination to leave what he should have to pay for, he set to, with a hearty will and good spirit, to finish what remained of the third bottle of Champagne; which, as he performed the pleasing task leisurely, occupied nearly one hour after his lordship had taken his leave.

As the last drop of the last glass drained into the doctor's mouth, he felt sleep's soothing power steal gradually over him :—he had before done his utmost to repulse its influence, and had partially succeeded; but now nature felt vanquished beneath the continued attack. Stretching himself composedly in the large chair which he occupied, he in a few seconds was engaged presenting his free-will offerings at the shrine of the oblivious god Somnus.

As the business-minding landlord felt it to be no business of his to keep awake, or awake out of sleep, his comfortable guest, he allowed him, without any disturbance, to sleep his sleep out.

During the profound state of unconsciousness into which

the doctor had fallen, he—as many others before and since his day have done—dreamed! and in that dream what strange and wild fantasies perplexed him. "Thieves! thieves!" escaped in muttered accents from his lips; "Murder!" and "Fire!" followed.

As if pursued by a legion of bloodthirsty bandits, the doctor strove to run; but an invisible hand held him and prevented his flight. He writhed and struggled in his roomy arm-chair, and then threw about his arms with strange velocity; and as he again shouted in louder tones than before, "Thieves! thieves!—murder!" he stretched forth his legs with a powerful action, as if a strong charge from a galvanic battery had been forced into his system, determining in his perturbed imagination to escape from his assailants, when the table, on which stood the remains of his Port-wine, with bottles, glasses, &c. &c., received the quick plunge, and in an instant the loud crash of bottles and glasses,—the fragments of which bestrewed the floor,—roused the sleeper from his slumber, and brought the landlord and two or three servants into the room.

"Thieves! thieves!" again shouted the doctor, standing upon his feet amidst the destruction he had produced; and then rubbing open his eyes and looking round him with the utmost consternation, he enquired, "What have I done?"

"What is the matter, Sir?" enquired mine host, for the darkness of the apartment prevented his perceiving at the moment the ruin which had been wrought.

"I have, I believe, been asleep for the last half-hour," returned the doctor, "and have been haunted by a most distressing dream;—I question if I have not done some little mischief—however, I will meet whatever expenses the damage done may come to. I feel happy at having escaped so well as I have from the robbers and murderers by whom I have been pursued. But what is the hour, landlord?" he enquired.

"Nearly half-past nine, Sir," returned mine host.

"Half-past nine!" roared his reverence,—"Never; it can't be,—you are jesting."

"I assure you, Sir," said the landlord, "I make a true report; 'tis *nearly* half-past nine."

"Astonishing!" returned the doctor.—"Why now, I perceive, the light has passed away, and it must be as you say. Is it possible I can have slept nearly *four* hours?"

" I cannot tell how long you have slept, Sir," answered
Boniface; " but I have looked in several times, and, finding
you fast asleep, did not feel myself warranted to wake you."

"This is most extraordinary," said the doctor.—" Never
in my life have I committed myself in such a way before.
Your wine must, certainly, have qualities in it of an unusual
character."

" My wine, Sir," replied the landlord, " is the most genuine in quality, and fresh from the wood. I can pledge all
I possess on the truth of my statement.

" Astonishing!" repeated the doctor, musing.—" It was
my full intention to have left three hours since for Lichfield;
but that is out of the question now, and I must from necessity
become your guest for the night."

" I shall be happy, Sir, to accommodate you," said the
landlord, " and, I flatter myself, your wishes will be fully
met—my accommodations are of the best kind. Gentlemen
of the highest respectability have favoured me with their company, and, without an exception, have professed themselves
gratified on leaving. Here, Mary!" shouted mine host,
placing his mouth close to the door, which he held ajar,
" bring some candles immediately."

" Before the ordered lights had shed their cheerful radiance
through the room, the table had been placed upon its own
foundation; and as the landlord departed to prepare a supper for the doctor, Mary appeared at the door with a pair of
mould candles.

" Well, I declare!" shouted the startled girl, as she stumbled over the fragments which still covered the floor, " here
is something vastly wrong. Whatever can have befallen this
'ere room?—if I doesn't think it is bewitched. Why, it was
only last week that our parson broke all the glasses on the
table in consequence of a quarrel with Mr. Mouldycrust, the
Overseer, *consarnin* a poor woman who was starved to death,
and about a new church rate, I think they called it; but, as
I never gets no time to go to the church, I understands as
much about it as a Hottentot; and as I can't read much, I
don't know if it is to be found in all the Bible;—but I dare
say it is, or the parson wouldn't wish it."

" Well, well, my good girl," said the doctor, " mind your
own business, talk less, and let those who are paid for it manage affairs above your comprehension."

" Talk less, Sir!" returned Mary, looking the doctor full

in the face with all the expression in her countenance of a woman who felt that one of her *highest* delights and native prerogatives was invaded by the rector's recommendations to her to hold her tongue,—" Hold my tongue, Sir!" she replied. " Well, things are coming to a pretty pass, indeed! Umph!—Poor people now are neither to think nor speak! 'Pon my word, if it ain't enough to drive all the people to America, where, as I understands, servants ain't servants, but are considered as good as their betters, and are allowed to talk just as much as they please, and no *contradiction*. I don't wish to talk, Sir, I assure you; I ain't in the habit of doing so;—nevertheless, it ain't pleasant to be told *not* to do it. I never likes to be *compulsioned* to *do* or *not* to do any thing. I suppose," she continued, commencing at the same time to gather up the fragments of the broken glasses, &c., " I suppose *talking* is all I shall get for clearing away this mess."

" What is your name, my good girl?" observed the doctor.

" My name, Sir, is Mary," she replied; " or if you please, Sir, ' *quiet* Mary,' as I am called."

" Well, Mary Quiet," said the doctor, " I—"

" No, Sir, if you please,—*quiet* Mary," interrupted the silent girl.

" *Quiet* Mary, then," returned the doctor, " here is a trifle for your trouble in clearing away this *mess*, which by accident I have caused;" and so saying, he handed her a shilling.

" Thank you, Sir," said Mary, dropping a curtsy, and giving a smile, which together, by many a connoisseur in those kind of things, would have been considered worth at least a score such pieces of silver.

" One thing remember, Mary," observed the doctor, as she retired;—" But for your *tongue* you would have had *twice* the sum you have received."

" Indeed, Sir," returned Mary, " Indeed, I am obliged to you; for the future," she added, mistaking the doctor's meaning, " I will be sure to attend to your advice: and when next I go into the company of a gentleman, I'll give up being *quiet*, and *talk* as much as I can; and then, perhaps, where I now get one shilling I shall get two." So saying, Mary curtsied again, and left the doctor alone, smiling at her simplicity and *cacoethes loquendi*.

CHAPTER XX.

" Take care, take care of your money-bags ho !
 The robbers are lurking about ;
Foul words and hard blows the caitiffs bestow,
 And fright with their horrible shout.

"Ho, ho ! but they're cowards, they flee, they flee,
 Although loudly 'revenge !' they cry,—
Up, up, and pursue them, for friends are we,
 And rather we'll perish than fly."

BORDER BALLADS.

THE doctor had just finished his breakfast on Saturday morning, and *quiet* Mary, after serving him, had retired for the purpose of desiring her master to send in his bill, when his worship prepared to meet the demand by taking his purse from his pocket. At the moment he did so, the landlord entered with a slip of paper, resembling in length a "bill of *fare*" rather than a "bill of *charge.*" As the eyes of the doctor fell upon his purse, he started and stared as if the fearful head of a basilisk had protruded from the silken net; while from his lips came forth an expression of mingled surprise and alarm.

" Bless me !" said his reverence, after a few seconds' pause, during which time he continued to gaze as if horror-stricken at the purse,—" Bless me ! what can all this mean ? Surely, as Mary said, this room must be troubled—at least I am."

"What is amiss, Sir ?" enquired the landlord, alarmed in his turn by the strange language and still stranger looks of his reverence.

" What's amiss ?" roared the divine,—" Why, my purse has undergone a change in colour, most extraordinary and unaccountable, since I came to your house yesterday afternoon—*then* it was *green,*—*now,* as you perceive, it is *yellow !*"

" I see the purse in your hand, Sir," returned the landlord, "is yellow, and so it must have been yesterday. You have made a mistake, Sir."

" No such thing," returned the doctor ; " I am positive what I state is correct: my purse, when I entered your house, was *green.*"

" You may soon satisfy your mind, Sir," resumed the landlord, "by referring to its contents,—if they have not undergone an equal change with the colour of the purse."

" Good," said the doctor; "mine had in it something
above twenty pounds in gold—this appears heavy : still the
change in its colour is astonishing.   I'll see, however, how
far the sum and character of its contents agree with what it
had in it last evening."

So saying, the doctor poured upon the table the contents
of the yellow purse, when, instead of gold,—

> " Forth roll'd a tide of bright but baser coin
> Than that which heads of majesty adorn :
> New farthings glitter'd on the shining table ;—
> With wild amaze, and loud as he was able,
> The owner shriek'd, and cried with words uncivil,
> ' The house is troubled, or by thieves or devil !' "

The lines we have quoted from the pen of a distinguished
bard of the olden times, as finely portray the result of the
exhibition as if they had been produced for the occasion.

" There !" exclaimed the doctor; "what think you now,
landlord ?"

" Why, I begin to think," returned mine host, " that I
smell a rat.   I am not to be bamboozled, depend upon it ;—
no, no, I am too wide awake for things of that sort.   Do you
suppose, now, you are going to play such a trick upon me ?"

" Bamboozled !—tricked !" exclaimed the doctor, jumping on his feet.

" Aye, aye,—be quiet, now," returned the mild and unmoved landlord, who really imagined the doctor was an ad-
venturous swindler from London, who was endeavouring to
play off a trick upon a country inn-keeper.—"Don't disturb
yourself," he added; "we'll make it all right.   You knew
as well before as now, all about your *yellow* purse, or your
green purse, or whatever else colour you please,—as well as
of its bright contents."

" Sir," retorted his reverence, with increasing warmth,
" do you mean to insinuate that I am a rogue, or that I—"

" I do not mean to *insinuate* any thing," returned Boniface, in the same cool determined way; but I do declare
plainly and without any *insinuation,* that my bill must be discharged.   I have not the pleasure of knowing you, and cannot, therefore, allow you to leave my house until a settlement
has taken place."

So greatly had the doctor been astonished by the transformation he had witnessed in the changing of his gold to
farthings, that a folded paper that had fallen from the purse

with the "small coin," had, until the present moment, escaped his notice. Now, however, it attracted his attention;
and, taking it up, he opened it, and to his utmost consternation read from it as follows :—

"*To the Reverend Dr. Titheum, Rector of Christchurch, and
Magistrate in the County of Hants.*

"Sir,—Notwithstanding your denial of having been in
my company before to-day, you will, no doubt, recollect the
time and place of our meeting when you have read this note.
I have been compelled to adopt the dress and character I have
assumed on the present occasion to prevent annoying delays
from those who might desire my company. For your Champagne to-day I thank you; as also for your prompt assistance
when I was about to fall: my object then was to exchange
purses with you, having enclosed this note in mine;—I need
not inform you I succeeded while leaning on your arm. I
hope the potion with which I have enriched your wine, will
take effect by sending you fast asleep for a few hours, as in
that case I shall be able to take a fresh dress and ride a few
miles distant.

"For all past favours, my dear Sir, accept my acknowledgments; and when next I have the pleasure of meeting you,
believe me I shall be most happy to prove how much and
how truly I am yours to serve.

"Lord Prigall,
Alias C. A. Montrose."

"P. S. I hope you will not forget to call at Filchit manor-
house, soon—ha! ha! ha!"

"There, Sir!" exclaimed the doctor; the eyes of whose
understanding were by this polite epistle immediately opened.
"There is an explanation of as dark and vile a transaction as
ever a gentleman was duped by;—but I am not in the 'commission of the peace' if this unparalleled impudent villain's
deserts shall not be fully met."

The very peculiar circumstances in which the doctor had
been, and was still placed, were soon explained, much more
to the satisfaction of the landlord than his own gratification.
The former trick which this *soi-disant* lord had played his
worship, and the loss he had now sustained, excited the best
feelings of mine host, who at once begged his reverence
would make himself perfectly easy concerning his bill, as the
amount could be remitted at his leisure; while to meet his

present necessities on his way home, he tendered the loan of whatever sum he might name.

"Necessity has no law," is an adage as common as rogues and thieves in London;—on the present occasion the reverend magistrate felt its influence : and, with whatever degree of reluctance he might have yielded to its power, yet, yield he did; and, acknowledging the kindness of the landlord, he accepted a proffered five pounds,—giving an order upon his banker for it and the amount he owed,—and then, having issued magisterial directions and commands for the pursuit of Lord Prigall, *alias* Charles Augustus Montrose, he once more made a movement towards home.

Claudius felt delighted beyond measure at the variety and beauty of the scenes through which he rode ; and whether he ascended the side of a lofty eminence, or descended into a valley, he felt equally gratified : while with both, and every thing beside, the doctor felt displeased and offended. His mind turned, with tormenting constancy, to the unprecedented circumstances through which he had passed, in consequence of the hoax that had been played upon him ; and while the insult to his dignity, and the losses he had sustained, stood full before his view, with all the aggravating circumstances which might yet arise from his journey to Chichester, he felt half frantic. Claudius, on the other hand, applauded himself for the ability he had displayed in the affair, and felt pleased alike with an escape from suspicion, and the enjoyment he had experienced.

With hard and silent riding,—for the doctor displayed no inclination to converse by the way,—they reached Titchfield in time for dinner ; having taken which, the doctor, as usual (notwithstanding his desire to reach home before night-fall), could not resist the strong inclination he felt to indulge his fleshly appetite with *one* half-pint of Port, and a small quantity of Indian weed.

While thus enjoying himself in the parlour, Claudius, who had managed long before the doctor commenced his feed, to satisfy the cravings of a hungry stomach, had strolled forth by the side of the river Aire,—which, to the great comfort and advantage of the dwellers in Titchfield, runs through the town,—and was surveying with pleasure the beauties of the place, and its admirable roadstead which was seen in the distance, with several vessels riding in Titchfield-bay, near the mouth of Southampton-water.

Having sauntered in this direction some time, our hero turned from his track for the purpose of making a circuitous tour back to the inn;—in so doing, he entered one of the narrow lanes with which the extensive parish abounds. He had not progressed far in the path he had chosen, which he perceived wound round to the church, before, in the most narrow part of the narrow road, he encountered a strange sort of being, who, as he approached, furnished ocular demonstration that the animal portion of him was the strangest part.

The personal appearance of this strange individual would have supplied the lamented and talented SEYMOUR with a rich pattern of Attic drollery, with which he might have embellished his truly comic scrap-book. His person was tall and thin, and, as a whole, singularly enough proportioned; or, rather, like an untrimmed crabstick, it had no proportions at all, except the proportions of deformity, and that, unquestionably, was strikingly prominent. His legs and arms were unusually long; the former of which useful appendages to a body might be said to resemble a pair of hop-poles, although far from being so straight as the most crooked of those supporters of useful plants : for his knees came into such intimate contact with each other, as might have given rise to a question in the mind of a stranger, if they were not actually united; while, on the contrary, his feet seemed to have a strong but indefinable antipathy to one another, in as much as they spread as far apart as the attachment of the knees would permit;—and then, as to length, the feet which bore the ponderous weight of Goliath's colossal form, must have been infant-sized understandings to them,—they were really and truly—*prodigious feet.*

Furthermore, the head of this "*rara avis*" of his species, which looked as if stuck upon a long slender protuberance from between his shoulders, and seemed to be as loosely set as a China mandarin's on an Italian image hawker's board, was very small, on the front of which was a face, long, pale, and thin, and as destitute of whisker, beard, or mustache, as the soft palm of a lady's waiting-maid. His eyes were of ample dimensions, and full of obliquation of vision. The crater-like aperture which served for a mouth, was almost literally from ear to ear; while his nose was a complete Pitt-ite one, sharp-pointed, up-turned, and of unusual dimensions.

᾽ The costume of this wonder in nature was as singular as his person, and appeared admirably adapted to display it, if not to the *best,* at least to the *fullest* advantage. The coat and vest which he wore *were,* or *had been* black ; but, evidently, their original occupants must have been of much shorter proportions than the present wearer. His trowsers were light drab-coloured ; but, unfortunately, they fitted him so tight, notwithstanding the slender character of his shanks, that every step he took threatened to burst asunder the tight-fitting garment ; while at the same time, they were so terribly curtailed in their length, that two-thirds of his slender calves protruded from the bottom of them.

When Claudius first caught sight of this non-descript-looking personage, he was distant from him about one hundred yards. So much was he under the influence of inebriation as to be utterly unable to maintain any thing like a perpendicular position. Sometimes he ran forward to save himself from falling, as if engaged in a chase after his own respectable nasal protuberance ; and then suddenly stopping, he staggered backwards almost as far and as fast.

Before our hero's eye encountered him, he was endeavouring to manage an old chaunt, and still he persevered in the attempt; but so barbarous was the nasal twang which accompanied a husky cracked voice, that the squeeking of a pig in a gate, or the wooing whine of a cat on a moonlight night, would have been considered by a connoiseur of sweet sounds, delectable harmony to it.—Thus it went on :—

> " That *I* rule the parish, who'll dare to deny ?
> No one in the parish is greater ;—
> I'll prove it as plain as the white of your eye,
> Nor seek the black art for a data.
> The little boys quake at my angry brow,
> And are dumb at the name of M'Larish :
> In a word or two more, I'll prove it just now,
> The schoolmaster's head of the parish.
>
> Now 'tis logic as plain as two and two's four,
> That the little boys rule their mammas ;
> And 'tis equally plain from the days of yore
> That the ladies rule all the dadas.
> Now, this being granted, the case is quite plain,
> As sure as my name is M'Larish,
> That in ruling the boys,—I say it again,—
> I rule—aye, the whole of the parish.
>
> At the school, or abroad, my name is rever'd—
> I'm great as a king in my station ;
> And if I'm not lov'd, why, at least, I am fear'd,
> And none can say more in the nation.

> All the little boys seek for the smile of my eye,
> The *ladies* praise Mr. M'Larish;—
> And *none* of their *husbands* will *dare* to deny
> That I am the head of the parish."

Thus braying, Mr. M'Larish continued to advance, reeling right and left like a becalmed ship in a heavy swell, until he was nearly in actual contact with Claudius; when suddenly stopping, as if some astounding vision waved him back, he managed for a moment, like another Apollyon, so to extend his legs and arms as to occupy the entire space of road, and then roared out in as authoritative a voice as he could command, "Who are you?—*Da locum melioribus*," he added, after a moment's pause, "or by my office I'll beat you *in puris naturalibus*."

Claudius's sides were so convulsed with laughter as to render all attempts at the required answer impossible; and hence—"Ha! ha! ha!" repeated over and over, was all that escaped him.

"Impudent dog!" shouted the infuriated M'Larish, mistaking Claudius for one of his pupils.—"I'll make every bone in your skin pay the forfeit' of your impertinence to-day. Give me your name!"

"Ha! ha! ha!" again roared Claudius;—"Will you sing another song if I tell you my name—eh! Mr. Head of the parish?—Ha! ha! ha!"

"Eh!—What's that?" said the pedagogue, dropping his outspread arms, as if the sound of our hero's voice, being strange to him, had suddenly driven away the mist of misconception by which his understanding had been beclouded, and staring full in his face,—"Who are you?" again he demanded.

"Why, I am a gentleman on my travels," replied Claudius.

"Now, by the spirit of Socrates, thou art a lying varlet," exclaimed Mr. M'Larish, hiccuping violently, "and I—(hiccup)—*I*, Mr. M'Larish, constable, clerk of the parish, and schoolmaster, apprehend thee as a rogue and a vagabond." So saying, he darted forward to execute his purpose, by seizing Claudius; but as his vision was rather confused, he seized a young tree which grew by the road side instead of our hero.

As might be supposed, the embrace was a rude one on the part of M'Larish, whose full-grown nose came more suddenly than he anticipated or enjoyed in contact with the rough bark of the sapling, and forth gushed a stream of crimson gore from the insulted organ. It did not require a moment's thought to determine whether or not he had missed his aim. He staggered back a few paces, and smeared the blood over his " very pale" face, giving it a complexion horrible to look upon.

" Sing me another song," said Claudius most provokingly, as he stood enjoying the mischief, " and I'll tell you who I am."

Once more the unsteady eye of the parish clerk, directed by the voice, caught an indistinct sight of our hero, and once again he prepared for a seizure.

" Thou imp of destruction !—Thou scoffer at honour, learning, and office !" roared Mr. M'Larish ;—I'll take thee, dead or alive." So determining, he drew a large clasp-knife from his pocket; which, having managed to open, to the great danger of losing the top of at least one finger, he brandished it furiously, rolling from side to side.—" Now," he added, " if you escape me, say that I am only *magni nominis umbra.*"

"Let me pass," said Claudius,—" Why do you stop my way ?"

" I stop you in the name of our sovereign ruler of blessed memory ;" and he re-commenced his efforts to lay hands upon Claudius, but with as little success as would have attended the attempt to grasp the wind, or to catch a sun-beam.

" Which side the road do you call yours ?" asked Claudius, as the functionary staggered from side to side.

" Which ?" hiccuped the constable ; " why, *both* to be sure," reeling at the same time in such a way as to make good his assertion.

" Are they so ?" said Claudius ;—" Well, then, as I can't stay here all day, I shall take the *middle;*" and so saying, he embraced, as he believed, a favourable opportunity to pass, and darted forward ; when, just at the moment, the head of the parish lurched from the side he had just taken to the centre,—the consequence was, that Claudius's head came in violent collision with M'Larish's magnificent mouth, and in a moment the unsteady pedagogue staggered backwards, and then measured his respectable length upon his mother-earth.

" Murder !—murder !—Thieves !—Help !—help !" roared the prostrate official, rolling about in deep sand, as if to ascertain in which quarter the ground lay.

" I'll go and send you some help," said Claudius, as he darted by him like a shot just discharged from a cannon, leaving Mr. M'Larish to shift for himself.

It was a fortunate circumstance for our hero that no help was at hand, or otherwise he might have been detained in a way, and for a longer time, than would have quite accorded with his liking. After a good run he succeeded in reaching the inn at the moment the doctor had rung for him.

"Claudius," said his worship, as he entered the room, "I intend leaving in a few minutes,—is all ready?"

"All *will be* ready, Sir, by the time you mention," replied Claudius.

"Good," said the rector,—" Good,—hem! Mind me, Claudius; I desire nothing may be said to any one concerning my journey or the business upon which I have been engaged,—you understand?"

"Oh yes, Sir," said Claudius; "and I will be sure and obey the wishes of your reverence."

"Very good," rejoined the doctor; "you shall not lose your reward."

It was a lovely afternoon, when his worship and Claudius crossed the bridge which spans the river Aire, in Titchfield, wending their way towards Christchurch; but, considering the distance they yet had to go, the doctor had certainly indulged himself somewhat too lengthily over his wine; so that the prospect appeared very fair of its being little short of midnight before they reached the rectory.

The moon had risen amidst rolling clouds, as they entered the long dreary forest of Ringwood, otherwise New Forest. The "spirit of the storm" appeared to be abroad; and as they pushed forward, it required no very powerful effort of imagination on the part of a superstitious person, to conceive that the sighings and moanings of the fitful gusts which blew amidst the branches of majestic trees, or rustled in the thick underwood below them, were the wailings of the unfortunate Rufus, whose blood Sir Walter Tyrrel shed here by accident.

It can scarcely be supposed that the reverend doctor was so weak, as that superstition annoyed his learned head; yet, some as learned as he was, have (in consequence of excessive morbid habits) been the slaves of such feelings;—generally, however, as information has been received, the spectral illusions of the imagination have ceased to exist. Admitting, however, that the doctor did rise above such weakness, still he did feel a chilling influence, very like superstitious fear, creep *over*, as the spirit of the Port he had taken, creeped *out* of him—in consequence whereof, without slackening his own pace greatly, he desired Claudius to keep close to him, by quickening Mayflower's action.

"You do not feel any thing like *fear,* I hope?" observed the doctor.

"Not in the least, Sir," replied our hero, most readily and truly.—"I have spent too many nights in a forest, Sir, to be alarmed by a few gusts of wind."

"Why, true,—true, child," returned the doctor; "so much for use; the homely adage is true, 'Use is second nature.' However, there is no need that you *should* fear here; I assure you the road we travel is perfectly safe. There are plenty of forest-keepers about, and passengers are almost constantly passing.—Bless me!" he exclaimed, starting almost out of his saddle.—"Did you hear that, Claudius?"

"I did not hear any thing, Sir," replied Claudius, "excepting the cracking of some of the limbs of the trees, which is usual in windy weather."

"Umph!" observed the doctor, looking about him.— "Never yield to fear; it makes an ill report of a man's principles,—all's right, I assure you;—there again," said his reverence, grasping more firmly the bridle,—"I certainly, as I am a living soul, heard something. I wish the moon would shine out clearly."

"I have travelled a lonelier road, many a darker night, Sir," observed Claudius, without regarding the rector's alarm, "and never met any thing worse than myself."

"Very likely, very likely, child," returned his worship. "You do not believe those idle tales, I hope, which foolish people tell to alarm children with."

"Tales, Sir!" said Claudius.

"Aye,—tales, child," answered the doctor, "respecting spirits—ghosts that is, and the like."

"No, indeed, Sir," returned our hero; "I place my trust in HIM whom the Indians call the GREAT SPIRIT; and I am sure he can protect me from all *little* ones."

"That's well, that's well," responded the divine; "and I assure you, there is no such thing as a—a—bless me, how excessively nervous I am getting!—Surely I heard the bushes parted then."

"No, Sir," said Claudius coolly, "nothing but the wind."

"I am not in the commission of the peace," said the magistrate, "if ever I take another journey like the present.

Oh, if I could catch the villain just now that dragged me from my home !—that is—" ,he added, checking himself, " the rascal who robbed me, and—and—not a fraction of the law's utmost severity should be abated to him—I'd punish him to the utmost extent."

A shrill whistle, as if at a short distance before our travellers, was, now distinctly heard; and, scarcely knowing what he did, the doctor reined in his horse.

" There !—there, Claudius !—Did you not hear that rogue's whistle ?" enquired his worship.

"'I heard a whistle, Sir," answered Claudius; " whether a rogue's or not I cannot say ; perhaps it was one of the keepers calling his dogs, or—"

" Stand !" interrupted a voice from behind, in a tone of thunder, and at the same instant two other wild-looking fellows presented themselves to the almost petrified doctor.

" What do you wish for, gentlemen ?" asked his worship, in a conciliatory tone.

"We wish to pay off an old score," replied one of the party, in a surly manner,—" We have been waiting for you and this youngster since last night; and now we've nabbed you, we mean to let you know it."

" Don't stand palavering there," said another of the gang; " knock the old *feller* over the head, and I'll manage the young 'un, I warrant you."

" Gentlemen !" exclaimed the rector, in the utmost trepidation, " ask what you will of me and I will cheerfully give it, only don't misuse me."

" You should learn to do as you'd be done by," replied a surly voice.—" Nobody wants mercy more than you hardhearted justices, what are the last to show it."

" Well, in the first place, hand over your chink," said the first speaker.

" Oh certainly, gentlemen! certainly!" returned the doctor.

" No words !" roared the ruffian, " but do as directed. Come,—quick ! quick ! or—" and he presented a cocked pistol at his worship's head, while one of his companions held the horse's bridle, as the doctor turned his pockets inside out, after delivering up their contents.

While the worthy personages referred to were discharging their professional duties with the doctor, another of the band attacked Claudius, with much less civility than his master had received at the hands of his attendants. Our hero, however,

bore not the assault with so much gentleness as the doctor. He had not yet so deeply studied the philosophy of non-resistance; and, withal, scorned the thought of yielding without making some effort at defence.

The encounter was so sudden and unexpected, that before our hero was aware of the presence of a third person, the hands of the marauder was actually upon him. In a little time he was dragged most unceremoniously from the back of Mayflower; but not without considerable opposition. During the scuffle he tore the mask which the fellow wore from his face, and at once recognised in the person of his assailant, an old acquaintance—the infamously renowned Philip M'Sheen, alias *Slipgibbet Phil!*

Claudius was fully aware of the strong antipathy, as well as the cause of it, which the Gypsy felt towards him; and made no doubt that his intentions concerning him were of the most deadly order : and while, therefore, he looked for the worst, he exerted himself to the extent of his strength to prevent the evil.

The contest, although unequal, from the size and fierceness of Slipgibbet compared with the youthful character of Claudins, was ably maintained on the part of our hero. The blood of Count Bolio ran in his veins, and scorning to strike so long as he could fight, or to ask mercy at the hand of an enemy by whom he knew it would be refused, he resolved to resist while he had ability to do so.

Twice was Claudius smitten to the ground by his furious and powerful antagonist, but he rose like another Antæus from his fall, each time appearing to gain fresh strength and vigour, and with as much alertness as Jack the Giant-killer is said to have done, he skipped from side to side and back-wards and forwards, and occasionally planted a blow so dexterously in different parts of the Gypsy's body, that the contest appeared likely to terminate in favour of the young pugilist.

During this time, the doctor was accommodating, although with no very good feeling, the *gentlemen,* who had told him he might do as he *pleased,* only they *would* have his purse ; after which they intended to punish him for sundry provocations, which several of their friends had received at his hands. The *only* way of escape from the threatened corporeal chastise-ment, which they assured him should be inflicted with *nettles* upon his bare breech, was, that he should solemnly swear

upon the gospel which he preached, that he would not hereafter, either by word or deed, by himself or in connexion
with others,—annoy, vex, or disturb, themselves or any of
their friends. The doctor trembled at every joint,—as indeed he had sufficient cause to do,—and, while his teeth chattered in his head, so that he could not speak a plain word, he
promised and vowed to *do*, or *not* to do—to *swear*, or *not* to
swear,—upon the Gospel or the Koran, just as the *gentlemen*
present might determine.

It is highly probable, that if those who read of the doctor's
miserable condition by the side of a cheerful fire, and, surrounded by smiling friends, feel disposed to laugh at the fears
which he suffered, and at his ready assent to the proposal
made to him, had been circumstanced as he was,—their hidden
parts about to be exposed, and a large bunch of stinging nettles ready to be applied to the bared extremity,—they would
have been driven to the extremity of their wits, or as readily
conceded to the terms proposed as his worship did; but the
change in condition is *every* thing. He who is stretching his
limbs in comfort before a blazing fire, enters not into the
pangs which those endure who are exposed to all the rigour
of a bitting winter's night; while the man who never felt the
want of a delicate dish, cannot properly sympathize with those
who are starving for the want of a morsel of bread.

Excuse this brief episode, gentle reader, and may you
profit by it.

The oath to which we have referred, was on the point of
being administered in due form, when a distant sound of carriage wheels was heard by the well-practised ear of those
English brigands. A significant and well-understood glance
passed from one to the other of the party as rapidly as
thought. In another moment a vehicle with two outriders
appeared in the distance, which, as the moon gleamed brightly
through an opening in the forest, it was evident approached
at a rapid rate.

Slipgibbet and his associate were fully aware they had not
sufficient force to venture a defence against the advancing
reinforcement; and therefore, beating a hasty retreat upon
the back and shoulders of the supplicating magistrate, they
fled into the thicket, and were lost amidst its thick foliage in
an instant.

The unexpected deliverance which his worship had experienced from the hands of those unmannerly and incensed

villains, had like to have proved fatal to him,—so sudden and
great was the transit which his spirit made from almost killing *alarm,* to almost killing *pleasure;* for on the arrival of the
carriage he found that he owed his second rescue from immi-
nent peril to his old friends, Lord Dashwood and Sir Marmaduke Varney; who, having protracted their stay in the
neighbourhood of Emsworth, were now returning to his lordship's mansion, which was only a few miles distant from the
doctor's residence.

Had it not been for the presence of mind, however, which
Claudius displayed on the occasion, before an explanation
had taken place, it is twenty to one that the doctor's fright
and nervous excitement would at once have been put an end
to by the lodgment of a bullet in some part of his body. .

"Who goes there?" demanded one of the outriders.

"*I—I—I,*" stammered out the doctor, not yet having recovered his speech; the 'loss of which had been occasioned
by his recent fright.

"Answer at once," continued the outrider, who took him
for another Turpin,—"Answer me at once, or you are a dead
man;" and he presented his pistol as he spoke.

"Hold!" shouted Claudius, who, in consequence of being
off his horse, had not at first been perceived—"It is Dr.
Titheum, the magistrate."

"Doctor the Devil," returned the fellow; "I'll doctor
him, and you too, in the twinkling of an eye, if either of you
dare to budge an inch."

"What's amiss there?" enquired Lord Dashwood, putting
his head out of the carriage window, as it drew up.

"Here are some robbers, your lordship, as I take it," replied the servant,—"I have challenged the feller on horseback, but he refuses to answer;—shall I fire, my lord?"

"'Pon my honour!" exclaimed Sir Marmaduke,—"For
gentlemen to be stopped in this kind of way. We had better pass on, my lord, I conceive, and leave the servants to
settle the affair. Positively, I can't endure the vile smell of .
powder,—foh!"

"No such thing, Sir Marmaduke," replied his lordship;
"I'll settle the affair with them in a short time," he added,
cocking his pistol.

The doctor, although he recognised the voices of his
friends, was so completely tongue-locked as to be unable to
make himself known; and to turn his horse's head he dared

not, lest the threat of the outrider should be executed. Claudius, however, as the " 'Pon my honour" of Sir Marmaduke fell upon his ear, ran towards the carriage to clear up the mystery.

"Approach another step," cried Lord Dashwood, "and this ball passes through your body."

" 'Pon my honour," rejoined Sir Marmaduke, as he shifted his seat, and held his head below the carriage window, expecting every moment to hear a whizzing ball from the supposed robber's pistol pass through the vehicle—" 'Pon my honour, this is extremely unpleasant.—"Be mild, my lord," he added, "and enquire what the gentlemen want."

"They want what they shall in a moment receive," returned Lord Dashwood, resolutely, if—"

"My Lord Dashwood, hold," exclaimed Claudius, as he appeared to be in the act of firing.

"Ah! who is it knows my name?" enquired his lordship; "I should know that voice;—who are you?—answer me, or—"

"I am Claudius, your lordship," returned our hero, Doctor Titheum's servant, and here is my master."

"Ha! ha! ha!" roared out Dashwood, lowering his pistol. —"So you and your master have taken up the honourable profession of highwaymen, have ye? ha! ha! ha!"

" 'Pon my honour," shouted Sir Marmaduke, raising his head most heroically, and looking as fearless as a steel-clad chieftain from the carriage window.—"This is very surprising. Why, how now, doctar,—Why don't you approach?— We only defend ourselves against robbers—'pon my honour; —You have no cause to fear us, I assure you;—Why don't you approach?"

"No, no," said Dashwood, convulsed with laughter, "you have no cause to fear us,—none in the least, my dear doctor."

"I feel happy, my lord," replied his reverence, once more recovering his speech, and changing his position,—"more happy than I can express, to meet you once more;—I have nearly been frightened to death, I assure you;—we have actually been beset by robbers."

"Ah! 'pon my honour," said Sir Marmaduke, as the doctor proceeded to state their recent unpleasant circumstances, "how extremely fortunate that we came up as we did: it is impossible to conjecture what would otherwise have been the consequence, 'pon my honour."

It was at once determined that the doctor should take his seat in the carriage, while his lordship's footman should mount his horse, and, in company with Claudius, bring up the rear. Matters were soon settled; Mayflower, who had retreated to a short distance as soon as Claudius was off his back, was easily caught, and as easily re-mounted by our hero, who, falling back, took his appointed place behind the carriage.

The doctor was soon comfortably seated by the side of Sir Marmaduke, and a *full* explanation, with several addenda, of his Quixotic adventure in the forest, was given, to the high entertainment of the friends as they proceeded with rapid pace towards home. The understanding which was entered into at Emsworth respecting visiting Clifton and its vicinity was confirmed; and without any further disaster or adventure, the doctor reached the rectory after an absence of *three* whole days, having in that time discharged some matters of grave and important character, of which the reader is already fully aware, being minus between forty and fifty pounds, enriched, however, with that which is more valuable than gold, —practical instruction in the fact taught by his own experience, namely, that *"a man greedy of honour is easily imposed upon."*

CHAPTER XXI.

"I tell you, man," the Parson cried,
"That none of all our race
As *we*,—whom all the world deride
Hold such a wretched place."

"*Indeed!*" cried Hodge, and scratch'd his head,—
"Then why such hardship brook?
I cannot tell, can you,—eh, Ned?"
"No!—but I'll ask the cook."

"You'll ask the cook! and why, pray, Ned?"
"Because, beyond a *book*,
Or *preaching*,—they love being *fed!*
Therefore,—I'll ask the cook."

REASONS FOR KEEPING PLACE.

Most authors who commit blunders,—and there are but few who do *not*,—either by putting *in* what should be left *out,* or leaving *out* what should have been put *in,*—most such gentlemen, we were about to observe, manage most dexterously to lay the blame of such blunders upon the broad and strong shoulders of their printers, by making, or *endeavouring* to make, the public believe that such errors are typographical mistakes. Now, *we* are more honest and honourable than so to act ;—let every beast bear his own burden, say we. Aye, gentle reader, we repeat it ; and the expression causes not a blush to tinge our cheeks ;—*we* are more honest and honourable than thus to act. We feel ready to acknowledge that there are things which might have been left *out* in the preceding parts of the present work;—we do not, intend, however, to *point* them *out;*—and there is *one* subject which should have been put *in* in the last chapter, and that is,—a solemn pledge on the part of Lord Dashwood and Sir Marmaduke Varney, made and confirmed to the Rev. Dr. Titheum,

> " Never to speak of that which they had *heard,*
> Or tell of what they with their eyes had *seen.*"

The plea set up by the worshipful divine while enjoining them to silence, was the same with that he had employed with Claudius, namely, the anxiety which he felt lest the statements which might be made should affect the health of Georgiana.

Well assured that in the silence of his friends he should be secured from the gibes and jeers which otherwise he might be called to endure, he went *boldly* into his house, as one who had performed a world of "important business ;"—and then, after making *brief* enquiry of those who were up, and giving *brief* replies to questions put to him, went *boldly* to bed.

Our hero, however, was not quite so fortunate as his master ; to him appertained not the same power as that possessed by the doctor, to speak or not to speak ; to *ask* questions, or to *reply* to those which were *asked,* as he might feel disposed ; for no sooner had he entered the kitchen than Sally, the housemaid, on one side, and Mistress Fatpan, the cook, on the other, saluted him with their incessant congratulations on his safe return,—a custom which Claudius thought

> " More honoured in the breach than in the observance ;"

which were followed up by a thousand questions concerning where he had been, and what he had seen and heard.

It is not always prudent for ladies in the presence of wooers to congratulate too kindly, or even at *all*, a second person of the masculine gender; jealousy is like tinder, a small spark sets it on fire. Joseph the butler felt so just then. "Jealousy," as one observes, "shot through his eye and wounded his peace,"—he noted with more attention than occasion called for, the familiar and joyous way in which Mistress Fatpan received our hero, and therefore urged Claudius to be quick and accompany him to the stable, to assist in attending to the horses.

"I insists upon it," said Mistress Fatpan, "that Claudius shall not go to the stables to-night; hasn't he had work enough already to-day? No, no, I sees no more reason in working a free horse to death, than in the white of an egg."

"For shame, Mister Joseph," echoed the housemaid, "you wouldn't think of taking the lad out again before he has had no *refreshingment*, would you?"

"Why, as to the matter of that," replied Joseph, whose eye was fixed upon the cook's as he spoke, and whose wrath he feared to rouse—"a little time couldn't harm him; we shall soon have done, and then—"

"Done or not done," exclaimed Mistress Fatpan, who was a perfect woman in meeting opposition by opposition—"or soon or late, *I* say he shall *not* go."

"I am obliged to you," said Claudius, turning to the best sort of *friends* a man can have, the females—"I am greatly obliged to you, but I can soon do what I have to do, and I don't feel too fatigued to attend to it."

"Well, but *we* insists upon it, you shall not go," returned the cook, who appeared to conceive that Mister Joseph had trounced too closely upon her prerogative of having her *own* way. "You shall not go,—Shall he, Sally?"

"*Sartenly* not," replied the housemaid; and laying hands on Claudius, they placed him in a chair between them, while Mister Joseph, half frantic at the attentions which he saw Mistress Fatpan lavish upon our hero, left the room in high dudgeon.

"I'm blest," exclaimed the butler as he departed, "if this doesn't beat all I ever comed a-near; I wonder what next."

"Now, Claudo," said the cook as soon as Joseph had disappeared, "now let us hear all about your journey."

Claudius laid his finger significantly upon his lips and remained silent.

" Why what do you mean?" exclaimed Sally, looking with surprise at our hero's action, " why don't you open your mouth, and tell us about the journey?"

" I'm dumb," replied Claudius.

" Dumb, dumb!" shouted Sally, " ha—ha—ha ! did any dumb person ever speak before, I wonder ? Come now," she added coaxingly, " I should so like to hear what you have seen."

" I'm blind," said Claudius.

" You're what ?" cried Mistress Sally.

" *Blind*," returned Claudius, " *stone* blind."

" You're *mad*, I rather think," retorted the housemaid, "Didn't you see nothing what's worth telling a body what is confined here from *Genvery* to *Disember* ? tell me now."

" I'm deaf," replied Claudius.

" You are a *booby*, that's what you are, to tantalize one so," cried Sally, " can you hear that ?"

" Oh yes," returned our hero, " perfectly well, never heard any thing better. Why, how you look at one, Mistress Sally, as if you were incredulous, or doubted my veracity ; but if you have any doubt about what I state, only ask the cook."

"*Ask the cook !*" cried the housemaid, nettled at what she considered our hero's obstinacy, " and pray what am I to ask the cook about ?"

" Why, ask if I am *not*, that is, if I am not *to be*, on all particular occasions, deaf, blind, and dumb."

About all that Claudius said there was a degree of mystery or incoherency which Sally, with all the depth of penetration upon which she prided herself, could not fathom, and simply for this reason : it so occurred that Sally did not happen to be present when Claudius received his first lesson from Mistress Fatpan, and therefore of course was ignorant of the instruction he had received on that occasion ; while, on the other hand, Claudius imagining that every servant in the doctor's establishment was acquainted with the particular course of scholastic drilling which the before-mentioned governess had adopted, naturally enough concluded that Sally understood it, and therefore referred her to that personage with the laconic direction—"Ask the cook."

Now it so happened,—and strange coincidences do sometimes take place—it so happened that at the moment Mistress Fatpan saw Joseph leave the kitchen, she expressed the wish that Claudius would furnish the particulars of his journey ;

and then, before he had time to reply, she hurried to her private store to procure a drop of her own well-beloved cordial for Claudius.

As we have already stated, the house was a *large* old-fashioned one, and the kitchen was of the same character, so that when Mistress Fatpan had entered her closet at the remotest part of the cooking apartment, the questions proposed by the anxious Sally, and the responses given by Claudius, were alike unheard by her: this explanation will account for the mystery which existed in the above recorded scene.

"Now, Claudo," said the good-natured cook, as she returned from the closet, bringing with her a bottle of cordial, alias cherry brandy,—"while I give you a treat of my rarest cordial, you shall treat us with an account of your journey. I dare say it has been full of *adventerings :* come now, drink, and tell us."

"Why I have been trying to get something out of him ever since you left us," said Sally, "but I cannot obtain a single word of information, except—'Ask the cook'—why he positively declares, and sticks to it as if it really was the case, that he is deaf, blind, and dumb."

"Ha, ha, ha," roared Mistress Fatpan, catching Claudius's meaning in the twinkling of an eye; "now that is *hexcellent*."

"What does he mean," enquired Sally, "about 'ask the cook?'"

Mistress Fatpan explained in her own luminous way, and added, "You are an *hexcellent scollard*, Claudo, only you makes a *little* mistake regarding times and places, as one may say. What I said about being blind, deaf, and dumb, only regards the *sarvents* and the kitchen; you are to hear *double*, to see *treble*, and to talk *a hundred times more*, respecting master and parlour folk.—Don't you see, Claudo,—eh?"

"Why not quite clearly," replied our hero, wishing to gain a moment's time and breath, that he might consider the best means of escape from the boring of the inquisitive cook and housemaid; for he well knew if a sentence escaped his lips touching any of the difficulties in which himself and the doctor had been placed, it would be multiplied *ad infinitum,* and in a few hours become an accredited tale through the whole parish; and therefore he had made up his mind not to communicate a word.

"Bless me!" rejoined the cook, "how dreadfully stupid you must be. Did I not tell you, you were to be blind, deaf, and dumb?"

"Yes, to be sure you did," interrupted our hero; "and I told Sally so,—did I not, Sally?"

"I don't know," replied the housemaid; "but I'll ask the cook."

"Well," continued Mistress Fatpan, "as I was saying, you are to be blind, deaf, and dumb, in the kitchen; but you must *hear* all you can,—you must *see* all you can,—and you must *tell* all you know, *consarning* the parlour, for the purpose of putting *us* on our guard : for, with *all* we can learn, it is a hard thing to trick masters now-a-days. Now you understand,—don't you?"

"Oh yes," said Claudius, "that's all quite plain;—aye, aye, I see it clearly now,—ha! ha! ha!"

"To be sure, you do," responded the cook;—"I knew you would. Here, drink this little drop of cordial, and then let's have the information."

Claudius received the presented glass, and swallowed half its contents, and then returned the remainder, gasping for breath, to Mistress Fatpan; who, laughing at the "poor little chicken," as she called him, kindly assisted our hero by drinking what he had left; after which, pouring out a *brimmer* for Sally, and another for herself, which they disposed of without making a wry face, they listened for Claudius's relation.

Calling to his aid all the invention he could muster, and giving what he had to say *multum in parvo,* he succeeded in accomplishing a most difficult task—satisfying the curiosity of the two ladies, without exposing his master or himself. The pleasantness of the journey,—the good entertainment they met with,—the friends they made,—the beauty of the city of Chichester,—its magnificent cathedral,—the tones of its organ, and other things equally instructive and entertaining, supplied Claudius with as much to say as was necessary; and by the time he had concluded his narration, Joseph entered from the stable, to whom the cook gave one of her winning smiles, as she handed him a glass of her cordial, observing—"Here, Joseph, *dear :* I'm glad you have returned. This will do you good." How powerful is "woman's witchery," and with what consummate skill do they accomplish their purposes,—a word—a *look*, from a female, if rightly applied, hushes at once the raging storm in the bosom of man. So now it was ; the smile and kind expression of Mistress Fatpan smoothed in an instant Joseph's wrinkled brow, and produced an amicable feeling between him and all present.

The Sabbath morning was about three hours old, when Claudius succeeded to obtain his discharge from the kitchen, and retired to bed ; where, in consequence of the previous day's ride, and the small quantity of brandy he had taken, he soon fell into a sound sleep, from which he did not wake until past ten o'clock ; and, in all probability, would have continued to sleep on even then, had he not been roused by a rough shaking from the strong hand of Sally, who was wishful to make the bed.

" Claudo, Claudo !" she called :—" What in the world is this,—are you going to sleep all day ?—Here's a fine piece of business ; the doctor has been up almost a quarter of an hour, and in a pretty temper he is, that I can tell you."

" What's the matter ?" asked Claudius, starting up in a fright.

" I don't know, exactly," replied the housemaid ; " but I'll ask the cook,—ha ! ha ! ha !"

" Eh,—what ?" returned Claudius, rubbing his eyes, which as yet were only half open.—" Why, what o'clock is it ?"

" I don't know, exactly," repeated the housemaid, sarcastically ; " but I'll ask the cook. However, I can tell you *one* thing,—the doctor is up, and you'll know all about it in a little time ;—he's in a precious temper for this blessed morning."

" Is he so?" returned Claudius, with indifference, " indeed, I'm glad to hear it ;—but has he enquired for me yet ?"

" I don't know," was the repeated and provoking reply of Sally ; " but," she added archly, as she left the room, " I'll ask the cook."

As soon as the housemaid left the apartment, Claudius left his bed ; and, with all the expedition he could command, proceeded to dress ; and in five minutes from the time he commenced, he had donned his clothes and was in the kitchen.

" Ha," yawned Claudius, " I fancy I have over-slept myself a little this morning."

" I fancy you have, and *not* a *little*, Mr. Claudo," returned the cook.—" Now, don't stand there yawning and stretching ; —I declare you'll give me the *garping*," added the cook, yawning.—" There now,—I shall do nothing else but garp, garp, garp, all day long."

" I hear the doctor's out of temper," observed Claudius.—
" What's the matter ?'

" Aye,—I fancy he is above a little out of temper ; even
Miss Georgiana can't please him."

" What is it all about ?" enquired our hero.

" Why, something consarning having to do duty to-day, I
fancy," returned Mistress Fatpan ; " and he's not in the humour for it,—and, for that matter, it is hard to say when he is.
Joseph took him a note this morning, as you warn't in the
way, which I understands comed from Mr. Milksop, his curate, who says (as Joseph says), he heard the doctor say,—
that he can't do duty to-day, because he had a *haxident* last
night, as he was going home from a party. He had taken a
leetle too much wine, and fell into a horsepond, and would
sartenly have been drowned hadn't it been for Dick Awle, the
shoemaker, who seed the haxident, and pulled the curate out,
and then led him home ;—however, he is laid up this morning, and can't leave his bed.—' Confound the church,' said
the doctor, as he read the note ; ' I wish it was at the
very——.' I won't say where he said, Claudo ;—but hark !
there's his bell,—run now, Claudo, and get your lecture."

" Aye,—make haste," cried Sally, who entered the kitchen
at the moment Claudius was leaving it,—" and if the doctor
asks you any hard question, tell him you'll ask the cook."

" Well, I declare," said Mistress Fatpan, " I'd rather have
a dozen Mondays in the week than one Sunday ; for what
with extra cooking on that day, for extra company, and the
extra bad temper in which the doctor is sure to be on a Sunday, it tires one off one's legs."

" Ah, that's true enough," returned Sally ; " I never saw
such doings, in all my born-days, as on a Sunday here : I
shall give warning, I'm certain, if things don't mend. If it
wasn't for Miss Georgiana I'm sure "the old gentleman" himself couldn't live here;—though, to be sure, we do see a bit
of fun now and then, and pretty often too, when the doctor
and some of the party gets fuddled, or falls out over the cards:
and, I must confess, that the extra trouble we have in clearing away their messes after overturning the tables and other
things, not very pleasant, some of the party pays by the
present of a few shillings,—and then, you know, you contrive
to fill a bottle or two from the remains of a Sunday's rout—
these little things make a small amends."

" To be sure," returned the cook ; " if it wasn't for these

'ere trifles, I couldn't stand it. But listen,—isn't Claudo catching it warmly?" and they both ran to the door to catch the sound of the doctor's voice.

The instant Claudius left the kitchen, he ran to receive his master's orders. As he opened the doctor's room door, he perceived him reading a letter, and talking to himself.

" Did you ring, Sir?" enquired Claudius.

" No, Sir," was the laconic reply, delivered with considerable asperity, while he re-folded his morning gown, and walked in violent agitation across the room. Claudius felt no particular wish that the tempest of the rector's wrath should burst upon himself, and therefore made a motion towards withdrawing.—" Where are you going, Sir?" said his reverence.

" I understood you did not want me, Sir," returned Claudius.

" You understood,—you have no business to understand, —nor any thing else," replied the doctor.—" Confound the church," he continued, as he again put his machine in motion.—" Yes, I did call you," he added, after the lapse of a few seconds, turning to our hero ; and once again he relapsed into a state of partial abstraction.—" Confound that fellow, Milksop ; I wish he had broken his neck before he had taken so much wine last night,—any other night would have been of no consequence ; but just now, when I am almost jaded to death. Well!" he exclaimed to Claudius, " Why do you not do as you are directed ?—How long am I to wait ?"

" I have not yet received any orders, Sir," returned Claudius.

" To do duty after three days of such unparalleled excitement as I have had to endure !" observed the rector, soliloquising,—" This is worse than a place in Purgatory. Let me have breakfast immediately,—do you hear ?—yes ;—ah,— breakfast,—and then,—do you hear ?—let Joseph go and direct the clerk to—to—what the deuce was I going to say ? —then—then—get me my breakfast."

Our hero bit his nether lip to suppress a laugh, which he could but ill conceal, and hasted to perform the doctor's bidding.

The required repast was soon spread before the divine, and Georgiana sat to do the honours of the table. During the whole of the meal the doctor continued, as he emptied his mouth, to give vent to the vexation of his spirit, in broken expletives; while his daughter, with the soothing softness of an angel, endeavoured to calm the irritation of his temper.

"Now, my dear papa," said the lovely girl, "do get your breakfast and dress; it is going on fast towards eleven o'clock."

"I tell you, child,". replied the doctor, "I don't feel disposed to do duty to-day, and yet, here I am compelled against my will to do it;—why, no scavenger in our streets, or pauper in the parish, but has a situation preferable to mine : they can at least do as they please, while I am compelled to attend to that for which I really have no inclination."

"Well; but consider now, my dear Pa—" said Georgiana, lovingly.

"Yes, yes ; consider,—it is all *very* proper to consider, my dear," interrupted the doctor ; "but what am I to consider ? —why, that I am obliged, like a West Indian Negro, to perform a task which I dislike."

Georgiana made repeated attempts to reason with her parent; but it wouldn't do : and how, indeed, could it be expected it would do ? Here was a gentleman—a learned gentleman,—a divine ! whose annual stipend was a mere *bagatelle*,—the price of an old song ;—nay, not so much ; for one, to wit, " *The Old English Gentleman*," not many years since, cost a *young Scotch Gentleman* nearly, or quite, *two thousand* pounds,—whereas, the salary of this worthy defender of the church fell short of eighteen hundred pounds a-year; yet, who, for this despicable trifle, was obliged to do the *unpleasant* duty of performing a service which would occupy nearly half an hour of his valuable time, almost every Sunday in the year,—except when attended to by his curate,—and now, too, when he wished to enjoy himself at home, he could obtain no remission of the *duty*. Look on, ye revilers of the deserving and the good, and weep ! Who, we ask, could but murmur and feel indignant under such distressing circumstances ? What scavenger, or pauper, or any thing else,—if any thing worse circumstanced than these can be,—would change places ?—who can reply to the question ?—Ask the cook.

After grumbling and eating, eating and grumbling, for half an hour, the doctor announced that his appetite was satisfied; and, as it now wanted only a quarter of an hour to eleven o'clock, at which time service was to commence, and as no alternative was presented, the doctor repaired to his room to dress for the performance of his *duty*.

When he again descended to the parlour, half a dozen pairs of shoes were placed before him, upon whose smooth surface Day and Martin had done wonders, in order that his reverence might make his election; but, out of that number, not a single pair suited him: it therefore remained a doubtful question, whether or not he should not be obliged to postpone the *duty* for a week, for the want of such a pair of shoes as suited his worship's fancy.

"Are there no other shoes in the house?" demanded the doctor.

"There is only one more pair, Sir," replied Claudius.

"Well, and why are they not brought?" asked his reverence; "they are the very pair I wish for."

"They are covered with mud, Sir," said Claudius.

"And why are they so?" exclaimed the doctor in a lofty key.

"In consequence, Sir, of my being from home the last three days," replied Claudius.—"I have not had time to clean more than six pairs, and two pairs of boots."

"Don't tell me about time, but go and clean them immediately," said the doctor;—"I'll have them and no other."

"I thought, Sir," said Claudius, "it being Sunday morning, your reverence—"

"What have I to do about Sunday morning?" exclaimed the divine; "I'll have my shoes cleaned whatever morning it is."

Claudius felt convinced that opposition would not succeed, and, therefore, made haste to cover the calf-skin with jet black.

It would have puzzled a learned professor in the art and mystery of cord-waining, or any other professor, to have distinguished between the shoes now brought and one or two other pairs which the doctor had refused;—but what of that? many others, besides Dr. Titheum, have made fools of themselves in a trifling matter—it was his *pleasure* to have those he did have, and that pleasure being met, he stepped into his carriage and was dragged to church.

When the noise of his chariot wheels was heard, as they rolled up to the vestry door, the minute-hand of the dial pointed to a quarter past eleven, notwithstanding that the hand had been put back one quarter of an hour before.

But who had most cause to complain, the waiting congregation which sat comfortably in lofty old-fashioned pews, which prevented their neighbours from observing if they were asleep or awake,—or the laborious doctor who had duty to perform?—Ask the cook.

His worshipful reverence bustled into the vestry, sat gracefully while his sacerdotals were put on, drank a glass of wine for his stomach's good, smacked his lips, and entered the reading-desk. The *first* part of the *duty* was soon despatched, and again the doctor walked statelily into the attiring room, to don his robes of inky colour, and take a second glass of Port; which having done, he prepared to finish his *laborious* and *unpleasant* duty.

The doctor had scarcely taken his seat in the rostrum, before he thrust his hand into the right hand pocket of his coat for his black-covered book, with the intention of bringing forth a delicious *morceau* for the edification of the people of his charge, on *meekness of temper*, but he found it not. He shifted his seat and dived deeper, until the ends of his fingers came in contact with the bottom of his pocket: still he could not feel it. The left hand repository underwent an equally severe scrutiny, but with no better success. His breast pocket in his coat, and every other place in which by possibility it could have obtained a lodgment, suffered the same process as a suspicious voyager from Calais or Boulogne would have to submit to at the Custom House at Dover; but, alas poor sermon! and alas, alas, poor doctor! the search was in vain.

"Confound the thing," broke from the reverend doctor's agitated lips, "what can have become of it? I certainly put a sermon into my pocket, and yet it is *possible* I may have made a mistake. Confound the thing," he repeated in a rather louder tone than before, "what in the name of patience am I to do?"

Fortunately for the doctor, and for the congregation too, the pipes of a powerful organ, and the still louder pipes of a bawling clerk, drowned the voice of the divine, and hence his wrathful exclamations were not heard.

After making two or three rather loud "hems," he succeeded in arresting the attention of one of the wardens, to whom he gave a significant beck, and in a brace of seconds the dapper Mr. Wiggins, peruke-maker and shaver extraordinary to the corporation, was at his elbow.

"Mr. Wiggins," said the doctor, "I'm in a confounded mess."

Page 245.—VIII.

"What's amiss, Sir?" enquired Wiggins, misunderstanding the doctor and snuffing like a beagle off scent—"what's amiss, Sir?"

"Why," whispered his reverence, "being short of time this morning, I came from home in a hurry, and—"

"Bless me, Sir!" interrupted the churchwarden, still on the wrong scent, and snuffing for an *expected* scent. "Had you not. better leave the pulpit awhile and get a change?"

"Get what?" exclaimed the doctor, in something like a loud whisper.

"A change, Sir, in the vestry," said Wiggins.

"I have nothing to change," returned his reverence.

"One can soon be obtained, Sir," responded the sympathizing warden.

"I tell you I have none to change," cried the doctor," if I had *any* sermon it would do, but I came from home without one."

"Whew!" returned Wiggins, "is that all, Sir?"

"All, all," said the doctor, "and is not that quite enough? What I wish is, that you would send or go to my house with all possible speed. Here is the key of my study: bring me the first sermon you can put your hands on; and, do you hear, Mr. Wiggins," added his reverence as his factotum was about to descend the pulpit stairs, "tell the clerk to sing the whole psalm, unless I direct to the contrary, which will give time."

"I will, Sir," replied Wiggins, and hasted on his mission.

During the above colloquy, the attentive congregation gaped with surprise at beholding Mr. Wiggins so elevated, and many were the surmises which took place as to the probable cause. A wag offered to wager a companion a pint of Sherry against a bottle of ginger beer, that the peruke-maker's head would turn giddy; while two young ladies came to the grave conclusion that a marriage was to have been solemnized, which his reverence had forgotten.

It happened most fortunately that the psalm upon which Mr. Splitlungs the clerk had fixed, was the one hundred and nineteenth, so that no danger existed of *soon* stopping for want of stanzas; moreover, as he was particularly fond, like most of his craft, of exercising his vocal powers, he felt no objection to the doctor's order; albeit, he did show a more than ordinary portion of the white of his eyes, as the direction was given, and 'turned a leaf or two to examine the extent of the psalm.

At the end of a quarter of an hour Mr. Wiggins returned to acquaint the doctor that he could not unlock his study door.

"Confound the door," said the doctor; "burst it then, burst it, Mr. Wiggins; a sermon I must have."

"I'll do it, Sir," said the warden, and was again skipping off."

"Yet, stop, stop," cried the rector, in a low whisper, "I fancy I have given you the wrong key; bless me, how came I to make such a blunder?—Why now I look at it, this is the key of my choice wine, which I trust to no'one;—there, Mr. Wiggins, that is the key of the study,—now be quick, and tell my servant Claudius to bring me one directly."

The churchwarden bowed and obeyed, and on went the singing. One by one the congregation grew husky, and gave up joining in what was any thing but melody, until at length few were found to possess lungs sufficient to assist the half-fatigued clerk, who every now and then threw up a look of beseeching character to the pulpit, and longed earnestly for the doctor's signal to close.

The usual time for pronouncing the benediction had some time elapsed, and many a *gude* housewife directed an anxious eye towards the dial in the front of the gallery, as they thought of their dinners, which they feared would be spoiled, or of boisterous husbands, who they feared would scold.

Presently in ran Claudius almost breathless, and hasted to put the black book into the rector's extended hand. A loud "hem!" from the doctor told the clerk to hold his noise. The rector used his handkerchief once or twice, and then, the organ having ceased its pealing sounds, rose in stately form, and, opening his manuscript, proceeded to read the text. All on a sudden the reverend doctor became distressingly husky: "hem" succeeded "hem," and yet the "hemming" brought no relief, until the "hems" became infectious, and went fairly, as regular as the responses, round the church.

What could have affected the doctor none knew but himself and Claudius, who, yielding once more to his inherent love of mischief, had carried matters too far on the present occasion; for instead of bringing his master a sermon, he had handed to him some hunting and drinking songs, at the composition of which, the doctor had been trying his hand. and which he had transcribed fairly into one of the books which had been made to write sermons in.   The first thing which caught his eye, on turning the black cover upon the velvet cushion, was the following exciting stanza :—

> "Come, fill, fill your glasses quite up to the brim,
>   And join in a chorus divine;
> While each quaffs a bumper to *it* and to *him*,
>   The smiling gay god of the wine.
> Hip! hip! hip! hurrah!   Hip! hip! hip! hurrah!
> The smiling gay god of the wine.'

Whatever trash, in the stead of scriptural instruction, Dr. Titheum had long been in the habit of serving to his flock, *this* at least would not do, and he was therefore obliged to yield to stern and uncompromising necessity; and hence, complaining of sudden indisposition, he gravely pronounced the benediction; the organ again struck up; the people, wondering at what they had *seen* rather than at what they had *heard*, retired from the church; while the doctor, happy to bring the matter to a close, stepped to the vestry and sipped his wine, and then rode home; and so ended the *laborious duty* of his reverence for the day, and for what longer period, depended upon the returning capabilities of his curate, or the obtaining other help.

CHAPTER XXII.

> Oh, 'tis a lovely place, I'm sure,
>   So full of London fashion;
> The men so neat, the maids demure—
>   Excepting those who *dash on.*
> And then I hear there's not a few
>   Who day to night are turning;
> Oh, let us go,—dear papa, do,
>   To visit BATH I'm burning.

ALL was busy bustle and perplexing preparation at the rectory of Christchurch on the morning of the Monday after the doctor's return from Chichester.   Two or three fashionable artists in the dress-making and millinery way, had been sent for, and were every moment expected by Miss Georgiana.

The occasion of the stirring excitement was not, as it is possible the reader may conjecture, an anticipated approach to the altar on the part of the rector's daughter, but an expected treat which to the ardent feelings of more than one in the doctor's family afforded almost equal pleasure : namely, "a trip to Bath."

Georgiana had reminded her papa, while sauntering with him on the Sunday evening round their delightful garden, of his promise to take her for an excursion on his return from his important business at Chichester.

"Well, well, Georgie," said the fond father, and all the affection and pride of a doting parent rushed to his heart as he looked at her, "where would you like to go ? that is, supposing I consent to be coaxed by you into a compliance with your desire."

"Why I have heard a great deal, papa," returned Miss Georgiana, "respecting Bath: some, indeed, say it is the most delightful city in England."

"Pshaw, pshaw, girl," exclaimed the doctor; "*who* says so, eh ?"

"Oh I have heard a great many people say so," replied Georgiana; "I can't remember their names this moment, but I am certain, papa, I have heard so; besides, I have read of it again and again, as being the place where Fashion has established her court, and where beauty and elegance are seen in her train; and being favoured by nature and art, it has acquired the distinguished pre-eminence which it so eminently maintains."

The enthusiasm with which Georgiana entered into her description of Bath, and the lofty panegyrics she lavished upon it, wrought so powerfully upon the doctor, whose love of sweet sounds has already been seen, that he actually stopped short in his walk, and stood gazing with admiration and surprise at his daughter, until she had exhausted her stock of heroics; or rather, without allowing her to proceed to the extent to which her enthusiastic temperament would have led her, he observed, as she paused a moment to take breath, "Well, well, Georgie, that's all exceedingly fine, but what then ?—*all* you say only proves, as your French folk would say, '*Avoir la langue deliée,*' your talk is all random trash."

"Now, indeed, papa, that's very cruel," replied Georgiana; "I'm sure if my tongue were not hung as well as it is, you would not like it so well as you sometimes say you do; and as for talking at random, how should I express my admiration of what I highly approve? If, however, you wish it, I will in future only use monosyllables, or reply to all questions by a wink or a nod."

"Bless thee, girl, bless thee," said the fond doctor affectionately, as he imprinted a kiss upon her glowing cheek, and looked upon her with a species of idolization, "you are a little arch wag, that's what you are, and think to cajole me into compliance with your wishes by telling me a fine tale.

"No, indeed, papa, I do not," replied the lovely girl; "but I should like to see Bath;" and she placed her beautiful forehead on her father's shoulder as she spoke, and pressed her cheek against his—"indeed I should."

"Should you indeed?" responded the doctor; "well, suppose I say I will gratify your wishes?"

"Why *then*," said Georgiana, "I'll do all in my power to prove that I appreciate your kindness."

"Then you shall have the opportunity," returned the rector, as he placed his arm within his daughter's, and recommenced his walk; "you shall have the opportunity, my Georgie; not that I for a moment question what you say, but that you may display it: you shall go to Bath, aye, and to Clifton too."

"Shall I indeed?" said the delighted girl; "then I'll commence my proof by pardoning the cruel reflection you just now threw out, respecting my tongue."

"Well, that's proof indeed," said the doctor; "ha, ha, ha! but shall I have no further proof?"

"Oh yes, papa," replied the young girl; "there's a seal of forgiveness," and she gave a kiss which might have been considered by some persons worth a hundred jaunts to Bath; "and besides which," she continued, "I'll ask a great many more favours before we go, and when we arrive at Bath—"

"Excellent," said the doctor, "excellent, ha, ha, ha! I think I must take care how I transgress again, if my absolution is to cost so much: why I question if a cardinal would not have absolved me of a much weightier offence for a less sum than it appears likely I shall have to pay:—but come," he continued, "let us see after supper;" and so saying, they went into the house.

The news of this intended excursion soon reached from Miss Georgiana's waiting-maid to every other servant in the family, and by no one was it listened to with more delight

than by Claudius. His elf-like spirit rejoiced at having a
fresh prospect presented of playing off some fresh tricks, as
well as having an opportunity of mingling with the inhabitants of this busy world, and taking notes of—

> " The foibles and the follies of the men
> Who stand as waymarks to the human race,
> In rank, and wealth, and influence, possessed;
> To warn them of the danger these create.—
> Or gaze, with eye of observation keen,
> Upon the vanities of woman-kind."

The mind of our hero was evidently of original and singular construction.   There were periods when a species of
philosophic abstractedness came over him, and then the
world and the world's vanities pleased him not: all appeared
" stale, flat, and unprofitable ;" under such moody feelings—
like Beattie's Edwin, or Byron's Childe Harold, he loved to
retire from his fellows, and frequently stole to some secluded
spot, where he might indulge in contemplations and reveries
suited to the temperament of his mind at the moment.   These
fits, however, for they were little else, were comparatively of
short duration ; the leading character of this wayward wight
was mischief-loving eccentricity.   To indulge in *this* propensity, he hesitated not to step never so much out of his way,
or to expose himself to consequences of a serious nature.
His wish appeared to be to learn men from *life* rather than
from *books*, and to gain a knowledge of character from personal observation instead of seeking it through the caricature
theories of the schools ; and hence, there was not any thing
singular in the delight which he experienced when the information referred to reached him.

As we have said, all was bustle and preparation at the
rectory on the Monday morning.   The ladies of the needle
had delayed coming at the precise moment Georgiana had
expected, and the consequence was, that a certain quantum
of peevishness, not usually displayed by her, appeared on
this *trying* occasion.

" This is really very provoking," observed the young lady
as she looked at her watch and found it was already at least
five minutes past the time at which the milliner and dress-
makers had promised to attend.   " Whatever can be the
cause of this annoying delay?" she added, walking from one
end of the room to the other.   " I suppose I must despatch
a courier after them, or I shall be disappointed in my prepa-

rations. So saying, she rang the bell, and Claudius, as the factotum of the establishment, entered : " Claudius," said his young mistress, " at what time did Miss Dressheads promise to be here ?"

" At ten, Miss," answered our hero.

" And the Misses Fashionfit ?" resumed the young lady.

" At the same time, Madam," replied Claudius.

" Certainly," said Georgiana, " so I understood; and it is now nearly *seven minutes* past the time,—bless me, how exceedingly provoking it is ! Run, Claudius, run directly, and say, if the ladies cannot come immediately, I must seek some other persons."

" I will, Miss," said Claudius.

" And, Claudius," continued Miss Georgiana," as you return, call on Mr. Calfskin, my shoemaker, and say I wish to see him in the course of the morning ;—or let me see,—aye, tell him to bring me a few pairs of satin slippers ; and as you pass Mr. Scentbox's, the perfumer, step in and desire him to send me some of his most fashionable perfumery ; and inform Mr. Silktwist, the draper, that I shall feel obliged by a sample of some of the last new dresses, and ribbons, and—but never mind, now, the other matters you can attend to when you come back :—now run, Claudius, make all possible haste, there's a good lad."

A smile from such a face as Miss Georgiana's, and *such* a smile as she now gave Claudius, would have been considered a reward for which any noble knight, during the chivalric days of our third Edward, would cheerfully have ventured limb and life ; nor was its magic influence entirely lost upon our hero ; the inspiring influence shot like quicksilver through his system, and with as active and graceful a motion as any knight-errant of the period referred to would have displayed in the cause of lady-love, he bowed his obedience to his young mistress, and vanished like a sprite to execute her commands.

Claudius had not left the house more than five minutes, before " rap, tap, tap, tap," and a violent pull at the door-bell, announced a visitor, and in a few seconds Miss Dressheads, the milliner, curtsied to Miss Georgiana.

This young lady had recently emigrated from the purlieus of Regent Street, and opened a flaming concern in Christchurch. The *cause* of this lady's leaving the metropolis had not transpired, maugre all the anxiety, and enquiry, and

o

surmising, which from her first appearance in the country had been on foot. All that was *known*, and many things were *guessed*, by certain well-disposed females, who looked serious, gave a palsied motion to their wise craniums, and turned up their eyes so as to display a considerable portion of the whites of them as they held converse concerning Miss Dressheads,—all that was *known*, as we have said, in the place where she had established, or was seeking to establish herself, was, that she had come, as aforesaid, from the metropolis, —that a dashing shop window, in which a dashing and large announcement was displayed, stating name, profession, with professions, and from whence she had come—displayed the most fashionable, and the newest fashions, that the *exterior* of a lady's head could require, or that the *interior* of *most* ladies' heads could conceive; so that all the fashionables in the place had fairly deserted the old standards, and had flocked—

"By fashion led, and swayed by prejudice,"

to the shop of the now celebrated Miss Dressheads from LONDON!

This was the sum total of all that was known of this fashionable milliner, and perhaps this was quite as much as was necessary to be known, both for the satisfaction and profit of either party. The "*bas bleus*" of the town were satisfied that having come from London, and having more-over a pretty good share of confidence (vulgar impudence), she must of course be just such a person as the town of Christchurch wanted in its present rising character, and, therefore, just such a person as they ought to patronise;— and above and beyond all this, the point which confirmed them in their high opinion of the superior taste, &c., of this lady adventurer was, that her charges were at least *double* the ordinary ones made by the old professionals in the place, although they had long been complained of as most exor-bitant, and *declared* to be perfectly ruinous by the economic wives who now patronised Miss Dressheads, and proved to be so by too many of their husbands.

"Good morning, Miss Titheum," said the dashing milli-ner, as she entered the apartment; "I fear I have a little ex-ceeded my time; but, really, I am so overwhelmed with en-gagements, that if I could for a short time dispose of myself at half a dozen places at the same time, I should not be able

to attend to the whole. I really fear I shall be obliged to return to London—my engagements, if persevered in, will certainly be the death of me. However," she continued,—for her
voluble powers were nothing impaired by her *numerous* and
killing engagements,—" However, I am proud to have put an
improved taste into motion, which was much wanted here. I
should hope the old-fashioned, common-place people who *call*
themselves milliners, will be able so far to improve upon my
hints, as to keep pace with the wants of the gentry;—but
what am I saying? my wishes can never be realized, that's
certain—the still antiquated formal habits which the *people*
here have so long indulged in, will never be put off; and
hence no lady will ever be able to obtain a bonnet or a cap, or
indeed a head-dress of any kind, fit to put on, unless some
superior hands in our line follow me here. Oh, by the bye,
my dear Miss Titheum, you were wishing to have a bonnet,
if I mistake not, precisely like the one I made for her Grace
the Duchess of Kent."

"Exactly so," replied Georgiana.

"I should like to see it," said Miss Dresshead *(aside)*, as
the play-people say.—" Well, Miss, you shall have it to your
liking. It is, however,—excuse me for merely naming it,—
it is *rather* an expensive thing; and yet, taking into the account the *fashion* and *quality*, nothing *out* of the way—nothing at all."

"About what sum, did you say?" enquired Georgiana.

"Why,—ah—something—ah—about—let me see—yes—
about, ah—ah—five guineas," returned Miss Dresshead.

"Five guineas!" exclaimed Georgiana, alarmed.

"Yes, Miss, *about* that," returned the London milliner,
with the utmost *sang-froid.*—" I have refused making one
this very morning, for a lady who wished one of the same
kind,—because the price didn't suit," she added aside,—
" that *you* might take the lead in the town."

"Five guineas!" repeated Georgiana, half mentally.

"By what time do you wish I should send it home, Miss?"
enquired the milliner.

"Why, *if* I were to have one of that kind, I should require it, without fail, early on Wednesday morning," replied
Georgiana.

"It shall be here on Tuesday night," returned Miss Dresshead; "one or two of my young ladies shall sit up the whole
of to-night upon it."

" Oh, by no means," said Georgiana ; " I could not think of such a thing on any account."

" What thing ?" enquired the milliner in apparent sur-prise.

" Why, as for young people to sit up the whole of a night on my account," replied Georgiana.

" Oh,—is that all, my dear Miss ?" rejoined Miss Dress-head,—" Why, we never think of allowing our young people in London to lie in bed above *two* nights in a week ;—we could never get on if we were, I assure you. But about the dress cap of which you were speaking : that, of course, is to be uniform," continued the ready-tongued milliner.

" Why, really, Miss Dresshead," said Georgiana, " I don't know what to say ; I almost fear to engage in that."

" Oh, my dear Miss Titheum," observed the garrulous lady, " that will not be a long price—I'll warrant it shall be the best British lace, and—"

"And at what price, Miss Dresshead ?" enquired Georgiana.

" Why, for such an article as you must have to match with the bonnet," said the milliner, " and, indeed, which will be indispensable for a lady at Bath,—it will be a mere song, I assure you : it shan't *exceed* four guineas—perhaps something less ;—it would, upon my honour, be dirt cheap at five."

Georgiana half shrieked at the sound ; but a little illumi-nating conversation from the London artiste concerning ap-pearances, fashion, rank, and a thousand other small matters, settled the point ; and, without waiting for any thing posi-tive, she again curtsied politely and retired : observing as she quitted the room,—" They shall be here, without fail, to-morrow evening. I wish you a very good morning, Miss Titheum."

The all-accomplished Miss Dresshead had imbibed the French proverb in its spirit ; although, perhaps, she had never seen it in black and white,—fashion must be supported, " *coute qui coute.*" She was aware that all she had to do with the young and the foolish, was to prove to them it was neces-sary, and she might serve in what she pleased. As we have seen, she had tried her skill at persuading very successfully with Georgiana ; while that young lady (like many others since her day) saw, while Miss Dresshead conversed with her, as she never before had done, the indispensable necessity of donning the top of the fashion at such a fashionable place as Bath : at the same time, she felt a certain unpleasant sensation attending the reflection of the expense she was incurring ; and the only relief she could obtain was, either to turn her mind to some other subject, or urge the fallacious argument,—necessary from circumstances.

Scarcely had the milliner made her exit, than the knocker and the bell kept up a constant medley, as the different tradesmen and callings appeared to present themselves and their commodities before the rector's daughter.

The two dress-makers were soon despatched with their commissions; for every garment, almost, in Georgiana's pretty large wardrobe required some alteration for Bath : while new ones were necessary to be prepared for the ball-room, the promenade, and the gardens.

Mr. Calfskin measured her tiny foot, for dancing and walking slippers ; and Scentbox, the perfumer, saturated the house with his various and recommended stores.

On no previous occasion did Georgiana welcome the close of day more heartily than at the present time ;—what with excitement of mind, and the fatigue of making so many arrangements, and giving directions to so many different persons, she was more than half indisposed. The thought of visiting, what she had been taught to believe, the most lovely and fashionable city in the country, intoxicated her mind, and rendered her doubly anxious to make suitable preparations for the memorable event. Had she believed the oft-quoted line, and acted up to her belief, that,

" Beauty, when unadorned, 's adorned the most,"

she would have escaped half the fatigue she endured. In truth, her own rich adorning, which nature had so liberally supplied, required no art or trickery of dress to set it off ;— ill indeed that it could do was to disfigure and deform, or conceal beauties by its quantity and glare, which it was foolishly enough supposed to give effect to. The ugly and the old alone require to be hid in costly finery ; and for them, fashion, as it is called, changes constantly its form and figure : while the young and beautiful, seduced by the adulation which fortune-seekers and coxcombs pay to dress, assume the same garb,

And veil their loveliness in coverings made
For beauty's apers, who require a shade ;
And so descend, where else they sure would rise—
Conquering the heart, e'en as they'd charm the eyes.

At length the morning of Wednesday came ; the preparations for the party's leaving the rectory had been duly made ; and at twelve o'clock the doctor and his daughter stepped into the carriage. Joseph took his seat on the box, and Claudius, with as much elevation of feeling as if he had been on the eve of taking a journey to the moon, or some equally novel tour, vaulted into, or upon, his place, behind the vehicle. " Click, click," and a gentle twig of the reins from Joseph, set the horses in motion, and off the visitors went towards Bath.

As nothing of any importance, worthy of being chronicled in this memoir, occurred on the road, we feel we have nothing to record ; and, therefore, while the party are pursuing their way towards " the city of Valetudinarians," as our Saxon progenitors called Bath, we shall step out before them and pay our editorial respects to Lady Bolio and her friends, who were already comfortably settled there.

CHAPTER XXIII.

Laius.	A nightingale say'st thou ? Yes, 'tis a nightingale ;
	Its warbling so enchants my list'ning ear,
	That I could swear it that sweet bird of night.
Ixion.	Or is it not like thunder ; at whose noise
	Poor mortals quake, and fear to list again ?
Laius.	Why, by my troth, 'tis very thunder-like !'
Ixion.	Aye, boy,—such is *woman's* tongue.—So soft
	When love it speaks, that then the nightingale
	It rivals ;—but, when passion moves its strings,
	The thunder's crash is a soft lute to it."

OTWAY.

" I TELL you, Doctor Leechum, I have made up my mind, and therefore go *I will.* If you refuse to accompany me, why it will be your own fault should any thing occur which you may not exactly approve of, and which your presence might have prevented. I dare say I shall find some person a *leetle* more gallant than my husband, who will not attempt to thwart me in any of my wishes : indeed I have been informed, and upon authority such as I feel no disposition to question, that there is no want of Chaperones in this delightful city. Oh, Dr. Leechum, Dr. Leechum, you did not always treat me thus cruelly ! there was a time when you prevented my wishing by anticipating every wish I could have felt ; but things have strangely changed since you have secured me in legal bond-age :—*now*, indeed, you strive to prevent my wishing, by attempting to crush every desire I have ; but I'll not be served so, by my womanhood I will not. I see that gentleness and meek submission suit you not, Sir ; I'll try another method, that I'will. Why, nearly two weeks have passed away since we came to Bath, and I have positively seen nothing !—no, not a single thing, excepting that I have been three times to the theatre, to one gala at Sydney garden, and,—let me think,—aye, to two dress balls ; with these *few* exceptions I have just seen nothing ! and now you are raising a thousand objections to my enjoying what above all other things I should delight in ;—but I have said it, *and go I will!* I have ordered my dress, and it will be here, I expect, in two hours' time."

So said Mrs. Leechum, while seated with her *dear* doctor, over the dessert. She had, as the lady very accurately stated, been in Bath *nearly* a fortnight, and during *all* that period she had only witnessed the *few* scenes of diversion of which a list has been furnished,—excepting a visit to Clifton, which by some means had escaped her tenacious memory.

The *gentle* altercation with which this chapter commences, arose from a wish which Mrs. Leechum had expressed to attend a masquerade that night, against which her husband had presumed, although uselessly, to raise his voice. For a full half-hour the point had been argued,—not fairly, we grant, for the doctor could only very occasionally put a word in,—during which time Lady Bolio was absent, changing her dress, which by accident had been considerably soiled by the overturning of a decanter of wine, the contents of which ran into her lap.

It is only necessary " *en passant*" to observe, that the gentle-tempered Mrs. Leechum hated nothing within the circumference of this naughty world, more cordially than *controversy;* at least she so said,—the reason for which we opine was, she disliked being *contradicted*. With the full inteution, therefore, to prevent controversy on the present occasion, she expressed her determination, calmly, distinctly, and fully, as already recorded.

" But, my *dear* Mrs. Leechum," returned the doctor mildly, still anxious to carry his point, yet fearing the consequences of seeming to oppose, " do consider, my love,—"

" What is it you intend, Doctor Leechum ?" enquired his excited lady, without allowing him to finish his sentence,—

" Do you wish that I should consider myself a child in lead-
ing-strings, or a prisoner under the serveillance of a jailor !"

" Neither, my dear," replied the doting doctor ; " all I
wish is that you would exercise your good sense, and—"

" I have exercised it," replied Mrs. Leechum, " and, *therefore*, it is that I determine to go."

" Yet, think of the impropriety, dear, of attending a
masquerade alone," reasoned the doctor ;—" What will be
said by ill-disposed persons who may hear of it ?"

" They will say," returned the lady, " that I displayed the
spirit of a woman in following my own will ; and that I did
right in doing so, when the gentleman who should have met
all my wishes without opposition, refused to escort me."

" I have told you, dear," replied the doctor, " that I detest such indiscriminate associations, and that to frequent
them is to patronise one of the most effective systems that evil
did ever suggest, to promote infidelity and vice.   What disgraceful assignations can be made openly and without shame,
to the ruin of reputation and a husband's peace, where the
blush of modesty is hid beneath a mask—while the professed
libertine pours into the ear of her he wishes to seduce, those
moral opiates, which, but for the garb that each has assumed,
he would not have dared to breathe."

" Monstrous ! Doctor Leechum, monstrous !" exclaimed
his wife, horrified at his observations.—" Your insinuations,
suspicions, and criminations, are positively dreadful,—I understand their import, I assure you, Sir ; but I'll convince
you I'm not the debased and profligate female you charge me
with being."

" Bless me, my dear !" returned the astonished Leechum,
opening wide his eyes, " you entirely misunderstand me,—I
was merely going to hint—"

" Such excessively *broad* hints, at least, might have been
omitted," observed Mrs. Leechum ; " but I tell you once for
all, Doctor Leechum, that go I *certainly will*, if only to prove
to you that your cruel insinuations and criminal suspicions,
are as much without foundation as they are destitute of good
principle ;—there now," continued the lady, as she perceived
the doctor was about to throw in a rejoinder, " it will be
quite as well if all this waste of breath is spared : my mind is
fixed,—I *will go !*"

Had Mrs. Leechum sat to the most distinguished scribe of
the present, or of any former age, her character could not

have been more graphically sketched than it is in the following pithy rhymes ;—at the same time let it be borne in mind
by the fair reader, that from its sweeping and universal application we heartily dissent :—

> " What man on earth has power or skill
> To change the torrent of a woman's will?
> For if she *will*, she *will*, you may depend on't;
> And if she *won't*, she *won't*, and there's an end on 't."

If for *one* moment we may be allowed to offer the reflection of a moralist on this part of our history, it would be
summed up in a short compass ; namely, that the constant
jarring and discord which existed between Dr. Leechum and
his lady, was the almost unavoidable result of a union in
which a disparity of ages existed. The tastes and views of
hilarious twenty-three can never be made to feel and enjoy
with the grave and sober habits of sixty. The cold blood
which flows in the veins of the latter, can never glow with
the generous heat which circulates through the system of
the former ; and hence, while one revels in all the hey-day
blithesomeness of cheerful spring, ever seeking delight, and
panting after fresh enjoyments ; the other, encased as it were
in the curdling winter of age, will possess neither inclination
nor power to relish pleasure themselves, or allow its enjoyment in reference to others. The impropriety of youth and
beauty uniting itself to age and wrinkles, must be evident to
all who will reflect for a moment—it is like placing

> " Arcadian beauty, or the tubal rose,
> 'Midst frozen deserts, and eternal snows;
> Or rudely daring, with an atheist hand,
> Perfection's works with infamy to brand ;
> Outraging nature ; and for ruin's cause,
> Make nature act oppose to her own laws."

At the moment that the doctor's young wife issued her
final determination, in rather harsh sounds to her lord's ears,
Lady Bolio re-entered the room.

"Oh my dear Lady Bolio," exclaimed Mrs. Leechum,
"how happy I am that you have returned ; I feel confident
that Dr. Leechum purposes to be the death of me."

"Why, what has occurred, my dear?" enquired Lady
Bolio, in something like alarm.

"I assure you, Lady Bolio," observed Leechum, "I was
merely hinting,—"

"No such thing, I assure your ladyship," interrupted

Mrs. Leechum—"no such thing, on the word of an op-pressed woman."

"Well, my dear," returned Lady Bolio, soothingly; "be composed, don't flurry yourself, I dare say all will soon be adjusted."

Now the soothing strain adopted by her ladyship, acted directly opposed to what was intended —that is, instead of calming, it excited the doctor's lady. She burst into a flood of tears, and looked a very Niobe, excepting only that she did not, as that lady is said to have done, weep herself into a statue; it became a grave question, however, even with Leechum himself, whether or not the lancet would not be required. The fact is most unquestionable, that the lady had *nearly* made up her mind to fall into violent hysterics, but revolving the matter in her mind, she thought it would not do, as in that case she should deprive herself of the plea-sure of talking, and perhaps of going to the masquerade that evening; and therefore she resolved *not* to faint, but state to Lady Bolio the cruel thraldom in which her husband held, or rather *wished* to hold her,—for hold her he could not.

"Am I not composed, Lady Bolio?" asked Mrs. Leechum, while her beautiful eyes poured out a fountain of tears, which rolled like pearls down her pretty cheeks—for pretty they were, although somewhat puffed up with excitement. "Do I flurry myself?" she continued; "Haven't I cause for my wretchedness?—Not a day, scarcely an hour, passes, but I am contradicted and opposed by the gentleman who is bound by love and honour to attend to my will in *every* thing. I'm sure I am not unreasonable in my desires; I *never* reply scarcely to any observation which he makes, or *insist* in the least matter to do my *own* pleasure. I make it my *constant study*, as your ladyship knows, to please him in every thing, and never so much as *whisper* a contradiction; and yet, *all* I can *do*, and *all* I patiently *suffer*, fails to secure for me any little indulgence, or, indeed, common respect.— Oh! oh! oh!"

Who could have withstood such a powerful appeal to the passions, as this pathetic speech, terminated as it was by choking grief, bursting forth in a heart-bursting "oh! oh! oh!"—who, we enquire, could have withstood such an appeal? No barbarian of the dark ages, whether Goth, Pict, or Vandal, or modern brute, who occupied a stall, or filled a throne,—

although proof has been given that such can bear much,—
yet neither of such gentlemen could have steeled their
.bosoms against it. How then could the gentle, kind-hearted,
trembling Dr. Leechum do so?—He looked upon his young
—his beautiful—his *dear* wife, and at once resolved, if only
to save her the frequent endurance of such torment, to allow
her to do *just* as she pleased.

"Well, my dear," observed Leechum, "allow me to hint
one thing—"

"No, no, no," exclaimed the calm and docile lady; "I'll
not hear *one* of your hints: you see, Lady Bolio," she continued, "You see how it is with your own eyes, and hear
how it is with your own ears; am I not most barbarously
dealt with?—Oh, that I should ever have sold my liberty to
one who knows not how to use me!"

Every thing that had transpired between Dr. and Mrs.
Leechum, had taken place during Lady Bolio's absence, and
therefore she was of necessity ignorant of the cause of dispute; and as neither of the party felt disposed to allow the
other, or to give themselves, the explanation she wished for,
she was completely at a loss how to act, or which side to
take.

"Now, Doctor Leechum," said her ladyship, "do permit
me to entreat you to—"

"Entreat him, indeed," exclaimed Mrs. Leechum,"—aye,
you may entreat him until doom's-day, but no other result
will follow than leaving him where you found him, I can
assure your ladyship. I have tried it again and again; I have
coaxed, and besought, and wept, but all in vain. Oh, that ever
I should have got married! but I'm determined to go."

"To go where?" enquired Lady Bolio, alarmed.

"Oh, hasn't he informed your ladyship?" returned Mrs.
Leechum.

"Informed me of what, my dear?" said Lady Bolio.

"Ah, there it is, your ladyship?" responded Mrs. Leechum,
—"there it is; he feels conscious of the wrong he does me,
and therefore he wishes to hide the cause of his opposition."

"But where is it, my dear, you hinted you were going?"
asked Lady Bolio.

"Why, to the masquerade to-night," replied Mrs. Leechum;
"no where else, I assure you."

"Ha! ha! ha! is that all?" roared Lady Bolio, surprised
that so small a matter should have led to so large a dispute.

—To the masquerade, and so you have been quarrelling all this time about a foolish masquerade, have you?—ha! ha! ha!'"

Once more the bright and expressive eyes of the doctor's spouse beamed with delight, as she heard Lady Bolio, as she imagined, take side with her.

"That is the whole of it, my dear Lady Bolio," said Mrs. Leechum; "I just stated, as mildly as possible, my wish to see the masquerade,—that is, if the doctor did not object, and he at once positively opposed my going."

"Well, now," said Lady Bolio, "let it be so; I'll take care and have a party this evening at home, and as the doctor wishes it, say you do not intend to go, and—"

"No, indeed," interrupted Mrs. Leechum; "if I could *submit* to any individual in the world, I am sure it would be to the counsel of your ladyship; but no, I have made up my mind to go, and I certainly *will*."

"Well then," returned Lady Bolio, jocosely, "*we* will certainly enjoy ourselves at home; promise me, my dear Mrs. Leechum, you will not be jealous."

"Jealous," echoed the lady, "jealous—ha, ha, ha!—no, indeed, Lady Bolio, *I* am not made of such inflammable materials; besides, in your ladyship's company, I could leave in perfect confidence even an Adonis."

"Really, my dear Mrs. Leechum, I *feel* the honour of your opinion," returned Lady Bolio, "and hope I shall never forfeit it: but suppose I were to accompany you to-night?"

"Oh, do so, my dear Lady Bolio," cried the doctor's gentle wife; "do so, and oblige me; I should, indeed I should, above all things be delighted with your company."

"Well, I do think I shall once more, and for the *last* time, indulge myself," returned her ladyship. "It is now, at least, twelve months since I attended a masquerade—but can't we persuade the doctor to accompany us?"

"Oh no, indeed you cannot; you cannot, upon my word," replied Mrs. Leechum, as if alarmed at the very idea of her husband's company with them.

"Well, I don't know, my dear," observed the doctor, meditatively; "I don't know,—as Lady Bolio purposes to go, and it will be obliging you, I think I will go."

"Aye, that's right, now," said Lady Bolio; "I knew he could be persuaded. Bless you, my dear," added her ladyship to Mrs. Leechum, the way to make husbands do as their wives wish them, is to speak good-temperedly, and treat them kindly."

Mrs. Leechum heard not the apostrophe of Lady Bolio; her ears had drunk in the words of her husband with as good a relish, almost, as the king of Denmark did the "juice of cursed hebenon," while

> "Sleeping within his orchard,
> His custom always in the afternoon;"

and therefore to him alone she replied.

"I am sure it would be highly improper if you did attend, Doctor Leechum; and because Lady Bolio's going," she added, "that's a compliment for me, certainly."

"I was merely going to hint," rejoined the doctor with agitation, for he perceived his lady's eye was again becoming alarmingly bright, "I was merely going to hint—".

"Yes, yes," said Mrs. Leechum," we are aware of it,—that, as Lady Bolio purposes to go, you will make one of the party. I think you had better not, doctor; indeed, I could not consent to it."

The king's *wish* expressed, is a *command* implied; and no loyal courtier would hesitate to attend it. Dr. Leechum was *not* a courtier, most certainly; neither, as certainly, was Mrs. Leechum a king,—more reasons than one prevented it; but her wish bore the same character, and Leechum acknowledged it.

"Umph," said the doctor to himself, for above his breath he dared not speak, for his peace's welfare: "*to what is not a married man obliged to submit!* not for *conscience*, but for *comfort's* sake." "Well, my dear," he continued, "I think, as you say, I had better not go; indeed, I have made up my mind not to do so."

"Have you so, love?" said the affectionate wife with an expressive look; "well, I suppose you must do as you please, you know I *never* wish to force your will."

"Oh, certainly not, certainly not," replied the doctor; and bit his lips.

"I have directed my dress, Lady Bolio, to be here by seven o'clock," observed Mrs. Leechum; hadn't your ladyship better make your selection, and send orders that the dress you may fix upon should be sent at the same time?"

The point was at once settled that it should be so, and the ladies retired instanter, regretting, of course, that the doctor would not consent to be of the party; and proceeded to make arrangements for their night's excursion, while Leech-um, for the purpose of drowning some rising feelings which had in them a considerable portion of mental gangrene, indulged himself more freely than he was wont to do, in drinking the health of all absent friends, not forgetting to pledge his own: so that by the time the masquerade dresses came home, this modern Æsculapius was almost in need of a stomach-pump to free his distended body from the large quantity of Port which he had swallowed.

A mathematical polemic, whose cranium gave the development of logical precision pretty largely, would be ready to enquire, supposing the question were mooted,—" Can evil produce good ?" To such we should feel disposed to reply, that *indirectly,* at least, it can : and our response would be founded upon the proof furnished in the doctor's case :—for had the leech not taken so large a quantity of wine as absolutely to incapacitate him to stand or go, he had fully made up his mind, after he had taken half a dozen glasses, to follow Lady Bolio and his wife to the masquerade. Now, had he so done, mischief incalculable would in all probability have been the result; for, elated as he then was with grape juice, as well as grievously afflicted with jealousy, he would have befooled himself in the room, and have annoyed the company: as it was, he escaped the mortification which after-reflection would have brought, while the maskers were preserved from the inconvenience.

The ladies were so fully engaged as almost, if not entirely, to have forgotten the doctor; and when they looked into the room, a few minutes before they left home, he was fast asleep, with his head lying on the table. The amiable partner of his joys and sorrows exulted to find her spouse so decidedly composed, and fearing lest her soft step should rouse him from his refreshing slumbers, she tripped back to her room, and put the final adorning on her own loved person. Precisely as the clock struck ten a pair of chairs were announced as being at the door, and forth the ladies sallied from their attiring apartments, and seating themselves in their snug boxes, were borne between two pairs of brawny shoulders each, to the masquerade.

CHAPTER XXIV.

" I've seen the day
That I have worn a visard, and could tell
A whispering tale in a fair lady's ear, .
Such as would please; 'tis gone, 'tis gone, 'tis gone."
CAPULET.

" A very picture of this motley world,
In antics strange, and wearing stranger garbs,
Rude and preposterous, and which sadly suit
The idle wearers who have donn'd them."
OTWAY.

THE spacious and elegant new assembly rooms in Bath—
than which none dedicated to pleasure in the kingdom are superior—blazed with light, so as almost to put day's meridian
glory to the blush. A considerable number of maskers had
already entered upon a variety of strange and grotesque antics
before Lady Bolio and the doctor's, now happy, wife arrived.
The latter entered the room richly habited as a wealthy Heiress
of Spain. Her dress and figure, which were really handsome,
attracted various eyes; the initiated into the mysteries of the
astronomy of fashion, gazed upon the young wife, as if a new
star had dropped from its orbit among them; while whis-
perings of admiration went round an apparent social party,
as she trode lightly to the sound of a guitar, which at the
moment was struck by a practised hand, as if to welcome
her entrée.

. Lady Bolio had been guided in her choice of the character she should assume, by the one which Mrs. Leechum had
taken, and, therefore, very appropriately selected that of a
Duenna; her gait, as well as the dress she wore, bespoke
the female guardian excellently well, and many were the
resolves which at that time were made by different individuals, that they would rob the duenna of her charge.

At a short distance from the door at which our heroines
entered, stood a character superlatively attractive. The rich
costume of a Knight of the Golden Fleece which he wore,
was splendid in the extreme, while the manly proportions of
his figure were admirably displayed by the dress which he had
donned; moreover there was, in the attitude he had assumed,
a gallant bearing, which could scarcely fail to attract the
attention of a romantic subject of the opposite sex.

As our Spanish heroine entered, the fixed gaze of the

Knight of the Golden Fleece was turned full upon her. The character which each sustained, appeared to challenge a display of knightly courtesy on one side, and of Spanish intrigue on the other. At a little remove from the knight, stood his page, who, as the heroines passed up the room, whispered the knight, familiarly, " 'Pon my honour, that's a beautiful creature—what say you, shall we carry her off?"

" Hush," returned the knight, " remember your character, you are my page, and *we* stand much upon etiquette."

" 'Pon my honour," returned the page, " that had completely escaped me—the beautiful Donna had driven every thing out of my head to make room for herself, 'pon my honour."

" Only attend my motions and do my bidding," replied he of the golden fleece, " and, all the world to a cracked dice, but I'll bear off the prize. In the first place, the good graces of the duenna must be secured; that object accomplished, the game will run smoothly. If they should prove ladies of condition—and I flatter myself I can judge pretty correctly on such a matter—and have any taste for ' shuffle and cut,' —being ladies of family, they *must* have,—why so much the better, for by that means two grand points may be obtained ; in the first place, my plans will be facilitated ; and, in the second, a few hundreds be bagged."

" 'Pon my honour," returned the page, " your knightship reasons well; neither the noble Marlborough, nor his gallant princely ally, ever devised their plans for the siege of a town or citadel with more promptitude and wisdom."

" If our success but equals theirs, we shall have cause of triumph," said the knight ; " until then we must *do* as well as *talk*."

As the knight and his page continued thus to converse, the heiress glided like a thing of air, round and through the splendid and magnificent room,

> " The admired of all beholders."

closely followed by her attendant, while the knight, like the very shadow of herself, was constantly by her side.

Waltzing had been pretty general for an hour or more, and the room was exceedingly crowded with company, when, overcome by the heat, the duenna complained to her fair mistress of indisposition, and appeared as if about to faint. No circumstance could have occurred more propitious for the Knight. His quick eye watched the presented opportunity, and with a graceful ease he improved it to his purpose.

With a respectful air, he approached the Duenna, like one well schooled in a knowledge of the whims and caprices of such important personages, and, in the most courtly style, proffered his assistance, which was graciously accepted.

Having led the lady to a seat, he turned to his page. "Lorenzo," he exclaimed, "haste with the fleetness of a courier dove, and obtain refreshment for this worthy lady."

"I will, Sir Gaston," answered the Page, and bowing low he retired.

"Sir Knight," observed the Duenna, "your gallantry merits other returns than from my poor hand it can receive."

"It ever behoves a knight, lady," returned he of the Golden Fleece, "and, above all knights, one of the distinguished order with which I stand connected, to protect oppressed ladies, and assist the afflicted."

"I thank you, Sir Knight," said the Duenna, "for your attentions; already I feel recovered."

The Page appeared as she spoke, with a glass of spring-water in one hand, and some fruit in the other. As, however, the Duenna had resolved not to unmask, the water was used in no other way than in merely wetting her lips slightly with it.

Whether the noble appearance of the Knight of the Golden Fleece, or his chivalrous attention to the Duenna, wrought most upon the Heiress, we pretend not to determine; but that he had secured for himself a place of no mean condition in the good grace of the lady is certain. She had listened to his addresses to her attendant with so much pleasure, as more than half to envy her situation; while the service he rendered her, which she noted with admiration, proved him "quite a ladies' man."

"For your kind attention, Sir Knight," observed the Heiress, with a tremulous voice, "you have made us your debtors;—how we shall discharge its amount I know not."

"Fair lady," returned the gallant knight, "your noticing them, such as they have been, would have over-paid their deserts had they been increased in number and quality a thousand fold. But if your own mind, fair lady, is not satisfied with such discharge, favour me with an opportunity to propose such means of payment as will, by receiving your ap. proval, make me your debtor."

"Such means, Sir Knight," returned the Heiress, "as I may command, and so far as I may with discreetness use, I shall feel happy to employ;—therefore, be pleased to name them, Sir."

"Your fair hand," said the Knight, as he took it right gal- lantly, and pressed it with such a grace to his lips as no lady could have objected to,—" Your hand, fair lady," he said, "in the dance which is now to commence."

The Heiress gave a significant glance at her duenna, and replied in perfect character : "I know not, Sir Knight, if I may, with propriety, accept the terms proposed ; and yet, I do confess, more difficult might have been named."

"Madam," said he of the Golden Fleece, addressing him- self to the Duenna, as the hint to do so was given him by the Heiress, "will you become my advocate on this occasion, and so bind me to your service, a true knight for ever ?"

A considerable period had elapsed since the ears of Lady Bolio had drunk in such sweet sounds as she now listened to. It is more than probable she would have offered but little ob- jection had her own hand been craved by the Knight, instead of her professed charge's. As it was, however, she,—as the duenna,—could not expect such request ; much less could she offer her company, especially while the Heiress stood by.

The Knight, by his polite attentions, had so far ingratiated himself into her good opinions, that she felt persuaded he filled such a station in society as would warrant such an ac- quaintance with him as might be innocently made at a masquerade ; and feeling, as she did, something like a desire to benefit by his protection and company during their stay in the rooms, she acceded to his wishes in reference to the Heiress.

"In truth, Sir Knight," replied the Duenna, "much as I fear me for Donna Rosabella, and although I love her good name dear as I value my own, yet, if on the honour of your order you will pledge yourself to protect her against all rude- ness, and to return her to my guardianship without doing her offence, I then might feel disposed to listen to your suit, and say to Donna Rosabella,—' Go.' "

"On the honour of a true knight I pledge me, lady," re- plied he of the Golden Fleece, " to all you name—I will with sword or lance, with limb and life, even to the death, protect the Lady Rosabella."

"Go then," said the Duenna; "I am satisfied—good pleasure speed you in the dance."

"'Pon my honour," said the Page to himself, who stood by, noticing all that passed, "that is magnificently done,—never saw an intrigue more brief, or more successful: the outposts having struck, the citadel must necessarily surrender soon,—that is, *comme it faut*, 'pon my honour. If now I could manage the Duenna;—but the character I have assumed,—confound it—already do I regret that I should have taken it—'tis excessively tormenting."

"Lorenzo," said the Knight, as, after taking the *now* cheerfully presented hand of the Heiress, he was on the point of leading her to the dance, "stand you by, and do your service to this worthy and honourable lady," pointing to the Duenna; "anticipate her wishes, and perform her pleasure as you value my favour."

"I will, Sir Gaston," replied the Page.—"I shall be happy, *most* happy, sweet lady," he continued, as he turned to the Duenna, "to receive and execute *any* commands with which it may please you to honour me,—'pon my honour."

"A most sensible and well-trained page," thought the Duenna to herself, and then added, addressing herself to the Knight's attendant, who stood before her,—"I shall avail myself of your master's courtesy, and your own very becoming attention, by desiring you to become my protector until the return of the party from the dance."

"'Pon my honour," half escaped the Page, as he bowed low before the Duenna, observing, "I feel superlatively honoured, Madam, by receiving your commands, and shall as proudly and as certainly protect you as my master would,—'pon my honour."

The dancers continued to beat time with their feet to the lively notes which issued from the instruments of a respectable orchestra; while the Duenna and the Page continued to converse. Donna Rosabella evinced her delight in the hilarity which prevailed, as well as her gratification in obtaining such a partner, by tripping it with more than wonted spirit

"On the light fantastic toe."

There was such a nameless winning about the addresses of the Knight, as well as nobleness in his figure and actions, as made the Heiress *almost* forget that she *was*, and at times *altogether* wish that she was *not,* a *"femme couverte."* She even went so far, while standing in familiar *tète-a-tète* at the bottom of the dance with her partner, as to draw a comparison,—an invidious one it must be allowed, and a dangerous one too,—between her *legal* lord, *alias* Dr. Leechum, and the gay young Knight of the Golden Fleece ; and, while her misguided passions decided in almost infinite preference of the Knight,

> " She wished
> That Heaven had made her such a man."

It was during one of those interesting intervals that the Knight, in terms redolent of attic gallantry, pressed the small hand of the Heiress, and observed,—" How happy, fair lady, must he be who is licensed to indulge the fond hope that one day he shall be privileged to call this fairy hand, as now perchance he does the heart that gives it pulsation, *his* OWN !— Oh, how magical that sound !—and, when allied with such inexpressibly dear and tender associations, perfectly transporting !"

The Lady Rosabella sighed deeply; but neither withdrew her hand or made reply.—" You sigh, fair lady," resumed the Knight,—" surely—"

" No, Sir Knight," returned the Heiress, confused,—" that is—'twas nothing—"

" Surely, lady," said the Knight, as if no reply had escaped the lips of the Heiress,—" Surely, one so young and beautiful as you must be, cannot already know grief;—your voice, your figure, all—"

" Sir Knight," interrupted the Heiress, rather pleased than otherwise with the compliments he was continuing to pour forth, and yet obliged to attempt to conceal her gratification, " Sir Knight, you flatter, and so may influence ; while, by your order, you are called upon to protect."

" No, fair lady," returned he of the Golden Fleece, in an impassioned tone, " by my honourable badge of knighthood, I swear—"

" Hush ! Sir Knight," said the Lady Rosabella, " I have not required an oath."

" Your pardon, lady," said the Knight, as he bent gracefully before her,—" Your pardon ;—but if there be truth in men of honour, I flatter not.—I feel my language is cold and powerless compared with the emotions of my heart : and such

emotions you only could have called into existence. But did
I hear you right, fair lady—said you I might *influence?*"

" I said it, Sir Knight," replied the Heiress;—"that is, I
should have said,—I mean, I intended to have said, that I—
I,—excuse me, Sir Knight," continued the lady, in the utmost confusion, " I have really forgotten *what* I intended to
have said."

" Then say what you have said over again," returned the
Knight, " for I could listen to your voice with feelings such
as the maiden of Verona experienced when, parting from her
lover,—she said,

" Parting is such sweet sorrow,
That I could say, ' good night,' 'till 't be to-morrow."

So long too could I listen to you ; and then, by fresh excited
longing influenced, I should crave you to commence again."

" Nay, nay, Sir Knight," returned the lady,—" now I possess full assurance that you do but flatter. Surely, a courtier's garb had better been donned by you than this same
knightly attire."

This was spoken in such sweet and pleasant tones, that the
reproof the words might seem to contain,—and, had they
been breathed from other lips, possibly *would* have conveyed,
—appeared rather to afford encouragement than repulse : so
the Knight considered them, and he proceeded in the same
romantic strain, until himself and the Heiress were so completely occupied with themselves as to forget the dance and
company ;—the consequence was, that although the champion
of the Golden Fleece and his fair partner were called for
once, and again,—they heard not the call : confusion followed,
and the dance abruptly closed.

The circumstance of the music ceasing, roused the pair
from their pleasing lethargy; and the Knight, taking the
hand of the Heiress, conducted her back to the Duenna, from
whom he received such acknowledgments as the favour he
had conferred might naturally call forth.

At this moment a sort of uproar was heard issuing from the
further end of the spacious apartment, the large folding-
doors were thrown open, and in danced a huge bear, to the
infinite terror of the ladies and the equal amusement of the
gentlemen. By the side of Sir Bruin walked a man, who
wore the costume of a wandering Italian, having a large three-
cornered hat upon his head, and a long pole in his right hand;

with which, by occasionally flourishing it, he kept the bear in order. In his left hand he held a strong cord, which, being attached to the muzzle of the bear, secured him from going beyond a determined distance from his master.

Upon the back of the rough animal was seated, dressed in full uniform, a full-grown monkey; who, as soon as he perceived the blaze of light by which he was surrounded immediately upon entering the room,—and the crowds of beauty, of which he appeared to be somewhat of a judge,—screamed with surprise and delight, and bounded about with as much alertness as if he had been an automaton rather than a thing of life.

"Stand up, Sir," said the keeper of the bear to his shaggy companion, who appeared little inclined to obey him;—"stand up, I say," repeated the man, accompanying his command with a stroke on his hind quarters by the pole which he held.

A loud growl, which shook the room, as well as the nerves of the ladies, and of some of the lady-like gentlemen, was returned by the bear in response; and then, rearing himself upon his hind paws, he roared again.

The keeper having placed the pole in the brute's grasp, he commenced dancing a most graceful canine fandango, shouldering at the same time the staff, with as much dexterity as a young recruit would a musket.

In the mean time, the monkey was performing a variety of tricks, which afforded much merriment to a large portion of the company, whose approximation to the antic-loving creature was at what was considered a safe distance. The bear and the monkey continued to dance round the room without the least opposition, followed by the keeper. Every step they took, and every time the bear growled, the female part of the company retired to a most respectful distance, and opened a pathway right and left to admit the dancing pair to pass on freely.

The Knight of the Golden Fleece had taken his seat beside the Heiress, the Duenna sat next her, and the Page stood in waiting before them.

"'Pon my honour," said the Knight's attendant to himself, trembling in his shoes as the quadrupeds approached his standing place, "how insufferably tormenting are such vulgar and boorish entertainments. Do you not feel alarmed, Madam?" he continued, addressing the Duenna.

".Oh no!" returned the lady, "not in the least; I admire the ability of the maskers—they enact their parts to admiration.

"Do they so, indeed?" observed the Page;—"'Pon my honour, I consider it a most offensive scene,—faugh!"

At this moment the eye of Chimpanzee appeared to catch sight of the Duenna, attracted, as it would seem, by her comely proportions, who sat in all the stateliness of conscious dignity; and, uttering a cry of pleasure, as if he considered her a "*bonne bouche*," he leaped fairly into her amply dimensioned lap, to the entire discomfiture of her equanimity of feeling, and the derangement of her dress. In the slight struggle which she made to free herself from the unwelcome intruder, her mask fell off, and Lady Bolio appeared in all her blushing comeliness before the gazing company;—Chimpanzee gazed too upon her countenance, but it was only for a moment; for, uttering a much louder scream than before, he leaped upon the bear's back, which continued to waddle round the room, occasionally growling: while the keeper held out his hat and received the subscriptions which were tossed into it, and then, making a respectful salam in concert with the bear and monkey, made his exit.

"'Pon my honour," said the Page, as his eyes followed with pleasure the receding brutes, " such vulgarity had better be confined to a bear-garden, than introduced into the company of ladies and gentlemen. How low must the tastes of the admirers of such exhibitions be—almost as debased as their's who played the bear and monkey—'Pon my honour."

"Hush!" said the Knight aside to his Page,—" Remember your character."

"Yes, yes," returned the Page, in the same under tone, " 'tis all very fine to say ' remember your character,'—I shall not soon forget it, I promise you; and when I next assume it, may a monkey or a bear kick me,—'Pon my honour."

The Heiress enjoyed the scene exceedingly,—feeling, as it is opined, perfectly safe beneath the protecting influence of a Knight of the Golden Fleece.

"Honoured lady," said the Knight, addressing the Duenna, "will you allow me the honour of attending yourself and the fair Donna Rosabella from the room?" as he perceived she wished to retire for the purpose of arranging her dress.—" Some refreshment by this time," he added, " must surely be required,—shall I be so far honoured?"

"Your continued politeness, Sir Knight," returned the

gratified Duenna, " lays me under increasing obligation ;—I really—"

" Madam," rejoined the Knight, eagerly, " he of the Golden Fleece feels it the pride of his heart to serve fair ladies ; and mine will be the obligation for your kind accept- ance of my services."

So saying, he presented his right arm to the Heiress, and his left to the Duenna, and neither thought proper to refuse the offer. Thus ably supported, the gallant Knight marched gracefully up the room, while the Page ran before to clear the way and open the door for his master.

The splendid tea-room adjoining the principal apartment, or assembly-room, had been tastefully fitted up as the supper- room, one end of which was divided by a delicate and beau- tiful screen, which presented to the company a charming entrance to a grotto, and conducted to a large recess, which served as a saloon where such refreshments as the maskers might require before supper, could be obtained; while the two card-rooms were devoted to the use of the ladies and gentlemen, for the purpose of changing or putting their dresses in order, as the cases might require.

To the door of the ladies' room the Knight accompanied Donna Rosabella and the Duenna, and then, sauntering back- wards and forwards, awaited their return.

" 'Pon my honour," observed the Page, advancing towards the Knight as soon as he was alone, " but you carry on your amour splendidly—one would take you to be a plenipoten- tiary extraordinary from the court of Cupid—'Pon my ho- nour."

" All goes on well," returned the Knight; " but don't for- get your character."

" 'Pon my honour," replied the Page, " but that is con- foundedly easily said, but outrageously unpleasant to attend to,—' mind your character,'—'Pon my honour ;—I protest by all that I most value—"

" That is," observed the Knight, pleasantly, " by *yourself* —eh, Lorenzo ?"

" Well, by myself,—and you will have it so," returned the Page,—" by myself I protest, I feel more than half inclined to doff the Page's garb and don a Domino—'Pon my honour."

" For shame, Lorenzo !" said the Knight; " for, don what you will, that shall be your name for the night, I promise you.—Don a Domino and desert your master !—Take off thy

mask and let me see thy blushes now,—fie! fie! upon thee;
—thou a honourable Page to a Knight of the Golden Fleece!
—no, no; play out thy part, man, for this evening, and we'll
share in the pleasures of conquest when we change our characters."

"Have you yet learned who the beautiful creature is, that
has placed herself under your knightly care?" enquired the
Page.

"Not yet," replied the Knight; "but I have learned what
is much more to the point—that she is not indifferent to my
person."

"Is she married, think you?" asked the Page.

"Married!—ha! ha! ha!—Married, said you?" returned
the Knight of the Golden Fleece.—"Why, in the name of my
honourable order, how am I to tell that, think ye?—and suppose she is,—what then?"

"Why *then*," replied the Page, "it is time you make up
your mind to—"

"Hush!" interrupted the Knight,—"They come,—see the
sun is rising.—Retire."

The ladies appeared at the door of the apartment as he
spoke—the Knight waited but a moment, and then stepped
up to them with the dignity of a sovereign, and again the
Heiress and the Duenna placed their slender wrists within
the presented arms of the cavalier of the Golden Fleece.

The Lady Rosabella was still in high spirits, and the Duenna's were improved since she had replaced her mask, and
re-adjusted,—as well as in a measure changed,—her dress,
and in such temper they were conducted,—nothing objecting,
—by the Knight to the saloon; from which, after spending
half an hour in taking refreshment, they returned to the apartment in which the company was still engaged in diversified
scenes of hilarity.

At the time of their return to the assembly-room, a party
was delighting a large circle by performing, with admirable
grace, an entire new dance, which received the appropriate
cognomen of "The Bath Waltz." The Knight, the Heiress,
and the Duenna, again resumed their seats. The Knight
pressed the hand of the fair Lady Rosabella as he led her to
her seat, and felt,—or imagined he did,—the pressure returned with equal warmth.

"And eyes met eyes at that soul-thrilling touch,—
The living glances spoke a language known

(Though mute the trembling lovers' burning lips),
Told more than language could have told,—and then
A bliss ecstatic, strong as flesh could bear,
Filled either bosom.''

While thus engaged, the dance terminated, and all eyes
were directed towards two persons who were habited as
Gipsy Girl and Boy. The Girl carried a light basket on her
arm, in which various small trinkets were disposed tastefully,
while the Boy held a bundle of ballads. The pair sauntered
into the room, with all the nonchalance of the characters they
had assumed, singing, as they advanced, the following

DUET.

Boy. From town to town we wend our way,
    I strive to please the ladies;
    In what respects, I need not say,—
    You well know what our trade is.

Girl. And *I* endeavour all I can
    To give the gent's some pleasure;
    But *how* I execute my plan,
    I'll tell when more at leisure.

Boy. In villages I ballads sell;
Girl. And I, pins, threads, and garters;
Both. { And, now and then, we fortunes tell,
    To mothers and their *darters.*

Boy. Come, gentle ladies, now, who will,
    I'll tell you what your fate is;
Girl. Come, sighing swains, and try *my* skill,
    I'll tell you who your mate is.

Boy. Who'll with some silver cross my hand?
Girl. Who'll buy my strong stay laces?
Both. { You've but to call, we're at command,
    To wait on smiling faces.

"Pon my honour," said the Page, as the gipsies finished
singing; "but that is a fine voice which this gipsy lass possesses."

The girl started, and, approaching the Page, asked—."Will
you have your fortune told, good gentleman?"

"Are you quite certain, my brunette divinity, that you can
tell it?" asked the Page.

"Cross my hand with a piece of silver," replied the Gipsy
Girl, "and I'll prove to you that I pretend to nothing more
than I can accomplish. I'll tell you the first letter of the
lady's name to whom you are now paying your attentions,
and whom you hope soon to lead to the altar."

"Ah! say you so, my pretty lass?" returned the Page;
"I'll wager this bauble," he continued, taking a handsome

diamond ring from his finger, "against your basket of trinkets, you cannot."

"No page of mine," observed the Knight, who had been listening attentively to the colloquy, "shall offer to wage or battle without performing his engagement. I'll hold the stakes," he continued; "if the Gipsy Girl accepts your offer, and will, as truth shall dictate, deliver both."

"So be it, Sir Knight," said the Gipsy Girl, making a low, although a somewhat uncourtly curtsy. "I agree to the terms; here is my basket."

"And here's my ring," observed the Page; and both were placed in the Knight's keeping.

"Give me your hand, Sir Page," said the Gipsy.

"There," said the Page, ungloving his right hand, and presenting it.

"Ah," exclaimed the girl, as she surveyed the lines upon it. "Here it is, as plain as fate can make it.—Do you yet repent your wager?" she added.

"Not I, 'pon my honour," replied the Page; "but I shrewdly guess you do."

"Shall I whisper in your ear, Sir Page," asked the girl, "or will you that I speak it out?"

"'Pon my honour," returned the Page, "how exquisitely polite you are. Speak it out so loud, at least, that my master may hear.'

"I will obey your bidding," returned the girl; "'tis F. Are you now satisfied?"

"Rightly told, and fairly won," said the Knight; "the prize is yours;" and he handed over the basket to the Gipsy Girl, and placed the ring on the fore-finger of her right hand.

"'Pon my honour," said the Page, "fairly beaten, I confess. 'Tis well you live in these days of toleration, or as certain as I have lost my ring, you'd be burned for a witch. But, tell me," he added in a whisper, "can you inform me, if I shall win the lady that I woo?"

To which the girl replied in a sort of recitative :—

> "Press firm your suit without despair,
> Let other maids alone :—
> He must contend, the crown who'd wear;
> The prize will be your own."

"'Pon my honour," said the Page, "but you are an exquisitely clever girl, you are, 'pon my honour; if it were

P 2.

not for that confounded mask of your's, I'd give you other pay.

To this the girl replied in the same tone :—

> "Sir Page, beware,
> And at length be wise,
> Your amours forbear,
> Or you'll lose your prize."

And so saying, she glided on without deigning to hold further converse.

"Will you, lady," said the Boy, approaching the Duenna, " will you, lady, allow me to tell your fortune ?"·

"Ha, ha, ha, returned the Duenna in high glee. " What think you, Sir Knight? dare I venture ?—your Page appears perfectly satisfied.—But *I* feel fully confident my stars are not so easily read. But there," she added, as she took a piece of gold from her purse, and placed it in the Gipsy Boy's hand, without waiting the Knight's reply,—" there is your fee, now for proof of your art."

The boy replied in the same way as the girl had done.

> " No ! no ears but thine
> My proof must hear ;
> Your feelings, not mine,
> I too much revere."

" In truth," said the Duenna, " you are a singular being : I already feel my curiosity excited, and yet I doubt if the cause of grief I have long felt can be told by you."

The boy replied as before.

> "Command my speech,
> I'll tell you true :
> As those who preach,
> Their hearers do."

" Well, well, speak out," said the Duenna. I command you !"

The boy remained silent, and only replied by an expressive shake of his head, and then, after a moment's pause, observed in an emphatic tone, "Your ear alone."

" Well," said the Duenna, bending her head forwards, as she spoke, to the boy's mouth, " now let me hear."

The boy whispered in the same singing tone,—

> " You've griev'd the year round
> For your lost son and heir ;
> He yet may be found,
> Bid adieu to despair."

The Duenna shrieked as the boy's words fell upon her ears, and falling back in her chair—she fainted. All was bustle and confusion in an instant, and while the attentions of the Knight, the Heiress, and the Page, were engaged in rendering the Duenna assistance, the Gipsy Girl and Boy glided like spirits from the room.

In a short time the Duenna was brought back to a state of consciousness. She opened her eyes, and looked wildly round, but evidently without meeting the object of her search.

"Were is he?" were the first words that escaped her lips.

"For whom do you enquire, Madam?" asked the Heiress.

"For that mysterious being,—the Gipsy Boy," replied the Duenna.

Every eye in the group turned to seek the person enquired for, but no one saw him.

"He has left the room, Madam," returned the Knight;—be composed, it was merely a masker's trick."

"Why, true," returned the Duenna, rousing, "it was as you say, Sir Knight, merely a masker's trick; and yet his knowledge—if knowledge he does possess—is singular; and, if a mere guess influenced his speech, why then 'twas equally strange."

"'Pon my honour," observed the Page, "I begin to fancy something above a trick has been played upon us. With your permission, Sir Gaston, I'll make enquiry respecting these same Gipsies. I will, 'pon my honour."

"O heed them not," returned the Knight; "the lady is better now. In a short time supper will be announced, and we shall meet them then, I warrant you."

The Duenna made an effort to rally, but her spirits continned to droop, and, at every renewed effort, the extra-excitement she was obliged to summon to her aid, only rendered her more weak, and she lost ground in proportion, and was after repeated struggles,

> "Against her quailing flesh,
> Which triumphed o'er her spirit,"

compelled, although with infinite unwillingness, to whisper her wish to the Heiress to retire.

Those who have entered into enjoyment such as the Heiress now revelled in, and with such spirit too as that lady did, need not be told how much she felt mortified at being disturbed in the very zenith of her delights. Still, she could not, with any show of consistency, offer any opposition to the expressed desire of her indisposed attendant.

So far, however, had the fascinating manners of the Knight of the Golden Fleece captivated her, that the principal regret she felt at leaving the assembly-room, arose from the disinclination she experienced at losing his society. While the Lady Donna Rosabella was borne away from the straightforward path of propriety by thus yielding to her passions, it became no very difficult task, on the part of the handsome cavalier, to obtain the consent of the Heiress to another meeting on the following evening. The assignation was duly made, and was to have taken place in Grosvenor Gardens, the dress which each purposed to wear having been very correctly, if not very consistently named.

On what a fearful precipice had not Mrs. Leechum's imprudence placed her. The ground upon which she stood appeared crumbling from beneath her feet, and threatened every moment to plunge her into an abyss whose bottom she could not discover, and from which no after-help could deliver her. Domestic peace, and fame, and honour, all were on the eve of being sacrificed, and all resulted from pursuing her *own* will in opposition to her husband's; by mixing in society where—alone, at least—she never ought to have been found. Severe and illiberal as the remarks of Dr. Leechum might have appeared in reference to masquerades, while viewed abstractedly, yet, when contemplated in connexion with the fearful circumstances in which his young wife now stood, they will only be considered of such a character as propriety called for.

The arrangement to which we have referred was frustrated, however, by an unlooked for accident, which was quite as agreeable to both the Knight and the Heiress, furnishing, as it did, an opportunity of meeting with less restraint.

Politeness of course dictated—if no other feeling had influenced—that the Knight should escort the ladies to the door of the assembly-room; having so done, their chairs were called, and into them the Heiress and the Duenna stepped, and off marched the chairmen with their load at a good round rate. The Knight continued to follow the Heiress's chair with his eyes, and she, to take a last look at her gallant cavalier, put the curtain aside, and looked with a neck as elongated as a crane's, towards the spot where he still stood in a most interesting attitude.

'Tis an almost threadbare adage, yet 'tis a saying which never since the days of its immortal author has been proved more *literally* correct than on the present occasion ; and therefore we use it, that—

"The course of true love never did run smooth."

Here it ran as *rough* as flint stones could make it. Thus it happened : unfortunately the spring which secured the door of the chair was defective, so that the moment the Heiress pressed against it, open it flew, and she fell out, like a harlequin in a pantomime taking a leap through the face of an eight-day clock ; but instead of falling like the chequer-clothed being upon a soft feather bed, she alighted upon hard and rough stones. A loud shriek broke from her lips, as she broke bond, which reached the ears of the chairmen who bore the Duenna, a short distance in the van, who, on turning their heads, beheld at once the disaster, and put down the chair in haste, in order to run to the prostrate lady's assistance ; but, unluckily, they made more *haste* than *good* speed, for the stones not being even upon which the sedan rested, before they had proceeded half a dozen steps, over it went, and the lusty Duenna soon found herself doubled up within the inclosure, like a subject for the knife of a dissector, which had newly been abstracted from its silent resting place.

The united screams of the prostrated ladies brought a crowd round them at a short notice, and many were the jests and jibes to which the ludicrous scene gave birth.

"For shame, Miss," said a drunken coal-heaver, to the Heiress, as he staggered to the spot from a pot-house he had just left. "For shame, Miss, to lay so pertic'larly un-decent, kicking up your petticoats at that ere rate ; vy don't you get up like a man, eh ?—I'm blow'd now, if my vife Nance vos for to do so, if I wou'dn't whack her like a sack." Then stooping down, he laid hold with his black hands of the lady's beautiful dress, observing, "Come, give us your flipper, my good un ;" and then staggering forwards, he made a false step, and fell completely over the prostrate Heiress into the chair, out of which she had just fallen.

The whole of this delectable scene was the work of a few seconds, and at the moment the coal-heaver had taken the place of Donna Rosabella in the chair, up came the Knight and his Page : the former lifted the Heiress in his arms, and bore her off, like a beautiful and valued prize, to the assembly-rooms, while the Page, by his master's orders, hastened to render such assistance to the Duenna, as her uncomfortable situation required.

By the united efforts of the Page and the chairmen, the sedan was righted, and the Duenna, more frightened than hurt, was conveyed back after the Lady Rosabella.

"'Pon my honour," said the Page, "but this is one of the most extraordinary affairs I ever met with,—I hope, Madam," he continued, as he walked by the side of the chair, "you have not received any serious injury."

"Oh no, Sir Page, none whatever," returned the Duenna; "at least, none that I am aware of," she added in a hurried tone; but how is my dear Mrs.——? that is, how is the Lady Rosabella?"

"Whew!" half whistled the Page, instead of replying to the Duenna's question, as the word *Mrs.* rung in his ear.— "Pon my honour, here's a fine scrape, I calculate, into which my Knight of the Golden Fleece has helped himself, and, for aught I know, has helped me too.—'Pon my honour—A duel in all probability will wind up the affair magnificently."

"Is the Lady Rosabella injured?" repeated the Duenna.

"'Pon my honour," returned the Page, "I cannot positively answer your question, Madam. I hope not, however —rather, I fancy not."

"Go on," bellowed out the coal-heaver, whose capacious body still lay in the bottom of the chair, while his head hung out on one side, and his legs on the other. "Go on, I says, Charley."

"Come, I say, old chap, make yourself scarce, will you?" said one of the chairmen, "or it may be you'll find yourself in the wrong box, soon."

"Go on, my fine box-carrier," again roared the Black Prince; "this is the first time I ever vos in one of these ere walking sentry boxes, and I'm blow'd if I don't have a ride like a gen'leman as I am; so go on, I says, and score it up to the ballas vipper."

"Vell, I plainly sees," observed one of the chairmen, "as how hargerment von't awale nothing vith this ere covey, so I'm dashed if I don't take another method to do the business."

So saying, he slipped the strap from his shoulders, in

which the ends of the bearing poles rested, and applying some quickly repeated and well-directed blows upon the coal-heaver's posteriors, that respectable gentleman thought it necessary to "toddle," as his tormentor exhorted him to do, to the tune of the rapidly descending bastinado, in double quick time.

Having in this way got rid of their *foul* fare, they hasted back to the room to seek after their *fair* fare, and soon found her in such a plight as at once assured them that it was "all up" with their fare.

"I say," whispered the Page, in the ear of his master, "be careful how you proceed in your amour. I feel an unconquerable objection to the unpleasant smell of powder,—'pon my honour."

"What mean you?" returned the Knight.

"I mean," resumed the Page, "that ever since I was nearly blowed up with squibs and crackers on a fifth of November, when I was about ten years of age, I have had an antipathy to bullets and such like, beyond any thing I can express,—'pon my honour."

"I entreat you, speak out," said the Knight. "What has occurred?—you have not been attacking the curs who surrounded the chair pugilistically, have you?

"No, 'pon my honour," returned the Page, "nothing of the kind, I assure you; but the Donna is a married woman, that's all, you understand now,—eh?—'pon my honour."

"She's an angel," returned the Knight, as he gazed fondly on her now unmasked face, and applied his lips to her's—as she lay still senseless in his arms. The soft salute, however, produced a wonderful effect; it roused the Heiress from the seeming lethargy into which she had fallen, without producing a positive return to consciousness; at least, she afterwards said so. She lifted her head languidly, and *then*, replaced it on the Knight's shoulder, while a pitiful, although musical sigh, broke from her heaving bosom; and *then*, threw her snow-white arms—quite unconsciously—round the cavalier's neck; and *then*,—but enough of particularizing, let the veil rest undisturbed on the remainder; just *then*, however, the Duenna entered the apartment from the attiring room, and, running up to the Lady Rosabella, exclaimed, "Oh, my dear, how very unfortunate we have been, this evening,—I fear you must be dreadfully hurt."

Once more the lovely Heiress opened her fine eyes, concerning which it might have been said, without overstepping the poetry of truth,

> "Alack! there .ies more peril in thine eyes,
> Than twenty of their swords."

"Where am I?" enquired the only semi-conscious lady.

"Be not alarmed, fair Lady," returned the Knight, still holding her, "no peril will befall you here."

"'Pon my honour," said the Page aside, "the lady appears remarkably well satisfied with her resting-place."

"Lorenzo," said the Knight, "desire my carriage to be in attendance—the ladies will, I hope, permit me the honour of seeing them safe home."

Before any objection could be urged by either of the ladies, if any they felt disposed to urge, the order was transferred to a footman, who waited without, and in an incredibly short space of time, the vehicle was announced. The Knight led the *fair* ones to the steps and handed them in, and then took his seat by the side of the Heiress; and as the Duenna appeared to require assistance, the Page was directed to afford that honourable personage all the aid in his power: the lady felt the polite attention of both the Knight and his Page, and with such acknowledgments as the occasion called for, accepted the proffered assistance, and the Page took his place accordingly—next the Duenna.

Lady Bolio's mansion was soon gained,—indeed, much sooner than Mrs. Leechum either expected, or desired; for ill as she *was*, or as she *might* have been, she would have preferred riding the whole of the day as she was, than return to the common-place duties of home, and her aged hus—but mum.

In consequence of the party still being in their masquerade dresses, the Knight declined entering the house that evening, but tenderly squeezing the hand of the Heiress, and receiving a return of the recognition, as a token of her sense of obligation, adieu was pronounced on either side, with the understanding that a call on the following day would not be considered intrusive on the part of the ladies.

CHAPTER XXV.

"Would you see this big world at a bird's-eye view,
  Or correct as in a galantie show,—
    With bustle and rout,
    Turns in and turns out,
Where all persons mix—Jews, Turks, and folk from Ashantee ho
    Repair without delay,
    For a week and a day,
    To a tavern or an inn
    (If your heads can bear the din,
And your pockets are well lined with Rhino) ;
    You'll see it to perfection,
    And perhaps upon reflection,
Your eyes may pour a flood of Brine-O."

OLD BALLAD.

THOSE persons who have ever visited the delightful city of Bath, whether in the pursuit of health or pleasure, with plenty of the needful in their purses, will scarce require information, as to where good accommodation, and fashionable luxuries blended with domestic comfort, may be obtained. If, however, from some unlucky circumstances, or untoward accident, the individuals to whom we refer (such as having been mis-directed, or not directed at all) may have been miserably domiciled, and worse attended and fed,—for the edification of such unfortunates, with whom we most sincerely sympathize,—on a future trip, as well as for the guidance of all others whom it may concern, we recommend to especial notice, the YORK HOUSE, in *York Buildings*, as an hotel of the very first class : being very capacious, very elegant, and very commodious, all which *very's* are *very* important things for one who has left—

"Home and all its pleasures,
For a land where strangers dwell ;
Kind attentions then, are treasures,
Richer far than tongue can tell."

No wines are better in flavour or quality,—beds cannot be softer, or rooms better ventilated :—while the charges do not exceed, and in many cases do not rival, those which the no-conscience gentry of very so-so travellers' lodges lay on, both *in* and *out* of London. The host is a gentleman who knows how to measure the length of the foot of each of his guests ; the hostess, for her good temper, good looks, and good sense, is worthy to fill the post of a lady of honour to any queen in the world, not excepting our own beautiful virgin Queen VICTORIA! while the servants, from he wot cleans boots, to the pretty chambermaid who supplies you with soft water, scented soap, and napkins white as the driven snow,—each display as much industry to please, as might reasonably be expected from those who are looking forward to be pleased themselves, by receiving a reward for their services.

At this very respectable hotel, Lord Dashwood, Sir Marmaduke Varney, and the ladies in their train, had billeted themselves; and here, also,—without knowing that his Lordship and party had fixed their quarters there,—Dr. Titheum and his daughter Georgiana, two days after them, hired apartments, purposing in the course of a few days to move onwards to Clifton.

The period of the doctor's arrival was the very night on which the masquerade, to which brief reference has been made, took place. The whole of the "fashionables" of Bath and its vicinity were on the tip-toe of expectation concerning it, and preparations had long been made by many for the occasion.

Fatigued as Georgiana was after the travel, still, the moment she was informed of the masquerade, all her lassitude, and the previous aching of her delicate limbs, appeared to pass off, as if some potent charm had been employed upon her. Her desire to attend it surpassed all expression, and especially as it was the last that would be held that season, and therefore was expected to be of more than ordinary splendour.

"Well, well, child," said the doctor, in reply to the earnest entreaties of his daughter that she might be permitted to go, "you are now as good as your word; you promised, I remember, before we left home, that if I would bring you to Bath, you would ask a great many more favours of me; and, in good faith, you are commencing with spirit, and without loss of time too. But how is it to be managed?" continued his reverence; "you must not go alone, that you are certain I can never allow; and to seek our friends this evening, would be exceedingly inconvenient, and in all probability, by this time, they are almost ready to set off, as without doubt they will attend."

"Can't you go with me, papa," said Georgiana.

"Me go, child?—Oh, no, no, no, certainly not," returned the doctor; "by no manner of means;—consider, my child, if *I* should be seen at a masquerade," he continued, "I should incur the displeasure of my diocesan,—and the preferment to which I look forward would be sacrificed for ever.—Oh, no, that's out of all question.

"Well, but who is to see you there, papa?" returned Georgiana; "at least, who is to recognise you in a mask?"

"Why true, child," returned the doctor, who, to tell the truth, wished as much as his daughter, to attend. "As you say a mask would effectually conceal me from observation, and I should not be the first of my cloth who ever wore a *mask!*—and as I am not known at Bath, either as being in the "commission of the peace," or the rector of Christchurch, —why, perhaps it might be managed."

"Oh, nothing could be more easily accomplished," returned the delighted girl; "only say I am to go, and I shall be almost wild with delight. Oh, it will be such a delightful treat!

"But how shall we manage to obtain dresses," observed the doctor, "without exciting suspicion?"

"Oh, I'll undertake to arrange that part of the business," answered Georgiana; "only tell me to do so, and it shall be done:—say so, *dear* papa,—shall I do it?"

"Well, I suppose I must treat you," returned the doctor; and yet I—"

"Oh, thank you, thank you," cried Georgiana, only regarding the first part of this brief speech,—"that is kind, now,—what character will you assume?"

"I shall make up my mind on that head," replied the doctor, when I learn what dresses can be obtained. I shall not feel surprised if the whole were engaged long before this late period."

"I'll ascertain that in a few minutes," observed Georgiana, and, ringing the bell, she desired Claudius might be sent in. Our hero entered, and Georgiana gave her orders to him, which were, that he should, with the greatest attention to secrecy, find out in what part of the town masquerade dresses might be obtained, and then, instantly to repair thither, and enquire if any remained unengaged; and if so, for what characters.

"Now, run quick, Claudius, and bring me word," said Georgiana; "there's a good lad; and I shall feel obliged to you."

"I'll do it as speedily as my legs will carry me, Miss," returned Claudius, and off he sped, like a swift-winged Mercury, bearing a commission from a conclave of gods.

While Claudius was thus engaged, running from street to street, in search of a masquerade-dress depôt, the doctor and his daughter set to with a good appetite upon a couple of boiled fowls, and the better part of a fine Westphalia ham, to assist the digestion of which, they used a strong decoction of the Arabian berry, whose refreshing qualities are said to have been discovered by a friar of a monastery, in a part of Arabia where the berry grew in wild abundance, in the following way :—During one of the solitary walks in which the good father frequently indulged, he observed the goats feeding upon the berries of the trees with great avidity, after which repast they became extremely brisk and alert. The thought struck him, that he would test the peculiar virtues of the berry upon the monks of his order, of whose lethargic propensities he had frequently had cause to complain. The trial proved successful, and from that period coffee is said to have been brought into general use.

At the expiration of a quarter of an hour, Claudius returned, reeking with perspiration like a fresh-skinned calf, and communicated the information, that only five dresses remained unengaged in the whole city; which were a male and female Gypsy dress, one for a Bear, one for his Keeper, and one for a Monkey.

"Ha, ha, ha!" roared the doctor, tickled in his fancy, as Claudius gave in the list *viva voce*. "There now, Georgie," he continued, as soon as he could command enough breath to speak, "you see it is all settled; to attend in either of these characters is impossible."

"I do not think so, papa," returned Georgiana, to whom all dresses were equal, and she might have thought, as all who would be present, voluntarily, would be alike ridiculous, it was of small consequence in what habit each person exposed his or her folly.

"Why surely, Georgie," responded the doctor, "you would not play the Bear, would you?"

"I am sure either character might be very well assumed," returned Georgie, "and sustained too, without much difficulty."

"What do you mean, Georgiana?" said the doctor, laying

down his knife and fork, and looking her full in the face; "there is, at least, none that *I* could assume."

"Why now, dear papa," said the coaxing girl, in her best winning style, "if you'll allow me to arrange matters, I'll soon make up a party, the best you can imagine."

"Thou art a wag, Georgie," said her fond father; "but come, let us hear your clever arrangement."

"Well, I'll tell you how it shall be," replied Georgiana. "Joseph, you know, can be the Bear, you can be his Keeper—there will be two characters *quite in character*—while Claudius can be the Monkey; and that, I think, will be in character too, for I am sure he is well-nigh as mischievous."

"Oh, never, never!" exclaimed the doctor; "cannot hear of it;—what! take our servants to the masquerade!—why it would be all over the county in a few hours."

"No, indeed, papa," said Georgiana, alarmed for her plan,—"I am certain it would not. I know I can bind to silence, as effectually as if they had lost their tongues, both Joseph and Claudius."

"Well, and what do you propose to assume?" asked the doctor.

"Oh, I'll be the Gypsy Girl," she replied; "and after Claudius has performed his part of the Monkey, he can become my associate as Gypsy Boy. I'm sure we shall do our parts well; and all Joseph will have to do, will be to *growl* loudly; you can *stir him up* with a pole, and desire him to dance when you please, you know. Now, I remember," added Georgiana, "while I was at school in France, there was a grand masquerade given in honour of the birth-day of a member of the reigning family, and on that occasion an English Bishop was present, and performed the part of a Bear to admiration: every one said that if his Grace had been born a Bear, he could not have done it better; while some added, that they were certain he had a good portion of the Bear in his nature, or he never could have *growled* so well as he did. And on that same occasion, an English Prince of the Blood Royal condescended to become his Keeper."

"Ha, ha, ha!" roared the divine. "I should have enjoyed the sight amazingly.—ha, ha, ha!"—he again burst forth, and then added, "Well, well, I suppose it must be as you propose; let the dresses be procured without loss of time, for even now we shall be late."

In this way the matter was finally settled. Claudius was

despatched for the costumes, which were sent without delay, and fitted to admiration. With what eclat they played their several parts in the Assembly-room has already been seen : there, as the reader is fully aware, Claudius disco- vered his lady mother by the falling of her mask, when, as a monkey, he leaped into her lap, without being himself recog- nised ;—and then, too, Georgiana, as the Gypsy Girl, per- ceived that the disguised as the Page was no other than Sir Marmaduke Varney, while she herself continued incog. It is barely necessary to state, that the Knight of the Golden Fleece was my Lord Dashwood—his lady, however, had not, as was first intended, accompanied him to Bath, in conse- quence of her being too far advanced in that state,

" As women wish to be who love their lords ;"

and for reasons best known to himself, his lordship did not press her to accompany him,—he might, perhaps, have thought her presence would have been a check upon his pleasurable pursuits and freaks of gallantry,—and therefore he went (as he much desired to do) without her.

It was fully calculated upon, that the wealthy Miss Fidget would have honoured the masquerade with her presence ;— such, however, was not the case—a serious domestic afflic- tion prevented : her beloved poodle, *Carlo*, was labouring under the pains of a sore throat, occasioned (as was believed) by his having kicked off his covering during the night ; at- tended by an extremely relaxed state of body. To have thought even of pleasure while this was the case, would, in Miss Fidget's opinion, have been a proof of insensibility of the most flagrant kind ; while the golden Duchess had been detained at the hotel in consequence of having indulged rather freely in large and frequent potations of her favourite drink—genuine Cognac. Hence she was carried to her bed, just at the time that Dashwood and Sir Marmaduke set off, in the character of the Knight and his Page, to the Assembly- room.

It was twelve o'clock on the following morning; when the musical ear of Sir Marmaduke caught the sound of an instru- ment in an opposite drawing-room to the one in which him- self and Dashwood, with the ladies, were taking breakfast. The tones of the instrument were beautifully liquid ; but that which to the practised organs of a connoisseur in sweet sounds would have rendered them doubly attractive, was the fact, that they were accompanied by the fine counter-tenor voice of a lady, who warbled with considerable effect the following interesting stanzas on

HOME.

" 'Tis *Home* where the heart is, wherever that be,
In city, in desert, on mountain, in dell ;
Not the grandeur, the numbers, the objects we see,
But that which we *love* is the magical spell.

'Tis this gives the cottage a charm and a grace,
Which the glare of a palace but seldom has known ;—
It is *this*, only this, and not station or place,
That gives being to pleasure, and makes it our own.

Like the dove from the Ark, a rest place to find,
In vain for enjoyment o'er nations we roam ;
HOME ONLY can yield solid joys to the mind,
And there where the heart is, there *only* is HOME !'

" 'Pon my honour !" exclaimed Sir Marmaduke, starting from his chair, as the sweet sounds to which he had listened with attention ceased,—"that voice is familiar to me,—an admirable performance, 'pon my honour.—You are a connoisseur, I believe, Miss Fidget," he added, turning complimentally to that lady ;—" What say you, Madam, to the execution of that beautiful and touching air ?"

Now it so happened, that almost all the ear for sounds with which nature had endowed Miss Fidget, was such as delighted only in listening to the yelping or barking of her dear Carlo. That this was a defect in nature for which no " loveliness of form, or shape, or air," could compensate, is unquestionable. There was, however, in the case of Carlo's mistress, one redeeming quality possessed,—that is, she did not, as not a few ignoramus's have done, set at defiance all human opinion, and pride herself upon her imperfection. It is possible she may have read some where, or some *when*, —as a thorough-bred Staffordshire Potter would say, the sentiment expressed by the poet,—

" The man that has not music in himself,—
That is not touch'd with concord of sweet sounds,
Is fit—*to be a slave-driver*."

and fancying its application to herself would be distressingly odious ; or recollecting, perchance, that the fashion of the day made it an indispensable part of a good education in a *young* lady to have a taste for music, and to be able to chat freely concerning *Sol, La, Me, Fa,* although she did not chance to possess an ear for " sweet sounds," she replied to Sir Marmaduke's question,—" O dear, yes, Sir Marmaduke, it is quite electrifying ;—only see,", she added, " I declare that dear Carlo has enjoyed it !"

" Why, positively," observed Dashwood, who knew the taste of the mistress and the dog to be about equal, " he looks better already."

" I should not feel at all surprised," added the Duchess in the same key, " if another such treat wouldn't entirely cure the sweet creature.   I wish, above all the world, I could obtain something to cure my head of the singular giddiness and nausea with which it is afflicted—I can't imagine what could have caused it."

" Oh! 'Pon my honour," observed Sir Marmaduke, "very distressing.   Pray, was your Grace up later than usual last evening ?"

" No, Sir Marmaduke," returned the Duchess, " not that I am aware of ;—I don't *exactly* know, indeed, at *what hour* I retired ; but it could not have been late."

" It would have been more singular than that your head aches," thought Lord Dashwood, " if your Grace *had known,* for I'll be sworn you could not have told the hour even if the clock at St. Paul's church had struck in your bedchamber."

Once more the fingers which had before struck the keys of the Piano so dexterously, ran sweetly over them ; and a fine bold symphony prepared the attentive listeners for something yet more delightful,—and then followed a profound stillness during a brief space ;—each one of the company appeared anxious to catch the notes as they issued from the instrument or the lips.

> " But when the stilly silence broke,
> As warbled forth her magic tongue ;
> It seem'd as if an angel spoke,
> Or some unearthly being sung.
>
> And yet, there was no effort made—
> No anxious striving to excel ;
> It was,—but language is not made
> To speak the powerful nameless spell."

Miss Fidget's dear Carlo even barked applause ; while Sir Marmaduke started from his chair with the intention of opening the door of the room to admit the sounds more freely

but, unfortunately, in so doing he *un*did all the order and harmony which up to that moment had prevailed, by drawing with him the cloth which covered the table, and with it the whole of the breakfast paraphernalia, not excepting

"The bubbling and loud hissing urn!"

What Muse immortal shall I invoke to supply a pen capable to write it ;—what mighty grasp of descriptive powers will be equal to the task; or what inventive genius furnish ability sufficient by tropes and figures to describe the scene which followed?

Carlo, who lay on a soft-cushioned chair by the side of his mistress, yelped furiously as he bounded from his resting-place with a scalded tail. Miss Fidget, overcome with terror for herself, and distress for her beloved Carlo, shrieked and fainted. The Duchess, into whose lap a plate of well-buttered toast had fallen, rushed with alarm from her seat ; and running her head directly into the face of Lord Dashwood, drew forth a crimson tide from his broken nose ; while the unfortunate author of the catastrophe, Sir Marmaduke, stood confounded on tip-toe amidst the scalding stream, and surrounded by the ruin which his untempered haste had produced.

The spacious apartment was literally strewed with fragments of splendid china, loaf-sugar, broken eggs, cream, toast, ham, &c. &c. Since the time that Nero stood upon his palace playing music, and gazed upon the conflagration of Rome, which his own hands or order had created, in order to raise a fresh persecution against the Christians,—never was such a scene presented.

The loud noise which the falling and breaking things caused, disturbed the musician, who ceased playing ; while mine host and two or three servants ran up to enquire the cause of the tremendous crash they had heard. At the instant the room-door in which the destruction had taken place was opened ; the door of the apartment immediately opposite, and in which the music had been heard, was likewise opened, and discovered Dr. Titheum and his daughter, who had run towards it, alarmed by what they had heard.

The instrumental and vocal performer was no other than Georgiana, who had, to please the doctor while at breakfast, played and sung. The quick eye of the rector's daughter discovered in an instant what had taken place. There stood

Sir Marmaduke, as stiff as if the wand of an enchanter, or the magic sword of a harlequin, had turned him into a sign-post; and there lay Miss Fidget.   Carlo still yelped, the Duchess continued to wipe the grease from her elegant morning dress, and my Lord Dashwood still bled profusely at the nose.

"Oh! papa," exclaimed Georgiana, "whatever can all this confusion mean?"

"Never since I have been in the ' commission of the peace,'" observed the doctor, "did I witness such a scene. Ah!" he continued, starting with surprise as he entered the room, "is that you, Sir Marmaduke?"

"Ah, my dear doc*tar*," returned the Knight, as if the spell by which he had been bound had, by the salute of the divine, been suddenly broken,—" happy to see you, 'pon my honour."

"Dr. Titheum!" exclaimed Lord Dashwood, as he heard him speak,—" are you here?—These are bloody times, doctor," he added; "but they are the consequences of *civil* wars."

"Here,—Claudius, Claudius!" cried Georgiana, who for the first time appeared to have discovered the state in which Miss Fidget lay.

"Yes, Miss," said Claudius, as he entered and surveyed the scene with high relish,—" Did you call?"

"I did, Claudius," said his young mistress.—"Make haste and assist me to raise Miss Fidget."

"'Pon my honour," observed Sir Marmaduke, most philosophically, "this is peculiarly unfortunate.   I hope you are not hurt, my dear Miss Fidget,—'pon my honour—"

"Oh, my poor Carlo!" sighed out Miss Fidget, faintly, as she opened her eyes;—" Is the dear creature hurt?"

"No, Madam," said Claudius, taking the still yelping brute in his arms, and pinching his tail, " he's only a little frightened."

"Bring him to me;" said the lady.

Claudius obeyed, and Miss Fidget pressed the dear companion of her virgin hours, with every demonstration of ardent affection, to her beating heart, and enquired, " Where are you hurt? tell me, my dear Carlo."

"Yelp, yelp, yelp," returned the poodle, as she touched his hind parts.

"Ah! his dear tail is hurt," sighed Miss Fidget.

"And my dress is completely spoiled," said the Duchess.

"And my nose is broken," said Lord Dashwood.

"And my foot is scalded," chimed in Sir Marmaduke, limping.

"And I am almost frightened out of my wits," added Georgiana, nearly bursting in her attempt to maintain her gravity.

Each one of the party appeared to think their individual case the most deplorable; but all seemed light as gossamer to Miss Fidget, compared to the affliction she felt for her beloved Carlo;—what was a *gown*, a *nose*, or a *foot*, when brought into competition with a poodle dog's *tail!*

"How has all this happened?" enquired the doctor.

"'Pon my honour, doc*tar*," said Sir Marmaduke, "it is difficult to determine; but I fancy Miss Georgiana has been the cause of the whole of it."

"Me, Sir Marmaduke!" shouted Georgiana,—"Me, did you say?—Why, I declare, Sir, you surprise me!—I little expected to find you in a jesting humour while your slippers are filled with boiling water,—ha! ha! ha!"

An explanation soon followed. The Duchess, who never took any thing seriously to heart,—except brandy,—laughed heartily over the affair, as she held up her beautiful dress, exclaiming,—"Who now will presume to deny that I am a *Greasian* Daughter?" and then, after making an apology to Lord Dashwood for having broken his nose, she retired to change her dress.

Sir Marmaduke made free with a bottle of Eau de Cologne, with which to refresh himself and Miss Fidget;—and then the party, accepting the invitation of the doctor, adjourned to his apartment to finish their breakfast with himself and daughter: during which time the servants gathered up the fragments, and put the room into order.

In a short time every face was arrayed in smiles, as if nothing had occurred to ruffle their placidity. The only drawback to the universal feeling of enjoyment which prevailed, was that which Dashwood and Sir Marmaduke experienced. The battered and swollen nose of the former, and the scalded foot of the latter, rendered it impossible for them to keep their appointment with the beautiful Heiress and her Duenna: they therefore managed to despatch a servant with a note, making such excuse, and offering such apology, as the accident they had met with would warrant.

"'Pon my honour," said Sir Marmaduke, "that was ex-

cessively unfortunate,—was it not?—However," he added,
" the felicity of meeting you, doc*tar*, and especially Miss
Titheum, has quite given me back my equanimity of spirits. Ah,—at what time did you reach Bath, pray?"

" Late last evening," returned the doctor.

" Ah,—'pon my honour," rejoined Sir Marmaduke, "that
was excessively unfortunate again,—was it not, my Lord?"

" A treat of no ordinary kind has been lost by you," observed Dashwood, addressing the rector and his daughter.

" How so, my Lord?" enquired Georgiana;—" Did any
thing take place last evening as rich as I have witnessed this
morning?"

" Infinitely surpassing it, I assure you," replied Dashwood,—" We had a masquerade."

" A masquerade!" echoed Georgiana;—" Oh, that must
have been delightful."

" Yes, 'pon my honour," said Sir Marmaduke, "a most
splendid one—never saw its equal;—you would have enjoyed
it, doc*tar*, 'pon my honour.—Company of the first order—
characters admirably sustained—perfect—delightful!"

" Was it so rich a treat, Miss Fidget?" asked Georgiana;
" I prefer the judgment of a lady rather than a gentleman's
on all occasions of taste; or—"

" Really I do not know, my dear," replied Miss Fidget;
" my poor Carlo was so unwell as to render it impossible
that I could attend."

" Perhaps your Grace could pleasure us with your opinion
of it," said Georgiana;—" your powers of description we all
know are unrivalled, and your judgment is in uniformity
with your descriptive powers."

" Thank you for your compliment, my dear," returned the
Duchess; " but, indeed I cannot oblige you—I did not attend,—was distracted with sick headache."

" Sorry to hear it," rejoined Georgiana,—" Then, of course,
you, my Lord, and Sir Marmaduke, were too gallant to leave
the ladies alone."

" Ah,—'pon my honour," yawned Sir Marmaduke, "we
had made such arrangements as to render it impossible to
remain away—exceedingly unfortunate; but so it was, 'pon
my honour,—was it not, my Lord?"

" Exactly so," replied Dashwood,—" Egad!" continued
his lordship, " I had almost forgotten it,—why, Sir Marmaduke had his fortune told, by a sly jade of a Gypsy."

"His fortune told!" shouted two or three voices,—"Ha! ha! ha!—his fortune told!"

"I dare say it was a most splendid one," returned Georgiana; "those kind of folk always take care to please those who are simple enough to become their *dupes.*"

"Umph!" said Sir Marmaduke; and then turning to Dashwood, observed,—"Better change the subject, 'pon my honour."

"Will you excuse me, Sir Marmaduke?" enquired the Duchess, who felt no inclination to linger any longer at the masquerade,—"Will you excuse me if I ask a favour of you?"

"Oh, certainly, your Grace," returned Sir Marmaduke; "it will afford me inexpressible gratification to meet your wishes in any way,—'pon my honour."

"Well, then," said the Duchess, "I am anxious to take the Duke a trifle from Bath, as I do from all places I visit, in order to please the youth,—and I know not what will suit my purpose better than a ring—"

"A ring!" cried Sir Marmaduke, mentally,—"Whew! —what next?—'Pon my honour."

"Now," continued the Duchess, "I have been greatly struck with the beauty and chastity of design which yours displays—perhaps you will oblige me with the loan of it for a pattern?"

"My ring, Madam?—certainly, your Grace," stammered out Sir Marmaduke, and bit his lips,—"with much pleasure, 'pon my honour; but,—"

"Yes, Sir Marmaduke," returned the Duchess, "the one you wore yesterday."

"Yesterday—my ring—'pon my honour—" continued to stammer the Knight,—"You said my ring,—confound it," he added aside, to Dashwood, "what shall I say?"

"Why, say the truth, that you lost it last night, to be sure," replied his lordship.

"Hem!—hem!—'Pon my honour," said Sir Marmaduke, "I regret that your Grace should have asked for the only thing which I have not the power to grant the loan of."

"Indeed!" returned the Duchess, with evident surprise, "I regret it too,—greatly regret it. It is, then, I suppose, a pattern which you are desirous to possess exclusively?"

"Not exactly so, 'pon my honour," returned the Knight;

"but the fact is—I—I lost it,—that is—yes—yes, I lost it last night."

" Lost that beautiful ring !" cried Miss Fidget.—" What, lost it from your finger, Sir Marmaduke ?"

" 'Tis true, 'pon my honour," returned the confused Knight.

" Then, I should doubt the respectability of the masquerade party," returned the Duchess.

" Oh, how very delightful it must have been," observed Georgiana, satirically,—" above any conception delightful, to have had your two arms pinioned by two strong ill-looking fellows, in the character of Inquisitors, while a third very kindly unhooped your finger, and transferred to his pocket your diamond ring,—very fine indeed,—ha ! ha ! ha !"

" Oh, exquisite !" rejoined the Duchess," as she marked the Knight's confusion ;—" This is *mask-queer-aid-ing,* and with a witness too."

" Well, ladies," continued Georgiana, " we have cause to bless our stars that we were not there."

" I'm sure I would not have been in such a scene for the world," observed Miss Fidget ;—" Do, pray, inform us how it happened, Sir Marmaduke."

" Aye,—do so," rejoined the doctor ; " and if my official influence can serve you, you have but to command it, Sir Marmaduke ; and I make no doubt we shall detect the thief."

" Why, doc*tar*," replied the Knight, " it was in this way —that is—" " Confound the thing, what shall I say ?") he again whispered to Lord Dashwood.

" Why, you lost it,—that's quite sufficient," answered his lordship, aside, " stick to that."

" Ah,—'pon my honour," returned Sir Marmaduke, " I cannot give any explanation—it was whisked away as if by a stroke of enchantment—it vanished from my finger ; but how, no one can tell ;—that is all I know about it, 'pon my honour."

" Oh, Sir Marmaduke," observed Georgiana, with befitting gravity of tone and look, " I do fear you are a naughty man —I do, indeed ;—now, was there not a lady in the case—eh ?"

" A lady !" shouted Miss Fidget.

" A lady !" rejoined Sir Marmaduke.

" Aye,—a *lady !*" said Georgiana,—" Now, do tell us who she was, and what she was, and—"

"No; 'pon my honour," said the Knight, "nothing of the kind—I never saw her before—that is,—I never heard such a question before."

"Indeed!" observed the Duchess, in a tone of credulity; however, I am sorry for your loss, *very* sorry; the pattern so pleased me."

"I have one," said Georgiana, "which has been greatly admired; *it* may, perhaps, suit your Grace;" and so saying, she drew her glove from her right hand, having carefully concealed the ring, and exhibited it,—"There," she added, "what says your Grace?"

Now, to all whom it may concern, be it known, that before the Duchess had risen to the dignified station which at this period she held, her Grace had been familiar with the stage; and now she appropriately displayed, both by word and action, her histrionic talents; for, as she continued to gaze on the ring which Georgiana still held, she exclaimed,

> "Durst I believe mine eyes
> I'd say I knew it,—and it was Sir Marmaduke's;"

to which Georgiana not less happily replied,—

> "Sir Marmaduke's, say'st thou?—Ah, it was Sir Marmaduke's."

"My ring!" exclaimed the Knight,—"my ring, Miss Georgiana! and possessed by you,—'pon my honour there is some perplexing mystery here."

"Indeed!" laughed Georgiana; and then assuming the tone and attitude of the Gypsy, she sung as on the past evening,

> "Sir Page, beware,
> And at length be wise;
> Your amours forbear,
> Or you'll lose your prize."

"'Pon my honour!" shouted Sir Marmaduke, "that's devilish clever,—ah,—beg pardon—ha! ha! ha!" he continued, while a simple look spread over his whole face, which was diffused with blushes, and exhibited a class of feelings which he evidently wished to conceal, yet knew not how.

"Why, what does all this mean, Sir Marmaduke?" enquired Miss Fidget, who, as she looked steadfastly into his face and beheld his confusion, felt something akin to jealousy agitate her tender bosom :—"There must be something amiss ; pray what is it ?"

"Oh, nothing ; positively nothing, 'pon my honour," returned Sir Marmaduke, doubly confused,—"that is—ah— as I said,—ha! ha! ha!—Confoundedly singular this, my Lord," he added, turning to Lord Dashwood.

"Why yes, rather so," returned his Lordship—ah,—a mere masquerade trick, Madam; nothing more, I assure you, Madam," he said, addressing Miss Fidget.

"A masquerade trick !" echoed the certain-aged lady,— "But you know, my Lord, when gentlemen flirt with ladies to such an extent as to lose their rings, a somewhat serious kind of *trick* must have been played."

"O these men! thése men!" shouted the Duchess, humorously,—who delighted in nothing so much as a right down lover's quarrel ;—"These men, Miss Fidget, are the destroyers of our peace. I know them well,—I wouldn't trust one that I valued a rush, the length of a rush out of my sight. Take my advice, Miss Fidget, and do as I do ; set your cap at as many as you feel disposed, and then take such one out of the lot as will best suit your purpose. Why, bless you," she continued, "if I had cared a button-top about my green-clad duke, I should have gone mad long ago; but no such thing—he wanted money, and I wanted a title ; I possessed the first and he the second, and so we agreed to put them together : I made him rich, and he made me a Duchess—dy'e see ?"

Miss Fidget pressed her dear Carlo to her heaving bosom, and declared, in the true spirit of Byron for his Newfoundlander,—"She never had but *one friend*, and Carlo was he."

Sir Marmaduke looked foolish, and attempted to explain, but failed most outrageously in the attempt. He stammered, hem'd and ha'd, said, unsaid, re-said, and then—was silent.

Lord Dashwood thought of the beautiful Heiress, and feared that his attentions to her might be disclosed by the fortune-teller ; while Georgiana, taking the ring from her finger, and approaching Sir Marmaduke, observed,—"Allow me, Sir Marmaduke, to restore this to its rightful owner ; and, for the satisfaction of all parties, permit me to give such an explanation of the whole affair as will, I am persuaded, satisfy all who are concerned in it.

The proposition was readily acceded to by Miss Fidget,

who really began to fear she should let the last offer slip, she
ever expected to receive ; while Sir Marmaduke, equally concerned, touching her large fortune, which he longed to handle,—felt delighted that one so able as Georgiana should undertake to set things right.

"'Pon my honour!" he exclaimed, brightening up, "I
feel superlatively obliged, Miss Titheum. Be assured," he
added, "my dear Miss Fidget, the satisfying of your mind
on a subject which, until explained, must appear mysterious,
is so greatly desired by me, that I feel beyond expression
happy that you will receive the explanation from one upon
whose word I feel assured you place implicit confidence, 'pon
my honour."

"Oh, Sir Marmaduke," sighed the lady, "of *your* honour and honourable intentions, I could have no possible
doubt; but you know, Sir Marmaduke, that an inexperienced *young* lady could but feel as I did in an affair of such
peculiar delicacy; but,—I beg pardon, my dear Miss Titheum;
do favour us with your statement : I feel a palpitation almost beyond endurance until I hear it. There now, dear
Carlo," continued the lady, "lay still a little,—there's a
sweet; and then I'll kiss you."

. Carlo, however, felt not inclined to wait; he was not a
wooer to be put off; he raised his scented face to his mistress, licked her blushing cheeks ; and, having received such
a salute as would have made some less favoured animal turn
rabid with delight, he wagged his tail, and again curled himself up in the *young* lady's lap.

The attention of the company being fully secured, Georgiana proceeded to sketch, in as sportive and graphic a way
as a shrewd wit might be supposed to do, as much of the
previous evening's entertainment as appeared to her necessary; and with which each appeared perfectly satisfied : a
hearty laugh went round the table, Sir Marmaduke forgot
his scalded foot, Lord Dashwood thought not upon his
broken nose, and Miss Fidget was so delighted to hear her
husband elect honourably acquitted, that, in the fulness of
her delight, she pronounced a solemn absolution upon the
head of the Knight for the offence of having overturned the
urn of boiling water upon the tail of her beloved Carlo.

CHAPTER XXVI.

> " Angels and ministers of grace, defend us !—
> Be thou a spirit of health, or goblin damn'd ;
> Bring with thee airs from heaven, or blasts from hell ;
> Be thy advent wicked or charitable,
> Thou com'st in such a questionable shape
> That I will speak to thee."
>
> HAMLET.

THE wine was circulating freely, and the mounting spirits of
Dr. Titheum and the Duchess led them into an argument
respecting the delectabilities of matrimony, to the infinite
entertainment of several of the party. As, however, it would
not accord with our purpose to give the whole of the argument,—maugre all the light and information it would throw
upon that frequently dark and intricate subject,—we shall
pass it over, and come at once to the hasty conclusion to
which one of the disputants came; although, certainly, altogether unconnected with the subject itself.

The Duchess insisted that either the divine was too old,
or too timid, to enter a second time the blissful estate of matrimony ! while the doctor, under the influence of a good
quantum of such excellent old Port as mine host of the York
House hotel, is deservedly celebrated for supplying his well-
paying guests with, rebutted the disreputable charge in great
good humour ; and offered to venture a couple of dozens of
the best wine that could be procured for money, against any
odds her Grace might feel disposed to state, that he would
get married,—aye, reader, 'twas boldly said; yet, said it was,
—he would get *married !* as soon as any one present: not
excepting Miss Fidget herself.

" It is a bet !" exclaimed the Duchess,—" I set four against
your two, doctor ;" adding,—" and the wine shall be used
upon the occasion,—that is, it shall be drunk on the happy
day that finds Miss Fidget a bride."

" To be sure, it shall," said the doctor,—" Wine ; plenty
of wine, and plenty of the best,—the *very* best sort is always
proper for a marriage feast—(hiccup !)—I can prove that, or
I'm not ' in the commission of the peace.' I can prove it
from—"

" When next you appear as a culprit at the altar," interrupted the Duchess, laughing ;—"Until then, doctor, we'll take it for granted it is proper."

"'Pon my honour," observed Sir Marmaduke, "I think, my dear Miss Fidget, we had better conclude our affair speedily, as such excellent preparation is making for the occasion, 'pon my honour I do."

"Oh, Sir Marmaduke!" exclaimed Miss Fidget, attempting to blush, "do, pray, pay some respect to my feelings. I dare say, however,—although I feel no wish to change my happy estate,—that I shall not play the prude upon the occasion; but when you—"

"Oh, I see! 'pon my honour, you are superlatively kind, Miss Fidget," interrupted Sir Marmaduke; "you are, 'pon my honour."

"Now, if we could fairly manage to procure a proper, handsome, gay, gallant, young marquis or lord, or something of that sort, for you, my dear Georgiana," observed the Duchess, jocosely, "we should have a day of wonders, such as the renowned Moore never foretold in his prophetic annual. However," continued her Grace, "I will make a note of this our engagement." So saying, she drew from a splendid crimson velvet reticule which hung on her arm, a small tablet, handsomely bound in blue morocco, fancifully decorated with mother-of-pearl, and confined with silver clasps, and wrote,—

"Mém. extraordinary.—Dr. Titheum to be married on the same day with Sir Marmaduke Varney, or forfeit two dozen wine. If ceremony performed at time stated, I lose twice the quantity,—there,—shall feel happy to fulfil my part of the engagement."

"Now, doctor, look out sharp," continued the Duchess, "and may you prosper."

"'Pon my honour, doctar," observed Sir Marmaduke, "but you are handsomely booked,—Ha! ha! ha! her Grace has you, 'pon my honour."

"Bless me!" exclaimed the Duchess, as her eye fell upon a memorandum in her tablet,—"Here is an engagement which I made a few days since, and to which I must attend this evening. I would not have forfeited my word in this case for fifty pounds. Will you not accompany me, my Lord?" she observed, applying to Dashwood.

"Should be most happy," returned his Lordship, "to accompany your Grace *any* where, had you not broken my nose."

" Oh, a fiddlestick with your nose !" cried her Grace, " it will do exceedingly well. There is nothing so uncommonly amiss with it ; besides, it is the best·you have, and will very well answer every purpose for which those sort of things are intended. The fact is simply this : the Manager of the Theatre here, by some unlucky circumstance, gained intelligence of my visit to Bath ; and, being well aware that I am always ready, when I can, to assist the profession, he waited upon me to request that I would allow him to announce a play, &c., this evening, under my especial patronage. Now, what *could* I say, but just what I *did* say ? that is, that I would accede to his wishes ; and, as I had a few friends with me, would engage that they should accompany me. A couple of boxes are waiting our pleasure, and not to fill them would be to cast disgrace upon my own patronage. Now, who among ye," she cried, turning to each of the party,

> ' Will shame my friendship in a cause like this ;
> Nor rally round me when I want your aid?
> Smile, all my friends, like generous Romans all,
> And tell me, as you smile, I have your hearts.'

Dr. Titheum, you will not desert me ?"

" Not I, in good truth," replied his reverence,—" I am not ' in the commission of the peace' if—(hiccup !)—I don't chaperone your Grace—(hiccup !)—*any* where you may desire."

" And I shall be delighted to visit the theatre," said Georgiana ; " I have heard so much of the beauty of the house, and of the superior character of the company, that to me it will be a positive treat."

" And Miss Fidget," said the Duchess, " you will—"

" Why, really," interrupted that lady, " I fear my dear Carlo is not sufficiently recovered to allow me to venture ; however, if Sir Marmaduke wishes it, I—"

" 'Pon my honour," returned the Knight, "I shall feel inexpressibly happy to accompany her Grace, and you, my dear Miss Fidget,—confound me if I shan't—'pon my honour."

Lord Dashwood saw and felt, that notwithstanding the battered state of his proboscis, he could not maintain his opposition solus ; and, therefore, as himself and other worthy members of the Upper House have frequently done, under the influence of petticoat government, he assented most heartily to the measure, and appeared ready to prove, that no question could have more fully accorded with his views, or more fully have met his wishes.

The engagement thus made, a little bustle followed in making preparation, and then away they rolled in their carriages to Orchard Street, leaving orders with their servants to be in attendance at a quarter past twelve, precisely; for, in consequence of some extra performances which were to be attended to that evening, they were aware it would be near one before the whole terminated.

Claudius and Joseph, in company with the servants of the other members of the party, had, before they were acquainted with the intentions of the Duchess and her train to visit the Theatre, planned for themselves an evening's entertainment, and experienced, therefore, an increased degree of pleasure at being left so completely at liberty to pursue their purpose until twelve o'clock, at least.

Now it was, that the mischief-loving propensity of our hero suddenly rose to its highest pressure; and, while a dozen happy souls of either gender were heartily regaling themselves with the best the kitchen afforded, and swallowing large quantums of Wiltshire ale, Claudius was racking his inventive brain to find some means by which,—like Yorick of old, who was wont with " gibes, gambols, songs, and flashes of merriment, to set the table in a roar,"—he might please himself and afford mirth to others.

A sufficient portion of strong ale had already been taken to make most, at the supper table, talk loudly, if not wisely; and ever and anon a din of opposing voices, from the soft but garrulous treble down to the ear-splitting base, sounded in the room, as if its present occupants had determined in their minds to rival, in discord and confusion, the scene which transpired at ancient Babel.

Among others who had been invited to this display of " high life below stairs," was a Mr. Muzzlechops, a precise, pedantic, would-be gentleman, a dresser of ladies' fronts, who railed loudly against the follies and vices of the age, and whose timely and spirited vituperations increased both in velocity and vehemence, as he poured increased portions of strong liquor down his thirsty throat.

Now, this same Mr. Muzzlechops had more than once dressed the head of Mrs. Plumpbottom, the fat cook, at the York Hotel; and thinking, doubtless, that if he could win the fat heart of the fat cook, he might, through her interest, succeed in obtaining a fat business in connexion with the Tavern—he, in common parlance, tried it on; and, from certain side looks, affable nods, winning smiles, &c., which the fat cook condescended to bestow upon her knight of the scissors and soap-suds, hoped to succeed.

On the evening in question, Mr. Muzzlechops had brought Mrs. Plumpbottom a beautiful new front: notice being duly given him that by some accident she had lost her former one. The new front he presented with a speech, which, with considerable labour, he had prepared for the occasion. The cook listened to his eloquent and elegant effusion with surprise, (the better half of which being perfectly unintelligible), received the front with pleasure, and, without feeling half so much for his *person* as for his *present,* she nevertheless invited him to make one of the party; which invitation, with undissembled pleasure, he accepted.

For the information of the reader it is proper to state, that Harry Whipcord, one of the coachmen from the Hotel, who drove a day coach from Bath to London—a smart and dashing chap, as most of those knowing coveys are in their way, —had long been smitten by the charms of Mrs. Plumpbottom's fine proportions, while a corresponding feeling possessed that fair damsel—at least she told him so; but who can believe a woman on such a subject?—for Harry's slap-up person. There was, she declared, such an *insinerwating* leer in his eye—such a *si-entiffic* turn in his elbow—such a grace in his handling the *rains* and the *vip,* that no feeling woman could look at him with indifference;—and then, his broad-brimmed hat, his handsome shawl-handkerchief bound round his neck, and his shining brown top-boots, were positively *captiwaiting.*

On this joyous evening, Harry was present, and felt not a little startled at seeing Mr. Muzzlechops, his rival, introduced to the company by the cook, as her *friend.*

Claudius soon learned how the cat jumped (as the Yorkshire man said when he tied a lighted cracker to her tail, and turned her loose into a China warehouse), and in a short time succeeded in securing the hearty concurrence of Harry Whipcord to make Mr. Muzzlechops the subject of at least part of their evening's amusement.

The loquacious barber (and few of that genus are often guilty of the sin of taciturnity) continued to swallow the ale with good relish, until his tongue appeared to have acquired a freedom of expression, as if moved in its operations by the power of steam.

"Mrs. Plumpbottom, I feels proud to drink your health," he observed, as he raised the tankard to his mouth, for about the fortieth time,—"Gentlemen and ladies all,—I begs pardon—*ladies* and gentlemen—the *felemile gendur* always takes the *pre-emisence*,—ladies and gentlemen all!" After taking a long and deep draught he replaced the vessel on the table, but so near the edge that it fell upon the floor, emptying its contents into the shoes of the housemaid, who sat next him.

"Confound your clumsy head!" exclaimed the girl:—and added, holding up first her right, and then her left foot, even with the table,—"See what a precious mess you have made my white stockings in."

"I axes pardon," said Muzzlechops, without much concern; and then drawing a dashing cambric handkerchief from his pocket, he flourished it awhile, blew his nose, wiped his mouth, and proceeded in his gastronimical exercise

"I zay," observed Giles Roughhead, the hostler, as he pushed a large piece of scalding-hot pudding into a crater-like mouth, and then returned it to his plate, spluttering with pain, while the tears flowed from his eyes.—"Danguns! how curst hot the pudding be's—I'ze slashed if I hant skotched my gums."

"If a person will be so greedy, among gentlemen and lad—no, I means *ladies* and gentlemen," observed Mr. Muzzlechops, "vy, vot else can be expected?" So saying, he thrust a spoonful of hot mock-turtle soup between his ivories, forgetting to blow it, which in as quick time as Giles's pudding had been ejected, not into his plate, however, but over the table.

"Well said, Mr. Muzzlechops!" roared Harry Whipcord, delighted to see his rival so punished;—"Wipe your eyes, my good man,—hook on the traces, and go it again, my hearty!"

Mr. Muzzlechops looked at Harry, but dared not make reply; then wiped his eyes and made a second apology.—"I hate wolgarity," he observed; "Mrs. Plumpbottom, oblige me with the tankard."

"Well," observed Giles again, "I guess ve is as happy as them 'ere folks at the Play."

" The Play !" exclaimed Mr. Muzzlechops; " oh, don't mention it,—the wolgar and degrading trash. I think's it is a shame that such 'ere things is tollerated in this 'ere country."

" And for vy ?" asked Giles.

" Because," replied Mr. Muzzlechops, "I do,—that's vy."

" Ha! ha! ha!" roared Joseph, who until this moment had been silent ;—" That is a reason, sure enough ; no milk girl could have given a better."

" Vell then," returned the barber, " if so be, I must be more *perticuller*,—I thinks they destroys the morals of the people. If those 'ere people who goes to the Play was to spend their wacant time, and spare money, in purchasing books and improving their mind, as I do, so much crime and ignorance wouldn't rebound."

" Vell, as to larnin," said Giles, " I don't mean to argufy with you consarning it ; I comed here to enjoy mysel', and dang me if I don't, spite o' all you larned chaps. I likes to make enquiries and observations, howsomdever. What is this 'ere play to-night ?"

" The ' Honey Moon,' " replied Claudius.

" The ' Honey Moon!' " shouted the barber,—" Vy, that must be a good sort of thing. Your health," he added, Mrs. Plumpbottom," winking,—" A good thing that ' Honey Moon.' "

" But that is not all," continued Claudius; " there's dancing, and singing, and a Farce ; and the whole concludes with a splendid Pantomime."

" A Pantomime !" exclaimed Muzzlechops; " Vy, whatever thing is that ? Please, hand me a little more of that 'ere fresh turreen of that 'ere fine soup, Mrs. Plumpbottom."

The fat cook attended the request of the barber ; and, diving the ladle deep in the reeking liquid, fished up something of a suspicious character ;—not having time, however, to examine it, she shot the whole into Mr. Muzzlechop's plate ; which, being well filled, he plunged his spoon into it, and then pushed part of its contents into his ample mouth, —the whole it could not receive,—when a convulsive roar, which threatened to end fatally with some of the party, rose from the whole as they perceived Mrs. Plumpbottom's lost front hanging, half in and half out, of the barber's mouth. The fact is, by some accident the ribbon which should have confined the glossy ringlets had snapped asunder, while the cook was attending a large saucepan of soup, and, unperceived by her, it had slipped into the greasy pool, from whence, after a few hours' boiling, it had been transferred to the tureen, and afterwards to the barber's plate, and subsequently to his mouth.

To record all that transpired from this singular circumstance, would occupy too much time and space; for a while it afforded a fund of amusement;—poor Muzzlechops groaned beneath the gibes which were thrown upon him; and at length, to change the subject, turned once more to the question he had formerly proposed,—of "what is a Pantomime?"

" What is it?" said Claudius,—" Why, did you never see one?"

" Never," replied the barber, " and suppose I never shall. I don't patronise sich things—still I should like to hear what they are. Mrs. Plumpbottom, could you oblige me with the information?"

" To be sure, I can," replied the cook; " they are things full of tricks, so suddenly performed as if a magician's wand had done it; and I do think there must be some dealings with the old un to do some of the things."

" Oh, no doubt of it," observed Mr. Muzzlechops,—" No doubt of it at all ;—it must be so."

" Why, they can change a wheelbarrow into a hackney-coach, and a cabbage into a gin shop," said the hostler ; " Ize seed it done with my own personal eyes."

" Ah," continued Harry Whipcord, " and more than that they can do ;—why, they have only to whistle in this sort of way, ' Whew !' and a fellow who just before was swaggering before your eyes, vanishes like a will o'the wisp."

" Wonderful !" had half escaped the extended jaws of Mr. Muzzlechops, when, as if the prince of the black art, whose authority and influence the barber had presumed to speak disparagingly of, determined to avenge himself on the audacions caitiff, his seat sprung suddenly from under him, while his unfortunate posteriors came in sudden and violent contact with the stone floor of the kitchen.

A fierce muscular movement, or spasmodic action, greatly resembling the effect of a strong galvanic operation upon a dead body, threw poor Muzzlechop's arms forward at the instant he was falling, and grasping hold of the table-cloth,—as a drowning man does at a straw,—he pulled the whole of the supply beneath which the table had groaned before, after him; and hot soup, boiling beef, and cooling ale, with a host of *eatables*, mingled strangely together like the elements of which our world was formed, while as yet all was chaos, and almost smothered the terrified dresser of ladies' fronts.

All was darkness and confusion, without form and void.— As soon as the first shock was over, Claudius, very good-naturedly, hasted to unpack the barber; but, whether by ac-cident or otherwise, has not transpired, he ran his hand against the chimney-back while running to render assistance, and bore away with him a quantity of soot; and then, while feeling after Mr. Muzzlechops, who groaned under a load of plates, dishes, and provisions, his sooty palm passed over his greasy face, and, in an instant, transformed him into a per-fect *fac-simile* of the unfortunate and abused Moor of Ve-nice.

As soon as lights were re-possessed, and confusion had partially subsided, it was ascertained that no very serious loss had been sustained. Mr. Muzzlechops was replaced in his chair, to the laugh-exciting observation of all present.

" Who are you?" asked Claudius, looking full in his face, —" What has brought you here?"

" Who am I?" returned the still trembling barber;—" Vy, really, I can hardly tell. However did all this happen?"

" Do you play Mungo, or Othello, or Zanga: or do you purpose to enact the part of Beelzebub himself to-night?" asked Joseph.

" Do I play what?" enquired Muzzlechops, confused by the loud laughter in which all joined, and the questions which were asked him, without understanding or conceiving the cause.

" Just step this way, Mr. Muzzlechops," said the house-maid, leading him towards a looking-glass which hung against the wall, " and I'll show you such a sight!—There," she added, pointing to the mirror, " did you ever see such a frightful thing before?"

" Bless me!" exclaimed Muzzlechops, starting back, as his eye caught the reflection of his own changed visage, which he scarcely recognised, " it is as you say, a frightful thing; that is,—ha! ha!" he added, taking another peep,—" I see,— ha! ha! ha!—Why, how came my face in sich a mess, I wonders?"

Mrs. Plumpbottom recommended an " *ablutation*," as she learnedly called the application of some soap and water to his face; and Mr. Muzzlechops acknowledged her attention with a polite congee, and accepted a proffered wooden bowl full of water, &c. &c., and in a few minutes,

"Richard was himself again!"

His face shone with its usual brilliancy; while his soiled dress, under the application of a hard brush, re-assumed their appearance of pristine elegance.

During the time the dresser of ladies' fronts and mower of bristles from gentlemen's chins, was engaged in the purification and improvement of his personal appearance and dress, the cook and her satellites were busy in clearing away the remains of supper, and placing chairs in order round the table, on which certain viands were now placed for the further regaling of the guests; together with earthen tubes for such as might feel disposed to make use of them.

It is scarcely necessary to mention the cause of the sudden descent of Mr. Muzzlechops; the reader will, in all probability, have anticipated it. Lest, however, any should not have been able to "catch the cue," for their special information be it stated, that Claudius, that wily, mischievous elf, had succeeded in attaching a strong piece of cord to one of the legs of the chair on which the barber was seated. Having so done, he retired with the other end of it to a remote corner of the roomy kitchen, and on a signal being given him by the jealous coachman,—who, by the bye, would have felt but little compunction if the neck of his unfortunate rival had been broken instead of his seat of importance being bruised,—gave a sudden pull, and, as has been seen, the half-fuddled artiste was overturned in the midst of his glory.

"Past eleven o'clock," had been said or sung, by the guardians of the night, through the length and breadth of the fair city of Bath; and the inhabitants, like good and honest citizens, had retired to seek the invigorating influence of

"Nature's kind restorer,—balmy sleep."

All was peace and quiet,—save in the houses of a few revellers, who appeared to indulge a strange propensity to invert the order of nature; or, influenced by a greedy desire (under the deceptive guise of soft and accommodating expressions employed by thousands to cheat themselves) to destroy their health and murder their souls, drained, amidst wild uproar, the wassal-bowl,—saving such exceptions, as we have said, all was peace and quiet.

Among the exceptions referred to, was the party in the kitchen of the York Hotel. They had each taken, not only *more* than enough to *satisfy* nature,

" Who in her claims is moderate ever,"

but sufficient to *offend* nature, and make their vilest passions turn rampant. It was at this point of time that Claudius determined once more to gratify his own inordinate love of mischief, as well as to meet the ardent wishes of Harry Whipcord, by making Mr. Muzzlechops appear ridiculous in the eyes of his mistress and the company.

In concert with that renowned personage, our hero soon completed sundry preparations for the execution of the scheme he had devised: Mr. Muzzlechops had now become pot-valiant; and, if his boasting statements had been credited, every one present would have believed that the redoubtable barber would, by his single arm, have put to flight a whole legion of foul spirits, or have driven, to his own gloomy regions, the foul fiend himself.

" I never yet seed a being, wissible or *in-wissible*," he exclaimed, pompously, " what I feared to encounter ;—and as for them 'ere fancies which some folks talks about, such as *ghosteses* and hobgoblins ; vy, bless you, I vos alvays too vell informed to admit the existance of any of um."

" It may be true," observed Claudius, " that you doubt their existence ; but it does not follow that spirits never do appear because *you* do not admit they do."

" Vy, that's werry good,—hexcellent, my lad !" returned Mr. Muzzlechops, fixing his large gogles, which appeared like two boiled gooseberries stuck in a quartern of dough, full upon our hero's face,—" That's *kappital ;* but still I means to maintain, that none but women and fools,—I begs pardon,—(hiccups)—I *concepts*, however, the present company ; —none, whatsomever,—I means to say, but fools and cowards, ever feared sich things."

" Very clever, indeed, Mr. Muzzlechops," observed Mrs. Plumpbottom,—" Then, of course, *you* never fear any spirits."

" What, me !—me !—Zedekiah Muzzlechops !—*me* fear !" returned the barber ;—"Ah, no,—yes ; I beg pardon; I do fear *some* spirits—a lady's ven she's not in a good temper : none beside, I promise you, Mrs. Plumpbottom. Vy, I'd go on tne darkest night whatever shined out of the blessed *firma-*

ment, into a churchyard *alone;* or, for that 'ere matter, into
a bone-house, and bring a pick-axe and spade,—aye, or a
jaw-bone, out of that 'ere place, and never fear."

"Indeed !" said Harry Whipcord, "I make no doubt but
you are a devilish bold fellow ; but a little braggish though.
Did you ever hear of the cellar under this kitchen being
haunted ?"

"Never, Sir," replied the barber, "and I denies it."

"Well, I have heard," continued Harry, "that there is a
small barrel of extra strong ale in one corner of that place,
which was brewed by an old waiter who was murdered in the
cellar, about twenty years ago ; and that when any one has
attempted to turn the tap in that barrel, old 'raw head,' as
he is called, has appeared in a flame of fire, and commanded
them to desist."

"Whew !" whistled Mr. Muzzlechops, looking at Mrs.
Plumpbottom with an heroic air, as if to offer himself as her
champion to drive the troubled spirit from her domain.—"I'll
wager you a guinea against a dump," said the barber, "that
I fetches,—with Mrs. Plumpbottom's *parmission*,—a jug full
of that 'ere ale, from that 'ere haunted barrel, in less than five
minutes."

"I'll cover your guinea that you don't," said Harry, immediately depositing the sum upon the table.

"Done," and "Done," like a pair of cock-fighters, was
pronounced by both, and the valiant barber prepared for the
fearful trial. Having taken a hearty draught at a glass of
rum-and-water, "to keep his courage up," he rose firmly
upon his pins.

"Hem !" said the hero of the hour,—"I am ready."
Bearing with him a light in one hand and a jug in the other,
he commenced descending a long flight of winding stairs,
which led to a large damp cellar below. No sooner had he
taken two steps of downward character, than the door above
him was closed with an ominous sound. This first shock to
his nerves tended partially to cause the spirit of the drink
he had swallowed, suddenly to evaporate, leaving him to
pursue his task unassisted by the aid of stimulants. Every
succeeding step increased his trepidation, as the old stairs
creaked beneath his tread, and the sound ran echoing in ter-
rifying response round the vacuum below.

Once and again he paused, and held the light above his
head,—all was silent, *painfully* silent ;—he could almost hear

the palpitations of his own bold heart, as it thumped against
his ribs as though it demanded egress. The rays of the taper
which he bore were not sufficient to dispel the thick and
palpable gloom which rested upon the distance. The pause
which he had made tended in a measure to remove the terror
which had fallen upon him, and down he went.

The bottom being at length gained, he once more paused,
and gazed wishfully and half fearfully round him, and presently espied the vessel out of which he was to procure the
forbidden ale. At this awful moment his thoughts happily
turned to Mrs. Plumpbottom; and, while the perspiration
oozed from his icy forehead, he thought his courage was in-
vigorated.

Slowly, and with marked steps, he approached the barrel,
and again paused and gazed round; and then, bending on
one knee, he placed the light on the stone floor, and was in
the act of placing his hand to the tap,—when a hollow and
deep sepulchral voice fell upon his ear, and demanded,—
"Who are you that dares presume to touch my ale?"

The barber's head turned mechanically towards the point
whence the sound proceeded—it was a dark recess on his
left hand, which he had not before perceived,—when, horror
of horrors!—the fearful apparition stood before him. A
long white garment, stained here and there with blood,
floated round the lower part of the figure; while, from his
eyeless sockets, fleshless nose, and hideously gaping jaws, a
flame issued, which gave an additionally fearful character to
the unearthly visitant.

The awe-struck barber stood not upon politeness at the
instant; and, therefore, without giving a reply to the question, he started upon his feet, and seized, without knowing
what he did, the candlestick, and at the same moment let the
jug fall from his enervated hand, which was dashed to pieces.

As if paralyzed by the awful sight, he stood a perfect picture of misery, gazing on the terrible vision—

> " His knotty and combined locks did part,
> And each particular hair did stand on end
> Like quills upon the fretful porcupine."

Slowly and solemnly the spectre shook its ghastly head,
and grinned a demon's grin at him. Muzzlechops groaned
with horror;—the Ghost appeared as if it would approach
him—when, springing from his Lot-like posture, he flew with

the fleetness of a lapwing up the numerous stairs, without feeling any or counting one; and bursting open the door, threw himself into the kitchen and fainted on the floor.

While proper applications are being made use of to restore the doughty barber to life and consciousness, we may, by a sort of episodical connecting link, review the back scenes of this farcical affair.

We have already stated, that Claudius and Harry Whipcord were in league—it was their *united* energies which gave perfection to the ghostly trick just played on the barber; although the honour of the projection of it belonged to the inventive brain of our hero alone.

Claudius had succeeded in drawing the conversation of the kitchen guests to the interesting and enlivening subject of ghosts and apparitions; and, having so done, proceeded to prepare a ghost, for the purpose of putting the boasted valour of the barber to the test.

Having procured a large turnip from a neighbouring greengrocer's, he scooped out the inside of it, leaving little more than the thick rind; and then having cut certain orifices upon it, rudely representing the eyes, nose, and mouth, of a human head, he placed it upon the handle of a worn-out mop, around which he wound in loose folds a sheet which had been supplied for the occasion by Harry Whipcord. For the purpose of rendering the appearance still more appalling, streaks of red ochre, representing flowing blood, were made upon the sheet.

The figure being thus prepared, Claudius proceeded to place it and himself in the best possible position, to give effect to the whole. A door which led from an adjoining closet admitted our hero into a dark recess, and there he took his stand, with a candle and dark lantern. The back part of the turnip having been cut away, he could with one hand hold his lighted taper behind the represented face, so as to give it effect, and, with the other, turn the whole figure as he pleased.

At the moment Muzzlechops was about to draw the ale, Claudius proposed the question which produced the effects already narrated. A moment's examination on the part of the dresser of ladies' fronts, would have led to a detection of the fraud; but fear having once gained the ascendancy of his reason and judgment, the consequences which followed were unavoidable.

A full quarter of an hour elapsed before poor Muzzle-chops opened his terrified eyes, and gazed wildly on the by-standers.

"Where is he?" he exclaimed in a phrenzied tone.

"Where's what?" asked Harry Whipcord, who revelled in the barber's terrors.

"The ghost, the ghost!" replied Muzzlechops; "I see'd him. Oh, how horribly he grinned!"

"Nonsense, man, nonsense," resumed Harry; "why, you don't believe in them ere things, do you?"

"I didn't once," said the barber, "but I do now, I have had *occull demonstra-shun*."

"Pshaw!" cried the coachman; "I thought you possessed a stouter heart."

"What do you mean?" asked the barber; "did *you* ever see a ghost?" he added, half raising himself and looking wildly.

"Never," said Harry, "and never shall, in my opinion; nor you either, I'll be bound."

"Yes, but I have, though—ugh!" cried the beautifier of chins, shrugging up his shoulders.

"I tell you it is no such thing," replied Harry; "and I'll prove it in a brace of winks."

So saying, he descended the cellar stairs, and returned immediately, bringing with him the face-formed turnip and the sheet.

"Look here, man," said Coachee, in a tone of triumph; "What think you of the ghost now I have stopped his wizzen for him?—ha, ha, ha!"

Mr. Muzzlechops felt greatly inclined to discredit his own eyes, and refused for a considerable time to allow his hand to come in contact with what he still believed to be the head of the ghost. At length, however,

"Confirmation, clear as Holy Writ,"

was possessed, and he joined the laugh in which the whole party was heartily indulging; and after shaking hands with his rival, left the house, declaring he would never again in-terfere between him and Mrs. Plumpbottom.

One by one the carousers departed, while those whose business called them to the theatre for their masters, put to their horses, and drove up to the door of the house as the clock struck twelve. After waiting nearly half an hour, the

parties appeared at the box door, from whence they stepped into their carriages, and returned home, wearied in body, but delighted with the entertainments of the evening.

———

CHAPTER XXVII.

"I've seen simplicity give place
To Fashion's meretricious grace,—
I've seen thee stoop to petty arts
For triumph o'er unvalued hearts,—
Envy, and vanity, and guile,
The secret springs of every smile;
While fearless confidence sits now
On that once blushing, timid brow.'

ANON.

THE note which Lord Dashwood and Sir Marmaduke Varney sent conjointly to Lady Bolio and Mrs. Leechum, containing an apology for their non-attendance at the period they had proposed, found those ladies in company with Dr. Leechum, in the drawing-room of the mansion in the Royal Crescent. Lady Bolio had not *yet* ceased to enjoy a flirtation, and, to Mrs. Leechum, such a thing seemed to be a sort of sunny spot, in what she called the dark map of her existence : such being the case, it can be no matter of astonishment that both were waiting on the tip-toe of expectation for the expected call of the Knight of the Golden Fleece, and his gentlemanly Page.

Lady Bolio had put a small extra quantity of rouge on her face, and arranged with more than ordinary care her purchased ringlets, in order to give effect; while Mrs. Leechum had stopped at least fifty times before a large mirror to enquire of its faithful reflection, if any additional stray lock could be allowed, by which to heighten her attractions.

"Well, my dear," observed Dr. Leechum to his sweet lady, "how were you entertained last evening ?"

"Why really, Dr. Leechum," returned his crooked rib, "I do not believe your equal lives for curiosity. Now, of what importance, I should like to be informed, can it be to you, *how* I enjoyed myself?—did you enjoy yourself? But I have no need to ask such a question, *you* always enjoy *yourself*."

"Why, yes, my love, tolerably well," replied the doctor;

"especially when you are absent," he added aside; "but I was merely going to observe—"

"Now, do pray, *merely* cease tormenting one so inces. santly," returned his lady. "The more you know, the more you desire to know:—you are like a horseleech, never sa. tisfied."

"And in order, therefore, that my desires may not be further excited," said the doctor, "you are determined not to let me know any thing."

"Exactly so," replied his wife, as she shook her pretty, plump, and bare shoulders, and turned from the doctor, as if the sight of him did not quite ravish her. "Bless me," she added, " it is very singular,—nearly one o'clock, and no call yet!"

"Do you expect a call, my love?" asked the doctor.

"There, again,—oh dear—oh dear!" sighed out the afflicted Mrs. Leechum. "Now, Lady Bolio, did ever you behold Dr. Leechum's equal at tormenting? I declare I am wearied out of my wits by replying to his endless interrogations."

Lady Bolio had been amusing herself in re-arranging a large and superb crape shawl, which was thrown carelessly over her shoulders; and so entirely had her mind been en- grossed by her important engagement, as scarcely to have heard the interesting tete-a-tete which had been held be- tween her friend and the doctor. On being directly appealed to, she turned from the mirror, without catching the whole of Mrs. Leechum's observation, or, indeed, understanding any part of it, and replied. "Why, yes, love, I suppose we may expect them in a few minutes; and really I have not often seen an equal to the Knight. I hope to have the pleasure, Dr. Leechum, to introduce you to two friends of mine presently."

"I feel obliged to your ladyship," returned Leechum,— " shall be most happy to meet any friends of Lady Bolio's."

"Oh! there can be no doubt of it," observed Mrs. Leech- um; "but I do think now, Dr. Leechum, if you were to take the stroll you were talking of, round the High Common, or just step through Orange Grove, and enjoy yourself for a few hours in the Pump Room, it would be beneficial to you."

"I shall feel much pleasure in taking the airing, love, which you recommend," returned the doctor, "and as soon as yourself and Lady Bolio are ready, will accompany you."

"Lady Bolio and myself are not going out this morning," said Mrs. Leechum, "it is quite impossible; last night has so fatigued us, that I am certain the least exertion would be more than we could bear."

"Here's a livery servant coming," observed Lady Bolio, as she gazed from the window, "with a note too,—some invitation to an evening party, I dare say."

"How troublesome people are just now," cried Mrs. Leechum peevishly; "why don't you go for your walk, Dr. Leechum? was ever any one tormented to the extent I am with a contrary husband? I tell you, Sir, to go out to-day is *impossible*."

The doctor took the *rather* broad hint that his dear wife wished for his absence, and with as much propriety as his duty told him he should display in the gratifying his *dear* wife in all her just wishes, he observed, "Well, well, my dear, as you *desire* it, I will go;" and, accordingly, he went to prepare for the walk Mrs. Leechum had—for reasons best known to herself—recommended.

"If you please, my lady," said a servant who appeared at the door, "there is a man in the hall, who states that he comes from Lord Dashwood with a note for Don Rosbell."

"From *Lord* Dashwood!" exclaimed Mrs. Leechum.

"Yes, madam," returned the servant, "that was the name, I'm sartin; and I told him that no sich person as Don Rosbell lived here, but he insisted this is the number he was to call at."

"Don Roshell!" said her ladyship, "you surely make a mistake—it must be Donna Rosabella;—bring up the note and let me see."

The servant bowed and withdrew, and in a moment returned with the billet-deux, and gave it into Lady Bolio's hand; on receiving it she read:—

"To the Ladies—Donna Rosabella, and her Honourable Duenna."

"Oh, it is quite right," observed Mrs. Leechum; "desire the servant to wait a moment, until we ascertain if any answer is required."

Lady Bolio broke open the note immediately, and read:—

"Lord Dashwood and Sir Marmaduke Varney, present their profound respects to the fair Donna Rosabella and her Honourable Duenna, and deeply regret that an accident this morning has rendered it impossible for them to enjoy the high gratification and honour they had contemplated, of paying their respects to the ladies in person.   At the earliest period, however, that present opposing circumstances shall have passed away, they hope to be indulged with the same permission as was granted them last evening, of enquiring after their health

"York Hotel, Bath."

"There is no answer," said Lady Bolio, to the servant, who entered at the sound of the bell,—"say so to the bearer of this note."

"I will, your ladyship," replied the servant, and withdrew.

"Lord Dashwood, and Sir Marmaduke Varney!" exclaimed Mrs. Leechum ; "well, I knew they were persons of some consequence.   I wonder which was Lord Dashwood."

"What can have happened so very important?" observed Lady Bolio, "as to prevent a call,—an accident they state—well it is of no consequence,—to us, at least,—of that I am certain."

"How very provoking it is to be so disappointed," cried Mrs. Leechum ; "I have been a doomed woman ever since I got married, that I have."

"Hush, my dear," said Lady Bolio, "here comes the doctor."

"Well, my dear," said Leechum, as he entered the apartment with his gold-headed cane, and equipped for the ramble which his wife had all but insisted on his taking,—"I am just going for my walk."

"Are you so, Dr. Leechum?" returned the lady pettishly; "well, one would have imagined you possessed sufficient politeness—although wanting in kindness and attention to your   wife —to ask if Lady Bolio and myself felt disposed to walk."

"To ask what?" exclaimed the doctor, opening his eyes widely, as though he supposed his ears had received a wrong sound.

"If we felt disposed to walk, Sir!" returned his gentle wife ; "surely I speak plainly."

"Why, I understood, my love," replied Leechum, "that neither Lady Bolio nor yourself could *possibly* go out to-day."

"Your understanding must be very obtuse, Sir," said Mrs. Leechum, "or you would have known better.   But I understand it all, I am aware that possession has induced satiety. I have thrown myself away, I feel I have; you wish to make a prisoner of me, and purpose, I dare say, to coop me up, as if I were a monster you were training for an exhibition."

"Now, indeed, my love, I did understand," observed Leechum pacifically, "that—"

"Yes, yes, I know it all," interrupted his wife; "I have my fears, I assure you, that while I, your too—too affectionate and docile wife, am immured at your pleasure, you are gallivanting with some other lady: it is very well, Sir," she continued, as she observed the doctor was about to reply,—'tis *very* well, I say; and I suppose you expect and wish it may last, do you not? But take care I do not turn to be what I fear your unkindness will drive me to,—the *most* gentle cannot always submit without a murmur."

"My dear love," said the doctor, maintaining a respectful distance, for fear of consequences, "now, really you said you could not go out to-day."

"I said no such thing, Dr. Leechum," returned his *most géntle* wife; "and, even if I had said so, what then?—it would have become you to have prevailed on me to walk, or if I had made up my mind not to go, you should have been contented to have remained at home, if only for the sake of appearances."

"Allow me to observe, my dear—" said the doctor,—

"Allow *me* to observe, Dr. Leechum, interrupted his *sweet* wife, that I don't choose to be so treated, and go I will. Lady Bolio," she added, "will you accompany me this morning for a stroll round York Buildings; or, at least somewhere?"

"I feel no objection, my dear," said her ladyship; "and since our expected visitors are not coming, I think we had better walk. But now, don't be vexed, my dear; Dr. Leechum will accompany us,—won't you?"

"I shall be most happy to do so," replied the Leech.

"Heigho!" sighed Mrs. Leechum, from the bottom of her heart —"Well, I suppose, as I am a wife—I suppose I *must* submit to it;—I am determined, nevertheless, to maintain the prerogative of a woman, if only for the honour of my sex, and because I am not *wanted* to go; *therefore*, I *will* go. Come, my dear Lady Bolio, shall we go and arrange? a little turn before dinner will quicken my appetite, which of late has become wretchedly bad."

"I think it will, my dear Mrs. Leechum," observed her ladyship,—"We shall soon return, doctor," she added, and withdrew with his lady to prepare for their walk.

At the end of a quarter of an hour,—during which time the doctor continued to pace the room, musing on the past, and comparing it with the present,—he laid his stick upon the table, and uncovered his head, and then seated himself on the sofa. Upon this "invention of luxury," Leechum spent another quarter of an hour, with something like patience; but as neither signs nor sounds gave indication of the return of the ladies, he began to feel a little pettish at being kept so long waiting, and once more he rose and paced the room.

Again and again he detected his hand wandering towards the bell-pull, to enquire the cause of the long delay: and then, suddenly starting from the action, as if he had been about to commit a deed of blood, he pursued his march.

How many times he "turned about and wheeled about," as he strode up and down the drawing-room, cannot with precision be stated. As, however, he was making one of his rotatory movements, his eye fell upon an object lying at one end of the sofa, which he had not before perceived: he approached and took it up. It proved to be a highly scented and beautifully folded note of the finest satin-paper, and of a tint such as connoisseurs in such matters would have pronounced, a maiden's blush.

"Umph!" said the doctor, as he placed his glasses bestride his olfactory protuberance, in order to examine the pretty thing more critically,—"What have we here?"

The address puzzled him not a little;—who could Donna Rosabella be; or what was meant by the Honourable Duenna? "Well," he soliloquized, "as no persons of such names reside in this house, it can belong to no one here;—it will not, therefore, be committing a breach of politeness if I just inspect the inside."

So thinking and half saying, he opened the billet-deux, and there read the apology of Lord Dashwood and Sir Marmaduke Varney, for not attending according to appointment. "Why, surely," said Leechum, "these cannot be the parties whom Lady Bolio expected; and yet, who else can they be?—But then, the address,—can all this be intended to blind my eyes?—Ha! ha! I must keep a look out,—I'll insist upon knowing the whole truth of this from Mrs. Leechum, or I'll—"

He had proceeded so far in expressing his mentally formed resolve, and still holding the epistle in his hand, when the door was suddenly thrown wide open, and in bounced Mrs. Leechum, having just before detected the loss of the note.

"So, Sir!" exclaimed the lady, snatching the scented paper from her husband's trembling hand,—"common politeness, one would have imagined, would have led you to leave any note you might chance to find in this room, unopened—"

"I was merely looking, my *dear*," returned he, agitated from head to foot, "I was merely looking at the beauty of the paper, &c."

"Your unbridled curiosity, Sir," replied Mrs. Leechum, "is unbounded;—no one beside yourself, Dr. Leechum, would so far have committed themselves."

"Well, my dear, don't allow yourself to be unduly excited," returned the doctor.

"Excited!" exclaimed the pacific lady,—"such treatment would excite any thing but a corpse. *You* know that no person in the world,—myself excepted,—would bear gently and peaceably what I have every day to endure ;—you will, indeed you will, drive me to commit myself."

"Well, my dear, now are you ready to walk ?" enquired Leechum, scarcely knowing what he said ; but thinking they had been long enough upon this tack, and wishing to change it.

"No, I am *not* ready," returned the lady, "nor shall I be ready to-day,—you have made me change my mind.—I shall go and undress, and—"

"Come, my dear," said Lady Bolio, who entered just then, "shall we set out ? I fear we have kept you waiting, Dr. Leechum ; but, you know, ladies cannot prepare to appear in public in a moment. Heighday !" she continued, observing Mrs. Leechum almost fainting on the sofa,—"What's amiss, my dear ?"

"Oh, ask the doctor," replied the lady, "he has been tormenting me, as usual."

"Allow me to observe," said Leechum.

"No ; I will not," interrupted his placid wife,—"Once for all, I will not go to-day ;—indeed, my dear Lady Bolio, I feel

that I am unable—I am too much excited; the fatigue would
be more than I could bear."

The doctor, very good-naturedly, so far sympathized with
his good-tempered wife, as to unite with her in opinion that
the fatigue would be too much for her : no sooner, however,
had he so done, than *she*, with equal good temper, took the
opposite position, and declared she felt persuaded that a walk
would be beneficial to her, and that nothing less than positive cruelty on the part of the doctor induced him to recommend her to remain at home. Lady Bolio acted as mode-
rator on the occasion; and, after about an hour and a half from
the time the first proposition to walk was made, the party
sallied forth ; and leaving the Royal Crescent, and turning
down Brook Street, they entered the Circus, out of which they
turned, by the way of Gay Street, directing their course towards
the usually crowded promenade for the elite, Milsom Street.

The scene of busy life which was here presented, the rich
exhibitions which every shop window displayed, and the
smiling and happy faces which appeared at every step, had
so powerful an influence and unexpected effect upon Mrs.
Leechum, as seemed really wonderful. She appeared another
creature at once ; and, entirely forgetting all the crushing circumstances which a few minutes before threatened to overwhelm her beneath their weight,—she positively looked good-
tempered and happy, and chatted most lovingly with her *dear*
husband.

It would be considered, I am aware, the very climax of
rudeness, and prove to a demonstration, not merely the want
of good breeding, but utter ignorance of the common cour-
tesies belonging to civilized life,—even to *hint* such a thing
as that Mrs. Leechum was influenced by so mean and selfish
a spirit as actuates most candidates for legislative honours,
who will smile and fawn, and promise and swear, until their
seats are secured ; and then, as Cromwell behaved towards
those who raised him to dignity and power, flog their consti-
tuents with rods of iron,—to *hint* such a thing, I say, would
be to call down the ire of the whole sex on one's head;—nevertheless, singular coincidences do *sometimes* occur ; and,
for which, no satisfactory reason can be given. So it chanced
to fall out now.

A handsome, or rather splendid pair of hand-screens and
ditto card-racks to match, were most tastefully displayed in
Marshall's library, and fancy shop window.

" Bless me !" exclaimed Mrs. Leechum, suddenly halting, " only look, Lady Bolio, what a superb pair of fire-screens is lying there."

"They are, indeed, *very* beautiful," returned her ladyship

" Oh, they exceed all I ever beheld," returned Mrs. Leechum ;—" Don't you think they are very sweet things, my *dear?*" she added, turning to her husband.

" Yes, *love,* they are pretty toys," returned Leechum, whose taste for such things was rather of a negative character.

" How I should like, them," observed the lady ; " our drawing-room, love, really would be improved by them ; indeed we actually want some such."

" Do you think so, *dear?*" cried the doctor, cautiously.

" Yes, *love;* indeed I do," returned his wife, looking unutterable things of kind and winning order in his face,— " Now do let me take them home,—shall I, *love ?*"

" Why, I think, dear," said Leechum, who had some strange misgivings that a long price would be required for them, and would, therefore, if he had *dared*, have denounced the thought of purchasing them,—" I think, *dear*, we should injure them before we reached home."

" Oh no, my *love*," returned his affectionate wife, " no danger of it, I assure you,—is there, Lady Bolio ?"

" Why no, my dear," replied her ladyship, " they can be well packed, and—"

" Certainly,—most certainly," said Mrs. Leechum ; " I'll take care of them. Come, let us inspect them."

The doctor held back, but it would not do ;—to refuse positively, would have been to insult his sensitive spouse, and might have produced consequences not *very* gratifying to himself, while, in the end, she would still have had her way ; and, therefore,

> " Though most unwilling on his part to do 't—
> While every feeling of his manly soul
> Hated the action which his foe proposed,
> And rose in arms to execrate the deed,"

he walked into Mr. Marshall's handsomely fitted and well-stocked shop.

The longed-for screens were produced, set off by all the embellishment of florid recommendation in which that gentleman excelled—and now the possession of them was indispensable to Mrs. Leechum's happiness. The card-racks were placed beside them, and she grew into ecstacies; but then, these were not the entire set. A splendid suit of porcelain vases formed a component part, and could not be separated. Such a display of workmanship, and such *useful* and unique articles, so far infatuated the affectionate lady, that she desired the whole might be packed up forthwith, and sent in the course of an hour, as per card, which she handed from her case.

"You have forgotten to enquire the price, my *love*," whispered the doctor.

"Oh right, my dear," returned Mrs. Leechum, "that had escaped me;—while Lady Bolio and myself look round the shop, you had better settle the account, *love*."

The doctor feared exceedingly that some other beautiful thing might strike her attention, and be equally indispensable to her happiness, if he allowed her to saunter a long while, and, therefore, hasted to cut short his visit to Marshall's.

"What is the amount of those articles?" asked the doctor, as he drew forth his purse.

"Thirty guineas, Sir," replied Mr. Marshall, with astonishing coolness,—"I always do my business on ready money principles, Sir; and, therefore, can afford to sell at least fifty per cent. below any other person in my line in Bath, or elsewhere."

"*Thirty guineas!*" issued from between Dr. Leechum's chattering teeth. The amputation of a leg or an arm would not have caused more pain than at this moment shot through his system; especially if the operation had been performed upon his *dear* Mrs. Leechum.

"That is a long price, Sir," observed Leechum at length, "and I fancy—"

"I assure you, Sir," said the adroit dealer, "you have a dead bargain."

"I imagine as much," returned the doctor; "*dead*, sure enough."

"Allow me to say, Sir," observed Mr. Marshall, "that I sold the fellow set to Lord Dashwood, a few days since, for an advance upon this sum of five guineas; but as it is the last I have,—I like to be at a word in my dealings,—I have put them in at the low price now named."

"Lord Dashwood!" fell upon the ear of Mrs. Leechum like magic tones, and she hasted from the other end of the shop, supposing that her *dear* husband was making enquiries respecting him.

"Don't be inquisitive, my *dear*," whispered Mrs. Leechum.

"I am not, my love," said the doctor; "I was merely hinting that the price was—"

"There, Sir," said the proprietor of the library, placing a receipt before Leechum;—"There is your receipt, Sir;—I feel obliged, and hope you will again honour me with your custom. Will you allow me, Madam," he continued, "to direct your attention to some new and elegant editions of some of the most popular authors, in various and splendid bindings? or this fancy stationery? or—"

The doctor trembled in his shoes, and gently hinted,— "My *love*, had we not better continue our little ramble?— what say you, Lady Bolio, shall we proceed?"

"As you please, doctor," returned her ladyship.

"Come then, my *love*," he observed, and, offering his arm to his kind lady, he hasted from the library, without so much as noticing the bowing proprietor.

Mrs. Leechum appeared in good spirits, and, what was more rare still, in good *temper*, as she passed up Milsom Street. So kindly, indeed affably, did she speak to the doctor, that he began to feel reconciled to his outlay of thirty guineas, as it appeared to have procured for him a respite at least from misery, in the amiability and affection which his wife displayed.

Never, perhaps, did the doggeral rhymes of old Verdun, the butler, receive a stronger exemplification, than in the case of Mrs. Leechum, when at the close of one of his stanzas, he observes,—

"To some people if you give
An *inch*, they'll take an *ell*."

The affectionate, and now really cheerful Mrs. Leechum, had not proceeded above one hundred yards from Marshall's library, before other attractive objects caught her attention, in the form of some newly imported and very superb Cashmere shawls; to which was attached a fanciful label, announcing them as the Queen's pattern. They were modestly declared to be unequalled by any thing that had *preceded* them, and unquestionably surpassed every thing that might *hereafter* be produced. This might have been considered by some persons as a touch of "puffing extraordinary;" the bait, however, was a gilded one, and, *therefore,* not a few swallowed it.

That Mrs. Leechum should have been captivated by the beauty and recommendation of the garments in question, was nothing singular; but even Lady Bolio felt moved at the sight of them, and so indeed did the doctor himself;—but, as the reader may opine without being marvellously sagacious,—in a very different way.

"Only just look here, *love*," said Mrs. Leechum, as her husband displayed strong evidence of a disposition to move on.

How to escape the snare which appeared spread before him, he could not divine;—he felt strongly inclined to be suddenly seized with a violent pain in the lower regions, and the declaration had risen to the thorax that it was indispensable he should withdraw for certain private reasons,—when the soft and harmonious tones of his young, and handsome, and languishing wife, turned his intention.

"Did you ever behold such a lovely pattern before?" asked Mrs. Leechum,—"eh, *love*."

"I don't profess to have any judgment in such things, my dear," returned the doctor; "but I fancy you have as handsome a one at home."

"Oh, my *love!*" shouted the lady; "look again, *dear;* you are certainly jesting with me."

The doctor appeared to think the *jest* would end seriously, and replied, cautiously,—"Well, my *dear*, I certainly *think* so."

"Now, that's very naughty of you, *love*," returned Mrs. Leechum, in notes of soft coaxing cadence,—"*If* I *could* be angry with you, I am sure I should be so now;—you know you are jesting with me,—now arn't you, *dear?*"

"Why, really, my dear Mrs. Leechum," observed Lady Bolio, who had been engaged making her critical observations upon the 'Queen's Pattern,' "I fancy I shall treat myself with one of them; not that I am in want of such an article, but they are so *very* beautiful."

"Well, I feel great pleasure that your ladyship's taste accords so exactly with my own in this case," returned Mrs. Leechum,—"Suppose we step in and examine them; or—"

"Allow me to hint, my dear," said the doctor.

"Yes, *love*," said his wife; and so saying, she entered the shop with Lady Bolio, while the doctor took the *hint* and followed.

The articles in request were displayed with all befitting attention to lofty recommendations on the part of a namby pamhy sort of *thing*, which wore the costume of a man; albeit the tones and action of the creature were perfectly womanish. If the doctor had dared to have done so, he would have thrust his gold-headed stick down the question-able gendered thing's throat, and thereby have put an end to the florid and persuading puffery, which sickened him at the heart: more reasons than one, however, withheld him, and he was obliged, if not *patiently*, at least, *silently*, to hear his *dear* wife echo the order of Lady Bolio, to send one of the invaluable and inimitable Cashmerian coverlids to No. — in the Royal Crescent.

"I'm quite *sure* you'll like to see me in it, *love*," observed the languishingly kind Mrs. Leechum to her spouse. "Won't you, dear?"

The doctor was obliged to allow "yes" to ooze from his parched throat, but it came forth with so bad a grace, that a bystander might have guessed the true expression of his feelings would have been,—"I'd as soon see you in your winding-sheets, if only to save the drum of my ear and my pocket."

Once more the *much-loved* husband was called upon to pull forth his pocket-book, and, with a grimace such as a severe spasmodic attack would produce, laid down a pair of ten-pound notes, while the puffer extraordinary assured the ladies that, unless two shawls had been taken, not a fraction could have been abated from twenty guineas, instead of pounds, each.

The fresh air which floated down Milsom Street appeared necessary to check the death-like perspiration which the doctor felt so oppressive as to threaten a fainting fit. On-wards they went and entered Bond Street, Mrs. Leechum continuing in the most happy and delightful flow of spirits, and regaling the doctor with a flood of tender expressions, delivered in the most tender tone and manner, while he, poor man, mused sadly over the fifty-one pound ten shillings, of which he found himself minus in the brief space of some-thing less than half an hour, and still trembling like an aspen leaf, whenever the sharp visual organs of his wife turned to any object of particular attraction.

They had progressed so far as Barratt's Library, intending to wind round to the right, by the way of Trim Street, into Barton Street, and from thence back to the Crescent, through the Circus, when the doctor's lady, whose head was turned

in another direction from the one in which she was proceeding, trode rather heavily upon the toes of a gentleman, who
was just leaving Mr. Barratt's depôt. Mrs Leechum was
proceeding in her expressions of regret for the accident,
while the sufferer begged she would not allow herself to feel
discomposed for a moment on his account, when the doctor,
who was at the distance of a few yards in advance, turned
on hearing a voice which he fancied he knew, and at once
beheld an old acquaintance in former years, and once a companion in his scholastic toils.

"My dear Sir," said the doctor, "I should know that
voice, or I am greatly mistaken."

"I know not, Sir," returned the stranger, "when or
where I can have been known by you; and yet, now I recollect me, your voice and person carry with them something
of 'Auld Lang Syne.'"

"I fancy it must be so," returned the doctor, whose heart
responded loudly and faithfully to the touch of friendship;
"your name, Sir, is Mornington, or I do forget myself."

"The same, good Sir, and your poor servant ever," returned Mornington, following up the doctor's quotation from
the "Prince of Denmark." "But in good faith, Sir," he
added, "my treacherous memory has, like a wide-meshed
sieve, allowed your name to escape me; but of that," continued Mornington, in a tone tinged with sadness, "there
can be little marvel, at least, on my part: the world, Sir, has
used me roughly, and where my too-confiding nature trusted
most confidently, there I have been most grievously de-
ceived."

"I am sorry to hear it," said the doctor in a tone of real
sympathy; "you were not wont to be either sad or moody,
when we spent our evenings in the vicinity of the City Road.

"Ah!" exclaimed Mornington, "I have it now; what,
Mr. Leechum, is it you?" and he seized the hand which the
doctor offered, with a degree of enthusiasm which proclaimed
more than language could have done, how *truly* and how
much he felt. "But those ladies," continued Mr. Mornington, turning to Lady Bolio and Mrs. Leechum.

A formal introduction instantly took place, and the doctor
placing his arm within Mornington's, insisted he should
spend the evening with them; to which he cheerfully consented, and forwards they went.

This was an event so entirely unexpected, that because of

its approximation to a romantic incident, the ladies felt delighted at it; for notwithstanding too much evidence was given that Mornington's exchequer was at a low ebb, there was about him something that interested the   and yet, there was nothing in Mornington's person or manners which is conceived to belong to what is called a ladies' man. But it has ever been proved, that where good sense coupled with good manners, and an honest face, are found, though, by untoward circumstances, associated with sorrow and necessity— the best feeling of a female heart has been exercised towards such: like angels of mercy, hovering about the paths of the unfortunate, they are found ever ready with open hand, and heart, and purse, to relieve and succour.

Mornington was of middle stature, rather thin, and of a semi-Hamite complexion. His contour intimated that he had been a child of misfortune, and a man of sorrow. Some circumstance of no common order had evidently touched the core of his being, of which, without doubt, he might have said,—

> "Oh! never, from that painful hour,
>   Has earthly joy been known;
> 'Midst crowds and charms which once had power,
>   I live uncharm'd—alone!
> A shade of what I might have been,
>   Is all that *is* of me;
> A thing of grief, where'er I'm seen,
>   Is all that I *can* be."

But when a theme was once touched upon into which he could enter—on which he *felt*—his whole countenance appeared as if irradiated with a glow of ethereal brightness. His large expressive eyes suddenly became

> "Bright as the morning star,"

and appeared to look into the souls of those with whom he conversed.

As they moved towards the Crescent, the doctor managed to give a brief account to the ladies of the intimacy which had long existed between himself and Mr. Mornington.

"And now," said Leechum, warming as he spoke, "I am persuaded that neither Lady Bolio, nor Mrs. Leechum, will allow you, my friend, to take your departure until you have satisfied them with such a sketch of your eventful history, as you may feel at liberty to give—I know it will interest them."

"Well, my dear Sir," returned Mornington, "as you are

aware that I was always ready, to the extent of my poor abilities, to gratify the ladies, I shall not forfeit my character in that respect now; and, as I have two days at my command, I shall feel most happy to spend them with you."

Each one of the party appeared equally delighted. Lady Bolio having " shook her years away,"—as the poet of the passions, HOME, would say,—tripped on with unwonted agility, while Mrs. Leechum was positively enchanting; and the doctor and Mornington so completely beguiled the way, that before they had imagined it, they had climbed the eminence on which the Royal Crescent stood, and were ushered into Lady Bolio's mansion.

As soon as convenient, the dinner was served; after which, while Port and Sherry gladdened the heart of each individual, the ladies,—having broken through the rules of etiquette by special request--that of leaving the gentlemen alone—immediately the cloth was removed,—sat to listen to Mr. Mornington's relation; the substance of which will be found in the following chapter.

CHAPTER XXVIII.

> " Such is the fate of Genius,—
> The scorn of witlings oft, or sport of fools !—
> While he (with sublimated mind, and eye
> Piercing the putrid film and murky gloom
> Which render stagnant other,—meaner minds,
> Whose only tact and exercise of thought
> Lies in their getting wealth ; which, like themselves,—
> Although it glares,—is cold and senseless still),
> Scatters an intellectual light around ;
> And, like the Sun benignant, warms and cheers ;
> Yet, like that orb, with cold neglect is left
> By soul-less ingrates.—Oh, son of Genius !
> I could weep for thee."
>
> MONODY ON CHATTERTON.

" IT is not necessary," commenced Mr. Mornington, " that I should be particular in supplying any information respecting my early days; of every particular relating to my juvenile pursuits, you, Sir, are already fully acquainted. For the information, however, of these kind ladies, it is proper that I should merely observe, that I was the first-born of parents whose memory is endeared to me by innumerable circumstances of unusual affection. My family was of considerable respectability in Kent, in which charming county my progenitors had resided a long period before my birth. As soon as I had passed through such preparatory course of instruction as qualified me for the university, I was sent to Dublin, where some of my most happy years were spent. Notwithstanding the many and great defects which then existed in that, as well as in most of the English universities, I did not participate in them; and for two reasons : first, because I had not at my command such funds as would enable me to launch forth into all the excesses generally indulged in them; and secondly,—and I may say chiefly,—because the gentleman who had been engaged as my tutor, was one whose honest pride consisted in making his pupils scholars, rather than pedants, and who knew how to blend the *suaviter in modo* with the *fortiter in re,* so as to divest the latter of every thing like ferocity by the tempering kindness of the former.

"It was at this seat of learning, doctor, that—as you remember,—I had the pleasure of first meeting you. You were, it is true, my senior by several years ; still we became friends, and to that friendship I then owed much.

" I devoted myself to severe study, prompted by an insatiable thirst of knowledge, and an unconquerable desire to excel. In those early days, botany, ornithology, and other branches of natural history, occupied much of my time, to the neglect, too often, of those professional studies which my friends designed I should pursue.

"How I passed through my university exercises, or with what stock of learning I left Dublin, is of little consequence to my narrative. I had found in too many instances, among young men making some pretensions to learning, that ribaldry was mistaken for humour; while not a few who were preparing for sacred duties, laughed at those whose chief stores of happiness were drawn from futurity. Such being the case, my mind naturally received a species of sceptical tinge ; not in the popular acceptation of that frequently mistaken word,— but in reference to men and their professions ;—hence I doubted frequently where I should have confided, and not less frequently committed the opposite blunder. Too often, I fear, like Goldsmith's philosophical vagabond, I pursued novelty at the expense of content, and gratification at the price of happiness.

"On my return home, a few months were spent by me in visiting, or receiving visits, instead of setting to at once, as I should have done, to the profession first intended for me. The consequence was, that at the end of half a year, my views and habits became changed,—the wholesome, not servile discipline which had been exercised over me at the university, had passed away. As one respectably learned, it was supposed I only had need to follow the tendency of my improved mind, and all would succeed prosperously: such, however, was not the case. The tastes and prejudices of certain young men of my acquaintance, and of others whose age ought to have been a guarantee for the correctness of their habits, were imperceptibly and as injuriously imbibed by me. I soon became restless in my feelings, and perplexed in my speculations. I ceased to be the happy being I had been; my mind could no longer be said to be fixed to any particular point.

"How long this state of things continued, I am not able distinctly to state; but, by a circumstance of singular character, a complete change, for a time at least, took place in my pursuits: I suddenly cut with my acquaintance, and became again a close student.

"I had from my boyhood felt an enthusiastic delight in theatrical representations; and even now, although so many years have elapsed, and so many strange and important changes have taken place, I can distinctly remember the rapture with which I have run to the little Theatre in my native town, where I have witnessed the present clever HARRY BEVERLY play the monkey in 'La Perouse;' or have witnessed the personation of Rolla by his father, and Cora by his mother; while COBHAM figured in all the glory of youth, as Alonzo, Alexander, and Glenalvon.

"Singular as it may appear, I had never then witnessed a performance in either of the patent houses. But now the fame of Master W. H. W. BETTY, or, as he was called, the 'Young Roscius,' drew me, as it did thousands of others, to London. I saw, admired, and wondered, and at once determined to become a candidate for histrionic honours. Full of this purpose, I returned home, and, as I have said, became a close student. As, however, no opportunity offered for me to don the sock and buskin, I resolved to write for others, and write I did; and as I scribbled for mere amusement, and not for gain, my performances were praised and accepted.

Here my literary career commenced—the *cacoethes scribendi* exerted its full influence over me, and I felt no pleasure equal to that which I experienced when busily engaged rummaging my mental wardrobe to find some trappings in which to dress the strange creations of my own brain. Thus, what I then did for amusement, laid a foundation for what I have been obliged to resort to since as a profession.

"But I will hasten on to what may be termed the most eventful, although by far the least creditable or pleasant part of my history. I settled in life, and settled, too, with prospects as bright and flattering as ever cheered the horizon of a human being's earthly prospects. But they were not less evanescent than beautiful; I never survey them (and I often do) without considering my subsequent sufferings as judicially permitted for my conduct then. Let no one after me consider perjury a venial offence, or imagine that the feelings of a sensitive and devoted female, are to be made the sport of a cold-hearted changeling with impunity; and yet mine was not change—no, no; bitter years of regret and unabated attachment, assure me it was infatuation,—madness;—I was trepanned, I,—but where am I wandering?—I will explain.

" It was a bright and beautiful summer's evening; when, as I was passing through my father's garden, I came unexpectedly in contact with a female. Whatever before had been my notions of female loveliness, I now felt they were incorrect; and that if any standard could be raised by which that arbitrary term might be defined, such an one stood before me. It was not simply in stature, symmetry, step, or complexion, that her fascination existed: these all appeared forgotten; and where, as on former occasions, my attention had been fixed by some particular grace or expression, I now was unable to make any selection—all seemed alike unequalled;—she appeared to me the prototype of Milton's Eve :—

> ' So lovely fair,
> That what seem'd fair in all the world, seem'd now
> Mean ; or in her summed up, in her contain'd,
> And in her looks ; which from that time infused
> Sweetness into my heart, unfelt before,
> And into all things by her inspir'd
> The spirit of love and amorous delight.'

" That I should feel anxious to know who this fair creature was, was natural, and it was soon gratified. She was only a visitor in the neighbourhood, and had called upon my mother at the request of the lady at whose house she was staying. After this we met frequently, and every succeeding meeting had the fatal tendency of robbing me completely of my peace. Soon I beheld the lovely girl with as ardent and pure a passion as mortal should feel towards mortal. At length, every assurance that modesty and truth could give, were furnished, that I loved not alone. A thousand instances of deep devoted attachment on her part are yet stored up in my memory; which, as I think on, crush me with a weight of grief scarcely endurable.

"Years passed on, and our acquaintance and friends talked expectingly of

> "Nuptial sanctity and marriage rites,

which they expected would soon take place, when—the thought is like a bolt of fire shot through my brain to scathe my being—a serpent, in female form, crossed my path, and coming between Amelia and myself, blasted my happiness for ever. Oh, how frequently have I reviewed that fatal moment with pangs unutterable; and then suddenly starting, as if roused from a fearful vision to endure the misery of dreadful reality,—I have enquired,—' Is it then true ?'—alas ! I have found it so. Between this woman and the artless Amelia, nature did never produce a greater dissimilarity. Shakspeare's comparison might here be instituted—

> " *That* was to *this*,
> Hyperion to a satyr."

Yet so it was, by a master-piece of art,—to perfect which were suited the *tone* of her *voice*, the *action* of her *body*, nay, the very *muscles* of her hated *face*,—she triumphed. Onwards I went to my ruin, as if unconscious of it,—meantime I saw the horrible chasm yawning to receive me. My infatuated passion over-ruled my judgment, but did not destroy it;—but to the sequel. After years of devoted affection, felt and returned, I resigned—abandoned ! the woman who *only* possessed my heart, and was united by *legal* bonds to one who acted as a demon to me afterwards. Still it is well ; I shudder, but dare not murmur.

" Scarcely had three short months elapsed after signing the fatal contract, when the mask was removed, which my wife, ere she became such, had worn. I now learned I had no HOME ! my *dwelling-place* became the most loathsome place. Now the soft and gentle tones of a voice which seemed incapable of reaching a loftier key, were changed to the ceaseless thundering of a Borean storm. Conviction fell with a withering blight upon me—I felt my evil situation, but knew not how to remedy it. Now it was that I saw a retributive hand in the sorrows I endured. The perjury of which I had been guilty to the deeply injured Amelia, was followed by punishment from the thing for whom I had sacrificed her happiness and health. To put away the more than half-distracting thoughts which harassed me, I seized—foolishly —madly seized the intoxicating cup, and added fire to flame.

"Oh, what a change had a few years wrought!—I stood confounded amidst ruin and desolation. Affairs at home grew worse and worse; and from a small quantity to cheer my spirits, as I foolishly supposed, I increased my draughts, until I became a settled drunkard! Under the influence of spirits, I gave security for a professed friend to a large amount. The sum for which I had unconsciously made myself responsible was demanded. To meet it I was convinced my whole property must be sacrificed. Stung to madness by my folly, and rendered desperate by my wife's insulting conduct—I ran to that which had already so deeply ruined me,—I staid not to examine the justness of the demand made upon me; but, in order to avoid present disgrace, and to escape the misery of beholding the distress of my beloved children,—for they were dear to me as my heart's blood,—I fled—fled from the place of my ruin; and scarcely knowing what I did, I crossed the British Channel, having no fixed plan before me, excepting a desire to leave my country, as I then thought, for ever.

"As soon as I arrived at Paris, I proceeded to the Rue de la Paix, and took up my residence at one of the best inns in that dissipated city, the Hotel Mirabeau. I had secured all the ready money I could lay my hand upon before I left home, which I found amounted to about two hundred and sixty pounds. Here I drank largely, anxious, if possible, to forget the past and hide the present and the future. With the feelings of a maniac, I rushed from the Hotel in the evening—I knew not to what point my steps were leading me, or what was my intention. I wandered on,—crossed the Place Louis XI., over the Pont Louis Seize, towards the bank of the Seine, and now destruction lay full before me. I approached the dark waters, in which, almost every night that passes, some one or more unhappy beings, rushing from the gaming tables or loathsome brothels of the Palais Royal, terminate their earthly sorrows.

"This was an awful crisis; the horrible suggestion stole upon me that it were better to die than live as I was doomed to do. I staggered nearer, and yet nearer,—I gained the margin of the water—an invisible power seemed to urge me on— a fearful desperation shot through my brain; the strong fumes of the ardent spirits I had drunk rendered me furious. I exclaimed as I rushed towards perdition,—'Thus will I end it.' At that moment I perceived a figure floating on the stream; it neared the spot where I stood—I seemed transfixed by some powerful necromantic spell, being alike unable to go forward or retreat. I stooped to lay hold of the object which had so singularly fixed my attention. It was the body of a woman,—oh! it was a ghastly sight!—I shuddered then —I shudder now. Murder had, without doubt, terminated the existence of one who was young and handsome. I was sobered in a moment;—my blood curdled in my veins as I gazed upon a gaping gash on the neck, from which even yet blood oozed out. The sound of approaching footsteps roused me from a partial stupor;—I feared to be charged with the black crime of murder, and I instantly sought to save what a few minutes before I appeared determined to destroy—my life! Creeping, like some guilty thing, I left the spot, and soon beheld the corpse conveyed to the building which is erected for the purpose of receiving the bodies found in the river.

"Once more I flew to ardent spirits, and drank until the proper exercise of my reason was gone; and in this state I wandered, more by instinct than understanding, to the first floor of the Palais Royal, and entered one of those spacious and splendid Pandemoniums whence many a frantic youth had issued, uttering fearful execrations on the hour that he first entered its infernal gates, and ended his course by an act of self-destruction.

"The dice were actively thrown, and polite invitations were tendered me to join the game. I did so,—won, and bet again and again; and again fortune seemed to favour me. Thus I continued to fill my pockets, until, feeling thirst pressing me, and elated at my success, I retired to that brilliant temple of luxury, the *Café des Milles Colonnes*: so called because its columns are reflected in glasses till they become

page 314-5

thousands,—and then I added intoxication to thirst. Now my *die* seemed cast indeed ; I strayed back to the place I had a short time since left, and in less than one hour, my winnings had returned to the pockets of those from whom they had proceeded, while my own money went with them. Thus, on the *first* night of this my last visit to Paris, I became, through intoxication, a *gambler*,—and, through gambling, a *beggar !*

"The grey mists of early dawn were still hanging around, when I awoke on the following morning, shivering with cold and damp like an aspen leaf. I started upon my feet with surprise, and, looking round, discovered that I had been reclining upon one of the chairs which are placed in the inside of the piazzas of the Palais Royal, and which, during the day, are let to dissipated loungers, with a newspaper, for a couple of sous each. A few moments' recollection sufficed to make me *feel* as much as I could recollect of my night's folly. But *how* I had left the gaming house, or by what means I had succeeded to place myself where I had, without doubt, remained a considerable time, I could by no effort explain or conceive.

"The hum of conversation which fell on my ear, soon increased to a noise ; for, as usual, the piazzas began to fill. Shame took hold of me, and, to avoid the gaze of my fellows, I hastily left the place. For two or three hours I strolled about the suburbs of the city, and mingled with crowds it was impossible to avoid. The cravings of nature became oppressive, and then the bitter thought that I was pennyless, nearly drove me to despair and madness. Without money, without a house, without a friend,—an exile from my country,— a ruined man fleeing from the myrmidons of the law, and seeking to avoid the pointing finger of scorn,—all this I was, what more could I be ? I was the dupe of hypocrisy and deception!

"One only piece of property remained to me in the world, —at least, that was available,—and that was a valuable watch. That it did remain was unaccountable ; yet so it was, and this to me appeared like a plank thrown out to a drowning man. A gleam of comfort darted athwart my gloomy mind as I felt it. My *immediate* wants might at least be met by the sum it would produce : of the *future* I dared not think. The first shop that caught my eye, at which it was likely I could exchange my time-piece for some pieces of gold, I entered, and found it was a thing of common occurrence for gentlemen, after spending a night in the Palais Royal, to raise funds in the same way. The bargain was soon struck, and with *nearly* one-third the worth of my watch, I entered a *restaurant;* the *carte* was handed me, and I made my selection.

" Having consumed sufficient to satisfy my appetite, and drunk half a bottle of wine, for which I paid four francs and twelve sous, I desired a strong tumbler of Brandy grog to be made me, and strove, while swallowing it, to put away the horrors of my now obtruding and distracting reflections; but in vain, they dwelt with me.

" Thus I passed one miserable week. At length, a powerful admonition in the shape of fast diminishing funds, warned me of the propriety of seeking a fresh supply; but how it was to be accomplished my inventive mind could not conceive. Day after day I strode through Paris, hoping to obtain some employment for my pen, but in vain. My applications met with a repulse in more instances than one.' So passed my time until the whole of my stock of money was contained in seven francs. What economy could do with this, perhaps I did do; but that could not make it last for ever: no, it diminished rapidly, and at length my *last* franc jingled upon the table of the *Café Montausier,*—for, from the most splendid accommodation which Paris could supply, I had sunk to the most wretched. I paid for my last meal; but how or where food or lodging was to be procured for the future, I could not conceive. Day passed, and night came with all the horrors of destitution, both of food and bed; for Parisians, like the dwellers in London, will no longer furnish supplies than *le prix* is produced.

"The beautiful plantations of the Champs Elysées seemed likely to afford me an asylum, and to those fine woods I wandered and took up my lodging. Soundly and sweetly I slept until the sun was high in the heavens of the following day. Again I strayed into the city of frivolity and dissipation; and, as I walked onwards, my eye caught an announcement which stated, that an English gentleman, who was about to take a tour, was in want of a servant. Menial as the situation was, I considered it preferable to starving. I applied for it, and was engaged. I was soon equipped in a dress suited to my new station, and in a short time left Paris with my master.

" With the rapidity of couriers we passed through Troyes, Dijon, and Besançon, to Lausanne; and from thence, after a

brief rest, moved at break of day for Chillon. If I did not
fear to exhaust your patience, I could linger here with delight to tell of the rich, sublime, and subduing charm of Swiss
scenery, where cottages, castles, churches, and villages, meet
the entranced view, and intersperse the luscious landscape.
Here, fertile vineyards greet the sight, and there, a handsome
chateau arrests the attention. Occasionally frowning perpendicular rocks of stupendous height, make a powerful impression on the mind; in whose deep beds the celebrated Rhone
dashed, foamed, and wound away, sending up sounds from
the deep abyss, loud and melancholy, which were again relieved by the tinkling of goatherds' bells, coming down from
the Alpine hills. The view from Villeneuve, which is at one
extremity of the lake of Geneva, is beyond all description
fine; the imagination of man can supply nothing equal to it.
So many bright associations are blended with the scenery as
to render it overpowering. From this point the chateau of
Chillon is seen to the utmost advantage, mouldering in its
own magnificence and idle uselessness. As it meets the eye,
the fate of the courageous, the patriotic, the virtuous Bon-
nivardt, the hero of liberty, the model of firmness, rushes
upon the mind,—and the prisoner of Chillon,

> 'Who, for his father's faith,
> Suffer'd chains, and courted death,'

stands before the creative imagination. Byron's Muse has
immortalized the place; with pure and happy expression, and
with a vigour and spirit which does honour to his own mighty
mind, he has sung his sufferings and his wrongs. Who can
but feel the charm of the latter part of his sonnet?

> 'Chillon! thy prison is a holy place,
>   And thy sad floor an altar;—for 'twas trod
>   Until his very steps have left a trace,
> Worn, as if thy cold pavement were a sod.
>   By *Bonnivardt!* May none those marks efface!
>   *For they appeal from tyranny to God!*'

"From this immortalized place we pushed across the
Simplon, terrible in grandeur; from whose giddy heights
we gazed on the captivating Val d'Ossalo; and passing
through several neat villages, and some very miserable ones,
entered Milan; a place justly famous for every thing but
liberty, which it has never properly known. After paying
all becoming respect to its magnificent amphitheatre, which

is capable of holding thirty thousand spectators, and surveying with admiration the splendid remains of those renowned masters, Leonardo da Vinci, Titian, and Bernardo
Zenale, and other interesting objects, we hasted on to the
gay and voluptuous city of Venice.   And here again my
highest wishes were gratified by the surveying of persons and
things, with which, by name, I had long been familiar

"Ferrara, Florence, Naples, the village Marochiano, and
the School of Virgil, were merely visited.   Rome was the
attractive spot to which our attention was directed; and
having taken up our abode in it, we remained a considerable
time.

"How lively a feeling is excited, and how powerful are its
workings in the breast of every lover of the fine arts, even by
the solitary mention of the cradle of History, Poetry, Music,
Painting, Sculpture, &c.,—ITALY :—every thing connected
with these scenes is blended with our youthful associations of
pleasure, delight, grandeur, glory, ecstacy.   Once the seat
of empire for the mistress of the whole world, although at
present the haunt of vice, and the throne of antichrist, it
will never lose its celebrity, until taste ceases to exist for
every thing that is great in antiquity or glorious in arts.
Every object of an inanimate kind even, whether dug from
the bowels of its flaming mountains, or fished up from the
Tiber, Po, or Adda, is conceived of as a gem by every vir-
tuoso : how could it be otherwise than that I should receive
more pleasure than I can express, when I stood upon the
ground whose praises all nations have sung, and whose fame
will only expire with the expiring groan of a dying world ?—
Yes, true and beautiful are the golden lines of ROGERS,—

> "For ever and for ever shalt thou be
> Unto the lover and the poet dear—
> Thou land of sun-lit skies, and fountains clear,
> Of temples and gay columns, waving woods, -
> And mountains, from whose heights the bursting floods
> Rush in bright tumult to the Adrian sea:
> O thou romantic ITALY !
> Mother of poetry, and sweet sounds."

"Having satisfied his curiosity here, my master determined
to visit Spain, and for that purpose embarked at the mouth
of that celebrated stream, the Tiber ; and, crossing the Medi-
terranean, landed at Cadiz.   But here our separation took
place; for, while enjoying an excursion in the bay, a sudden
gust caught the boat in which he was; she heeled on her lar-

board gunwale, filled, and sunk; and all on board, excepting only myself, perished.

" Once more I was literally thrown upon the world, having nothing. The whole of my late master's papers were under my care; and, while I was carelessly turning over some newspapers which had been recently received from England, I saw, to my inexpressible astonishment, an announcement of my wife's death, connected with a paragraph which referred to my sudden departure from home some years before, under the presumption, as it was supposed, that my entire property had been forfeited in consequence of my having become security for a false friend. It added, that the document had been examined when the demand was made, and found in some legal point informal; in consequence of which, what I had left had been enjoyed by my wife and family until her death, and would now, in all probability, be placed under the care of the Lord Chancellor, unless I should, if living, soon return and prevent it.

" Such intelligence was electrical. I soon changed my dress, and in two months from that time I again pressed my dear children to my heart. I found, however, that my property had wasted materially; but in a little time I procured a situation of the greatest respectability; and all things bid fair that I might yet be happy and prosperous; but alas! it was not so,—death entered my family, and tore from my arms the delight of my eyes, in the person of a dear, dear girl! Another sickened, and with menacing attitude the fell destroyer appeared fast approaching her. Nothing, I was sure, would save her life but a removal; and, therefore, to remove I determined.

" Before this period I had become acquainted with one who had professed the greatest interest in my welfare. Again and again he had besought me to remove to the vicinity of his mansion, in the country; assuring me of all the aid he could render me both by influence and property. Upwards of a year had passed, during which time his importunities had been continued, when I informed him, in the confidence of friendship, that I required a trifling sum to free me from a few obligations which pressed upon me; and if he could supply that upon loan, I would accede to his pressing wishes, and remove. Without hesitation he did so, for to accomplish any purpose upon which his heart was bent, nothing would retard him.

"Such treatment as I received from himself and others, upon my settling where he had wished me, made me feel confident I was fixed for life. But soon the flattering scene passed away, and the fallacy of resting upon human friendship was, when too late, discovered. The person to whom I refer was the keeper of a private asylum for insane persons, —you, it is possible, have never heard his name even,— would I had not,—it is *Wildolett—*"

"Wildolett!" exclaimed Lady Bolio, and the doctor and his wife together.

"Yes, Wildolett," returned Mr. Mornington; "but why?"

"Surely, I have heard that name," observed Mrs. Leechum; "but no, no; it cannot be the same;—excuse me, Sir : we met a gentleman of that name, recently, at Devizes."

"It is the same, Madam," resumed Mornington ; "there he is well known—would that I had known him as well before I listened to his specious promises, as I have since done. He is a villain, Madam, one of the darkest grain,—*a stabber in the dark—a robber of families—the changeling of an hour*— a pompous braggadocian, whose darling expression of ' Rhodomontade,' is fully characteristic of that part of the man. But I beg pardon, I will hasten to a close with my too prolix tale.

"A few months only had passed after I had located in the vicinity of F——ton House, the residence of my would-be-considered honest and disinterested friend, Mr. Wildolett, when such a falling off took place as I could scarcely have conceived to have been within the range of possibility; although not a few had prognosticated it. The fact is, he had a particular object to accomplish, but of which I, until after he had employed me as his tool, was not aware. He panted for official supremacy in the place, which, on the ground of qualification and character, had long been possessed by another. His little soul

' Hated the excellence it could not reach,'

and he determined by some means—and to him it mattered not what their character might be—

'Though dark as Erebus, and vile and low
As fiends could practise from the realms below,'

to oust the gentleman who now held the station, after which he panted, and get himself inaugurated.

"There is a degree of subtlety about some rogues which is

really astonishing;—they have a tact and method of their own which none can imitate, while a steady, patient, circumlocutory plotting is resorted to by them; which, while it lulls the suspicions of those upon whom they are about to work, generally accomplishes their purpose. Thus it was, in the principles and practices of the present honourable gent. No way appeared so likely to him, by which to effectuate his design, as through my influence, and that influence he determined to obtain.

"The disposal of the office in question was not, indeed, vested in me; but from the station which I removed into Wiltshire to fill, I had little more to do than signify my wish in the matter, and it would be attended to.

"My removal having taken place, the canting, fawning sycophant commenced the enaction of his part. Like another Lord Protector in spirit, without possessing a hundredth part of his intelligence,—for it was merely the worst part of that great man's character which he possessed,—like him, he deplored that things were as they were; and hinted an improvement could never take place until a change in official influence was effected; but, at the same time, most solemnly protested against ever taking office himself, even if besought to do so.

"Oh, the darkness of that man's soul!—the deep-grained hypocrisy with which he acted! He had professed himself my friend,—my devoted friend. He had, professionally, served me. He had watched my every want, and anticipated my every wish,—and wherefore? O the climax of deception! that he might the more easily and entirely gain my confidence, and obtain, as he might desire, my ear and heart.

"He commenced his operations with the skill of a miner, cautiously and covertly approaching the point at which he purposed to spring his mine. With words of ambiguity he gently hinted at the vileness of the character of the gentleman whom he wished to supplant; his entire unfitness for office; the ill favour in which he stood with all about him; the joy that would be diffused if he were ejected; the— enough,—his inuendos were poured forth with the readiness of a master. I was a stranger to the place and to the libelled individual;—the robber of his fair fame aped the part of Dr. Cantwell excellently,—nay, he aped it not at all; he was to the very life what that well-known character had been made by the creative energy of the poet.

"Too fully and too fatally the fellow succeeded ; a change was effected, and he—*he* who had solemnly vowed never to fill the post, jumped at its possession, and occupied the chair. His triumph seemed complete—his soul's desire was accomplished ; and now, a change,—a sudden change,—came on. I saw, when too late, that I had been duped. He soon became cool in his attentions, and distant in his manners ; or with a degree of vulgar familiarity, diametrically opposed to the respectful courtesy which had before characterized his manners towards me, he evidently was determined to make me *feel* I was his *debtor!* He did make me feel it, for on that point I was most sensitive ;—he insulted me, meanly,—and in the most cowardly way insulted me, in the persons of my children. I felt my thraldom, and was compelled silently to submit,—with poor Romeo I was ready to exclaim,

'Break, my heart, for I must hold my tongue.'

"Once and again, however, I claimed at his hands sums which he held in trust for me, from those whose officer he had now become. The response to the demand, however, suited not his purpose. I grew troublesome to him, and he determined to rid himself of one whose eyes began to be opened to the part he had been, and still was, playing.

"Now came the climax of his dark plotting mind ;—he framed with ingenuity a tale, and caused it to be circulated by certain family agents, which at once stabbed my good name, and made me a thing little short of a beggar. I appealed to the laws of my country for protection and restitution ; and, had I possessed funds, could have *purchased* that justice which I sought for in vain without money. What could I do ?—the stigma rested upon my character ; and because I possessed not the means to obtain redress, there, like a plague-spot, it continued : and, while the execrations of the many fell upon my persecutor, by not a few I was held as guilty, and I was doomed to endure the consequences.

"Of all the miseries, merely of an earthly nature, which a man can know, poverty appears the greatest. A man may be infected with a disease which makes him loathsome both to himself and others ; yet, money can make his society delightful ;—every infirmity under which human nature can groan may he endure—money can conceal the infirmity, or can change the defect to a positive embellishment—he may be a knave of the first quality, whom society ought to shun and execrate, and yet money will form an apology for him, and make his presence welcome, even where the appearance of evil, it might have been supposed, would have been studiously avoided. ' *Non compos mentis*' may be his state ; in plain English, a very fool, whose ignorance may be declared by every word he utters, and in every action he performs ; but money will turn his folly into racy wit, and his soporific ignorance into oracular wisdom ;—in short, the only unpardonable and intolerable sin is *poverty !* Mind, and integrity, and real worth, because associated with indigence, is obliged to suffer

> ' The stings and arrows of outrageous fortune,
> Or else to bear the whips and scorns of time,
> The oppressor's wrong,—the proud man's contumely.
> ....the law's delay,
> The insolence of office, and the spurns
> That patient merit of the unworthy takes.'

" All this *I* now felt,—bitterly felt. I was necessitated to leave the town, into which but a short time before, that man, —if he be a man,—who was now the cause of my removal, had ushered me with the sound of music. Like the first murderer, I was consigned to wander forth and seek a subsistence for myself and my children elsewhere. My establishment was broken up, and my property brought to the hammer—at an immense sacrifice, I need not say. I looked upon my children, and felt only as a father could feel. Oh misery !—misery !—they were suddenly and unexpectedly thrown upon the world. I now turned for a living to that which had long been my favourite recreation,—authorship. And here again I felt the cruelty of Wildolett : the library which I possessed, and which, in the profession upon which I was compelled to enter, appeared indispensable that I should retain,—this friend, this devoted and disinterested friend of the mad-house,—demanded and possessed as security for the sum he had advanced to me upon loan, as an inducement to me to take up my abode near his asylum, and serve his purposes ; but

> ' He won not his honours well,
> And did not wear them long.'

He was ejected from his villanously obtained office, while a special vote was recorded against him that he was *unfit for the office.*

S

" Situated as I now was, I had no resource left me but to repair to the emporium of every thing estimable and execrable—London! I did so, and with all possible expedition entered upon the miseries of a literary career, professionally. While I wrote gratuitously, my compositions had been received with pleasure and applause; but now, being obliged to write for food, they were treated with indifference, and in not a few cases rejected. I have sold to a bloated mercenary bookseller, who was revelling in abundance at the expense of authors' brains, a volume for fifty or sixty shillings! for which I ought to have received as many pounds.

" I was yet a novice in my new profession; I knew not the art and trickery of the business upon which I had entered. I applied week after week, and month after month, for literary engagements, fondly hoping to succeed, until hope being delayed made my heart completely sick. I lived upon the little I had possessed until the whole of that little was gone, and all I retained in the world was what I stood upright in, and in that *all* a coat was not included.

" At length the gloom broke away, I obtained an engagement, and what I produced was applauded,—highly applauded; but then it was with difficulty I could obtain my money for what I had written. Often have I wandered in the Park and about London, hungry and faint, and the only solace I had, if such can be so called, was to reflect that the immortal *Johnson*, and his unfortunate friend *Savage*, had many a time traversed the streets of the city during whole nights for want of a bed.

" Whether sheer barbarity, ignorance, or forgetfulness, be the cause or not, it would, perhaps, be unfair to determine; but I have known it many a time and oft, that I have entered the shop of the man for whom I had written, and who was at the time my debtor for pounds, when I have been allowed to stand the gazing-stock of customers and porters, until every fibre of my system has been stretched to their utmost tension by strong excitement; and then, with coldness which good manners could not approve, the small sum he has felt disposed to pay, has been doled out as if it had been a subscription to some unpopular charity fund.

" At this time my residence was a small dark smoky upper room, in a narrow dark passage, something in point of size and furniture, like that which Kirke White so graphically describes as having been his study at Cambridge,

with this no very slight difference,—the annoyance of squall-
ing children, quarrelling females, and drunken men, which by
day and by night I had often to endure.

" I have frequently contemplated the change in my circumstances, until I have been reduced to a state little short of
what would have fitted me to have become a worthy inmate
of my worthy and well-beloved friend Wildolett's establishment.

" At length a brighter day dawned. I became known
among the initiated literati—the *trade* found me out, and I
obtained such engagements as rendered me increasingly comfortable. I am now rising in my new profession. I feel
something very like happiness ; but that I fear I never shall
know again—

> ' I have a secret sorrow here,'

an indefinable presentiment which assures me that happiness
has fled my bosom for ever !—the current of my being seems
soured. The deception I have experienced has rendered me,—
what naturally I was not, a suspicious thing. I have become a species of misanthrope—my only ambition now is to
see my children provided for, and placed above the cold contempt, or chilling pity, of those who once made a semi-idol
of their father : that felicitous object granted me, and I shall
be satisfied. Hope still urges to the pursuit of that for
which I constantly sigh, and incessantly labour ; and, while
I feel grateful for the care Providence has exercised over
me and mine until the present hour, I hesitate not to
trust in the paternal protection of HIM who is the Father
of us all. I have learned some useful lessons, which I hope
never to forget, from the treatment I have experienced
at the hands of Wildolett ; and, although I sincerely pity his
despicable character, I shall feel it a duty I owe to society, to
warn others against his deceptions ; and, while malevolent
feelings are banished from my breast, I shall, in stronger language than he will approve, make such disclosures concerning him and his establishment, as he does not expect ; and,
by so doing, make the public acquainted with facts of which
they ought not to remain ignorant."

Here Mornington closed his somewhat prolix narrative.
The doctor offered his condolence to his old friend for his
past mishaps, while he congratulated him upon his brighter
prospects.

" Only think of that barefaced canting old fellow!" exclaimed Mrs. Leechum ;—" Well, I protest, he would only meet his deserts if, for two days in every week during a whole year, he was to be placed in the stocks on Devizes Green—I'm sure I should not pity him,—should you, my dear Lady Bolio ?"

" Such despicable creatures, my dear," answered her ladyship, " are beneath our notice ; and yet, while they swarm around us as they do, it does appear necessary, to prevent the mischief they delight ever to be doing, that some strong measures should be taken for that purpose. I think the course Mr. Mornington intends pursuing, is the best that can be adopted : his knowledge of the man and of his ways will empower him to do two services at one time,—punish the vile aggressor for his infamous conduct, and warn the public against his notorious practices."

Every thing that could be done to render Mr. Mornington's stay at Bath pleasant was resorted to ; and when the time arrived which rendered it necessary he should leave, some substantial proofs were presented him that his visit had been enjoyed by his kind friends ; while a promise was received from him that he would, whenever an opportunity offered, spend some time with them, at their residence in Devonshire.

CHAPTER XXIX.

" Come gather round me, murky night,
  And hide the deed from heav'n's clear light.
  My ring, my purse, my gold and all,
  For service rendered, gratis ;
  She seiz'd,—then fled beyond my call—
  Oh, think now what my fate is !"

CUNNINGHAM.

SEVERAL days had passed since the distressing circumstances, gravely detailed in a preceding chapter, took place, when the tail of Miss Fidget's dear Carlo was scalded, the nose of Lord Dashwood was bruised and battered, Sir Marmaduke had stood up to his ancles in boiling water, &c. &c., during which time, neither Dashwood, Sir Marmaduke, nor the doctor, had strolled one hundred yards from the York

Hotel. Not only had his lordship's nasal protuberance continued dreadfully swollen, but a pair of black eyes had been superadded, a natural consequence of the blow he had received from the thick head of the Duchess; while the Knight's foot was still sore from the scalding ablution. These causes prevented the before-mentioned personages from enjoying the delightful excursions on which they had confidently calculated: in the mean time his reverence had been confined to his chamber by a severe attack of cholick, as the doctor confidently believed, by too great an abstinence from such decoctions of brandy as he loved, and swallowing too large portions of those celebrated waters, the honour of the discovery of which, the ancient Bathonians most sagely maintained, belonged to King Bladud and his foul-scurfed pigs; but which monstrous legend the present eminently enlightened race reject with as much scorn as a lover of true history would a wild and fictitious Canterbury tale.

But while the male portion of our Bath visitors were thus confined to their hotel, the ladies indulged themselves with such pleasures as the various public walks and accommodating lounges of the city and vicinity so abundantly supply. Here the golden Duchess might be seen passing along the fashionable crowded way, with as much dignity of step and demeanour as if she had derived her being in a direct and uncorrupted line from the celebrated Charlemagne, instead of standing connected—(as by marriage she did)—remotely, it is admitted, to the scarcely less popular character,—*Nell Gwynne*;—while Miss Fidget, bearing in her arms her dear Carlo, appeared only to experience enjoyment, as she believed her canine darling was happy.

As the just mentioned pair of important personages moved on, noticed and bowed to by numbers in the throng, in consequence of the fame which the Duchess from various causes had acquired, Georgiana enjoyed a good-tempered and kind *tête-a-tête* in the rear, with her servant Claudius. Frequent intercourse with our hero had led the young lady to think less meanly, or rather more favourably, of his talents, than heretofore she had done;—there was to her something half engaging in his ready witted replies to her questions, and the shrewd observations which he made in reference to subjects on which she wished for information.

Had not our hero worn his master's livery, it is a hundred to one but some scandal-loving personages might have been

censorious enough to have hinted that the sweet and fine
bright eyes of Georgiana were turned too often and too tenderly towards the handsome young man, or that he was
allowed to walk too near her person. As it was, however,
little danger existed on that head; not only was his costume
a sufficient guarantee for full propriety of conduct on either
side, but the familiar associations and unrestrained inter-
change of thoughts, common between ladies of ton and their
liveried attendants, gave full sanction for Georgiana's conduct, and caused that to pass unnoticed among the votaries
of fashion, which in an uninitiated village would have supplied matter for a week's consternation and a month's gossip,
amongst prudish old maids and precise order-loving ma-
trons.

It was on one such occasion as has just been referred to,
that an incident occurred, which, however serious to the parties concerned, afforded no small measure of amusement to
those who were only spectators of the scene.

One of the favourite and almost daily walks of the ladies
was Grosvenor Gardens; here they sauntered through delightful groves, wandered down serpentine walks, rested in
shady bowers, or lost themselves in artfully formed laby-
rinths, looking and feeling as if they had been resident spirits of this fairy realm.

"Claudius!" shouted the Duchess, as she took her seat
in as beautiful a grotto as any dweller in the coral caves of
ocean would wish to inhabit,—"Claudius, I say."

No responsive sound came forth from the called one, and
good reason there was for it; he was not within the reach of
her voice, although the lungs of her Grace were by no means
deficient in strength, or spared upon the occasion.

"How very annoying this is," observed Miss Fidget, "to
be obliged to shout thus for a servant."

"I wish," resumed her Grace, "I had desired one of my
servants to be in attendance; but then to have such a posse
of menials around me is almost as irksome as to be altogether destitute.—I find that every servant, my dear Miss
Fidget, is a spy upon the actions of those they serve; and it
is not always quite agreeable to fill the world with information through such a medium; and you can neither render
servants blind or dumb;—to be sure, I do manage mine
pretty well, I pay them liberally, and now and then a present
is thankfully received."

Now, it is quite certain, that Miss Fidget heard every word of this somewhat lengthy speech; but then, she did not feel its force—she either did not do that in the presence of her servants which she would blush to have made known, or otherwise she was less sensitive respecting the world's opinion than the golden Duchess; and, therefore, as though she had not heard her friend's observations, she turned again to the subject her Grace had started, and enquired—"Wherever can he have gone?—and Georgiana too,—why, I declare, we have lost them both! Georgiana,—my dear Georgiana," cried the anxious Miss Fidget.

"Oh, don't trouble yourself, my dear Miss Fidget," observed her Grace, soothingly, "she is not far off, depend on it; and, as Claudius is with her, no harm will befal her—his presence will be a sufficient protection for Georgie, against the rudeness of others; while of himself, of course, there can be no danger. My walk," continued the Duchess, "has excited such a degree of thirst and languor, that I really must take some refreshment. This is a most delightful spot for the purpose. What would you prefer, Miss Fidget?"

"Why, really, your Grace must excuse me," returned the sensitive lady, "I could not think of taking any thing in a public garden."

"Why, my dear Miss Fidget!" exclaimed the Duchess, opening wide her eyes, and looking what she felt,—positively amazed at her delicately nerved companion,—"what do you mean?"

"Oh, I should feel ready to die with confusion!" returned Miss Fidget; "indeed I should, if any persons were to see me taking refreshment in such a place."

"Pooh, pooh!" returned the Duchess, whose delicacy on such points was not quite so transparent as Miss Fidget's;—"Now, I protest, that I feel almost ready to die for want of something, and shall soon give up the ghost altogether if I do not obtain it! Not take refreshment in a public garden! ha! ha! ha!—Excuse me, my dear Miss Fidget; but only think how excessively foolish it is to indulge in such feelings. Oh, here comes a waiter,—that's fortunate;—now tell me what I shall desire him to bring to us."

"Now really, my dear Duchess," simpered out the blushing young lady, "you must excuse me—indeed, you must."

"Tut!—tut," returned her Grace,—"Here,—waiter!"

"Yes, Madam," said John, putting his hand very politely

to his unbonneted head, and then giving the white napkin
which he carried in his hand an extra turn round his arm.

" Bring this lady a glass of hot port-negus, and let me
have a tumbler of brandy-and-water—I feel very disposed to
flatulency, and am obliged to have recourse to Cognac medicine."

" I will attend to your order immediately, Madam," returned John; and making a graceful salam, he vanished like
a sprite.

As the order fell from the lips of the Duchess, Miss Fidget
almost shrieked with alarm, and would, in all probability,
have fainted from surprise, if it had been quite convenient.

" Negus and brandy-and-water !" observed Miss Fidget;
" why, surely your Grace is going—"

" To have what nature requires," said the Duchess, taking
up and finishing Miss Fidget's deliberate observation.—" Depend upon it, my dear friend, that it is one of the greatest
follies of which we poor innocent women are guilty, to be influenced by the opinions of lookers on, rather than by the
dictates of nature and common sense ;—however," added her
Grace, in such a good-natured manner that even Miss Fidget
could not return the charge, " I bless my stars that I have
lived *in* the world long enough to laugh at its weaknesses, and
set at defiance all it pleases to say : if I had not so done, I
should have gone mad, or have died of a broken heart long
ago."

However strong, and however proper, the dissenting feelings of Miss Fidget might have been to the loose philosophy
which the rhapsody of the Duchess contained, she, as we
have said, replied not to it. The *title* of her Grace frittered
away the obnoxiousness of her sentiments; while the finished
sang froid of her manner, carried more force in it than the
strongest argument would have contained, although it had
been delivered by the mouth of a sage, or had issued from the
chair of philosophy.

The steaming beverage was soon placed before the ladies,
and her Grace seized the drink she loved, and paid such respectful compliments to it, as proved it was to her a most
welcome friend; while Miss Fidget gently pressed the glass
of negus with her thin lips, and then replaced it on the
waiter.

" Well, the negus is really excellent," observed Miss Fidget, sipping it again and again.

" I should not have supposed it," returned the Duchess, " if you had not said so."

" Is is, upon my word," repeated the *young* lady, and she ventured to dip deeper than she had done before, by a good mouthful. '

" Well, now, that does look a little more like it," observed her Grace; " I can't endure to see persons sip, sip, sip, and then hear them speak of that which a stranger might conceive to be medicine of the most nauseous kind, in terms of high eulogy;—however, it is not my way of doing things," she added, and again drew hard upon her glass, until something less than one-third of its recent contents remained.

" Now, be quiet, dear Carlo," cried Miss Fidget to her bosom friend, as he elevated his nose to her face, and then applied his milk-white tongue to her lips, and kissed from them such portions of the negus as yet might adhere to them. " Oh fie, fie! Carlo, that's very rude," she continued; " you have really forgotten yourself this morning;—I really can't allow such liberties."

Whether Carlo misunderstood the soft tones in which his mistress's reproof was given, supposing they were intended as an invitation to a further participation with her of the port-negus or not, is uncertain,—Carlo never stated,—but no sooner had Miss Fidget's tongue ceased to wag, than Carlo leaped from her lap upon the table, wagged his tail, and, to the consternation of both the ladies, overturned both the glasses, which, coming in rude contact with each other, were dashed into a hundred pieces.

" Oh! the brute!" exclaimed the Duchess, raising her hand at the same moment, with the evident intention of administering summary chastisement on the offending quadruped.

" For heaven's sake!" shouted the terrified Miss Fidget, seizing her Grace's up-raised arm,—" What is your Grace going to do?"

" Going to do!" returned the Duchess, who felt the influence of the drink she had taken warming her spirit, and who deplored that even a small quantity of the much-loved liquor should be wasted; " why to punish the nasty brute for what he has done, certainly."

Such language applied to her *dear* Carlo, was more than the delicate nerves of the excited Miss Fidget could bear; and, without further preface than a loud shriek of anguish, she went off into strong hysterics.

Carlo, the ungrateful Carlo, whose ill-mannerly conduct had been the cause of the distressing scene, unmindful both of the sympathy which his mistress had displayed towards him, and the lamentable condition in which she now lay, continued to stand quite unconcerned amidst the ruins he had made, and ever and anon applied his tongue to the united streams of the brandy-and-water and port-wine negus.

The alarming shriek which had issued from Miss Fidget's lips was heard to a considerable extent in the gardens, and crowds of either sex rushed to the secluded grotto from whence the sounds had proceeded.

Among several others who pushed forward to render assistance to the unfortunate lady, were two individuals who rendered themselves particularly conspicuous by the extraordinary sympathy they displayed, and the activity with which they lent their aid. One of these was a female of the most dashing exterior; the other a dandified mustachioed person of the opposite gender. The lady bent over Miss Fidget with sisterly solicitude, and almost drowned her with cold ablutions, which fell from between her beautiful ringed fingers, as if proceeding from a spacious shower bath. As, however, Miss Fidget did not feel disposed to " come to" too easily, the lady chafed the palms of her hands, and loosened some of her garments, which appeared, in her judgment, too confined for her difficult respiration.

After the lapse of some ten or twenty minutes, a profound sigh from the heaving bosom of the still unconscious lady, gave notice of her return to life. The announcement was listened to with evident attention by the officious lady; who, as it would seem, scorned the thought of being thanked for doing a kind action; she, therefore, resigned Miss Fidget to the arms of the Duchess; and, pressing through the surrounding crowd, vanished from view.

The compassion which had swayed the breasts of the bystanders so long as Miss Fidget continued in her state of stupor, was succeeded by very different feelings as she opened her eyes, and enquired with the first breath she drew fairly, for her dear Carlo. Her face exhibited so ludicrous a spectacle, as to set at defiance the most morbid-souled being present, to maintain any thing like gravity. The beautiful tints which had, a short time previously, given to her countenance the appearance of a Peri's youth and beauty, had by the unceremonious application of lavender water, hartshorn, and various other reviving liquids, been partially washed away, leaving only such grotesque streaks as the once celebrated Joey Grimaldi never had the art to lay upon his strangely metamorphosed physiognomy. Her head-dress had also been deranged to such an extent, that the beautiful auburn ringlets which had depended, with grace and regularity, down her lily and coral-coloured cheeks, were entirely displaced, and the grey and scanty covering which grew upon her cranium, most annoyingly obtruded itself before the eyes of the spectators.

The Duchess, as well she might, felt unutterable things, and would rather have given the weight of Carlo in golden coin, than have been placed in the unpleasant circumstances in which she found herself. It is true, that on many previous occasions she had been gazed upon by thousands of persons, while some unfortunate had fainted in her arms; but *then* it was only the mimicking of the thing, while this was reality—and *then*, too, she was only a player—and now she was a DUCHESS!

"Where is my dear Carlo?" enquired Miss Fidget, as soon as her tongue could be put in motion.

"Don't disturb yourself, my dear Miss Fidget," whispered her Grace, "he is safe enough, I make no doubt."

"Safe enough!" reiterated the lady; "but where is the dear creature?"

"Who does the *old* lady want?" asked a young wag who heard her enquiry.

"Who?" echoed his companion, "why, her chaperoni, to be sure,—where the devil can the fellow have gone?—it is devilish rude to leave an old woman in such a mess;—if she was a score or two younger I should feel inclined to take his place; but as it is,—why, Hooky Walker is my name."

Miss Fidget's ears received the ungrateful sounds; and, if the glance of her eye could have performed the action which poets say ladies' eyes sometimes do,—shoot out fire!—the base maligner of her youth and beauty would, without benefit of clergy, have been destroyed;—but her look, although fierce as an untamed tiger's, was perfectly harmless: and hence—

"The heartless mockers at a lady's age,
Whom whips and scourges, minister'd by rage,
Might, without pity, round the world chastise
Before the gaze of men's approving eyes,"

were suffered to escape without loss of life or limb.

Anxious to escape the annoyance to which she was exposed by senseless and unfeeling curiosity, in the grotto, the
Duchess proposed an adjournment to the Hotel connected
with the gardens, to which proposition Miss Fidget, without
a syllable of opposition, assented; and, with a little assistance, she was soon domiciled in that splendid establishment.

During the whole of this time, Miss Georgiana and Claudius continued absent; and, had the Duchess and her friend
been aware of the cause of their long delay, of whatever other
feelings they might have been the subjects, surprise at least
would not have possessed them.

. The day was one of those soft subduing ones, such as even
in our almost constantly variable clime is sometimes known,
which throws a spell over the spirits; and, before the victim
of soft passion is aware, renders him half a voluptuary in
feeling. The young blood of our hero and heroine mounted
rapidly under the influence of animal magnetism. The place
in which they sauntered, as well as the character of the day,
seemed under the special auspices of Venus, or some of her
busy satellites.

Quite unconscious that the Duchess and Miss Fidget had
left the path in which they continued to lounge, Georgiana
moved on, with Claudius close behind her. A sudden strange
palpitation on her left side, which spread an unusual tremor
over her whole frame, was suddenly experienced by the lovely
girl.

> " And yet, in truth, it was a pain,
>   So mystically pleasing,
> That, like the maid who wished again
>   For Hero's frown'd-at teasing.
> She rather would have weep'd about it,
> Than lived a single hour without it."

"What can this mean?" she enquired of herself, and the
response was, "What can this mean?"

Her snow-white kerchief dropped unconsciously from her
hand, and on she passed. The converse she had held with
Claudius had so engaged her, that she was lost to every thing
beside. Our hero perceived the scented cambric—he eagerly
caught it from its low condition, and hasted to return it to
his mistress.

Whether there was any thing unusually polite in his manner on the occasion, or whether his eye looked brighter, or
the tones of his voice were softer, as he said, with a gentle
inclination of the body,—" Your handkerchief, Miss;" the

young lady herself has never reported;—she felt, however, as if his voice, his eye, and his manner, were all different from any former time.

"Thank you, Claudius," she said, as she received the presented beautifully embroidered property; "I am *very* much obliged to you,—did I drop it?"

"You did, Miss," returned Claudius, and again appeared inclined to drop behind; but Miss Georgiana did not appear inclined to allow him to do so.

"Claudius," said the young lady, in tones of soul-subduing cadence, and stopped.

"Yes, Miss," returned our hero, bowing gracefully.

"Pray, Claudius, will you oblige me?" enquired Georgiana, in trembling accents, "by,—that is,—will you be so kind as to tell me if you can keep a secret?"

"If, Miss, it is to serve you," said Claudius, "I feel assured you may trust me, whatever its character may be; and no one shall, without your permission, be the wiser for it."

"Oh, you are very, *very* kind, Claudius!" rejoined Georgiana,—"indeed you are, and I don't know how I shall make you such a return as it deserves."

"I fear, Miss Georgiana," returned Claudius, "your kindness overrates my merits;—I am sure there is not any thing in my power that I should not feel most happy to do to serve you; while your approval of my doings would be an ample recompense for the service I might render."

With a look which none but a Stoic thrice baptized in ascetic inanity, could have withstood, and in a tone which a deaf man only could have been indifferent to, Georgiana gazed on Claudius and replied:—"Oh, Claudius! *dear* Claudius! I cannot help thinking, and I have done so a long time, what a pity it is that you were not born a gentleman; but if you had been, I perhaps should never have seen you; and then I should have lost the pleasure which I have often felt while conversing with you. Do you feel quite comfortable in your present situation? if not, let me know, and all *I* can do to render you happy I shall feel a pleasure in doing;—indeed, to serve *you*, will be serving myself."

"In my situation, Miss," returned Claudius, "I could not be otherwise than happy so long as I have the honour of serving you."

"Indeed, Claudius!" said Georgiana, trembling with emo-

tion,—" what do you mean?" she continued eagerly,—" Do
tell me," and forgetting time, place, and circumstances,—she
unconsciously laid hold of his hand, and, with her taper fingers, gently pressed it.

"I only mean, Miss," answered Claudius, " that you are
so very kind and good-natured, that it is a pleasure to attend
to any order you issue."

"Is that *all* now, dear Claudius?" asked Georgiana,—
"Are you quite *sure*, that is all?—Did you never feel the
same pleasure in seeing any other person?"

" Oh, never,—never, I assure you, Miss," returned Claudius;—" Indeed, I never did serve any one before that I cared
about serving.—Oh, yes; there was one," continued our
hero, and a sigh escaped him.

"There was *one*," cried Georgiana, and her face changed
from a beautiful, luscious carmine glow, to a deep death-
like paleness;—"There was one!—when, dear Claudius,—
who was she?"

There was a hurriedness in the young lady's tone and ac
tion that really alarmed Claudius; and, although he was far
from a novice in certain matters relating to the passions, yet
he scarcely dared venture to give such an interpretation of
the present incident as circumstances seemed to warrant.

"Bless me! Miss Georgiana," exclaimed Claudius, with
real alarm, as he looked on her face, " you are not well!
allow me to lead you to yonder seat—you are, perhaps,
fatigued, Miss, and a little rest will recruit your strength."

So saying, and without any opposition on the part of the
lady, Claudius conducted his kind mistress to the place referred to. It was a beautiful alcove, so thickly covered by
the matted tendrils of various vines, as effectually to exclude
the strong rays of the sun, which now glowed in all the power
of meridian glory; while a soft breeze gently moved the
leaves of the flowering shrubs which grew in rich luxuriance
all around, rendering it such a spot as a romance writer
would have fixed upon for the retreat of a sighing woe-begone
lady-love and gallant knight; or, as the fit abode for a penitent hermit, or rigid anchorite.

Scarcely had she taken her seat, while Claudius stood before her as if to receive her commands, than she resumed the
subject, and enquired,—" *Who* was she, Claudius?—do tell
me; that is, if you can;—I mean the person you referred to
just now,—how long since was it?"

" Allow me to fetch you some refreshment, Miss," said Claudius, perceiving that the paleness of Georgiana's cheek was increased rather than diminished.

" Thank you, Claudius," returned the lady, " but I do not require any ;—can you oblige me by replying to my question ?"

" It was my mother !" replied Claudius, and a sigh once more escaped him.

" Your mother, dear Claudius!" exclaimed Georgiana, and the mounting rose of health began instantly to enliven her cheek, and her eyes assumed their wonted calm brilliancy,—" Your mother, was it; and no one else ?—Haven't you sometimes, now, felt pleasure in serving other ladies ?"

" I always feel pleasure in doing what I can for any one, Miss," replied Claudius ; " but I never feel so *much* pleasure as in serving you."

" Oh, Claudius !" sighed the ingenuous Georgiana, " you have made me so happy by your statement, that I almost fancy I could love you for it,—that is—I feel so much interested in your welfare that,—you understand me, Claudius, —any thing I can do to serve you, I shall feel most happy to attend to."

Another look accompanied this declaration, which carried away even Claudius from the distant reserve he had hitherto maintained; and which it now became fully evident Georgiana felt anxious should be dispensed with.

While timidity is the natural result and almost constant associate of love, there are, nevertheless, moments when boldness throws off all restraint, and displays the strength of the affections in a way which the most daring could not at other times exhibit. This mysterious and perhaps indefinable operation of the passions was now experienced by Claudius. The tones of Georgiana's voice—the beamings of her luscious eye—the character of the questions she had proposed,—all appeared to unite to produce the effect referred to.

" You have asked me, Miss Georgiana," said our hero, as he leaned over the seat on which she reclined,—" You have asked me if I could keep a secret—I have assured you I can, and will keep any you may honour me with the keeping of; —may I now be permitted to respond the question ?"

" To be sure you may, dear Claudius," returned Georgiana ;—" ask me *any* question you may think it proper to propose, and I will be as candid as yourself."

"Well, then," continued Claudius, "will you be offended if I ask—can you keep a secret?"

"Angry!" replied Georgiana,—"No, indeed, I will not; but what secret do you wish I should keep, and from whom?" she enquired, eagerly; at the same time encouraging Claudius by a smile of assurance, which incredulity itself might have believed.

"The secret," said Claudius, "is an important one, and I wish you to keep it from *every* one."

"Well, then, I promise you," returned Georgiana, "*I will keep it*—any thing for you I will cheerfully undertake to perform."

Claudius bowed his head gently towards Miss Georgiana's ear, and seizing, tremulously, one of her fairy hands, he put his lips to her's, and then, throwing himself before her on one knee, exclaimed :—"Can you keep the secret, dear Georgiana, that I love you,—dearly love you?"

The hand which Claudius had taken remained still in his, —a slight pressure was returned like a gentle vibration from a fine-toned and skilfully touched instrument—a rich glow of rose-like tinting mantled the maiden's cheeks—while the index of her soul's high feelings spoke unutterable things. In accents which told how sincere her declarations were, she replied,—"I will, Claudius,—indeed, I will keep your secret; be equally careful you don't betray mine. But rise," she continued; "dear Claudius, rise; if any one should discover you in such a position, we should have both our secrets at once betrayed."

Claudius obeyed his mistress's bidding, and once again pressed the unobjecting lips of Georgiana.

"Oh! how unfortunate it is," said Georgiana, "that I cannot, as I am sure I gladly would, receive that support from you which I now feel I need; but alas! I dare not."

"That may hereafter be," returned Claudius, "and without fear or shame. I *now*, dear Georgiana, feel for the *first* time, ashamed of my garb and station;—but I shall not always wear the one, or fill the other."

"What do you mean?" enquired Georgiana, eagerly; "surely you do not intend to leave us—do you?"

"Oh no,—no, indeed, I do not," replied Claudius;— "never, never;—but I am not what I seem to be—hereafter you will know more—will know all,—at present I cannot explain even what I would."

"Ah!" said Georgiana, starting,—"Not what you seem to be!—What?"

"Nay, dear Georgiana," interrupted Claudius, in a style of eloquent persuasion which his young mistress could not resist, "press me no further now;—but will not your absence excite alarm," he continued, "and, perhaps, suspicion?"

"True,—true, Claudius," returned Georgiana, starting up, "I had forgotten that. Bless me! what can have become of her Grace and Miss Fidget?—we must seek them instantly." So saying, she stepped forwards, and Claudius falling once more into his serving station, followed.

The Duchess and Miss Fidget, as we have seen, had reached the Hotel; where, after the lapse of a few minutes, —during which time the fury of the excited lady had considerably passed away,—the first discovery she made was that she had lost, from the forefinger of her left hand, a diamond ring of great value; and in the next moment she ascertained that her purse, containing sundry gold pieces, and certain "promises" to pay from the Bank of England, to a handsome amount, had departed from her reticule. But these losses, heavily as they were felt by the lady, were as completely forgotten as if with the feelings of a sage philosopher she had received the Bard of Avon's well-known lines:—

"Who steals my purse, steals *trash*—'tis something, nothing;
'Twas mine, 'tis his, and has been slave to thousands."

But it was not so: oh no, she valued the *trash*, but another valued thing out-valued it.

Great and small are what mathematicians call comparative terms; and, however great a loss may be in itself, something still greater by estimation, or fictitious value, may be lost, making that which before was considered great, almost despicable: so it was now, for Miss Fidget discovered that her Carlo, her dear, dear Carlo, had,—as she believed,—been most feloniously and inhumanly torn from her fond embrace!

The wailings and lamentations of a large company, composed of either sex, from the Emerald Isle, at a wake, is a sufficiently dolorous and hipping affair; but their fiend-like howlings and demoniacal expressions of grief might be considered, by a lover of the fine arts, as the music of the spheres compared with the wild and unearthly expressions of sorrow which Miss Fidget gave utterance to, as she called, but called in vain, for her dear, her sweet, her precious Carlo !

In the midst of this delectable scene, Miss Georgiana presented herself before the astonished Duchess. A few words explained, so far as Miss Georgiana thought necessary, the cause of her absence ; and then the occasion of the distress which at present existed, was naturally enquired into.

" Oh ! my dear Georgiana !" exclaimed the broken-hearted Miss Fidget, wringing her hands in agony, " I have lost my dear Carlo !"

" Lost Carlo !" returned Georgiana ;—" Why, you haven't, surely, done any thing of the kind ?"

" It is true, I assure you, my dear," observed the Duchess, who was solacing herself from a bumper of her favourite beverage,—" Poor Carlo has made his exit ; but how, or where, we can't say ; he has finished his part, that appears certain," and she briefly touched upon the delicious scene in the grotto.

" Well, now, is that *all ?*" enquired Georgiana, with a most provokingly unfeeling look and tone, addressing Miss Fidget ; " now do, pray, dry your eyes, my dear Miss."

" Is that all !" re-echoed the lady, looking at Georgiana as if she had been gazing upon some fearful abortion of nature ; " What more could I lose ?" enquired the lady.

" Ha ! ha ! ha !" laughed Georgiana, with all the causticity of biting malice ;—" Will you promise me, now," she enquired, in a graver tone, " to be my true and sincere friend from this day forward—helping me out of all kind of scrapes into which I may chance to fall, and assisting me from every difficulty by which I may be surrounded, if I find Carlo for you ?"

" Oh yes,—yes, my dear Georgiana, I will be any thing, do any thing, promise *every* thing," said Miss Fidget, " on such condition."

" Well, then, Claudius has got him safe enough," returned Georgiana.

" Where,—where is he ?" shouted the anxious lady ;— " Oh ! let me press the dear creature to my heart !"

" Which do you mean ?" asked Georgiana, half jestingly, half jealously.

" Why, dear Carlo, certainly," replied Miss Fidget.

" Oh, that you shall do directly," said Georgiana ; and ringing the bell, Claudius entered with Carlo in his arms.

The moment Miss Fidget saw him, she rushed towards her

bosom friend, and enfolded the unconcerned and unthankful canine favourite in her arms; and, lavishing a host of kisses and a long string of tender epithets upon him, in one moment forgot as entirely all her grief, as if she had only been mourning for having become a widow, as another suitor made his appearance.

Now, for the information of the reader, it is necessary to state, that the lady who had, in so very active a manner, rendered her important assistance to Miss Fidget in the grotto, had paid a visit to Bath, purposely with the intention of paying,—as opportunity might offer,—her respects to the superfluous ornaments or cash of some of the many who, like herself, were visiting there; but who, *unlike* herself, had more money than wits. The mustachioed dandified gentleman was her *friend*, or her *livery-servant*, or the *Count* her husband, or her dear *brother*, as occasion might require.

Now, as no situation is better adapted for the display of the mystery of the *black art*,—which such "*respectables*" are ever ready to exhibit,—than a crowd, whether gathered by accident, or assembled by an affray,—the parties in question attended with alacrity to the call of Miss Fidget; and rushing, with many others, to the spot, the *lady* beheld with pity the fainting fair one, and hasted to her aid. The blazing ring upon her finger caught her keen eye in a moment; and, as it might, perchance, prevent the circulation of the blood in that part of her system, she managed with peculiar dexterity to unhoop Miss Fidget's finger, while chafing her hands, and with equal skill succeeded in transporting the purse from Miss Fidget's reticule into her own. How she left has been explained; for to remain to receive the acknowledgments of those whom she assisted, was a thing she never made a practice of doing.

The gentleman, who on this occasion was "the Count her husband," took a particular fancy to Carlo; and, as he appeared unnoticed by any one, and might, if so left, be injured, he considerately and carefully placed him beneath his mackintosh, and marched off with his countess.

The scene we have narrated, between Georgiana and Claudius, had just terminated, and the happy pair had nearly reached the head of the avenue, when they abruptly encountered the Count and his lady, who were walking to the tune of "Fly swift as Lightning," to the grand point of egress from the gardens. At this very moment Carlo popped his head from beneath the mustachioed gentleman's mackintosh, and was, at the first glance, recognised by Claudius; who immediately called out, " Carlo, Carlo;" when the sagacious brute, uttering a yelp of recognition on his part, leaped from the arms of his new protector and ran to our hero.

Either the Count had not time to stay, or judged it more consistent with the dignity of his character not to do so; and, therefore, while Claudius was engaged in raising Carlo from the ground, and presenting him to Georgiana, the fashionable pair made their exit. A little enquiry on the part of Claudius led to the discovery of the ladies in the Hotel, and the restoration of the stupid poodle to his doting and disconsolate mistress followed.

If the whole party did not feel agreeably gratified with the results of their morning's walk, each felt it time to wend their way towards home for dinner ; and, without one objecting voice, they accordingly returned to York Buildings ; a mutual understanding having taken place that the several secrets which they possessed, should be studiously preserved from every other person.

CHAPTER XXX.

> " Ah ! I remember well the man ;
> As well as any thing I can ;—
> His looks, attire, and bon-ton grace,
> With every pimple on his face.
> His splendid snuff-box, cane, and capers ;
> His parchment rolls, and rolls of papers :
> But better than his looks, gait, clothes,
> I recollect his *bottle nose.*"

"'Pon my honour !" exclaimed Sir Marmaduke, as the ladies retired after dinner, " I think it is almost time, Dashwood, that we paid our promised visit ;—your nose looks particularly well again, and my foot is as sound as ever. What say you,—shall we stroll there to-day—eh ? 'Pon my honour I think, after our long confinement, it would be superlatively beneficial."

Little as Dashwood regarded common opinion, or the comments which the herd, as he called the community at large, might please to make upon any part of his conduct, still, for reasons of a private nature, he appeared on the present occasion to feel no disposition to let Dr. Titheum into the secret of his masquerade amour; and, therefore, without replying to Sir Marmaduke's question, he simply gave him a significant wink across the table, as he tossed off his glass.

The doctor had been so busily engaged in swallowing the grape juice, as not to be able to perceive so diminutive an action as a wink; but the accompanying one, that of tossing off the wine, he twigged instantly; and, as naturally as a company of soldiers follow the motions of a fugleman, his reverence imitated Dashwood by again emptying his own glass. Having so done, he observed as he re-filled,—" The ladies appear fatigued with their morning's ramble; and as you, gentlemen, think of walking, and I have no particular wish to sit alone, I think I shall take a stroll myself, and take a few notes of the conduct of the people of this city. At what hour in the evening will you join me in a hand at Whist?"

" Why really, doctor," returned Dashwood, " that is not quite easy to determine: we have a call to make which, certainly, is of no particular importance; but still, we may be detained longer than we at present anticipate. I should suppose we shall return by eleven,—what say you, Sir Marmaduke?"

" By eleven!" exclaimed the Knight, " 'Pon my honour! have you forgotten Miss Fidget? I am as thoughtless a fellow on those points as need be; but you appear to surpass me in this splendid accomplishment, for a man of ragged fortunes, in an almost infinite degree—'pon my honour."

" Well, I must plead guilty to the charge, my dear Sir Marmaduke," returned his lordship; " but your memory will become less tenacious on these points, as you feel the shackles of matrimony press upon you. I *am* a married man *you* know, and *I* know; and, therefore, every excuse can be made for me on that head. If I were laying my bait for a splendid fortune, as—but mum—why, without doubt, I should be as attentive and as thoughtful, and as every thing else, as other people;—but, marriage,—oh, that's a confounded change-making thing—'tis, Sir Marmaduke, I assure you; very convenient at *certain* times, but devilishly awkward at others."

" Oh, true,—true, 'pon my honour," returned Sir Marmaduke; " I fancy that circumstances make a slight difference, —I do, 'pon my honour;—is it not quite natural it should do so, doc*tar?*"

" Oh, quite so," replied the divine, " quite so—(hiccup)—
but at the same time, allow me to say, not quite correct—
(hiccup)—a little attention should be paid after—(hiccup)—
confound the wind, I must wash it down;" so saying, he
drank his glass,—" As I was observing, a little . attention
should be paid after as well as before marriage. I don't
mean to insinuate—(hiccup)—that a gentleman is not to enjoy himself with a friend ; or that he is always to have his
lady—(hiccup)—hanging on his arm,—no, no; that would be
to invert the order of nature, and to pervert the very design
and institution of marriage; which, as I hold it, was for man's
comfort ;—but still I maintain that—that—pshaw ! what was
I saying ?—oh ; I maintain—that wine, if taken in proper
proportions, is conducive to health and comfort; and, therefore,—(hiccup)—"

" We were attending to your dissertation on matrimony,
doctor," observed Dashwood ; " however, I approve most
heartily of your digression; it is the way that most of our
present celebrated orators proceed in their arguments ; and i*
tells well, it confounds the listeners, and applause follows :
for the multitude always applaud that most which they understand least."

" Ha! ha! ha!" roared the doctor, good-humouredly ;
" I like your wit, Dashwood ; that's what I call genuine
'Attic'—(hiccup).—Matrimony was the subject,—was it ?
Ha! ha! ha!—Well, I was marrying wine at the time, and we
generally love to talk of that we love ;—but a truce to jesting—I'll fill to the brim for a special occasion, and go back
to matrimony."

As the doctor said, so he did ; and, to say the truth, he
did *more* than he *said,* for he overrun the brim, to the perfect saturation,—if not complete spoliation,—of the splendid
table-cover ; and then, taking the overflowing glass in his
hand, he drank,—as the liquor ran down his finger into his
coat-sleeve,—" Here's a speedy termination to your courting
engagement, Sir Marmaduke ; and after matrimony has been
committed—(hiccup),—with your permission I'll furnish you
with a lecture on sundry points connected with your conduct
as a married man."

Sir Marmaduke made a profound bow to the doctor, and
offered a suitable reply to his philanthropic wish and ghostly
offer ; and then, after himself and Dashwood had taken a few

more glasses of wine, they sallied forth, leaving the doctor to enjoy himself with his pipe and bottle.

So long as his reverence had company, he found sufficient employment in conversation, and occasionally blowing a cloud, and swallowing a glass of wine ; but when left alone, he was obliged to resort to other engagements to preserve himself from the misery of *ennui;* and as none were more convenient or more welcome than the bottle, he applied to it, and continued so actively to pay his devoirs to it, that he soon became unsteady in his seat; while his tongue, had he attempted to use it, would most certainly, and most abominably, have marred the king's English.

The doctor's large proboscis glowed like the celebrated Alexandrine Pharos of old ; or, to adopt the every-day language of the multitude, his bottle nose was as red as a capsicum ; while the large pimples, which plentifully bestudded his cheeks, appeared like so many beautiful garnets of more than ordinary brilliancy.

Thus equipped for the occasion, he proceeded to leave the York, for the purpose of taking notes of the conduct of the people of Bath. Having reached the door of the Hotel without any other injury than a slip down two or three stairs upon his hinder parts was calculated to occasion, the doctor appeared likely to suffer a lengthy detention,—not from John Doe, or Richard Roe, however, or any of that annoying and uncivil fraternity; but from a singular controversy which arose in his own mind as to whether he should turn right or left; or if the straight-forward line should be proceeded in or any other direction should be selected by him.

How long the opposition of his fancy might have been maintained against his wishes to proceed, is impossible to determine, if a circumstance had not occurred which at once settled the contested point.

Greatly as the tithe-extorting system had hardened the heart and vitiated the best feelings of the doctor, rendering him a very Caligula in spirit compared with what he would otherwise have been, still there were periods and occasions when the natural urbanity of his heart broke from the shackles which a degrading system had forged ; and he appeared, on such occasions, a truly worthy personage ; for then it was that he became a species of prototype of the charming Rector whom Goldsmith drew, who.

" Pointed to brighter worlds, and led the way."

This chanced to be one of those rational intervals of the doctor's, when the cormorant cravings of the hireling priest fell before the better feelings of the man ; and now an object, which called into full play the exercise of his sympathies, stood before his vision.

An interesting-looking young female, whose face still bore the evidences of having once been handsome,—although now sadly changed,—appeared at a short distance from the spot where the doctor stood. In her arms she carried an infant, apparently a few months old ; while at her side hung another, not much more than twelve months its senior. The countenances of each of the children, as well as their mother's, afforded too much proof that want, if not ill-treatment, had been endured by them. The poor woman's clothes, which had once been good, were now few and wretched,—" the shreds and patches of their former selves,"—while the little one by her side had scarcely a shoe to cover its feet, or a whole garment upon its partially exposed body.

" Well, my good woman," said the doctor, as she approached him, with the evident intention of passing on, " where are you hurrying so fast ?"

" I am going after my husband, Sir," replied the female, in a tone and manner which declared she had seen better days.

" Would it not be better for you to remain at home," asked the doctor, " and make yourself and children comfortable ?"

" Make them comfortable, Sir !" returned the female, and tears coursed down her cheeks as she gazed upon each ;— " They might have been so, Sir," she added, " if their father had loved them as I do."

" Is it possible," asked the doctor, " that their father can do other than love them ?—I am sure they are very pretty."

" If he did love them, Sir," she replied, " he would not spend every farthing he obtains in drink, and leave us destitute of every thing at home."

" And can he possibly do so ?" enquired the doctor.

" He can,—he does, Sir," rejoined the weeping mother.

" I hate drunkards," observed the doctor, hiccuping rather more freely than a perfectly sober man might be supposed to do ; " and especially I detest such as foolishly waste their property to the injury of their families ;—if he were a gentleman now, and could afford it, why—then—(hiccup)—it would be pardonable; but—(hiccup)—how long did you say you had been married?"

"I have been married nearly two years, Sir," replied the woman.

"And what profession or calling, pray, is your husband?" asked the divine.

"He is a carpenter, Sir," replied the female.

"And is he in work?" enquired his reverence.

"He was, Sir, while he kept sober; for he is an excellent workman," rejoined the woman, "and can then earn sufficient to keep us all comfortable,—at least he once did so,—but, Sir, he has so addicted himself to drinking lately, that he has been turned out of his employ; or if he obtains any work by chance, he is never sober until he has spent his last sixpence."

"Have you ever reasoned mildly and good-temperedly with him," enquired the doctor, "and endeavoured to show him how wrong he is acting—eh?"

"Yes, Sir, I have done so until he will hear me no longer," replied the female.

"And what apology does he offer for his conduct?" interrogated the doctor.

"Why, Sir, he says his betters do the same thing," replied the woman; "and therefore, he says, he has a right to do so too. I know, Sir, the excuse is a foolish one; but then, Sir, you know all drunkards make fools of themselves."

"True, true," rejoined the doctor, with a hard hiccup. "Your's is a very distressing case," he added, without displaying any anxiety to pursue the subject further.—"I pity you," he said, shaking his head with great gravity; "and if he was in my jurisdiction, I'm not in the 'commission of the peace' if I would not visit his transgressions with such punishment as the law adjudges the righteous award of such characters. There," continued his reverence, as he drew his purse-string,—"There is something for you.—Go home, now; and, as Shakspeare says,

"Buy some food, and get thee into flesh."

The poor woman burst into tears as she received the few shillings, which in her destitute circumstances appeared a fortune to her; and dropping a low curtsy as she turned away, with the intention of acting upon the doctor's recommenda-

T

tion, she exclaimed with a pathos which must have made even the doctor's heart leap,—"Heaven's blessing rest upon you for your bounty, kind Sir!"

The thought suddenly entered the head of the divine, that perhaps he might be able to render some service to the poor woman's husband, and he therefore called her back.—"Stay a moment, my good woman," he said;—"Did you not tell me you were going in pursuit of your husband?"

"Yes, Sir," she replied; "I was going to endeavour to persuade him to return home."

"Then you know where to find him?" observed the doctor.

"I have no doubt, Sir, but he is where all his days and nights are spent when he has any money," returned the woman.

"And where is that?" asked his reverence.

"At that house yonder, in Oxford Row," said the sorrowing wife, pointing in the direction to which she referred.

"Very well," said the doctor,—"very well: now go home and make yourself and dear children comfortable; and when your husband may return, don't scold,—that is not the way to win him—be kind—be affectionate. The kindness and affection of a woman's heart will win the most refractory husband, if properly employed; while ill-temper and passion may ruin the kindest and best. Go and be wise."

Once more the grateful woman dropped a curtsy, and prayed for a blessing upon his reverence; and in a few moments was, with her children, out of sight.

"So," said the doctor, "I'll see if I can't produce something like reformation in this place—(hiccup).—I feel surprised the magistracy here do not exercise their delegated authority to cause the lower orders among the people to desist from their drinking propensities—(hiccups). Drunkenness is a villanous and destructive vice;—moreover, it is an offence against the state; it therefore should he put a stop to amongst the lower orders. Gentlemen have a license to do what those beneath them should not think of; although, by the bye, I would punish every one who drank to intoxication."

As the doctor thus sagely soliloquized, he proceeded up the street in the direction the woman had pointed out, hiccuping as he went. As, however, he had neglected to enquire both for the name of the house and of the individual whom he had purposed in his own mind to cure, he felt himself bewildered how to proceed: for, in the first place, more pot-houses than one stared him in the face, and each house had its full share of customers. He acknowledged to himself that he had been very remiss in his enquiries, and felt that the benevolent plan he had purposed to pursue, must, in consequence of his own neglect, be abandoned.

After turning and winding, up one street and down another, until it would have been impossible for his reverence to have determined at what point of the compass the York Hotel stood from the way he was walking, his course was stopped by a flamingly decorated gin-palace; which, from its magnitude and garnishings, attracted his special notice.

While he stood gazing upon this species of Pandemonium, with feelings almost as confused as those possessed by the Knight of De la Mancha, when he was preparing to attack the windmill,—the doors were thrown open, and he perceived that its roomy interior was filled with a motley group of men, women, and children, many of whom appeared like walking bundles of rags, although a few might be seen who were decently attired. Some were reeling before a long counter, and spilling half the burning liquid which they attempted to raise to their lips; while others were quarrelling in different parts of the drunkard's den, and several sallow-visaged, hollow-eyed wretches were huddled together like swine upon the filthy floor.

The doors had been opened for the purpose of giving egress to a party which was reeling from it. Now the doctor thought he felt himself moved by the Spirit to commence his Quixotic career,—and, without doubt, the spirit of the port he had taken, had produced the effect noticed,—and, accordingly, striding up to the individuals referred to, striking, at the same time, his gold-headed cane with more than usual violence upon the stones (as if to announce his approach, and prepare the party for his reception), he opened the siege in the most heroic style.

"Hem!" said the doctor, elevating his head and pushing forward his chest.

"Hem—hem!" echoed a wag of the party, and wiped his nose with the cuff of his jacket.

"You appear particularly merry—(hiccup)—my fine fellows," added the doctor.

"Eh?" observed one of the party,—"Who are you?" as he reeled forward, as if he intended to make a battering-ram of his head against the doctor's body; and then suddenly righting, like a ship brought up by a heavy sea, he placed his arms a-kimbo, and exclaimed,—"Oh, I see!" and then turning to one of his companions, he added, elbowing him scientifically,—"Look here, Bill; I'm blowed if this ain't one of the fellers who eats up all our yarnings, like the caterpillars which the Bible tells us of, and the locusts, and them 'ere other things—eh? Ain't he a fine chap?"

This was a sort of attack which his reverence, in the 'commission of the peace,' never thought of; and he was, in consequence, taken all aback, as a sailor would have said, had he been placed in similar circumstances. He stood for a while with his eyes and mouth wide open, gazing upon the pot-valiant and liquor-eloquent personage before him; and instead of commencing, as he had intended, the assault, and so playing the part of the offensive, he was obliged to change his position and act on the defensive.

"Young man," observed the doctor, addressing the most juvenile of the party, "do you know who I am?"

"To be sure we do," returned the graceless wight; "at least by the cut of your gib, we guesses you are a parson."

"I am so," returned Titheum, "and I am also in the 'commission of the peace.'"

"Are you so?" said another of the group;—"Then it's a pity you doesn't know better not to break it, by 'costing us honest people in the way you did. Doesn't we yarn our bobs and browns by the sweat of our brow, and ain't we got a right to spend them as we likes—eh, old chap?—vy, you never sweats a 'air from one blessed year's end to another, for all you gets,—and yet you does what you likes with it."

"I had no intention to offend you," returned the doctor, in a somewhat milder tone than he had at first assumed; "my object was to endeavour to persuade you—(hiccup)—to—(hiccup)—to give up drinking."

"Oh, my eyes and limbs!" shouted another,—"Dost hear that, Bill? well, that beats the feller who cautioned the countryman against thieves as he picked his pocket! Give up drinking!—I ain't much of a hand at the Bible, more to my shame; for I read it through and through when I was at school; but I thinks I can give you a text,—what say you, old thrums;—vill you compound it for me—eh?"

"*Ex*pound it—(hiccup)—I suppose you mean," said the doctor.

"Vell, expound, or compound, or any other pound; it s all the same thing," returned the fellow,—"Vill you,—what do you call it?"

"Expound," said Bill, assisting his companion's memory.

"Aye, expound,—vill you expound it?" continued the interrogator.

"Certainly; I shall be ready to—(hiccup)—inform you," replied the doctor.—"What is it?"

"Vy it is this," returned the fellow, looking most archly in the doctor's face, '*Fisishon, heal yourself!*'—Eh? That's something near the mark, howsomever."

The doctor felt the reproof; while the companions of the proposer of the question set up a loud and discordant laugh, as they beheld the triumph of their champion.

"Vell said, Mike!" shouted one of them;—"That's a poser, at all events; he hasn't had sich a nut to crack this many a day. Vy, I'm blest if you ain't completely floored him;—go it again, my hearty!—I think as how you ought to be made a Member of Parliament, for you'd beat a whole bench of bishops with your hargaments."

Happily for the doctor, he soon regained his usual equanimity of temper and feeling, and returned with renewed vigour to the charge.

"I tell you, my good fellows," he observed, "you are too fond of the bottle—(hiccup),—and if you don't—(hiccup)—refrain speedily, your sun will set in darkness."

"Well, you have one comfort, old chap," returned the chief speaker, "vich none of us has; and that is,—what do you think it is now—eh?" he asked abruptly, observing the doctor was paying particular attention to his sage observations.

"I can't tell," returned his reverence, "I am listening to learn."

"Well, it is this," continued the fellow:—"You'll never want a *bottle* while you have a *nose*." The ludicrous allusion to the doctor's full-sized and now highly coloured nasal protuberance had the effect the speaker designed, in setting the whole party into another roar of laughter.—"And I'll tell you what," continued the fellow, "notwithstanding we don't understand much about your larned metaphogs, yet ven our sun goes out, vy we shall only have to put a forsforous match within half a yard of your conk, and we shall have a light directly."

" You're growing impertinent," said the doctor, his choler beginning to rise; " and I'm not in the ' commission of the peace' if I don't make you repent it." So saying, and allowing his passion to get the better of his reason, he raised his gold-headed cane in threatening attitude, and seemed as if about to employ it upon the refractory sons of the church, in the same way as the Roman Catholic clergy, are wont to do, in order to bring their disciples to submission; but the spirit of the Englishman,—or some other kind of spirit,—rose within the threatened party; and one of them, having at the moment a rather large quid of tobacco in his mouth, managed, with beastly dexterity, to shoot a stream of its very essence into the doctor's face, to the instant disfiguration of his physiognomy, and the almost blinding of his eyes; and then,—without further ceremony, as his reverence dropped his gold-headed cane, and prepared to apply his handkerchief to his visual organs to clear away the irritating filth from them,—the party seized him most rudely, and, bearing him to a horse-trough, were in the act of immersing his whole body in the dirty bath, when his cries of—" Help! help!—Thieves!—Murder!" brought unexpected and very seasonable aid to his rescue.

" Halloo!—villains!" shouted a voice at a short distance; " What! are you not contented with committing a robbery, but you must add murder to it, at this early hour of the evening?"

" 'Pon my honour!" exclaimed a second voice, " this is particularly unpleasant;—one may as well retire to that throat-cutting State, Venice, at once, as to come to this vile city—'pon my honour!"

" Here—Police! Police!" shouted the first voice, at the same time advancing and laying hold of one of the fellows. But as, in London, you may frequently split your lungs before one of those worthy personages can be found, when really wanted,—so now: not a single protector of the people, or guardian of the night, was within hearing. Of this, however, the insurgents were not aware; but, supposing a posse of the "Force" was coming down upon them, staff in hand, they, dropped the struggling doctor on the stones, and knocking down one of the persons who had disturbed them, they took to their heels and fled.

" 'Pon my honour!" exclaimed the person who had most unceremoniously been overturned by a sledge-hammer kind of fist being placed a few inches below the region of the chest,—"This is beyond all endurance—'tis barbarous, 'pon my honour!"

"Whose voice is that?" enquired the doctor, as he managed to get upon his hands and knees; his ears rather than his eyes directing him; for they were still half-blinded by the tobacco juice.

"Who the devil have we here?" exclaimed the other person,—"Why, by all that's marvellous, it is Dr. Titheum!"

"Aye,—it is, indeed!" groaned out his reverence,—"But to whom am I indebted for this timely rescue?"

"Ha! ha! ha!" burst from the lips of the first speaker; "This is an adventure and no mistake."

"'Pon my honour," sighed his friend, "I fear I have injured my back by this unlucky fall. Who did you say?" he continued; "why, 'pon my honour, yes, as I hope soon to enter the sublimated region of matrimony, it is indeed the worthy doctar."

In a little time his reverence succeeded in partially cleansing his face; and then, looking up to his friends, at once recognised Dashwood and Sir Marmaduke. The pleasure of the doctor, as he made the discovery, exceeded all bounds; for not only had he trembled least a renewal of the murderous attempt upon his person should be repeated, but, having lost all knowledge of where he was, he feared considerable difficulty existed to his fiuding,—in any thing like reasonable time,— his way to the Hotel.

After a hasty but hearty greeting, the friends, locked arm / and arm, proceeded towards the "York," each furnishing to the other such information as remained in part a mystery, connected with their singular meeting.

The reader is already aware, that Lord Dashwood and Sir Marmaduke Varney had fully purposed to pay their promised visit to the "Donna" and her "Duenna." For this purpose they left their Hotel an hour or two before, and in a short time after setting out, found themselves at the residence of the ladies, in the Royal Crescent.

If Dashwood had been fascinated by Mrs. Leechum, when he beheld her in the character of "Donna Rosabella," his admiration of her person and manners,—for both, when she pleased, were good,—exceeded what he had before felt, as he gazed upon her in the quiet of a splendid drawing-room.

Dr. Leechum received the gentlemen as the friends

of Lady Bolio, and Mrs. Leechum welcomed them most heartily, as highly esteemed and most noble signiors.

The moments of this visit flew with unwonted celerity,—at least Mrs. Leechum thought so ; and before she had entirely recovered from the perturbation into which the announcement of Lord Dashwood had thrown her, the proposal was made by Sir Marmaduke to depart. Mrs. Leechum troubled not herself to enquire, or rather to *think*, if Dashwood were a Benedictine or not; nay, she almost forgot that she was herself really and truly married to Dr. Leechum.

The gallantry of Lord Dashwood was excessive, and yet it did not appear to exceed the bounds of fashionable attention. The limits of these bounds, indeed, are difficult to define ;—and, perhaps, if examined by the critical eye of prudence, propriety, or even rectitude, they would be found to overstep exceedingly the limits of consistency; leading, in not a few instances, to positive criminality. What his Lordship *said* and *looked*, appeared to be just what good breeding and lordly courtesy dictated ; and, *therefore*, Mrs. Leechum listened to his conversation, and returned his looks with infinite satisfaction to herself, to the pleasure of Dashwood, and not *greatly* to the offence of the doctor himself ;—at least, whatever he felt or thought, he presumed not to *say* any thing.

Before Dashwood and Sir Marmaduke left the Royal Crescent, they gave a pressing invitation, accompanied by a fervent hope, that they might be favoured by the ladies and Dr. Leechum, to dine with the ladies of their party and themselves, on the following day, at the York Hotel. No very strong objections were urged against the proposition ; and with the understanding that the case was settled, the adventurers were returning home elated at the success of their visit, when they unexpectedly encountered the doctor, as has been narrated, and saved him from being plunged over head and ears into the horse-trough.

The arrangement which had been made was soon communicated to the whole party, each of whom seemed gratified with the expected visit.

" Now, doctor," observed the Duchess, " my wager quakes : if the report be correct which his Lordship has given, Lady Bolio is the very person for your money. I should not wonder if we have a double wedding now before we leave Bath."

" My dear Duchess," observed Miss Fidget, attempting to

blush, as the eye of her Grace leered towards her, at the close of her observation, "Do pray think what you are saying, and spare my sensitive feelings."

"I do think, my dear friend," replied her Grace, "and therefore I speak. When is the happy day fixed for Sir Marmaduke?" she continued, appealing to the Knight.

"'Pon my honour," returned Sir Marmaduke, "your Grace is too severe upon us,—you are, 'pon my honour!"

"Oh, I dare say, you are a pair of very bashful personages!" retorted the Duchess.—"Now I'll give you a toast—here's—"

"Now do, pray, spare me!" exclaimed Miss Fidget.

"And I must cry your mercy, also," said the doctor.

"'Pon my honour," chimed in Sir Marmaduke, "we had better unite our forces and attack her Grace *en masse*,—we had, 'pon my honour."

"Well, well," said the Duchess, "I'll sound a retreat then, and *spare* ye all."

The whole evening went off with cheerfulness,—Miss Fidget was more than usually easy,—Georgiana thought fondly of Claudius, and wished he had been a gentleman,—the Duchess drank her brandy-and-water, and the gentlemen their wine,—and, at a late hour, the party separated for the night.

CHAPTER XXXI.

> "But farewell compliment,
> Dost thou love me? I know thou wilt say 'aye!'
> And I shall take thy word;—yet, if thou swear'st,
> Thou may'st prove false: at lover's perjuries,
> They say, Jove laughs...............
> If thou dost love, pronounce it faithfully;
> Or, if you think I am too quickly won,
> I'll frown and be perverse, and say thee 'nay,'
> So thou wilt woo; but else not for the world.
> In truth,—I am too fond."
>
> JULIET.

AT an earlier hour than was usual with the doctor, he left his chamber and descended to his sitting-room. As he approached the door his ears were saluted by sounds from within, which startled him. Without giving himself time to think on the impropriety of becoming an eves-dropper, he applied his ear close to the key-hole, when the sounds were repeated. In consequence, however, of their being low and indistinct, they came in such disjointed and fragmentized parcels, as left him at a loss to conceive what could be their import.

"Surely," he thought, "that is Georgiana's voice; but with whom can she be conversing at so early an hour,—and wherefore in such a low and whispering manner?"

Again he placed his sound-receiving organ close to the small aperture; and holding his breath in till he was scarce able to breathe, for fear of being discovered, he caught the words,—"No, dear Georgiana, I assure you."

"That is not the voice of a woman," thought the doctor; "Who can it be?"

Suddenly the thought rushed through his mind, that his ardent wishes in reference to Georgiana and Sir Marmaduke might yet be realized;—and, as the rapid impression came, he experienced a rapture he could scarce contain. He hastily ran over in his memory the attentions which he now fancied he had seen the Knight pay to his daughter during the last two or three days; and allowed not a darkening question to blot the bright disk of the pleasing reverie.

In the height of his ecstatic emotions, the following brief colloquy broke on his ear,—"I can no longer conceal the truth," said Georgiana, "although I feel I ought to blush so directly to acknowledge it,—I love you—I have long done so!"

"Dearest Georgiana," returned another voice, "if I had dared to presume so far, I should, long since, have ventured to assure you of my deep and devoted attachment; but, you are aware—"

"Do not name it," interrupted Georgiana,—"I am aware, —painfully aware of the difficulties in which we are both placed; but we must endeavour to devise some way by which to break down the barrier that at present exists."

"That will, I hope, be a task of little difficulty," returned the other; "but at present it cannot be done;—insurmountable difficulties, my love, he in the way."

"Our secret must be preserved most carefully," said Georgiana."

"By me it shall be most sacredly kept," returned the male voice.

" It's all right," thought the doctor, rubbing his hands in
ecstacy ;—" It's all right,—Miss Fidget stands in the way,—
only Miss Fidget; but that difficulty may be got over, so Sir
Marmaduke himself thinks.   They intend to keep it a secret
from every one—ha! ha! ha!" he chuckled to himself.—
" They little know how difficult it is to deceive a justice of
the peace.   Well, they shall know that I can keep a secret;
—I'll surprise them, and assure the lovers of my sanction—
Sir Marmaduke shall be convinced that it will afford me more
pleasure than I can express to call him son-in-law."

Full of the benevolent purpose of rendering his daughter
and Sir Marmaduke happy, as well as to have a hearty laugh
at the slight confusion into which his presence would throw
them, he opened the room-door and stepped in.   So gently
did he accomplish his object, and so completely absorbed
were the lovers in each other's company, that they perceived
not his entrance.

He had not proceeded three paces, however, on tip-toe,
before his progress was stopped as suddenly as if the power
of motion had suddenly been taken from his limbs.   There
sat Georgiana on the sofa, and there too was,—*not* Sir Marmaduke Varney, but the gentle livery-clad *Master Claudius !*
One arm of our hero entwined his young mistress's slender
waist, while one of her beautiful hands was locked in his.

" Dear Georgiana !" had just trembled from the lips of
Claudius, receiving the response of " Dear Claudius !" from
Georgiana, as their lips came in close and affectionate contact,
and a long, fervent, burning kiss proved how much the
youthful lovers felt,—when, almost bursting with disappoint-
ment and rage, his reverence seized our hero ; and, tearing
him from the fond embrace of his mistress, hurled him to a
remote part of the room.

" So !" exclaimed the doctor, while a saliva flowed from his
quivering lips, in as white a foam as would have issued from
the extended jaws of a rabid mastiff,—" So ! this is very
fine !—very fine, indeed !"

Claudius felt in a very awkward predicament, and looked
as he felt ; while Georgiana, uttering a piercing shriek, fainted
in her father's arms.

" You artful villain !" exclaimed his reverence, presenting
his clenched fist at Claudius,—" leave this place instantly,
and let me never again set my eyes upon you ; or I'm not
in the ' commission of the peace' if I don't pound you into a
jelly !"

Claudius felt half disposed to proclaim himself at once the son of Lady Bolio; but judging it better for a short time longer to remain *incog.*, he held his tongue. Still to leave his mistress in such a state as he now saw her, was maddening to think on even; and, therefore, without attending to the kind admonition of the doctor, in order to escape being jellyized, he enquired,—" Will your worship allow me to fetch some cold water, or—?"

" If you do not instantly obey me," thundered the doctor, " and leave this place, I'll make you feel the weight of my infuriated displeasure."

" But, Sir," continued Claudius, " Miss Georgiana requires some assistance."

" Scoundrel!" roared the doctor, at the same moment laying the insensible girl on the sofa, and seizing our hero;— " Begone, I say!" and without further ceremony ejected him from the apartment.

The object of his anger being removed, all the affection of the doctor's heart rushed towards his beloved Georgiana; and as he again pressed her to his bosom, he almost forgot the folly of which she had been guilty.

" My dear Georgiana," said the doctor to his daughter, as soon as she was sufficiently recovered, " how could you so greatly forget yourself as to allow your passions to wander to a livery servant ?—if he had been any thing else I could have excused it; for, I confess, there is something about the lad that has pleased me,—he is shrewd, intelligent, and of quick parts;—moreover, his personal appearance is not to be objected to; but then, he is still what he is,—and whatever kind of excellence, or however diversified the talents of any one moving in such a sphere, they form no recommendation of them to a lady; at least they should not. If this should be known, Georgiana, by our friends, what would be said ? your prospects in life would be ruined for ever."

Georgiana replied to the doctor's address by a flood of tears, connected with strong symptoms of again departing for a while from a state of consciousness. The doctor trembled lest such a circumstance should be repeated; and, therefore, in a coaxing strain observed, as he kissed her pale cheek,— " Well, well, now I see you are sorry for it;—it was a slip of youth, and I shall take no more notice of the matter. Come, rouse up, and be yourself again. Come, oblige me with a little music while breakfast is preparing."

" Indeed, papa, you must excuse me this time," said Georgiana, faintly.

" But, indeed, I will not," returned the doctor, playfully; —". If you don't instantly play me a tune, and give me a little ballad, I'll not promise you shall be of our party to-day at dinner."

" You know I would play and sing too, most cheerfully, if I could," returned Georgiana; " but my head aches sadly, and I cannot."

" I'll have no excuse this morning," said the doctor; " I wish to get my spirits up in order to receive our visitors with becoming decorum—so play you must!--Here," he continued, " this little thing won't hurt you;—come now, Georgie—it will suit you exactly, I'm certain."

Georgiana, though sad at heart, felt pleased that her father felt disposed to carry off the matter in the way proposed; and finding that no excuse would avail her, she seated herself upon her music-stool, and sung as her father wished,

" APART FROM THOSE WE LOVE!

" How lonely are the hours
  Of each returning day;
Though bustling crowds around us throng,
  And suitors homage pay.
Though pleasures court our smile,
  Their transports cannot move;
For sadness still will fill the soul
  Apart from those we love!

The joys which once we knew,
  Bring madness to the brain;
As reason whispers, while we think,
  ' Such ne'er will come again.'
Each object once enjoyed,
  Grows hateful, and we prove
With anguish,—seeking rest is vain
  Apart from those we love!

A smile, indeed, may play
  Upon the ashy cheek,
Like a sun-beam dancing round a tomb,
  And falsehood's language speak.
Still sadness from the soul
  Will ne'er again remove;
Unchang'd by place, unmov'd by time,—
  Apart from those we love!"

At the end of the song breakfast was set on; and without the slightest reference to Claudius, the repast was finished; after which they withdrew, in order to spend a few hoursbefore the toilet, in order to prepare themselves to receive, with due form and dignity, their expected visitors.

The mind of poor Georgiana was torn by a thousand conflicting passions : love for Claudius, obedience to her parent, and her own respectability and credit, by turns put in their claims. But love is a subtle casuist, and seldom fails to carry his point : on the present occasion he did so triumphantly ; and hence, while the Duchess and Miss Fidget were rouging, curling, padding, and patching, Georgiana was placing herself in such positions as she supposed the most likely in which to meet Claudius. Still she saw him not ;— again and again she shifted her station ; but alas ! with no better success.

Being entirely ignorant of what had taken place during the time she lay fainting on the sofa, she imagined the object of her affection avoided meeting her by design ; and then the fear, the maddening fear possessed her, lest he should, from the discovery her father had made, cool in his affections towards her. Full of such alarm, and scarcely knowing what she did, she rang the bell, and when a servant entered she desired that Claudius should wait upon her to carry a letter to the post.

"I will carry it, Miss, if you please," was the reply.

"Thank you," returned Georgiana, "I have not written yet ; but I wish Claudius to be in readiness."

"We haven't seen him, Miss, since the first of the morning," replied the servant.

"Not seen him !" exclaimed Georgiana, with strong feeling; and then suddenly checking herself, she observed,—"You had better seek him, and say I wish him to convey a message for me."

"I will, Miss," said the servant, and left the room.

"Not seen him !" Georgiana repeated to herself, with emphasis, as she paced the room.—"Where can he be ?—surely he has not left the house ;—oh ! no, no ; that I think he would not do ; and yet,—not seen him !" she continued to muse ;—"Where, oh ! where can he be ?"

At the end of half an hour the servant returned ; Georgiana observed him with peculiar emotion, and enquired,— "Well, have you delivered my message to Claudius ?"

"No, Miss," returned the servant ; "I have sought for him every where, and can't find him ; and I have enquired of the other servants respecting him, and all of them say they know nought about him."

Georgiana was obliged to do violence to her feelings; and with as much apparent indifference as she could display, she dismissed the servant, although the actual state of her mind bordered closely on distraction.

Amidst the chaos of thought of which she now became the subject, she happily maintained so much collectedness as to be aware of the necessity under which she was laid to keep her secret to herself; and the best way to do so, she felt assured, and prevent the prying suspicions of those by whom she was surrounded, was to give no cause to them; and, therefore, she repaired to her dressing-room in hopes of calming the tempest of her mind by engaging in the—(to her)—distasteful but requisite preparations for receiving company.

CHAPTER XXXII.

> " *Mer.* ....We must have you dance.
> *Rom.* Not I, believe me; you have dancing shoes,
>   With nimble soles,—I have a soul of lead,
>   So stakes me to the ground, I cannot move.
> *Mer.* You are a lover: borrow Cupid's wings,
>   And soar with them above a common bound.
> *Rom.* I am too sore empierced with his shaft,
>   To soar with his light feathers; and so bound,
>   I cannot bound a pitch above dull care;
>   Under love's heavy burden do I sink."
>
> SHAKSPEARE.

THE clock of the Abbey church was striking six as Lady Bolio's carriage drove up to the door of the York Hotel, and in a moment Lord Dashwood, Sir Marmaduke Varney, and Dr. Titheum, were in attendance, to escort the ladies to the drawing-room. Mrs. Leechum leaned on the arm of Lord Dashwood, and "tripped like a fairy," as they passed along the hall, and ascended the noble and easy flight of stairs leading to a grand suite of rooms on the first floor. Dr. Titheum had the good fortune to please Lady Bolio at first sight; who thought him a very proper man, and honoured him so far as to accept his offered assistance; while Sir Marmaduke, in close confabulation with Leechum, brought up the rear. The introduction to the other parts of the party followed in due form; and, after a few slight arrangements had been made,

connected with the ladies' attire, at a little before seven, dinner was served.

While others were engaged in the actual and active discus-
sion of solids and fluids, Georgiana appeared half vacant.
Every time a servant entered the room, her head and eyes
were turned in the direction of the door, expecting that Claudius would make his appearance; but she was disappointed
—he came not.

"Will you allow me the honour, Madam," said Lord Dashwood, addressing himself to Mrs. Leechum, "to take a glass
of wine with you?"

"With great pleasure, my lord," answered the smiling
lady, and they accordingly pledged each other.

"Now, my dear Carlo," observed Miss Fidget to her dear
companion, "that is very rude;—I can't, indeed, allow you
to eat out of my plate before company."

"'Pon my honour," said Sir Marmaduke, "I fear Master
Carlo is rather troublesome, my dear Miss Fidget; will you
permit me to take charge of him while you dine,—I will be
superlatively careful of him, 'pon my honour."

"Oh, you are *very* kind, Sir Marmaduke," replied Miss
Fidget.—"I am *sure* you would be as careful of him as of
myself; and if I dared to trust him to any one's care, it would
be to *your's*, Sir Marmaduke."

"Oh, 'pon my honour you flatter me," returned the Knight,
—"you do positively;—still I protest, by all that's beautiful,
you speak the truth,—you do, 'pon my honour."

While Miss Fidget and the Knight continued to hold sweet
intercourse, the Duchess launched out in all the freedom of
easy converse, and displayed such a vein of good-humour,
and such a fund of general information, while conversing
with Dr. Leechum, as not merely gratified that worthy professional, but diverted his mind from what, in all probability,
would otherwise have spoiled his dinner,—the particular attentions which Dashwood paid to his young and gentle wife.

Dr. Titheum and Lady Bolio appeared to have established
themselves on the best possible terms with each other;—indeed, more than once the thought entered her Ladyship's
head, that she had been too hasty in determining *never*
again to change her state,—matrimonially considered,—for
she felt disposed to flatter herself that she had already made
an impression upon the tender passions of his reverence.

Poor Georgiana alone appeared alone; and she was *alone*

indeed in her feelings !—she could not have been more so had she changed situations with Alexander Selkirk, or Philip Quarl. It is true, she joined occasionally in the general conversation which took place, and with a spirit and vivacity which delighted Lady Bolio ; but if those who best knew her had noticed the way in which she did so, they would have been convinced she was a mere performer, on that occasion, of what at other times was her natural character.

All soon became unrestrained good-humour and innocent hilarity ; jest succeeded jest, and one repartee was only the precursor of a string of others. The Duchess evidently enjoyed the port-wine,—Mrs. Leechum was delighted with Lord Dashwood,—Lady Bolio thought Dr. Titheum the most agreeable man she had ever met with,—

> " And wished
> That heaven had made her such a man ;"

while, what with the attentions of Sir Marmaduke to Miss Fidget, and her own attentions to Carlo, that lady managed to .be perfectly composed, until the signal was given for withdrawing to the ball-room. Leechum alone appeared neglected, and poor Georgiana forlorn; but, as in the great world in which we exist, every one has enough to do to look to themselves without being greatly affected by the cares of others ; so in this miniature universe each one was so fully occupied in their own pursuits, that little attention was paid to others.

" 'Pon my honour !" exclaimed Sir Marmaduke, " this is one of the most-felicitous parties I ever had the honour to meet,—I suppose we must give all the credit to the ladies— eh, doctar?"

" You *suppose*, Sir Marmaduke !" returned the doctor, whose eloquence on the present occasion was only exceeded by his politeness and gallantry ; both of which were stimulated by the large and frequent potations in which he had indulged.—" You *suppose*, Sir Marmaduke !—and why *suppose?* —is not every thing that is delightful on earth rendered so by the ladies ? and in reference to the present party,—why, their fascinations would enliven a dungeon ! I'm not in the ' commission of the peace' if I should not have enjoyed the Bastille itself in such society."

" 'Pon my honour," returned Sir Marmaduke, " I stand corrected,—that is, *reprimanded* for my obtuseness of imagination and want of feeling ;—your observations, doc*tar*, strike me as being irrefutably correct; they do, 'pon my honour. In such society, as you justly observe, a dungeon would be transformed to a fairy palace; it would, 'pon my honour." So saying, the Knight extended his hand in order to give energy to his eloquent echo of the doctor, when, unfortunately, it came in collision with the lancet-like teeth of Miss Fidget's bosom companion, who,—either bent upon mischief, or mistaking the perfumed forefinger of his electmaster for some dainty morsel intended for mastication,—very unceremoniously closed his jaws upon it, until the blood gushed from several lacerations.

Sir Marmaduke kicked and shouted, and Carlo maintained his grasp; while Miss Fidget, in very gentle and entreating language, requested her dear poodle to relinquish his hold upon the quivering flesh; but which, notwithstanding, he appeared very indisposed to do.

"Oh fie, fie, Carlo!" exclaimed Miss Fidget, after the extrication had been effected, "that is very rude of you,—how could you think of committing such an act?"

"Who would have supposed, Sir Marmaduke," observed the Duchess, "that you would have put your finger in the poor thing's mouth?—ha! ha! ha!—He appears very anxious to claim intimate connexion,—how very sagacious he is."

"'Pon my honour," said the Knight, as he bound the maimed member in his snow-white handkerchief, "this is a confoundedly awkward affair."

"Well, really, Sir," observed Lady Bolio, "I feel, for my own part, that you have a claim upon our strongest sympathies; for had it not been for the very polite compliments you were paying us ladies, the accident would not have occurred."

Sir Marmaduke placed his right hand under his left breast, indicating how much he felt the compliment of her Ladyship; and observed, as he bowed low,—"'Pon my honour, I feel honoured by your observation, Madam; I do, 'pon my honour."

"Allow me the pleasure, Lady Bolio," said Titheum, as he presented his arm, "to escort your Ladyship to the ballroom."

"Oh, you are *very* kind, Dr. Titheum," returned her Ladyship;—"really, your polite attentions this evening will render me your everlasting debtor!" and she took his arm.

"I hope not *quite* so long, Madam," rejoined the doctor,

very significantly, which her Ladyship, evidently, well understood ; but of which she appeared anxious to make the doctor believe she was ignorant.

"Why, what *reason,* doctor, have you to *hope* not ?" enquired her Ladyship.—"How *can* I make return for your *very* polite attentions ?"

"Your Ladyship will, perhaps, allow me the pleasure of enquiring after your health," returned the doctor, "on some future occasions, as an off-set."

"Oh, that will be only to increase my obligations," replied Lady Bolio ; "I shall by that means get deeper in debt."·

"Perhaps, then," said the doctor, "your Ladyship will feel inclined, on some future day, to discharge the whole at once, by—"

"How ?" said her Ladyship.

The doctor would have given the required explanation, but at that moment they entered the ball-room, although they had stepped as deliberately as propriety would allow ; and Sir Marmaduke exclaimed,—"Come, doc*tar,* I want a little of your help, 'pon my honour ; Miss Fidget declines dancing to-night, and Miss Georgiana refuses to be my partner ; that is confoundedly awkward,—is it not, doc*tar?*"

"Georgiana, my dear," said the doctor, "what is amiss ; are you not well to-night?—Come, come ; surely you will not refuse Sir Marmaduke for a partner ?"

"Really, dear papa," replied Georgiana, "I must be excused ;—I do not refuse because Sir Marmaduke has been kind enough to ask me for his partner ; but I cannot dance to-night ; indeed I cannot,—I feel somewhat unwell."

The doctor's mind was so completely engrossed with the thoughts of Lady Bolio, as absolutely to have forgotten the affair between Georgiana and Claudius, although it had so recently occurred ; and, therefore, receiving the excuse which his daughter had offered as perfectly correct,—and in truth it was so, for she was not well,—he did not further press her on the point.

Happily for Sir Marmaduke, a bumper of brandy-and-water had so far elevated the spirits of the Duchess, that without ceremony she paired with him ; while, shortly after, Miss Fidget changed her mind, and lent her maiden hand to Dr. Leechum ; and the whole company, save and except Georgiana and Carlo, were soon in motion.

Before the company broke up, which did not take place until some time after

"Bright Phœbus had mounted his car in the east,"

it became very evident to every one present, that the chances were on the side of strong probability, that something would issue between Lady Bolio and Dr. Titheum from the visit; while, if Dr. Leechum's countenance had been taken as an index of his thoughts and feelings, it would have been imagined that his suspicions were strongly excited that something which he might object to would take place from it, between his dear, sweet-tempered lady and Lord Dashwood.

An excess of enjoyment of any kind leads to satiety : we are not constitutioned so as to endure an uninterrupted course of pleasure. The present party felt it ; and, although some one or two pairs would, perhaps, have been able to bear each other's company an hour or two longer, the general feeling displayed was, a desire to separate, and separate they did ; and in the same order as they entered the Hotel they now departed from it; previous to which, however, a positive engagement had been made for a return of the visit on that day week, at Lady Bolio's mansion, in the Royal Crescent ; and with this understanding, " Good night," and " Good night," sounded from each of the group : and then her Ladyship's carriage bowled over the stones at a rapid rate towards her residence.

" Now, is not Lord Dashwood a charming creature ?" asked Mrs. Leechum of Lady Bolio, as soon as they entered the drawing-room.—" I do positively think I shall dream of him."

" Why yes," replied Lady Bolio, in a rather indifferent sort of tone, "he is in *his* way well enough."

" In *his* way !" cried Mrs. Leechum ;—" Why, my dear Lady Bolio, what do you mean ?"

" Why, I mean," replied her Ladyship in the same key, " he is a very nice-looking personage,—plenty of humour, very full of gallantry, and all that sort of thing."

" Well," exclaimed Mrs. Leechum, " and what would your Ladyship wish a gentleman should be ?"

" Oh, I don't wish for *any thing*, not I," returned Lady Bolio ;—" but what think you of Dr. Titheum ?"

" What do I think of *him ?*" replied Mrs. Leechum.

" Aye," continued her Ladyship, " of *him*. If I could

make a conquest there I do think I should be induced, with a *leetle* persuasion, to promise to—' *obey.*' "

"Ha! ha! ha!" burst from the doctor's lady;—"Well, now, that is just what I expected ; it is, I assure you,—and I feel no hesitation in saying, you have made a *hit* there.   I only wish I could be as certain of having made an impression upon Lord Dashwood."

"My dear!" exclaimed Leechum, no longer able to listen in silence, "what are you saying ;—do you indeed forget that *I* am your husband ?"

"No, Sir, I do not forget it," returned the lady.—"Pray what, allow me to ask, do you intend to insinuate by *such* a question ?"

"Oh nothing, my love! nothing, I assure you," replied the trembling doctor ; "I was merely going to hint—"

"You *did hint*, Sir, I think," interrupted his lately amiable-spirited rib,—"You did *hint* something that reflected no credit upon me ; and what, *therefore*, was not *very* complimentary to yourself."

"No, my dear," returned Leechum, "upon my word, I merely intended to hint that—"

"I will not hear any more such *hints*, Sir," roared the lady.   "Do you wish to *hint* that I am in love with Lord Dashwood ?   Cannot a lady feel a warm respect for an amiable man without loving him ?   Oh! Lady Bolio, never get married!" she continued,—"You see how I have sold my liberty : I can *go* no where,—I can be free, that is, *polite* to no one, but this gentleman is hinting, and,—oh, I am wild!—I am distracted!—I shall go raving mad, I know I shall, to be so inhumanly treated !"

"Now, be calm, my dear Mrs. Leechum," observed Lady Bolio, "and, I dare say, when Lord Dashwood pays us his visit, all will be set right."

"Oh certainly, certainly, my dear," responded Leechum, "I shall be most happy to see his Lordship,—' hanged and quartered !' he whispered to himself.

"Why true, as you say, my dear Lady Bolio," rejoined Mrs. Leechum, "the time will soon come round when we shall again be favoured with a visit; and then, I dare say, Dr. Leechum will be fully satisfied that his *hints* are unnecessary, and his suspicions ridiculous or idle."

"Umph!" thought Leechum,—"Very likely;" and then addressing his lady, he observed,—"Well, my love, I suppose it will be so; all would have been well if you had permitted me to hint—"

"I think you had better retire, Dr. Leechum," said his lady, with a look full of meaning ; " I wish to have a few moments' conversation with Lady Bolio ; I suppose I may be allowed *that* privilege without being suspected."

If the unfortunate doctor had felt, disposed to offer a re- monstrance, he dared not to have done so ;—nay, if Lord Dashwood, instead of Lady Bolio, had been the person with whom she desired a few moments' conversation, it would have been as good for his health and peace that he had swal- lowed every tooth in his head, as to have given a single *hint* of objection.

"Certainly, my love! certainly,—you are at full liberty," said Leechum; " but allow me to hint, my dear, that I think you require rest; and, therefore, the sooner you follow me—"

"I shall do so, Sir, when *I* think it is necessary," returned his obedient and sweet-tempered spouse; " I suppose you understand *that* hint ?" she added with a sagely significant nod of the head. It was evident he *did* understand it, for without another hint he bade Lady Bolio " Good morning," and re- tired to muse over the delectabilities of matrimony.

"Well, now, my dear Lady Bolio," said Mrs. Leechum, as soon as the doctor had fairly vanished, " may I trust you with a secret ?"

"Oh, most certainly," replied her Ladyship.

"And will you keep it most sacredly," asked Mrs. Leechum, " and give me your candid advice ?"

"I will do both if you desire it," replied Lady Bolio.

"Well, then," said Mrs. Leechum, " Lord Dashwood has pressed me to meet him for an hour to-morrow afternoon."

"Lord Dashwood has !" exclaimed Lady Bolio, in strong surprise.

"Yes," returned the doctor's rib; " shall I do so?"

"By no means, my love," replied her Ladyship; " it would, in my opinion, be highly improper. I give you my candid opinion."

"Well, but it is an affair of importance," returned Mrs. Leechum, " and his Lordship assured me—"

"I dare say it is," rejoined Lady Bolio; " it *should* be something of importance that should induce a married lady to meet a married lord by appointment."

" Well, but," said Mrs. Leechum, " Dr. Titheum is to be present."

" Dr. Titheum !" exclaimed her Ladyship,—" Indeed ! Oh, that alters the case."

" Yes, and you were to accompany me," said Mrs. Leechum.

" Oh, well then ; I can have no objection," observed Lady Bolio,—" none whatever ;—go, certainly. What do you imagine is the object of the meeting,—is any thing proposed ?"

" Nothing, whatever, that I know of," returned Mrs. Leechum ; " but, I suppose, *you* are not *entirely* ignorant,— are you now ?"

" Upon my honour !" said her Ladyship, " I know nothing about it;—but do you suppose, my dear, that Dr. Titheum will be disposed to be agreeable,—that is, you know—"

" Bless your Ladyship !" returned Mrs. Leechum, " I am sure you may make what you please of the doctor."

" Well, certainly, that is saying a great deal," responded Lady Bolio.

" I wish I had the power to make as much of Lord Dashwood," sighed Mrs. Leechum.

" At what hour are we to meet the gentlemen ?" enquired her Ladyship, without attending to Mrs. Leechum's sigh, or fervently expressed wish.

" At eight in the evening," replied Mrs. Leechum.

" Well, my dear, we must make some excuse for our absence," said Lady Bolio. " You may depend on me, —I'll accompany you. Adieu !" So saying, they separated, each filled with the utmost anxiety respecting the expected meeting.

CHAPTER XXXIII.

" She sigh'd as they met,—gave a look full of pleasure,—
Would have blush'd if she could,—Love had stolen the measure.
  Then a lady-like curtsy she dropp'd ;—
The swain took the hint, and, with passion ecstatic,
Seized her beautiful hand, and with action erratic,
  Kiss'd her lips,—and the question popp'd !
' Who can refuse a swain so killing ?'
She said,—then sigh'd,—' to wed I'm willing.'
Thus strangely woo'd, and strangely won,
The morrow saw the parties one !"

WOOING A LA MODE.

THE utmost extent of period that either Dashwood, Dr. Titheum, or Lady Bolio, proposed to remain at Bath when first they entered it, was ten days; that time, however, was already over-run, and still they felt, for very special reasons, fully disposed to remain a week or two longer. The only one of the party that had grown tired of its gaiety was Georgiana. She felt assured that Claudius had left the city; but to what extent her father had been concerned in his departure, she did not so much as conjecture. Her heart no longer beat in unison with the merry sounds which struck upon her ear; neither was she captivated by the gawdy sights which played before her eye: she had become emphatically—a "joyless one."

Sir Marmaduke felt himself so bound to Dashwood, that he cared not to leave before his Lordship; while neither Miss Fidget nor the Duchess were disposed to depart alone and unattended.

It now became evident that Sir Marmaduke began seriously to think of his expected union with Miss Fidget; and, to say the truth, that lady knew no just cause or impediment why the ceremony which would *legally* and for life unite their fortunes, should not forthwith be attended to; although the pride of womanhood prevented her from giving her thoughts utterance.

Thus affairs stood when the meeting related in the preceding chapter took place. Dashwood, who perceived from the first that the reverend doctor was smitten, either by the person, or property, or title of Lady Bolio,—and that that lady had herself far from outlived her amorous feelings, or platonic sensibility,—determined in some way, as circumstances might offer, to accomplish his own ends in reference to Mrs. Leechum, through their means.

In pursuance of the resolve which Dashwood had formed, he managed most dexterously, on the evening above referred to, to solicit Mrs. Leechum to favour him with a meeting on the afternoon of the following day;—from this proposition, however, the lady shrunk alarmed; for, notwithstanding the folly and impropriety with which she had been and was still chargeable, any thing that wore the appearance of positive criminality she shuddered to think on, and turned from with disgust.

She was not, however, aware to what a fearful extent she was working to weaken, if not entirely overthrow, the virtuous principles which yet influenced her, by encouraging such a person as Lord Dashwood in his visits; or by cherishing for a moment such a feeling as had already taken too strong hold upon her. She allowed herself most inconsistently and foolishly,—we might have said, criminally!—to institute a comparison between *old* Dr. Leechum, as she now in her own mind called her husband, and the young, gay, and courteous Lord Dashwood: the result was, as might have been confidently expected, both in reference to her peace and prudence—it destroyed the one and undermined the other. As we have stated, however, she shrunk from Dashwood's request to meet him alone;—he therefore proposed, that if Lady Bolio would accompany her, he would engage that Dr. Titheum should be his companion on the occasion. To this Mrs. Leechum saw no objection; and, accordingly, promised, upon condition that Lady Bolio did not object, it should be so; but that on no account would she meet him if Dr. Titheum were not in company. How far Lady Bolio consented to the arrangement has been seen; while the proposal, when made by Dashwood to Titheum, was caught at by his reverence with as much eagerness as himself, or many of his cloth, would have sprung at a mitre. The divine felt little doubt of success in bearing away the titled widow, with the assistance of such powerful auxiliaries as his Lordship and Mrs. Leechum; who was, as his Lordship assured him, entirely in his interest.

If diplomas had been issued from the groves of Venus with which to reward her subjects according to their skill in intrigue, Dashwood would unquestionably have received, long

before this period, that of M. A. He was as great an adept
in the art as a perfect gamester is in dealing cards to his own
advantage; or a political tactician in proving what no one
understands, and what he does not himself believe.

To render all that might take place perfectly natural, and
to lull any thing like suspicion to sleep, Dashwood had managed to concoct a sufficient reason for the absence of himself
and the doctor for an hour or two after eight o'clock; and,
having so arranged the affair, he waited with anxiety the
appointed time.

Sir Marmaduke, who had been informed that his Lordship
and the doctor would have occasion to leave the Hotel for a
short time in the evening, felt a secret rejoicing that it was to
be so, as he determined to "screw his courage to the sticking-
post," and press Miss Fidget to allow an early day to be
named for their nuptials.

The time had nearly come, when Mrs. Leechum, accompanied by Lady Bolio, each suitably attired, descended to the
drawing-room. Mrs. Leechum took one more approving,
lingering look at her person in the mirror which adorned the
chimney-piece, to see if any thing more could be done to
render herself as attractive as she *could* be; and then turning
to her Ladyship, she enquired,—"Are you quite ready, my
dear Lady Bolio?"

"Quite so, my dear," replied her Ladyship;—"We will,
if you please, set out immediately."

"May I enquire," observed Leechum, "where you ladies
intend to walk so late in the day?"

"We are going *out*," returned Mrs. Leechum, most
obligingly.

"I am aware of that, my love," said Leechum; "but
where, my dear?"

"Where now?" echoed his lady,—"Did the world ever
witness Dr. Leechum's fellow! Thus it is from day to day;
morning, noon, and night!"

"Well, my love," returned the doctor, "I was merely
going to hint, that—"

"To *hint!*—oh, how I *abhor* those hints!" said Mrs.
Leechum; "I shall be driven to desperation by them!"

"Shall you be long gone?" enquired her trembling lord.

"We shall be gone until we have performed our business,
of course," returned the lady. "But, bless me!" she added,
"I had forgotten myself;—if I stand answering all the

useless, and indeed impertinent questions which Dr. Leechum may feel disposed to press upon one, I shall not leave before midnight. Come, Lady Bolio," continued the amiable and placid fair one, " shall we make our exit ?" But her Lady-ship had already taken her leave; and, therefore, shutting the door with rather strong action, she hurried after and joined Lady Bolio in the hall; and then, after giving her companion her arm, they drew their veils closely over their faces, and walked towards the place of assignation.

How wonderful are the events which flow from trivial and apparently insignificant causes. The romance of history need not be sifted to prove our position;—indeed, a simple *title* given to each, would form no mean volume in point of bulk, without entering into detail. The every-day occur-rences of human life supply, to an attentive observer of things as they are, proofs more than sufficient to our purpose. So too it happened in the case of Lady Bolio and Dr. Titheum. Claudius's quarrel with his Tutor, Mr. Ferule, led to his elopement; *that,*—in connexion with his lady-mother's pla-tonic affection for the pedagogue, produced illness,—in order to the re-establishment of health she repaired to Bath, and at a masquerade meets with Dashwood and Sir Marmaduke;— this singular occurrence brought about another,—and then our assignation follows. The result of the whole may pos-sibly be, an engagement which will cause a revolution in family concerns, whose consequences will run on *ad in-finitum.*

But we are anticipating concerning important matters, for which it is possible we shall not receive so much as the thanks of the reader. It will doubtless be better to state, that, anxious as the ladies were to attend to their part of the appointment, the gentlemen were not the shadow of a shade behind them. In fact, before the time had come, Dashwood and the doctor had spent a full half-hour in sauntering round the spot; which, to their fevered imagination, seemed quad-rupled.

At length, two figures, closely veiled, made their appear-ance, and in the twinkling of an eye Dashwood exclaimed, " Egad they are here, doctor!—Now prepare your artillery; give no quarter, and the citadel must surrender."

" Are you certain," asked the doctor, " that yonder females are Lady Bolio and Mrs. Leechum."

" Am I certain, doctor ?" returned his Lordship,—" Ha!

ha! ha!—Why, bless you, I can scent game farther than
many others can see it!"

"Indeed!" ejaculated the doctor, not precisely catching
the meaning of his Lordship's trope,—"That is very extraordinary."

" ' 'Tis true, 'pon my honour,' as Sir Marmaduke would
say," returned Dashwood. "But to business, doctor; to
business: while I strive to lead Mrs. Leechum aside to give
you the opportunity; you understand—eh?—second my en-
deavours, and saunter to such a distance as you think will
answer your purpose; then press home the question,—' to be
or not to be.' It would not be quite agreeable, perhaps, to
remain within hearing;—ladies are, or pretend to be, delicate
on certain points."

"I am not in the 'commission of the peace,'" observed
the doctor, "if I do not follow your counsel."

"Enough!" said the crafty lord;—"Remember, no quarter—now for the attack—hem!" So saying, he advanced at
a double quick pace towards the ladies, leaving the doctor
considerably in the rear; and, with all the freedom and fondness of an acknowledged suitor, seized the hand of Mrs.
Leechum, and exclaimed,—"Madam, a thousand thanks for
this unmerited act of condescension! I am your debtor for
life! Your servant, Lady Bolio; most happy to see your
Ladyship. My good friend, Dr. Titheum, has been dying
with anxiety for the arrival of this hour, in order to pay his
respects to you."

"Lady Bolio," said the doctor, who at this moment joined
the party, "I am happy to perceive that your last night's
fatigue has not been too great for you."

"You are *very* kind, doctor," returned her Ladyship;
"but who would not make a little effort to accompany a
friend?"

"True, true," responded the doctor; "you are all kindness, Lady Bolio! indeed you are. Allow me to render you
some assistance," he continued, presenting his arm, which
with suitable acknowledgments Lady Bolio cheerfully accepted.

"Dearest Madam!" exclaimed Dashwood, as he placed
Mrs. Leechum's arm within his, and gently led her away,
"instruct me how to express my acknowledgments for this
favour."

"Oh, your Lordship places too much value upon trifles,"
returned Mrs. Leechum. "But did you not state that you

page 437.

wished to make a communication of importance to mé?"
she added with a bland smile.

"I did, loveliest of women!" returned Dashwood.

"Now, you really must desist from flattery, my Lord," said
Mrs. Leechum, whose ears drank in the sweet sounds with
pleasure inexpressible,—"you must, indeed; or I shall call
you a naughty man."

"Flattery!" exclaimed Dashwood;—"Hold me guiltless
of such a despicable spirit, I beseech you, sweetest of your
sex!"

"Well, well," returned Mrs. Leechum, "I'll see what I
can do. But this important communication," she continued;
"Woman-like," she added, smiling, "you perceive, my curiosity is excited."

Dashwood was an old practitioner, and feared by a too
sudden or too specific declaration, to mar what he had so
well begun; and, therefore, hesitated to state positively a
passion which he, as a man of honour, should have scorned
to cherish. "Can you be ignorant of it," he enquired,
"dearest Rosabella? for by that name you will, I hope, allow
me the pleasure of calling you."

"Why, you have done so," returned Mrs. Leechum;
"but if it will afford you any gratification, why, I see nothing in a name; and, therefore,—but I am, indeed, ignorant
of the communication; which,—bless me!" she continued,
as she looked round, "where is Lady Bolio? Are we then
alone?"

"Be not alarmed, dear Rosabella!" said Dashwood,
"while I am near you no danger can befall you. I would
with my life—"

"It is not danger I fear," returned Mrs. Leechum; "but
where can her Ladyship and the doctor have gone?"

"Why, you know, dear Rosabella," resumed his Lordship, "the doctor has a little business to arrange with Lady
Bolio."

"Has he so?" observed Mrs. Leechum;—"Oh then, I
suppose, *that* is the *important* communication! But, *really*,
we must seek them."

Dashwood would have urged her to proceed, but it would
not do; and, therefore, he turned back, and in a few minutes
the doctor and Lady Bolio were discovered, in a position
which left no doubt of the pleasure they experienced in each
other's society. To state *all* that the doctor had stated to

Lady Bolio, or to narrate *all* that Lady Bolio said in reply, even supposing that we possessed the power, would be unnecessary;—it is enough to state, that the doctor had so well attended to the tuition of Dashwood, and so fully improved the opportunity afforded him; and, to the infinite satisfaction of Lady Bolio, had so plainly declared his passion for her, that she, poor lady,—tired of the lonely estate of widowhood, and willing to render others happy to the extent of her power,—received the statements and listened to the declaration with courtesy; and, in the end, acknowledged she was not insensible to the doctor's attentions, or inflexible where compliance would make herself what she had long sighed to be—a happy wife.

As soon as Dashwood discovered the parties, he again attempted to draw Mrs. Leechum aside, but in vain; all he could do was to whisper soft sayings in her ear,—and, assuredly, with much more freedom than propriety sanctioned, pressed her hand.

After accompanying the ladies as near the Royal Crescent as, without exciting suspicion, they dared do, they bade them farewell.

> " With looks and actions, such as lovers give,
> Who vow that only in Love's arms they live;
> They breath'd their vows, and vowed those vows were true:
> Then vowed again, and sigh'd—'adieu! adieu!'"

There is an old-fashioned and well-known piece of advice which our metaphor-loving forefathers have supplied us with; which, if carried into all the affairs of human life, would be found highly beneficial;—it is, to " *make hay while the sun shines.*"   In such case, Shakspeare's beautiful declaration would not so frequently lie unproved, or prove, so often as it does, a mere dead letter,—when he states,

> "There is a tide in every man's affairs,
> Which, taken at the full, leads on to fortune."

Now, Sir Marmaduke chanced to think with the poet on this very important occasion; and, therefore, he determined to prove how far the high tide of his affairs would now lead on to fortune—a thing which he very much stood in need of. Moreover, he appeared to have a vivid perception of the importance of the advice above referred to, as well as an understanding of its import; and, therefore, he made up his mind to act upon it: hence, while Dashwood and the doctor were busily engaged with Mrs. Leechum and the Duchess, he availed himself of the sunny opportunity to press his point with Miss Fidget.

" 'Pon my honour," commenced the Knight, " your exquisite kindness, Miss Fidget, has rendered me one of the happiest of men ; it has, 'pon my honour."

" Oh, dear Sir Marmaduke !" sighed Miss Fidget, " I pray *don't* mention it,—the pleasure has, I assure you, been mutual."

" 'Pon my honour," continued the Knight, " you electrify me with delight by saying so !—you do, 'pon my honour. May I be allowed to say, my dear Miss Fidget, that—I—I— 'pon my honour."

" Oh, certainly, Sir Marmaduke," replied the lady, " I shall be happy to attend to any thing you may be disposed to say."

" 'Pon my honour," thought Sir Marmaduke, " that is what Othello would have called a *hint*, and I will speak upon it."—" Well, then, dear Madam," he continued, " when, allow me to enquire, may I calculate upon the entrancing felicity of leading you to the—altar ?"

" Oh, Sir Marmaduke !" returned the lady, evincing at the same time very strong symptoms of a disposition to " go off" again ; but, whether from an exuberance of delight at hearing that a probability existed of things being soon brought to a close ; or whether, from an excess of maiden coyness, the reader is left to form his own opinion—so it was. The Knight perceived the effect his address had produced, and observed,—" 'Pon my honour, Miss Fidget, are you unwell, or has my abruptness affected you so greatly ?"

" Oh, you are very sympathizing, Sir Marmaduke," returned the lady : " but *such* a question, you must be aware, could not fail to produce an effect upon a *young* and *inexperienced* female. You have so embarrassed me that I really do not know what reply to make to your *very* serious question. ' Now do, pray, lie still Carlo,' " continued Miss Fidget, " I really cannot attend to you just now."

Sir Marmaduke, in the trepidation of his feelings, did not observe the name of the animal pronounced to whom Miss Fidget was addressing herself ; but, catching only the latter part of her observation, he imagined it to be addressed to himself ; and quaking for the success of his suit and the loss of a splendid fortune, should that suit fail, he felt that a desperate effort must be made to carry this point; and, therefore, throwing himself into such a posture as proud beauty delights to behold the "lords of creation" in,—at their feet,—he exclaimed with a vehemence which the most absorbing passion for her person could scarcely have exceeded,—"'Pon my honour, Miss Fidget, you will annihilate me by your words! Loveliest of women, revoke that expression! Oh, say not that you cannot attend to me now! but raise me from despair by directing me to rise from your feet with the cheering assurance that you will listen to my suit, and render my agonized but devoted and adoring heart happy!"

"Oh, Sir Marmaduke!" sighed out the compassionate Miss Fidget, "you overwhelm me with confusion,—such a degree of ardent passion I never supposed I could inspire! Rise, Sir Marmaduke,—rise;—I cannot endure the sight of one so worthy as yourself being placed in such a situation; but, I assure you, you have entirely mistaken me."

"Mistaken you!" exclaimed Sir Marmaduke, still kneeling, increasingly alarmed. "Mistaken you,—did you say? Have I then cherished the fond hope until now of being made the happiest of men, only to be rendered the most miserable?—'Pon my honour, I shall become a maniac!"

"Rise, Sir Marmaduke, and hear me," rejoined the lady.

"Never!" shouted the Knight; "Never will I quit this attitude until—"

"Well, I will consent to what you propose," interrupted Miss Fidget, "only do get up. I say again, you have mistaken me; it was not to you I said I could not attend, but to my dear little Carlo."

"'Pon my honour," exclaimed Sir Marmaduke, jumping upon his feet, and taking one of the passive hands of Miss Fidget, upon which he imprinted half a score of kisses, "you have given me new life,—ha! ha! ha! It was Carlo to whom you spoke—was it? Very singular, 'pon my honour! Will you allow me to name this day week for the—"

"Oh, do spare me!" interrupted the sensitive *young* lady. "Do, Sir Marmaduke, consider my feelings—my inexperience!"

"'Pon my honour!" observed the Knight, in an impassioned tone; while his eyes looked with a pleasing softness which Miss Fidget could not resist. "Shall I wait until tomorrow for your reply; or will you appoint a longer period?"

"Oh, Sir Marmaduke," said the lady, "you are aware how much power you possess over our poor weak sex ;—'wait until to-morrow,' said you? why, really now—" 'Do be quiet a short time, Carlo, or I shall scold you,—indeed I shall. Well, then,' she continued episodically, as Carlo applied his tongue to her lip ;—' there now, let that do for the present.' "Until to-morrow, Sir Marmaduke?" she added with quickness,—"Why no ; excuse my blushes,—let it be as you have said—this day week—I consent to—"

"A thousand thanks!" exclaimed Sir Marmaduke with rapture, before whose vision a princely fortune appeared already to float. "This day week, then, I shall be made the happiest of mortals! I shall, 'pon my honour." So saying, he presumed to salute the *young* lady in a similar way that Carlo had before done ; but, whether the first or second animal's salute was most valued, is difficult to determine.

So far Sir Marmaduke had gained his point ; and, notwithstanding Miss Fidget's maiden coyness, it was fully evident her gratification was not less than the Knight's, at the nearness of the period when she should change both her name and station. Her countenance was illuminated with such a measure of animating delight, as might have led a believer in the marvellous to suppose that some restoring process had passed upon her, by which youth had been recommunicated to her system.

The celebrated Rochefoucault asserts, that "many men would never have been in love, if they had never heard of love." Now, however correct and shrewd this remark may be in reference to the masculine, it is not less so in reference to the feminine gender : perhaps in ninety-nine cases out of a hundred it would be found, upon close investigation, that the perusal of some namby-pamhy sentimental love-story at a boarding-school, or the reading of some romance or novel, instead of handling the needle, or finding engagement in some domestic matters,—has excited the imagination, and roused the passions, until every dustman almost has appeared an Adonis, and each member of the coarse blue "Force," a knight in search of adventure.

But, in the above quoted learned writer's observation, we opine, a positive admission is made that such a thing or passion as love does exist, and may really and truly be experienced. Now, rare as the existence of the genuine all-absorbing passion may be ; or if, indeed, in no former instance it had ever before been felt, it did most certainly at the present time exercise a most powerful—not to say tyrannical—sway over the spirits of Georgiana; the heart's core of whose being appeared filled with the delectable poison.

From being one of the most cheerful, she sunk into one of the most sad of her species; and, while prospects fair and bright cheered the onward path of the doctor and Sir Marmaduke, as well as of their cheerfully-consenting lady-loves, she mourned over her own wretchedness; which, as she reflected upon, seemed to increase. "*Why* had Claudius left, and whither had he fled?" were to her natural questions; but for which she could find no reasonable or satisfactory reply. She dared not make enquiry of the doctor for the absentee, and none of the servants belonging to the Hotel knew any thing of him.

At one moment the distracting thought rushed through her brain, that Claudius understood not the passion which consumed her being, or that he felt it not for her; while, at the next, the pleasing assurance appeared to possess her, that the affection of her soul was reciprocated by our hero.

"But what could he mean," she thought to herself, "by saying he was not what he seemed to be, and that I should know all hereafter? Oh, what would I not give to have these mysteries removed,—to see him again; or even to know he was well, and had not forgotten me!"

These reflections had scarcely come to a close, as she sat alone in her room, when a gentle tapping at the door announced a visitor. "Come in," said Georgiana, and the door slowly opened, and a singular-looking old person, clad in the costume of a woman, but "bearded like a pard," appeared, bearing in her hand a somewhat bulky bundle.

"Pray, lady," said the visitant, dropping a curtsy, "if I may make so bold, can you inform me where I may meet with the young lady I want?"

"Unless I am furnished with her name or description," replied Georgiana, smiling, "I fear I shall not be able to direct you. From whom do you come, and what business, may I ask?"

"Aye,—true, true," replied the woman, without attending to the questions, "that had escaped me; and so for the matter of that has the name too, I fancy;—let me think a moment,—aye, sure enough," she continued, after a few moments' pause, "it is as I thought—gone—quite gone—I fear I am getting old. Ah me!—there was a time when I

could ha' remembered the names of all the kings and queens of England from,—ah! that is gone too; but—"

" Well, my good woman," rejoined Georgiana, " if it will not be betraying any trust imposed upon you, acquaint me with the name of the person from whom you have come; as I suppose some person has sent you; and I may then, perhaps, be able to give you the information you seek."

" Why, there it is again," returned the old woman; " I don't know who it is that has sent me. However, he is as nice a young gentleman, as one may say, as this good city of Bath contains."

" A young gentleman," observed Georgiana; " oh, then I fear I shall not be able to serve you. I do not know any one here to whom a young gentleman would send;—but what, may I ask, is the nature of your business?"

" Oh, as to that," returned the female, " I haven't forgotten it, lady;—oh no, bless you! if I had been entrusted with untold gold, it would have been safe, I warrant you,—nobody ever yet knew old Jannet to wrong a person of a farthing."

" I am not calling your honesty in question," returned Georgiana, who bore with the old woman's garrulity as an infirmity to which she was aware her sex and old age were equally subject. " My only object is to attain a clue, if possible, to the person you want, in order to direct you."

" Kind lady," said Jannet, " you put me, for all the world, in mind of a sweet gentlewoman I used to serve when I was young,—she was so good-tempered and so obliging, and—"

" Well, now," said Georgiana, smiling, " if you will be so obliging as to tell me what the nature of your business is, so far as will be proper for you to do, I will then serve you if I can."

" My business is very soon done, kind lady," replied the old woman;—" I have only to deliver this parcel and this letter to the person I want, and then go home again,—that's all, lady."

" Will you allow me to look at the outside of the letter?" asked Georgiana, " it is, most likely, directed."

" Aye, that it is, sure enough," said Jannet, without presenting the billet; " but I dare not *show* it even to any but the lady it is for."

" Indeed!" said Georgiana, and a sudden thought impressed her that it was possible, barely possible, it might come from Claudius;—it was, however, but a thought, and one of the most transient kind: still she felt,—as females always do when a secret is in the way,—more than ever anxious to know who the sought for person could be.

"Now I think on it," said Jannet, "may be the parcel will tell you, for I was told any body might look at it."

"If so," returned Georgiana, "let me see the direction on it."

"Yes, lady; here it is," said the old woman, as she presented it.

"Bless me!" said Georgiana, as she read the name,— "from whom does the parcel come?"

"I am sure, lady," returned Jannet, with as much ease as if she had received a score years' tuition in the trade of intrigue from an experienced Spanish Duenna —"I am sure, lady, you'll excuse me for not being able to tell; but a nicer young gentleman I never set my eyes on. However, do you know the person for whom it is directed?"

"It is for my papa," replied Georgiana.

"For your papa, lady!" said Jannet,—"Pray, what may his name be?"

"Dr. Titheum," answered Georgiana.

"As sure as my name be Jannet, that is the very name!" said the old woman in ecstacy; "I knowed I should remember it again when I heard it."

"May I ask," said Georgiana, "if the note is for Dr. Titheum?"

"Oh, bless you! no, lady," said Jannet; "for quite a different sort of a person," and she looked round very cautiously, as if to satisfy herself that no person was within hearing. "I suppose I may tell you,—it is for the doctor's daughter; and, as you are that lady, why there it is." And so saying, she placed the parcel on the table, and the letter in Georgiana's hand; and then, dropping another curtsy, before Georgiana could recover from her surprise, left the room and quitted the Hotel.

"From whom can this come?" thought Georgiana, "and so much secrecy about it to;—and then this parcel for my papa, from a young gentleman, she said; I wish I had not taken it. However, as I have done so, why I may as well learn, if I can, from whom it comes." So saying, she broke the seal; and then, while her hand so trembled as to render it scarcely possible for her to read a line, she cast her eyes to the bottom of it, and saw—"CLAUDIUS."

In the first burst of her feelings she pressed the paper to her lips with fervour; and then, doubting the correctness of her vision, she again examined the magic letter; on which subject, having rendered assurance doubly sure, she deposited the dear epistle in her bosom, and flew to her chamber to peruse its contents. Turning the key in the lock to prevent all intrusion, she drew forth the *billet-doux* from its palpitating and sacred depository, and read as follows:—

" Inexpressibly Dear Georgiana,

" Language is not sufficiently expressive to tell all I feel, or to declare with what strength of passion I love you! Since my departure from the Hotel,—the cause of which I presume, you are fully acquainted with,—I have been beyond measure wretched. The time, however, I fondly hope, will be comparatively short when the secrecy which now from necessity rests upon my conduct, will be removed, and I shall be able to express my passion for you without fear or disguise.

" I have thrown off the garb of a servant, and assumed a plain dress. The livery, which belongs to your father, I have returned. Where I am at present you must pardon me for not stating, and believe that wherever I am, and however situated, I shall remain unchanged,

" Your's devotedly,

" CLAUDIUS."

" Dear Claudius!" broke unconsciously from Georgiana's lips, as she finished this peculiarly welcome effusion. " Yes, I will endeavour to be happy now; but where can he be,—how is he situated? How foolish I was to allow the old woman to leave without enquiring further; but if I had done so, it is highly probable she would have given me no information; and, as Claudius appears to wish to remain in secret a while, I should do him wrong by endeavouring to penetrate a mystery he wishes should for a time continue."

Once more she pressed the dear scrawl to her lips, and impressed a host of warm kisses on it; and then opening a private drawer in her escritoir, deposited it among rich scents and precious relics.

CHAPTER XXXIV.

———

" Speak you of joys, or talk of pleasure,
   Which sordid souls, to avarice sold,
Experience 'midst their hoarded treasure,
   While gazing on their bags of gold?

Compar'd with her's,—who fondly dreaming
   Of bliss, as hastes her wedding-day,—
Their's is distress—a bliss but seeming ;
   While her's is rapture,—ecstacy !"

LANGHORNE.

"WHY, what in the name of wonder has taken place within this last four-and-twenty hours ?" observed the Duchess, as the party surrounded the breakfast-table, on the following morning. "Something, I am positive, has occurred, which more than ordinarily interests Miss Fidget."

"That interests me !" returned that lady,—*really* doing that for once which she had frequently, on former occasions, attempted to do, but failed to accomplish,—deeply blushing ;—"What can your Grace imagine has taken place ?"

"Why, the question is a fair one," returned the Duchess, "and challenges a fair reply. I'll double the bet with Sir Marmaduke, if he'll take the odds, which I made with Dr. Titheum, touching a certain important matter, that he has popped the question—to—"

"'Pon my honour," exclaimed the Knight, " your Grace challenges like a hero,—you do, 'pon my honour."

"But does Sir Marmaduke, like a hero, boldly accept the challenge ?" rejoined the Duchess.

"Now really, my dear Duchess !" exclaimed Miss Fidget, —"What is it you mean ?"

"A straight-forward question again," returned the Duchess, " and it shall have a kindred answer,—I mean—"

"Now, 'pon my honour," interrupted Sir Marmaduke. "your Grace must excuse,—that is—" "My dear Miss Fidget, you are spilling your tea."

"Now, I appeal to Lord Dashwood, and to you, Dr. Titheum, without excepting you, my dear Georgiana, if I have done more; nay, even so much,—than echo to certain questions by certain persons proposed."

"Ha! ha! ha!" burst from both the gentlemen to whom the appeal had been made, at the broad humour displayed by the Duchess, and the evident confusion which suffused with blushes the faces of Sir Marmaduke and Miss Fidget.

"What say you?" continued the Duchess, addressing the same party;—"Guilty, or not guilty?"

"Guilty," broke from each of the gentlemen's lips; while Georgiana sighed 'deep, but not loud,' and felt she too was guilty—of loving Claudius to distraction.

"'Pon my honour!" said Sir Marmaduke, recovering himself in a measure, and in the same degree joining in the Duchess's pleasantry,—"I suppose, Miss Fidget, that as our case has been thus summarily dealt with, it will be as well, in order that the ends of justice may be answered, that we make a free, true, and full confession,—I do, 'pon my honour."

"What have we to confess, Sir Marmaduke?" enquired Miss Fidget.—"I really am not aware that we are guilty of any—"

"Certainly not," observed Dashwood, in a tone of Attic jocularity;—"Certainly not, my dear friend; we acquit Miss Fidget of all participation in the guilt of a certain action, which on strong presumptive evidence has been proved to have taken place between Sir Marmaduke Varney and the said Miss Fidget; and convict her merely of listening attentively to certain statements made by the said Sir Marmaduke Varney, and at the time feeling high gratification at the propositions of which Sir Marmaduke has not so much as attempted a proof of being innocent."

"'Pon my honour!" exclaimed Sir Marmaduke, laughing heartily;—"your Lordship's gallantry in so completely exculpating the lady, is only equalled by your unparalleled ingenuity. I do confess that I have been bold enough to implore Miss Fidget to make me happy—"

"And, of course," interrupted the Duchess, "Miss Fidget, in the overflowing goodness of her heart, has consented on certain understood conditions, not necessary now to be named,—to do so."

"'Pon my honour," returned the Knight, "your Grace is always infallibly correct in your judgment: like an angel in another sphere, she has condescended to lend a propitious ear to my petition, and has consented to take me under her special patronage."

"In a very short time, I presume and *hope ?*" observed Dashwood.

"Just so, 'pon my honour," returned Sir Marmaduke.

"Aye, to be sure," returned the Duchess, chuckling with delight. "Now where, I should like to know, was the necessity for all this humming and haing ;—why not at once say : 'Friends all, wish us joy ; or, joy with us in the joy we feel ;—the days of our miserable single loneliness are about to close : at the end of one week we summon each and every one of you to meet us at our bridal banquet.'—Ha ! ha ! ha ! Why, bless you," continued her sportive Grace, "I knew the meaning of your bright and smiling eyes the moment I saw them ; and unless my calculations are as erroneous as the speculations of a weather almanack-maker, the walk of his Lordship and the doctor, last evening, was far from an unpleasant one."

"Whew!" thought the doctor, wincing,—"What's coming now ?"

"The walks of Bath," said Dashwood, "can scarcely fail to afford pleasure."

"No more can *some* of the ladies in Bath," returned the Duchess ; and then humming a few lines from an old ballad, she continued,—

> "A little bird whispered a tale in mine ear,
> Listen to me, listen to me ;—
> Who though silent as death,—unseen was near-
> Love's ecstacies to hear and see.
> The moon above was bright ;
> Each lover's heart was light,
> And no rough blast howl'd rudely by.
> Their eyes a language spoke
> Though neither silence broke,
> Which told they lov'd right tenderly."

"'Pon my honour, doc*tar,*" observed Sir Marmaduke, "there appear to be more secrets than one in the world ; perhaps your Lordship can explain."

"Oh certainly, certainly," returned Dashwood, who was never taken aback in affairs of this nature ; "nothing more easy. Her Grace begins to tremble for her wager,—nothing more—"

"And not without good cause either," remarked the Duchess, looking most significantly at the doctor.

"I shall be happy to be empowered to call upon your Grace for the wine at the time Sir Marmaduke has referred to," observed the doctor; " but I fear the forfeit will be mine to pay. However," he added, " I'll do my best, and until I am fully beaten, will not fully despair."

" 'Pon my honour, doc*tar*," observed Sir Marmaduke, " you have illuminated me marvellously,—you have, 'pon my honour;—but how her Grace," continued the Knight, " has obtained certain information,—as it appears beyond the shadow of a doubt she has,—completely confounds me,—it does, 'pon my honour."

" Ha! ha! ha!" roared the Duchess, as heartily as any lady that ever cried, " Fish O!" from Billingsgate. " Why, bless you, Sir Marmaduke, did you not know that I keep up an uninterrupted intercourse with the court of the patron and queen of sighing swains and melting maidens? You surely did not imagine that I foreswore all right and privilege to such society when I *condescended*,—as you would very properly say,—to take the falcon Knight under my patronage;—no, no, I assure you; my interest has thereby increased rather than diminished. But a truce to jesting," continued her Grace; " I know as much about the business as is necessary; and that my information is correct, you attempt not to deny,—how I obtained my knowledge,

' It little boots, my friends, to know ;
But the great teacher, *Time*, may show.' "

" That your Grace's information is very extensive," observed Georgiana, who until now had remained a silent listener, " every one must allow; still there are secrets which even your communicative informants have not revealed to you."

" Of that, my dear," returned the Duchess, " there can be no question, so long as I remain ignorant of the cause that has thrown sadness into a spirit which, until recently, might have been received as a faithful counterpart of Momus himself."

Georgiana bit her lips, and more than half wished she had perforated her tongue ere she had spoken so unadvisedly as she had done;—her feelings for the moment triumphed over her judgment;—a case, by the bye, of no very singular or uncommon occurrence among young ladies of a certain age and under certain peculiar circumstances; but which, nevertheless, seldom produces other consequences than those of sorrow and regret.

It is a known fact, that Georgiana had been influenced by a desire to learn if the Duchess, in the extensiveness and variety of her knowledge on points connected with courtship and matrimony, possessed any information relative to Claudius, touching his departure from the Hotel, and present place of residence. No sooner, however, had the words,—which she had intended as a *feeler*,—escaped her lips, than she felt she had done wrong in permitting them to do so: she consoled herself, however, with the assurance that the Duchess was not in possession of her secret.

Carlo, the immortal Carlo, happily relieved Miss Titheum from a slight embarrassment, into which her own foolish observation, and the Duchess's reply, had thrown her; for at this very instant the attention of all present was suddenly caught away from every thing else than master Carlo's violation of the rules of good breeding.

We intend not to insinuate that there is any thing extraordinary in a puppy's behaving rudely, because such things are of every day occurrence,—puppies, in the *form* of gentlemen even, swarm around us, who, in instances of the most flagrant order, prove themselves but " brutes o' their breed." Every day's Police report presents fresh instances of ill-mannered puppyism; while, either because they are puppies, or because they are *genteel* puppies, the heavy pains and penalties with which puppies of under character would be visited, are made to fall with lighter influence upon them;—the dispensers of the law treat their semi-rabid compeers with all befitting lenity; but, as Byron once said, in reference to Coleridge's "Lines to a Young Ass,"

" 'A fellow-feeling makes us wondrous kind."

But, as we have stated, Miss Fidget's dear Carlo, without either merit or blame on his part, did, by a freak of his fancy, relieve Georgiana from distressing embarrassment, by suddenly leaping from the soft warm lap of his devoted mistress upon the breakfast-table; by which action he not only deranged the tea and coffee paraphernalia, but *demolished* several pieces of valuable china.

"Carlo, my dear Carlo!" shouted Miss Fidget,—"What are you doing?"

" What has he not *done?*" reiterated Dashwood.

" Yelp! yelp! yelp!" returned the brute, as the hot water annoyed his tender face; and then, without waiting for a pressing invitation from Miss Fidget to return, he bounded back to his snug reposing place, as if nothing had occurred, save and except that his shaggy extremities were dripping wet; but which slight inconvenience was soon arranged by the application of his mistress's cambric to his saturated parts.

"My poor dear Carlo!" exclaimed Miss Fidget, pressing him at the same time to her heaving bosom;—"How uncomfortable you have made yourself. It will be next to a miracle, Sir Marmaduke," she added, turning to that gentleman, "if he does not take a dreadful cold from this accident."

"'Pon my honour," returned the Knight, "he has given me a warming; I'm sure I trembled in every joint of me, lest my feet should experience a fresh scalding,—I did, 'pon my honour."

"I think," whispered Dashwood to Sir Marmaduke, "the best thing we can do for the nasty brute, will be to make him into a pie for your bride elect;—what think you to have him served up as a treat of novel and extraordinary character on your wedding-day—eh? I'll do the thing."

"Hush!" returned the Knight; "if a whisper of your murderous design was to reach Miss Fidget's ear, I should be disappointed in my sanguine expectation,—I should, 'pon my honour."

"Why, much as the lady wishes to become a bride," returned Dashwood, "I think with you, Sir Marmaduke, she would sacrifice such a superior lord, even as yourself will make, to her devoted attachment for Carlo, and give up a husband for a poodle."

"'Pon my honour," whispered the Knight, "the conclusion to which you so readily come is a singular, but, I believe, no less correct one;—but no matter, let me secure the main chance, and then boil, or bake, or roast, or stew, Carlo as you will, and I'll not thwart the volatile whim of your Lordship."

"By the bye," observed the Duchess, "what has become of our smart little Claudius?"

> "What's in a name?—That which we call a rose,
> By any other name would smell as sweet."

So said Miss Juliet, of Veronean celebrity;—and, certainly, so far as a rose or any other flower is concerned, she said true,—a change of name would not affect the scent:

> "The fragrant violet still would perfume shed,
> Though deadly nightshade were the name it bore."

But in a *name* there *is* an importance,—a magic,—an influence of mighty character. Miss Georgiana felt *all* this at the mention of Claudius's name by the Duchess—her colour went and came with rapid. alternation ; while a nervous tremour spread over her whole frame to such an extent, as, in all probability, no other name would or could have occasioned.

The doctor was not quite ready with a reply to the Duchess's question ; and, therefore, her Grace continued,— " I have taken a fancy to Claudius, doctor, and feel inclined to make an overture for his services, supposing you would not object to part with him, and he felt no reluctance to change situations."

" I am not able to reply to your Grace's proposition," stammered the doctor ; " you had better, perhaps, see the youth, and make your own proposals to him. I can assure you, *I* shall feel most happy to meet, so far as I can, your Grace's wishes."

Whether the room had suddenly become surcharged with heat, or whether from any other unexplained cause, is not necessary for the chronicler of these events to determine ;— certain it is, however, that Georgiana experienced a difficulty in breathing to a very painful extent, as the conversation thus abruptly terminated.   Her hopes, which had been sanguine, of hearing some further particulars concerning Claudius, were suddenly destroyed. The particular cause of his leaving the Hotel, and whether his departure had been voluntary or otherwise—to what extent her papa was concerned in it— where he was now residing, and if a chance existed of soon seeing him,—were points upon which she expected to have received satisfactory information ; but alas ! the doctor's quaintness put a termination to further converse on the matter, and threw her an immense distance back into the regions of perplexity, and on the precincts of despair.

The Duchess, as has been seen, had caused most of the party to run the gauntlet of her raillery and wit to such an extent, that the eggs stood untouched and the ham uneaten ; while sundry other dainty nic-nacs, calculated and intended to coax their delicate appetites, had been changed half a dozen times, and still they remained cold and spoiled, in consequence of the attention of the company being so completely pre-engaged by her facetious Grace.

Once more the Duchess was on the point of hurling her

satirical shaft at the doctor, when he was mercifully delivered
from the intended sore infliction by the entrance of a servant,
who stated that a gentleman below requested an immediate
interview with his reverence, on business of great importance.

. "So!" said the doctor ;—"What kind of a person is this
gentleman—eh ?"

". A real gentleman, Sir," replied the servant, as he turned
over a half-crown in his trowsers pocket, which he had received to make the announcement.

"Indeed !" said the doctor, with doubtful cadence ;' whose
mind involuntarily turned to a *real* gentleman, whom he had
had any thing but the pleasure of meeting before at Havant
and Corsham. Confident, however, that he should never
again become the " dupe," as he termed it, of rogues and
vagabonds, he directed the servant to show the gentleman
into his sitting-room; to which,—after making a suitable
apology for leaving the breakfast-table,—he immediately
walked.

There certainly must be something not common to other
seats, in a great arm-chair ; as also, in a dignified and imposing attitude assumed ; or unquestionably such things,—
like large wigs with many tails,—would not be so much delighted in as they without question are, by certain dignitaries
in the clerical and legal professions.

Dr. Titheum, beyond all question, delighted in a roomy
imposing-looking chair, in which he could with perfect ease
disport his capacious body : hence one had been, by special
desire, placed in his sitting-room.

Scarcely had the doctor thrown himself, on the present
occasion, into the said imposing-looking seat, and properly
adjusted his garments, and his limbs, and his wig, before the
door of the apartment opened, and the servant ushered in
the already referred-to gentleman.

In person, the stranger was of rather small dimensions ;
but there was such a perfect symmetry in all his parts that the
doctor at once felt prepossessed in his favour. His eyes were
sharp and penetrating, yet, as restless as a man's might be
supposed to be who expected, every moment to be,—what by
most persons will be understood,—" tapped upon the shoulder." His dress was in the very height of the fashion; albeit,
a close inspector of that respectable fraternity that occupy
both sides of a long street in the vicinity of Tower Hill,—
'yclept " Rag Fair,"—would at once have declared they were

not quite as "good as new,"—but then, his address was case itself. Every muscle of his countenance, as well as every member of his body, appeared to be influenced according to the expressions he was uttering. He was neither stiff nor formal,—as though he had been a mere cast-iron sort of man, —on the one hand ; neither did he, on the other, display the attitudes, or make the grimaces of one upon whom a powerful galvanic shock was operating; but, as has been intimated, he was "free and easy," and "evidently at home" with his company.

"I have the honour," said the stranger, drawing his right foot from the ancle of forty-five, and bending his body with graceful gravity.—"I have the honour of addressing the Rev. Dr. Titheum, if I am not greatly mistaken."

"That is my name, Sir," returned the doctor, evidently pleased with the respectful and graceful manner of the visitor.

"And," continued the stranger, with another profound inclination of his body, "a magistrate for the county of Hants, if I am not greatly mistaken."

"I have the honour to be in the 'commission of the peace,' Sir, and very much at your service," said the doctor, elevating at the same time his head, and extending his elbows; while a " hem" of dignified accent accompanied the action.

"I am an entire stranger to your worship," observed the gentleman, "if I am not greatly mistaken."

"I have not the pleasure of recollecting you, Sir," returned the doctor,—"May I enquire—"

"True, true; very true, Sir,—if I am not very greatly mistaken," interrupted the visitor. "However, Sir, your name, character, and official celebrity, are known to myself. I have long been an admirer of your learning, piety, and benevolence."

"Hem !" said the doctor, to whom the essence of flattery was as pleasant to his brain as an Olympus-formed pile of Arabian spices would have been to his olfactory organs.

"It is so, Sir, I solemnly protest, if I am not greatly mistaken," rejoined the stranger.

"I beg your pardon, Sir," said the doctor, starting from his chair,—"Pray be seated, Sir."

The stranger, who until now had stood bowing before his worship, with as much readiness as if he had for half a century been a close student of Chesterfield's sage admonitions, immediately did as the doctor requested ; which having done, he observed,—"You are, Sir, if I am not greatly mistaken, an enlightened and liberal patron of the arts—and—"

"You are correct, Sir," returned the doctor hastily; " I feel proud to give, when I can, a helping hand to genius ; though the truth is, unfortunately, we have but little of true genius in the present day ; although I am happy at the rapid advancement which our country is making in every thing great, good, and useful."

"Indeed !" thought the stranger ; not being able exactly to reconcile the different parts of the doctor's observations. However, he *said* nothing, and the doctor proceeded.

"May I have the honour of being made acquainted with the name of the gentleman whose knowledge of myself is so extensive ?" "and whose flattery," he might have added, " is so highly agreeable."

"Oh ! my dear Sir, I beg ten thousand pardons," returned the visitor, "for my remissness in not presenting my card before ; but you will excuse it, if I am not greatly mistaken."

"Don't mention it, Sir," replied the doctor, as he received the presented card, upon which was engraved, " R. W. B. S. RACKBRAIN, F. R. S., L.L. D., &c.

"That will be satisfactory," observed Mr. Rackbrain, as the doctor surveyed the card attentively, "if I am not greatly mistaken."

"Oh, perfectly so, Sir,—perfectly so," returned the doctor.

"Now, Sir," observed Mr. Rackbrain, "as to the object of my visit ;—you will allow me to state it, if I am not greatly mistaken."

"I shall consider myself favoured, Sir, by the communication," answered the doctor.

"Well then, *Doctor* Titheum," observed the Fellow of the "Royal Society, &c. &c.," with great gravity, and laying particular emphasis on his reverence's honorary title, " I flatter myself I have done perfectly right in what I have done,—indeed, I am confident of it, if I am not greatly mistaken."

"I cannot question it," responded the doctor.

"I have, Dr. Titheum," continued Mr. Rackbrain, "passed by a host of noble and illustrious personages to wait upon yourself."

"I feel honoured, Sir," said the doctor.

"I could lay before you, Dr. Titheum," added Mr. Rackbrain, taking, as he spoke, a large bundle of letters from his pocket, which were confined by a piece of red tape.—" I could lay before you, Dr. Titheum, a host of letters from men who lay claim to titles and honours which, if I am not greatly mistaken, their thick heads never won.   Men, Sir," continued the academician, warming as he proceeded, "who, through the interest of interested friends and a few pounds, have procured D. D.'s, and M. A.'s, and F. R. S.'s, but who never knew how to write a line of good English, or possessed the ability to construe a single passage in Tacitus, Ovid, or Livy; and are as ignorant of the cosmogony or creation of the world, as a Dutch boor, or a Russian serf.   But, Sir," added Rackbrain, "if I am not greatly mistaken, I am straying from the point—"

" I beg you will make no apology, Sir," observed the doctor; " your correct view, and clear statement of things, charm me."

" Well, Sir, as I was saying," resumed Mr. Rackbrain, " these men have requested, petitioned I might say, to have the honour of that which I am certain Dr. Titheum alone merits."

" Sir!" exclaimed the doctor, elevated beyond all bounds at the compliment of the " Fellow of the Royal Society;" as well as delighted with the profundity of his learning, without understanding the fecundity of his wit—" you over-rate my poor abilities."

" Excuse me, Sir," returned Mr. Rackbrain, "I greatly under-rate them, if I am not greatly mistaken."

" And pray, Sir," enquired the doctor, " what may be the nature of the honour you have so handsomely reserved for me ?"

" It is no honour at all, Sir," replied Mr. Rackbrain, " if I am not greatly mistaken;—it is merely what your distinguished abilities claim, and what will receive an honour from, rather than confer honour upon you."

" Indeed !" said Dr. Titheum, in an ecstacy.

" I have, it is well known, Sir, in the higher circles," continued Mr. Rackbrain, " invented a writing fluid of unheard-of and invaluable properties ; and which to Divines, Magistrates, and Schoolmasters, will be an inestimable treasure. Indeed, Sir, without vanity I may say, its advantages will be felt by the whole world.   I am about to establish a company in shares of twenty pounds each, to be denominated, ' The Newly Invented and Incomparable Writing Fluid Joint Stock Company,' of which, Sir, I wish you to become the patron."

"Sir," replied Titheum, "I fear you are pressing an honour upon me I do not deserve."

"My dear doctor," returned the inventor of the incomparable writing fluid, "allow me to say, you *alone* are worthy to fill the office. Here," he continued, as he unrolled a long paper, "is a list of distinguished personages, at the head of which I shall have the gratification of placing your name, if I am not greatly mistaken."

Such a splendid galaxy of dignity and talent was not frequently seen as that upon which the doctor now gazed, to stand at the head of which afforded more pleasure to the mind of him in the "commission of the peace,' than to have been placed at the head of one thousand times the number on a battle-field; although as celebrated as any which either ancient or modern history records.

"I shall be proud to stand associated with such a list of worthies," said the doctor. "Perhaps you will oblige me with a brief description of the peculiar properties of your incomparable writing fluid?"

"Undoubtedly," returned Mr. Rackbrain; "I shall feel pleasure in so doing. From its peculiar properties and,—if I am not greatly mistaken,—I might say, magic character, it will save an incalculable measure of trouble and time. Our divines, whose time,—*as you well know, doctor,*—is so much engaged by a variety of innocent and necessary engagements, —such as a hunt now and then, and a race occasionally; or upon whose shoulders the weighty concerns of magisterial matters are made to press, so heavily as to leave neither time nor inclination to compose sermons,—such, I say, will only have to dip a common pen into my fluid, and then hold the nib of the said pen to paper, and discourses of the most orthodox character, in language of the most beautiful construction, will flow forth without the labour of thought or the possession of knowledge."

"Wonderful!" exclaimed the doctor.

"You will say so, Sir," responded the inventor, "when you have proved it, if I am not greatly mistaken."

"Undoubtedly I shall," said the divine.

"The numerous errors in theology, which are now so flagrant," resumed Rackbrain, "and the barbarous style of composition which is now so common among the professors of our colleges, and the candidates for a mitre, will by my fluid be completely removed; while magistrates who are as ignorant of the jurisprudence of our country as Laplanders, or Chinese mandarins,—will merely have to adopt the process I have already named, and verdicts, plain, prompt, and correct, will be seen on the paper."

" Wonderful!" again shouted the doctor.

" It is true, on my honour," returned Mr. Rackbrain. " You will perceive at once, doctor, how many false imprisonments, which ignorance and misconception have occasioned, will be prevented by my incomparable writing fluid "

" I perceive it quite clearly," said the doctor.

" Bless me !" exclaimed Mr. Rackbrain, as he looked at his gold repeater;—" My time is gone; I have to call next upon the Right Hon. Lord Dondoodle, whose name will follow yours, doctor."

The doctor took the hint, which Mr. Rackbrain evidently intended for him, and observed,—" I suppose, as president of this ' Joint Stock Company,' I must prove my admiration of the invention, and I shall do so most heartily. I intend to take three shares,—shall I give you a cheque on my banker, or—"

" That will do, Sir," replied the inventor, " if you make it payable at sight."

" Certainly," returned Dr. Titheum; and taking the pen to write an order payable at sight for sixty pounds, which Mr. Rackbrain received with a becoming expression of obligation, &c., and safely deposited in his pocket-book.

It was a singular circumstance that the doctor did not think of trying the incomparable writing fluid, when writing the cheque; in the hurry of his elated feelings, however, it escaped him, and the inventor himself was evidently too modest to press it upon him.

" By the bye," observed the doctor, as Mr. Rackbrain was bowing from the room,—" I had forgotten,—I have two or three friends in another room ; suppose you wait upon them, they will gladly take shares, I'm certain."

" If I am not greatly mistaken," returned the Fellow of the Royal Society, " I must leave with all possible haste,— my time is already gone."

" I am sorry for it," said the doctor; "however, I'll manage it for you : you are about to make a call, you stated,— where shall we be able to send to you in,—say half an hour?"

" Where ?" responded Mr. Rackbrain,—" If I am not greatly mistaken, I shall then be with his lordship at the

White Hart Tavern. Good morning, Sir," and with as much alertness as if he had himself been a hart, he bounded away.

The doctor re-joined his friends in the breakfast-room, and with a short preface informed them of the wonderful discovery into the secret of which he had just been initiated. The intention of the inventor to form a joint stock company, and the dignity to which himself was to be raised, formed ample occasion for the exercise of all the eloquence he possessed ; but when he announced the amount of each share, and pressed Dashwood and Sir Marmaduke to take shares with all possible despatch, his Lordship burst into a loud laugh, and exclaimed,—" Excellent !—superlatively excellent !—Did you ever," he continued, appealing to the Knight, "Did you ever hear a better hoax than this which the doctor wishes to play upon us ?"

" Never, 'pon my honour," replied Sir Marmaduke.

" Upon the honour of a gentleman," resumed the doctor, who began to think they questioned his statements, " I am not attempting to hoax you ;—I have taken three shares myself, for which I have given a cheque upon my banker for sixty pounds."

" 'Pon my honour !" exclaimed Sir Marmaduke ; " Are you indeed not jesting ?"

" Not I, indeed," replied the doctor. "The invention is most wonderful."

" If you are not attempting to hoax us," replied Dashwood, " you are regularly hoaxed yourself, and no mistake." " What thinks your Grace ?" he continued, appealing to the Duchess.

" The doctor's done brown," replied her Grace, laconically.

" If you will allow me, doctor," said Dashwood, " I'll prove to you, in less than ten minutes, you are hoaxed."

" Indeed !" said the doctor, most incredulously,—" By what means, pray ?"

" Simply by sending a servant to the White Hart with an enquiry how long Lord Dondoodle,—who, by the bye, I never before heard of,—has been there ; and to request that Mr. Rackbrain would favour us with his company."

" Good !" said the doctor ; " Let it be so ; and will you promise to take a share each if I am correct ?"

" I'll pledge myself to take half-a-dozen," replied Dashwood.

"And I," said the Duchess, "will engage for half a score."

A servant was despatched to make the enquiries suggested by Dashwood; and in a few minutes he returned, stating that no person of the name either of Dondoodle or Rackbrain had ever been at the White Hart.

"'Pon my honour," exclaimed Sir Marmaduke, "you are regularly done, doc*tar*."

"I begin to think I am," returned his reverence.

Lord Dashwood suggested the propriety of sending off express to his banker to stop the payment of the cheque, and detain the person who might present it. The doctor saw the propriety of the advice, and accordingly adopted it; while the ladies withdrew to their apartments for the purpose of making arrangements for their morning's walk.

CHAPTER XXXV.

Arnago.   Is't but the coinage of your fertile brain,
Bearing the show and mimicing of truth,
Without its substance ;—or but an idle tale
By tongues of gossips forg'd and vended too ?
Alphida.   No, it has the voucher of these eyes and ears ;—
I gaz'd upon it,—though at first I deem'd
'Twas but a phantasy of fever'd sleep.
I heard the rating of one noisy dame;
The laughing merriment which the other felt;
And pitied, from my soul, he who *was* wed,
And scarcely less the one prepar'd *to be so.*"

THE DOUBLE PAIR.

ARBOUZIM, the Wise, at that period of life when most men feel the greatest love to the world, fled from its false joys and positive sorrows, to seek after permanent happiness in solitude, meditation, and prayer. He lived as most misanthropists do, but was not one himself. He loved and sympathized with his fellow-men, and ever felt happy when by his counsel or assistance he could alleviate the wretchedness or add to the comfort of any.

Multitudes flocked, at different times, to Arbouzim's lonely retreat, for the purpose of seeking instruction—among others Gunoy, the Unfortunate, repaired thither. His eye was sunken through care, and premature age rested upon his form and features in consequence of sorrow.

"My son," said Arbouzim, as he met him, "wherefore are you sad?"

"My sorrows are multiplied," returned Gunoy. "The chief spring from whence I looked for pleasant waters in this valley of mourning, has proved but a well of bitterness."

"Fix your attention on one object alone," said Arbouzim, "and even to the sacrifice of all others determine upon its possession: for all others possessed without it, will advantage you nothing; while with it, although all else desert you, happiness will be yours."

"Name it," cried Gunoy.

"*Peace!*" exclaimed Arbouzim,—"*Peace at* HOME!"

"Enough!" ejaculated Gunoy;—"I'll return to my habitation; and, although my wife is as a well of bitter waters to me, for twelve months I'll follow your advice, and determine to attain, at whatever expense,—*peace!*"

Now, we are not sure that Dr. Leechum had ever seen, or even heard of, the advice of Arbouzim, or the determination of Gunoy; but that he possessed the spirit of the latter is certain, and appeared closely to follow his determination.

On the evening, and at the hour that Lady Bolio and Mrs. Leechum left the Royal Crescent to fulfil their appointment with Dr. Titheum and Lord Dashwood, Dr. Leechum was busily engaged in investigating the opposing qualities of different acids, in order to ascertain by what means the most fearful and destructive might be neutralized, so as to be rendered harmless; hoping that while so engaged, some fortunate thought might be given him from his patron saint, by which he might understand how to qualify a far worse and more destructive poison to men's peace than were the compounds he was examining to men's lives.

Having completed his task, without obtaining, however, a solution of the latter problem, he descended to the sitting-room; and finding it still empty, he rang the bell and enquired of the servant if her mistress was not yet returned: receiving an answer in the negative, he began to feel a degree of unpleasantness for which he could not account. He looked out upon the scene before him, and perceived the moon was already high in the heavens.

"Where can Lady Bolio and Mrs. Leechum be until this hour?" thought the doctor,—"Surely," he said to himself, "Mrs. Leechum cannot be in company with,—oh, no no," he cried aloud, as if the thought which had suddenly, like an

erratic flash of lightning, entered his mind, was too horrible
to dwell upon,—much more give utterance to, " Lady
Bolio is with her, and all must be well."

Now the apartment in which the doctor sat, or rather paced
with hurried step, while engaged in these deep, although by
no means delightful, cogitations,—commanded a very extensive and equally pleasant prospect over the gay city of
Bath ; together with the wide range of opposite hills which
formed a species of majestic back-ground to the soft and
sleeping picture : at the same time, the room was so situated
as to prevent those who were within from seeing any one approach the house, until within a short distance from it.

Already the perturbation of the doctor's mind had tended
to enervate his infirm body ;—he seated himself near the window ; and, as if moonstruck, was musing in a melancholy
state of feeling on the instability of all created things, and
revelling in that exquisite kind of delight which the thoughts
of the miseries of matrimony might be supposed to give birth
to, and especially in the experience of one

"Who writhed himself beneath the scorpion lash,
And sighed for change, which but, to think upon,
Quickened the agony of the pangs he bore ;"

when, at this well-timed moment, a mysterious-looking figure
suddenly stood before the window ; and, like an ancient
sybil, muttered some unintelligible sentences in the doctor's
hearing.

Although, as we have said, the moon shone brightly, still,
the deep shadow in which the figure stood, prevented the
possibility of distinguishing its features ; or, indeed, determining with any thing like accuracy, by the garments which
covered it, the sex to which it belonged—or if

"The sepulchre
Had ope'd its ponderous and marble jaws
To cast it up again."

At the first appearance of the form the doctor started in
considerable alarm ; but, presently recovering himself, he
enquired who it was, and what was its business. A few singular gestures gave evidence that the interrogations were understood ; and then, after pausing a few seconds,

"It lifted up its head, and did address
Itself to motion, and began to speak,

by uttering, in a semi-singing tone, the following reply :—

> "I come not to answer questions now;
> To beg or to steal, or to borrow;
> But tiue, as if bound by a Palmer's vow,
> To save from disgrace and dishonour!"

"Oh! my prophetic soul!" half uttered the doctor, placing himself in a respectful attitude before the "revealer of hidden things," and listening with profound attention, as if unwilling to allow a single word to pass by the drum of his ear.

"Listen!" said the figure emphatically.

"I will," replied the doctor.

The assurance and manner of the doctor appeared to satisfy the mysterious visitant; and, in the same tone as before, it continued—

> "Beware, beware of jealousy;
> Let prudence be your guide;
> Yet mingle *care* with *courtesy*—
> Watch o'er, watch o'er your bride.
> A gay young lord
> Plots ruin abroad;
> And now, while the moon shines bright,
> A deed may do,
> Which they both may rue:
> Beware, beware!—Good night.".

"Stay!" exclaimed the doctor, in a high state of excitement, as the figure appeared about to glide away.

Whether extreme good nature in the earthly or unearthly visitant, or the authoritative tone which the doctor assumed on the occasion, produced the effect, we profess not to determine;—but stay the figure did.. As, however, the doctor appeared too much confused to know *why* he had detained the form, as he said nothing, the figure itself very politely enquired, by observing,—

> "Hastily speak your wish, and say
> Wherefore do you wish my stay?
> What further knowledge would you gain?
> Speak!—All I can I will explain."

"Tell me," cried the doctor, "where is my wife now?" The visitant replied,—

> "That I could, but may not show.
> *Who* should like a husband *know?*
> To *you* belong the joy and duty
> Of watching over wedded beauty."

"Tell me," continued Leechum, while drops of perspiration, somewhat less than mill-stones, oozed from every pore of his agitated body.—" Tell me, mysterious stranger, has an assignation to-night taken place between my wife and—"

The invoked being sent forth, somewhat abruptly, the following response :—

" What will it avail to know,
That which can but heighten woe ?
Fare thee well!—I now must go.
Yet ere I depart,
To lighten your heart,
One secret I'll tell,
Take heed to it well,
Your wife still is true
To wedlock and you.
Though airy and light,
If managed aright,
She still may be won,
From ways she should shun.
The hard task is thine;
Ther. strive to combine
The husband and lover,
And never discover
Ill-temper or spleen ;
Or jealousy mean.
Arraign not her will ;
Her wishes fulfil.
Of *titles* beware—
No more I declare.
Hark !—Footsteps I hear ;
The ladies are near.
I shall meet you again
When the skies are fair.
So my counsels attend,
· And beware !—beware !"

So saying, the figure waved its hand, and like a thing of air, glided away.

" This is very mysterious," thought the doctor, as he sunk back in the chair which he occupied. " I have done wrong," he added, " in listening to this babbler ; or have I been dreaming ?—No ; I am awake,—wide awake. This strange figure must be one of those impudent impostors who infest our country, to the injury of the simple and the ruin of the unwary ;—but I am not of that character—no no ; I'll not be imposed upon."

For a few moments the doctor paused, as if lost amidst the bewilderings of his own reflections, and then continued :—
" 'Tis very mysterious !—This strange Being replied to my questions like one who knew more than he felt disposed to reveal. ' Of titles beware,' he said ; yet am I not to discover 'jealousy,' nor to ' oppose her will.' Umph !—that I have .

long proved an idle and unprofitable attempt. A woman's will, and a bar of steel, are two things very hard to bend."

The agitation of Leechum's feelings, as he continued to think over a variety of things connected with his own experieuce and prospects, became painfully oppressive : he rose from his chair, and with a view of tranquillizing his mind, traversed the spacious apartment, muttering to himself as he did so,—" Of titles beware."

The seeming cabilistic expression had escaped his lips for the twentieth time, when a tremendous knocking at the street-door, and a violent pulling at the bell, announced some other visitor ; and as the *style* of announcement would say,—of some importance.

" Who have we now ?" thought the doctor, stopping midway in his walk. His suspense on that head was of short duration ; for before he had resumed his walk, the door of the apartment opened, and in walked his dear, dear wife, and Lady Bolio.

There the doctor continued to stand, as if deprived of motion ; while from his lips the warning words came forth unconsciously,—" Of titles beware."

" Well, I'm sure, Dr. Leechum," observed his gentle spouse, " this is a fine welcome !—is it not ? Why, whatever do you mean ?—Am I always to be served thus when I return home, after making all possible dispatch on business of importance ?"

" Dr. Leechum," observed Lady Bolio, in a tone of such ineffable sweetness as seemed to indicate the unusual tranquillity, or rather joyousness of her spirit,—" I have a secret to tell you."

" A *secret !*" exclaimed the doctor, as if that word had contained a charm sufficiently strong to break the spell which had bound him, and calm his perturbed spirit. " Well, se-crets abound now-a-days ;—I should like to hear your Lady-ship's vastly."

" Should you, *Sir?*" interrupted his sweet lady ;—" Perhaps I could tell you a secret you would *not* like to hear."

" Indeed, my love," returned the doctor, " then I hope *you* will not reveal it."

" We have been out, Sir," observed Mrs Leechum.

" That I am aware of, my love," rejoined the doctor ; " there is no secret in that."

" We have returned again," added the lady, evidently

anxious to say something, without knowing *what* to say, or what she *wished* to say.

" *Of that,* too, I am aware, my love," returned the doctor, —"there is no secret in that."

" Tell me, Dr. Leechum," cried his placid wife; " am I to understand that you intend to insult me by your emphasis?"

" Oh, by no means, my love," replied the doctor; " I would not offend you for the world."

" I suppose not, Sir," rejoined the lady, with sufficient asperity of look and tone; " but a much less thing than a world would induce you to do it."

" Now tell me, my love," said the doctor, in such a tone of fondness as might have been sufficient to have won the heart of the most obdurate of the softer sex, but which did not appear to affect the hard heart of Mrs. Leechum in the least degree,—" Tell me, my love, *where* you have been walking this evening?"

" Did any one ever hear such rudeness!" exclaimed Mrs. Leechum, addressing Lady Bolio, and apparently shocked at her husband's want of decorum.—" I shall do no such thing; curiosity always implies a suspicious or a mean mind: I don't choose to patronize either," she replied.

" With *whom* have you been walking, may I enquire, my dear?" enquired Leechum.

" No, Sir," returned the lady; "that is,—what do you mean, Sir?—Monstrous!—horrible!—What, Sir!" she continued, almost in a scream,—" What do you mean to insinuate?—Have I not been in company with Lady Bolio?"

" Yes, my love," returned the doctor, " I know you have; but," he thought to himself,—" ' Of titles beware!' What *can* that mean?"

" Now, if you'll promise to keep a secret for a little while, Dr. Leechum, I'll tell you *all* about it," said Lady Bolio.

" In mercy's sake!" shouted Mrs. Leechum, " all about what, Lady Bolio?"

" All about *my* secret," replied Lady Bolio.—" Don't be alarmed, my dear," she added, aside,—" I can keep *your* secret."

" As you please, Lady Bolio," added Mrs. Leechum, relieved from a mountain load of alarm.—" But, *I* think, curiosity ought not to be satisfied."

" Well, Dr. Leechum," continued Lady Bolio, " what say you?"

"I promise you, on the honour of a man of honour," replied Leechum, "to keep your secret."

"Well then," said Lady Bolio, drawing a face of feigned sorrow, "I have committed myself, this evening,—sadly committed myself."

"What do I hear!" exclaimed the doctor, trembling from head to foot, and expecting to hear a disclosure of things touching his own and Mrs. Leechum's honour.—"What do I hear!", he repeated, and the strange figure's mystic words rushed into his mind,—

"Your wife still is true
To wedlock and you."

"Perhaps," he thought, "the Sybil was mistaken;—it must be so." Once more he repeated,—"What do I hear?"

"Why," returned Lady Bolio, with a still sorrowful face, "that I have committed myself this evening; but," she added, "you promised to keep my secret."

"Yes, yes," cried the half distracted doctor, "I'll keep it —that is,—and has Mrs. Leechum committed herself too?"

"Not this evening," replied Lady Bolio gravely,—"She committed herself some time since."

"Mrs. Leechum has committed herself,—has she?" ejaculated the doctor, with a phrenzied air.

"Me, Sir!" cried the lady;—"Me committed myself!— What do you mean, Sir?—Did you ever know me to commit myself?—Have I not always behaved in the most exemplary manner?—Oh! you cruel man!"

"Now, will you hear my penitential confession?" enquired Lady Bolio.

"I am anxious to hear it," replied the doctor; "most anxious."

"Well then," said Lady Bolio, "as I before said,—so I again state,—I have committed myself this evening,—I have allowed myself to be persuaded,—aye, Dr. Leechum," continned her Ladyship, "you may well stare, while you hear me, at my time of life, make such a humiliating confession,— I have allowed myself to be persuaded to promise once more to enter into a matrimonial connexion."

"And is that *all?*" asked Leechum, gasping for breath; —"Is that *all,* Lady Bolio?"

"Is that *all?*" responded her Ladyship; "and is not that sufficient, think you, doctor?"

" Of titles beware," thought Leechum.—" This, then, is what the strange Being referred to ;—he has mistaken Lady Bolio for Mrs. Leechum. Oh, it is plain,—I see it all. A matrimonial engagement." At length he exclaimed,—" Well, well, Lady Bolio, I am happy to hear it ; and, I presume, with Lord Dashwood !" for the doctor was ignorant that Dashwood had already committed himself,—in a matrimonial engagement.

"No such thing, I assure you," interrupted Mrs. Leechum. " With Lord Dashwood, indeed ! - Why with Lord Dashwood pray, Sir ?"

" And why not, my love ?" enquired Leechum.

" Because I should not ap—that is," stammered out the lady,—" he has too much respect for—pshaw !" she added, " how provokingly inquisitive you are ;—because he is married already."

" Whew !" cried the doctor,—" Is he so ?—I beg his Lordship's pardon, my love ;—but with whom, then, is it that Lady Bolio has *committed* herself in the way she has stated ?"

" What do you say to Dr. Titheum ?" asked Lady Bolio.

" Dr. Titheum !" shouted Leechum ;—" Why, the very man ; a better choice could not have been made—admirable ! Lord Dashwood is not a patch upon him,—I would rather see you married to Dr. Titheum's little finger, than Lord Dashwood's whole body."

" Oh ! you insensible, degrading monster !" shouted Mrs. Leechum.

" What, in the name of wonder, do you mean, my dear love ?" asked Leechum ; " I merely hinted my opinion— nothing more ;—I may be wrong, I confess it."

" *Wrong* indeed !" said his lady, with emphasis. " Oh, the taste of some people !"

" Well, I am happy to hear *you* approve my choice, Dr. Leechum," observed Lady Bolio, evidently anxious to prevent Mrs. Leechum from letting her own secret out.

" I do most heartily approve it," rejoined Leechum. " But how came it about this evening,—is it not rather a sudden thing ?"

" Aye ; there it is," said his sweet lady ; " there it is,— ever prying into secrets with which he can have no possible business."

" I merely enquired, my love," returned her placid lord, " for the purpose of hinting—"

" Oh, how I abhor those abominable and everlasting *hintings!*" shouted Mrs. Leechum.—" I tell you, Dr. Leechum, we met the doctor this evening."

" No, love, you did not;—indeed, dear, you didn't," returned her spouse, trembling at her kindling eye. "Until this moment you have not so much as *mentioned* the meeting, I assure you, love."

" Well, if I did not before, I have done so *now,* and that is sufficient," replied Mrs. Leechum.

" Oh, quite so, love,—quite so," returned the doctor.

" Well, so it was, Dr. Leechum," resumed Lady Bolio ; " we met the doctor; and, as I have stated, I have positively accepted him; and, I suppose shall, before many years, cease to be Lady Bolio."

" Delightful !" exclaimed the doctor.—" Many years, say yon?—aye, before many days, I should hope : I do not approve of protracted engagements ; and particularly at a certain age."

" One would imagine not," interrupted Mrs. Leechum ; " and, therefore, it was, that you were so killingly pressing to secure me. Heigho ! Fool that I was !—If I had calculated upon consequences better, I should now have been,— but the sacrifice is made, and the subject will not bear reflection,—it positively will not. I must think of something else, or Dr. Leechum's cruelty will drive me mad."

" Think, my love, of being Lady Bolio's bridesmaid," said Leechum, soothingly; "and think, too, in what way I can meet your wishes to make you happy, and I will do it."

" I have no doubt of it, Sir," returned the lady ; " so you said before I resigned my liberty ; and you have kept your word, have you not ?—I must and *will* have my own will, Dr. Leechum."

" So you shall, my love," returned her husband; " and allow me to hint, that—"

" I'll have no more *hints,*" said Mrs. Leechum, with a *little* vehemence. " Shall we retire, Lady Bolio, and throw off some of our dress, and, if possible, escape being *hinted* at?"

" With all my heart, love," replied her Ladyship, and they accordingly withdrew.

Leechum felt his mind considerably relieved by Lady Bolio's statement; although he still feared there was something at which the dark expressions of the singular visitant had hinted, which related to Mrs. Leechum, not yet ex-

plained.   He thought, however, that no better plan could be
pursued by him, than to allow Mrs. Leechum to follow, unrestrained, her own wayward fancies ; and meet, so far as he
could, her unbending will; and by so doing, strive to win her
to himself.   Having so determined in his own mind, he
waited the return of the ladies, hoping to learn more from
Lady Bolio, respecting his wife and her Ladyship's approaching marriage.

CHAPTER XXXVI.

" The secret is out !
    All mystery is over ;
The news spreads about;
    All plainly discover,
What none until now
    Had even once *thought* on—
That chance,—nothing more,—
    A marriage had brought on."

MYSTERIES MADE PLAIN.

WE are not aware that a satisfactory reason has yet been
given for the singular and instantaneous manner with which
some persons have been gifted with an extraordinary measure
of penetration, who before could scarcely comprehend by
what means two and two make four.   But, upon a simple
statement being made of circumstances that have occurred,
or that are on the eve of taking place, they at once see clearly
how one thing acted upon, or in connexion with another, by
the production of certain results ; and then are able to trace
most sc entifically,—nor less dogmatically,—the connexion between certain understood causes and palpable effects.   How
any one could possibly be so ignorant as not to have seen,
as they did long before, what would follow previous combi-
nations,—is to them, with all their wisdom, matter of astonishment.

    Now we are not aware, as we have said, that any *satisfac-
tory* reason has been given for this sudden, this,—we had
almost said,—intuitive and truly wonderful possession of
penetration !   That reasons have been given we are fully
aware ; but it is not reasons merely to which we refer, which
are easily enough given for any and every thing, but a satis-

factory one. If, however, no attempt at elucidation had been made on this momentous subject, it is one thousand to a unit but the reader would have comprehended it, without any other aid than his own good sense ;—but enough of irony. It is, really amusing to hear the penetration to which some ignoramuses lay claim ; because, after certain results have followed some known causes, they have been able to deter- mine that such causes would naturally produce such results. So it happened in the case of Dr. Titheum and Lady Bolio : the moment the secret came out,—and that was only a few hours after the meeting of the parties on the evening referred to in a preceding chapter,—every one saw, without so much as a mote of doubt obscuring their mental visions, that such a consummation would follow the masquerade meeting : *how* they discovered the connexion between that meeting and the connexion of the parties in question, we have not been able to discover ; but the marvels of second sight may not yet have ceased.

It was no longer attempted to be concealed, that Lady Bolio and Dr. Titheum had contracted with each other ; and that at no very remote period the reverend gentleman would lead his blushing (query ?) bride to the altar.

This circumstance gave a new feature to almost all the en- gagements of the party at the York Hotel : and, as it had before been agreed, that on a given day the above-named party would return the visit paid them by the members of the family from the Royal Circus, some thought that that day would be, above all other days, a proper one for the so- lemn occasion. To be sure, the time was short ; but what then? why, " a *bad* job cannot be too soon got over," thought Lord Dashwood; and " a *good* one cannot be too soon per- formed," observed Sir Marmaduke. However, on this point it was,—according to the immutable laws by etiquette esta- blished,—left to the ladies to determine *when* and *where* the delectable ceremony should take place.

" Well now, really, Dr. Titheum," observed the Duchess, " you have fairly taken me in."

" No, on my honour, your Grace !" exclaimed the doctor.

" If," resumed the Duchess, " some prior engagement was made, or some understanding existed between yourself and Lady Bolio, I still maintain you have taken me in ; and, if nothing of the kind existed, why you must be a marvel- lously clever man, that's all, doctor."

" If such *must* be the case," returned the doctor, " why, then, as your Grace very graciously states, I *am* a marvellously clever man—and, indeed, being as I am, and long have been ; in the ' commission of the peace,' bespeaks me to be possessed of something more than ordinary sense."

" Why true," returned her Grace, " as you observe, doctor ;—and, as in the case of your own experience, it certainly is true, that being in the ' commission of the peace' bespeaks you to be possessed of something more than *ordinary sense*, yet, you know, it does not always follow,—I could write down in a dozen minutes twice that number of gentlemen who are in the ' commission of the peace,' in whose experience the argument holds not good. Indeed I have sometimes thought, that the greatest numskulls have been sought out, upon whose heads to place the Tom-fool's cap of office."

" I beg your Grace will cease to speak evil of dignitaries," observed the doctor with peculiar gravity.—" Render honour to whom honour is due."

" Oh, I cry your reverence's pardon!" returned the Duchess, laughing ; " I speak not evil of dignities, but of clowns and witlings ; and as to rendering honour to whom honour is due, why, bless you, I am the most rigid stickler for the maintenance of the doctrine under the sun ;—but then, doctor, you cannot suppose that because a man's head is adorned with a cap and bells, I must, therefore, bow down at the soles of his feet, and cry ' Hail, mighty Cæsar !' No no ; I am sure you know better, doctor. *Yourself I honour, and your office too !*"

" Well well," returned the doctor, " I will not contend with your Grace ; I admit you are *very* near correct."

" I am happy to find you are a convert to the right," continued her Grace ; " and now, doctor, as you are about to enter another ' commission' soon, I hope it will also be a ' commission of *peace*,' and then you will hold a *double* ' commission of the peace.' "

" Good !" exclaimed the doctor ;—" Benevolent ever are the thoughts and wishes of your Grace !"

" 'Pon my honour !" exclaimed Sir Marmaduke, who entered at the moment. " But these wise men of Bath are particularly officious."

" What has happened, Sir Marmaduke," enquired Dashwood, " of so extraordinary a character as to excite your particular attention, and rouse your wrath ?"

" 'Pon my honour," returned the Knight, "if it were not for certain cogent reasons, the confidence of these wise-acres, should for once be disappointed. There," continued Sir Marmaduke, taking a paper from his pocket and handing it to Dashwood,—" read, and inform yourself,—'pon my honour!"

His Lordship took the presented paper, and read the following offensive article ; which, because of its importance, was placed in a conspicuous part of the paper :—

" In the course of a few days, two marriages in high life will take place in our city. Sir Marmaduke Varney will lead the *accomplished* and wealthy Miss Fidget to the hymeneal altar ; and the Rev. Dr. Titheum, Rector of Christchurch, Hants, will be honoured at the same time with the hand of the distinguished Lady Bolio."

" Well," enquired Dashwood, " and what is there so *particularly* objectionable in all this, Sir Marmaduke ? To lead an *accomplished* and *wealthy* young lady to the altar of Hymen, is certainly better than *being led* to the altar of sacrifice."

" 'Pon my honour," returned the Knight, "there your *Lud*ship says true;—still, I protest—"

" Pshaw !" returned Dashwood; " I wish your chance had fallen to my lot;—but *entre nous*," continued his Lordship giving an understood wink to the Knight,—" Accomplished and *wealthy*—eh ? Those," he added, in a higher key, "who live by communicating news, must keep both ears open to catch it as it flies."

" 'Pon my honour," returned the Knight, " I feel indignant at the liberty the rascal of an editor has taken with my own and Miss Fidget's name,—I do, 'pon my honour ; and, but for a certain reason, I would immediately institute proceedings against the fellow, and punish him for it, although it should cost me a thousand pounds."

" Nay, Sir Marmaduke," said Miss Fidget, who felt gratified with the paragraph, rather than offended, and particularly with the " *accomplished*" part of it,—" don't, I entreat you, allow yourself to feel annoyed by the trivial circumstance,—for *my* sake, take no notice of it."

" For *your* sake, my *dear* Miss Fidget, I will forego my wrath," replied Sir Marmaduke ;—" *but* for your sake my revenge should have been in proportion to the liberty taken."

" And for *my* sake," added the doctor, " let the offence pass by in silence. I am in the ' commission of the peace' you know, and it would ill accord with my character and office to allow the peace to be broken on such an occasion."

"And I'll venture to say," chimed in the Duchess, laughing, "that neither of the ladies referred to will be offended with the *period* that is announced."

"Pray, Sir Marmaduke," enquired Lord Dashwood, "will you consider me rude if I ask how soon you intend to leave Bath, after the ' consummation devoutly to be wished for' has taken place ?"

"Oh no, 'pon my honour," replied the gallant Knight. "We shall, I think, repair immediately to my estate in Sussex."

"The devil you will!" interrupted Dashwood, aside.

"Yes, 'pon my honour," returned Sir Marmaduke, in the same by-tone.

"What! before you have purchased it—eh?" said Dashwood.

"I have struck the bargain, you know," replied the Knight, "and shall *pay* for *it*, and wipe off a few odd things immediately my claims are legalized."

"Oh, oh,—I see right, and mum!" rejoined Dashwood, with a significant application of the fore-finger of his right hand to the left side of his nasal protuberance. "You intend immediately to visit Sussex, do you, Sir Marmaduke?" he continued aloud.

"Yes, 'pon my honour," said the Knight; "at least such is my intention,—that is, of course, supposing this lady does not object, without whose entire pleasure I can do nothing, 'pon my honour."

"I feel perfectly willing to acquiesce in any thing that Sir Marmaduke may think proper to propose or do," observed the "accomplished" Miss Fidget, in the true spirit of a lady who was *not* married, but who hoped *soon* to be, and who then would feel at full liberty to make such fresh arrangements in the trifling concern of "*obeying*" as might suit her convenience.

"Well and properly spoken," said the doctor, with an approving smile. "Sir Marmaduke, I congratulate you on your highly flattering prospects. The woman whose good sense leads her cheerfully to yield up her own will to the *lawful* will of her husband, ensures his happiness and her own comfort and respectability. I shall be happy to find, what I confidently expect, a counterpart of the 'accomplished' and correctly determining Miss Fidget in Lady Bolio."

Miss Fidget and Sir Marmaduke expressed, at the same time, their sense of the compliment paid them by the doctor, and responded to his wish, that all he expected he might find in Lady Bolio.

"Now do you really think it is *quite* proper," rejoined the Duchess, addressing herself to the doctor, "that a lady should give up *all* her will to her husband?"

"Your Grace has heard my opinion on that head," returned his Reverence." "I say not that a lady's will should be sacrificed to the caprice or spleen of a brute, because he bears the form of a man; but however rude and unreasonable a man may be, nothing, depend on it, will ever be gained by a lady's opposing her husband's rudeness, merely for the purpose of having her will."

"Indeed!" returned her Grace; "then you hold it quite right, doctor, that we poor things should quietly adopt the doctrine of passive obedience and non-resistance to the lords of creation; and like a spaniel, whose fondness for his master is said to increase with the ill-treatment he receives at his hands, we are to cringe to, and love dearly, and be very, very submissive, to those who know not how to treat us?"

"Your Grace, I am certain, does not believe that I think any such thing," returned the doctor. "I hold, as the vilest monster that incumbers our earth, the man who treats not a kind and affectionate woman with a full return of all that is kind and affectionate: nevertheless, when the case so happens, I think—nay, I am as sure as that I am in the 'commission of the peace'—that a lady will possess her own will more, by not seeming to seek it, than by open violence demanding, what she may even justly consider to be her right."

"'Pon my honour," exclaimed Sir Marmaduke," your statements, doctor, are as interesting as an homily. Do you not think they are superlatively excellent, and unobjectionably correct, Miss Fidget?"

"Certainly I do," replied the lady.

"Well, well," said her Grace, "we shall see what your thoughts are upon the subject this day twelvemonth; if, however," she added with something like seriousness, "your opinion then is what now it is, ours will not disagree. I think you are quite correct, doctor, though heaven knows what I should think or do, if I had not always my own will."

CHAPTER XXXVII.

" All were amaz'd he stay'd so long,
    And some the statement taunted;
While others vow'd the statement wrong,
    Which said a stranger wanted.

But oh, it was, alas, too true,
    That one who pity flaunted;
Whose soul compassion never knew,
    Indeed, the poor Gent. wanted."

THE EXCITEMENT.

THERE is an old adage which states, "There's many a slip between the cup and the lip." However near the cup may have been brought to the lip, it may, before the union actually takes place, be dashed away.

A circumstance now occurred in the experience of Sir Marmaduke, which made it appear very likely that he would soon possess a practical confirmation of the truth of the said saying: for near as be had come to quaffing the delectable goblet of delight, which the *wealthy* Miss Fidget had almost rendered him certain of enjoying, still a doubt existed if he would ever taste it.

It has already been stated, that the Knight's finances were far from being in a flourishing condition, and that his exclusive object in wishing to marry Miss Fidget was for the purpose of replenishing his exchequer. His debts of honour had been heavy, but he had never failed to discharge them, not from a sense of honour, but because, unless he had so done, he would have been black-balled, and, neither on the turf, nor at the billiard or card-table, would he have been able to hold up his head, and cry to any noble or ignoble challenge, " I take you, Sir."

But there were other debts, and sweeping ones, too, which ought to have been considered debts of honour, which he never *honoured;* repeated applications had been made to him by needy, yet honest tradesmen, but to all and every such application, Sir Marmaduke gave *promises* to pay, but *no payment.*

At length the patience of some two or three was entirely exhausted; they pressed their demands with what Sir Marmaduke pronounced rudeness—*alias* earnestness, and then pressed into the Knight's hand a very suspicious-looking kind of paper, which assured him that evasion could no longer avail, but that, within a certain specified time, he must either pay or go to quod. Now to do the former he *could* not, and to do the latter he did not approve, and therefore he determined he *would* not: from these circumstances it was that he became increasingly anxious to settle matters with Miss Fidget, whose funds were ample, but which funds he feared, should his need of them become known too soon, would for ever be locked from his touch.

One perplexing difficulty now existed, and that was the means to be adopted to retain his liberty until the lady had taken him " for better for worse." The time prescribed to him was so short as to render it impossible he could, within the period, win Miss Fidget to his purpose. Lord Dashwood had long been his confident—and, indeed, to that worthy he was under some heavy obligations; to him he communicated the dilemma into which he was thrown, and by his advice the visit to Bath was taken, in order to get out of the way.

The dogs of the law are perfect blood hounds in scent ; no matter which way the wind blows, their olfactory organs are so sensitive that their hunted game is sure to be discovered, though they burrow " e'en a mile deep."

How could Sir Marmaduke Varney expect to escape? As all others do. The well-known line of Young—

" All men think all men mortal but themselves"—

true as it is, is not more so, than that every man, circumstanced as Sir Marmaduke was, believes himself an excepted one, and although all others may be found, themselves are safe from detection.

The conversation recorded above, between the Duchess, the doctor, &c., was progressing with spirit ; Sir Marmaduke, full of confidence that at the end of another week he should be able, with a plentiful supply of funds, to sport it handsomely, talked largely, and was proceeding to lay down plans and purposes in the most lively manner, when a servant entered the room, and, with a profound bow, observed,

" A gentleman, Sir Marmaduke, has just enquired for you below."

" A gentleman," observed the Knight—" 'pon my honour ! what kind of a gentleman?"

"A very old one, Sir," replied the servant. "His hair, Sir, is as vite as this 'ere napkin."

"'Pon my honour!" returned Sir Marmaduke, "and how looking?"

"Like a lord, Sir," answered the servant. "Rather short, Sir, thin, and powdered."

"'Pon my honour!—Ah," continued the Knight, "I see, my neighbour, Squire Turnabout, a little while since a flaming Tory—then a Whig—and now an out and out Radical, but withal a worthy fellow, and a warm friend. Ah! 'pon honour, shall have the pleasure of introducing an old, intimate, and wealthy friend. I have expected him a full week, but he is so changeable that I had given him up. 'Pon my honour—rather close, but can come out. Show the gentleman up," he continued, "with my best respects. 'Pon my honour—this is fortunate."

"He has left, Sir," returned the servant.

"Left!" exclaimed Sir Marmaduke. "Why did you allow him to leave?—'Pon my honour!"

"He stated he was in a great hurry, Sir," answered the serving man, "but said he should be happy if you could call upon him at his hotel in half an hour, or earlier if possible."

"At his hotel!" shouted Sir Marmaduke. "'Pon my honour, and which may his hotel be?"

"The Vhite Lion, Sir, in the market-place," returned the servant."

"'Pon my honour," observed the Knight, "he is a very crusty old fellow, and must be humoured." "I am under small obligation to him," he whispered to Dashwood.

"Are you so?" said Dashwood; "then by all means keep in for the time with him."

"Shall I step and insist upon his joining us?" asked the Knight.

"Certainly," observed the doctor, "you cannot indeed do less."

"By all means," said Miss Fidget.

"It will only be acting respectfully to an *old* friend," echoed the Duchess.

"'Pon my honour," said Sir Marmaduke, "I'll do as you all recommend. To *send,* I am certain, would be of no avail; —he must be humoured, 'pon my honour. I'll return in a few seconds.

' No business can detain me long from you.' "

So saying, he set *off*, and the party he had left set *to* discussing sundry points connected with the expected matrimonial ceremony.

The first half hour passed away without much notice being taken of the Knight's long absence;—the second was drawing to a close, and still he did not appear. Miss Fidget began to feel a *little* uneasy,—poor Carlo even offended his mistress by offering a chaste salute. So true it is, that small things, and even such as at other times affords pleasure, yields but offence when the mind is not at ease.

" Where can Sir Marmaduke stay so long?" observed Miss Fidget, with considerable anxiety, as the third half hour commenced, during the whole of which time he had been invisible to her adoring eyes. " I begin to think something has occurred of an unpleasant nature."

" Oh, there is no cause of alarm, Madam," returned Dashwood; " I'll be bound for his safety.

" But how are we to account for his outrageously long delay?" said the Duchess; " surely *this* expression of tenderness accords not with the burning anxiety of a lover."

" Let us think favourably of Sir Marmaduke," observed the doctor; " for although *we* are not able to explain why he has been so long absent, he, doubtless, will be able to do so on his return, to the satisfaction of the lady most concerned."

" Oh, no doubt," returned the Duchess; " you, gentlemen, are exceedingly skilful at giving satisfactory reasons."

At this moment a servant entered the room, and delivered a note to Lord Dashwood, and then withdrew.—Offering an apology for so doing,—his Lordship rose and walked towards the window; when, to his surprise and consternation, he read as follows :—

" My Dear Dashwood,
" I have been regularly trapped,—I have, 'pon my honour. Make some excuse for me; and with all dispatch hasten to the White Lion, and meet yours, 'pon my honour,
" Most truly, but
" Most unfortunate,
" VARNEY."

" Here's a precious mess !" thought his Lordship to himself; not daring to give utterance to his reflections. "What shall I do?—If this comes out, it will be all U-P with this marriage affair; and then,—farewell; a long and eternal farewell to all my hopes of recovering the few thousands in . which Sir Marmaduke stands indebted to me. That won't do ;—no no, a scheme must be hit upon,—oh, I have it. Hem!" he added, after a few moments' thought,—" I have it, by Jove!" and then turning to the company with perfect indifference in his manner, he observed,—" Sorry to say, that for a few minutes I must leave you, ladies;—this note is from an intimate friend, who has just arrived in Bath, extremely ill. By the time I return, I dare say, Sir Marmaduke will be here, and the '*satisfactory reason*' will have been given. To the care and gallantry of my reverend friend I leave you.— Adieu !"

Profoundly bowing, his Lordship left the room, and hasted to learn in what condition Sir Marmaduke stood. Of Sir Marmaduke's departure from the York Hotel, to meet his friend Squire Turnabout, the reader has been informed. No sooner did he reach the well-known establishment, the "White Lion," than he made inquiries for the Squire. As, however, the gentleman had not announced his name, Sir Marmaduke was obliged to send up his own to the gentle- man, whose appearance so exactly answered the description which he gave of the person after whom he was seeking. In less than two minutes he was informed by the servant it was all right ; and then was, with all befitting ceremony, ushered into the room. The gentleman rose to receive him, politely handed him a chair, shut the door of the apartment, turned the key in the lock, and then turned it into his pocket. Sir Marmaduke felt astonished.

" 'Pon my honour," said the Knight, " I beg ten thou- sand pardons ! I have made a mistake I perceive."

" No apologies, my dear Sir," returned the stranger, who did not happen to be Squire Turnabout, " it is all right I assure you;—your name, I believe, is Sir Marmaduke Varney ?"

" Quite correct, 'pon my honour," returned the Knight.

" So I judged," returned the stranger. " *Very* happy to meet you, Sir," he added, deliberately, removing as he spoke a white peruke from his head, and whiskers to match from his face. " I think you recollect your old friend, Solomon Feritfox ?"

" 'Pon my honour!" exclaimed Sir Marmaduke, astounded at finding himself enclosetted with a Sheriff's officer ; " What does all this mean ?"

" Oh, to oblige you with an explanation will be no trouble,"
returned Solomon, with a broad grin, " if so be you *need* it ;
but I guess it's all quite unnecessary. The fact is, Sir Marmaduke, I knew no method by which to have the pleasure of
an interview with you but by assuming a·disguise; this you
see I have done ;—and, as I thought it better you should call
at *my* hotel,—that our meeting might be private,—rather
than that I should wait upon you at *yours,* where we might
have been annoyed by persons whose company we didn't wish
for,—why, I used the little trickery which we great men allow
one to another,—you understand me ?"

" 'Pon.my honour," said Sir Marmaduke, " am I then to
consider myself your prisoner ?"

" Exactly so," returned Feritfox,—" just guessed it."

The Knight offered to pawn his honour that he would pay
or surrender at the end of one week, if Mr. Solomon Feritfox
would allow him to go at large until that time; as he had an
affair of importance on hand, which could not possibly be
done without him ; but he had so frequently done the same
thing to the same parties, that he now refused to take the
pledge for the amount of security required.

After arguing the case and shifting his position for nearly
one hour and a half, the Knight determined to write to Lord
Dashwood; and the note which the reader has seen was immediately penned by him and despatched by a servant, with
strict injunctions to place it in Lord Dashwood's own hand.

The man of the law and Sir Marmaduke were still in close
and earnest conversation, when the voice of Dashwood at the
door put a termination to it.

One would have supposed, judging from the actions of Solomon Feritfox, that however fully he might have believed
the truth of the common saying, " there is honour among
rogues," he did not think there was any among noblemen,
or otherwise he conceived they were rogues of deeper grain
and blacker character than those of ordinary stamp; for, before he opened the door at the loud demand of Dashwood,
whose authoritative tone appeared to have no more influence
upon him than water upon a duck's back,—he very deliberately took from his pocket a bright little pistol, to the great
annoyance of the Knight, whose antipathy to those kind of
playthings has already been seen,—and having examined the
priming, cocked it, and so seemed to say,—" No rescue, if
you please, without money or bond."

As soon as 'his Lordship was admitted, and learned how matters stood, he gave Feritfox his own security for his friend, and so freed him from the vice-like gripe from which he could not have delivered himself.

"Away," said Dashwood to the Knight, "with all speed to the York Hotel. But stay,—what excuse can we offer for your absence; and, especially, for your not introducing your *friend?* I suppose you have no particular wish that Mr. Solomon Feritfox should accompany you?"

" 'Pon my honour," exclaimed the Knight, "I had much rather his satanic majesty went with me: I have an insuperable aversion to gentlemen of Mr. Feritfox's profession,—I have, 'pon my honour."

"What's to be done?" said Dashwood, thoughtfully.— "To let the ladies into this secret won't do.—Oh, I have it, my boy! Your point with Miss Fidget *must* be carried, and then I shall leave you to go alone—eh?"

" 'Pon my honour," returned the Knight, "your *Lud-*ship's kindness is marvellous!—'tis, 'pon my honour, and shall not be forgotten.

"Well, this you must do," returned Dashwood,—"throw a spoonful or two of Port over your leg, bind your handkerchief round it, and then we'll take a coach from the door to our hotel: you must make a few wry faces as you enter the room, limp confoundedly,—and state that, going to see your friend start, five minutes after you reached the White Lion, one of the wheels of his carriage caught your leg and injured it,—that you have been detained by a doctor, who has examined it,—that nothing of consequence has taken place,— and that you did not, until you were obliged, write to me for fear of alarming the ladies. I'll be at your back and support you, and soon make all right,—do you see?"

" 'Pon my honour," said Sir Marmaduke, "your powers of invention are wonderful,—your head would be an honour to a chancellor's wig; while the woolsack would receive grace and dignity by your filling it,—'tis true, 'pon my honour."

"Those points we'll settle another time," returned Dashwood, laughing heartily at Sir Marmaduke's conceit, "at present we have business to settle which will be of more importance to you than either of the offices you have mentioned is to the nation."

" 'Pon my honour, that's true," replied Sir Marmaduke

"Here goes, then, to attend to the first part of your advice." So saying, he stained his white silk hose with a small quantity of Port-wine, and then bound round the apparently injured part with his handkerchief; thus assuming the semblance of injury, and limping to the very life, the Knight and his Lordship left the White Lion, and were driven in a hackney-coach to the York Hotel.

"Well," exclaimed Dashwood, as he entered the room where the party still sat in grave debate respecting the unaccountable absence of Sir Marmaduke, "has the absentee returned yet?"

"He has not," replied Miss Fidget, almost fainting from excitement. "Something, I feel certain, has happened of a serious nature."

"Now, don't allow yourself to be alarmed, Madam," returned Dashwood; "I have come to announce—"

"Ah!" exclaimed Miss Fidget,—"Come to announce what?"

"Why, that a *trifling* accident has occurred," replied his Lordship; "but—"

"Oh!" shrieked the sensitive *young* lady, betraying *more* emotion than she wished; although much *less* than she felt. "Tell me, I implore your Lordship, what has happened?—Where is he?"

"Oh, he is in the next room," replied Dashwood, with the utmost indifference. "Now don't be alarmed, I repeat; I came before to prepare you; and now, with your permission, I'll introduce Sir Marmaduke."

In a moment the gallant Knight made his appearance, displaying such novel contortions of physiognomy as well-nigh overcame the assumed gravity even of Dashwood; while his limping gait was so inimitable, that no pensioner in Chelsea College, or Greenwich Hospital, with one of his calves shot away, could have done it better;—in fact, he played his part to the very life.

An explanation of the serious affair was soon given, according to the plan laid down by Dashwood: no one present expressed a wish to examine the wound, which was a fortunate circumstance; while his Lordship, with all the assurance of a man of honour, vouched for the truth of Sir Marmaduke's statement.

"How exceedingly fortunate it was," observed Miss Fidget, "that the leg was not broken."

" Yes, indeed, observed the Duchess, " or that Sir Marmaduke was not killed upon the spot."

" If such had been the case," sighed Miss Fidget, " what should I have done ?"

" Why, in that case," said the doctor, " your marriage must certainly have been postponed ; and I should have been deprived of the pleasant company upon which I have fondly calculated when leading Lady Bolio to the altar."

So much sympathy as a real accident would scarcely have received, was lavished upon the Knight: each person appeared anxious to minister to his comfort ; while Miss Fidget hoped most fervently (although she did not express her hopes) that Sir Marmaduke's accident would not prove of so serious a nature as to render a postponement of the wished-for nuptial ceremony necessary.

———

CHAPTER XXXVIII.

" A wanderer now he seem'd,
      As if his race to shun ;
   Him, some a robber deemed ;
      Yet still in secret, one
Sigh'd ceaseless for him ;—nor once thought the maid,
Like a good angel, round her path he stray'd."

J. YOUNG.

" WHERE can Claudius be ?" had issued from the lips of poor Georgiana at least a score of times, every day, since his departure from the York Hotel ; but the implied desire to obtain information received only the annoying echo,— " Where can Claudius be ?"

It is at least a *possible* case that the reader may have thought with Georgiana,—" Where can Claudius be ?" That the language of desire has been so frequently expressed, or so powerfully felt by the reader as by Georgiana, is what cannot be reckoned upon ;—still, for the satisfaction of their minds, we shall introduce a short episodical chapter on the subject, and show where and in what way Claudius disposed of himself.

Immediately upon our hero's leaving the room in which the doctor had detected him in such interesting engagement with his daughter, he repaired to the apartment he had occupied, in connexion with his fellow-servant, as a sleeping-room; and taking from his box a few pounds which he had saved from his wages, or which at different times he had received as presents from those for whom he had done " some service," he thrust the whole into a brown holland bag,—lacking as he did a purse,—and then deposited his store safely in his pocket.

Having managed that important business, he sallied forth from the Hotel with as sorrowful a heart as ever Knight-errant possessed when separated, by some untoward circumstance, from his beloved Dulcinia.

Such was the perturbed state of his feelings, occasioned by the sudden and unlooked-for change in his situation and fortunes, that without any thing definite in view, he wandered on until he had reached the outskirts of the picturesque village of Claverton, when a small portion of reason came to his aid, under whose influence he attempted to arrange something like a plan for his future course. Still his unsettled and confused mind was unable to fix on any thing,—and on he went.

Already he had passed through the above-named romantic place, from which the Claverton Down takes it name,—a spot which will long be hallowed in the memory of the sons and friends of genius, from its celebrated, although somewhat eccentric rector, the ingenious RICHARD GRAVES, the friend of the poet SHENSTONE, and the author of the " Spiritual Quixote," and other interesting works,—when, suddenly turning, he stood and gazed upon the city he was leaving; and which, in his warm and strong imagination, contained a treasure of far more value than the mines of Golconda, or the wealth of a world, in the person of Georgiana.

" Shall I," exclaimed our hero, " thus tamely resign her whose heart I evidently possess, because I have been repulsed by her father? or shall I at once make known who I am, and crave forgiveness at the hands of my mother?—No," he continued after a pause,—" No; at present I will not do so; yet I will watch the movements of the doctor, and seek occasionally to gain a glimpse of my dear Georgiana."

Having closed this brief soliloquy,—like another Whittington when fleeing from London,—Claudius turned back to Bath. In a short time he succeeded in purchasing such a change of dress as his purpose required, and again retired to the vicinity of the city; and in a retired spot, beneath an embowering hedge, changed his costume; and then, having made as snug a bundle of his livery as he could manage to do, trudged off to seek a lodging suitable to his finances.

The soft calm hour of eventide had come as Claudius strolled down Westgate Buildings, gazing at every paper he saw exhibited in various windows, and on every board hung out at different houses, anxious to find "A furnished room to let." He had already seen several announcements of " Lodgings for Gentlemen," and " Gentlemen done for," handsomely printed on embossed cards, or beautifully written ; but whatever the feelings of Claudius might have been on the subject, his modesty or prudence deterred him from making application at any such places.

" For *Gentlemen*," thought Claudius, " that is, indeed, an ambiguous term,—by it, I suppose is meant, at Bath, those who have plenty of money, and a good stock of impudence, —such as can pay well for what they have, and who will not, with too much rigidity, investigate the particular items of charges tendered to them : my funds, however, will not allow me so to act; and, therefore, I must seek something of a humbler character."

Still on he went, and at length ventured to announce himself at a house where "Lodgings for single *men*," was exhibited, and where a *knocker*,—a distinction worthy of especial note,—instead of a *bell*, was the instrument to be employed for the purpose ;—the latter appeared pretty generally to be appended to mansions of more imposing exterior than the one at the door of which he had presumed to knock. In the twinkling of an eye, the door was opened by a girl, of whom Claudius enquired,—" Have you not a lodging to let for a single man ?"

" Yes," returned the girl, " for a *man* we have."

" Well," said Claudius, " I wish to form an engagement for such,—can I see it?"

" Oh, I don't know," returned the female churl, eyeing Claudius most suspiciously, and particularly directing her scrutinizing visual orbs to the bundle which contained his livery wardrobe ; " but I'll ax my Misses if you'll stand there awhile."

" Very good," said Claudius ; "I'll do so."

" If you please, Marm !" shouted the girl to her mistress, in a tone that compelled Claudius to hear every word, " here's a lad at the door what is axing arter the 'partment; but I don't like his looks,—in the first place, he ain't a man."

".Not a man!" roared the lady housekeeper; "Why, what is he?"

"Why, he is only a lad, as I said, Marm," rejoined the girl; "but besides that 'ere, he has got a large bundle under his arm, which, I thinks, looks very suspicious."

"So it does, Fan," rejoined the mistress; from whose accents Claudius now guessed that the lady was no friend to the wholesome rules of the Temperance Society,—"Howsomever," she added, "I'll take a peep at him myself."

After the lapse of a few minutes, Claudius was confronted by the lady of the house. She appeared to be approaching fast towards sixty; but her dress was such as a girl of sixteen might very prudently have worn;—it was *very* fashionable, but not *very well* put on,—her face looked as if a quarter of a pound of carmine had been lavished upon it; but whether occasioned more by the application of that beauty-destroying daub, or by the swallowing of large quantities of ardent spirits, is not certain;—but there she stood, or rather attempted to stand, for

> " She heel'd like a ship in a furious storm,
>   And could not for a moment stand still;
>   Now backwards, now forwards, and then on each side,
>   She stagger'd, though much against will."

"Well, Sir," commenced the lady, "and pray what may your pleasure be?"

"I understand from the card in your window, Madam," replied Claudius, "that you have a lodging to let for a single man."

"You understand!" echoed the lady,—"and pray do you always understand, when you wait upon a lady, to enquire for lodgings?"

"Why, to say the truth," returned Claudius, "I have never before been compelled to do so."

"Eh?" observed the lady, very knowingly;—"Never *what*, did you say?—I hope you are an honest person. Where do you come from?"

"I suppose that can be of no consequence to you, Madam," answered Claudius, with a respectful tone.

"You suppose!" cried the lady, in rather a loud key; "but, I tell you, it makes *all* the consequence; and neither you nor any one else shall, without proper reference, have my lodging."

"Then I wish you a very good evening, Madam," said Claudius, turning to go.

"Not quite so fast, *Sir*," returned the lodging-house-keeping lady, at the same time laying rather unceremoniously hold on the nether part of his coat,—"Not quite so fast, if you please, Sir!—I have my suspicions about me. Pray who are you, where did you come from, and what have you in that bundle?"

"Who am I?" returned Claudius, possibly thinking it right to begin with the first of her many questions.

"Aye,—*who* are you?" responded the lady. "None of your mocking, if you please : I say I have my suspicions of you. I shall send for a constable and have you locked up ;— I have no doubt but you have robbed some one of that bundle."

On the score of honesty our hero, of course, felt himself perfectly safe ; but as he felt no disposition to submit to such an investigation as would of necessity follow an incarceration in a common prison, he contemplated the best way to cut the affair, and saw none so proper as *cutting* off ; and, accordingly, freeing the tail of his coat by a dexterous movement of his body from the grasp of his detainer,—by which action he also, without intention, completely floored the lady,—he closed the door after him, and, with the fleetness of a lapwing, fled from the spot.

"Which way shall I turn now," thought our hero, "or where seek for a lodging?—I shall almost fear to knock at another door, lest I escape not so well. To be suspected of being a thief is *bad* enough, but to be pushed into a felon's cell would be, beyond all comparison, *worse*."

By this time Claudius strayed to a yet humbler part of the city,—or rather beyond the city itself, on the Bristol road,— when in the window of a low white-washed cottage, whose appearance indicated cleanliness and comfort, he espied, in very humble characters, "A Lodging for a Single Man."

"Well," thought our hero, "I'll make another venture; —surely I shall not be suspected in this place of being a robber."

Opening a little gate which led through a small plot of garden-ground neatly laid out and full of flowers, he walked up to the door ; and, as neither knocker nor bell was affixed to it, he applied his knuckles to the pannels, and presently the door was opened by an aged form, who, dropping a curtsy to Claudius, enquired what he pleased to want.

"Have you not, my good woman," said our hero, " a lodging to let ?"

" Oh yes, Sir," returned the clean and antique personage, "it is a homely, but clean and wholesome one. I am a lone widow woman, and have been so, come the twenty-sixth of next month, seven years. My husband—rest his soul—was one of the kindest and best a woman ever knew,—he built this cottage, Sir, and by frugality and the proceeds of industry, we managed to lay by a trifle, on which I now, with the help of a lodger occasionally, manage to live. I was only seventeen when I married."

To what extent the old lady's garrulous powers would have led her, if Claudius had not mildly enquired if he could see the lodging, is impossible to say.

"Oh, Sir, I beg your pardon!" said the old woman ;— "Do please to walk in ; and if so be it will suit you, I shall feel glad to make you as comfortable as I can." So saying, she walked in, and Claudius followed. "You see, Sir," she re-commenced, as she passed from the front to the backroom, and from thence ascended a narrow staircase which led to the room it was intended he should occupy,—"You see, Sir, mine is, as I said, very humble ; but, I hope, wholesome and clean."

" I like the appearance much," said Claudius ; for the kind open-heartedness of the old woman rather pleased than otherwise ; "all I require is something of the kind you describe."

" Well, then, I am sure I can suit you," returned the old woman. "There," she added, as she opened a small door, "that is the room which I let when I can get a decent kind of a person."

Claudius entered ;—it was perfectly unique in its character —two chairs, a table, a wash-hand-stand, and a small bedstead, formed the chief portions of the furniture : there was, indeed, a small piece of drugget beside the bed, and a fender before the fire-place, but no superfluities ;—still, upon the whole cleanliness was impressed,—indeed, to such an extent, that, as the old woman had said more than once, "you might eat your victuals off the floor."

"This will do excellently well," said Claudius ;—"What are your terms ?"

"Why, Sir," returned the old woman, "I always have two shillings a week for this room; and when I do for the lodger I has ninepence more."

"Two shillings and ninepence a week, then, is what you ask for lodging and cooking?" said Claudius.

"Exactly so, Sir," replied the dame; "but then I always—"

Claudius feared she was going to say,—"I always have a reference,"—and, if so, he was convinced he should have to go "further a field" for a lodging; to prevent which he interruptingly replied,—"Well, I shall give you three shillings a week; and here," he added, taking out his purse, "here are twelve shillings, which will be one month's pay, in advance,—will that satisfy you?"

"O bless you, Sir!" said the old woman, curtsying half-a-dozen times without stopping, as she received the money, "I never desires more than I says; of course I am satisfied. I'll take care you shall be as happy as may be while you are my lodger;—I felt certain, when first I set eyes on you, that you was a gentleman,—and now you have proved it with a witness, as my poor husband would have said,—rest his soul. Ah! Sir, he was such a husband!—my loss when he died was—"

"I don't doubt it," said Claudius, as the old woman was again about to supply an explanation which he did not require, and could not have understood. "I am to consider myself your lodger then, and this as my apartment?"

"Just so, Sir," returned the old woman. "Would you like that I should provide something for your supper?"

This interesting suggestion met with Claudius's unqualified approval, and his landlady was accordingly despatched to purchase the needful; while our hero was left, without any suspicion of his being a thief, in full and quiet possession.

Early on the following morning, Claudius stood before a small glass which was attached by a brass ring to the wall of his chamber, and therein he surveyed his person with as much scrutiny as if to ascertain whether it were his own self or another person;—this, however, was not his object,—he merely wished to determine in his own mind, if the disguise he had assumed was of such a character as might with reason be calculated upon as sufficient to screen him from the observation and knowledge of those whom he had formerly served : little doubt upon the point existed, and he therefore determined to watch the movements of his master and Georgiana, and act as circumstances might dictate.

His first determination was to send back his livery to the doctor; but how to do it he was at a loss to decide. At length, however, he resolved to try his old landlady. " Could you do me a service," enquired Claudius, " this evening ?"

" Could I ?" responded the old woman,—" Aye, Sir,—if any person in the world can render a gentleman a service, Jannet can. Why, bless you, Sir, I was always considered the best hand at doing odd jobs for gentlemen in the whole parish."

" And you are then ready to serve me, Jannet ?" asked Claudius ;—" I do not desire your service without rewarding y u,—I shall be glad to satisfy you for that which I wish you to do."

" You will never find a person more willing to serve you, Sir," returned Jannet,—" as for reward, why, I think I have received it already."

" And can you keep a secret ?" asked Claudius ?

" No one can do it better in the parish," responded the old lady. " I could give you a hundred instances, if necessary— but—"

" Well, well," said Claudius, " what I wish you to do is to carry a bundle and letter for me to the York Hotel ;—the letter must be delivered by you into the hand of the young lady to whom it is addressed, and to no other person ; and this you must manage to do when no one sees you."

" Aye, aye !" exclaimed Jannet, looking archly in our hero's face,—" I see it all,—I see it ;—yes, yes, trust me, Jannet will do the business for you to your entire satisfaction."

" I do believe it," said Claudius, and he proceeded to give her such directions as were necessary—the sequel is already known. Jannet *did* deliver the letter to Georgiana ; and then, as Claudius desired her, left the hotel without discovering either the abode or name of her employer.

At the time that Jannet set off on her expedition, Claudius left the cottage for the purpose of diverting his mind by a stroll in the vicinity of the city. He had walked nearly two hours, when he thought of returning to learn the success of Jannet's mission. The moon was already shining bright in the heavens—the evening was as beautiful and fair as ever the happy lovers of paradise knew 'ere man's first act of disobedience

"Brought death into our world, with all its woe."

The retired spot he had selected, or rather to which, without choice or intention, he had sauntered, appeared sacred to meditation.   Silence reigned so supreme that the hum of the grasshopper could be heard; and the faint buz which arose from the dwellers in the city came upon the ear like the indistinct sounds of music from another sphere.

Onward our hero walked, wrapt in deep reverie, and revolving in his own mind his future course of action. Whether his lady mother was still in Bath or not, he had not been able to learn,—that the lady who was with her at the masquerade was Dr. Leechum's wife, he had no doubt in his mind; still he had no assurance beyond his own conviction on that head, —if they still remained in the city, where could they reside,— and if they continued so long, for what purpose ? These were thoughts which rather perplexed than satisfied ;—he made up his mind, at length, that, come what might, he would endeavour to ascertain if Lady Bolio still continued in Bath; and if so, *where* she resided, and then seek a fit opportunity to present himself before her, and crave her forgiveness.

Such were the cogitations and such the resolves of Claudius's mind, when the sound of voices at no great distance roused him from his meditations : an angle in the place had placed him in deep shade, from which he could see in the moon's bright beams two persons approaching. They drew near to where he stood; and with almost overwhelming astonishment he discovered Lord Dashwood and Dr. Titheum.

To leave the spot on which he stood without being seen by them was impossible, and, therefore, he felt disposed rather to cringe still further into shade to avoid detection.

"We are yet early," observed Dashwood, "at least a quarter of an hour before the appointed time."

"Are you certain they will come ?" enquired the doctor.

"Don't fear that," returned his Lordship ; "ladies never disappoint in such affairs,—they, dear souls, are always punctual."

"So," thought Claudius,—"an assignation ;—then I may learn something which may guide me in my future proceedings."

His Lordship and the doctor walked on, and then sauntered back again, furnishing Claudius with an opportunity to shift his position, so as with better advantage to mark the whole of the business.

"Here they are, doctor," at length he heard Dashwood exclaim; and, at the same moment, looking in the direction to which the expecting gentlemen bent their eyes, he perceived two females approaching. Dashwood, as the reader is aware, ran to meet them, and the doctor followed.

In a few minutes the doctor returned with one of the ladies bearing on his arm; when, as they approached the place of his concealment, he beheld the well-known person of his mother!

"Good heavens!" thought Claudius, "what can this mean?—my mother here, and in company with the father of my Georgiana;—but I will learn the whole." So saying, he stole, cautiously, close to the seat which in a short time they occupied, and there over-heard the tale of love the doctor had to tell, and listened to the response which fell from the lips of his mother.

"Where are Mrs. Leechum and Lord Dashwood?" at length enquired Lady Bolio.

"Mrs. Leechum!" exclaimed Claudius, mentally, "and with Lord Dashwood, too!—this must be made known."

"They are not far off, Madam," replied the doctor.

"I would not that Dr. Leechum knew of his lady being here for all the world," said Lady Bolio.

"There is no fear of it, Madam," returned the doctor; "he is quietly enjoying himself in the Royal Crescent, be assured."

"In the Royal Crescent," said Claudius,—"So!—then I'll haste to acquaint him of a part, at least, of this affair. Shall I frustrate the intentions of the doctor with my mother by the means with which this discovery has possessed me?" thought our hero; "or shall I allow his wishes to be realized?—Let me see,—a slight trick would settle the matter; but then I might, and in all probability should, lose my dear Georgiana,—that I cannot think of;—besides, I have no great objection to the doctor; he is at least as good as most doctors, and much better than many. Well, I suppose I must consent to it, and at a fit time I will let him know what a son-in-law he has;—but, for Dr. Leechum, I'll put him on his guard." So saying, Claudius flew back to his lodgings, in order to obtain such a disguise as the wardrobe of his landlady might be able to furnish; of whom he felt assured he should be able to obtain the loan for a small consideration.

The art of transformation had been acquired by our hero during the period of his Gypsy profession ;—it was not, therefore, a difficult task to arrange the materials he could obtain in such a way as to give an appearance to his person of the most singular character.

Of the way in which Claudius introduced himself to Dr. Leechum, as well as of the conversation he held with him, the reader has already been informed ; at the end of which he seemed, to the doctor's excited and distracted feelings, to

> " Exhale into the thin air;
> Or, like an unsubstantial thing, to pass
> Into the heavens, or earth, whence he had come."

So, however, he did not; but, like a being of flesh and blood, slunk further into shade, and then hasted to change his garb; which having completed, he scrawled a note in haste, detailing in it, in obscure phraseology, the meeting which had taken place between Dashwood and the doctor and two ladies,—which, having sealed, he directed to her Grace the golden Duchess, confident in what way she would use it; and then, trusting to his change of dress and a large shawl-neckerchief wound round his neck for a prevention of recognition, he carried it to the York Hotel, and delivered it to a servant in attendance, by whom it was forwarded to her Grace. In what way the Duchess employed the scrawl, and the effects it produced, need not be repeated ;—and, although the Duchess herself was as ignorant of the person from whom the information had come as any other person in the company, yet all gave her credit for knowledge which perfectly astounded them.

"Bless me, Sir !" exclaimed Jannet, as she entered the room with some boiling water for Claudius's breakfast, "have you heard the news ?"

"So much news is stirring in this busy city," returned Claudius, "that it is impossible to stir abroad without hearing something fresh ; but to what do you refer ? I suppose it is not any thing in which either you or myself is concerned."

"Why, as to the matter of that," replied Jannet, "I suppose not :—there is, indeed, little that concerns me, now-a-days. Heigho !—I can remember well the time that every

thing seemed to concern me,—that is, when my poor husband,—rest his soul,—was living ;—oh, Sir, if you had known
him,—he was so kind! I remember once, we had taken it
into our heads to enjoy ourselves—"

"Well, but the news, Jannet, which you just now referred
to," interrupted Claudius.

"Aye, aye;—true, true," responded Jannet; "that had
nearly escaped me ;—I never speak of my poor husband, Sir,
but I forget every thing else,—and then I find my memory
fails me. Oh, Sir! when so many years have passed over
your head as I have lived, vast changes will be experienced
by you. There is your water, Sir," she added : "if you wish
for any thing, and will be so kind as to knock, you shall have
it in a moment. Every thing that I can do to make you feel
quite comfortable, I shall be happy to do." So saying, Jannet dropped a curtsy, and was retiring without communicating
the information of which she was so full when first she entered the room : other matters had, for the moment, engaged
her, and of course that was forgotten.

"You have not yet told me the news, Jannet," observed
Claudius,—"I am waiting to hear it."

"Bless me !" exclaimed Jannet, "how dull I'm growing;
—sure enough, I had forgotten it. Well, we are going to
have two grand weddings in the city in a few days,—at least,
so it is stated in the paper. I hope they may be as happy
ones as mine was; but there are few to be found now-a-days,
like my dear husband,—rest his soul,—he was so kind and
affectionate—"

"And who are the parties, Jannet?" asked Claudius.

"Why, I have forgotten the name of one of the gentlemen," replied Jannet; "and, indeed, that is no wonder, it
was so strange a name that it would puzzle any head half
the age of mine to remember it. I do wonder how it is that
people get such very odd names ;—do you not think it
would be much better, Sir, if so be all those strange outland-
ish names were done away with? My dear husband,—rest
his soul,—used sometimes to think mine was rather singular
—that is, Jannet Heckwickmondyke; but you know, Sir,
it was my father's name,—and, for the matter of that, I think
a very good one."

"Very good !" responded Claudius; "But what is the
person's name that you recollect, who is about to be married,
and that has caused some excitement ?"

"Why, what would you think, Sir?" asked Jannet.

"Nay," said Claudius, "that is impossible."

"Only try and guess, Sir," continued Jannet, with great simplicity.

"I tell you it is impossible," returned Claudius.

"Well, then, I'll tell you," said Jannet,—"the very person to whom I took your parcel yesterday."

"What! Dr. Titheum?" asked Claudius.

"The very same, Sir," returned Jannet, "as sure as my name is Jannet."

"Indeed!" exclaimed Claudius. "And, pray, do you recollect the lady's name?"

"Why, there it is again," observed Jannet, "as I said before, people will have such very strange names,—let me see —it is Lady somebody, I am quite certain; but—deary me! deary me! how strange it is,—I can't think of the other part; no, not if it was to save my life."

"Should you know it if you were to hear it?" asked Claudius.

"Aye, that I should directly," replied Jannet; "I was always famed for recollecting names after they were mentioned. I could mention a strange circumstance—"

"Was it Lady Bolio?" asked Claudius.

"Lady Bolio,—yes, sure enough, that was the very name," returned Jannet. "Some one is knocking, I hear," continued the old lady. "If you want any thing, Sir, call, and I'll attend upon you immediately." Thus saying, she curtsied, and left Claudius to his reflections.

"All then is settled," said our hero, "and I am shortly to have a father-in-law. I suppose the other distinguished personages are Sir Marmaduke and Miss Fidget. Well, be it so,—I'll watch the motions of the parties, and, if possible, be,—although not invited,—a party at the ceremony, or a guest at the nuptial banquet. Georgiana will feel surprised at meeting a brother in her lover; and, I suppose, the doctor will feel less disposed than before to expel me from the room; —at all events, I'll try it on, and enjoy the sport of the thing."

With all reasonable despatch he swallowed his breakfast, and hastily attired himself; and then set forth to gather such information as would enable him to lay down his plans for future operations.

CHAPTER XXXIX.

" The smiling morn,—as if to greet
  Love's vot'ries,—broke in brightness;
And forth they came for marriage meet,
  In robes of virgin whiteness.
The bride, upon that happy day,
  Promised to *love* and to—*obey!*"

THE BRIDAL.

A HOST of professionals crowded into the Royal Crescent in pursuance of directions sent by Lady Bolio to some of the first artists in Bath, that she might be waited upon to receive orders for dresses of various descriptions, suited to her rank and the memorable occasion upon which they were to be used.

"Oh, how I envy you," observed Mrs. Leechum, "on this joyous occasion!"

"And why so, my dear?" enquired Lady Bolio; "I can assure you I wish the affair was over."

"Why so, Lady Bolio?" replied Mrs. Leechum. "Surely your Ladyship does not intend to sport with my wretched-ness."

"Not I, upon my honour," returned Lady Bolio; "but I see no reason why you should envy me. Really now, my dear, the feelings I must necessarily endure are not so *very* delightful."

"Oh, as to the feelings," said Mrs. Leechum, "I would endure a thousand such feelings for the pleasure of being married over again."

"Consider, my dear Mrs. Leechum," continued her Lady-ship, "that, being wedded, you had better suppress than give license to such feelings."

"It is well for your Ladyship so to talk," returned the doctor's lady; "but to be bound to a person,—*such* a person as I am,—one who is everlastingly inventing fresh plans to annoy and torment! Oh! it is past all endurance."

"Suppose, now," said Lady Bolio, "you could this moment be free to receive an offer from any gentleman who might feel disposed to make it,—would you really accept such freedom?"

"Would I?" exclaimed Mrs. Leechum, with a feeling of strong excitement. "Never did a captive leave his prison-house with half the delight that I should feel at such an event !"

" Well, but you must acknowledge," resumed Lady Bolio " that the doctor is very kind and obliging sometimes."

" Sometimes," responded Mrs. Leechum, " and these times are—

    ' Like angel-visits, few and far between.' "

" But then, you know, my dear," said Lady Bolio, " you might give yourself away to some one whose kindness would never be repeated after the honey-moon had ceased ;—now I have got all this to prove."

" Well, but, my dear lady," continued Mrs. Leechum, "would not the attention that I give to the doctor, and the ease with which I give up every point to him, and all that sort of thing, win any man but him to allow me to do as I pleased ? Now I'll tell you, Lady Bolio,—and I do so, not merely to show you what my own determinations are if ever I am so happy as to be led a second time to the altar,—but to advise you as a friend,—I will never again humour any man as I have done Dr. Leechum,—I have, positively, spoiled him and injured myself by over indulgence. No, no, Lady Bolio ; have your own way in *every* thing,—allow of no contradictions,—make the doctor, the moment you are married, feel the terror of your eye,—rule him properly, and you may then have some chance of holding such a rank as every woman should hold—that of independence, and of making your husband, what every husband should be, a thing of convenience."

" If I dissent from you, my dear Mrs. Leechum, it is not, believe me, for the purpose of dissenting, but from conviction : I should think that man unworthy the name of husband,—and, certainly, should blush to own such a one to be mine,—who did not maintain that dignity and station which reason and nature have given to him."

" What !" exclaimed Mrs. Leechum, in high alarm, " are you really going to give up your will then to the caprice of a man ; and—?"

" I am going to promise at the altar," replied Lady Bolio, " to love, honour, and obey, and I hope to do what I promise ;—but here comes the doctor,"—" Good morning, doctor," continued her Ladyship :—" You have, I hope, enjoyed your walk ?"

"I have done so to a certain extent," replied Leechum; "but should have done so in a much greater degree if my dear Mrs. Leechum had been with me."

"There now, my dear," said Lady Bolio, turning to Mrs. Leechum, 'what think you of that? Why, half the professed gallants in the good city of London would have forgotten to pay such a compliment to a wife."

"A compliment, indeed!" returned the lady; "I wish for something more than mere compliment."

"Well, my love," said the doctor, "I assure you I should have been happy beyond measure if you had been with me this morning."

"I don't believe one word of it, Sir," returned his good-tempered lady; "you know you are never so well pleased as when you can get out by yourself,—at least, as when you can leave me at home, and wander about where you please and with whom you please."

"Now, my dear Mrs. Leechum," rejoined the doctor, "you do me wrong;—you can't but be aware that I am never so much delighted as when you are in a good—that is, when—"

"When what, Sir?" interrupted the lady, with warmth; "Do you intend to impugn my character?—I insist upon knowing what you were going to say."

"Only, my love," said the doctor, "when you are in a good temper; and wish ever—"

"Am I not *always* in a good temper?" demanded the meek lady. "Answer me, you vile defamer!" she continued, as her spouse hung fire, awed by her roused and indignant spirit. "Answer me, I say, Sir."

"Why yes, love," he at length stammered;—"yes, you are pretty well."

"Pretty well,—pretty well, said you, Sir?" repeated Mrs. Leechum, swelling like a certain animal is said to have done at an ox, in order to attain to its size, but which burst in the experiment. "There, Lady Bolio," added the choaking lady, "did you *ever* hear any thing equal to that?—This, you perceive, is the result of being easy and gentle, and humouring that gentleman at a time when I ought to have asserted my rights,—this is my reward for being *too* gentle and *too* indulgent; allowing Dr. Leechum to enjoy his will, when I should have insisted upon having my own."

"Allow me, my love, just to hint one thing," said Leechum, beseechingly.

"Oh, that *hinting* propensity!" shrieked the lady,—"I abhor it,—I will hear no more." So saying, she rushed from the room, leaving the doctor as stationary with surprise and alarm, as Lot's wife, or an Egyptian pyramid. Lady Bolio followed in order to sooth her, and the leech remained *solus*.

"This is most extraordinary," thought the doctor, as soon as he was capable of thinking. "What is the 'head and front of my offending?' I have allowed Mrs. Leechum to have her way in every thing, until she appears positively crazed with having her way so much. The approaching festival must not be marred by our private feuds, otherwise I would make a change—an instant and radical change; let the ceremony pass over which binds the contracted parties as tightly as I am bound, and then may I be bound for New South Wales, or some of the back settlements of Australia, on a fourteen years' apprenticeship, if I don't let Mrs. Leechum know that I will be lord of the ascendant."

While matters were thus moving on harmoniously at the Royal Crescent, the inmates of the York Hotel were actively engaged in making arrangements for the day of legal binding.

"How confoundedly long the days have grown," observed Sir Marmaduke to his friend Dashwood,—"they have, 'pon my honour."

"Don't be impatient, my boy," returned his Lordship, "you'll soon wish they had stood still for ever, or I am mistaken;—to be sure, you'll have at least *one* soothing consideration upon which to meditate after the *fatal* act has taken place,—that of having procured a handsome fortune at the price of your liberty."

"'Pon my honour!" exclaimed Sir Marmaduke,—"My liberty, my lord,—I don't understand you—no, 'pon my honour, I don't."

"Ha! ha! ha!" roared Dashwood,—"One week after marriage, and Lady Varney will instruct you on the subject: farewell then to hunting, coursing, a rubber now and then, and an occasional flirtation."

"'Pon my honour," said Sir Marmaduke, as if just awaking from a gratifying dream to experience all the horrors of an approaching execution. "Does it then follow necessarily, that having made Miss Fidget, Lady Varney, I must at once and entirely abandon all my recreations?"

"Does it *not* follow?" returned Dashwood;—why, to be sure it does. Then you must become a staid, serious, sedate kind of gentleman; as, for instance, I am."

" 'Pon my honour," cried the Knight; " as your _Lud_-ship _is !_—Well, that will do,—I will consent to matrimony on the condition that I enjoy equal freedom with yourself, 'pon my honour."

" Bravo !" shouted Dashwood,—" Bravo, my boy ! That's a display of spirit a little stretch beyond what I had looked for. For my own part," continued his Lordship, " I would rather marry Miss Fidget's poodle and her money, and have my liberty, than Miss Fidget herself, and forfeit so distinguished a blessing."

" 'Pon my honour," rejoined Sir Marmaduke, " your _Lud_-ship is excessively facetious this morning ; however, I agree perfectly with you,—your observations are as sage as a philosopher's,—they are, 'pon my honour."

" Hush !" cried Dashwood, " here comes the lady."

" Now really, my dear Miss Fidget," observed the Duchess, upon whose arm the bride-elect leaned, " you must get over this nonsense ; indeed you must. Oh ! here is Sir Marmaduke and his Lordship, too ;—there now, I shall turn you over to them if you do not promise me to rise above such weakness," she whispered to the lady.

" Are you unwell, Madam ?" enquired Dashwood, approaching Miss Fidget with seeming great concern.

" Only a slight head-ache this morning, my Lord," returned Miss Fidget.

" 'Pon my honour," observed Sir Marmaduke, with a face shrouded upon the instant in gloomy sadness, " inexpressibly sorry to hear it. Can I render you any help ?"

" Oh, yes," said the Duchess, laughing ; " you, I think, are the cause of the whole of it."

" 'Pon my honour !" returned the Knight ;—" I the cause ! Pray explain, or I shall go wild with anxiety,—I shall, 'pon my honour !"

" Now, my dear Duchess," interrupted Miss Fidget, " do regard my feelings."

" I promise you I will," said her Grace, " upon the condition I have named. To make all this fuss, indeed, about getting married,—ha! ha! ha! For shame! my dear Miss Fidget—for shame! Why, I should not make so much ado about it, if I had the business to attend to every New-year's day."

The spirit displayed by the Duchess appeared to inspire Miss Fidget with fresh courage ; and, with something like nerve, she looked forward to the nuptial morn.

Time moved on its axis with its usual celerity; and, although the fevered anxiety of certain parties disposed them to think otherwise, still on it went, and brought with it at length the much-desired and long-wished-for morning of the day upon which the knot, which it was believed death only would render dissoluble, would be tied.

After considerable and close thought, and a variety of opinions on the subject, it had been determined that the ceremony should be performed in the abbey-church; and, also, that the whole party should return from thence to the York Hotel, at which place a sumptuous dinner was to be provided.

At a much earlier hour than she was accustomed to rise, Miss Fidget raised her head from its downy resting-place, and sighed most piteously as she thought of the arduous duties to which she would that day have to attend.

"My dear Carlo," said the affectionate lady, as she embraced him with more than usual warmth; "to-day thy mistress gives herself to one who has promised to be thy friend as well as her's,—if I could entertain a doubt to the contrary, even now, for thy sake I would refuse to accompany him to the altar. But how shall I dispose of you to-day?—must I take you with me to where my vows are to be registered; or shall I leave you in the care of my servant?"

"Yelp! yelp!" returned Carlo, most sagaciously, without any definite reply being furnished, but which Miss Fidget as sagaciously interpreted to be a reply in the affirmative.

"Well, dear," said the affectionate mistress, "you shall accompany me; I will not go without you."

This interesting colloquy was broken up by the appearance of the Duchess and Georgiana; who, as the bridesmaids of Miss Fidget, came to announce themselves as her attendants.

"Oh, my dear Georgiana!" exclaimed Miss Fidget, bursting into tears, and looking very much as if disposed to "go off," "I never shall be able to get through this day!"

"Nonsense!" returned the Duchess; "I tell you, my dear, it positively is nothing. Now, I am quite sure, Georgiana would not make so much fuss about saying, *I will.*—You will be able to say it without any labour in a little time, I make no doubt;—only let Sir Marmaduke contradict your pleasures, or thwart your purpose once or twice, and you are not a woman if '*I will !*' or '*I will not !*' don't issue from your lips freely enough."

"Ah!" thought Georgiana, "if I stood in the same connexion this morning, with my dear Claudius, as Miss Fidget does with Sir Marmaduke, I'm sure I should be too happy to *think* even of the painful part of the duty."

The rolling of Lord Dashwood's carriage up to the door of the York Hotel announced the time of departure for the cathedral; and once-more the sensitive nerves of Miss Fidget received a fearful shock. As, however, due care had been taken to give a strong colour to her bloomless cheeks, no change in countenance could be perceived.

The Duchess had employed all her powers of rhetoric, but in vain, to persuade the accomplished bride to leave Carlo at home,—go he must. She hugged the shaggy brute to her breast; and, supported by her maids, descended the stairs, and in a moment was hid from the gaping crowd within the closely drawn blinds of the carriage.

The doctor and his party had reached the church some minutes before Sir Marmaduke drove up, and were awaiting their arrival, with the dignitary who was to perform the office, in the vestry.

Having sipped a little wine to keep their spirits up, they proceeded gravely towards the altar; and then the very reverend functionary commenced the ceremony—the doctor and Lady Bolio leading the van. These having been in due form pronounced man and wife, Sir Marmaduke led the trembling Miss Fidget to the rails of the communion-table, and there solemnly promised all that was required of him. One or two blunders excepted on the part of the Knight, all went off well; and these occurred principally from his habit of pledging his honour to every thing: as, for instance, when asked, "Wilt thou have this woman?" &c., he quite unconsciously responded, "I will, 'pon my honour." As, however, it was considered an infirmity in the gallant Knight rather than an intended slight or insult upon the ceremony, it was allowed to pass without observation by the worthy divine.

Never before that day was so splendid a banquet, or so distinguished à party, seen at the York Hotel. Sir Marmaduke was determined the thing should be done handsomely, and especially so as he had that day stepped into a particularly handsome fortune; while the taste and love of exhibition in a regal style, which possessed and influenced the Duchess in all her movements, and to whom, in connexion with Dashwood, the direction of the present affair was left,—rendered

it quite certain that no half-and-half measures would be tolerated on the occasion.

It was, as has been stated, a splendid set-out. Sir Marmaduke was in his element,—all with him was dash and
splash; while Miss Fid—we beg her Ladyship's pardon,—
Lady Varney, endured the fatigue and other things like a
hero; even Carlo appeared to understand that something
out of the usual order of things had happened; and, therefore, seemed to suppose he had a license to take a few more
than ordinary liberties. The doctor and his bride smiled
graciously on all, and returned without affectation of assumed
bashfulness the kindly wishes and hearty gratulations which
were addressed to them from every quarter.

Georgiana looked upon the festive scene with thoughtful-
ness; and although her musing mood did not degenerate into
gloomy sadness, still the hilarity with which she would once
have hailed such an occasion, had departed from her.

At this moment an unusual noise, close to the door of the
apartment on the outside, caught the attention of the whole
party. Some words of altercation followed, as if the servants
in attendance were opposing the entrance of some one who
sought to do so.

"What can this mean?" exclaimed Sir Marmaduke, his
countenance undergoing a change as he spoke. "'Tis very
extraordinary, 'pon my honour."

"Some one who would be an unwelcome intruder, I should
imagine," responded Dashwood, directing a significant
glance towards Sir Marmaduke. The Knight caught the expressive look, and appeared fully to understand it.

"'Pon my honour," returned Sir Marmaduke, "'tis
strange. To what period did the date of the bond extend?"
he enquired of Dashwood.

"The bond!" exclaimed two or three voices.

"To what bond do you refer, love?" asked Lady
Varney.

"'Pon my honour!" answered the Knight;—"What was
it, my Lud?"

"Oh, a mere trifle," replied that statesman-like worthy,
who was ever ready with an answer for every question, and
had at his tongue's end an excuse, or evasion, for every case
of difficulty: "A poor man whom Sir Marmaduke has kindly
served, and who promised that he would redeem his security
to-day or to-morrow."

'Such an action, so performed, Sir Marmaduke, reflects the highest honour upon your character," observed the doctor, "and deserves a compliment elegant and durable as that paid by Pope to his benevolent friend, Ralph Allen, Esq., who formerly possessed the handsome property on the right of Claverton Down, called 'Prior Park,' which owns the noble Hawarden for its lord—

'Let humble Allen with ingenuous shame,
Do good by stealth, and blush to find his fame.' "

" 'Pon my honour," had just issued from Sir Marmaduke's lips, as the preface to a speech in which he purposed to acknowledge the *intended* compliment of the doctor; but which was, as the reader is aware, every thing the reverse,—when a yet louder noise, accompanied by a scuffle, was heard, and then a report as if more than one head had come in contact with some neighbouring wainscoting followed, which was again followed by the opening of the door of the room, and in rushed an elegant-looking young man, followed by a posse of servants who had attempted, but in vain, to prevent his entrance.

"My mother!—my mother!" burst from the lips of the intruder, as he threw himself at the feet of Mrs. Titheum. "Can you pardon the waywardness of your repentant son?"

" 'Pon my honour!" exclaimed Sir Marmaduke,—"What does all this mean?"

"My dear,—my long-lost Claudius!" exclaimed the fond mother, enfolding the supplicant in her arms.

"Claudius!" cried the doctor, starting in amazement. "Is it possible?—What! my livery servant transformed into my son-in-law!"

Little more than the first exclamation uttered by Claudius had been heard by Georgiana;—the delight and wonder of the maid entirely overpowered her, and she swooned in the arms of the Duchess. Claudius beheld his beloved mistress —now by marriage his sister,—die away; and, without waiting for the pardon he had solicited at the hands of his mother, hurried to relieve the Duchess of her lovely burden.

A short time sufficed to restore order,—the servants, of course, retired at the instant the doctor waved his hand for them to do so,—and Claudius, being placed on the left hand of his mother, with Georgiana beside him, proceeded to amuse the company by recounting some of the leading scenes of his

z

peregrinations, with which all expressed themselves astonished and delighted.

"'Pon my honour," exclaimed Sir Marmaduke, with high
delight of tone and countenance,—relieved from the fear
which beset him, that Mr. Solomon Feritfox had made him
a final call;—"this is, indeed, particularly wonderful! Mr.
Claudius," he continued, as he presented his hand to our
hero, "I congratulate you with all my heart,—I do, 'pon my
honour,—your adventures have been very extraordinary."

"And no one," observed Dr. Titheum, "could hit upon
a better plan to gain information of men and manners. I am
not in the 'commission of the peace' if I do not recommend
its adoption to all the junior branches of my connexions. If it
were generally pursued it would be an important improvement
upon the course pursued by our sprigs of nobility;—if instead of migrating to foreign shores, and picking up just as
much of the customs and habits of their inhabitants as tends
to make them libertines and atheists, they were to read the
living chronicles, which in every grade of society are open to
their inspection in their own country, they would by such
means understand human nature better, and, of course, be
more fully qualified to legislate for the benefit of the community, and for the promotion of the interests and glory of the
land."

"Bravo!" cried Dashwood,—"and what would you recommend to the candidates for sacred functions and ecclesiastical honours?"

"Umph!" said the doctor, pouring down a glass of wine
to brighten his intellects. "I think the best study for those
who desire to be perfect in the science of anatomy, is the
human frame,—connecting, of course, such practice with a
diligent investigation of the works of the wise and learned of
by-gone ages."

"Exactly so," observed Dr. Leechum.

"And by parity of reasoning," said Dashwood, "I suppose I am to infer, that a close study of human nature, connected with a thoughtful perusal of the productions of sound
and good theologians, is the course you would recommend
to such candidates, instead of—"

"That is precisely my view of the subject," interrupted
the doctor, without allowing his Lordship to make such observations as in all probability, he opined, would reflect upon
a large proportion of his cloth.

" Then it appears, doctor,' resumed Dashwood, " you would recommend a radical change in long-established customs."

" So far as customs are opposed to the views I have named," said the doctor, " I would certainly do so."

" I propose, gentlemen," cried the Duchess, " that unless his Lordship and the doctor pay a little more respect to the ladies by changing their *subject*,—a heavy fine shall be laid upon each of them."

" 'Pon my honour," responded Sir Marmaduke, " that is shrewdly said by your Grace ;—I second the proposition,—I do, 'pon my honour."

" To prevent the trouble of putting it to the vote," said Dashwood, " we plead guilty of a breach of order; and, craving the pardon of the house, promise never in the same way to offend again."

So passed the hours of this memorable day, the night of which was closed by a splendid ball, at which Claudius and Georgiana shone forth the stars of the brilliant circle ; while Lord Dashwood and Mrs. Leechum, to the no small annoyance of the worthy leech, flirted with broad hilarity.

The period at length came when a separation of the parties was determined on ; and, after having spent so many weeks in each other's company, the sound of adieu fell not pleasantly upon the ear. Mrs. Leechum positively shed tears, not a few, although she contrived to conceal them, as the final pressure of her hand was felt from Dashwood ;—while the doctor appeared to rejoice as he drove from the hotel with his amiable wife ; hoping, that being thereby freed from the suspicious attentions of a titled one, the lady might pay a little more attention to her too much neglected husband.

Dr. Titheum and his family remained a day beyond any of the others,—not for his own pleasure exactly, but at the request of Claudius, whose grateful heart swelled with desire to reward, in some measure, the services performed and the kindness shown to him, by his old landlady, Jannet.

Accompanied by Georgiana, and arrayed in a suit more becoming his change of fortune than he had before been seen in, he walked to the lowly cottage of the kind-hearted widow. He had already by a note informed her, that his absence from his lodging was occasioned by business, in order to prevent the alarm which otherwise she might have felt for his safety; but at the same time assured her that in a few days he should return.

z 2

The joy of Jannet at seeing Claudius was excessive; but when he informed her that his object in calling was to make her some return for the services she had rendered him, and to take his leave of her, the old woman burst into tears, and wept like an infant. Georgiana employed her art to sooth her, and after some time succeeded; and then, having placed a substantial evidence of their gratitude in Jaunet's hand, they retired from the humble dwelling, followed by the blessings of the widow.

On the return of Claudius and Georgiana to the York, they found every thing had been prepared for their departure during their absence; and without any other delay than some trifling change in dress occasioned, they commenced their journey towards the doctor's residence at Christchurch.

To follow our travellers through the whole line of road they journeyed, or to notice every circumstance which took place on the way, and at the several places at which they halted, is neither necessary nor intended; it will suffice to state, that without any accident the whole party reached the Rectory in safety, and were received with every demonstration of pleasure which sincerity could display, by the several dependants of the doctor.

The change which had taken place in the character and station of Claudius produced feelings of astonishment and delight in every member of the establishment, by whom he had ever been a great favourite; while with a generous kindness, such as a noble heart alone could feel, our hero returned the salutes they gave.

It was soon determined that a *fête* of a splendid character should mark the event, and numerous cards of invitation were despatched to the " respectables" of the neighbourhood, among which Claudius did not fail to number the generous Farmer Primrose and family, to whose kindness he had formerly owed so much. The attendance of the party was highly gratifying, and the entertainments of the evening interesting and unique. Claudius and Georgiana appeared as the presiding spirits of the time, while all seemed equally astonished and delighted with the sketch which was furnished them of the—"*Rambles of Claudius Bolio.*"

THE END.